Detectives
A to Z

EDITED BY

Frank D. McSherry, Jr.,
Martin H. Greenberg,
&
Charles G. Waugh

BONANZA BOOKS
New York

Published 1985 by Bonanza Books, distributed by Crown Publishers, Inc., 225 Park Avenue South, New York, New York 10003

Printed and bound in the United States of America

Library of Congress Cataloging-in-Publication Data
  Main entry under title:
  Detectives A–Z.
  1. Detective and mystery stories. I. McSherry, Frank D. II. Greenberg, Martin Harry. III. Waugh, Charles.
PN6120.95.D45D47 1985   808.83'872   85-17115
Book design by Jane Treuhaft
ISBN: 0-517-49004-8
h g f e d c b a

ACKNOWLEDGMENTS

MacDonald—Copyright © 1960 by Ross MacDonald. Reprinted by permission of Harold Ober Associates, Incorporated.

Chesterton—Reprinted by permission of Miss D. E. Collins and AP Watt Ltd.

McBain—Copyright © 1956, by Ed McBain, © renewed 1984 by Ed McBain. Reprinted by permission of John Farquharson Ltd.

"Why Shoot a Corpse?" by John K. Butler. Copyright 1938 Blazing Publications, Inc. All rights reserved. Originally published in *Dime Detective Magazine,* May 1938. Copyright 1938 by Popular Publications, Inc. Copyright renewed © 1966 by Popular Publications, Inc. Reprinted by special arrangement with Blazing Publications, Inc., proprietor and conservator of the respective copyrights and successor-in-interest to Popular Publications, Inc.

Carr—Copyright © 1958 by John Dickson Carr. Reprinted by permission of Harold Ober Associates, Incorporated.

MacDonald—Copyright © 1947 by The American Mercury, Inc. Reprinted by permission of Doubleday & Company, Inc., and Collins Publishers, London.

Wellen—Copyright © 1975 by H.S.D. Publications, Inc. Reprinted by permission of the author.

De la Torre—Copyright © 1947 by Lillian de la Torre. Copyright renewed © 1975 by Lillian de la Torre. Reprinted by permission of Harold Ober Associates, Incorporated.

Nebel—Reprinted by permission of Mrs. Frederick Nebel.

Hoch—Copyright © 1975 by Edward D. Hoch. First published in *Ellery Queen's Mystery Magazine*. Reprinted by permission of the author.

Simenon—Copyright © 1953 by Georges Simenon. From *Maigret et les Petits Cochons Sans Queue*. Reprinted by permission of the author.

Pronzini—Copyright © 1980 by Bill Pronzini. First published as a limited edition by Waves Press, Richmond, VA. Reprinted by permission of the author.

Gores—Copyright © by Joe Gores. First appeared in *Ellery Queen's Mystery Magazine*. Reprinted by permission of the author.

Gilbert—Copyright © 1969 by Michael Gilbert. First appeared in *Ellery Queen's Mystery Magazine*. Reprinted by permission of Curtis Brown Ltd.

Queen—Copyright © 1935; renewed © 1963 by Ellery Queen. Reprinted by permission of the agents for the author's estate, the Scott Meredith Literary Agency, Inc., 845 Third Ave., New York, NY 10022

Mortimer—Copyright © 1981 by John Mortimer. Reprinted by permission of Viking Penguin Inc.

Charteris—Copyright 1933 by Leslie Charteris. Reprinted by permission of the author.

Ball—Copyright © 1972 by John Ball. Reprinted by permission of the author.

Asimov—Copyright 1954 by Fantasy House, Inc.; copyright renewed © 1982 by Isaac Asimov. Reprinted by permission of the author.

Stout—Copyright 1945, 1946, 1947, 1949 by Rex Stout. Copyright renewed © 1972 by Rex Stout. From *Trouble in Triplicate* by Rex Stout. Reprinted by permission of Viking Penguin Inc.

Hoch—Copyright © 1985 by Edward D. Hoch. Reprinted by permission from the author.

Anderson—Copyright © 1964 by Paul and Karen Anderson. Reprinted by permission of the author and his agents, the Scott Meredith Literary Agency, Inc., 845 Third Ave., New York, NY 10022.

Gardner—Copyright 1931 by Red Star News Co., © renewed 1959 by Erle Stanley Gardner. (Originally titled "The First Stone.") Reprinted by permission of The Erle Stanley Gardner Trust.

CONTENTS

I FEEL A MURDER COMING ON...

WHAT IS THE greatest pleasure? A romantic evening with a lovely woman, the rose-colored candlelight gleaming on wineglasses and silver? Winning the gold medal at the Olympic games? A gourmet dinner in a fancy restaurant? Whatever your answer is, it will change with time and your mood.

But one pleasure never changes, from childhood to old age, and that's reading a story that fits the mood you're in. How satisfying that is! And that's why series characters—from the immortal Sherlock Holmes to the Saint—have always been so popular in mystery, or any other, fiction. A reader familiar with any series character, and the type of story in which he appears, with its own particular atmosphere and ambience, will always reach for another in the series, knowing it will satisfy his craving. This satisfaction enhances his enjoyment of the story and increases his fondness for series detectives.

Are you in the mood to exercise your deductive abilities? Then turn to Ellery Queen and the impossible crime he faces in ''The Lamp of God.'' During a winter's night, the big Black House, three stories tall, all of solid granite, disappears without a sound. Gone too, without a trace, is the fortune in gold hidden in it by a dying millionaire.

Are you, perhaps, in an armchair-detective mood, pleasantly physically tired but mentally full of energy? Turn to Dr. Sam: Johnson, and his adventure in a cleaner, greener land, the England of more than two centuries ago, as he faces the real-life mystery of ''The Disappearing Servant Wench.'' On New Year's Day in 1753, Elizabeth Canning, a respectable girl, vanishes as if into thin air and returns a month later to accuse a band of gypsies of kidnapping her. What is the real story? Aided by the fabulous Black Stone of Dr. Dee, the great inventor of the dictionary sets out to uncover the truth by power of reason alone. "Sir, man is the master, not by reason of . . . shovels, but by virtue of the vision in his head."

Or if you're in the mood for a hard-boiled story of tough, fast action, turn to Kennedy and Cap McBride. Their exploits in "Take It and Like It" are set in the Roaring Twenties when jazz nightclubs rattled to the roar of tommy guns, and Capone and his gangsters ruled the roost.

For those in the mood for something new, we've included Tricky Enright, whose case "Why Shoot a Corpse?", is reprinted for the first time in this collection; and too-little-known exploits of more familiar sleuths, among them Prof. Augustus S.F.X. Van Dusen, the Thinking Machine. His case of "The Phantom Motor," written in the dawn of the Automobile Age, poses a painful puzzle for the police. They see a crazed speedster—going nearly forty miles an hour!—roaring night after night, headlights blazing, into a sunken road, never coming out at the other end, though both ends are watched and guarded.

And there's much, much more! There are *twenty-six* series detectives in this collection, one for each letter of the alphabet, from Archer (Lew) to Zoom (Sidney). Their adventures have been chosen for their variety, ranging from a short-short such as "Drumbeat" to novellas such as "The Lamp of God" and "Instead of Evidence." Each detective has his own distinctive style, from suave to seedy.

Sample the twenty-six moods. Pick the detective who fits yours, and while the cold rain drums on the windowpane in the night, sit by the fire in comfort and enjoy the longest-lasting pleasure. Be my guest.

I feel a murder coming on . . .

FRANK D. MCSHERRY, JR.
McAlester, Oklahoma
1985

MIDNIGHT BLUE
Ross MacDonald

I T HAD RAINED in the canyon during the night. The world had the colored freshness of a butterfly just emerged from the chrysalis stage and trembling in the sun. Actual butterflies danced in flight across free spaces of air or played a game of tag without any rules among the tree branches. At this height there were giant pines among the eucalyptus trees.

I parked my car where I usually parked it, in the shadow of the stone building just inside the gates of the old estate. Just inside the posts, that is—the gates had long since fallen from their rusted hinges. The owner of the country house had died in Europe, and the place had stood empty since the war. It was one reason I came here on the occasional Sunday when I wanted to get away from the Hollywood rat race. Nobody lived within two miles.

Until now, anyway. The window of the gatehouse overlooking the drive had been broken the last time that I'd noticed it. Now it was patched up with a piece of cardboard. Through a hole punched in the middle of the cardboard, bright emptiness watched me—human eye's bright emptiness.

"Hello," I said.

A grudging voice answered: "Hello."

The gatehouse door creaked open, and a white-haired man came out. A smile sat strangely on his ravaged face. He walked mechanically, shuffling in the leaves, as if his body was not at home in the world. He wore faded denims through which his clumsy muscles bulged like animals in a sack. His feet were bare.

I saw when he came up to me that he was a huge old man, a head taller than I was and a foot wider. His smile was not a greeting or any kind of a smile that I could respond to. It was the stretched, blind grimace of a man who lived in a world of his own, a world that didn't include me.

"Get out of here. I don't want trouble. I don't want nobody messing around."

"No trouble," I said. "I came up to do a little target shooting. I probably have as much right here as you have."

His eyes widened. They were as blue and empty as holes in his head through which I could see the sky.

"Nobody has the rights here that I have. I lifted up mine eyes unto the hills and the voice spoke and I found sanctuary. Nobody's going to force me out of my sanctuary."

I could feel the short hairs bristling on back of my neck. Though my instincts didn't say so, he was probably a harmless nut. I tried to keep my instincts out of my voice.

"I won't bother you. You don't bother me. That should be fair enough."

"You bother me just *being* here. I can't stand people. I can't stand cars. And this is twice in two days you come up harrying me and harassing me."

"I haven't been here for a month."

"You're an Ananias liar." His voice whined like a rising wind. He clenched his knobbed fists and shuddered on the verge of violence.

"Calm down, old man," I said. "There's room in the world for both of us."

He looked around at the high green world as if my words had snapped him out of a dream.

"You're right," he said in a different voice. "I have been blessed, and I must remember to be joyful. Joyful. Creation belongs to all of us poor creatures." His smiling teeth were as long and yellow as an old horse's. His roving glance fell on my car. "And it wasn't you who come up here last night. It was a different automobile. I remember."

He turned away, muttering something about washing his socks, and dragged his horny feet back into the gatehouse. I got my targets, pistol, and ammunition out of the trunk, and locked the car up tight. The old man watched me through his peephole, but he didn't come out again.

Below the road, in the wild canyon, there was an open meadow backed by a sheer bank which was topped by the crumbling wall of the estate. It was my shooting gallery. I slid down the wet grass of the bank and tacked a target to an oak tree, using the butt of my heavy-framed twenty-two as a hammer.

While I was loading it, something caught my eye—something that glinted red, like a ruby among the leaves. I stooped to pick it up and found it was attached. It was a red-enameled fingernail at the tip of a white hand. The hand was cold and stiff.

I let out a sound that must have been loud in the stillness. A jay bird erupted from a manzanita, sailed up to a high limb of the oak, and yelled down curses at me. A dozen chickadees flew out of the oak and settled in another at the far end of the meadow.

Panting like a dog, I scraped away the dirt and wet leaves that had been loosely piled over the body. It was the body of a girl wearing a midnight-blue sweater and skirt. She was a blonde, about seventeen. The blood that congested her face made her look old and dark. The white rope with which she had been garrotted was sunk almost out of sight in the flesh of her neck. The rope was tied at the nape in what is called a granny's knot, the kind of knot that any child can tie.

I left her where she lay and climbed back up to the road on trembling knees. The grass showed traces of the track her body had made where someone had dragged it down the bank. I looked for tire marks on the shoulder and in the rutted, impacted gravel of the road. If there had been any, the rain had washed them out.

I trudged up the road to the gatehouse and knocked on the door. It creaked inward under my hand. Inside there was nothing alive but the spiders that had webbed the low black beams. A dustless rectangle in front of the stone fireplace showed where a bedroll had lain. Several blackened tin cans had evidently been used as cooking utensils. Gray embers lay on the cavernous hearth. Suspended above it from a spike in the mantel was a pair of white cotton work socks. The socks were wet. Their owner had left in a hurry.

It wasn't my job to hunt him. I drove down the canyon to the highway and along it for a few miles to the outskirts of the nearest town. There a drab green box of a building with a flag in front of it housed the Highway Patrol. Across the highway was a lumberyard, deserted on Sunday.

"Too bad about Ginnie," the dispatcher said when she had radioed the local sheriff. She was a thirtyish brunette with fine black eyes and dirty fingernails. She had on a plain white blouse, which was full of her.

"Did you know Ginnie?"

"My younger sister knows her. They go—they went to high school together. It's an awful thing when it happens to a young person like that. I knew she was missing—I got the report when I came on at eight—but I kept hoping that she was just off on a lost weekend, like. Now there's nothing to hope for, is there?'' Her eyes were liquid with feeling. ''Poor Ginnie. And poor Mr. Green.''

''Her father?''

''That's right. He was in here with her high school counselor not more than an hour ago. I hope he doesn't come back right away. I don't want to be the one that has to tell him.''

''How long has the girl been missing?''

''Just since last night. We got the report here about 3 A.M., I think. Apparently she wandered away from a party at Cavern Beach. Down the pike a ways.'' She pointed south toward the mouth of the canyon.

''What kind of a party was it?''

''Some of the kids from the Union High School—they took some wienies down and had a fire. The party was part of graduation week. I happen to know about it because my young sister Alice went. I didn't want her to go, even if it was supervised. That can be a dangerous beach at night. All sorts of bums and scroungers hang out in the caves. Why, one night when I was a kid I saw a naked man down there in the moonlight. He didn't have a woman with him either.''

She caught the drift of her words, did a slow blush, and checked her loquacity. I leaned on the plywood counter between us.

''What sort of girl was Ginnie Green?''

''I wouldn't know. I never really knew her.''

''Your sister does.''

''I don't let my sister run around with girls like Ginnie Green. Does that answer your question?''

''Not in any detail.''

''It seems to me you ask a lot of questions.''

''I'm naturally interested, since I found her. Also, I happen to be a private detective.''

''Looking for a job?''

''I can always use a job.''

''So can I, and I've got one and I don't intend to lose it.'' She softened the words with a smile. ''Excuse me; I have work to do.''

She turned to her shortwave and sent out a message to the patrol cars that Virginia Green had been found. Virginia Green's father heard it as he came in the door. He was a puffy gray-faced man with red-rimmed eyes. Striped pajama bottoms showed below the cuffs of his trousers. His shoes were muddy, and he walked as if he had been walking all night.

He supported himself on the edge of the counter, opening and shutting his mouth like a beached fish. Words came out, half strangled by shock.

"I heard you say she was dead, Anita."

The woman raised her eyes to his, "Yes. I'm awfully sorry, Mr. Green."

He put his face down on the counter and stayed there like a penitent, perfectly still. I could hear a clock somewhere, snipping off seconds, and in the back of the room the L.A. police signals like muttering voices coming in from another planet. Another planet very much like this one, where violence measured out the hours.

"It's my fault," Green said to the bare wood under his face. "I didn't bring her up properly. I haven't been a good father."

The woman watched him with dark and glistening eyes ready to spill. She stretched out an unconscious hand to touch him, pulled her hand back in embarrassment when a second man came into the station. He was a young man with crew-cut brown hair, tanned and fit-looking in a Hawaiian shirt. Fit-looking except for the glare of sleeplessness in his eyes and the anxious lines around them.

"What is it, Miss Brocco? What's the word?"

"The word is bad." She sounded angry. "Somebody murdered Ginnie Green. This man here is a detective and he just found her body up in Trumbull Canyon."

The young man ran his fingers through his short hair and failed to get a grip on it, or on himself. "My God! That's terrible!"

"Yes," the woman said. "You were supposed to be looking after her, weren't you?"

They glared at each other across the counter. The tips of her breasts pointed at him through her blouse like accusing fingers. The young man lost the glaring match. He turned to me with a wilted look.

"My name is Connor, Franklin Connor, and I'm afraid I'm very much to blame in this. I'm counselor at the high school, and I was supposed to be looking after the party, as Miss Brocco said."

"Why didn't you?"

"I didn't realize. I mean, I thought they were all perfectly happy and safe. The boys and girls had pretty well paired off around the fire. Frankly, I felt rather out of place. They aren't children, you know. They were all seniors, they had cars. So I said good night and walked home along the beach. As a matter of fact, I was hoping for a phone call from my wife."

"What time did you leave the party?"

"It must have been nearly eleven. The ones who hadn't paired off had already gone home."

"Who did Ginnie pair off with?"

"I don't know. I'm afraid I wasn't paying too much attention to the kids. It's graduation week, and I've had a lot of problems—"

The father, Green, had been listening with a changing face. In a sudden yammering rage his implosive grief and guilt exploded outward.

"It's your business to know! By God, I'll have your job for this. I'll make it *my* business to run you out of town."

Connor hung his head and looked at the stained tile floor. There was a thin spot in his short brown hair, and his scalp gleamed through it like bare white bone. It was turning into a bad day for everybody, and I felt the dull old nagging pull of other people's trouble, like a toothache you can't leave alone.

The sheriff arrived, flanked by several deputies and an HP sergeant. He wore a western hat and a rawhide tie and a blue gabardine business suit which together produced a kind of gun-smog effect. His name was Pearsall.

I rode back up the canyon in the right front seat of Pearsall's black Buick, filling him in on the way. The deputies' Ford and an HP car followed us, and Green's new Oldsmobile convertible brought up the rear.

The sheriff said: "The old guy sounds like a looney to me."

"He's a loner, anyway."

"You never can tell about them hoboes. That's why I give my boys instructions to roust 'em. Well, it looks like an open-and-shut case."

"Maybe. Let's keep our minds open anyway, Sheriff."

"Sure. Sure. But the old guy went on the run. That shows conscious-ness of guilt. Don't worry, we'll hunt him down. I got men that know these hills like you know your wife's geography."

"I'm not married."

"Your girl friend, then." He gave me a sideways leer that was no gift. "And if we can't find him on foot, we'll use the air squadron."

"You have an air squadron?"

"Volunteer, mostly local ranchers. We'll get him." His tires squealed on a curve. "Was the girl raped?"

"I didn't try to find out. I'm not a doctor. I left her as she was."

The sheriff grunted. "You did the right thing at that."

Nothing had changed in the high meadow. The girl lay waiting to have her picture taken. It was taken many times, from several angles. All the birds flew away. Her father leaned on a tree and watched them go. Later he was sitting on the ground.

I volunteered to drive him home. It wasn't pure altruism. I'm incapable of it. I said when I had turned his Oldsmobile:

"Why did you say it was your fault, Mr. Green?"

He wasn't listening. Below the road four uniformed men were wrestling a heavy covered aluminum stretcher up the steep bank. Green watched them as he had watched the departing birds, until they were out of sight around a curve.

"She was so young," he said to the back seat.

I waited, and tried again. "Why did you blame yourself for her death?"

He roused himself from his daze. "Did I say that?"

"In the Highway Patrol office you said something of the sort."

He touched my arm. "I didn't mean I killed her."

"I didn't think you meant that. I'm interested in finding out who did."

"Are you a cop—a policeman?"

"I have been."

"You're not with the locals."

"No. I happen to be a private detective from Los Angeles. The name is Archer."

He sat and pondered this information. Below and ahead the summer sea brimmed up in the mouth of the canyon.

"You don't think the old tramp did her in?" Green said.

"It's hard to figure out how he could have. He's a strong-looking old buzzard, but he couldn't have carried her all the way up from the beach. And she wouldn't have come along with him of her own accord."

It was a question, in a way.

"I don't know," her father said. "Ginnie was a little wild. She'd do a thing *because* it was wrong, *because* it was dangerous. She hated to turn down a dare, especially from a man."

"There were men in her life?"

"She was attractive to men. You saw her, even as she is." He gulped. "Don't get me wrong. Ginnie was never a *bad* girl. She was a little headstrong, and I made mistakes. That's why I blame myself."

"What sort of mistakes, Mr. Green?"

"All the usual ones, and some I made up on my own." His voice was bitter. "Ginnie didn't have a mother, you see. Her mother left me years ago, and it was as much my fault as hers. I tried to bring her up myself. I didn't give her proper supervision. I run a restaurant in town, and I don't get home nights till after midnight. Ginnie was pretty much on her own since she was in grade school. We got along fine when I was there, but I usually wasn't there.

"The worst mistake I made was letting her work in the restaurant over the weekends. That started about a year ago. She wanted the money for clothes, and I thought the discipline would be good for her. I thought I could keep an eye on her, you know. But it didn't work out. She grew up too fast, and the night work played hell with her studies. I finally got the word from the school authorities. I fired her a couple of months ago, but I guess it was too late. We haven't been getting along too well since then. Mr. Connor said she resented my indecision, that I gave her too much responsibility and then took it away again."

"You've talked her over with Connor?"

"More than once, including last night. He was her academic counselor, and he was concerned about her grades. We both were. Ginnie finally pulled through, after all, thanks to him. She was going to graduate. Not that it matters now, of course.

Green was silent for a time. The sea expanded below us like a second blue dawn. I could hear the roar of the highway. Green touched my elbow again, as if he needed human contact.

"I oughtn't to've blown my top at Connor. He's a decent boy, he means well. He gave my daughter hours of free tuition this last month. And he's got troubles of his own, like he said."

"What troubles?"

"I happen to know his wife left him, same as mine. I shouldn't have borne down so hard on him. I have a lousy temper, always have had." He hesitated, then blurted out as if he had found a confessor: "I said a terrible thing to Ginnie at supper last night. She always has supper with me at the restaurant. I said if she wasn't home when I got home last night that I'd wring her neck."

"And she wasn't home," I said. And somebody wrung her neck, I didn't say.

The light at the highway was red. I glanced at Green. Tear tracks glistened like small tracks on his face.

"Tell me what happened last night."

"There isn't anything much to tell," he said. "I got to the house about twelve-thirty, and, like you said, she wasn't home. So I called Al Brocco's house. He's my night cook, and I knew his youngest daughter Alice was at the moonlight party on the beach. Alice was home all right."

"Did you talk to Alice?"

"She was in bed asleep. Al woke her up, but I didn't talk to her. She told him she didn't know where Ginnie was. I went to bed, but I couldn't sleep. Finally I got up and called Mr. Connor. That was about one-thirty. I thought I should get in touch with the authorities, but he said no, Ginnie had enough black marks against her already. He came over to the house and waited for a while and then we went down to Cavern Beach. There was no trace of her. I said it was time to call in the authorities, and he agreed. We went to his beach house, because it was nearer, and called the sheriff's office from there. We went back to the beach with a couple of flashlights and went through the caves. He stayed with me all night. I give him that."

"Where are these caves?"

"We'll pass them in a minute. I'll show you if you want. But there's nothing in any of the three of them."

Nothing but shadows and empty beer cans, discarded contraceptives, the odor of rotting kelp. I got sand in my shoes and sweat under my collar. The sun dazzled my eyes when I half-walked, half-crawled, from the last of the caves.

Green was waiting beside a heap of ashes.

"This is where they had the wienie roast," he said.

I kicked the ashes. A half-burned sausage rolled along the sand. Sand fleas hopped in the sun like fat on a griddle. Green and I faced each other over the dead fire. He looked out to sea. A seal's face floated like a small black nose cone beyond the breakers. Farther out a water skier slid between unfolding wings of spray.

Away up the beach two people were walking toward us. They were small and lonely and distinct as Chirico figures in the long white distance.

Green squinted against the sun. Red-rimmed or not, his eyes were good. "I believe that's Mr. Connor. I wonder who the woman is with him."

They were walking as close as lovers, just above the white margin of the surf. They pulled apart when they noticed us, but they were still holding hands as they approached.

"It's Mrs. Connor," Green said in a low voice.

"I thought you said she left him."

"That's what he told me last night. She took off on him a couple of weeks ago, couldn't stand a high school teacher's hours. She must have changed her mind."

She looked as though she had a mind to change. She was a hard-faced blonde who walked like a man. A certain amount of style took the curse off her stiff angularity. She had on a madras shirt, mannishly cut, and a pair of black Capri pants that hugged her long, slim legs. She had good legs.

Connor looked at us in complex embarrassment. "I thought it was you from a distance, Mr. Green. I don't believe you know my wife."

"I've seen her in my place of business." He explained to the woman: "I run the Highway Restaurant in town."

"How do you do," she said aloofly, then added in an entirely different voice: "You're Virginia's father, aren't you? I'm so sorry."

The words sounded queer. Perhaps it was the surroundings; the ashes on the beach, the entrances to the caves, the sea, and the empty sky which dwarfed us all. Green answered her solemnly.

"Thank you, ma'am. Mr. Connor was a strong right arm to me last night. I can tell you." He was apologizing. And Connor responded:

"Why don't you come to our place for a drink? It's just down the beach. You look as if you could use one, Mr. Green. You, too," he said to me. "I don't believe I know your name."

"Archer. Lew Archer."

He gave me a hard hand. His wife interposed. "I'm sure Mr. Green and his friend won't want to be bothered with us on a day like this. Besides, it isn't even noon yet, Frank."

She was the one who didn't want to be bothered. We stood around for a minute, exchanging grim, nonsensical comments on the beauty of the day. Then she led Connor back in the direction they had come from. Private Property, her attitude seemed to say: Trespassers will be fresh-frozen.

I drove Green to the Highway Patrol station. He said that he was feeling better, and could make it home from there by himself. He thanked me profusely for being a friend in need to him, as he put it. He followed me to the door of the station, thanking me.

The dispatcher was cleaning her fingernails with an ivory-handled file. She glanced up eagerly.

"Did they catch him yet?"

"I was going to ask you the same question, Miss Brocco."

"No such luck. But they'll get him," she said with female vindictiveness. "The sheriff called out his air squadron, and he sent to Ventura for bloodhounds."

"Big deal."

She bridled. "What do you mean by that?"

"I don't think the old man of the mountain killed her. If he had, he wouldn't have waited till this morning to go on the lam. He'd have taken off right away."

"Then why did he go on the lam at all?" The word sounded strange in her prim mouth.

"I think he saw me discover the body, and realized he'd be blamed."

She considered this, bending the long nail file between her fingers. "If the old tramp didn't do it, who did?"

"You may be able to help me answer that question."

"Me help you? How?"

"You know Frank Connor, for one thing."

"I know him. I've seen him about my sister's grades a few times."

"You don't seem to like him much."

"I don't like him, I don't dislike him. He's just blah to me."

"Why? What's the matter with him?"

Her tight mouth quivered, and let out words: "*I* don't know what's the matter with him. He can't keep his hands off of young girls."

"How do you know that?"

"I heard it."

"From your sister Alice?"

"Yes. The rumor was going around the school, she said."

"Did the rumor involve Ginnie Green?"

She nodded. Her eyes were black as fingerprint ink.

"Is that why Connor's wife left him?"

"I wouldn't know about that. I never even laid eyes on Mrs. Connor."

"You haven't been missing much."

There was a yell outside, a kind of choked ululation. It sounded as much like an animal as a man. It was Green. When I reached the door, he was climbing out of his convertible with a heavy blue revolver in his hand.

"I saw the killer," he cried out exultantly.

"Where?"

He waved the revolver toward the lumberyard across the road. "He poked his head up behind that pile of white pine. When he saw me, he ran like a deer. I'm going to get him."

"No. Give me the gun."

"Why? I got a license to carry it. And use it."

He started across the four-lane highway, dodging through the moving patterns of the Sunday traffic as if he were playing parcheesi on the kitchen table at home. The sounds of brakes and curses split the air. He had scrambled over the locked gate of the yard before I got to it. I went over after him.

* * *

Green disappeared behind a pile of lumber. I turned the corner and saw him running halfway down a long aisle walled with stacked wood and floored with beaten earth. The old man of the mountain was running ahead of him. His white hair blew in the wind of his own movement. A burlap sack bounced on his shoulders like a load of sorrow and shame.

"Stop or I'll shoot!" Green cried.

The old man ran on as if the devil himself were after him. He came to a cyclone fence, discarded his sack, and tried to climb it. He almost got over. Three strands of barbed wire along the top of the fence caught and held him struggling.

I heard a tearing sound, and then the sound of a shot. The huge old body espaliered on the fence twitched and went limp, fell heavily to the earth. Green stood over him breathing through his teeth.

I pushed him out of the way. The old man was alive, though there was blood in his mouth. He spat it onto his chin when I lifted his head.

"You shouldn't ought to of done it. I come to turn myself in. Then I got ascairt."

"Why were you scared?"

"I watched you uncover the little girl in the leaves. I knew I'd be blamed. I'm one of the chosen. They always blame the chosen. I been in trouble before."

"Trouble with girls?" At my shoulder Green was grinning terribly.

"Trouble with cops."

"For killing people?" Green said.

"For preaching on the street without a license. The voice told me to preach to the tribes of the wicked. And the voice told me this morning to come in and give my testimony."

"What voice?"

"The great voice." His voice was little and weak. He coughed red.

"He's as crazy as a bedbug," Green said.

"Shut up." I turned back to the dying man. "What testimony do you have to give?"

"About the car I seen. It woke me up in the middle of the night, stopped in the road below my sanctuary."

"What kind of car?"

"I don't know cars. I think it was one of them foreign cars. It made a noise to wake the dead."

"Did you see who was driving it?"

"No. I didn't go near. I was ascairt."

"What time was this car in the road?"

"I don't keep track of time. The moon was down behind the trees."

Those were his final words. He looked up at the sky with his sky-colored eyes, straight into the sun. His eyes changed color.

Green said: "Don't tell them. If you do, I'll make a liar out of you. I'm a respected citizen in this town. I got a business to lose. And they'll believe me ahead of you, mister."

"Shut up."

He couldn't. "The old fellow was lying anyway. You know that. You heard him say yourself that he heard voices. That proves he's a psycho. He's a psycho killer. I shot him down like you would a mad dog, and I did right."

He waved the revolver.

"You did wrong, Green, and you know it. Give me that gun before it kills somebody else."

He thrust it into my hand suddenly. I unloaded it, breaking my fingernails in the process, and handed it back to him empty. He nudged up against me.

"Listen, maybe I did do wrong. I had provocation. It doesn't have to get out. I got a business to lose."

He fumbled in his hip pocket and brought out a thick sharkskin wallet. "Here. I can pay you good money. You say that you're a private eye; you know how to keep your lip buttoned."

I walked away and left him blabbering beside the body of the man he had killed. They were both victims, in a sense, but only one of them had blood on his hands.

Miss Brocco was in the HP parking lot. Her bosom was jumping with excitement.

"I heard a shot."

"Green shot the old man. Dead. You better send in for the meat wagon and call off your bloody dogs."

The words hit her like slaps. She raised her hand to her face, defensively. "Are you mad at me? Why are you mad at me?"

"I'm mad at everybody."

"You still don't think he did it."

"I know damned well he didn't. I want to talk to your sister."

"Alice? What for?"

"Information. She was on the beach with Ginnie Green last night. She may be able to tell me something."

"You leave Alice alone."

"I'll treat her gently. Where do you live?"

"I don't want my little sister dragged into this filthy mess."

"All I want to know is who Ginnie paired off with."

"I'll ask Alice. I'll tell you."

"Come on, Miss Brocco, we're wasting time. I don't need your permission to talk to your sister, after all. I can get the address out of the phone book if I have to."

She flared up and then flared down.

"You win. We live on Orlando Street, 224. That's on the other side of town. You will be nice to Alice, won't you? She's bothered enough as it is about Ginnie's death."

"She really was a friend of Ginnie's, then?"

"Yes. I tried to break it up. But you know how kids are—two motherless girls, they stick together. I tried to be like a mother to Alice."

"What happened to your own mother?"

"Father—I mean, she died." A greenish pallor invaded her face and turned it to old bronze. "Please. I don't want to talk about it. I was only a kid when she died."

She went back to her muttering radios. She was quite a woman, I thought as I drove away. Nubile but unmarried, probably full of un-tapped Mediterranean passions. If she worked an eight-hour shift and started at eight, she'd be getting off about four.

It wasn't a large town, and it wasn't far across it. The highway doubled as its main street. I passed the Union High School. On the green playing field beside it a lot of kids in mortarboards and gowns were rehearsing their graduation exercises. A kind of pall seemed to hang over the field. Perhaps it was in my mind.

Farther along the street I passed Green's Highway Restaurant. A dozen cars stood in its parking space. A couple of white-uniformed waitresses were scooting around behind the plate-glass windows.

Orlando Street was a lower-middle-class residential street bisected by the highway. Jacaranda trees bloomed like low small purple clouds among its stucco and frame cottages. Fallen purple petals carpeted the narrow lawn in front of the Brocco house.

A thin, dark man, wiry under his T-shirt, was washing a small red Fiat in the driveway beside the front porch. He must have been over fifty, but his long hair was as black as an Indian's. His Sicilian nose was humped in the middle by an old break.

"Mr. Brocco?"

"That's me."

"Is your daughter Alice home?"

"She's home."

"I'd like to speak to her."

He turned off his hose, pointing its dripping nozzle at me like a gun.

"You're a little old for her, ain't you?"

"I'm a detective investigating the death of Ginnie Green."

"Alice don't know nothing about that."

"I've just been talking to your older daughter at the Highway Patrol office. She thinks Alice may know something."

He shifted on his feet. "Well, if Anita says it's all right."

"It's okay, Dad," a girl said from the front door. "Anita just called me on the telephone. Come in, Mister—Archer isn't it?"

"Archer."

She opened the screen door for me. It opened directly into a small square living room containing worn green frieze furniture and a television set which the girl switched off. She was a handsome, serious-looking girl, a younger version of her sister with ten years and ten pounds subtracted and a pony tail added. She sat down gravely on the edge of the chair, waving her hand at the chesterfield. Her movements were languid. There were blue depressions under her eyes. Her face was sallow.

"What kind of questions do you want to ask me? My sister didn't say."

"Who was Ginnie with last night?"

"Nobody. I mean, she was with me. She didn't make out with any of the boys." She glanced from me to the blind television set, as if she felt caught between. "It said on the television that she was with a man, that there was medical evidence to prove it. But I didn't see her with no man. Any man."

"Did Ginnie go with men?"

She shook her head. Her pony tail switched and hung limp. She was close to tears.

"You told Anita she did."

"I did not!"

"Your sister wouldn't lie. You passed on a rumor to her—a high school rumor that Ginnie had had something to do with one man in particular."

The girl was watching my face in fascination. Her eyes were like a bird's, bright and shallow and fearful.

"Was the rumor true?"

She shrugged her thin shoulders. "How would I know?"

"You were good friends with Ginnie."

"Yes. I was." Her voice broke on the past tense. "She was a real nice kid, even if she was kind of boy crazy."

"She was boy crazy, but she didn't make out with any of the boys last night."

"Not while I was there."

"Did she make out with Mr. Connor?"

"No. He wasn't there. He said he was going home. He lives up the beach."

"What did Ginnie do?"

"I don't know. I didn't notice."

"You said she was with you. Was she with you all evening?"

"Yes." Her face was agonized. "I mean no."

"Did Ginnie go away, too?"

She nodded.

"In the same direction Mr. Connor took? The direction of his house?"

Her head moved almost imperceptibly downward.

"What time was that, Alice?"

"About eleven o'clock, I guess."

"And Ginnie never came back from Mr. Connor's house?"

"I don't know. I don't know for certain that she went there."

"But Ginnie and Mr. Connor were good friends?"

"I guess so."

"How good? Like a boy friend and a girl friend?"

She sat mute, her birdlike stare unblinking.

"Tell me, Alice."

"Afraid of Mr. Connor?"

"No. Not him."

"Has someone threatened you—told you not to talk?"

Her head moved in another barely perceptible nod.

"Who threatened you, Alice? You'd better tell me for your own protection. Whoever did threaten you is probably a murderer."

She burst into frantic tears. Brocco came to the door.

"What goes on in here?"

"Your daughter is upset. I'm sorry."

"Yeah, and I know who upset her. You better get out of here or you'll be sorrier."

He opened the screen door and held it open, his head poised like a dark and broken ax. I went out past him. He spat after me. The Broccos were a very emotional family.

I started back toward Connor's beach house on the south side of town but ran into a diversion on the way. Green's car was parked in the lot beside his restaurant. I went in.

The place smelled of grease. It was almost full of late Sunday lunchers seated in booths and at the U-shaped breakfast bar in the middle. Green himself was sitting on a stool behind the cash register counting money. He was counting it as if his life and his hope of heaven depended on the colored paper in his hands.

He looked up, smiling loosely and vaguely. "Yes, sir?" Then he recognized me. His face went through a quick series of transformations and settled for a kind of boozy shame. "I know I shouldn't be here working on a day like this. But it keeps my mind off my troubles. Besides, they steal you blind if you don't watch 'em. And I'll be needing the money."

"What for, Mr. Green?"

"The trial." He spoke the word as if it gave him a bitter satisfaction.

"Whose trial?"

"Mine. I told the sheriff what the old guy said. And what I did. I know what I did. I shot him down like a dog, and I had no right to. I was crazy with my sorrow, you might say."

He was less crazy now. The shame in his eyes was clearing. But the sorrow was still there in their depths, like stone at the bottom of a well.

"I'm glad you told the truth, Mr. Green."

"So am I. It doesn't help him, and it doesn't bring Ginnie back. But at least I can live with myself."

"Speaking of Ginnie," I said. "Was she seeing quite a lot of Frank Connor?"

"Yeah. I guess you could say so. He came over to help her with her studies quite a few times. At the house, and at the library. He didn't charge me any tuition, either."

"That was nice of him. Was Ginnie fond of Connor?"

"Sure she was. She thought very highly of Mr. Connor."

"Was she in love with him?"

"In love? Hell, I never thought of anything like that. Why?"

"Did she have dates with Connor?"

"Not to my knowledge," he said. "If she did, she must done it behind my back." His eyes narrowed to two red swollen slits. "You think Frank Connor had something to do with her death?"

"It's a possibility. Don't go into a sweat now. You know where that gets you."

"Don't worry. But what about this Connor? Did you get something on him? I thought he was acting queer last night."

"Queer in what way?"

"Well, he was pretty tight when he came to the house. I gave him a stiff snort, and that straightened him out for a while. But later on, down on the beach, he got almost hysterical. He was running around like a rooster with his head chopped off.''

"Is he a heavy drinker?''

"I wouldn't know. I never saw him drink before last night at my house.'' Green narrowed his eyes. "But he tossed down a triple bourbon like it was water. And remember this morning, he offered us a drink on the beach. A drink in the morning, that isn't the usual thing, especially for a high school teacher.''

"I noticed that.''

"What else have you been noticing?''

"We won't go into it now,'' I said. "I don't want to ruin a man unless and until I'm sure he's got it coming.''

He sat on his stool with his head down. Thought moved murkily under his knitted brows. His glance fell on the money in his hands. He was counting tens.

"Listen, Mr. Archer. You're working on this case on your own, aren't you? For free?''

"So far.''

"So go to work for me. Nail Connor for me, and I'll pay you whatever you ask.''

"Not so fast,'' I said. "We don't know that Connor is guilty. There are other possibilities.''

"Such as?''

"If I tell you, can I trust you not to go on a shooting spree?''

"Don't worry,'' he repeated. "I've had that.''

"Where's your revolver?''

"I turned it in to Sheriff Pearsall. He asked for it.''

We were interrupted by a family group getting up from one of the booths. They gave Green their money and their sympathy. When they were out of hearing, I said:

"You mentioned that your daughter worked here in the restaurant for a while. Was Al Brocco working here at the same time?''

"Yeah. He's been my night cook for six-seven years. Al is a darned good cook. He trained as a chef on the Italian line.'' His slow mind, punchy with grief, did a double-take. "You wouldn't be saying that he messed around with Ginnie?''

"I'm asking you.''

"Shucks, Al is old enough to be her father. He's all wrapped up in his own girls, Anita in particular. He worships the ground she walks on. She's the mainspring of that family.''

"How did he get on with Ginnie?"

"Very well. They kidded back and forth. She was the only one who could ever make him smile. Al is a sad man, you know. He had a tragedy in his life."

"His wife's death?"

"It was worse than that," Green said. "Al Brocco killed his wife with his own hand. He caught her with another man and put a knife in her."

"And he's walking around loose?"

"The other man was a Mex," Green said in an explanatory way. "A wetback. He couldn't even talk the English language. The town hardly blamed Al, the jury gave him manslaughter. But when he got out of the pen, the people at the Pink Flamingo wouldn't give him his old job back—he used to be chef there. So I took him on. I felt sorry for his girls, I guess, and Al's been a good worker. A man doesn't do a thing like that twice, you know."

He did another slow mental double-take. His mouth hung open. I could see the gold in its corners.

"Let's hope not."

"Listen here," he said. "You go to work for me, eh? You nail the guy, whoever he is. I'll pay you. I'll pay you now. How much do you want?"

I took a hundred dollars of his money and left him trying to comfort himself with the rest of it. The smell of grease stayed in my nostrils.

Connor's house clung to the edge of a low bluff about halfway between the HP station and the mouth of the canyon where the thing had begun: a semi-cantilevered redwood cottage with a closed double garage fronting the highway. From the grapestake-fenced patio in the angle between the garage and the front door a flight of wooden steps climbed to the flat roof which was railed as a sun deck. A second set of steps descended the fifteen or twenty feet to the beach.

I tripped on a pair of garden shears crossing the patio to the garage window. I peered into the interior twilight. Two things inside interested me: a dismasted flattie sitting on a trailer, and a car. The sailboat interested me because its cordage resembled the white rope that had strangled Ginnie. The car interested me because it was an imported model, a low-slung Triumph two-seater.

I was planning to have a closer look at it when a woman's voice screeked overhead like a gull's:

"What do you think you're doing?"

Mrs. Connor was leaning over the railing on the roof. Her hair was in curlers. She looked like a blonde Gorgon. I smiled up at her, the way that Greek whose name I don't remember must have smiled.

"Your husband invited me for a drink, remember? I don't know whether he gave me a rain check or not."

"He did not! Go away! My husband is sleeping!"

"Ssh. You'll wake him up. You'll wake up the people in Forest Lawn."

She put her hand to her mouth. From the expression on her face she seemed to be biting her hand. She disappeared for a moment, and then came down the steps with a multi-colored silk scarf over her curlers. The rest of her was sheathed in a white satin bathing suit. Against it her flesh looked like brown wood.

"You get out of here," she said. "Or I shall call the police."

"Fine. Call them. I've got nothing to hide."

"Are you implying that we have?"

"We'll see. Why did you leave your husband?"

"That's none of your business."

"I'm making it my business, Mrs. Connor. I'm a detective investigating the murder of Ginnie Green. Did you leave Frank on account of Ginnie Green?"

"No. No! I wasn't even aware—" Her hand went to her mouth again. She chewed on it some more.

"You weren't aware that Frank was having an affair with Ginnie Green?"

"He wasn't."

"So you say. Others say different."

"What others? Anita Brocco? You can't believe anything *that* woman says. Why, her own father is a murderer, everybody in town knows that."

"Your own husband may be another, Mrs. Connor. You might as well come clean with me."

"But I have nothing to tell you."

"You can tell me why you left him."

"That is a private matter, between Frank and me. It has nothing to do with anybody but us." She was calming down, setting her moral forces in a stubborn, defensive posture.

"There's usually only the one reason."

"I had my reasons. I said they were none of your business. I chose for reasons of my own to spend a month with my parents in Long Beach."

"When did you come back?"

"This morning."

"Frank called me. He said he needed me." She touched her thin breast absently, pathetically, as if perhaps she hadn't been much needed in the past.

"Needed you for what?"

"As his wife," she said. "He said there might be tr—" Her hand went to her mouth again. She said around it: "Trouble."

"Did he name the kind of trouble?"

"No."

"What time did he call you?"

"Very early, around seven o'clock."

"That was more than an hour before I found Ginnie's body."

"He knew she was missing. He spent the whole night looking for her."

"Why would he do that, Mrs. Connor?"

"She was his student. He was fond of her. Besides, he was more or less responsible for her."

"Responsible for her death?"

"How dare you say a thing like that!"

"If he dared to do it, I can dare to say it."

"He didn't!" she cried. "Frank is a good man. He may have his faults, but he wouldn't kill anyone. I know him."

"What are his faults?"

"We won't discuss them."

"Then may I have a look in your garage?"

"What for? What are you looking for?"

"I'll know when I find it." I turned toward the garage door.

"You mustn't go in there," she said intensely. "Not without Frank's permission."

"Wake him up and we'll get his permission."

"I will not. He got no sleep last night."

"Then I'll just have a look without his permission."

"I'll kill you if you go in there."

She picked up the garden shears and brandished them at me—a sick-looking lioness defending her overgrown cub. The cub himself opened the front door of the cottage. He slouched in the doorway groggily, naked except for white shorts.

"What goes on, Stella?"

"This man has been making the most horrible accusations."

His blurred glance wavered between us and focused on her. "What did he say?"

"I won't repeat it."

"I will, Mr. Connor. I think you were Ginnie Green's lover, if that's the word. I think she followed you to this house last night, around midnight. I think she left it with a rope around her neck."

Connor's head jerked. He started to make a move in my direction. Something inhibited it, like an invisible leash. His body slanted toward me, static, all the muscles taut. It resembled an anatomy specimen with the skin off. Even his face seemed bone and teeth.

I hoped he'd swing on me and let me hit him. He didn't. Stella Connor dropped the garden shears. They made a noise like the dull clank of doom.

"Aren't you going to deny it, Frank?"

"I didn't kill her. I swear I didn't. I admit that we—that we were together last night, Ginnie and I."

"Ginnie and I?" the woman repeated incredulously.

His head hung down. "I'm sorry, Stella. I didn't want to hurt you more than I have already. But it has to come out. I took up with the girl after you left. I was lonely and feeling sorry for myself. Ginnie kept hanging around. One night I drank too much and let it happen. It happened more than once. I was so flattered that a pretty young girl—"

"You fool!" she said in a deep, harsh voice.

"Yes, I'm a moral fool. That's no surprise to you, is it?"

"I thought you respected your pupils, at least. You mean to say you brought her into our own house, into our own bed?"

"You'd left. It wasn't ours any more. Besides, she came of her own accord. She wanted to come. She loved me."

She said with grinding contempt: "You poor, groveling ninny. And to think you had the gall to ask me to come back here, to make you look respectable."

I cut in between them. "Was she here last night, Connor?"

"She was here. I didn't invite her. I wanted her to come, but I dreaded it, too. I knew that I was taking an awful chance. I drank quite a bit to numb my conscience—"

"What conscience?" Stella Connor said.

"I have a conscience," he said without looking at her. "You don't know the hell I've been going through. After she came, after it happened last night, I drank myself unconscious."

"Do you mean after you killed her?" I said.

"I didn't kill her. When I passed out, she was perfectly all right. She was sitting up drinking a cup of instant coffee. The next thing I knew, hours later, her father was on the telephone and she was gone."

"Are you trying to pull the old blackout alibi? You'll have to do better than that."

"I can't. It's the truth."

"Let me into your garage."

He seemed almost glad to be given an order, a chance for some activity. The garage wasn't locked. He raised the overhead door and let the daylight into the interior. It smelled of paint. There were empty cans of marine paint on a bench beside the sailboat. Its hull gleamed virgin white.

"I painted my flattie last week," he said inconsequentially.

"You do a lot of sailing?"

"I used to. Not much lately."

"No," his wife said from the doorway. "Frank changed his hobby to women. Wine and women."

"Lay off, eh?" His voice was pleading.

She looked at him from a great and stony silence.

I walked around the boat, examining the cordage. The starboard jib line had been sheared off short. Comparing it with the port line, I found that the missing piece was approximately a yard long. That was the length of the piece of white rope that I was interested in.

"Hey!" Connor grabbed the end of the cut line. He fingered it as if it was a wound in his own flesh. "Who's been messing with my lines? Did you cut it, Stella?"

"I never go near your blessed boat," she said.

"I can tell you where the rest of that line is, Connor. A line of similar length and color and thickness was wrapped around Ginnie Green's neck when I found her."

"Surely you don't believe I put it there?"

I tried to, but I couldn't. Small-boat sailers don't cut their jib lines, even when they're contemplating murder. And while Connor was clearly no genius, he was smart enough to have known that the line could easily be traced to him. Perhaps someone else had been equally smart.

I turned to Mrs. Connor. She was standing in the doorway with her legs apart. Her body was almost black against the daylight. Her eyes were hooded by the scarf on her head.

"What time did you get home, Mrs. Connor?"

"About ten o'clock this morning. I took a bus as soon as my husband called. But I'm in no position to give him an alibi."

"An alibi wasn't what I had in mind. I suggest another possibility, that you came home twice. You came home unexpectedly last night, saw the girl in the house with your husband, waited in the dark till the girl came out, waited with a piece of rope in your hands—a piece of rope you'd cut from your husband's boat in the hope of getting him punished for what he'd done to you. But the picture doesn't fit the frame, Mrs. Connor. A sailor like your husband wouldn't cut a piece of line from his own boat. And even in the heat of murder he wouldn't tie a granny's knot. His fingers would automatically tie a reef knot. That isn't true of a woman's fingers."

She held herself upright with one long, rigid arm against the doorframe.

"I wouldn't do anything like that. I wouldn't do that to Frank."

"Maybe you wouldn't in daylight, Mrs. Connor. Things have different shapes at midnight."

"And hell hath no fury like a woman scorned? Is that what you're thinking? You're wrong. I wasn't here last night. I was in bed in my father's house in Long Beach. I didn't even know about that girl and Frank."

"Then why did you leave him?"

"He was in love with another woman. He wanted to divorce me and marry her. But he was afraid—afraid that it would affect his position in town. He told me on the phone this morning that it was all over with the other woman. So I agreed to come back to him." Her arm dropped to her side.

"He said that it was all over with Ginnie?"

Possibilities were racing through my mind. There was the possibility that Connor had been playing reverse English, deliberately and clumsily framing himself in order to be cleared. But that was out of far left field.

"Not Ginnie," his wife said. "The other woman was Anita Brocco. He met her last spring in the course of work and fell in love—what *he* calls love. My husband is a foolish, fickle man."

"Please, Stella. I said it was all over between me and Anita, and it is."

She turned on him in quiet savagery. "What does it matter now? If it isn't one girl it's another. Any kind of female flesh will do to poultice your sick little ego."

Her cruelty struck inward and hurt her. She stretched out her hand toward him. Suddenly her eyes were blind with tears.

"Any flesh but mine, Frank," she said brokenly.

Connor paid no attention to his wife.

He said to me in a hushed voice:

"My God, I never thought. I noticed her car last night when I was walking home along the beach."

"Whose car?"

"Anita's red Fiat. It was parked at the viewpoint a few hundred yards from here." He gestured vaguely toward town. "Later, when Ginnie was with me, I thought I heard someone in the garage. But I was too drunk to make a search." His eyes burned into mine. "You say a woman tied that knot?"

"All we can do is ask her."

We started toward my car together. His wife called after him:

"Don't go, Frank. Let him handle it."

He hesitated, a weak man caught between opposing forces.

"I need you," she said. "We need each other."

I pushed him in her direction.

It was nearly four when I got to the HP station. The patrol cars had gathered like homing pigeons for the change in shift. Their uniformed drivers were talking and laughing inside.

Anita Brocco wasn't among them. A male dispatcher, a fat-faced man with pimples, had taken her place behind the counter.

"Where's Miss Brocco?" I asked.

"In the ladies' room. Her father is coming to pick her up any minute."

She came out wearing lipstick and a light beige coat. Her face turned beige when she saw my face. She came toward me in slow motion, leaned with both hands flat on the counter. Her lipstick looked like fresh blood on a corpse.

"You're a handsome woman, Anita. Too bad about you."

"Too bad." It was half a statement and half a question. She looked down at her hands.

"Your fingernails are clean now. They were dirty this morning. You were digging in the dirt last night, weren't you?"

"No."

"You were, though. You saw them together and you couldn't stand it. You waited in ambush with a rope, and put it around her neck. Around your own neck, too."

She touched her neck. The talk and laughter had subsided around us. I could hear the tick of the clock again, and the muttering signals coming in from inner space.

"What did you use to cut the rope with, Anita? The garden shears?"

Her red mouth groped for words and found them. "I was crazy about him. She took him away. It was all over before it started. I didn't know what to do with myself. I wanted him to suffer."

"He suffering. He's going to suffer more."

"He deserved to. He was the only man—" She shrugged in a twisted way and looked down at her breast. "I didn't want to kill her, but when I saw them together—I saw them through the window. I saw her take off her clothes and put them on. Then I thought of the night my father— when he—when there was all the blood in Mother's bed. I had to wash it out of the sheets."

The men around me were murmuring. One of them, a sergeant, raised his voice.

"Did you kill Ginnie Green?"

"Yes."

"Are you ready to make a statement?" I said.

"Yes. I'll talk to Sheriff Pearsall. I don't want to talk here, in front of my friends." She looked around doubtfully.

"I'll take you downtown."

"Wait a minute." She glanced once more at her empty hands. "I left my purse in the—in the back room. I'll go and get it."

She crossed the office like a zombie, opened a plain door, closed it behind her. She didn't come out. After a while we broke the lock and went in after her.

Her body was cramped on the narrow floor. The ivory-handled nail file lay by her right hand. There were bloody holes in her white blouse and in the white breast under it. One of them had gone as deep as her heart.

Later Al Brocco drove up in her red Fiat and came into the station.

"I'm a little late," he said to the room in general. "Anita wanted me to give her car a good cleaning. Where is she, anyway?"

The sergeant cleared his throat to answer Brocco.

All us poor creatures, as the old man of the mountain had said that morning.

Father Brown

THE SIGN OF THE BROKEN SWORD

G. K. Chesterton

THE THOUSAND ARMS of the forest were gray, and its million fingers silver. In a sky of dark green-blue-like slate the stars were bleak and brilliant like splintered ice. All htat thickly wooded and sparsely tenanted countryside was stiff with a bitter and brittle frost. The black hollows between the trunks of the trees looked like bottomless, black caverns of that Scandinavian hell, a hell of incalculable cold. Even the square stone tower of the church looked northern to the point of heathenry, as if it were some barbaric tower among the sea rocks of Iceland. It was a queer night for anyone to explore a churchyard. But, on the other hand, perhaps it was worth exploring.

It rose abruptly out of the ashen wastes of forest in a sort of hump or shoulder of green turf that looked gray in the starlight. Most of the graves were on a slant, and the path leading up to the church was as steep as a staircase. On the top of the hill, in the one flat and prominent place, was the monument for which the place was famous. It contrasted strangely with the featureless graves all round, for it was the work of one of the greatest sculptors of modern Europe; and yet his fame was at once forgotten in the fame of the man whose image he had made. It showed, by touches of the small silver pencil of starlight, the massive metal figure of a soldier recumbent, the strong hands sealed in an everlasting worship, the great head pillowed upon a gun. The venerable face was bearded, or rather whiskered, in the old, heavy Colonel Newcome fashion. The uniform, though suggested with the few strokes of simplicity, was that of modern war. By his right side lay a sword, of which the tip was broken off; on the left side lay a Bible. On glowing summer afternoons wagonettes came full of Americans and cultured suburbans to see the sepulchre; but even then they felt the vast forest land with its one dumpy dome of churchyard and church as a place oddly dumb and neglected. In this freezing darkness of mid-winter one would think he might be left alone with the stars. Nevertheless, in the stillness of those stiff woods a wooden gate creaked, and two dim figures dressed in black climbed up the little path to the tomb.

So faint was that frigid starlight that nothing could have been traced about them except that while they both wore black, one man was enormously big, and the other (perhaps by contrast) almost startlingly small. They went up to the great graven tomb of the historic warrior, and stood for a few minutes staring at it. There was no human, perhaps no living, thing for a wide circle; and a morbid fancy might well have wondered if they were human themselves. In any case, the beginning of their conversation might have seemed strange. After the first silence the small man said to the other:

"Where does a wise man hide a pebble?"

And the tall man answered in a low voice: "On the beach."

The small man nodded, and after a short silence said: "Where does a wise man hide a leaf?"

And the other answered: "In the forest."

There was another stillness, and then the tall man resumed: "Do you mean that when a wise man has to hide a real diamond he has been known to hide it among sham ones?"

"No, no," said the little man with a laugh, "we will let bygones be bygones."

He stamped his cold feet for a second or two, and then said: "I'm not thinking of that at all, but of something else; something rather peculiar. Just strike a match, will you?"

The big man fumbled in his pocket, and soon a scratch and a flare painted gold the whole flat side of the monument. On it was cut in black letters the well-known words which so many Americans had reverently read: "Sacred to the Memory of General Sir Arthur St. Clare, Hero and Martyr, who Always Vanquished his Enemies and Always Spared Them, and Was Treacherously Slain by Them At Last. May God in Whom he Trusted both Reward and Revenge him."

The match burnt the big man's fingers, blackened, and dropped. He was about to strike another, but his small companion stopped him. "That's all right, Flambeau, old man; I saw what I wanted. Or, rather, I didn't see what I didn't want. And now we must walk a mile and a half along the road to the next inn, and I will try to tell you all about it. For

Heaven knows a man should have a fire and ale when he dares tell such a story.''

They descended the precipitous path, they relatched the rusty gate, and set off at a stamping, ringing walk down the frozen forest road. They had gone a full quarter of a mile before the smaller man spoke again. He said: ''Yes; the wise man hides a pebble on the beach. But what does he do if there is no beach? Do you know anything of that great St. Clare trouble?''

''I know nothing about English generals, Father Brown,'' answered the large man, laughing, ''though a little about English policemen. I only know that you have dragged me a precious long distance to all the shrines of this fellow, whoever he is. One would think he got buried in six different places. I've seen a memorial to General St. Clare in Westminster Abbey. I've seen a ramping equestrian statue of General St. Clare on the Embankment. I've seen a medallion of St. Clare in the street he was born in, and another in the street he lived in; and now you drag me after dark to his coffin in the village churchyard. I am beginning to be a bit tired of his magnificent personality, especially as I don't in the least know who he was. What are you hunting for in all these crypts and effigies?''

''I am only looking for one word,'' said Father Brown. ''A word that isn't there.''

''Well,'' asked Flambeau; ''are you going to tell me anything about it?''

''I must divide it into two parts,'' remarked the priest. ''First there is what everybody knows; and then there is what I know. Now, what everybody knows is short and plain enough. It is also entirely wrong.''

''Right you are,'' said the big man called Flambeau cheerfully. ''Let's begin at the wrong end. Let's begin with what everybody knows, which isn't true.''

''If not wholly untrue, it is at least very inadequate,'' continued Brown; ''for in point of fact, all that the public knows amounts precisely to this: The public knows that Arthur St. Clare was a great and successful English general. It knows that after splendid yet careful campaigns both in India and Africa he was in command against Brazil when the great Brazilian patriot Olivier issued his ultimatum. It knows that on that occasion St. Clare with a very small force attacked Olivier with a very large one, and was captured after heroic resistance. And it knows that after his capture, and to the abhorrence of the civilized world, St. Clare was hanged on the nearest tree. He was found swinging there after the Brazilians had retired, with his broken sword hung round his neck.''

"And that popular story is untrue?" suggested Flambeau.

"No," said his friend quietly, "that story is quite true, so far as it goes."

"Well, I think it goes far enough!" said Flambeau; "but if the popular story is true, what is the mystery?"

They had passed many hundreds of gray and ghostly trees before the little priest answered. Then he bit his finger reflectively and said: "Why, the mystery is a mystery of psychology. Or, rather, it is a mystery of two psychologies. In that Brazilian business two of the most famous men of modern history acted flat against their characters. Mind you, Olivier and St. Clare were both heroes—the old thing, and no mistake; it was like the fight between Hector and Achilles. Now, what would you say to an affair in which Achilles was timid and Hector was treacherous?"

"Go on," said the large man impatiently as the other bit his finger again.

"Sir Arthur St. Clare was a soldier of the old religious type—the type that saved us during the Mutiny," continued Brown. "He was always more for duty than for dash; and with all his personal courage was decidedly a prudent commander, particularly indignant at any needless waste of soldiers. Yet in this last battle he attempted something that a baby could see was absurd. One need not be a strategist to see it was as wild as wind; just as one need not be a strategist to keep out the way of a motor-bus. Well, that is the first mystery; what had become of the English general's head? The second riddle is what had become of the Brazilian general's heart? President Olivier might be called a visionary or a nuisance; but even his enemies admitted that he was magnanimous to the point of knight errantry. Almost every other prisoner he had ever captured had been set free or even loaded with benefits. Men who had really wronged him came away touched by his simplicity and sweetness. Why the deuce should he diabolically revenge himself only once in his life; and that for the one particular blow that could not have hurt him? Well, there you have it. One of the wisest men in the world acted like an idiot for no reason. One of the best men in the world acted like a fiend for no reason, That's the long and the short of it; and I leave it to you, my boy."

"No, you don't," said the other with a snort. "I leave it to you; and you jolly well tell me all about it."

"Well," resumed Father Brown, "It's not fair to say that the public impression is just what I've said, without adding that two things have happened since. I can't say they threw a new light; for nobody can make sense of them. But they threw a new kind of darkness; they threw the darkness in new directions. The first was this. The family physician of the St. Clares quarrelled with that family, and began publishing a violent series of articles, in which he said that the late general was a religious maniac; but as far as the tale went, this semed to mean little more than a religious man. Anyhow, the story fizzled out. Eveyone knew, of course, that St. Clare had some of the eccentricities of puritan piety. The second incident was much more arresting. In the luckless and unsupported regiment which made that rash attempt at the Black River there was a certain Captain Keith, who was at that time engaged to St. Clare's daughter, and who afterwards married her. He was one of those who were captured by Olivier, and, like all the rest except the general, appears to have been bounteously treated and promptly set free. Some twenty years afterwards this man, then Lieutenant-Colonel Keith, published a sort of autobiography called 'A British Officer in Burmah and Brazil.' In the place where the reader looks eagerly for some account of the mystery of St. Clare's disaster may be found the following words: 'Everywhere else in this book I have narrated things exactly as they occurred, holding as I do the old-fashioned opinion that the glory of England is old enough to take care of itself. The exception I shall make is in this matter of the defeat by the Black River; and my reasons, though private, are honorable and compelling. I will, however, add this in justice to the memories of two distinguished men. General St. Clare has been accused of incapacity on this occasion; I can at least testify that this action, properly understood, was one of the most brilliant and sagacious of his life. President Olivier by similar report is charged with savage injustice. I think it due to the honor of an enemy to say that he acted on this occasion with even more than his characteristic good feeling. To put the matter popularly, I can assure my countrymen that St. Clare was by no means such a fool nor Olivier such a brute as he looked. This is all I have to say; nor shall any earthly consideration induce me to add a word to it.' "

A large frozen moon like a lustrous snowball began to show through the tangle of twigs in front of them, and by its light the narrator had been able to refresh his memory of Captain Keith's text from a scrap of printed paper. As he folded it up and put it back in his pocket Flambeau threw up his hand with a French gesture.

"Wait a bit, wait a bit," he cried excitedly. "I believe I can guess it at the first go."

He strode on, breathing hard, his black head and bull neck forward, like a man winning a walking race. The little priest, amused and interested, had some trouble in trotting beside him. Just before them the trees fell back a little to left and right, and the road swept downwards across a clear, moonlit valley, till it dived again like a rabbit into the wall of another wood. The entrance to the farther forest looked small and round, like that black hole of a remote railway tunnel. But it was within some hundred yards, and gaped like a cavern before Flambeau spoke again.

"I've got it," he cried at last, slapping his thigh with his great hand. "Four minutes' thinking, and I can tell your whole story myself."

"All right," assented his friend. "You tell it."

Flambeau lifted his head, but lowered his voice. "General Sir Arthur St. Clare," he said, "came of a family in which madness was hereditary; and his whole aim was to keep this from his daughter, and even, if possible, from his future son-in-law. Rightly or wrongly, he thought the final collapse was close, and resolved on suicide. Yet ordinary suicide would blazon the very idea he dreaded. As the campaign approached the clouds came thicker on his brain; and at last in a mad moment he sacrificed his public duty to his private. He rushed rashly into battle, hoping to fall by the first shot. When he found that he had only attained capture and discredit, the sealed bomb in his brain burst, and he broke his own sword and hanged himself."

He stared firmly at the gray façade of forest in front of him, with the one black gap in it, like the mouth of the grave, into which their path plunged. Perhaps something menacing in the road thus suddenly swallowed reinforced his vivid vision of the tragedy, for he shuddered.

"A horrid story," he said.

"A horrid story," repeated the priest with bent head. "But not the real story."

Then he threw back his head with a sort of despair and cried: "Oh, I wish it had been."

The tall Flambeau faced round and stared at him.

"Yours is a clean story," cried Father Brown, deeply moved. "A sweet, pure, honest story, as open and white as that moon. Madness and despair are innocent enough. There are worse things, Flambeau."

Flambeau looked up wildly at the moon thus invoked; and from where he stood one black tree-bough curved across it exactly like a devil's horn.

"Father—father," cried Flambeau with the French gesture and stepping yet more rapidly forward, "do you mean it was worse than that?"

"Worse than that," said the priest like a grave echo. And they plunged into the black cloister of the woodland, which ran by them in a dim tapestry of trunks, like one of the dark corridors in a dream.

They were soon in the most secret entrails of the wood, and felt close about them foliage that they could not see, when the priest said again:

"Where does a wise man hide a leaf? In the forest. But what does he do if there is no forest?"

"Well, well, " cried Flambeau irritably, "what does he do?"

"He grows a forest to hide it in," said the priest in an obscure voice. "A fearful sin."

"Look here," cried his friend impatiently, for the dark wood and the dark saying got a little on his nerves; "will you tell me this story or not? What other evidence is there to go on?"

"There are three more bits of evidence," said the other, "that I have dug up in holes and corners; and I will give them in logical rather than chronological order. First of all, of course, our authority for the issue and event of the battle is in Olivier's own dispatches, which are lucid enough. He was entrenched with two or three regiments on the heights that swept down to the Black River, on the other side of which was lower and more marshy ground. Beyond this again was gently rising country, on which was the first English outpost, supported by others which lay, however, considerably in its rear. The British forces as a whole were greatly superior in numbers; but this particular regiment was just far enough from its base to make Olivier consider the project of crossing the river to cut it off. By sunset, however, he had decided to retain his own position, which was a specially strong one. At daybreak next morning he was thunderstruck to see that this stray handful of English, entirely unsupported from their rear, had flung themselves across the river, half by a bridge to the right, and the other half by a ford higher up, and were massed upon the marshy bank below him.

"That they should attempt an attack with such numbers against such a position was incredible enough; but Olivier noticed something yet more extraordinary. For instead of attempting to seize more solid ground, this mad regiment, having put the river in its rear by one wild charge, did nothing more, but stuck there in the mire like flies in treacle. Needless to say, the Brazilians blew great gaps in them with artillery, which they could only return with spirited but lessening rifle fire. Yet they never broke; and Olivier's curt account ends with a strong tribute of admiration for the mystic valor of these imbeciles. 'Our line then advanced finally,' writes Olivier, 'and drove them into the river; we captured General St. Clare himself and several other officers. The colonel and the major had both fallen in the battle. I cannot resist saying that few finer sights can have been seen in history than the last stand of this extraordinary regiment; wounded officers picking up the rifles of dead soldiers, and the general himself facing us on horseback bareheaded and with a broken sword.' On what happened to the general afterwards Olivier is as silent as Captain Keith.''

''Well,'' grunted Flambeau, ''get on to the next bit of evidence.''

''The next evidence,'' said Father Brown, ''took some time to find, but it will not take long to tell. I found at last in an almshouse down in the Lincolnshire Fens an old soldier who not only was wounded at the Black River, but had actually knelt beside the colonel of the regiment when he died. This latter was a certain Colonel Clancy, a big bull of an Irishman; and it would seem that he died almost as much of rage as of bullets. He, at any rate, was not responsible for that ridiculous raid; it must have been imposed on him by the general. His last edifying words, according to my informant, were these: 'And there goes the damned old donkey with the end of his sword knocked off. I wish it was his head.' You will remark that everyone seems to have noticed this detail about the broken sword blade, though most people regard it somewhat more reverently than did the late Colonel Clancy. And now for the third fragment.''

Their path through the woodland began to go upward, and the speaker paused a little for breath before he went on. Then he continued in the same business-like tone:

''Only a month or two ago a certain Brazilian official died in England, having quarrelled with Olivier and left his country. He was a well-known figure both here and on the Continent, a Spaniard named Espado; I knew him myself, a yellow-faced old dandy, with a hooked nose. For various private reasons I had permission to see the documents he had left; he was a Catholic, of course, and I had been with him towards the end. There was nothing of his that lit up any corner of the black St. Clare business, except five or six common exercise books filled with the diary of some English soldier. I can only suppose that it was found by the Brazilians on one of those that fell. Anyhow, it stopped abruptly the night before the battle.

''But the account of that last day in the poor fellow's life was certainly worth reading. I have it on me; but it's too dark to read it here, and I will give you a résumé. The first part of that entry is full of jokes, evidently flung about among the men, about somebody called the Vulture. It does not seem as if this person, whoever he was, was one of themselves, nor even an Englishman; neither is he exactly spoken of as one of the enemy.

It sounds rather as if he were some local go-between and non-combatant; perhaps a guide or a journalist. He has been closeted with old colonel Clancy; but is more often seen talking to the major. Indeed, the major is somewhat prominent in this soldier's narrative; a lean, dark-haired man, apparently, of the name of Murray—a north of Ireland man and a Puritan. There are continual jests about the contrast between this Ulsterman's austerity and the conviviality of Colonel Clancy. There is also some joke about the Vulture wearing bright-colored clothes.

"But all these levities are scattered by what may well be called the note of a bugle. Behind the English camp and almost parallel to the river ran one of the few great roads of that district. Westward the road curved round towards the river, which it crossed by the bridge before mentioned. To the east the road swept backwards into the wilds, and some two miles along it was the next English outpost. From this direction there came along the road that evening a glitter and clatter of light cavalry, in which even the simple diarist could recognize with astonishment the general with his staff. He rode the great white horse which you have seen so often in illustrated papers and Academy pictures; and you may be sure that the salute they gave him was not merely ceremonial. He, at least, wasted no time on ceremony, but, springing from the saddle immediately, mixed with the group of officers, and fell into emphatic though confidential speech. What struck our friend the diarist most was his special disposition to discuss matters with Major Murray; but, indeed, such a selection, so long as it was not marked, was in no way unnatural. The two men were made for sympathy; they were men who 'read their Bibles'; they were both the old Evangelical type of officer. However this may be, it is certain that when the general mounted again he was still talking earnestly to Murray; and that as he walked his horse slowly down the road towards the river, the tall Ulsterman still walked by his bridle rein in earnest debate. The soldiers watched the two until they vanished behind a clump of trees where the road turned towards the river. The colonel had gone back to his tent, and the men to their pickets; the man with the diary lingered for another four minutes, and saw a marvellous sight.

"The great white horse which had marched slowly down the road as it had marched in so many processions, flew back, galloping up the road towards them as if it were mad to win a race. At first they thought it had run away with the man on its back; but they soon saw that the general, a fine rider, was himself urging it to full speed. Horse and man swept up to them like a whirlwind; and then, reining up the reeling charge, the general turned on them a face like flame, and called for the colonel like the trumpet that wakes the dead.

"I conceive that all the earthquake events of that catastrophe tumbled on top of each other rather like lumber in the minds of men such as our friend with the diary. With the dazed excitement of a dream, they found themselves falling—literally falling—into their ranks, and learned that an attack was to be led at once across the river. The general and the major, it was said, had found out something at the bridge, and there was only just time to strike for life. The major had gone back at once to call up the reserve along the road behind; it was doubtful if even with that prompt appeal help could reach them in time. But they must pass the stream that night, and seize the heights by morning. It is with the very stir and throb of that romantic nocturnal march that the diary suddenly ends."

Father Brown had mounted ahead; for the woodland path grew smaller, steeper, and more twisted, till they felt as if they were ascending a winding staircase. The priest's voice came from above out of the darkness.

"There was one other little and enormous thing. When the general urged them to their chivalric charge he half drew his sword from the scabbard; and then, as if ashamed of such melodrama, thrust it back again. The sword again, you see."

A half-light broke through the network of boughs above them, flinging the ghost of a net about their feet; for they were mounting again to the faint luminosity of the naked night. Flambeau felt truth all round him as an atmosphere, but not as an idea. He answered with bewildered brain: "Well, what's the matter with the sword? Officers generally have swords, don't they?"

"They are not often mentioned in modern war," said the other dispassionately; "but in this affair one falls over the blessed sword everywhere."

"Well, what is there in that?" growled Flambeau; "it was a twopence colored sort of incident; the old man's blade breaking in his last battle. Anyone might bet the papers would get hold of it, as they have. On all these tombs and things it's shown broken at the point. I hope you haven't dragged me through this Polar expedition merely because two men with an eye for a picture saw St. Clare's broken sword."

"No," cried Father Brown, with a sharp voice like a pistol shot; "but who saw his unbroken sword?"

"What do you mean?" cried the other, and stood still under the stars. They had come abruptly out of the gray gates of the wood.

"I say, who saw his unbroken sword?" repeated Father Brown obstinately. "Not the writer of the diary, anyhow; the general sheathed it in time."

Flambeau looked about him in the moonlight, as a man struck blind might look in the sun; and his friend went on, for the first time with eagerness:

"Flambeau," he cried, "I cannot prove it, even after hunting through the tombs. But I am sure of it. Let me add just one more tiny fact that tips the whole thing over. The colonel, by a strange chance, was one of the first struck by a bullet. He was struck long before the troops came to close quarters. But he saw St. Clare's sword broken. Why was it broken? How was it broken? My friend, it was broken before the battle."

"Oh!" said his friend, with a sort of forlorn jocularity; "and pray where is the other piece?"

"I can tell you," said the priest promptly. "In the north-east corner of the cemetery of the Protestant Cathedral at Belfast."

"Indeed?" inquired the other. "Have you looked for it?"

"I couldn't," replied Brown, with frank regret. "There's a great marble monument on top of it; a monument to the heroic Major Murray, who fell fighting gloriously at the famous Battle of the Black River."

Flambeau seemed suddenly galvanized into existence. "You mean," he cried hoarsely, "that General St. Clare hated Murray, and murdered him on the field of battle because—"

"You are still full of good and pure thoughts," said the other. "It was worse than that."

"Well," said the large man, "my stock of evil imagination is used up."

The priest seemed really doubtful where to begin, and at last he said again:

"Where would a wise man hide a leaf? In the forest."

The other did not answer.

"If there were no forest, he would make a forest. And if he wished to hide a dead leaf, he would make a dead forest."

There was still no reply, and the priest added still more mildly and quietly:

"And if a man had to hide a dead body, he would make a field of dead bodies to hide it in."

Flambeau began to stamp forward with an intolerance of delay in time or space; but Father Brown went on as if he were continuing the last sentence:

"Sir Arthur St. Clare, as I have already said, was a man who read his Bible. That was what was the matter with *him*. When will people understand that it is useless for a man to read his Bible unless he also reads everybody else's Bible? A printer reads a Bible for misprints. A Mormon reads his Bible, and finds polygamy; a Christian Scientist reads his, and finds we have no arms and legs. St. Clare was an old Anglo-Indian Protestant soldier. Now, just think what that might mean; and, for Heaven's sake, don't cant about it. It might mean a man physically formidable living under a tropic sun in an Oriental society, and soaking himself without sense or guidance in an Oriental Book. Of course, he read the Old Testament rather than the New. Of course, he found in the Old Testament anything that he wanted—lust, tyranny, treason. Oh, I dare say he was honest, as you call it. But what is the good of a man being honest in his worship of dishonesty?

"In each of the hot and secret countries to which the man went he kept a harem, he tortured witnesses, he amassed shameful gold; but certainly he would have said with steady eyes that he did it to the glory of the Lord. My own theology is sufficiently expressed by asking which Lord? Anyhow, there is this about such evil, that it opens door after door in hell, and always into smaller and smaller chambers. This is the real case against crime, that a man does not become wilder and wilder, but only meaner and meaner. St. Clare was soon suffocated by difficulties of bribery and blackmail; and needed more and more cash. And by the time of the Battle of the Black River he had fallen from world to world to that place which Dante makes the lowest floor of the universe."

"What do you mean?" asked his friend again.

"I mean *that*," retorted the cleric, and suddenly pointed at a puddle sealed with ice that shone in the moon. "Do you remember whom Dante put in the last circle of ice?"

"The traitors," said Flambeau, and shuddered. As he looked around at the inhuman landscape of trees, with taunting and almost obscene outlines, he could almost fancy he was Dante, and the priest with the rivulet of a voice was, indeed, a Virgil leading him through a land of eternal sins.

The voice went on: "Olivier, as you know, was quixotic, and would not permit a secret service and spies. The thing, however, was done, like many other things, behind his back. It was managed by my old friend Espado; he was the bright-clad fop, whose hook nose got him called the

Vulture. Posing as a sort of philanthropist at the front, he felt his way through the English Army, and at last got his fingers on its one corrupt man—please God!—and that man at the top. St. Clare was in foul need of money, and mountains of it. The discredited family doctor was threatening those extraordinary exposures that afterwards began and were broken off; tales of monstrous and prehistoric things in Park Lane; things done by an English Evangelist that smelt like human sacrifice and hordes of slaves. Money was wanted, too, for his daughter's dowry; for to him the fame of wealth was as sweet as wealth itself. He snapped the last thread, whispered the word to Brazil, and wealth poured in from the enemies of England. But another man had talked to Espado the Vulture as well as he. Somehow the dark, grim young major from Ulster had guessed the hideous truth; and when they walked slowly together down that road towards the bridge Murray was telling the general that he must resign instantly, or be court-martialled and shot. The general temporized with him till they came to the fringe of tropic trees by the bridge; and there by the singing river and the sunlit palms (for I can see the picture) the general drew his sabre and plunged it through the body of the major.''

The wintry road curved over a ridge in cutting frost, with cruel black shapes of bush and thicket; but Flambeau fancied that he saw beyond it faintly the edge of an aureole that was not starlight and moonlight, but some fire such as is made by men. He watched it as the tale drew to its close.

''St. Clare was a hell-hound, but he was a hound of breed. Never, I'll swear, was he so lucid and so strong as when poor Murray lay a cold lump at his feet. Never in all his triumphs, as Captain Keith said truly, was the great man so great as he was in this last world-despised defeat. He looked coolly at his weapon to wipe off the blood; he saw the point he had planted between his victim's shoulders had broken off in the body. He saw quite calmly, as through a club windowpane, all that must follow. He saw that men must find the unaccountable corpse; must extract the unaccountable sword-point; must notice the unaccountable broken sword—or absence of sword. He had killed, but not silenced. But his imperious intellect rose against the facer; there was one way yet. He could make the corpse less unaccountable. He could create a hill of corpses to cover this one. In twenty minutes eight hundred English soldiers were marching down to their death.''

The warmer glow behind the black winter wood grew richer and brighter, and Flambeau strode on to reach it. Father Brown also quickened his stride; but he seemed merely absorbed in his tale.

"Such was the valor of that English thousand, and such the genius of their commander, that if they had at once attacked the hill, even their mad march might have met some luck. But the evil mind that played with them like pawns had other aims and reasons. They must remain in the marshes by the bridge at least till British corpses should be a common sight there. Then for the last grand scene; the silver-haired soldier-saint would give up his shattered sword to save further slaughter. Oh, it was well organized for an impromptu. But I think (I cannot prove), I think that it was while they stuck there in the bloody mire that someone doubted—and someone guessed."

He was mute a moment, and then said: "There is a voice from nowhere that tells me the man who guessed was the lover . . . the man to wed the old man's child."

"But what about Olivier and the hanging?" asked Flambeau.

"Olivier, partly from chivalry, partly from policy, seldom encumbered his march with captives," explained the narrator. "He released everybody in most cases. He released everybody in this case."

"Everybody but the general," said the tall man.

"Everybody," said the priest.

Flambeau knit his black brows. "I don't grasp it all yet," he said.

"There is another picture, Flambeau," said Brown in his more mystical undertone. "I can't prove it; but I can do more—I can see it. There is a camp breaking up on the bare, torrid hills at morning, and Brazilian uniforms massed in blocks and columns to march. There is the red shirt and long black beard of Flambeau, which blows as he stands, his broad-brimmed hat in his hand. He is saying farewell to the great enemy he is setting free—the simple, snow-headed English veteran, who thanks him in the name of his men. The English remnant stand behind at attention; beside them are stores and vehicles for the retreat. The drums roll; the Brazilians are moving; the English are still like statues. So they abide till the last hum and flash of the enemy have faded from the tropic horizon. Then they alter their postures all at once, like dead men coming to life; they turn their fifty faces upon the general—faces not to be forgotten."

Flambeau gave a great jump. "Ah," he cried. "You don't mean—"

"Yes," said Father Brown in a deep, moving voice. "It was an English hand that put the rope round St. Clare's neck; I believe the hand that put the ring on his daughter's finger. They were English hands that dragged him up to the tree of shame; the hands of men that had adored him and followed him to victory. And they were English souls (God pardon and endure us all!) who stared at him swinging in that foreign sun on the green gallows of palm, and prayed in their hatred that he might drop off it into hell.''

As the two topped the ridge there burst on them the strong scarlet light of a red-curtained English inn. It stood sideways in the road, as if standing aside in the amplitude of hospitality. Its three doors stood open with invitation; and even where they stood they could hear the hum and laughter of humanity happy for a night.

''I need not tell you more,'' said Father Brown. ''They tried him in the wilderness and destroyed him; and then, for the honor of England and of his daughter, they took an oath to seal up for ever the story of the traitor's purse and the assassin's sword blade. Perhaps—Heaven help them—they tried to forget it. Let us try to forget it, anyhow; here is our inn.''

''With all my heart,'' said Flambeau, and was just striding into the bright, noisy bar when he stepped back and almost fell on the road.

''Look there, in the devil's name!'' he cried, and pointed rigidly at the square wooden sign that overhung the road. It showed dimly the crude shape of a sabre hilt and shortened blade; and was inscribed in false archaic lettering, ''The Sign of the Broken Sword.''

''Were you not prepared?'' asked Father Brown gently. ''He is the god of this country; half the inns and parks and streets are named after him and his story.''

''I thought we had done with the leper,'' cried Flambeau, and spat on the road.

''You will never have done with him in England,'' said the priest, looking down, ''while brass is strong and stone abides. His marble statues will erect the souls of proud, innocent boys for centuries, his village tomb will smell of loyalty as of lilies. Millions who never knew him shall love him like a father—this man whom the last few that knew him dealt with like dung. He shall be a saint; and the truth shall never be told of him, because I have made up my mind at last. There is so much good and evil in breaking secrets, that I put my conduct to a test. All these newspapers will perish; the anti-Brazil boom is already over; Olivier is already honored everywhere. But I told myself that if anywhere, by name, in metal or marble that will endure like the pyramids, Colonel Clancy, or Captain Keith, or President Olivier, or any innocent man was wrongly blamed, then I would speak. If it were only that St. Clare was wrongly praised, I would be silent. And I will.''

They plunged into the red-curtained tavern, which was not only cozy, but even luxurious inside. On a table stood a silver model of the tomb of

St. Clare, the silver head bowed, the silver sword broken. On the walls were colored photographs of the same scene, and of the system of wagonettes that took tourists to see it. They sat down on the comfortable padded benches.

"Come, it's cold," cried Father Brown; "let's have some wine or beer."

"Or brandy," said Flambeau.

Steve Carella

NIGHTSHADE
Ed McBain

THE MORNING HOURS of the night come imperceptibly here. It is a minute before midnight on the peeling face of the hanging wall clock, and then it is midnight, and then the minute hand moves visibly and with a lurch into the new day. The morning hours have begun, but scarcely anyone has noticed. The stale coffee in soggy cardboard containers tastes the same as it did thirty seconds ago, the spastic rhythm of the clacking typewriters continues unabated, a drunk across the room shouts that the world is full of brutality, and cigarette smoke drifts up toward the face of the clock where, unnoticed and unmourned, the old day has already been dead for two minutes.

Then the telephone rings.

The men in this room are part of a tired routine, somewhat shabby about the edges, as faded and as gloomy as the room itself, with its cigarette-scarred desks and its smudged green walls. This could be the office of a failing insurance company were it not for the evidence of the holstered pistols hanging from belts on the backs of wooden chairs painted a darker green than the walls. The furniture is ancient, the typewriters are ancient, the building itself is ancient—which is perhaps only fitting since these men are involved in what is an ancient pursuit, a pursuit once considered honorable. They are law enforcers. They are, in the mildest words of the drunk still hurling epithets from the grilled detention cage across the room, dirty rotten pigs.

The telephone continues to ring.

The little girl lying in the alley behind the theater was wearing a belted white trench coat wet with blood. There was blood on the floor of the alley, and blood on the metal fire door behind her, and blood on her face and matted in her blonde hair, blood on her miniskirt and on the lavender tights she wore. A neon sign across the street stained the girl's ebbing life juices green and then orange, while from the open knife wound in her chest the blood sprouted like some ghastly night flower, dark and rich, red, orange, green, pulsing in time to the neon flicker—a grotesque psychedelic light show, and then losing the rhythm, welling up with less force and power.

She opened her mouth, she tried to speak, and the scream of an ambulance approaching the theater seemed to come from her mouth on a fresh bubble of blood. The blood stopped, her life ended, the girl's eyes rolled back into her head.

Detective Steve Carella turned away as the ambulance attendants rushed a stretcher into the alley. He told them the girl was dead.

"We got here in seven minutes," one of the attendants said.

"Nobody's blaming you," Carell answered.

"This is Saturday night," the attendant complained. "Streets are full of traffic even *with* the damn siren."

Carella walked to the unmarked sedan parked at the curb. Detective Cotton Hawes, sitting behind the wheel, rolled down his frost-rimmed window and said, "How is she?"

"We've got a homicide," Carell answered.

The boy was 18 years old, and he had been picked up not ten minutes ago for breaking off car aerials. He had broken off twelve on the same street, strewing them behind him like Johnny Appleseed planting radios; a cruising squad car had spotted him as he tried to twist off the aerial of a 1966 Cadillac. He was drunk or stoned or both, and when Sergeant Murchison at the muster desk asked him to read the Miranda-Escobedo warning signs on the wall, printed in both English and Spanish, he could read neither.

The arresting patrolman took the boy to the squadroom upstairs, where detective Bert Kling was talking to Hawes on the telephone. Kling signaled for the patrolman to wait with his prisoner on the bench outside the slatted wooden rail divider, and then buzzed Murchison at the desk downstairs.

"Dave," he said, "we've got a homicide in the alley of the Eleventh Street Theater. You want to get it rolling?"

"Right," Murchison said, and hung up.

Homicides are a common occurrence in this city, and each one is treated identically, the grisly horror of violent death reduced to routine by a police force that would otherwise be overwhelmed by statistics. At the muster desk upstairs Kling waved the patrolman and his prisoner into the squadroom, Sergeant Murchison first reported the murder to Captain Frick, who commanded the 87th Precinct, and then to Lieutenant Byrnes, who commanded the 87th Detective Squad. He then phoned Homicide, who in turn set into motion an escalating process of notification that included the Police Laboratory, the Telegraph, Telephone and Teletype Bureau at Headquarters, the Medical Examiner, the District Attorney, the District Commander of the Detective Division, the Chief of Detectives, and finally the Police Commissioner himself. Someone had thoughtlessly robbed a young woman of her life, and now a lot of sleepy-eyed men were being shaken out of their beds on a cold October night.

Upstairs, the clock on the squadroom wall read 12:30 A.M. The boy who had broken off twelve car aerials sat in a chair alongside Bert Kling's desk. Kling took one look at him and yelled to Miscolo in the Clerical Office to bring in a pot of strong coffee. Across the room the drunk in the detention wanted to know where he was. In a little while they would release him with a warning to try to stay sober till morning.

But the night was young.

They arrived alone or in pairs, blowing on their hands, shoulders hunched against the bitter cold, breaths pluming whitely from their lips. They marked the dead girl's position in the alleyway, they took her picture, they made drawings of the scene, they searched for the murder weapon and found none, and then they stood around speculating on sudden death. In this alleyway alongside a theater the policemen were the stars and the celebrities, and a curious crowd thronged the sidewalk where a barricade had already been set up, anxious for a glimpse of these men with their shields pinned to their overcoats—the identifying *Playbills* of law enforcement, without which you could not tell the civilians from the plainclothes cops.

Monoghan and Monroe had arrived from Homicide, and they watched dispassionately now as the Assistant Medical Examiner fluttered around the dead girl. They were both wearing black overcoats, black mufflers, and black fedoras; both were heavier men than Carella, who stood between them with the lean look of an overtrained athlete, a pained expression on his face.

"He done some job on her," Monroe said.

Monoghan made a rude sound.

"You identified her yet?" Monroe asked.

"I'm waiting for the M.E. to get through," Carella answered.

"Might help to know what she was doing here in the alley. What's that door there?" Monoghan asked.

"Stage entrance."

"Think she was in the show?"

"I don't know," Carella said.

"Well, what the hell," Monroe said, "they're finished with her pocketbook there, ain't they? Why don't you look through it? You finished with that pocketbook there?" he yelled to one of the lab technicians.

"Yeah, anytime you want it," the technician shouted back.

"Go on, Carella, take a look."

The technician wiped the blood off the dead girl's bag, then handed it to Carella. Monoghan and Monroe crowded in on him as he twisted open the clasp.

"Bring it over to the light," Monroe said.

The light, with a metal shade, hung over the stage door. So violently had the girl been stabbed that flecks of blood had even dotted the enameled white underside of the shade. In her bag they found a driver's license identifying her as Mercy Howell of 1113 Rutherford Avenue, Age 24, Height 5'3", Eyes Blue. They found an Actors Equity card in her name, as well as credit cards for two of the city's largest department stores. They found an unopened package of Virginia Slims, and a book of matches advertising an art course. They found a rat-tailed comb. They found $17.43. They found a package of Kleenex, and an appointment book. They found a ballpoint pen with shreds of tobacco clinging to its tip, an eyelash curler, two subway tokens, and an advertisement for a see-through blouse, clipped from one of the local newspapers.

In the pocket of her trench coat, when the M.E. had finished with her and pronounced her dead from multiple stab wounds in the chest and throat, they found an unfired Browning .25 caliber automatic. They tagged the gun and the handbag, and they moved the girl out of the alleyway and into the waiting ambulance for removal to the morgue. There was now nothing left of Mercy Howell but a chalked outline of her body and a pool of her blood on the alley floor.

"You sober enough to understand me?" Kling asked the boy.

"I was never drunk to begin with," the boy answered.

"Okay then, here we go," Kling said. "In keeping with the Supreme Court decision in Miranda versus Arizona we are not permitted to ask you any questions until you are warned of your right to counsel and your privilege against self-incrimination."

"What does that mean?" the body asked. "Self-incrimination?"

"I'm about to explain that to you now," Kling said.

"This coffee stinks."

"First, you have the right to remain silent if you so choose," Kling said. "Do you understand that?"

"I understand it."

"Second, you do not have to answer any police questions if you don't want to. Do you understand that?"

"What the hell are you asking me if I understand for? Do I look like a moron or something?"

"The law requires that I ask whether or not you understand these specific warnings. *Did* you understand what I just said about not having to answer?"

"Yeah, yeah, I understood."

"All right. Third, if you do decide to answer any questions, the answers may be used as evidence against you, do you—?"

"What the hell did I do, break off a couple of lousy car aerials?"

"Did you understand that?"

"I understood it."

"You also have the right to consult with an attorney before or during police questioning. If you do not have the money to hire a lawyer, a lawyer will be appointed to consult with you."

Kling gave this warning straight-faced even though he knew that under the Criminal Procedure Code of the city for which he worked, a public defender could not be appointed by the courts until the preliminary hearing. There was no legal provision for the courts *or* the police to appoint counsel during questioning, and there were certainly no police funds set aside for the appointment of attorneys. In theory, a call to the Legal Aid Society should have brought a lawyer up there to the old squadroom withing minutes, ready and eager to offer counsel to any indigent person desiring it. But in practice, if this boy sitting beside Kling told him in the next three seconds that he was unable to pay for his own attorney and would like one provided, Kling would not have known just what the hell to do—other than call off the questioning.

"I understand," the boy said.

"You've signified that you understand all the warnings," Kling said, "and now I ask you whether you are willing to answer my questions without an attorney here to counsel you."

"Go fly a kite," the boy said. "I don't want to answer nothing."

So that was that.

They booked him for Criminal Mischief, a Class-A Misdemeanor defined as intentional or reckless damage to the property of another person, and they took him downstairs to a holding cell, to await transportation to the Criminal Courts Building for arraignment.

The phone was ringing again, and a woman was waiting on the bench just outside the squadroom.

The watchman's booth was just inside the metal stage door. An electric clock on the wall behind the watchman's stool read 1:10 A.M. The watchman was a man in his late seventies who did not at all mind being questioned by the police. He came on duty, he told them, at 7:30 each night. The company call was for 8:00, and he was there at the stage door waiting to greet everybody as they arrived to get made up and in costume. Curtain went down at 11:20, and usually most of the kids was out of the theater by 11:45 or, at the latest, midnight. He stayed on till 9:00 the next morning, when the theater box office opened.

"Ain't much to do during the night except hang around and make sure nobody runs off with the scenery," he said, chuckling.

"Did you happen to notice what time Mercy Howell left the theater?" Carella asked.

"She the one got killed?" the old man asked.

"Yes," Hawes said. "Mercy Howell. About this high, blonde hair, blue eyes."

"They're all about that high with blonde hair and blue eyes," the old man said, and chuckled again. "I don't know hardly none of them by name. Shows come and go, you know. Be a hell of a chore to have to remember all the kids who go in and out that door."

"Do you sit here by the door all night?" Carella asked.

"Well, no, not all night. What I do, I lock the door after everybody's out and then I check the lights, make sure just the work light's on. I won't touch the switchboard, not allowed to, but I can turn out lights in the lobby, for example, if somebody left them on, or down in the toilets— sometimes they leave lights on down in the toilets. Then I come back here to the booth, and read or listen to the radio. Along about two o'clock I check the theater again, make sure we ain't got no fires or nothing, and then I come back here and make the rounds again at four o'clock, and six o'clock, and again about eight. That's what I do."

"You say you lock this door?"

"That's right."

"Would you remember what time you locked it tonight?"

"Oh, must've been about ten minutes to twelve. Soon as I knew everybody was out."

"How do you know when they're out."

"I give a yell up the stairs there. You see those stairs there? They go up to the dressing rooms. Dressing rooms are all upstairs in this house. So I go to the steps, and I yell 'Locking up! Anybody here?' And if somebody yells back, I know somebody's here, and I say, 'Let's shake it, honey,' if it's a girl, and if it's a boy, I say, 'Let's hurry it up, sonny.'"The old man chuckled again. "With this show it's sometimes hard to tell which's the girls and which's the boys. I manage, though," he said, and again chuckled.

"So you locked the door at ten minutes to twelve?"

"Right."

"And everybody had left the theater by that time?"

"'Cept me, of course."

"Did you look out into the alley before you locked the door?"

"Nope. Why should I do that?"

"Did you hear anything outside *while* you were locking the door?"

"Nope."

"Or at any time *before* you locked it?"

"Well, there's always noise outside when they're leaving, you know. They got friends waiting for them, or else they go home together, you know—there's always a lot of chatter when they go out."

"But it was quiet when you locked the door?"

"Dead quiet," the old man said.

The woman who took the chair beside Detective Meyer Meyer's desk was perhaps 32 years old, with long straight black hair trailing down her back and wide brown eyes that were terrified. It was still October, and the color of her tailored coat seemed suited to the season, a subtle tangerine with a small brown fur collar that echoed an outdoors trembling with the colors of autumn.

"I feel sort of silly about this," she said, "but my husband insisted that I come."

"I see," Meyer said.

"There are ghosts," the woman said.

Across the room Kling unlocked the door to the detention cage and said, "Okay, pal, on your way. Try to stay sober till morning, huh?"

"It ain't one thirty yet," the man said, "the night is young." He stepped out of the cage, tipped his hat to Kling, and hurriedly left the squadroom.

Meyer looked at the woman sitting beside him, studying her with new interest because, to tell the truth, she had not seemed like a nut when she first walked into the squadroom. He had been a detective for more years than he chose to count, and in his time had met far too many nuts of every stripe and persuasion. But he had never met one as pretty as Adele Gorman with her well-tailored, fur-collared coat, and her Vassar voice and her skillfully applied eye makeup, lips bare of color in her pale white face, pert and reasonably young and intelligent—but apparently a nut besides.

"In the house," she said. "Ghosts."

"Where do you live, ma'am?" he asked. He had written her name on the pad in front of him and now he watched her with his pencil poised and recalled the lady who had come into the squadroom only last month to report a gorilla peering into her bedroom from the fire escape outside. They had sent a patrolman over to make a routine check, and had even called the zoo and the circus (which coincidentally was in town, and which lent at least some measure of credibility to her claim), but there had been no gorilla on the fire escape, nor had any gorilla recently escaped from a cage. The lady came back the next day to report that her visiting gorilla had put in another appearance the night before, this time wearing a top hat and carrying a black cane with an ivory head. Meyer had assured her that he would have a platoon of cops watching her building that night, which seemed to calm her at least somewhat. He had then led her personally out of the squadroom and down the iron-runged steps, and through the high-ceilinged muster room, and past the hanging green globes on the front stoop, and onto the sidewalk outside the station house. Sergeant Murchison, at the muster desk, shook his head after the lady was gone, and muttered, "More of them outside than in."

Meyer watched Adele Gorman now, remembered what Murchison had said, and thought: *Gorillas in September, ghosts in October.*

"We live in Smoke Rise," she said. "Actually, it's my father's house, but my husband and I are living there with him."

"The address?"

"MacArthur Lane—number three hundred seventy-four. You take the first access road into Smoke Rise, about a mile and a half east of Silvermine Oval. The name on the mailbox is Van Houten. That's my father's name. Willem Van Houten," She paused and studied him, as though expecting some reaction.

"Okay," Meyer said, and ran a hand over his bald pate. He looked up and said, "Now, you were saying, Mrs. Gorman—"

"That we have ghosts."

"Uh-huh. What kind of ghosts?"

"Ghosts. Poltergeists. Shades. I don't know," she said, and shrugged. "What kinds of ghosts are there?"

"Well, they're your ghosts, so suppose you tell me," Meyer said.

The telephone on Kling's desk rang. He lifted the receiver and said, "Eighty-seventh, Detective Kling."

"There are two of them," Adele said.

"Male or female?"

"One of each."

"Yeah," Kling said into the telephone, "go ahead."

"How old would you say they were?"

"Centuries, I would guess."

"No, I mean—"

"Oh, how old do they look? Well, the man—"

"You've seen them?"

"Oh, yes, many times."

"Uh-huh," Meyer said.

"I'll be right over," Kling said into the telephone. "You stay there." He slammed down the receiver, opened his desk drawer, pulled out a holstered revolver, and hurriedly clipped it to his belt. "Somebody threw a bomb into a store-front church. One-seven-three-three Culver Avenue. I'm heading over."

"Right," Meyer said. "Get back to me."

"We'll need a couple of meat wagons. The minister and two others were killed, and it sounds as if there're a lot of injured."

"Will you tell Dave?"

"On the way out," Kling said, and was gone.

"Mrs. Gorman," Meyer said, "as you can see, we're pretty busy here just now. I wonder if your ghosts can wait till morning."

"No, they can't," Adele said.

"Why not?"

"Because they appear precisely at two forty-five A.M. and I want someone to see them."

"Why don't you and your husband look at them?" Meyer said.

"You think I'm a nut, don't you?" Adele said.

"No, no, Mrs. Gorman, not at all."

"Oh, yes you do," Adele said. "I didn't believe in ghosts either—until I saw these two."

"Well, this is all very interesting, I assure you, Mrs. Gorman, but really we do have our hands full right now, and I don't know what we can do about these ghosts of yours, even if we did come over to take a look at them."

"They've been stealing things from us," Adele said, and Meyer thought: *Oh, we have got ourselves a prime lunatic this time.*

"What sort of things?"

"A diamond brooch that used to belong to my mother when she was alive. They stole that from my father's safe."

"What else?"

"A pair of emerald earrings. They were in the safe, too."

"When did these thefts occur?"

"Last month."

"Isn't it possible the jewelry's been mislaid?"

"You don't mislay a diamond brooch and a pair of emerald earrings that are locked inside a wall safe."

"Did you report these thefts?"

"No."

"Why not?"

"Because I knew you'd think I was crazy. Which is just what you're thinking right this minute."

"No, Mrs. Gorman, but I'm sure you can appreciate the fact that we—uh—can't go around arresting ghosts," Meyer said, and tried a smile.

Adele Gorman did not smile back. "Forget the ghosts," she said, "I was foolish to mention them. I should have known better." She took a deep breath, looked him squarely in the eye, and said, "I'm here to report the theft of a diamond brooch valued at six thousand dollars, and a pair of earrings worth thirty-five hundred dollars. Will you send a man to investigate tonight, or should I ask my father to get in touch with your superior officer?"

"Your father? What's he got to—"

"My father is a retired Surrogate's Court judge," Adele said.

"I see."

"Yes, I hope you do."

"What time did you say these ghosts arrive?" Meyer asked, and sighed heavily.

Between midnight and 2:00 the city does not change very much. The theaters have all let out, and the average Saturday night revelers, good citizens from Bethtown or Calm's Point, Riverhead or Majesta, have come into the Isola streets again in search of a snack or a giggle before heading home. The city is an ant's nest of after-theater eateries ranging from chic French cafés to pizzerias to luncheonettes to coffee shops to hot-dog stands to delicatessens, all of them packed to the ceilings because Saturday night is not only the loneliest night of the week, it is also the night to howl. And howl they do, these good burghers who have put in five long hard days of labor and who are anxious now to relax and enjoy themselves before Sunday arrives, bringing with it the attendant boredom of too much leisure time, anathema for the American male.

The crowds shove and jostle their way along The Stem, moving in and out of bowling alleys, shooting galleries, penny arcades, strip joints, night clubs, jazz emporiums, souvenir shops, lining the sidewalks outside plate-glass windows in which go-go girls gyrate, or watching with fascination as a roast beef slowly turns on a spit. Saturday night is a time for pleasure for the good people of Isola and environs, with nothing more on their minds than a little enjoyment of the short respite between Friday night at 5:00 and Monday morning at 9:00.

But along around 2:00 A.M. the city begins to change.

The good citizens have waited to get their cars out of parking garages (more garages than there are barber shops) or have staggered their way sleepily into subways to make the long trip back to the outlying sections, the furry toy dog won in the Pokerino palace clutched limply, the laughter a bit thin, the voice a bit croaked, a college song being sung on a rattling subway car, but without much force or spirit. Saturday night has ended, it is really Sunday morning already, and the morning hours are truly upon the city—and now the denizens appear.

The predators approach, with the attendant danger of the good citizens getting mugged and rolled. The junkies are out in force, looking for cars foolishly left unlocked and parked on the streets, or—lacking such fortuitous circumstance—experienced enough to force the side vent with a screwdriver, hook the lock button with a wire hanger, and open the door that way. There are pushers peddling their dream stuff, from pot to speed to hoss, a nickel bag or a twenty-dollar deck; fences hawking their stolen goodies, anything from a transistor radio to a refrigerator, the biggest bargain basements in town; burglars jimmying windows or forcing doors with a celluloid strip, this being an excellent hour to break into apartments, when the occupants are asleep and the street sounds are hushed.

But worse than any of these are the predators who roam the night in search of trouble. In cruising wedges of three or four, sometimes high but more often not, they look for victims—a taxicab driver coming out of a cafeteria, an old woman poking around garbage cans for hidden treasures, a teenage couple necking in a parked automobile—it doesn't matter. You can get killed in this city at any time of the day or night, but your chances for extinction are best after 2:00 A.M. because, paradoxically, the night people take over in the morning. There are neighborhoods that terrify even cops in this lunar landscape, and there are certain places the cops will not enter unless they have first checked to see that there are two doors, one to get in by, and the other to get out through, fast, should someone decide to block the exit from behind.

The Painted Parasol was just such an establishment.

They had found in Mercy Howell's appointment book a notation that read: *Harry, 2:00 A.M. The Painted Parasol;* and since they knew this particular joint for exactly the kind of hole it was, and since they wondered what connection the slain girl might have had with the various unappetizing types who frequented the place from dusk till dawn, they decided to hit it and find out. The front entrance opened on a long flight of stairs that led down to the main room of what was not a restaurant, and not a club, though it combined features of both. It did not possess a liquor license, and so it served only coffee and sandwiches; but occasionally a rock singer would plug in his amplifier and guitar and whack out a few numbers for the patrons. The back door of the—hangout?—opened onto a sidestreet alley. Hawes checked it out, reported back to Carella, and they both made a mental floor plan just in case they needed it later.

Carella went down the long flight of steps first, Hawes immediately behind him. At the bottom of the stairway they moved through a beaded curtain and found themselves in a large room overhung with an old Air Force parachute painted in a wild psychedelic pattern. A counter on which rested a coffee urn and trays of sandwiches in Saran Wrap was just opposite the hanging beaded curtain. To the left and right of the counter were perhaps two dozen tables, all of them occupied. A waitress in a black leotard and black high-heeled patent-leather pumps was swiveling between and around the tables, taking orders.

There was a buzz of conversation in the room, hovering, captured in the fold of the brightly painted parachute. Behind the counter a man in a white apron was drawing a cup of coffee from the huge silver urn. Carella and Hawes walked over to him. Carella was almost six feet tall, and he weighed 180 pounds, with wide shoulders and a narrow waist and the hands of a street brawler. Hawes was six feet two inches tall, and he weighed 195 pounds bone-dry, and his hair was a fiery red with a white streak over the left temple where he had once been knifed while investigating a burglary. Both men looked like exactly what they were— fuzz.

"What's the trouble?" the man behind the counter asked immediately.

"No trouble," Carella said. "This your place?"

"Yeah. My name is Georgie Bright, and I have already been visited, thanks. Twice."

"Oh? Who visited you?"

"First time a cop named O'Brien, second time a cop named Parker. I already cleared up that whole thing that was going on downstairs?"

"What whole thing going on downstairs?"

"In the Men's Room. Some kids were selling pot down there, it got to be a regular neighborhood supermarket. So I done what O'Brien suggested, I put a man down there outside the toilet door, and the rule now is only one person goes in there at a time. Parker came around to make sure I was keeping my part of the bargain. I don't want no narcotics trouble here. Go down and take a look if you like. You'll see I got a man watching the toilet."

"Who's watching the man watching the toilet?" Carella asked.

"That ain't funny," Georgie Bright said, looking offended.

"Know anybody named Harry?" Hawes asked.

"Harry who? I know a lot of Harrys."

"Any of them here tonight?"

"Maybe."

"Where?"

"There's one over there near the bandstand. The big guy with the light hair."

"Harry what?"

"Donatello."

"Make the name?" Carella asked Hawes.

"No," Hawes said.

"Neither do I."

"Let's talk to him."

"You want a cup of coffee or something?" Georgie Bright asked.

"Yeah, why don't you send some over to the table?" Hawes said, and followed Carella across the room to where Harry Donatello was sitting with another man. Donatello was wearing gray slacks, black shoes and socks, a white shirt open at the throat, and a double-breasted blue blazer. His long blondish hair was combed straight back from the forehead, revealing a sharply defined widow's peak. He was easily as big as Hawes, and he sat with this hands folded on the table in front of him, talking to the man who sat opposite him. He did not look up as the detectives approached.

"Is your name Harry Donatello?" Carella asked.

"Who wants to know?"

"Police officers," Carella said, and flashed his shield.

"I'm Harry Donatello. What's the matter?"

"Mind if we sit down?" Hawes asked, and before Donatello could answer, both men sat, their backs to the empty bandstand and the exit door.

"Do you know a girl named Mercy Howell?" Carella asked.

"What about her?"

"Do you know her?"

"I know her. What's the beef? She underage or something?"

"When did you see her last?"

The man with Donatello, who up to now had been silent, suddenly piped, "You don't have to answer no questions without a lawyer, Harry. Tell them you want a lawyer."

The detectives looked him over. He was small and thin, with black hair combed sideways to conceal a receding hairline. He was badly in need of a shave. He was wearing blue trousers and a striped shirt.

"This is a field investigation," Hawes said drily, "and we can ask anything we damn please."

"Town's getting full of lawyers," Carella said. "What's *your* name, counselor?"

"Jerry Riggs. You going to drag *me* in this, whatever it is?"

"It's a few friendly questions in the middle of the night," Hawes said. "Anybody got any objections to that?"

"Getting so two guys can't even sit and talk together without getting shook down," Riggs said.

"You've got a rough life, all right," Hawes said, and the girl in the black leotard brought their coffee to the table, and then hurried off to take another order. Donatello watched her jiggling as she swiveled across the room.

"So when's the last time you saw the Howell girl?" Carella asked again.

"Wednesday night," Donatello said.

"Did you see her tonight?"

"No."

"Were you supposed to see her tonight?"

"Where'd you get that idea?"

"We're full of ideas," Hawes said.

"Yeah, I was supposed to meet her here ten minutes ago. Dumb broad is late, as usual."

"What do you do for a living, Donatello?"

"I'm an importer. You want to see my business card?"

"What do you import?"

"Souvenir ashtrays."

"How'd you get to know Mercy Howell?"

"I met her at a party in The Quarter. She got a little high, and she done her thing."

"What thing?"

"The thing she does in that show she's in."

"Which is what?"

"She done this dance where she takes off all her clothes."

"How long have you been seeing her?"

"I met her a couple of months ago. I see her on and off, maybe once a week, something like that. This town is full of broads, you know—a guy don't have to get himself involved in no relationship with no specific broad."

"What was your relationship with *this* specific broad?"

"We have a few laughs together, that's all. She's a swinger, little Mercy," Donatello said, and grinned at Riggs.

"Want to tell us where you were tonight between eleven and twelve?"

"Is this still a *field* investigation?" Riggs asked sarcastically.

"Nobody's in custody yet," Hawes said, "so let's cut the legal jazz, okay? Tell us where you were, Donatello."

"Right here," Donatello said. "From ten o'clock till now."

"I suppose somebody saw you here during that time."

"A *hundred* people saw me."

A crowd of angry black men and women were standing outside the shattered window of the storefront church. Two fire engines and an ambulance were parked at the curb. Kling pulled in behind the second engine, some ten feet away from the hydrant. It was almost 2:30 A.M. on a bitterly cold October night, but the crowd looked and sounded like a mob at an afternoon street-corner rally in the middle of August. Restless, noisy, abrasive, anticipative, they ignored the penetrating cold and concentrated instead on the burning issue of the hour—the fact that a person or persons unknown had thrown a bomb through the plate-glass window of the church.

The beat patrolman, a newly appointed cop who felt vaguely uneasy in this neighborhood even during his daytime shift, greeted Kling effusively, his pale white face bracketed by earmuffs, his gloved hands clinging desperately to his nightstick. The crowd parted to let Kling through. It did not help that he was the youngest man on the squad, with the callow look of a country bumpkin on his unlined face; it did not help that he was blonde and hatless; it did not help that he walked into the church with the confident youthful stride of a champion come to set things right. The crowd knew he was fuzz, and they knew he was Whitey, and they knew, too, that if this bombing had taken place on Hall Avenue crosstown and downtown, the Police Commissioner himself would have arrived behind a herald of official trumpets.

This, however, was Culver Avenue, where a boiling mixture of Puerto Ricans and Blacks shared a disintegrating ghetto, and so the car that pulled to the curb was not marked with the Commissioner's distinctive blue-and-gold seal, but was instead a green Chevy convertible that belonged to Kling himself; and the man who stepped out of it looked young and inexperienced and inept despite the confident stride he affected as he walked into the church, his shield pinned to his overcoat.

The bomb had caused little fire damage, and the firemen already had the flames under control, their hoses snaking through and around the overturned folding chairs scattered around the small room. Ambulance attendants picked their way over the hoses and around the debris, carrying out the injured—the dead could wait.

"Have you called the Bomb Squad?" Kling asked the patrolman.

"No," the patrolman answered, shaken by the sudden possibility that he had been derelict in his duty.

"Why don't you do that now?" Kling suggested.

"Yes, sir," the patrolman answered, and rushed out. The ambulance attendants went by with a moaning woman on a stretcher. She was still wearing her eyeglasses, but one lens had been shattered and blood was running in a steady rivulet down the side of her nose. The place stank of gunpowder and smoke and charred wood. The most serious damage had been done at the rear of the small store, farthest away from the entrance door. Whoever had thrown the bomb must have possessed a good pitching arm to have hurled it so accurately through the window and across the fifteen feet to the makeshift altar.

The minister lay across his own altar, dead. Two women who had been sitting on folding chairs closest to the altar lay on the floor, tangled in death, their cloths still smoldering. The sounds of the injured filled the room, and then were suffocated by the overriding siren-shriek of the second ambulance arriving. Kling went outside to the crowd.

"Anybody here witness this?" he asked.

A young man, black, wearing a beard and a natural hair style, turned away from a group of other youths and walked directly to Kling.

"Is the minister dead?" he asked.

"Yes, he is," Kling answered.

"Who else?"

"Two women."

"Who?"

"I don't know yet. We'll identify them as soon as the men are through in there." Kling turned again to the crowd. "Did anybody see what happened?" he asked.

"I saw it," the young man said.

"What's your name, son?"

"Andrew Jordan."

Kling took out his pad. "All right, let's have it."

"What good's this going to do?" Jordan asked. "Writing all this stuff in your book?"

"You said you saw what—"

"I saw it, all right. I was walking by, heading for the pool room up the street, and the ladies were inside singing, and this car pulled up, and a guy got out, threw the bomb, and ran back to the car."

"What kind of a car was it?"

"A red Volkswagen."

"What year?"

"Who can tell with those VWs?"

"How many people in it?"

"Two. The driver and the guy who threw the bomb."

"Notice the license-plate number?"

"No. They drove off too fast."

"Can you describe the man who threw the bomb?"

"Yeah. He was white."

"What else?" Kling asked.

"That's all," Jordan replied. "He was white."

There were perhaps three dozen estates in all of Smoke Rise, a hundred or so people living in luxurious near-seclusion on acres of valuable land through which ran four winding, interconnected, private roadways. Meyer Meyer drove betwen the wide stone pillars marking Smoke Rise's western access road, entering a city within a city, bounded on the north by the River Harb, shielded from the River Highway by stands of poplars and evergreens on the south—exclusive Smoke Rise, known familiarly and derisively to the rest of the city's inhabitants as "The Club."

MacArthur Lane was at the end of the road that curved past the Hamilton Bridge. Number 374 was a huge gray-stonehouse with a slate roof and scores of gables and chimneys jostling the sky, perched high in gloomy shadow above the Harb. As he stepped from the car, Meyer could hear the sounds of river traffic, the hooting of tugs, the blowing of whistles, the eruption of a squawk box on a destroyer midstream. He looked out over the water. Reflected lights glistened in shimmering liquid beauty—the hanging cables, the dazzling reds and greens of signal lights on the opposite shore, single illuminated window slashes in apartment buildings throwing their mirror images onto the black surface of the river, the blinking wing lights of an airplane overhead moving in watery reflection like a submarine. The air was cold, and a fine piercing drizzle had begun several minutes ago.

Meyer shuddered, pulled the collar of his coat higher on his neck, and walked toward the old gray house, his shoes crunching on the driveway gravel, the sound echoing away into the high surrounding bushes.

The stones of the old house oozed wetness. Thick vines covered the wall, climbing to the gabled, turreted roof. He found a doorbell set over a brass escutcheon in the thick oak doorjamb, and pressed it. Chimes sounded somewhere deep inside the house. He waited.

The door opened suddenly.

The man looking out at him was perhaps 70 years old, with piercing blue eyes; he was bald except for white thatches of hair that sprang wildly from behind each ear. He wore a red smoking jacket and black trousers, a black ascot around his neck, and red velvet slippers.

"What do you want?" he asked immediately.

"I'm Detective Meyer of the Eighty-seventh—"

"Who sent for you?"

"A woman named Adele Gorman came to the—"

"My daughter's a fool," the man said. "We don't need police here." And he slammed the door in Meyer's face.

The detective stood on the doorstep feeling somewhat like a horse's neck. A tugboat hooted on the river. A light snapped on upstairs, casting an amber rectangle into the dark driveway. He looked at the luminous dial of his watch. It was 2:35 A.M. The drizzle was cold and penetrating. He took out his handkerchief, blew his nose, and wondered what he should do next. He did not like ghosts, and he did not like lunatics, and he did not like nasty old men who did not comb their hair and who slammed doors in a person's face. He was about to head back for his car when the door opened again.

"Detective Meyer?" Adele Gorman said. "Do come in."

"Thank you," he said, and stepped into the entrance foyer.

"You're right on time."

"Well, a little early actually," Meyer said. He still felt foolish. What the hell was he doing in Smoke Rise investigating ghosts in the middle of the night?

"This way," Adele said, and he followed her through a somberly paneled foyer into a vast dimly lighted living room. Heavy oak beams ran overhead, velvet draperies hung at the window, the room was cluttered with ponderous old furniture. He could believe there were ghosts in this house, he could believe it.

A young man wearing dark glasses rose like a specter from the sofa near the fireplace. His face, illuminated by the single standing floor lamp, looked wan and drawn. Wearing a black cardigan sweater over a whiter shirt and dark slacks, he approached Meyer unsmilingly with his hand extended—but he did not accept Meyer's hand when it was offered in return.

Meyer suddenly realized that the man was blind.

"I'm Ralph Gorman," he said, his hand still extended. "Adele's husband."

"How do you do, Mr. Gorman," Meyer said, and took his hand. The palm was moist and cold.

"It was good of you to come," Gorman said. "These apparitions have been driving us crazy."

"What time is it?" Adele asked suddenly, and looked at her watch. "We've got five minutes," she said. There was a tremor in her voice. She looked suddenly very frightened.

"Won't your father be here?" Meyer asked.

"No, he's gone up to bed," Adele said. "I'm afraid he's bored with the whole affair, and terribly angry that we notified the police."

Meyer made no comment. Had he known that Willem Van Houten, former Surrogate's Court judge, had not wanted the police to be notified, Meyer would not have been here either. He debated leaving now, but Adele Gorman had begun to talk again.

" . . . is in her early thirties, I would guess. The other ghost, the male, is about your age—forty or forty-five, something like that."

"I'm thirty-seven," Meyer said.

"Oh."

"The bald head fools a lot of people."

"Yes."

"I was bald at a very early age."

"Anyway," Adele said, "their names are Elisabeth and Johann, and they've probably been—"

"Oh, they have names, do they?"

"Yes. They're ancestors, you know. My father is Dutch, and there actually were an Elisabeth and Johann Van Houten in the family centuries ago, when Smoke Rise was still a Dutch settlement."

"They're Dutch. Um-huh, I see," Meyer said.

"Yes. They always appear wearing Dutch costumes. And they also speak Dutch."

"Have you heard them, Mr. Gorman?"

"Yes," Gorman said. "I'm blind, you know—" he added, and hesitated, as though expecting some comment from Meyer. When none came, he said, "But I have heard them."

"Do you speak Dutch?"

"No. My father-in-law speaks it fluently, though, and he identified the language for us, and told us what they were saying."

"What *did* they say?"

"Well for one thing, they said they were going to steal Adele's jewelry, and they did just that."

"Your *wife's* jewelry? But I thought—"

"It was willed to her by her mother. My father-in-law keeps it in his safe."

"Kept, you mean."

"No, keeps. There are several pieces in addition to the ones that were stolen. Two rings and also a necklace."

"And the value?"

"Altogether? I would say about forty thousand dollars."

"Your ghosts have expensive taste."

The floor lamp in the room suddenly began to flicker. Meyer glanced at it and felt the hackles rising at the back of his neck.

"The lights are going out, Ralph." Adele whispered.

"Is it two forty-five?"

"Yes."

"They're here," Gorman whispered. "The ghosts are here."

Mercy Howell's roommate had been asleep for nearly four hours when they knocked on her door. But she was a wily young lady, hip to the ways of the big city, and very much awake as she conducted her own little investigation without so much as opening the door a crack. First she asked them to spell their names slowly. Then she asked them their shield numbers. Then she asked them to hold their shields and I.D. cards close to the door's peephole, where she could see them. Still unconvinced, she said through the locked door, "You just wait there a minute."

They waited for closer to five minutes before they heard her approaching the door again. The heavy steel bar of a Fox lock was lowered noisily to the floor, a safety chain rattled on its track, the tumblers of one lock clicked open, and then another, and finally the girl opened the door.

"Come in," she said, "I'm sorry I kept you waiting. I called the station house and they said you were okay."

"You're a very careful girl," Hawes said.

"At this hour of the morning? Are you kidding?" she said.

She was perhaps 25, with her red hair up in curlers, her face cold-creamed clean of makeup. She was wearing a pink quilted robe over flannel pajamas, and although she was probably a very pretty girl at 9:00 A.M. , she now looked about as attractive as a Buffalo nickel.

"What's your name, Miss?" Carella asked.

"Lois Kaplan. What's this all about? Has there been another burglary in the building?"

"No, Miss Kaplan. We want to ask you some questions about Mercy Howell. Did she live here with you?"

"Yes," Lois said, and suddenly looked at them shrewdly. "What do you mean *did*? She still *does*."

They were standing in the small foyer of the apartment, and the foyer went so still that all the night sounds of the building were clearly audible all at once, as though they had not been there before but had only been summoned up now to fill the void of silence. A toilet flushed somewhere, a hot-water pipe rattled, a baby whimpered, a dog barked, someone dropped a shoe. In the foyer, now filled with noise, they stared at each other wordlessly, and finally Carella drew a deep breath and said, "Your roommate is dead. She was stabbed tonight as she was leaving the theater."

"No," Lois said, simply and flatly and unequivocally. "No, she isn't."

"Miss Kaplan—"

"I don't give a damn what you say, Mercy isn't dead."

"Miss Kaplan, she's dead."

"Oh, God," Lois said, and burst into tears.

The two men stood by feeling stupid and big and awkward and

helpless. Lois Kaplan covered her face with her hands and sobbed into them, her shoulders heaving, saying over and over again, "I'm sorry, oh, God, please, I'm sorry, please, oh poor Mercy, oh my God," while the detectives tried not to watch.

At last the crying stopped and she looked up at them with eyes that had been knifed, and said softly, "Come in. Please," and led them into the living room. She kept staring at the floor as she talked. It was as if she could not look them in the face, not these men who had brought her the dreadful news.

"Do you know who did it?" she asked.

"No. Not yet."

"We wouldn't have wakened you in the middle of the night if—"

"That's all right."

"But very often, if we get moving on a case fast enough, before the trail gets cold—"

"Yes, I understand."

"We can often—"

"Yes, before the trail gets cold," Lois said.

"Yes."

The apartment went silent again.

"Would you know if Miss Howell had any enemies?" Carella asked.

"She was the sweetest girl in the world," Lois said.

"Did she argue with anyone recently? Were there any—"

"No."

"—any threatening telephone calls or letters?"

Lois Kaplan looked up at them.

"Yes," she said. "A letter."

"A *threatening* letter?"

"We couldn't tell. It frightened Mercy, though. That's why she bought the gun."

"What kind of gun?"

"I don't know. A small one."

"Would it have been a .25 caliber Browning?"

"I don't know guns."

"Was this letter mailed to her, or delivered personally?

"It was mailed to her. At the theater."

"When?"

"A week ago."

"Did she report it to the police?"

"No."

"Why not?"

"Haven't you seen *Rattlesnake*?" Lois said.

"What do you mean?" Carella said.

"*Rattlesnake*. The musical. The show Mercy was in."

"No, I haven't."

"But you've heard of it."

"No."

"Where do you live, for God's sake? On the moon?"

"I'm, sorry, I just haven't—"

"Forgive me," Lois said immediately. I'm not usually—I'm trying very hard to—I'm sorry. Forgive me."

"That's all right," Carella said.

"Anyway, it's a big hit now but—well there was trouble in the beginning, you see. Are you *sure* you don't know about this? It was in all the newspapers."

"Well, I guess I missed it," Carella said. "What was the trouble about?"

"Don't *you* know about this either?" she asked Hawes.

"No, I'm sorry."

"About Mercy's dance?"

"No."

"Well, in one scene Mercy danced the title song without any clothes on. Because the idea was to express—the hell with what the idea was. The point is that the dance wasn't at all obscene, it wasn't even sexy! But the police *missed* the point, and closed the show down two days after it opened. The producers had to go to court for a writ or something to get the show opened again."

"Yes, I remember it now," Carella said.

"What I'm trying to say is that nobody involved with *Rattlesnake* would report *anything* to the police. Not even a threatening letter."

"If she bought a pistol," Hawes said, "she would have *had* to go to the police. For a permit."

"She didn't have a permit."

"Then how'd she get the pistol? You can't buy a handgun without first—"

"A friend of hers sold it to her."

"What's the friend's name?"

"Harry Donatello."

"An importer," Carella said.

"Of souvenir ashtrays," Hawes said.

"I don't know what he does for a living," Lois said, "but he got the gun for her."

"When was this?"

"A few days after she received the letter."

"What did the letter say?" Carella asked.

"I'll get it for you," Lois said, and went into the bedroom. They heard a dresser drawer opening, the rustle of clothes, what might have been a tin candy box being opened. Lois came back into the room. "Here it is," she said.

There didn't seem much point in trying to preserve latent prints on a letter that had already been handled by Mercy Howell, Lois Kaplan, and the Lord knew how many others. But nonetheless Carella accepted the letter on a handkerchief spread over the palm of his hand, and then looked at the face of the envelope. "She should have brought this to us immediately," he said. "It's written on hotel stationery, we've got an address without lifting a finger."

The letter had indeed been written on stationery from The Addison Hotel, one of the city's lesser-known fleabags, some two blocks north of the Eleventh Street Theater, where Mercy Howell had worked. There was a single sheet of paper in the envelope. Carella unfolded it. Lettered on the paper in pencil were the words:

PUT ON YOUR
CLOSE, MISS!

The avenging Angel

The lamp went out, the room was black.

At first there was no sound but the sharp intake of Adele Gorman's breath. And then, indistinctly, as faintly as though carried on a swirling mist that blew in wetly from some desolated shore, there came the sound of garbled voices, and the room grew suddenly cold. The voices were those of a crowd in endless debate, rising and falling in cacophonous cadence, a mixture of tongues that rattled and rasped. There was the sound, too, of a rising wind, as though a door to some forbidden landscape had been sharply and suddenly blown open to reveal a host of corpses incessantly pacing, involved in formless dialogue.

The voices rose in volume now, carried on that same chill penetrating wind, louder, closer, until they seemed to overwhelm the room, clamoring to be released from whatever unearthly vault contained them. And then, as if two of those disembodied voices had succeeded in breaking away from the mass of unseen dead, bringing with them a rush of bone-chilling air from some world unknown, there came a whisper at first, the whisper of a man's voice, saying the single word "Ralph!"—sharp-edged and with a distinctive foreign inflection.

"Ralph!"—and then a woman's voice joining it saying, "Adele!'—pronounced strangely and in the same cutting whisper.

"Adele!''—and then "Ralph!'' again, the voices overlapping, unmistakably foreign, urgent, rising in volume until the whispers commingled to become an agonizing groan—and then the names were lost in the shrilling echo of the wind.

Meyer's eyes played tricks in the darkness. Apparitions that surely were not there seemed to float on the crescendo of sound that saturated the room. Barely perceived pieces of furniture assumed amorphous shapes as the male voice snarled and the female voice moaned above it.

And then the babel of other voices intruded again, as though calling these two back to whatever grim mossy crypt they had momentarily escaped. The sound of the wind became more fierce, and the voices of those numberless pacing dead receded, and echoed, and were gone.

The lamp sputtered back into dim illumination. The room seemed perceptibly warmer, but Meyer Meyer was covered with a cold clammy sweat.

"Now do you believe?'' Adele Gorman asked.

Detective Bob O'Brien was coming out of the Men's Room down the hall when he saw the woman sitting on the bench just outside the squadroom. He almost went back into the toilet, but he was an instant too late; she had seen him, so there was no escape.

"Hello, Mr. O'Brien,'' she said, and performed an awkward little half-rising motion, as though uncertain whether she should stand to greet or accept the deference due a lady. The clock on the squadroom wall read 3:02 A.M. but the lady was dressed as though for a brisk afternoon's hike in the park—brown slacks, low-heeled walking shoes, beige car coat, a scarf around her head. She was perhaps 55, with a face that once must have been pretty, save for the overlong nose. Green-eyed, with prominent cheekbones and a generous mouth, she executed her abortive rise, and then fell into step beside O'Brien as he walked into the squadroom.

"Little late in the night to be out, isn't it, Mrs. Blair?'' O'Brien asked. He was not an insensitive cop, but his manner now was brusque and dismissive. Faced with Mrs. Blair for perhaps the seventeenth time in a month, he tried not to empathize with her loss because, truthfully, he was unable to assist her, and his inability to do so was frustrating.

"Have you seen her?" Mrs. Blair asked.

"No," O'Brien said. "I'm sorry, Mrs. Blair, but I haven't."

"I have a new picture—perhaps that will help."

"Yes, perhaps it will," he said.

The telephone was ringing. He lifted the receiver and said, "Eighty-seventh, O'Brien here."

"Bob, this's Bert Kling over on Culver—the church bombing."

"Yeah, Bert."

"Seems I remember seeing a red Volkswagen on that hot-car bulletin we got yesterday. You want to dig it out and let me know where it was snatched?"

"Yeah, just a second" O'Brien said, and began scanning the sheet on his desk.

"Here's the new picture," Mrs. Blair said. "I know you're very good with runaways, Mr. O'Brien—the kids all like you and give you information. If you see Penelope, all I want you to do is tell her I love her and am sorry for the misunderstanding."

"Yeah, I will," O'Brien said. Into the phone he said, "I've got two red VWs, Bert, a sixty-four and a sixty-six. You want them both?"

"Shoot," Kling said.

"The sixty-four was stolen from a guy named Art Hauser. It was parked outside eight-six-one West Meridian."

"And the sixty-six?"

"Owner is a woman named Alice Cleary. Car was stolen from a parking lot on Fourteenth."

"North or South?"

"South. Three-o-three South."

"Right. Thanks, Bob," Kling said, and hung up.

"And ask her to come home to me," Mrs. Blair said.

"Yes, I will," O'Brien said. "If I see her, I certainly will."

"That's a nice picture of Penny, don't you think?" Mrs. Blair asked. "It was taken last Easter. It's the most recent picture I have. I thought it would be helpful to you."

O'Brien looked at the girl in the picture, and then looked up into Mrs. Blair's green eyes, misted now with tears, and suddenly wanted to reach across the desk and pat her hand reassuringly, the one thing he could not do with any honesty. Because whereas it was true that he was the squad's runaway expert, with perhaps 50 snapshots of teenagers crammed into his bulging notebook, and whereas his record of finds was more impressive than any other cop's in the city, uniformed or plainclothes, there wasn't a damn thing he could do for the mother of Penelope Blair who had run away from home last June.

"You understand—" he started to say.

"Let's not go into that again, Mr. O'Brien," she said, and rose.

"Mrs. Blair—"

"I don't want to hear it," Mrs. Blair said, walking quickly out of the squadroom. "Tell her to come home. Tell her I love her," she said, and was gone down the iron-runged steps.

O'Brien sighed and stuffed the new picture of Penelope into his notebook. What Mr. Blair did not choose to hear again was the fact that her runaway daughter Penny was 24 years old, and there was not a single agency on God's green earth, police or otherwise, that could force her to go home again if she did not choose to.

Fats Donner was a stool pigeon with a penchant for Turkish baths. A mountainous white buddha of a man, he could usually be found at one of the city's steam emporiums at any given hour of the day, draped in a towel and reveling in the heat that saturated his flabby body. Bert Kling found him in an all-night place called Steam-Fit.

Kling sent the masseur into the steam room to tell Donner he was there, and Donner sent word out that he would be through in five minutes, unless Kling wished to join him. Kling did not wish to join him. He waited in the locker room, and in seven minutes' time, Donner came out, draped in his customary towel, a ludicrous sight at any time, but particularly at 3:30 A.M.

"Hey!" Donner said. "How you doing?"

"Fine," Kling said. "How about yourself?"

"Comme-çi, comme-ça," Donner said, and made a seesawing motion with one fleshy hand.

"I'm looking for some stolen heaps," Kling said, getting directly to the point."

"What kind?" Donner said.

"Volkswagens. A sixty-four and a sixty-six."

"What color?"

"Red."

"Both of them?"

"Yes."

"Where were they heisted?"

"One from in front of eight-six-one West Meridian. The other from a parking lot on South Fourteenth."

"When was this?"

"Both last week sometime. I don't have the exact dates."

"What do you want to know?"

"Who stole them."

"You think it's the same guy on both?"

"I don't know."

"What's so important about these heaps?"

"One of them may have been used in a bombing tonight."

"You mean the church over on Culver?"

"That's right."

"Count me out," Donner said.

"What do you mean?"

"There's a lot guys in this town who're in *sympathy* with what happened over there tonight. I don't want to get involved."

"Who's going to know whether you're involved or not?" Kling asked.

"The same way *you* get information, they get information."

"I need your help, Donner."

"Yeah, well, I'm sorry on this one," Donner said and shook his head.

"In that case I'd better hurry downtown to High Street."

"Why? You got another source down there?"

"No, that's where the D.A.'s office is."

Both men stared at each other—Donner in a white towel draped around his belly, sweat still pouring from his face and his chest even though he was no longer in the steam room, and Kling looking like a slightly tired advertising executive rather than a cop threatening a man with revelation of past deeds not entirely legal. They stared at each other with total understanding, caught in the curious symbiosis of law breaker and law enforcer, an empathy created by neither man, but essential to the existence of both. It was Donner who broke the silence.

"I don't like being coerced," he said.

"I don't like being refused," Kling answered.

"When do you need this?"

"I want to get going on it before morning."

"You expect miracles, don't you?"

"Doesn't everybody?"

"Miracles cost."

"How much?"

"Twenty-five if I turn up one heap, fifty if I turn up both."

"Turn them up first. We'll talk later."

"And if somebody breaks my head later?"

"You should have thought of that before you entered the profession," Kling said. "Come on, Donner, cut it out. This is a routine bombing by a couple of punks. You've got nothing to be afraid of."

"No?" Donner asked. And then, in a very professorial voice, he uttered perhaps the biggest understatement of the decade. "Racial tensions are running high in this city right now."

"Have you got my number at the squadroom?"

"Yeah, I've got it," Donner said glumly.

"I'm going back there now. Let me hear from you soon."

"You mind if I get dressed first?" Donner asked.

The night clerk at The Addison hotel was alone in the lobby when Carella and Hawes walked in. Immersed in an open book on the desk in front of him, he did not look up as they approached. The lobby was furnished in faded Victorian: a threadbare Oriental rug, heavy curlicued mahogany tables, ponderous stuffed chairs with sagging bottoms and soiled antimacassars, two spittoons resting alongside each of two mahogany paneled supporting columns. A genuine Tiffany lampshade hung over the registration desk, one leaded glass panel gone, another badly cracked. In the old days The Addison had been a luxury hotel. It now wore its past splendor with all the style of a dance-hall girl in a moth-eaten mink she'd picked up in a thrift shop.

The clerk, in contrast to his antique surroundings, was a young man in his mid-twenties, wearing a neatly pressed brown tweed suit, a tan shirt, a gold and brown rep tie, and eyeglasses with tortoise-shell rims. He glanced up at the detectives belatedly, squinting after the intense concentration of peering at print, and then he got to his feet.

"Yes, gentlemen," he said. "May I help you?"

"Police officers," Carella said. He took his wallet from his pocket, and opened it to where his detective's shield was pinned to a leather flap.

"Yes, sir."

"I'm Detective Carella, this is my partner, Detective Hawes."

"How do you do? I'm the night clerk—my name is Ronald Sanford."

"We're looking for someone who may have been registered here two weeks ago," Hawes said.

"Well, if he was registered here two weeks ago," Sanford said, "chances are he's still registered. Most of our guests are residents."

"Do you keep stationery in the lobby here?" Carella asked.

"Sir?"

"Stationery. Is there any place in the lobby where someone could walk in off the street and pick up a piece of stationery?"

"No, sir. There's a writing desk there in the corner, near the staircase, but we don't stock it with stationery, no, sir."

"Is there stationery in the rooms?"

"Yes, sir."

"How about here at the desk?"

"Yes, of course, sir."

"Is there someone at this desk twenty-four hours a day?"

"Twenty-four hours a day, yes, sir. We have three shifts. Eight to four in the afternoon. Four to midnight. And midnight to eight A.M."

"You came on at midnight, did you?"

"Yes, sir."

"Any guests come in after you started your shift?"

"A few, yes, sir."

"Notice anybody with blood on his clothes?"

"Blood? Oh, no, sir."

"Would you have noticed?"

"What do you mean?"

"Are you generally pretty aware of what's going on around here?"

"I try to be, sir. At least, for most of the night. I catch a little nap when I'm not studying, but usually—"

"What do you study?"

"Accounting."

"Where?"

"At Ramsey U."

"Mind if we take a look at your register?"

"Not at all, sir."

He walked to the mail rack and took the hotel register from the counter there. Returning to the desk he opened it and said, "All of our present guests are residents, with the exception of Mr. Lambert in two hundred and four, and Mrs. Grant in seven hundred and one."

"When did they check in?"

"Mr. Lambert checked in—last night, I think it was. And Mrs. Grant has been here four days. She's leaving on Tuesday."

"Are these the actual signatures of your guest?"

"Yes, sir. All guests are asked to sign the register, as required by state law."

"Have you got that note, Cotton?" Carella asked, and then turned again to Sanford. "Would you mind if we took this over to the couch there?"

"Well, we're not supposed—"

"We can give you a receipt for it, if you like."

"No, I guess it'll be all right."

They carried the register to a couch upholstered in faded red velvet. With the book supported on Carella's lap they unfolded the note that Mercy Howell had received, and began to compare the signatures of the guests with the only part of the note that was not written in block letters—the words, *The Avenging Angel*.

There were 52 guests in the hotel. Carella and Hawes went through the register once, and then started through it a second time.

"Hey," Hawes said suddenly.

"What?"

"Look at this one."

He took the note and placed it on the page so that it was directly above one of the signatures:

PUT ON YOUR
CLOSE, MISS!

The Avenging Angel

Timothy Allen Ames

"What do you think?" he asked.

"Different handwriting," Carella said.

"Same initials," Hawes said.

Detective Meyer Meyer was still shaken. He did not like ghosts. He did not like this house. He wanted to go home to his wife Sarah. He wanted her to stroke his hand and tell him that such things did not exist, there was nothing to be afraid of, a grown man? How could he believe in poltergeists, shades, Dutch spirits? Ridiculous!

But he had heard them, and he had felt their chilling presence, and had almost thought he'd seen them, if only for an instant. He turned with fresh shock now toward the hall staircase and the sound of descending footsteps. Eyes wide, he waited for whatever new manifestation might present itself. He was tempted to draw his revolver, but he would appear foolish to the Gormans. He had come here a skeptic, and he was now at least *willing* to believe, and he waited in dread for whatever was coming down those steps with such ponderous footfalls—some ghoul trailing winding sheets and rattling chains? Some specter with a bleached skull for a head and long bony clutching fingers dripping the blood of babies?

Willem Van Houten, wearing his red velvet slippers and his red smoking jacket, his hair still jutting wildly from behind each ear, his blue eyes fierce and snapping, came into the living room and walked directly to where his daughter and son-in-law were sitting.

"Well?" he asked. "Did they come again?"

"Yes, Daddy," Adele said.

"What did they want this time?"

"I don't know. They spoke Dutch again."

Van Houten turned to Meyer. "Did *you* see them?" he asked.

"No, sir, I did not," Meyer said.

"But they were *here*," Gorman protested, and turned his blank face to his wife. "I heard them."

"Yes, darling," Adele assured him. "We *all* heard them. But it was like that other time, don't you remember? When we could hear them even though they couldn't quite break through."

"Yes, that's right," Gorman said, and nodded. "This happened once before, Detective Meyer." He was facing Meyer now, his head tilted quizzically, the sightless eyes covered with their black glasses. When he spoke his voice was like that of a child seeking reassurance. "But you *did* hear them, didn't you, Detective Meyer?"

"Yes," Meyer said. "I heard them, Mr. Gorman."

"And the wind?"

"Yes, the wind, too."

"And felt them. It—it gets so cold when they appear. You did feel their presence, didn't you?"

"I felt something," Meyer said.

Van Houten suddenly asked, "Are you satisfied?"

"About what?" Meyer said.

"That there are ghosts in this house? That's why you're here, isn't it? To ascertain—"

"He's here because I asked Adele to notify the police," Gorman said.

"Why did you do that?"

"Because of the stolen jewelry," Gorman said. "And because—"
He paused. "Because I've lost my sight, yes, but I wanted to—to make
sure I wasn't losing my mind as well."

"You're perfectly sane, Ralph," Van Houten said.

"About the jewelry—" Meyer said.

"*They* took it," Van Houten said.

"Who?"

"Johann and Elisabeth. Our friendly neighborhood ghosts."

"That's impossible?"

"Because ghosts—" Meyer started, and hesitated.

"Yes?"

"Ghosts—well, ghosts don't go around stealing jewelry. I mean,
what use would they have for it?" he said lamely, and looked at the
Gormans for corroboration. Neither of the Gormans seemed to be in a
substantiating mood. They sat on the sofa near the fireplace, both
looking glum.

"They want us out of this house," Van Houten said. "It's as simple as
that."

"How do you know?"

"Because they said so."

"When?"

"Before they stole the necklace and the earrings."

"They told this to you?"

"To me and to my children. All three of us were here."

"But I understand the ghosts speak only Dutch."

"Yes, I translated for Ralph and Adele."

"And then what happened?"

"What do you mean?"

"When did you discover the jewlery was missing?"

"The instant they were gone."

"You mean you went to the safe?"

"Yes, and opened it, and the jewelry was gone."

"We had put it in the safe not ten minutes before that," Adele said.
"We'd been to a party, Ralph and I, and we got home very late, and
Daddy was still awake, reading, sitting in that chair you're in this very
minute. I asked him to open the safe, and he did, and he put the jewlery in
and closed the safe and . . . and then *they* came and . . . and made their
threats."

"What time was this?"

"The usual time. The time they always come. Two forty-five in the
morning."

"And you say the jewelry was put into the safe at what time?"

"About two-thirty," Gorman said.

"And when was the safe opened again?"

"Immediately after they left. They only stay a few moments. This time they told my father-in-law they were taking the necklace and the earrings with them. He rushed to the safe as soon as the lights came on again—"

"Do the lights always go off?"

"Always,"Adele said. "It's always the same. The lights go off, and the room gets very cold, and we hear these strange voices arguing." She paused. "And then Johann and Elisabeth come."

"Except that this time they didn't come," Meyer said.

"And one other time," Adele said quickly.

"They want us out of this house," Van Houten said, "that's all there is to it. Maybe we ought to leave. Before they take *everything* from us."

"Everything? What do you mean?"

"The rest of my daughter's jewelry. And some stock certificates. Everything that's in the safe."

"Where *is* the safe?" Meyer asked.

"Here. Behind this painting." Van Houten walked to the wall opposite the fireplace. An oil painting of a pastoral landscape hung there in an ornate gilt frame. The frame was hinged to the wall. Van Houten swung the painting out as though opening a door, and revealed the small, round, black safe behind it. "Here."

"How many people know the combination?" Meyer asked.

"Just me," Van Houten said.

"Do you keep the number written down anywhere?"

"Yes."

"Where?"

"Hidden."

"Where?"

"I hardly think that's any of your business, Detective Meyer."

"I'm only trying to find out whether some other person could have got hold of the combination somehow."

"Yes, I suppose that's possible," Van Houten said. "But highly unlikely."

"Well" Meyer said, and shrugged. "I don't really know what to say. I'd like to measure the dimensions, placement of doors and windows, things like that. For my report." He shrugged again.

"It's rather late, isn't it?" Van Houten said.

"Well, I *got* here rather late," Meyer said, and smiled.

"Come, Daddy, I'll make us all some tea in the kitchen," Adele said. "Will you be long, Detective Meyer?"

"It may take a while."

"Shall I bring you some tea?"

"Thank you, that would be nice."

She rose from the couch and then guided her husband's hand to her arm. Walking slowly beside him, she led him past her father and out of the room. Van Houten looked at Meyer once again, nodded briefly, and followed them out. Meyer closed the door behind them and immediately walked to the standing floor lamp.

The woman was 60 years old, and she looked like anybody's grand-mother, except that she had just murdered her husband and three children. They had explained her rights to her, and she had told them she had nothing to hide and would answer any questions they asked her. She sat in a straight-backed squadroom chair, wearing a black cloth coat over blood-stained nightgown and robe, her handcuffed hands in her lap, her hands unmoving on her black leather pocketbook.

O'Brien and Kling looked at the police stenographer, who glanced up at the wall clock, noted the time of the interrogation's start as 3:55 A.M., and then signaled that he was ready whenever they were.

"What is your name?" O'Brien asked.

"Isabel Martin."

"How old are you, Mrs. Martin?"

"Sixty."

"Where do you live?"

"On Ainsley Avenue."

"Where on Ainsley?"

"Six hundred fifty-seven Ainsley."

"With whom do you live there?"

"With my husband Roger, and my son Peter and daughters Anne and Abigail."

"Would you like to tell us what happened tonight, Mrs. Martin?" Kling asked.

"I killed them all," she said. She had white hair, a fine aquiline nose, brown eyes behind rimless spectacles. She stared straight ahead of her as she spoke, looking neither to her right nor to her left, seemingly alone with the memory of what she had done not a half hour before.

"Can you give us some of the details, Mrs. Martin?"

"I killed *him* first."

"Who do you mean, Mrs. Martin?"

"My husband."

"When was this?"

"When he came home."

"What time was that, do you remember?"

"A little while ago."

"It's almost four o'clock now," Kling said. "Would you say this was at, what, three thirty or thereabouts?"

"I didn't look at the clock," she said. "I heard his key in the door, and I went in the kitchen, and there he was."

"Yes?"

"There's a meat cleaver I keep on the sink. I hit him with it."

"Why did you do that, Mrs. Martin?"

"Because I wanted to."

"Were you arguing with him, is that it?"

"No. I just went over to the sink and picked up the cleaver, and then I hit him with it."

"Where did you hit him, Mrs. Martin?"

"On his head and on his neck and I think on his shoulder."

"You hit him three times with the cleaver?"

"I hit him a lot of times. I don't know how many."

"Were you aware that you were hitting him?"

"Yes, I was aware."

"You knew you were striking him with a cleaver."

"Yes, I knew."

"Did you intend to kill him with the cleaver?"

"I intended to kill him with the cleaver."

"And afterwards, did you know you had killed him?"

"I knew he was dead, yes."

"What did you do then?"

"My oldest child came into the kitchen. Peter. My son. He yelled at me, he wanted to know what I'd done, he kept yelling at me and yelling at me. I hit him too—to get him to shut up. I hit him only once, across the throat."

"Did you know what you were doing at the time?"

"I knew what I was doing. He was *another* one, that Peter."

"What happened next, Mrs. Martin?"

"I went in the back bedroom where the two girls sleep, and I hit Annie with the cleaver first, and then I hit Abigail."

"Where did you hit them, Mrs. Martin?"

"On the face. Their faces."

"How many times?"

"I think I hit Annie twice, and Abigail only once."

"Why did you do that, Mrs. Martin?"

"Who would take care of them after I was gone?" Mrs. Martin asked of no one.

"There was a long pause, then Kling asked, "Is there anything else you want to tell us?"

"There's nothing more to tell. I done the right thing."

The detectives walked away from the desk. They were both pale. "Man," O'Brien whispered.

"Yeah," Kling said. "We'd better call the night D.A. right away, get him to take a full confession from her."

"Killed four of them without batting an eyelash," O'Brien said, and shook his head, and went back to where the stenographer was typing up Mrs. Martin's statement.

The telephone was ringing. Kling walked to the nearest desk and lifted the receiver. "Eighty-seventh, Detective Kling," he said.

"This is Donner."

"Yeah, Fats."

"I think I got a lead on one of those heaps."

"Shoot."

"This would be the one heisted on Fourteenth Street. According to the dope I've got it happened yesterday morning. Does that check out?"

"I'll have to look at the bulletin again. Go ahead, Fats."

"It's already been ditched," Donner said. "If you're looking for it try outside the electric company on the River Road."

"Thanks, I'll make a note of that. Who stole it, Fats?"

"This is strictly *entre nous*," Donner said. "I don't want *no* tie-in with it *never*. The guy who done it is a mean little guy—rip out his mother's heart for a dime. He hates blacks, killed one in a street rumble a few years ago, and managed to beat the rap. I think maybe some officer was on the take, huh, Kling?"

"You can't square homicide in this city, and you know it, Fats."

"Yeah? I'm surprised. You can square damn near anything else for a couple of bills."

"What's his name?"

"Danny Ryder. Three-five-four-one Grover Avenue. You won't find him there now, though."

"Where *will* I find him now?"

"Ten minutes ago he was in an all-night bar on Mason, place called Felicia's. You going in after him?"

"I am."

"Take your gun," Donner said."

There were seven people in Felicia's when Kling got there at 4:45. He cased the bar through the plate-glass window fronting the place, unbuttoned the third button of his overcoat, reached in to clutch the butt of his revolver, worked it out of the holster once and then back again, and went in through the front door.

There was the immediate smell of stale cigarette smoke and beer and sweat and cheap perfume. A Puerto Rican girl was in whispered consultation with a sailor in one of the leatherette-lined booths. Another sailor was hunched over the juke box thoughtfully considering his next selection, his face tinted orange and red and green from the colored tubing. A tired, fat, 50-year-old blonde sat at the far end of the bar, watching the sailor as though the next button he pushed might destroy the entire world. The bartender was polishing glasses. He looked up when Kling walked in and immediately smelled the law.

Two men were seated at the opposite end of the bar.

One of them was wearing a blue turtleneck sweater, gray slacks, and desert boots. His brown hair was clipped close to his scalp in a military cut. The other man was wearing a bright orange team jacket, almost luminous, with the words *Orioles, S.A.C.* lettered across its back. The one with the crewcut said something softly, and the other one chuckled. Behind the bar a glass clinked as the bartender replaced it on the shelf. The juke box erupted in sound, Jimi Hendrix rendering *All Along the Watchtower*.

Kling walked over to the two men.

"Which one of you is Danny Ryder?" he asked.

The one with the short hair said, "Who wants to know?"

"Police officer," Kling said, and the one in the orange jacket whirled with a pistol in his hand. Kling's eyes opened wide in surprise, and the pistol went off.

There was no time to think, there was hardly time to breathe. The explosion of the pistol was shockingly close, the acrid stink of cordite was in Kling's nostrils. The knowledge that he was still alive, the sweet rushing clean awareness that the bullet had somehow missed him was only a fleeting click of intelligence accompanying what was essentially a reflexive act.

Kling's .38 came free of its holster, his finger was inside the trigger guard and around the trigger, he squeezed off his shot almost before the gun had cleared the flap of his overcoat, fired into the orange jacket and threw his shoulder simultaneously against the chest of the man with the short hair, knocking him backward off his stool. The man in the orange jacket, his face twisted in pain, was leveling the pistol for another shot.

Kling fired again, squeezing the trigger without thought of rancor, and then whirled on the man with the short hair, who was crouched on the floor against the bar.

"Get up!" he yelled.

"Don't shoot!"

"Get *up*!"

He yanked the man to his feet, hurled him against the bar, thrust the muzzle of his pistol at the blue turtleneck sweater, ran his hands under the armpits and between the legs, while the man kept saying over and over again, "Don't shoot, please don't shoot."

He backed away from him and leaned over the one in the orange jacket.

"Is this Ryder?" he asked.

"Yes."

"Who're you?"

"Frank Pasquale. Look, I—"

"Shut up, Frank," Kling said. "Put your hands behind your back. Move!"

He had already taken his handcuffs from his belt. He snapped them onto Pasquale's wrists, and only then became aware that Jimi Hendrix was still singing, the sailors were watching with pale white faces, the Puerto Rican girl was screaming, the fat faded blonde had her mouth open, the bartender was frozen in midmotion, the tip of his bar towel inside a glass.

"All right," Kling said. He was breathing harshly. "All right," he said again, and wiped his forehead.

Timothy Allen Ames was a potbellied man of 40, with a thick black mustache, a mane of long black hair, and brown eyes sharply alert at 5:05 in the morning. He answered the door as though he'd been already awake, asked for identification, then asked the detectives to wait a moment, closed the door, and came back shortly afterward, wearing a robe over his striped pajamas.

"Is your name Timothy Ames?" Carella asked.

"That's me," Ames said. "Little late to be paying a visit, ain't it?"

"Or early, depending on how you look at it," Hawes said.

"One thing I can do without at five A.M. is humorous cops," Ames said. "How'd you get up here, anyway? Is that little jerk asleep at the desk again?"

"Who do you mean?" Carella asked.

"Lonnie Sanford, or whatever his name is."

"Ronald—Ronnie Sanford."

"Yeah, him. Always giving me trouble."

"What kind of trouble?"

"About broads," Ames said. "Acts like he's running a nunnery here, can't stand to see a guy come in with a girl. I notice he ain't got no compunctions about letting *cops* upstairs, though, no matter *what* time it is."

"Never mind, Sanford, let's talk about you," Carella said.

"Sure, what would you like to know?"

"Where were you between eleven twenty and twelve tonight?"

"Right here."

"Can you prove it?"

"Sure. I got back here about eleven o'clock, and I been here ever since. Ask Sanford downstairs—no, he wasn't on yet. He don't come on till midnight."

"Who *else* can we ask, Ames?"

"Listen, you going to make trouble for me?"

"Only if you're in trouble."

"I got a broad here. She's over eighteen, don't worry. But, like, she's a junkie, you know? But I know you guys, and if you want to make trouble—"

"Where is she?"

"In the john."

"Get her out here."

"Look, do me a favor, will you? Don't bust the kid. She's trying to kick the habit, she really is. I been helping her along."

"How?"

"By keeping her busy," Ames said, and winked.

"Call her."

"Bea, come out here!" Ames shouted.

There were a few moments of hesitation, then the bathroom door opened. The girl was a tall plain brunette wearing a short terrycloth robe. She sidled into the room cautiously, as though expecting to be struck in the face at any moment. Her brown eyes were wide with expectancy. She knew fuzz, she knew what it was like to be arrested on a narcotics charge, and she had listened to the conversation from behind the closed bathroom door; and now she waited for whatever was coming, expecting the worst.

"What's your name, Miss?" Hawes asked.

"Beatrice Norden."

"What time did you get here tonight, Beatrice?"

"About eleven."

"Was this man with you?"

"Yes."

"Did he leave here at any time tonight?"

"No."

"Are you sure?"

"I'm, positive. He picked me up about nine o'clock——"

"Where do you live, Beatrice?"

"Well, that's the thing, you see," the girl said. "I been put out of my room."

"So where'd he pick you up?"

"At my girl friend's house. You can ask her, she was there when he came. Her name is Rosalie Dawes. Anyway, Timmy picked me up at nine, and we went out to eat, and we came up here around eleven."

"I hope you're telling us the truth, Miss Norden," Carella said.

"I swear to God, we been here all night," Beatrice answered.

"All right, Ames," Hawes said, "we'd like a sample of your handwriting."

"My *what*?"

"Your handwriting."

"What for?"

"We collect autographs," Carella said.

"Gee, these guys really break me up," Ames said to the girl. "Regular night-club comics we get in the middle of the night."

Carella handed him a pencil and then tore a sheet from his pad. "You want to write this for me?" he said. "The first part's in block lettering."

"What the hell is block lettering?" Ames asked.

"He means *print* it," Hawes said.

"Then why didn't he say so?"

"Put on your clothes, Miss," Carella said.

"What for?" Beatrice said.

"That's what I want him to write," Carella explained.

"Oh."

"Put on your clothes, Miss," Ames repeated, and lettered it onto the sheet of paper. "What else?" he asked, looking up.

"Now sign it in your own handwriting with the following words: The Avenging Angel."

"What the hell is this supposed to be?" Ames asked.

"You want to write it, please?"

Ames wrote the words, then handed the slip of paper to Carella. He and Hawes compared it with the note that had been mailed to Mercy Howell:

PUT ON YOUR CLOTHES,
MISS.

The Avenging Angel

PUT ON YOUR
CLOSE, MISS!

The Avenging Angel

"So?" Ames asked.

"So you're clean," Hawes said.

At the desk downstairs, Ronnie Sanford was still immersed in his accounting textbook. He got to his feet again as the detectives came out of the elevator, adjusted his glasses on his nose, and said, "Any luck?"

"Afraid not," Carella answered. "We're going to need this register for a while, if that's okay."

"Well—"

"Give him a receipt for it, Cotton," Carella said. It was late, and he didn't want a debate in the lobby of a rundown hotel. Hawes quickly made out a receipt in duplicate, signed both copies, and handed one to Sanford.

"What about this torn cover?" Hawes asked belatedly.

"Yeah," Carella said. There was a small rip on the leather binding of the book. He fingered it briefly now, then said, "Better note that on the receipt, Cotton.'' Hawes took back the receipt and, on both copies, jotted the words ''Small rip on front cover.'' He handed the receipts back to Sanford.

''Want to just sign these, Mr. Sanford?'' he said.

''What for?'' Sanford asked.

''To indicate we received the register in this condition.''

''Oh, sure,'' Sanford said. He picked up a ballpoint pen from its desk holder, and asked, ''What do you want me to write?''

''Your name and your title that's all.''

''My title?''

''Night Clerk, The Addison Hotel.''

''Oh, sure,'' Sanford said, and signed both receipts. ''This okay?'' he asked. The detectives looked at what he had written.

''You like girls?'' Carella asked suddenly.

''What?'' Sanford asked.

''Girls,'' Hawes said.

''Sure. Sure, I like girls.''

''Dressed or naked?''

''What?''

''With clothes or without?''

''I—I don't know what you mean, sir.''

''Where were you tonight between eleven twenty and midnight?'' Hawes asked.

''Getting—getting ready to come to—to work,'' Sanford said.

''You sure you weren't in the alley of the Eleventh Street Theater stabbing a girl named Mercy Howell?''

''What? No—no, of course not. I was—I was home—getting dressed—'' Sanford took a deep breath and decided to get indignant. ''Listen, what's this all about?'' he said. ''Would you mind telling me?''

''It's all about this,'' Carella said, and turned one of the receipts so that Sanford could read the signature:

Ronald Sanford
Night Clerk
The Addison Hotel

''Get your hat,'' Hawes said. ''Study hall's over.''

* * *

It was 5:25 when Adele Gorman came into the room with Meyer's cup of tea. He was crouched near the air-conditioning unit recessed into the wall to the left of the drapes; he glanced up when he heard her, then rose.

"I didn't know what you took," she said, "so I brought everything."

"Thank you," he said. "Just a little sugar is fine."

"Have you measured the room?" she asked, and put the tray down on the table in front of the sofa.

"Yes, I think I have everything I need now," Meyer said. He put a spoonful of sugar into the tea, stirred it, then lifted the cup to his mouth. "Hot," he said.

Adele Gorman was watching him silently. She said nothing. He kept sipping his tea. The ornate clock on the mantelpiece ticked in a swift whispering tempo.

"Do you always keep this room so dim?" Meyer asked.

"Well, my husband is blind, you know," Adele said. "There's really no need for brighter light."

"Mmm. But your father reads in this room, doesn't he?"

"I beg your pardon?"

"The night you came home from that party. He was sitting in the chair over there near the floor lamp. Reading. Remember?"

"Oh. Yes, he was."

"Bad light to read by."

"Yes, I suppose it is."

"I think maybe those bulbs are defective," Meyer said.

"Do you think so?"

"Mmm. I happened to look at the lamp, and there are three one-hundred-watt bulbs in it, all of them burning. You should be getting a lot more light with that much wattage."

"Well, I really don't know about such—"

"Unless the lamp is on a rheostat, of course."

"I'm afraid I don't even know what a rheostat is."

"It's an adjustable resistor. You can dim your lights or make them brighter with it. I thought maybe the lamp was on a rheostat, but I couldn't find a control knob anywhere in the room." Meyer paused. "You wouldn't know if there's a rheostat control in the house, would you?"

"I'm sure there isn't," Adele said.

"Must be defective bulbs then," Meyer said, and smiled. "Also, I think your air conditioner is broken."

"No, I'm sure it isn't."

"Well, I was just looking at it, and all the switches are turned to the 'On' position, but it isn't working. So I guess it's broken. That's a shame, too, because it's such a nice unit. Sixteen thousand BTUs. That's a lot of cooling power for a room this size. We've got one of those big old price-fixed apartments on Concord, my wife and I, with a large bedroom, and we get adequate cooling from a half-ton unit. It's a shame this one is broken."

"Yes. Detective Meyer, I don't wish to appear rude, but it is late—"

"Sure," Meyer said. "Unless, of course, the air conditioner's on a remote switch, too. So that all you have to do is turn a knob in another part of the house and it comes on." He paused. "*Is* there such a switch somewhere, Mrs. Gorman?"

"I have no idea."

"I'll finish my tea and run along," Meyer said. He lifted the cup to his lips, sipped the tea, glanced at her over the rim, took the cup away from his mouth, and said, "But I'll be back."

"I hardly think there's any need for that," Adele said.

"Well, some jewelry's been stolen—"

"The ghosts—"

"Come off it, Mrs. Gorman."

The room went silent.

"Where are the loudspeakers, Mrs. Gorman?" Meyer asked. "In the false beams up there? They're hollow—I checked them out."

"I think perhaps you'd better leave," Adele said slowly.

"Sure," Meyer said. He put the teacup down, sighed, and got to his feet.

"I'll show you out," Adele said.

They walked to the front door and out into the driveway. The night was still. The drizzle had stopped, and a thin layer of frost covered the grass rolling away toward the river below. Their footsteps crunched on the gravel as they walked slowly toward the automobile.

"My husband was blinded four years ago," Adele said abruptly. "He's a chemical engineer, there was an explosion at the plant, he could have been killed. Instead, he was only blinded." She hesitated an instant, then said again, "Only blinded," and there was such a sudden cry of despair in those two words that Meyer wanted to put his arm around her, console her the way he might his daughter, tell her that everything would be all right come morning, the night was almost done, and morning was on the horizon.

But instead he leaned on the fender of his car, and she stood beside him looking down at the driveway gravel, her eyes not meeting his. They could have been conspirators exchanging secrets in the night, but they were only two people who had been thrown together on a premise as flimsy as the ghosts that inhabited this house.

"He gets a disability pension from the company," Adele said, "they've really been quite kind to us. And, of course, I work. I teach school, Detective Meyer. Kindergarten. I love children." She paused. She would not raise her eyes to meet his. "But—it's sometimes very difficult. My father, you see—"

Meyer waited. He longed suddenly for dawn, but he waited patiently, and heard her catch her breath as though committed to go ahead now however painful the revelation might be, compelled to throw herself on the mercy of the night before the morning sun broke through.

"My father's been retired for fifteen years." She took a deep breath, and then said, "He gambles, Detective Meyer. He's a horse player. He loses large sums of money."

"Is that why he stole your jewels?" Meyer asked.

"You know, don't you?" Adele said simply, and raised her eyes to his. "Of course you know. It's quite transparent, his ruse, a shoddy little show really, a performance that would fool no one but—no one but a blind man." She brushed at her cheek; he could not tell whether the cold air had caused her tears. "I really don't care about the theft; the jewels were left to me by my mother, and after all it was my father who bought them for her, so it's—it's really like returning a legacy. I really don't care about that part of it. I'd have *given* the jewelry to him if only he'd asked, but he's so proud, such a proud man. A proud man who—who steals from me and pretends that ghosts are committing the crime.

"And my husband, in his dark universe, listens to the sounds my father puts on tape and visualizes things he cannot quite believe and so he asks me to notify the police because he needs an impartial observer to contradict the suspicion that someone is stealing pennies from his blind man's cup. That's why I came to you, Detective Meyer. So that you would arrive here tonight and perhaps be fooled as I was fooled at first, and perhaps say to my husband, 'Yes, Mr. Gorman, there *are* ghosts in your house.'"

She suddenly placed her hand on his sleeve. The tears were streaming down her face, she had difficulty catching her breath. "Because, you see, Detective Meyer, there *are* ghosts in this house, there really and truly are. The ghost of a proud man who was once a brilliant judge and who is now a gambler and a thief; and the ghost of a man who once could see, and who now trips and falls in the darkness.''

On the river a tugboat hooted. Adele Gorman fell silent. Meyer opened the door of his car and got in behind the wheel.

"I'll call your husband tomorrow,'' he said abruptly and gruffly. "Tell him I'm convinced something supernatural is happening here.''

"And will you be back, Detective Meyer?''

"No,'' he said. "I won't be back, Mrs. Gorman.''

In the squadroom they were wrapping up the night. Their day had begun at 7:45 P.M. yesterday and they had been officially relieved at 5:45 A.M.; but they had not left the office yet because there were questions still to be asked, reports to be typed, odds and ends to be put in place before they could go home. And since the relieving detectives were busy getting *their* approaching workday organized, the squadroom at 6:00 A.M. was busier than it might have been on any given afternoon, with two teams of cops getting in each others' way.

In the Interrogation Room, Carella and Hawes were questioning young Ronald Sanford in the presence of the Assistant District Attorney who had come over earlier to take Mrs. Martin's confession, and who now found himself listening to another one when all he wanted to do was go home to sleep. Sanford seemed terribly shocked that they had been able to notice the identical handwriting in *The Addison Hotel* and The Avenging Angel—he couldn't get over it. He thought he had been very clever in misspelling the word ''Clothes,'' because then they would think some illiterate had written it, not someone who was studying to be an accountant.

He could not explain why he had killed Mercy Howell. He got all mixed up when he tried to explain that. It had something to do with the moral climate of America, and people exposing themselves in public, people like that shouldn't be allowed to pollute others, to foist their filth on others, to intrude on the privacy of others who wanted to make something of themselves, studying accounting by day and working in a hotel by night, what right had these other people to ruin it for everybody else?

Frank Pasquale's tune, sung in the Clerical Office to Kling and O'Brien, was not quite so hysterical, but similar to Sanford's nonetheless. He had got the idea together with Danny Ryder. They had decided between them that the blacks in America were taking jobs away from decent hardworking people who only wanted to be left alone, what right did they have to force themselves on everybody else? So they had decided to bomb the church, just to show them they couldn't get away with it, not in America. He didn't seem terribly concerned over the fact that his partner was lying stone-cold dead on a slab at the morgue, or that their little Culver Avenue expedition had cost three people their lives, and had severely injured a half dozen others. All he wanted to know, repeatedly, was whether his picture would be in the newspaper.

At his desk Meyer Meyer started to type up a report on the Gorman ghosts, then decided the hell with it. If the lieutenant asked him where he'd been half the night, he would say he had been out looking for trouble in the streets. The Lord knew there was enough of *that* around, any night. He pulled the report forms and their separating sheets of carbon paper from the ancient typewriter, and noticed that Detective Hal Willis was pacing the room anxiously, waiting to get at the desk the moment he vacated it.

"Okay, Hal," he said, "it's all yours."

"*Finalmente!*" Willis, who was not Italian, said.

The telephone rang.

The sun was up when they came out of the building and walked past the hanging green "87" globes and down the low flat steps to the sidewalk. The park across the street shimmered with early-morning autumn brilliance, the sky above it was clear and blue. It was going to be a beautiful day.

They walked toward the diner on the next block, Meyer and O'Brien ahead of the others, Carella, Hawes, and Kling bringing up the rear. They were tired, and exhaustion showed in their eyes, in the set of their mouths, in the pace they kept. They talked without animation, mostly about their work, their breaths feathery and white on the cold morning air.

When they reached the diner, they took off their overcoats and ordered hot coffee and cheese Danish and toasted English muffins. Meyer said he thought he was coming down with a cold. Carella told him about some cough medicine his wife had given one of the children. O'Brien, munching on a muffin, glanced across the diner and a young girl in one of the booths. She was wearing blue jeans and a bright-colored Mexican serape, and she was talking to a boy wearing a Navy pea jacket.

"I think I see somebody," he said, and he moved out of the booth past Kling and Hawes, who were talking about the newest regulation on search and seizure.

The girl looked up when he approached the booth.

"Miss Blair?" he said. "Penelope Blair?"

"Yes," the girl answered. "Who are you?"

"Detective O'Brien," he said, "Eighty-seventh Precinct. Your mother was in last night, Penny. She asked me to tell you—"

"Flake off, cop," Penelope Blair said. "Go stop a riot somewhere."

O'Brien looked at her silently for a moment. Then he nodded, turned away, and went back to the table.

"Anything?" Kling asked.

"You can't win 'em all," O'Brien said.

C. Auguste Dupin

THE MURDERS IN THE RUE MORGUE
Edgar Allan Poe

What song the Syrens sang, or what name Achilles assumed
when he hid himself among women, although puzzling ques-
tions, are not beyond all conjecture.

SIR THOMAS BROWNE

THE MENTAL FEATURES discoursed of as the analytical, are, in themselves, but little susceptible of analysis. We appreciate them only in their effects. We know of them, among other things, that they are always to their possessor, when inordinately possessed, a source of the liveliest enjoyment. As the strong man exults in his physical ability, delighting in such exercises as call his muscles into action, so glories the analyst in that moral activity which *disentangles*. He derives pleasure from even the most trivial occupations bringing his talent into play. He is fond of enigmas, of conundrums, hieroglyphics; exhibiting in his solutions of each a degree of *acumen* which appears to the ordinary apprehension praeternatural. His results, brought about by the very soul and essence of method, have, in truth, the whole air of intuition.

The faculty of re-solution is possibly much invigorated by mathematical study, and especially by that highest branch of it which, unjustly, and merely on account of its retrograde operations, has been called, as if *par excellence,* analysis. Yet to calculate is not in itself to analyze. A chess player, for example, does the one, without effort at the other. It follows that the game of chess, in its effects upon mental character, is greatly misunderstood. I am not now writing a treatise, but simply prefacing a somewhat peculiar narrative by observations very much at random; I will, therefore, take occasion to assert that the higher powers of the reflective intellect are more decidedly and more usefully tasked by the unostentatious game of draughts than by all the elaborate frivolity of chess. In this latter, where the pieces have different and *bizarre* motions, with various and variable values, what is only complex, is mistaken (a not unusual error) for what is profound. The *attention* is here called powerfully into play. If it flag for an instant, an oversight is committed,

101

resulting in injury or defeat. The possible moves being not only manifold, but involute, the chances of such oversights are multiplied; and in
nine cases out of ten, it is the more concentrative rather than the more
acute player who conquers. In draughts, on the contrary, where the
moves are *unique* and have but little variation, the probabilities of
inadvertence are diminished, and the mere attention being left comparatively unemployed, what advantages are obtained by either party are
obtained by superior *acumen*. To be less abstract, let us suppose a game
of draughts where the pieces are reduced to four kings, and where, of
course, no oversight is to be expected. It is obvious that here the victory
can be decided (the players being at all equal) only by some *recherché*
movement, the result of some strong exertion of the intellect. Deprived
of ordinary resources, the analyst throws himself into the spirit of his
opponent, identifies himself therewith, and not unfrequently sees thus, at
a glance, the sole methods (sometimes indeed absurdly simple ones) by
which he may seduce into error or hurry into miscalculation.

Whist has long been noted for its influence upon what is termed the
calculating power; and men of the highest order of intellect have been
known to take an apparently unaccountable delight in it, while eschew-
ing chess as frivolous. Beyond doubt there is nothing of a similar nature
so greatly tasking the faculty of analysis. The best chess-player in
Christendom *may* be little more than the best player of chess; but
proficiency in whist implies capacity for success in all those more
important undertakings where mind struggles with mind. When I say
proficiency, I mean that perfection in the game which includes a comprehension of *all* the sources whence legitimate advantage may be
derived. These are not only manifold, but multiform, and lie frequently
among recesses of thought altogether inaccessible to the ordinary understanding. To observe attentively is to remember distinctly; and, so far,
the concentrative chessplayer will do very well at whist; while the rules
of Hoyle (themselves based upon the mere mechanics of the game) are
sufficiently and generally comprehensible. Thus to have a retentive
memory, and proceed by "the book" are points commonly regarded as
the sum total of good playing. But it is in matters beyond the limits of
mere rule that the skill of the analyst is evinced. He makes, in silence, a
host of observations and inferences. So, perhaps, do his companions;
and the difference in the extent of the information obtained, lies not so
much in the validity of the inference as in the quality of the observation.
The necessary knowledge is that of *what* to observe. Our player confines
himself not at all; nor, because the game is the object, does he reject

deductions from things external to the game. He examines the countenance of his partner, comparing it carefully with that of each of his opponents. He considers the mode of assorting the cards in each hand; often counting trump by trump, and honor by honor, through the glances bestowed by their holders upon each. He notes every variation of face as the play progresses, gathering a fund of thought from the differences in the expression of certainty, of surprise, or triumph, or chagrin. From the manner of gathering up a trick he judges whether the person taking it, can make another in the suit. He recognizes what is played through feint, by the air with which it is thrown upon the table. A casual or inadvertent word; the accidental dropping or turning of a card, with the accompanying anxiety or carelessness in regard to its concealment; the counting of the tricks, with the order of their arrangement; embarrassment, hesitation, eagerness, or trepidation—all afford, to his apparently intuitive perception, indications of the true state of affairs. The first two or three rounds having been played, he is in full possession of the contents of each hand, and thenceforward puts down his cards with as absolute a precision of purpose as if the rest of the party had turned outward the faces of their own.

The analytical power should not be confounded with simple ingenuity; for while the analyst is necessarily ingenious, the ingenious man is often remarkably incapable of analysis. The constructive or combining power, by which ingenuity is usually manifested, and to which the phrenologists (I believe erroneously) have assigned a separate organ, supposing it a primitive faculty, has been so frequently seen in those whose intellect bordered otherwise upon idiocy, as to have attracted general observation among writers on morals. Between ingenuity and the analytic ability there exists a difference far greater, indeed, than that between the fancy and the imagination, but of a character very strictly analogous. It will be found, in fact, that the ingenious are always fanciful, and the *truly* imaginative never otherwise than analytic.

The narrative which follows will appear to the reader somewhat in the light of a commentary upon the propositions just advanced.

Residing in Paris during the spring and part of the summer of 18—, I there became acquainted with a Monsieur C. Auguste Dupin. This young gentleman was of an excellent, indeed of an illustrious family, but, by a variety of untoward events, had been reduced to such poverty that the energy of his character succumbed beneath it, and he ceased to bestir himself in the world, or to care for the retrieval of his fortunes. By courtesy of his creditors, there still remained in his possession a small remnant of his patrimony; and, upon the income arising from this, he managed, by means of a rigorous economy, to procure the necessaries of life, without troubling himself about its superfluities. Books, indeed, were his sole luxuries, and in Paris these are easily obtained.

Our first meeting was at an obscure library in the Rue Montmartre, where the accident of our both being in search of the same very rare and very remarkable volume, brought us into closer communion. We saw each other again and again. I was deeply interested in the little family history which he detailed to me with all that candor which a Frenchman indulges whenever mere self is his theme. I was astonished, too, at the vast extent of his reading; and, above all, I felt my soul enkindled within me by the wild fervor, and the vivid freshness of his imagination. Seeking in Paris the objects I then sought, I felt that the society of such a man would be to me a treasure beyond price; and this feeling I frankly confided to him. It was at length arranged that we should live together during my stay in the city; and as my worldly circumstances were somewhat less embarrassed than his own, I was permitted to be at the expense of renting, and furnishing in a style which suited the rather fantastic gloom of our common temper, a time-eaten and grotesque mansion, long deserted through superstitions into which we did not inquire, and tottering to its fall in a retired and desolate portion of the Faubourg St. Germain.

Had the routine of our life at this place been known to the world, we should have been regarded as madmen—although, perhaps, as madmen of a harmless nature. Our seclusion was perfect. We admitted no visitors. Indeed the locality of our retirement had been carefully kept a secret from my own former associates; and it had been many years since Dupin had ceased to know or be known in Paris. We existed within ourselves alone.

It was a freak of fancy in my friend (for what else shall I call it?) to be enamored of the night for her own sake; and into this *bizarrerie*, as into all his others, I quietly fell; giving myself up to his wild whims with a perfect *abandon*. The sable divinity would not herself dwell with us always; but we could counterfeit her presence. At the first dawn of the morning we closed all the massy shutters of our old building; lighting a couple of tapers which, strongly perfumed, threw out only the ghastliest and feeblest of rays. By the aid of these we then busied our souls in dreams—reading, writing, or conversing, until warned by the clock of the advent of the true Darkness. Then we sallied forth into the streets, arm in arm, continuing the topics of the day, or roaming far and wide until a late hour, seeking, amid the wild lights and shadows of the populous city, that infinity of mental excitement which quiet observation can afford.

At such times I could not help remarking and admiring (although from his rich ideality I had been prepared to expect it) a peculiar analytic ability in Dupin. He seemed, too, to take an eager delight in its exercise—if not exactly in its display—and did not hesitate to confess the pleasure thus derived. He boasted to me, with a low chuckling laugh, that most men, in respect to himself, wore windows in their bosoms, and was wont to follow up such assertions by direct and very startling proofs of his intimate knowledge of my own. His manner at these moments was frigid and abstract; his eyes were vacant in expression; while his voice, usually a rich tenor, rose into a treble which would have sounded petulantly but for the deliberateness and entire distinctness of the enunciation. Observing him in these moods, I often dwelt meditatively upon the old philosophy of the Bi-Part Soul, and amused myself with the fancy of a double Dupin—the creative and the resolvent.

Let it not be supposed, from what I have just said, that I am detailing any mystery, or penning any romance. What I have described in the Frenchman was merely the result of an excited, or perhaps of a diseased, intelligence, but of the character of his remarks at the periods in question an example will best convey the idea.

We were strolling one night down a long dirty street, in the vicinity of the Palais Royal. Being both, apparently, occupied with thought, neither of us had spoken a syllable for fifteen minutes at least. All at once Dupin broke forth with these words:

"He is a very little fellow, that's true, and would do better for the *Théâtre des Variétés*."

"There can be no doubt of that," I replied, unwittingly, and not at first observing (so much had I been absorbed in reflection) the extraordinary manner in which the speaker had chimed in with my meditations. In an instant afterward I recollected myself, and my astonishment was profound.

"Dupin," said I, gravely, "this is beyond my comprehension. I do not hesitate to say that I am amazed, and can scarcely credit my senses. How was it possible you should know I was thinking of —?" Here I paused, to ascertain beyond a doubt whether he really knew of whom I thought.

"—— of Chantilly," said he, "why do you pause? You were remarking to yourself that his diminutive figure unfitted him for tragedy."

This was precisely what had formed the subject of my reflections.

Chantilly was a *quondam* cobbler of the Rue St. Dennis, who, becoming stage-mad, had attempted the *rôle* of Xerxes, Crébillon's tragedy so called, and been notoriously Pasquinaded for his pains.

"Tell me, for Heaven's sake," I exclaimed, "the method—if method there is—by which you have been enabled to fathom my soul in this matter." In fact, I was even more startled than I would have been willing to express.

"It was the fruiterer," replied my friend, "who brought you to the conclusion that the mender of soles was not of sufficient height for Xerxes *et id genus omne.*"

"The fruiterer!—you astonish me—I know no fruiterer whomsoever."

"The man who ran up against you as we entered the street—it may have been fifteen minutes ago."

I now remembered that, in fact, a fruiterer, carrying upon his head a large basket of apples, had nearly thrown me down, by accident, as we passed from the Rue C—— into the thoroughfare where we stood; but what this had to do with Chantilly I could not possibly understand.

There was not a particle of *charlatânerie* about Dupin. "I will explain," he said, "and that you may comprehend all clearly, we will first retrace the course of your meditations, from the moment in which I spoke to you until that of the *rencontre* with the fruiterer in question. The larger links of the chain run thus—Chantilly, Orion, Dr. Nichols, Epicurus, Stereotomy, the street stones, the fruiterer."

There are few persons who have not, at some period of their lives, amused themselves in retracing their steps by which particular conclusions of their own minds have been attained. The occupation is often full of interest; and he who attempts it for the first time is astonished by the apparently illimitable distance and incoherence between the starting-point and the goal. What, then, must have been my amazement, when I heard the Frenchman speak what he had just spoken, and I could not help acknowledging that he had spoken the truth. He continued:

"We had been talking of horses, if I remember aright, just before leaving the Rue C——. This was the last subject we discussed. As we crossed into this street, a fruiterer, with a large basket upon his head, brushing quickly past us, thrust you upon a pile of paving-stones collected at a spot where the causeway is undergoing repair. You stepped upon one of the loose fragments, slipped, slightly strained your ankle, appeared vexed or sulky, muttered a few words, turned to look at the pile, and then proceeded in silence. I was not particularly attentive to what you did; but observation has become with me, of late, a species of necessity.

"You kept your eyes upon the ground—glancing, with a petulant expression, at the holes and ruts in the pavement, (so that I saw you were still thinking of the stones,) until we reached the little alley called Lamartine, which has been paved, by way of experiment, with the overlapping and riveted blocks. Here your countenance brightened up, and, perceiving your lips move, I could not doubt that you murmured the word 'stereotomy,' a term very affectedly applied to this species of pavement. I knew that you could not say to yourself 'stereotomy' without being brought to think of atomies, and thus of the theories of Epicurus; and since, when we discussed this subject not very long ago, I mentioned to you how singlarly, yet with how little notice, the vague guesses of that noble Greek had met with confirmation in the late nebular cosmogony, I felt that you could not avoid casting your eyes upward to the great *nebula* in Orion, and I certainly expected that you would do so. You did look up; and I was now assured that I had correctly followed your steps. But in that bitter *tirade* upon Chantilly, which appeared in yesterday's '*Musée*,' the satirist, making some disgraceful allusions to the cobbler's change of name upon assuming the buskin, quoted a Latin line about which we have often conversed. I mean the line

Perdidit antiquum litera prima sonum.

I had told you that this was in reference to Orion, formerly written Urion; and, from certain pungencies connected with this explanation, I was aware that you could not have forgotten it. It was clear, therefore, that you would not fail to combine the two ideas of Orion and Chantilly. That you did combine them I saw by the character of the smile which passed over your lips. You thought of the poor cobbler's immolation. So far, you had been stooping in your gait; but now I saw you draw yourself up to your full height. I was then sure that you reflected upon the diminutive figure of Chantilly. At this point I interrupted your meditations to remark that as, in fact, he *was* a very little fellow—that Chantilly—he would do better at the *Théâtre des Variétés*."

Not long after this, we were looking over an evening edition of the *Gazette des Tribunaux*, when the following paragraphs arrested our attention.

EXTRAORDINARY MURDERS

This morning, about three o'clock, the inhabitants of the Quartier St. Roch were roused from sleep by a succession of terrific shrieks, issuing, apparently, from the fourth story of a house in the Rue Morgue, known to be in the sole occupancy of one Madame L'Espanaye, and her daughter, Mademoiselle Camille L'Espanaye. After some delay, occasioned by a fruitless attempt to procure admission in the usual manner, the gateway was broken in with a crowbar, and eight or ten of the neighbors entered, accompanied by two *gendarmes*. By this time the cries had ceased; but, as the party rushed up the first flight of stairs, two or more rough voices, in angry contention, were distinguished, and seemed to proceed from the upper part of the house. As the second landing was reached, these sounds, also, had ceased, and everything remained perfectly quiet. The party spread themselves and hurried from room to room. Upon arriving at a large back chamber in the fourth story, (the door of which, being found locked, with the key inside, was forced open,) a spectacle presented itself which struck every one present not less with horror than with astonishment.

The apartment was in the wildest disorder—the furniture broken and thrown about in all directions. There was only one bedstead; and from this the bed had been removed, and thrown into the middle of the floor. On a chair lay a razor, besmeared with blood. On the hearth were two or three long and thick tresses of gray human hair, also dabbled with blood, and seeming to have been pulled out by the roots. Upon the floor were found four Napoleons, an ear-ring of topaz, three large silver spoons three smaller of *metal d'Alger,* and two bags, containing nearly four thousand francs in gold. The drawers of a *bureau,* which stood in one corner, were open, and had been, apparently, rifled, although many articles still remained in them. A small iron safe was discovered under the *bed* (not under the bedstead). It was open, with the key still in the door. It has no contents beyond a few old letters, and other papers of little consequence.

Of Madame L'Espanaye no traces were here seen; but an unusual quantity of soot being observed in the fireplace, a search was made in the chimney, and (horrible to relate!) the corpse of the daughter, head downward, was dragged therefrom; it having been thus forced up the narrow aperture for a considerable distance. The body was quite warm. Upon examining it, many excoriations were perceived, no doubt occasioned by the violence with which it had been thrust up and disengaged. Upon the face were many severe scratches, and, upon the throat, dark bruises, and deep indentations of finger nails, as if the deceased had been throttled to death.

After a thorough investigation of every portion of the house without farther discovery, the party made its way into a small paved yard in the rear of the building, where lay the corpse of the old lady, with her throat so entirely cut that, upon an attempt to raise her, the head fell off. The body, as well as the head, was fearfully mutilated—the former so much so as scarcely to retain any semblance of humanity.

To this horrible mystery there is not as yet, we believe, the slightest clew.

The next day's paper had these additional particulars:

THE TRAGEDY IN THE RUE MORGUE

Many individuals have been examined in relation to this most extraordinary and frightful affair, [the word *'affaire'* has not yet, in France, that levity of import which it conveys with us] but nothing whatever has transpired to throw light upon it. We give below all the material testimony elicited.

Pauline Duborg, laundress, deposes that she has known both the deceased for three years, having washed for them during that period. The old lady and her daughter seemed on good terms—very affectionate toward each other. They were excellent pay. Could not speak in regard to their mode or means of living. Believed that Madam L. told fortunes for a living. Was reputed to have money put by. Never met any person in the house when she called for the clothes or took them home. Was sure that they had no servant in employ. There appeared to be no furniture in any part of the building except in the fourth story.

Pierre Moreau, tobacconist, deposes that he has been in the habit of selling small quantities of tobacco and snuff to Madame L'Espanaye for nearly four years. Was born in the neighborhood, and has always resided there. The deceased and her daughter had occupied the house in which the corpses were found, for more than six years. It was formerly occupied by a jeweller, who under-let the upper rooms to various persons. The house was the property of Madame L. She became dissatisfied with the abuse of the premises by her tenant, and moved into them herself, refusing to let any portion. The old lady was childish. Witness had seen the daughter some five or six times during the six years. The two lived an exceedingly retired life—were reputed to have money. Had heard it said among the neighbors that Madame L. told fortunes—did not believe it. Had never seen any person enter the door except the old lady and her daughter, a porter once or twice, and a physician some eight or ten times.

Many other persons, neighbors, gave evidence to the same effect. No one was spoken of as frequenting the house. It was not known whether there were any living connections of Madame L. and her daughter. The shutters of the front windows were seldom opened. Those in the rear were always closed, with the exception of the large back room, fourth story. The house was a good house—not very old.

Isidore Musèt, gendarme, deposes that he was called to the house about three o'clock in the morning, and found some twenty or thirty persons at the gateway, endeavoring to gain admittance. Forced it open, at length, with a bayonet—not with a crowbar. Had but little difficulty in getting it open, on account of its being a double or folding gate, and bolted neither at bottom nor top. The shrieks were continued until the gate was forced—and then suddenly ceased. They seemed to be screams of some person (or persons) in great agony—were loud and drawn out, not short and quick. Witness led the way up stairs. Upon reaching the first landing, heard two voices in loud and angry contention—the one a gruff voice, the other much shriller—a very strange voice. Could distinguish some words of the former, which was that of a Frenchman. Was positive that it was not a woman's voice. Could distinguish the words 'sacré' and 'diable.' The shrill voice was that of a foreigner. Could not be sure whether it was the voice of a man or a woman. Could not make out what was said, but believed the language to be Spanish. The state of the room and of the bodies was described by this witness as we described them yesterday.

Henri Duval, a neighbor, and by trade a silver-smith, deposes that he was one of the party who first entered the house. Corroborates the testimony of Musèt, in general. As soon as they forced an entrance, they reclosed the door, to keep out the crowd, which collected very fast, notwithstanding the lateness of the hour. The shrill voice, this witness thinks, was that of an Italian. Was certain it was not French. Could not be sure that it was a man's voice. It might have been a woman's. Was not acquainted with the Italian language. Could not distinguish the words, but was convinced by the intonation that the speaker was an Italian. Knew Madam L. and her daughter. Had conversed with both frequently. Was sure that the shrill voice was not that of either of the deceased.

—Odenheimer, restaurateur. —This witness volunteered his testimony. Not speaking French, was examined through an interpreter. Is a native of Amsterdam. Was passing the house at the time of the shrieks. They lasted for several minutes—probably ten. They were long and loud—very awful and distressing. Was one of those who entered the building. Corroborated the previous evidence in every respect but one. Was sure that the shrill voice was that of a man—of a Frenchman. Could not distinguish the words uttered. They were loud and quick—unequal—spoken apparently in fear as well as in anger. The voice was harsh—not so much shrill as harsh. Could not call it a shrill voice. The gruff voice said repeatedly, 'Sacré,' ' diable,' and once 'mon Dieu.'

Jules Mignaud, banker, of the firm of Mignaud et Fils, Rue Deloraine. Is the elder Mignaud. Madame L'Espanaye had some property. Had opened an account with his banking house in the spring of the year—(eight years previously). Made frequent deposits in small sums. Had checked for nothing until the third day before her death, when she took out in person the sum of 4000 francs. This sum was paid in gold, and a clerk sent home with the money.

Adolphe Le Bon, clerk to Mignaud et Fils, deposes that on the day in question, about noon, he accompanied Madame L'Espanaye to her residence with the 4000 francs, put up in two bags. Upon the door being opened, Mademoiselle L. appeared and took from his hands one of the bags, while the old lady relieved him of the other. He then bowed and departed. Did not see any person in the street at the time. It is a by-street—very lonely.

Willaim Bird, tailor, deposes that he was one of the party who entered the house. Is an Englishman. Has lived in Paris two years. Was one of the first to ascend the stairs. Heard the voices in contention. The gruff voice was that of a Frenchman. Could make out several words, but cannot now remember all. Heard distinctly '*sacré*' and '*mon Dieu.*' There was a sound at the moment as if of several persons struggling—a scraping and scuffling sound. The shrill voice was very loud—louder than the gruff one. Is sure that it was not the voice of an Englishman. Appeared to be that of a German. Might have been a woman's voice. Does not understand German.

Four of the above-named witnesses being recalled, deposed that the door of the chamber in which was found the body of Mademoiselle L. was locked on the inside when the party reached it. Every thing was perfectly silent—no groans or noises of any kind. Upon forcing the door no person was seen. The windows, both of the back and front room, were down and firmly fastened from within. A door between the two rooms was closed but not locked. The door leading from the front room into the passage was locked, with the key inside. A small room in the front of the house, on the fourth story, at the head of the passage, was open, the door being ajar. This room was crowded with old beds, boxes, and so forth. These were carefully removed and searched. There was not an inch of any portion of the house which was not carefully searched. Sweeps were sent up and down the chimneys. The house was a four-story one, with garrets (*mansardes*). A trap-door on the roof was nailed down very securely— did not appear to have been opened for years. The time lapsing between the hearing of the voices in contention and the breaking open of the room door was variously stated by the witnesses. Some made it as short as three minutes—some as long as five. The door was opened with difficulty.

Alfonzo Garcio, undertaker, deposes that he resides in the Rue Morgue. Is a native of Spain. Was one of the party who entered the house. Did not proceed up stairs. Is nervous, and was apprehensive of the consequences of agitation. Heard the voices in contention. The gruff voice was that of a Frenchman. Could not distinguish what was said. The shrill voice was that of an Englishman—is sure of this. Does not understand the English language, but judges by the intonation.

Alberto Montani, confectioner, deposes that he was among the first to ascend the stairs. Heard the voices in question. The gruff voice was that of a Frenchman. Distinguished several words. The speaker appeared to be expostulating. Could not make out the words of the shrill voice. Spoke quick and unevenly. Thinks it the voice of a Russian. Corroborates the general testimony. Is an Italian. Never conversed with a native of Russia.

Several witnesses, recalled, here testified that the chimneys of all the rooms on the fourth story were too narrow to admit the passage of a human being. By 'sweeps' were meant cylindrical sweeping-brushes, such as are employed by those who clean chimneys. These brushes were passed up and down every flue in the house. There is no back passage by which any one could have descended while the party proceeded up stairs. The body of Mademoiselle L'Espanaye was so firmly wedged in the chimney that it could not be got down until four or five of the party united their strength.

Paul Dumas, physician, deposes that he was called to view the bodies about daybreak. They were both then lying on the sacking of the bedstead in the chamber where Mademoiselle L. was found. The corpse of the young lady was much bruised and excoriated. The fact that it had been thrust up the chimney would sufficiently account for these appearances. The throat was greatly chafed. There were several deep scratches just below the chin, together with a series of livid spots which were evidently the impression of fingers. The face was fearfully discolored, and the eyeballs protruded. The tongue had been partially bitten through. A large bruise was discovered upon the pit of the stomach, produced, apparently, by the pressure of a knee. In the opinion of M. Dumas, Mademoiselle L'Espanaye had been throttled to death by some person or persons unknown. The corpse of the mother was horribly mutilated. All the bones of the right leg and arm were more or less shattered. The left *tibia* much splintered, as well as all the ribs of the left side. Whole body dreadfully bruised and discolored. It was not possible to say how the injuries had been inflicted. A heavy club of wood, or a broad bar of iron—a chair—any large, heavy, and obtuse weapon would have produced such results, if wielded by the hands of a very powerful man. No woman could have inflicted the blows with any weapon. The head of the deceased, when seen by witness, was entirely separated from the body, and was also greatly shattered. The throat had evidently been cut with some very sharp instrument—probably with a razor.

Alexandre Etienne, surgeon, was called with M. Dumas to view the bodies. Corroborated the testimony and the opinions of M. Dumas.

Nothing further of importance was elicited, although several other persons were examined. A murder so mysterious, and so perplexing in all its particulars, was never before committed in Paris—if indeed a murder has been committed at all. The police are entirely at fault—an unusual occurrence in affairs of this nature. There is not, however, the shadow of a clew apparent.

The evening edition of the paper stated that the greatest excitement still continued in the Quartier St. Roch—that the premises in question had been carefully re-searched, and fresh examinations of witnesses instituted, but all to no purpose. A postscript, however, mentioned that Adolphe Le Bon had been arrested and imprisoned—although nothing appeared to criminate him beyond the facts already detailed.

Dupin seemed singularly interested in the progress of this affair—at least so I judged from his manner, for he made no comments. It was only after the announcement that Le Bon had been imprisoned, that he asked me my opinion respecting the murders.

I could merely agree with all Paris in considering them an insoluble mystery. I saw no means by which it would be possible to trace the murderer.

"We must not judge of the means," said Dupin, "by this shell of an examination. The Parisian police, so much extolled for *acumen*, are cunning, but no more. There is no method in their proceedings, beyond the method of the moment. They make a vast parade of measures; but, not unfrequently, these are so ill-adapted to the objects proposed, as to put us in mind of Monsieur Jourdain's calling for his *robe-de-chambre— pour mieux entendre la musique*. The results attained by them are not unfrequently surprising, but, for the most part, are brought about by simple diligence and activity. When these qualities are unavailing, their schemes fail. Vidocq, for example, was a good guesser, and a persevering man. But, without educated thought, he erred continually by the very intensity of his investigations. He impaired his vision by holding the object too close. He might see, perhaps, one or two points with unusual clearness, but in so doing he, necessarily, lost sight of the matter as a whole. Thus there is such a thing as being too profound. Truth is not always in a well. In fact, as regards the more important knowledge, I do believe that she is invariably superficial. The depth lies in the valleys where we seek her, and not upon the mountain-tops where she is found. The modes and sources of this kind of error are well typified in the contemplation of the heavenly bodies. To look at a star by glances—to view it in a side-long way, by turning toward it the exterior portions of the *retina* (more susceptible of feeble impressions of light than the interior), is to behold the star distinctly—is to have the best appreciation of its lustre—a lustre which grows dim just in proportion as we turn our vision *fully* upon it. A greater number of rays actually fall upon the eye in the latter case, but in the former, there is the more refined capacity for comprehension. By undue profundity we perplex and enfeeble thought; and it is possible to make even Venus herself vanish from the firmament by a scrutiny too sustained, too concentrated, or too direct.

"As for these murders, let us enter into some examinations for ourselves, before we make up an opinion respecting them. An inquiry will afford us amusement," [I thought this an odd term, so applied, but said nothing] "and besides, Le Bon once rendered me a service for which I am not ungrateful. We will go and see the premises with our own eyes. I know G———, the Prefect of Police, and shall have no difficulty in obtaining the necessary permission."

The permission was obtained, and we proceeded at once to the Rue Morgue. This is one of those miserable thoroughfares which intervenes between the Rue Richelieu and the Rue St. Roch. It was late in the afternoon when we reached it, as this quarter is at a great distance from that in which we resided. The house was readily found; for there were still many persons gazing up at the closed shutters, with an objectless curiosity, from the opposite side of the way. It was an ordinary Parisian house, with a gateway, on one side of which was a glazed watch-box, with a sliding panel in the window, indicating a *loge de concierge*. Before going in we walked up the street, turned down an alley, and then, again turning, passed in the rear of the building—Dupin, meanwhile, examining the whole neighborhood, as well as the house, with a minuteness of attention for which I could see no possible object.

Retracing our steps we came again to the front of the dwelling, rang, and having shown our credentials, were admitted by the agents in charge. We went up stairs—into the chamber where the body of Mademoiselle L'Espanaye had been found, and where both the deceased still lay. The disorders of the room had, as usual, been suffered to exist. I saw nothing beyond what had been stated in the *Gazette des Tribunaux*. Dupin scrutinized every thing—not excepting the bodies of the victims. We then went into the other rooms, and into the yard; a *gendarme* accompanying us throughout. The examination occupied us until dark, when we took our departure. On our way home my companion stepped in for a moment at the office of one of the daily papers.

I have said that the whims of my friend were manifold, and that *Je les ménageais:*—for this phrase there is no English equivalent. It was his humor, now, to decline all conversation on the subject of the murder, until about noon the next day. He then asked me, suddenly, if I had observed any thing *peculiar* at the scene of the atrocity.

There was something in his manner of emphasizing the word "peculiar," which caused me to shudder, without knowing why.

"No, nothing *peculiar*," I said; "nothing more, at least, than we both saw stated in the paper."

"The *Gazette*," he replied, "has not entered, I fear, into the unusual horror of the thing. But dismiss the idle opinon of this print. It appears to me, that this mystery is considered insoluble, for the very reason which should cause it to be regarded as easy of solution—I mean for the *outré* character of its features. The police are confounded by the seeming absence of motive—not for the murder itself—but for the atrocity of the murder. They are puzzled, too, by the seeming impossibility of reconciling the voices heard in contention, with the facts that no one was discovered upstairs but the assassinated Mademoiselle L'Espanaye, and that there were no means of egress without the notice of the party ascending. The wild disorder of the room; the corpse thrust, with the head downward, up the chimney; the frightful mutilation of the body of the old lady; these considerations, with those just mentioned, and others which I need not mention, have sufficed to paralyze the powers, by putting completely at fault the boasted *acumen*, of the government agents. They have fallen into the gross but common error of confounding the unusual with the abstruse. But it is by these deviations from the plane of the ordinary, that reason feels its way, if at all, in its search for the true. In investigations such as we are now pursuing, it should not be so much asked 'what has occurred,' as 'what has occurred that has never occurred before.' In fact, the facility with which I shall arrive, or have arrived, at the solution of this mystery, is in the direct ratio of its apparent insolubility in the eyes of the police."

I stared at the speaker in mute astonishment.

"I am now awaiting," continued he, looking toward the door of our apartment—"I am now awaiting a person who, although perhaps not the perpetrator of these butcheries, must have been in some measure implicated in their perpetration. Of the worst portion of the crimes committed, it is probable that he is innocent. I hope that I am right in this supposition; for upon it I build my expectation of reading the entire riddle. I look for the man here—in this room—every moment. It is true that he may not arrive; but the probability is that he will. Should he come, it will be necessary to detain him. Here are pistols; and we both know how to use them when occasion demands their use.''

I took the pistols, scarcely knowing what I did, or believing what I heard, while Dupin went on, very much as if in a soliloquy. I have already spoken of his abstract manner at such times. His discourse was addressed to myself; but his voice, although by no means loud, had that intonation which is commonly employed in speaking to some one at a great distance. His eyes, vacant in expression, regarded only the wall.

''That the voices heard in contention,'' he said, ''by the party upon the stairs, were not the voices of the women themselves, was fully proved by the evidence. This relieves us of all doubt upon the question whether the old lady could have first destroyed the daughter, and afterward have committed suicide. I speak of this point chiefly for the sake of method; for the strength of Madame L'Espanaye would have been utterly unequal to the task of thrusting her daughter's corpse up the chimney as it was found; and the nature of the wounds upon her own person entirely precludes the idea of self-destruction. Murder, then, has been committed by some third party; and the voices of this third party were those heard in contention. Let me now advert—not to the whole testimony respecting these voices—but to what was *peculiar* in that testimony. Did you observe any thing peculiar about it?''

I remarked that, while all the witnesses agreed in supposing the gruff voice to be that of a Frenchman, there was much disagreement in regard to the shrill, or, as one individual termed it, the harsh voice.

''That was the evidence itself,'' said Dupin, ''but it was not the peculiarity of the evidence. You have observed nothing distinctive. Yet there *was* something to be observed. The witnesses, as you remark, agreed about the gruff voice; they were here unanimous. But in regard to the shrill voice, the peculiarity is—not that they disagreed—but that, while an Italian, an Englishman, a Spaniard, a Hollander, and a Frenchman attempted to describe it, each one spoke of it as that *of a foreigner*. Each is sure that it was not the voice of one of his own countrymen. Each likens it—not to the voice of an individual of any nation with whose language he is conversant—but the converse. The Frenchman supposes it the voice of a Spaniard, and 'might have distinguished some words *had he been acquainted with the Spanish.*' The Dutchman maintains it to have been that of a Frenchman; but we find it stated that '*not understanding French this witness was examined through an interpreter.*' The Englishman thinks it the voice of a German, and '*does not understand German.*' The Spaniard 'is sure' that it was that of an Englishman, but 'judges by the intonation' altogether, '*as he has no knowledge of the*

English.' The Italian believes it the voice of a Russian, but *'has never conversed with a native of Russia.'* A second Frenchman differs, moreover, with the first, and is positive that the voice was that of an Italian; but, *not being cognizant of that tongue*, is, like the Spaniard, 'convinced by the intonation.' Now, how strangely unusual must that voice have really been, about which such testimony as this *could* have been elicited!—in whose *tones*, even, denizens of the five great divisions of Europe could recognize nothing familiar! You will say that it might have been the voice of an Asiatic—of an African. Neither Asiatics nor Africans abound in Paris; but, without denying the inference, I will now merely call your attention to three points. The voice is termed by one witness 'harsh rather than shrill.' It is represented by two others to have been 'quick and *unequal*.' No words—no sounds resembling words—were by any witness mentioned as distinguishable.

"I know not," continued Dupin, "what impression I may have made, so far, upon your own understanding; but I do not hesitate to say that legitimate deductions even from this portion of the testimony—the portion respecting the gruff and shrill voices—are in themselves sufficient to engender a suspicion which should give direction to all farther progress in the investigation of the mystery. I said 'legitimate deductions'; but my meaning is not thus fully expressed. I designed to imply that the deductions are the *sole* proper ones, and that the suspicion arises *inevitably* from them as the single result. What the suspicion is, however, I will not say just yet. I merely wish you to bear in mind that, with myself, it was sufficiently forcible to give a definite form—a certain tendency—to my inquiries in the chamber.

"Let us now transport ourselves, in fancy, to this chamber. What shall we first seek here? The means of egress employed by the murderers. It is not too much to say that neither of us believe in praeternatural events. Madame and Mademoiselle L'Espanaye were not destroyed by spirits. The doers of the deed were material and escaped materially. Then how? Fortunately there is but one mode of reasoning upon the point, and that mode *must* lead us to a definite decision. Let us examine, each by each, the possible means of egress. It is clear that the assassins were in the room where Mademoiselle L'Espanaye was found, or at least in the room adjoining, when the party ascended the stairs. It is, then, only from these two apartments that we have to seek issues. The police have laid bare the floors, the ceiling, and the masonry of the walls, in every direction. No *secret* issues could have escaped their vigilance. But, not trusting to *their* eyes, I examined with my own. There were, then, *no* secret issues. Both doors leading from the rooms into the passage were securely locked, with the keys inside. Let us turn to the chimneys. These, although of ordinary width for some eight or ten feet above the hearths, will not admit, throughout their extent, the body of a large cat. The impossibility of egress, by means already stated, being thus absolute, we are reduced to the windows. Through those of the front room no one could have escaped without notice from the crowd in the street. The murderers *must* have passed, then, through those of the back room. Now, brought to this conclusion in so unequivocal a manner as we are, it is not our part, as reasoners, to reject it on account of apparent impossibilities. It is only left for us to prove that these apparent 'impossibilities' are, in reality, not such.

"There are two windows in the chamber. One of them is unobstructed by furniture, and is wholly visible. The lower portion of the other is hidden from view by the head of the unwieldy bedstead which is thrust close up against it. The former was found securely fastened from within. It resisted the utmost force of those who endeavored to raise it. A large gimlet-hole had been pierced in its frame to the left, and a very stout nail was found fitted therein, nearly to the head. Upon examining the other window, a similar nail was seen similarly fitted in it; and a vigorous attempt to raise this sash failed also. The police were now entirely satisfied that egress had not been in these directions. And, *therefore*, it was thought a matter of supererogation to withdraw the nails and open the windows.

"My own examination was somewhat more particular, and was so for the reason I have just given—because here it was, I knew, that all apparent impossibilities *must* be proved to be not such in reality.

"I proceeded to think thus— *a posteriori*. The murderers *did* escape from one of these windows. This being so, they could not have refastened the sashes from the inside, as they were found fastened—the consideration which put a stop, through its obviousness, to the scrutiny of the police in this quarter. Yet the sashes *were* fastened. They *must*, then, have the power of fastening themselves. There was no escape from this conclusion. I stepped to the unobstructed casement, withdrew the nail with some difficulty, and attempted to raise the sash. It resisted all my efforts, as I had anticipated. A concealed spring must, I now knew, exist; and this corroboration of my idea convinced me that my premises, at least, were correct, however mysterious still appeared the circumstances attending the nails. A careful search soon brought to light the hidden spring. I pressed it, and, satisfied with the discovery, forbore to upraise the sash.

"I now replaced the nail and regarded it attentively. A person passing out through this window might have reclosed it, and the spring would have caught—but the nail could not have been replaced. The conclusion was plain, and again narrowed in the field of my investigations. The assassins *must* have escaped through the other window. Supposing, then, the springs upon each sash to be the same, as was probable, there *must* be found a difference between the nails, or at least between the modes of their fixture. Getting upon the sacking of the bedstead, I looked over the head-board minutely at the second casement. Passing my hand down behind the board, I readily discovered and pressed the spring, which was, as I had supposed, identical in character with its neighbor. I now looked at the nail. It was as stout as the other, and apparently fitted in the same manner—driven in nearly up to the head.

"You will say that I was puzzled; but, if you think so, you must have misunderstood the nature of the inductions. To use a sporting phrase, I had not been once 'at fault.' The scent had never for an instant been lost. There was no flaw in any link of the chain. I had traced the secret to its ultimate result,—and that result was *the nail*. It had, I say, in every respect, the appearance of its fellow in the other window; but this fact was an absolute nullity (conclusive as it might seem to be) when compared with the consideration that here, at this point, terminated the clew. 'There *must* be something wrong,' I said, 'about the nail.' I touched it; and the head, with about a quarter of an inch of the shank came off in my fingers. The rest of the shank was in the gimlet-hole, where it had been broken off. The fracture was an old one (for its edges were incrusted with rust), and had apparently been accomplished by the blow of a hammer, which had partially imbedded, in the top of the bottom sash, the head portion of the nail. I now carefully replaced this head portion in the indentation whence I had taken it, and the resemblance to a perfect nail was complete—the fissure was invisible. Pressing the spring, I gently raised the sash for a few inches; the head went up with it, remaining firm in its bed. I closed the window, and the semblance of the whole nail was again perfect.

"This riddle, so far, was now unriddled. The assassin had escaped through the window which looked upon the bed. Dropping of its own accord upon his exit (or perhaps purposely closed), it had become fastened by the spring; and it was the retention of this spring which had been mistaken by the police for that of the nail,—farther inquiry being thus considered unnecessary.

"The next question is that of the mode of descent. Upon this point I had been satisfied in my walk with you around the building. About five feet and a half from the casement in question there runs a lightning-rod. From this rod it would have been impossible for any one to reach the window itself, to say nothing of entering it. I observed, however, that the shutters of the fourth story were of the peculiar kind called by Parisian carpenters *ferrades*—a kind rarely employed at the present day, but frequently seen upon very old mansions at Lyons and Bordeaux. They are in the form of an ordinary door (a single, not a folding door), except that the upper half is latticed or worked in open trellis—thus affording an excellent hold for the hands. In the present instance these shutters are fully three feet and a half broad. When we saw them from the rear of the house, they were both about half open—that is to say, they stood off at right angles from the wall. It is probable that the police as well as myself, examined the back of the tenement; but, if so, in looking at these *ferrades* in the line of their breadth (as they must have done), they did not perceive this great breadth itself, or, at all events, failed to take it into due consideration. In fact, having once satisfied themselves that no egress could have been made in this quarter, they would naturally bestow here a very cursory examination. It was clear to me, however, that the shutter belonging to the window at the head of the bed, would, if swung fully back to the wall, reach to within two feet of the lightning-rod. It was also evident that, by exertion of a very unusual degree of activity and courage, an entrance into the window, from the rod, might have been thus effected. By reaching to the distance of two feet and a half (we now suppose the shutter open to its whole extent) a robber might have taken a firm grasp upon the trellis-work. Letting go, then, his hold upon the rod, placing his feet securely against the wall, and springing boldly from it, he might have swung the shutter so as to close it, and, if we imagine the window open at the time, might even have swung himself into the room.

"I wish you to bear especially in mind that I have spoken of a *very* unusual degree of activity as requisite to success in so hazardous and so difficult a feat. It is my design to show you first, that the thing might possibly have been accomplished:—but, secondly and *chiefly,* I wish to impress upon your understanding the *very extraordinary*—the almost praeternatural character of that agility which could have accomplished it.

"You will say, no doubt, using the language of the law, that 'to make out my case,' I should rather undervalue, than insist upon a full estimation of the activity required in this matter. This may be the practice in law, but it is not the usage of reason. My ultimate object is only the truth.

My immediate purpose is to lead you to place in juxtaposition, that *very unusual* activity of which I have just spoken, with the *very peculiar* shrill (or harsh) and *unequal* voice, about whose nationality no two persons could be found to agree, and in whose utterance no syllabification could be detected.''

At these words a vague and half-formed conception of the meaning of Dupin flitted over my mind. I seemed to be upon the verge of comprehension, without power to comprehend—as men, at times, find themselves upon the brink of remembrance, without being able, in the end, to remember. My friend went on with his discourse.

''You will see,'' he said, ''that I have shifted the question from the mode of egress to that of ingress. It was my design to convey the idea that both were effected in the same manner, at the same point. Let us now revert to the interior of the room. Let us survey the appearances here. The drawers of the bureau, it is said, had been rifled, although many articles of apparel still remained within them. The conclusion here is absurd. It is a mere guess—a very silly one—and no more. How are we to know that the articles found in the drawers were not all these drawers had originally contained? Madame L'Espanaye and her daughter lived an exceedingly retired life—saw no company—seldom went out—had little use for numerous changes of habiliment. Those found were at least of as good quality as any likely to be possessed by these ladies. If a thief had taken any, why did he not take the best—why did he not take all? In a word, why did he abandon four thousand francs in gold to encumber himself with a bundle of linen? The gold *was* abandoned. Nearly the whole sum mentioned by Monsieur Mignaud, the banker, was discovered, in bags, upon the floor. I wish you therefore, to discard from your thoughts the blundering idea of *motive*, engendered in the brains of the police by that portion of the evidence which speaks of money delivered at the door of the house. Coincidences ten times as remarkable as this (the delivery of the money, and murder committed within three days upon the party receiving it), happen to all of us every hour of our lives, without attracting even momentary notice. Coincidences, in general, are great stumbling-blocks in the way of that class of thinkers who have been educated to know nothing of the theory of probabilities—that theory to which the most glorious objects of human research are indebted for the most glorious of illustration. In the present instance, had the gold been gone, the fact of its delivery three days before would have formed something more than a coincidence. It would have been corroborative of this idea of motive. But, under the real circumstances of the case, if we are to suppose gold the motive of this outrage, we must also imagine the perpetrator so vacillating an idiot as to have abandoned his gold and his motive together.

"Keeping now steadily in the mind the points to which I have drawn your attention—that peculiar voice, that unusual agility, and that startling absence of motive in a murder so singularly atrocious as this— let us glance at the butchery itself. Here is a woman strangled to death by manual strength, and thrust up a chimney head downward. Ordinary assassins employ no such mode of murder as this. Least of all, do they thus dispose of the murdered. In this manner of thrusting the corpse up the chimney, you will admit that there was something *excessively outré*—something altogether irreconcilable with our common notions of human action, even when we suppose the actors the most depraved of men. Think, too, how great must have been that strength which could have thrust the body *up* such an aperture so forcibly that the united vigor of several persons was found barely sufficient to drag it *down!*

"Turn, now, to other indications of the employment of a vigor most marvellous. On the hearth were thick tresses—very thick tresses—of gray human hair. These had been torn out by the roots. You are aware of the great force necessary in tearing thus from the head even twenty or thirty hairs together. You saw the locks in question as well as myself. Their roots (a hideous sight!) were clotted with fragments of the flesh of the scalp—sure token of the prodigious power which had been exerted in uprooting perhaps half a million of hairs at a time. The throat of the old lady was not merely cut, but the head absolutely severed from the body: the instrument was a mere razor. I wish you also to look at the *brutal* ferocity of these deeds. Of the bruises upon the body of Madame L'Espanaye I do not speak. Monsieur Dumas, and his worthy co-adjutor Monsieur Etienne, have pronounced that they were inflicted by some obtuse instrument; and so far these gentlemen are very correct. The obtuse instrument was clearly the stone pavement in the yard, upon which the victim had fallen from the window which looked in upon the bed. This idea, however simple it may now seem, escaped the police for the same reason that the breadth of the shutters escaped from them— because, by the affair of the nails, their perceptions had been hermetically sealed against the possibility of the windows having ever been opened at all.

"If now, in addition to all these things, you have properly reflected upon the odd disorder of the chamber, we have gone so far as to combine the ideas of an agility astounding, a strength superhuman, a ferocity brutal, a butchery without motive, a *grotesquerie* in horror absolutely alien from humanity, and a voice foreign in tone to the ears of men of many nations, and devoid of all distinct or intelligible syllabification. What result, then, has ensued? What impression have I made upon your fancy?''

I felt a creeping of the flesh as Dupin asked me the question. "A madman," I said, "has done this deed—some raving maniac, escaping from a neighboring *Maison de Santé*."

"In some respects," he replied, "your idea is not irrelevant. But the voices of madmen, even in their wildest paroxysms, are never found to tally with that peculiar voice heard upon the stairs. Madmen are of some nation, and their language, however incoherent in its words, has always the coherence of syllabification. Besides, the hair of a madman is not such as I now hold in my hand. I disentangled this little tuft from the rigidly clutched fingers of Madame L'Espanaye. Tell me what you can make of it."

"Dupin!" I said, completely unnerved; "this hair is most unusual— this is no *human* hair."

"I have not asserted that it is," said he; "but, before we decide this point, I wish you to glance at the little sketch I have here traced upon this paper. It is a *fac-simile* drawing of what has been described in one portion of the testimony as 'dark bruises and deep indentations of finger nails' upon the throat of Mademoiselle L'Espanaye, and in another (by Messrs. Dumas and Etienne) as a 'series of livid spots, evidently the impressions of fingers.'

"You will perceive," continued my friend, spreading out the paper upon the table before us, "that this drawing gives the idea of a firm and fixed hold. There is no *slipping* apparent. Each finger has retained— possibly until the death of the victim—the fearful grasp by which it originally imbedded itself. Attempt, now, to place all your fingers, at the same time, in the respective impressions as you see them."

I made the attempt in vain.

"We are possibly not giving this matter a fair trial," he said. "The paper is spread out upon a plane surface; but the human throat is cylindrical. Here is a billet of wood, the circumference of which is about that of the throat. Wrap the drawing around it, and try the experiment again."

I did so; but the difficulty was even more obvious than before. "This," I said, "is the mark of no human hand."

"Read now," replied Dupin, "this passage from Cuvier."

It was a minute anatomical and generally descriptive account of the large fulvous Ourang-Outang of the East Indian Islands. The gigantic stature, the prodigious strength and activity, the wild ferocity, and the imitative propensities of these mammalia are sufficiently well known to all. I understood the full horrors of the murder at once.

"The description of the digits," said I, as I made an end of reading, "is in exact accordance with this drawing. I see that no animal but an Ourang-Outang, of the species here mentioned, could have impressed the indentations as you have traced them. This tuft of tawny hair, too, is identical in character with that of the beast of Cuvier. But I cannot possibly comprehend the particulars of this frightful mystery. Besides, there were *two* voices heard in contention, and one of them was unquestionably the voice of a Frenchman."

"True; and you will remember an expression attributed almost unanimously, by the evidence, to this voice,—the expression, '*mon Dieu!*' This, under the circumstances, has been justly characterized by one of the witnesses (Montani, the confectioner) as an expression of remonstrance or expostulation. Upon these two words, therefore, I have mainly built my hopes of a full solution of the riddle. A Frenchman was cognizant of the murder. It is possible—indeed it is far more than probable—that he was innocent of all participation in the bloody transaction which took place. The Ourang-Outang may have escaped from him. He may have traced it to the chamber; but, under the agitating circumstances which ensued, he could never have recaptured it. It is still at large. I will not pursue these guesses—for I have no right to call them more—since the shades of reflection upon which they are based are scarcely of sufficient depth to be appreciable by my own intellect, and since I would not pretend to make them intelligible to the understanding of another. We will call them guesses, then, and speak of them as such. If the Frenchman in question is indeed, as I suppose, innocent of this atrocity, this advertisement, which I left last night upon our return home, at the office of *Le Monde* (a paper devoted to the shipping interest, and much sought by sailors), will bring him to our residence."

He handed me a paper, and I read thus:

CAUGHT—*In the Bois de Boulogne, early in the morning of the* ——*inst.* (the morning of the murder), *a very large tawny Ourang-Outang of the Bornese species. The owner (who is ascertained to be a sailor, belonging to a Maltese vessel) may have the animal again, upon identifying it satisfactorily, and paying a few charges arising from its capture and keeping. Call at No.—— Rue——, Faubourg St. Germain—au troisiême.*"

"How was it possible," I asked, "that you should know the man to be a sailor, and belonging to a Maltese vessel"

"I do *not know* it," said Dupin. "I am not *sure* of it. Here, however, is a small piece of ribbon, which from its form, and from its greasy appearance, has evidently been used in tying the hair in one of those long *queues* of which sailors are so fond. Moreover, this knot is one which few besides sailors can tie, and it is peculiar to the Maltese. I picked the ribbon up at the foot of the lightning-rod. It could not have belonged to either of the deceased. Now if, after all, I am wrong in my induction from this ribbon, that the Frenchman was a sailor belonging to a Maltese vessel, still I can have done no harm in saying what I did in the advertisement. If I am right, a great point is gained. Cognizant although innocent of the murder, the Frenchman will naturally hesitate about replying to the advertisement—about demanding the Ourang-Outang. He will reason thus:—'I am innocent; I am poor; my Ourang-Outang is of great value—to one in my circumstances a fortune of itself—why should I lose it through idle apprehensions of danger? Here it is, within my grasp. It was found in the Bois de Boulogne—at a vast distance from the scene of that butchery. How can it ever be suspected that a brute beast should have done the deed? The police are at fault—they have failed to procure the slightest clew. Should they even trace the animal, it would be impossible to prove me cognizant of the murder, or to implicate me in guilt on account of that cognizance. Above all, *I am known*. The advertiser designates me as the possessor of the beast. I am not sure to what limit his knowledge may extend. Should I avoid claiming a property of so great value, which it is known that I possess, I will render the animal at least, liable to suspicion. It is not my policy to attract attention either to myself or to the beast. I will answer the advertisement, get the Ourang-Outang, and keep it close until this matter has blown over.'"

"Be ready," said Dupin, "with your pistols, but neither use them nor show them until at a signal from myself."

The front door of the house had been left open, and the visitor had entered, without ringing, and advanced several steps upon the staircase. Now, however, he seemed to hesitate. Presently we heard him descending. Dupin was moving quickly to the door, when we again heard him coming up. He did not turn back a second time, but stepped up with decision, and rapped at the door of our chamber.

"Come in," said Dupin, in a cheerful and hearty tone.

A man entered. He was a sailor, evidently,—a tall, stout, and muscular-looking person, with a certain daredevil expression of countenance, not altogether unprepossessing. His face, greatly sunburnt, was more than half hidden by whisker and *mustachio*. He had with him a huge oaken cudgel, but appeared to be otherwise unarmed. He bowed awkwardly, and bade us "good evening," in French accents, which, although somewhat Neufchatelish, were still sufficiently indicative of a Parisian origin.

"Sit down, my friend," said Dupin. "I suppose you have called about the Ourang-Outang. Upon my word, I almost envy you the possession of him; a remarkably fine, and no doubt a very valuable animal. How old do you suppose him to be?"

The sailor drew a long breath, with the air of some intolerable burden, and then replied, in an assured tone:

"I have no way of telling—but he can't be more than four or five years old. Have you got him here?"

"Oh, no; we had no conveniences for keeping him here. He is at a livery stable in the Rue Dubourg, just by. You can get him in the morning. Of course you are prepared to identify the property?"

"To be sure I am, sir."

"I shall be sorry to part with him," said Dupin.

"I don't mean that you should be at all this trouble for nothing, sir," said the man. "Couldn't expect it. Am very willing to pay a reward for the finding of the animal—that is to say, anything in reason."

"Well," replied my friend, "that is all very fair, to be sure. Let me think!—what should I have? Oh! I will tell you. My reward shall be this. You shall give me all the information in your power about these murders in the Rue Morgue."

Dupin said the last words in a very low tone, and very quietly. Just as quietly, too, he walked toward the door, locked it, and put the key in his pocket. He then drew a pistol from his bosom and placed it, without the least flurry, upon the table.

The sailor's face flushed up as if he were struggling with suffocation. He started to his feet and grasped his cudgel; but the next moment he fell back into his seat, trembling violently, and with the countenance of death itself. He spoke not a word. I pitied him from the bottom of my heart.

"My friend," said Dupin, in a kind tone, "you are alarming yourself unnecessarily—you are indeed. We mean you no harm whatever. I pledge you the honor of a gentleman, and of a Frenchman, that we intend you no injury. I perfectly well know that you are innocent of the atrocities in the Rue Morgue. It will not do, however, to deny that you are in some measure implicated in them. From what I have already said, you must know that I have had means of information about this matter—means of which you could never have dreamed. Now the thing stands thus. You have no reason for concealment. On the other hand, you are bound by every principle of honor to confess all you know. An innocent man is now imprisoned, charged with that crime of which you can point out the perpetrator.''

The sailor had recovered his presence of mind, in a great measure, while Dupin uttered these words; but his original boldness of bearing was all gone.

''So help me God!'' said he, after a brief pause, ''I *will* tell you all I know about this affair;—but I do not expect you to believe one half I say—I would be a fool indeed if I did. Still, I *am* innocent, and I will make a clean breast if I die for it.''

What he stated was, in substance, this. He had lately made a voyage to the Indian Archipelago. A party, of which he formed one, landed at Borneo, and passed into the interior on an excursion of pleasure. Himself and a companion had captured the Ourang-Outang. This companion dying, the animal fell into his own exclusive posession. After a great trouble, occasioned by the intractable ferocity of his captive during the home voyage, he at length succeeded in lodging it safely at his own residence in Paris, where, not to attract toward himself the unpleasant curiosity of his neighbors, he kept it carefully secluded, until such time as it should recover from a wound in the foot, received from a splinter on board ship. His ultimate design was to sell it.

Returning home from some sailor's frolic on the night, or rather in the morning, of the murder, he found the beast occupying his own bedroom, into which it had broken from a closet adjoining, where it had been, as was thought, securely confined. Razor in hand, and fully lathered, it was sitting before a looking-glass, attempting the operation of shaving, in which it had no doubt previously watched its master through the keyhole of the closet. Terrified at the sight of so dangerous a weapon in the possession of an animal so ferocious, and so well able to use it, the man, for some moments, was at a loss what to do. He had been accustomed, however, to quiet the creature, even in its fiercest moods, by the use of a whip, and to this he now resorted. Upon sight of it, the Ourang-Outang sprang at once through the door of the chamber, down the stairs, and thence, through a window, unfortunately open, into the street.

The Frenchman followed in despair; the ape, razor still in hand, occasionally stopping to look back and gesticulate at his pursuer, until the latter had nearly come up with it. It then again made off. In this manner the chase continued for a long time. The streets were profoundly quiet, as it was nearly three o'clock in the morning. In passing down an alley in the rear of the Rue Morgue, the fugitive's attention was arrested by a light gleaming from the open window of Madame L'Espanaye's chamber, in the fourth story of her house. Rushing to the building it perceived the lightning-rod, clambered up with inconceivable agility, grasped the shutter, which was thrown fully back against the wall, and, by its means, swung itself directly upon the headboard of the bed. The whole feat did not occupy a minute. The shutter was kicked open again by the Ourang-Outang as it entered the room.

The sailor, in the meantime, was both rejoiced and perplexed. He had strong hopes of now recapturing the brute, as it could scarcely escape from the trap into which it had ventured, except by the rod, where it might be intercepted as it came down. On the other hand, there was much cause for anxiety as to what it might do in the house. This latter reflection urged the man still to follow the fugitive. A lightning-rod is ascended without difficulty, especially by a sailor; but, when he had arrived as high as the window, which lay far to his left, his career was stopped; the most that he could accomplish was to reach over so as to obtain a glimpse of the interior of the room. At this glimpse he nearly fell from his hold through excess of horror. Now it was that those hideous shrieks arose upon the night, which had startled from slumber the inmates of the Rue Morgue. Madame L'Espanaye and her daughter, habited in their night clothes, had apparently been occupied in arranging some papers in the iron chest already mentioned, which had been wheeled into the middle of the room. It was open, and its contents lay beside it on the floor. The victims must have been sitting with their backs toward the window; and, from the time elapsing between the ingress of the beast and the screams, it seems probable that it was not immediately perceived. The flapping to of the shutter would naturally have been attributed to the wind.

As the sailor looked in, the gigantic animal had seized Madame L'Espanaye by the hair (which was loose, as she had been combing it), and was flourishing the razor about her face, in imitation of the motions of a barber. The daughter lay prostrate and motionless; she had swooned. The screams and struggles of the old lady (during which the hair was torn from her head) had the effect of changing the probably pacific purposes of the Ourang-Outang into those of wrath. With one determined sweep of its muscular arm it nearly severed her head from her body. The sight of blood inflamed its anger into phrenzy. Gnashing its teeth, and flashing fire from its eyes, it flew upon the body of the girl and embedded its fearful talons in her throat, retaining its grasp until she expired. Its wandering and wild glances fell at this moment upon the head of the bed, over which the face of its master, rigid with horror, was just discernible. The fury of the beast, who no doubt bore still in mind the dreaded whip, was instantly coverted into fear. Conscious of having deserved punishment, it seemed desirous of concealing its bloody deeds, and skipped about the chamber in an agony of nervous agitation; throwing down and breaking the furniture as it moved, and dragging the bed from the bedstead. In conclusion, it seized first the corpse of the daughter, and thrust it up the chimney, as it was found; then that of the old lady, which, it immediately hurled through the window headlong.

As the ape approached the casement with its mutilated burden, the sailor shrank aghast to the rod, and, rather gliding than clambering down, hurried at once home—dreading the consequences of the butchery, and gladly abandoning, in his terror, all solicitude about the fate of the Ourang-Outang. The words heard by the party upon the staircase were the Frenchman's exclamations of horror and affright, commingled with the fiendish jabbering of the brute.

I have scarcely any thing to add. The Ourang-Outang must have escaped from the chamber, by the rod, just before the breaking of the door. It must have closed the window as it passed through it. It was subsequently caught by the owner himself, who obtained for it a very large sum at the *Jardin des Plantes*. Le Bon was instantly released, upon our narration of the circumstances (with some comments from Dupin) at the *bureau* of the Prefect of Police. This functionary, however well disposed to my friend, could not altogether conceal his chagrin at the turn which affairs had taken, and was fain to indulge in a sarcasm or two about the propriety of every person minding his own business.

"Let him talk," said Dupin, who had not thought it necessary to reply. "Let him discourse; it will ease his conscience. I am satisfied with having defeated him in his own castle. Nevertheless, that he failed in the solution of this mystery, is by no means that matter for wonder which he supposes it; for, in truth, our friend the prefect is somewhat too cunning to be profound. In his wisdom is no *stamen*. It is all head and no body, like the pictures of the Goddess Laverna—or, at best, all head and shoulders, like a codfish. But he is a good creature after all. I like him especially for one master stroke of cant, by which he has attained his reputation for ingenuity, I mean the way he has '*de nier ce qui est, et d' expliquer ce qui n' est pas.*' "

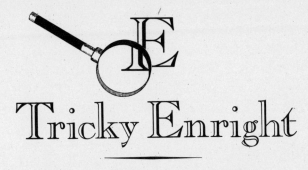

Tricky Enright

WHY SHOOT A CORPSE?
John K. Butler

CHAPTER ONE
The Man Who Was Doomed to Die

IT MUST HAVE been about a quarter past eleven when I drifted into the Little Brown Jug. That's a saloon on the corner of Main and Leavenworth. I was the only customer in the place.

Mike shook hands with me across the bar. "Glad to see you, Mr. Osborne," he said.

He never used my right name. That was what I liked about him. He was an intelligent bartender.

I boosted myself to a bar stool and inquired: "How's it going, Mike?"

"Not so good, Mr. Osborne." His face twisted into a glum grimace as he poured me a rye. "Business is slow these days. That damn D.A. again."

"Up to his old tricks?"

"Yeah. Clamping down all over town. Yesterday he closed the horse-shop across the street. Hell, it's getting so nobody can make a decent living any more."

He poured himself a drink to solace his troubles, leaned fat forearms on the bar and talked to me.

With the D.A. on the warpath, knocking over chisel joints and gunning after rackets, all the smart boys and gals ducked out of town on "vacations." That left such haunts as the Little Brown Jug without customers.

"It's a hell of a situation," Mike said sourly.

A cold draft of air swept into the room at my back and I glanced into the bar mirror. A party of three had come through the swing doors. They took a table across the room and Mike waddled around the end of the bar to take their orders.

I recognized the two men right away. One was Lester Lamia, a big shot in the horse racket. He looked thin and sick, and he carried his right arm in a sling. I remembered he was out of the hospital only a few weeks.

The other man was his bodyguard, Foghorn Noonan. I'd never seen the woman before.

She was young, a blonde. She wore a red cape, no hat, and drops of rain sparkled like hundreds of tiny diamonds in her hair. She had nice lips and eyes, smiling at Lamia. I watched her in the mirror and liked her.

Mike bent over the table, shook his head apologetically, as though the girl had requested some drink he couldn't make.

Then Foghorn Noonan scraped back his chair. "I'll pick up a bottle at the liquor store," he said in his deep nasal voice.

Foghorn was one of the heftiest men I've even seen outside a wrestling-ring—built like a Sierra locomotive. He made a swell bodyguard because his appearance alone was enough to scare away the average tough boy. He stood six foot four, heavily planted, as though he grew right up from the ground. He wore an Army automatic under each armpit, yet he was so big you didn't notice them—unless his coat happened to slip back.

He grinned at Les Lamia and the blonde, grinned at Mike. His teeth were obviously false. Sometimes I wondered what had become of the originals. The other guy must've been good.

He clapped his hat on, pushed through the swing doors, and I watched his big shadow pass the steamy front window, walking down the sidewalk in the rain.

Mike returned to the bar, setting up a glass and a bottle. "That's Les Lamia," he whispered to me, pointing briefly with a fat thumb. "Nice guy. One of my regular customers. He looks kinda sick these days. Somebody tried to bump him."

I nodded. In the mirror I saw Lamia leave the table and go over to the electric phonograph. He had quite a limp in his left leg. I watched him finger a nickel into the slot, saw the record jerk out mechanically, behind plate glass, and move down to the rotating disc. When an orchestra began to play, the blonde squealed with joy and slapped her palms together in time to the music.

Les Lamia came over to the bar and tossed down the drink Mike had poured for him.

"Hi, Les," I said. I'd met him a year ago on a party at Johnny Dominick's.

"Hello, there!" he greeted cordially, and his eyes—sickly-looking, weary from the long session in the hospital—searched my face, trying to recall where he'd seen it before.

"Johnny Dominick's," I said.

"Sure," he nodded, "sure! I remember you well. How's it going?"

I could tell he didn't know me from Adam's lost rib, so I coached him. "Enright—Tricky Enright."

"Sure. You didn't have to tell me. I knew you as soon as I came into the place."

He was sort of a nice guy. I guess most people like him. He was a racketeer from way back in bootleg days. Now it was the horse racket, which he played as square as you can play any racket.

"How you feeling these days, Les?"

He shrugged his shoulders. "Pretty good—considering." He grinned. "I'm sort of dancing around the edge of the frying-pan and trying to keep out of the fire."

I knew what he meant. He'd already been spotted twice.

The first time was last April. He'd been driving alone down Wilshire Boulevard when a Tommy-gun cut loose at him from a following car. Lamia swung his sedan sharply off the street into a filling-station and smashed a pair of gasoline pumps. You could smell gas around there for days. The guy with the Tommy-gun scrammed without scoring a hit. Lousy shooting if you ask me.

The cops grilled Lamia for several weeks, wanting to know who had tried to gun him and why, but he wouldn't talk. He said it was all a mistake.

A month later Les came out of a restaurant on Vermont Avenue and they blazed at him with shotguns. Slugs tore through his left arm, smashed his hip, chipped the knee-cap. He spent seven months in St. Thomas Hospital under armed guard.

Again the cops grilled him, and again they learned nothing. He laughed and joked with the law and all the reporters.

"Just another mistake," he said.

I looked at him now, at the bar in the Little Brown Jug, and realized what a sick man he was—sick, worried, maybe a little afraid.

I said: "I've got a guess what your trouble is, Les. Any harm guessing?"

He eyed me thoughtfully, and I went on: "You and Johnny Dominick got along swell when Johnny operated the horse-shops in the Hollywood district and you kept over on your own side of town. Everything was peaceful. But when you started to open places along Hollywood Boulevard, Johnny got sore. He's been spitting at you with Tommy-guns and shotguns. I always figured you were smart enough to stick to your own territory. What's the answer? A dame?''

He laughed and slapped me on the back. "Not bad—for guessing. Hey, Mike! Set up another for my pal!''

Mike filled my glass and moved away down the bar. I toasted Les and said to him: "One guess was good enough to buy me a drink, so I'll try another. Any harm in guessing again?''

He frowned. "Go ahead.''

"O.K. Here it is. Shotgun slugs banged you in the left side, in the left arm. But it's your right arm that you've got in a sling. So my guess is that you're packing a rod under the sling.''

He looked at me for a long time. I couldn't tell anything by his face. His eyes narrowed. His lips compressed into a tight line. Then he laughed.

"I'll be damned! Hey, Mike! Fill it up again for my pal.''

While Mike was getting the bottle, Les showed me the gun. The silk sling covered it nicely. All he had to do was yank back the silk with his left hand, and there it was—a neat snub-barrel .38 gripped in his right fist. He had to carry it there because his left arm was still stiff. He never figured anybody would notice which arm wore the sling.

I said: "I've reached my limit on the drinks, but I'll try another guess, and if I'm right I'll take a rain check. All set?''

"Let's have it.''

"O.K. I've already guessed that you moved into Johnny Dominick's territory because of a woman. I don't know who she is, but I'll bet my last buck it isn't the blonde with you tonight.''

He stared at me in amazement. "How do you know it isn't this one?''

"Because if you were warm enough over a woman to jump Johnny Dominick, you wouldn't leave the heart-throb sitting alone at a table while you gabbed with a bum at the bar.''

He laughed in a surprised way. Then he slapped me on the back, not very hard. I guess his left arm was still pretty sore.

"Nice guessing,'' he told me. "This blonde is a nurse I had when I was in St. Thomas Hospital. She's a good kid, and I only take her out so I can repay her for all she done for me while I was sick. She's got another guy. And me, I've got another woman. I just take her out to give her a good time.''

I said: "Did she order some drink Mike didn't have?"

"Yeah. She ordered Italian Galliano. Mike never even heard of it. So I sent Foghorn down the block to buy a bottle." He eyed me sharply. "Say! There you go guessing again. Hell, you ought to be a cop. You guess better than any cop I ever met."

I laughed and pretended that me being a cop was a very funny idea. He thought I was a hood. He'd have fallen right off the stool if he'd known who I really was.

"Listen," I said, "aren't you scared to be alone—I mean without your bodyguard?"

He shook his head. "I got this gun. And anyway Foghorn'll be back in a minute with the Galliano. And anyway, nobody won't hurt me for another month yet."

I stared at him. "Another month?"

"Sure. The town's hot. The D.A.'s running around like a Boy Scout at a fire, and nobody wants to make the town any hotter than it is already. I'm plenty safe. None of the boys'll bother me for another month, anyway."

"How about after the month?"

He shrugged. "We all got to take it someday, don't we?"

I tossed down the rest of my drink. "Why don't you lam out?" I suggested.

"Lam?" His mouth twisted into a cynical grin, while he stared vacantly at the bottles on the shelves. "Where the hell could I lam to?" He gave a futile shrug. "I'm all washed up. All I got's another month. Then it's curtains for Lamia. I'm practically a corpse now."

I tried to laugh it off. "What the hell, Les. Another month and things'll be different."

"Different? It won't be no different, Tricky. They'll get me just as sure as I'm sitting here. But I still got a month. They won't monkey with me while the town's hot. After that —what the hell?"

I shrugged. "If you want to look at it that way."

"Sure," he said. "Why not? As the fellow says—here today, gone tomorrow." He shook hands with me briefly. "Well, so long, Tricky. Glad to see you again. Be seeing you."

"Sure," I told him. "Thanks for the drinks."

In the mirror I watched him return to the table where the blonde waited. He smiled at her. She said something friendly, in a whisper, and patted his left arm. Then he laughed. He'd gotten a grip on himself and acted just as though he had a whole lifetime before him.

I kept watching until the bartender spoke to me. "You want another rye, Mr. Osborne?"

The short man came in first. When I heard the door open I thought it'd be Foghorn Noonan with the Galliano for Lamia's blonde.

Then I saw in the mirror it wasn't Noonan. He was much too short. And it wasn't a bottle he carried—it was a revolver. He wore a big overcoat and his hat was yanked low over his eyes.

He went straight to the table, walking in fast long strides. Lamia saw him coming, opened his mouth. The girl screamed. The short man clouted her on the side of the head, knocking her halfway across the room. He didn't pay any more attention to her.

"Hello, you son-of-a——!" he snapped at Les Lamia, his lips smirking.

It all took only a couple of seconds.

Les, with his mouth still open, shoved back his chair. He started to get his gun out of concealment in the fake sling, started to get up.

The short man shot him three times in the chest.

Les went backwards off the chair with his mouth still open and his gun still hidden in the sling.

The second man barged through the swing doors as the shots sounded. This one was tall. He wore a raincoat, a cap, and a mask. He carried a machine-gun cradled in his arms, and he let fly as he walked into the room.

The saloon suddenly became filled with deafening sound. The last thing I saw was a weird tableau—the blonde on the floor, screaming, Les Lamia on the floor, sprawled over a broken chair, while the short man pumped three more bullets into his chest and kicked his face to see if he was dead—the tall man in the raincoat spraying machine-gun bullets all over the room. Then the lights went out.

I dived head first over the bar and landed on top of Mike who was already hiding. He gave a grunt as my weight plopped down on him. "Geez!" he said, and tried to sock me.

"Easy, Mike," I yelled in his ear. "It's me."

The Tommy-gun kept chattering and I heard the mirror go to pieces, heard bottles on the shelves explode like clay targets on a shooting-range. Liquor and broken glass came showering down in the dark. Splinters of glass cut my hand, got under me, and I felt it grinding into my knees.

Then the machine-gun stopped. Everything was dark and suddenly silent. I remembered a time when I'd been in a movie theater and the film broke, and everybody waited in the darkness for the show to continue. Mike and I didn't move. Nobody moved. We waited tensely for the show to go on.

I heard a voice shout: "O.K! He's dead! Let's get the hell out of here!"

Running shoes pounded on the floor, continued into the street. The door of an automobile slammed and a motor growled under abrupt acceleration.

I peeked over the top of the bar at about the same time Mike did. Mike had a flashlight. He focused the white beam across the room and we saw the blonde.

She wasn't screaming now. She wasn't at all hysterical. She knelt there beside the dead body of Lester Lamia, going through his pockets, frisking him. I saw her take a packet of papers from his overcoat, and I yelled: "Hey, sister! Cut that!"

The glare of the flash and the boom of my voice, coming together, startled her. She fumbled the packet. But inside of a split second she'd scooped it up, and fled through the swing doors into the rain.

I vaulted the bar to go after her, and I was doing fine until I got halfway across the room. Then my shoes skidded on a dark wet stain that oozed over the floor near Lamia's body. I sat down hard.

Mike called: "It was two guys, Enright! A short guy and a tall guy! I seen 'em plain, Tricky!"

In the excitement, he'd forgotten he was supposed to call me by the name of Osborne.

Maybe you wonder why I let myself get mixed up in this at all. According to the newspapers, I'm sought by every law-enforcement agency in the state. You can even see my picture on the wall in your neighborhood post office—along with the announcement that I'm wanted for complicity in a mail-truck robbery outside Auburn on May 4, 1937. I'm also wanted as a Folsom fugitive, and for questioning on the murder of a store keeper in Grass Valley.

All that is a bunch of baloney.

My criminal reputation is just a blind to cover my real work as undercover operator working directly out of the Governor's office. My salary comes from a Secret Service fund allotted each year to the State Attorney General for private investigations, and my name isn't entered on any payroll list. In fact, no records are kept at all, because my life as well as my job depends on absolute secrecy.

This killing of Lester Lamia, in the Little Brown Jug, was just a new job for me. It had happened right before my eyes, and there were plenty of angles about it I couldn't understand.

In the first place, while Les admitted he was a target in a gang war, he firmly believed he had a month more to live before they turned the hose on him. And I felt he was right in believing that nobody, not even Johnny Dominick, would pull a gang killing while the D.A. was clamping down the lid all over the county. Racketeers are, after all, business men. They don't like to stir up more trouble in a community when a certain amount of trouble is already stirred up.

Yet Les had been bumped off—in spite of the reform wave—a month before he expected it. If Johnny Dominick had pulled the job, then Johnny was behaving very unlike himself. He was a peace-loving racketeer who'd never bump a guy while the town was hot, when it would hurt his own business or embarrass the district attorney.

I couldn't figure it.

But as it was part of my job to figure killings I got up and went chasing after the blonde.

CHAPTER TWO
Smart Blonde

IT WAS RAINING harder now. The street looked empty except for a night-owl trolley that had stopped halfway down the block. The motor-man and conductor stood on the back platform, along with three or four passengers. Apparently they'd heard the shooting for they were looking back at the beer parlor.

I glanced both ways on Main, but didn't catch sight of the blonde. I ducked around the corner and saw a lone figure hurrying away up Leavenworth. I recognized the red cape as she passed under a street lamp and called: "Hey, sister!"

She flashed one quick look over her shoulder and broke into a run, turning the next corner.

I turned it a second later and saw her getting into a taxi at the curb. I knew the cab must've been waiting to pick her up, because this was Las Flores Lane, a street with nothing on it but darkened warehouses, and no cabby would take a stand there unless he'd been ordered to wait for a fare.

He must have been waiting for quite a while in the rain because the motor was cold and he had to step on the starter twice. On the second try, I reached the cab, wrenched open the door, and piled into the back seat beside the blonde.

It was like landing in a cage with a wildcat. She beat me in the face with her handbag, kicked my shins, knocked my hat off, took a fistful of hair from my scalp, and was starting to go to work with her fingernails when I managed to catch hold of her wrists. She tried to bite the back of my hand.

I kept an eye out for the driver. He'd slipped off the front seat and was standing beside the car with a tire tool for a club. It was a good weapon, all right, but he just stood there looking surprised, worried, undecided.

The girl called to him: "Help! I don't know this man! Driver, please—"

I pulled her down close to me and whispered: "Listen, baby, you can't get rid of me that way. I'll stick till the cops come. Then I'll tell 'em you scrammed out of the Little Brown Jug after Les Lamia was killed. You don't want that, do you?"

She calmed down right away. And just as she calmed down the driver got busy and socked me on the back of the head with the tire tool.

I ducked, whirled. The driver tried to sock me again and my shoe caught him above the belt. It was more of a shove than a kick, but there was enough force in it to send him in a backward run. He tripped and sat down hard on the wet sidewalk.

As he was getting to his feet, the blonde's manner changed abruptly. She spoke to him in a sweetly apologetic voice. "I'm sorry this happened, driver. It's all my fault. This is my husband. We had a quarrel, and I was trying to get away from him. It's all right now. We'll pay double fare." She squeezed my hand. "Won't we, Albert?"

The driver approached cautiously. He didn't appear very convinced. I slipped him a sawbuck and said: "My wife and I are sorry this happened."

He tossed the tire tool into the front seat and brushed water off his pants. "O.K.," he grumbled sullenly. "When she yelled, I figured you for some bum trying to attack her. I didn't know you was her husband."

"We'll still pay double fare," I said. "No hard feelings?"

He shook his head, half-grinned, and got into the front seat. "No hard feelings. I'm sorry I conked you."

"Let's forget all about it," I suggested. "Give me your cab number, and if I can ever turn any business your way, I'll do it."

"It's Seventy-six," he told me.

"I'll remember. Now just drive us out toward Westlake Park. The wife and I want to talk." I rolled the window up.

The blonde didn't look at me. She held the handbag on her lap, toying nervously with the clasp. Her voice was soft, with a tremor in it. "So you're not a policeman, or a detective?"

"No more than my name's Albert or I'm your husband."

"Why are you after me?"

"I want to find out why you lit out as soon as Lamia was bumped."

Her shoulders gave a little shiver. "I didn't have anything to do with it. I'd only met Mr. Lamia casually. I was trying to avoid trouble."

I said: "It was nice that you had the cab waiting over here on Las Flores Lane."

She glared at me indignantly. "That has a nasty implication! I just happened to find the taxi standing there."

I lit a cigarette. "Oh, yeah. Shall I check with the driver?"

She began to cry into her hands, softly, all hunched over. "I'm telling the truth. If you'll leave me alone, I'll do anything. I'll even pay you a hundred dollars."

"How about telling me your name?"

She looked up at me, her eyes flooded with tears. Her lips trembled. "My name's Rose O'Brien."

I said: "Why not tell me your real name? I know you were a nurse for Les Lamia when he was in St. Thomas Hospital. I can find you again through the hospital. Or I can let the cops find you."

That got her crying again. Finally she said her name was Rose O'Shaughnessy. She was afraid if anybody at St. Thomas learned she'd been out with a gangster when he got bumped off, she'd lose her job at the hospital.

"Won't you help me?" she pleaded.

"You mean will I keep my mouth shut about seeing you with Les Lamia?"

"Yes."

"How about Noonan?"

"Oh, that's all right. Foghorn won't tell. I went out with them with the understanding I could run away if any trouble started. I'm sure Foghorn won't drag me into it."

"How about Mike?"

"Mike?"

"Yeah, the bartender at the Jug. He saw you with the party."

She nodded slowly. "That's true. But he wouldn't know me. And anyway, Mr. Lamia said the people at the Little Brown Jug were the kind who never talked. He said you could throw a bomb in the Little Brown Jug, and when the police came to investigate only the bartender would be there. And the bartender would say it was just a big firecracker, and that he'd been alone in the place when it went off."

I grinned. "So it's just me you're worried about?"

She patted my hand in an affectionate way, smiling at me through tears. "I'm not worried about you. I don't even know your name, but I know I can trust you. You won't drag me into it, will you?" She gave my hand a little squeeze. "I can make it worth your while if you don't."

I'm cynical. I said: "How much worth?"

"You mean money?"

I shrugged. "For the time being, let's figure in dollars. It helps to keep the books straight."

She looked at me as though she were seeing me for the first time. "Well, if it's money you mean—well, I have to see a friend of mine first. I can't pay you right now. But by morning I think I can make it five hundred dollars. Will five hundred dollars keep the books straight?

"It'll help."

"You can trust me about that," she said. "I've got to play fair with you, or else you can make enough trouble so I'll lose my job."

I nodded without saying anything.

"And I know I can trust you," she added. She looked out the window. We were passing over Wilshire through Westlake Park. It was very dark out there, the rain falling hard. "Let's stop at the Town House," she said.

I had the driver take us to the Town House. We got out in the rain, and I wanted the taxi to wait, but Rose O'Shaughnessy insisted she had to talk to me about something. She said I could call another cab later, so I paid this one off—like a sucker. It was five minutes before I realized what a fast one she'd pulled.

I'd figured she lived at the Town House. After the cab had gone she admitted she didn't.

"In case that driver overheard us talking," she explained, "I thought we should get rid of him. We'll separate here. And I'll look for you tomorrow up at the hospital. I'll have the money for you."

That was O.K. I still hadn't gotten next to how she'd tricked me.

I said: "There's just one other thing, Rose. After Les Lamia was shot, and while the lights were out, you frisked his pockets."

She stared at me speechlessly, as if she didn't know what I was talking about.

"I saw you take something," I said. "I yelled at you to cut it out. But when you scrammed, you had some papers. Don't try to kid me." I extended my hand. "Let's have a look at them."

Her eyes were innocent. Too innocent. "You must be mistaken. I didn't take anything."

"Come on," I said, "fork over. Otherwise, I might still call the cops."

She shook her head. "I'm not holding out," she said. "I'll prove it." She took me by the hand.

There was a delivery alley running down the side of the apartment building. We went in there, just a few steps, and she raised her arms over her head.

"You can search me. I don't want you to think you can't trust me. Go ahead and search me."

I started to search her, still not realizing what a sucker I was. I went through the pockets of her coat, felt around the collar and the hem. I wrinkled up the garment in a way that would let me know if anything had been concealed in the lining.

Once I hesitated.

She said: "Go right ahead. I want you to be sure."

So I did a frisking job which, if done at police headquarters, would require the services of a matron.

I thought I was being nobody's sucker and that I'd locate the packet of papers in the next few seconds. Then, suddenly, I got the idea. I looked up, saw her hands over her head, and missed something. I tried to figure out what it was. Then I knew.

"Do you trust me now?" she inquired softly, without sarcasm.

"Absolutely," I told her, and tried not to show any sarcasm either.

"You know I'm being honest with you?"

"Sure," I said. "I'm sorry I tried to frisk you at all. My mistake. I just wanted to check up."

"That's quite all right. We must trust each other."

There was something smug in her voice now. Evidently she still regarded me as a sucker. She'd pulled a fast one, all right.

I shook hands with her in front of the Town House.

"I'll look for you tomorrow at the hospital," she told me sweetly. "Right now I'll step into the lobby and call another cab. Good luck to you."

I said good-night to her and strolled to the corner.

As soon as I rounded it, out of her sight, I ran like hell.

There was an all-night drug store up at Western Avenue, four or five blocks away. I ran for it so fast I lost my hat.

CHAPTER THREE
Taxi Trouble

THE WARMTH OF the drug store smacked me as if I'd barged into a Turkish bath. A clerk sat behind the soda fountain reading a paper. Otherwise, the store was empty.

"Phone?" I inquired.

He jerked a thumb toward the back of the store, and I raced past a counter cluttered with hot water bottles and jammed myself into the booth, closed the folding door.

I fumbled a nickel into the slot and dialed Mission 22-22. That was the cab company. I asked to be connected with the dispatcher, and I told him: "Look—this is very important. About ten minutes ago my wife and I paid off one of your cabs, but we left something behind. My wife forgot her handbag."

The dispatcher's voice came smoothly polite over the telephone. "Certainly, sir. We're glad to assist you. Our drivers return all articles found in our vehicles to the Lost and Found Department. If you'll come down to our main office in the morning and identify the article. . . ."

"Hey!" I cut in. "My wife wants her handbag tonight! I remember the number of the cab. It was Seventy-six. We took the cab at Las Flores and Leavenworth and rode to the Town House. As soon as the driver checks in, tell him I'm waiting at Wilshire and Western. And I want the bag. I can describe it."

"We're glad to be of service to our customers," said the dispatcher. "However, it's a rule of the company to report all lost articles to the Lost and Found Department."

"Nuts to your damn Lost and Found Department," I told him impatiently. "My wife wants her handbag tonight. I'm willing to pay for the driver's trip. And if he doesn't remember me—and if I can't identify the bag to his satisfaction—he doesn't have to turn it over. Isn't that fair enough?''

The dispatcher cleared his throat. "Certainly, sir. I'll send Seventy-six to Wilshire and Western the moment he checks in."

"O.K. And here's something else. In case my wife calls you about the bag, tell her not to worry. Tell her we've already taken care of it."

"Certainly, sir."

I rang off.

It was hot in the booth. I opened the folding door to let some air in and sat there and smoked. I killed a cigarette, popped another nickel in the slot and called the cab company again. This time the dispatcher didn't sound so courteous. I explained I was the party who'd called a short while ago about the lost handbag, and that I was calling back to learn if he'd dispatched the cab yet.

His answer was a sullen "Yes." No *sir* attached to it. Then he said: "Look here, there seems to be some sort of difficulty about this bag. I want you to understand that while the company makes every effort to assist customers in the matter of articles left in our vehicles, we accept no responsibility. In case of two parties demanding return of an article—"

"Begin at the beginning," I interrupted. "What's the trouble?"

He seemed pretty worried—and annoyed. He said: "I took your word that you had a claim on the article left in Seventy-six. I dispatched the driver to Wilshire and Western about three minutes ago. Then, just a moment later, your wife called. I mean your ex-wife."

"Ex-wife?"

"Yes. When I told her I'd sent out the cab to deliver the bag to you on your identification, she became wildly angry. She explained that she had divorced you and that you had no right to claim the bag, and that out driver had no right to turn it over to you. She demands that I call back that driver, or she'll sue."

I wiped sweat off my forehead. Rose O'Shaughnessy had certainly made a play to keep that packet of papers away from me. Leaving her bag in the taxi had been a neat stunt. She thought I wouldn't notice she no longer had it. Of course she'd planned to have the bag returned to her by the cab company as soon as she'd gotten rid of me.

"Have you reached the driver?" I yelled into the phone.

"No, but I'm dispatching another driver to stop him. The handbag will not be turned over. This is a job for our legal department."

I got out of there so fast I didn't even bother to hang up the phone.

* * *

It was a break for me that a cab had a stand at the intersection, and that it wasn't out on a call.

I piled in and said to the hacker: "My wife left a handbag in Number Seventy-six. He's on the way to bring it to me, but I want to meet him. Let's go back over Wilshire."

The taxi cruised back across Westlake, on along the boulevard, but no other taxi showed up. We passed only a single car, a police prowler, in ten blocks.

I'd just about given up the idea, believing that Seventy-six had been turned back, or had taken some other route, when a pair of lights came toward us through the rain. My driver winked his lamps three times. The oncoming lights returned the wink and the cabs stopped opposite each other.

My driver called: "Seventy-six?"

"Yeah."

"I got a fare here who says his wife left a handbag, and we come along hunting you."

"I got the bag," said Seventy-six.

That was music to my ears. I paid off the driver who'd brought me from Western, and crossed the street to where Seventy-six stood beside his hack with a pocket flash. He threw the beam briefly into my face.

"Remember me?" I asked.

"Sure. Does your head hurt?"

"It's sore. You've got a nice swing with a tire tool."

He laughed and said: "You, brother, don't need no tool. You got feet like a pile driver."

We were on good terms as I climbed into the rear seat. I guess he remembered the tenner and the double fare. He gave me the handbag.

"How's your wife?"

"Fine—though we seem to have little arguments now and then."

"Don't we all."

I told him to return me to the Town House. That seemed like the right place to get rid of him. He'd naturally conclude I was going home to my wife.

While we drove I kep an eye out the rear for the cab I knew the dispatcher had chasing Seventy-six.

I held the handbag down between my knees, so the driver couldn't see what I was doing in his mirror. In the bag I found the usual collection of feminine cosmetics, a small purse with coins and a few dollar bills and a driver's license made out to *Rose O'Shaughnessy—Occupation, nurse—Age, 24.*

I also found the packet of papers. They were letters in lavender envelopes addressed in green ink to Lester A. Lamia, with various street addresses under the name in Los Angeles, Palm Springs, Lake Arrowhead, and Miami Beach, Florida.

I didn't take the letters from the envelopes. I'd have plenty of time for that later. I just replaced the rubber band around the packet, stuffed everything into the handbag, and slipped the bag into my coat pocket.

At that moment, there was a sound like a tire bursting, only louder—and right at my ear.

The gun was close—so close that the pressure of the powder gas knocked out the left-hand window of the cab as though somebody had smashed it with a rock. Jagged glass clattered and tinkled, and a piece as thin as a razor knifed into my cheek and stayed there.

In a short crazy ride, we skidded into the curb, bounced away from it, and locked fenders with a sleek black coupe running along beside us. Then the fenders broke free with a wrench of metal, and we skidded against the curb again, sideswiped a lamp post and put out all our lights.

I'd been asleep at the switch and hadn't seen the coupe come up behind and overtake us. Nor had I seen the gun. I guess my driver hadn't noticed either.

Anyway, it was too late to do much now. Until we brought up against the lamp post, I'd been thrown around the back of the cab like dice in a chuck-a-luck cage. Naturally, I carry a gun—a 38/44—but I wore it in an open case on my left hip and didn't have a chance in the world to produce it.

The coupe skidded on the wet pavement, nosed into the curb. A big guy had already jumped out of it, and he stood beside our taxi with that glass-smashing cannon in his fist. The muzzle came through the opening which had recently been a window as I was getting up off the floor, punched me in the mouth and split my upper lip against my teeth.

"Don't try anything!" the guy advised. "Just remember it's better to be a live coward than a dead hero."

The driver up front swung around suddenly. Maybe he thought he'd get in some work with the tire tool. I don't know just what he had in mind and the big guy didn't wait to find out. He banged him on the side of the head with the gun—a hard blow. The driver's head jerked and he slipped down lifelessly under the wheel.

I still hadn't had a chance. That gun was covering me again in a second.

The guy said: "Get out. And bring that handbag with you."

I got out, and a voice from the coupe put skids under the protests I had on the tip of my tongue. "That's him, Stan! He must have it—or else the driver still has."

I recognized the voice of Rose O'Shaughnessy, coming from the shadowy figure at the wheel of the coupe.

I glanced both ways, hoping an automobile would come along. It didn't have to be a police car. I'd have settled for a couple of night-rounding drunks in a Model T. But nothing showed. You'd think we were on a cowpath in the toolies instead of a major boulevard in the city.

Stan was frisking me, and he called to the girl: "You'd better get going quick. You don't want to be chased."

"I'll wait."

"No," he barked, "get going. A police car could catch you inside of a dozen blocks."

"How about you?"

"I'll get away on foot. Don't worry about me."

She backed the car from the curb. I tried to read the license number, but it was no go. They'd smeared mud over half the plate.

She swung the coupe around, went down a dark narrow street off Wilshire in second gear. One of the fenders was banging against a tire.

In the front seat of my cab the driver moaned loudly, constantly, in a peculiar snoring rhythm. I thought he might be dying, but I couldn't do anything for him with that gun on me.

The big guy reached into my coat with his left hand and found the handbag. My heart began to bump. This was the right time—but I had to play it exactly right.

His hand dug deeper in my pocket trying to get the bag out and I twisted sharply. It was as if his hand had been caught in a trap. My twist pulled him off balance and the gun jerked away from me. While he was off balance, I slugged him.

My blow had been too short, too quick. It glanced along his jawbone, peeling skin from my knuckles, and we both slipped on the wet pavement and went down in a heap.

It was a crazy fight. He was plenty strong, tall, and heavy in the shoulders. I had the edge when we spilled, with his left hand trapped in my pocket. But when we hit the pavement, he tore it free and chopped me a short one in the stomach.

I rolled over against him and slugged him with rights and lefts, kept trying to get a hand on the gun. He fired twice—missed me twice. Then he scrambled to his feet like an acrobat, quickly, going backward and away from me.

I dived at his legs, spilled him, and the gun went off again like a firecracker somebody had secretly planted in my left ear. I crawled over him, and it turned into a wrestling match. He had both his hands on the butt of his gun. I had both mine on the six-inch barrel.

We stayed locked like that for several seconds, putting every ounce of our strength into moving that gun—he to turn it on me, I to prevent him. But we just stayed locked.

Far over on Wilshire, beyond the park, a police siren cried through the night.

He snapped suddenly: ''We've got to go! You don't want us picked up by cops, do you?''

''No.''

''Let's go then.''

''Who gets the gun?'' I asked.

There we were, sprawled on the wet pavement, in the dark, neither of us giving an inch. And both of us wanting to scram before the cops came, both of us wanting the handbag, and neither willing to trust the other with the gun.

''We got to hurry!'' he said. His voice was breathless, and not just from the exertion of the fight either. ''Have you got a gun on you?''

''No,'' I lied.

''Then I'll tell you what. I'll fire the last shells out of this one. Then we'll go our separate ways.''

''Who keeps the handbag?''

He snorted impatiently. ''The hell with that. You can have it.''

''Along with the letters?''

''Sure.''

The siren sounded closer, coming fast over Westlake. He triggered the gun six times. Twice it exploded. Four times the hammer clicked on empty cases.

''There you are,'' he said, and let me take the revolver away from him without further struggle.

We got to our feet and he cast a nervous look along Wilshire toward Westlake. While his head was turned I slugged him right on the button with the barrel of the gun.

You might call that a double-cross. I don't care much what you call it. I was in a tough game, and I couldn't afford to pull my punches.

He fell flat on his back, but he still wasn't out. He tossed and pitched, groggily, trying to get to his feet. There was a lot of strength in the guy.

I frisked him for his wallet, threw his gun at him, and hoofed along Wilshire to the corner. When I got there, I looked back. He was up and running like hell across the street in long bounds. He intended to get away, all right.

Four white lights and a red spot sped up Wilshire—the police car.

The cops wouldn't learn much. They'd find a smashed cab, a slugged driver who might eventually tell them about a husband and wife, a lost handbag, and a shooting. I figured that was about as far as the police could go.

And as I hoofed my way in the night, going down rainy streets, past dark apartment houses, I felt kind of good.

CHAPTER FOUR
Letters in Lavender

I GOT BACK to my hotel on North Main at three A.M. The night clerk greeted me pleasantly. "Good-morning, Mr. Osborne," he said.

He didn't notice the cut on my cheek, the welt on my forehead, the blood along my jaw. He didn't notice that my pants had big triangular rips at the knees, revealing knee-caps as raw as hamburger in a butcher's window. He didn't even notice that I carried a woman's handbag. He just handed me my room key, smiled politely at the cracked plaster of the lobby ceiling, and completely overlooked my appearance.

He was that kind of clerk—it was that kind of hotel.

I went upstairs and parked for nearly an hour in a tubful of steaming hot water. It helped. Rose O'Shaughnessy's hefty boy-friend had given me quite a work-over when we tussled for the gun on Wilshire Boulevard, and I discovered a lot of places where I couldn't recall being hit.

I doctored myself with liniment and iodine, hit the hay at four A.M., and didn't wake up till noon.

Otto, the bellboy, brought me up a pot of coffee and the latest edition of the *Examiner*.

The killing of Lester Lamia occupied most of the front page. There was a flash photo, taken inside the Little Brown Jug, showing Les lying on the floor, beside the tipped-over chair, his mouth open.

The news story said a lot and concluded nothing. A high police official was quoted as saying the crime had been perpetrated, obviously, "by professional killers imported from the East." The high official added: "Eastern hoodlums shall not be tolerated in Southern California!" He further stated that police were working on "certain secret evidence which cannot be divulged at the present time," and he promised, with dramatic firmness, that arrests would be made within twenty-four hours.

It was sheer baloney—the same old song and dance. I went over the paper carefully and knew the Law was in the dark.

I read an interview with Mike Gorsuch, the bartender at the Jug. Mike admitted there had been a customer in the bar at the time of the shooting, but he said he'd never seen the man before. That covered me. Mike covered himself by insisting that he wasn't able to identify the killers. As far as Mike knew, or as far as he admitted to the police, the killers had been four mysterious guys in brown overcoats. I said Mike was a smart barkeep.

I searched all through the paper and couldn't find a single reference to the blonde, Rose O'Shaughnessy. Mike hadn't mentioned her. And neither had Foghorn Noonan.

Noonan, identifying himself as Lamia's bodyguard, had offered reasonable proof that he'd been down the block at the time of the shooting buying a bottle of special liquor for his boss. The cops released him after five hours' questioning.

On the second page I found an item to the effect that police had questioned a certain party known as Johnny Dominick. Dominick, the paper hinted, had long been "suspected" of large-scale gambling and racketeering activities in Southern California. He was even "suspected" of having been an enemy of Les Lamia. In fact, the Law went so far as to intimate that it might have been Johnny Dominick's gang who, twice before, had made attempts on Les Lamia's life.

However, police were not filing any formal charges against him at the present time, nor had they any reason, they said, to implicate him in the fatal shooting of Lamia. They had merely extended an invitation to Johnny to "come downtown and talk it over." And Johnny had accepted—cheerfully.

I could picture Johnny at Headquarters. He had always been an immaculate and fastidious dresser. I could see him sitting there, in a freshly pressed gray suit, a silk handkerchief peeping smartly from his breast pocket, while sweating detectives threw questions at him. Johnny, calm and smiling, wagging his head sadly over the affair, telling them what a terrible thing crime was, and how he wished, as a law-abiding citizen, that he could somehow aid them in clearing up the case.

I tossed away the paper and got dressed. Then I sent off a code telegram to the Governor telling him I was working on the Lamia case. It wasn't addressed to him, of course, or even to the Capitol. I had a special method for communicating with either the Governor or the State Attorney General.

Then I sat down and went through the packet of letters I'd acquired from the blonde. There were over a dozen of them, written on lavender stationery with green ink, all addressed to Lester A. Lamia. They were love-letters, most of them very hot stuff.

A woman who signed herself ''Ella''—and sometimes ''Ella Brewster''—told Les how much she loved him. She told him in very plain language. She referred to places where they'd met, and she suggested places where they might see each other again. They'd been together, secretly, in a good many places, including a hotel at Santa Barbara and an auto camp outside Palm Springs.

From the way the letters were written, even a moron could reason that ''Ella Brewster'' had a husband who—if he learned about it—would undoubtedly object to his wife's loving attachment to Lamia.

Four of the letters had return addresses on them—

Mrs. Conrad Brewster
1404 Mountain Drive
Beverly Hills
California

I checked with the city directory and learned that Conrad H. Brewster was in the oil business. I checked with *Who's Who in America* and learned that Brewster was fifty-eight years old and President of the Sierra Oil Company of California. I called a friend of mine in the oil business. He told me that Brewster owned two thirds of the stock in the Sierra Company, received a salary of fifty thousand a year, and lived in a Beverly Hills mansion with his wife, Ella, who had a figure like Mae West's and a record of three previous marriages.

I tucked the letters in my pocket and examined the wallet I'd swiped from Rose O'Shaughnessy's boy-friend out there on Wilshire Boulevard. According to his driver's license, he went by the name of Stanley Flynn. I recalled that Rose had called him "Stan." The license described him as six-foot-two, red hair, blue eyes, weighing two hundred and ten pounds. That was the guy all right.

Other cards in the wallet revealed that he was employed as an interne at St. Thomas Hospital. He was an osteopath—which helped explain his hefty physique and the fact that I'd found him such a tough baby to tussle with.

I stowed the wallet in my pocket, along with the letters, finished my dressing, and put on my rod. Then I got a hat and a raincoat and shoved off.

The Weather Bureau had foreseen clearing skies, with moderate westerly winds carrying the storm inland and leaving a bright afternoon for Los Angeles County. Consequently, there were no clearing skies, no moderate winds—westerly or otherwise—and the afternoon was the darkest, stormiest, rainiest of the season.

I'd rented a sedan from a "U-drive" Agency on Spring Street, but to get to Beverly Hills I should have rented a boat.

Gutters ran full, pouring minor floods into the intersections. In places where drains had become clogged, the water had formed muddy lakes, from curb to curb, and cars were stalled. Cops rerouted traffic, and girls in transparent raincoats stood squealing on the corners, jumping back when passing automobiles splashed their stockings.

I drove out Wilshire to Beverly Hills, and went north on a wide residential avenue lined with giant palms.

Rain came down in gray sheets. Lawns were soggy and gray, like swamps, and no matter where you looked, there was water.

I drove through Beverly to Mountain Drive. It was a steep climb on a narrow twisting road. I had to take it in low gear. 1404 was the last house up the hill. I parked in front, fished the lavender love letters from my pocket and concealed all but three of them under the seat of the sedan. Then I hiked up a long flight of concrete steps and rang the bell.

By the swank look of the place, you'd expect an English butler to answer the door. Or at least a Filipino boy in a starched white coat. But the guy who answered my ring wasn't English, wasn't a Filipino, wasn't a servant. He didn't look like he owned the place, either.

He was about medium height and was built heavy through the shoulders. His suit needed pressing—his nails needed a manicure—his face needed a shave. He chewed the soggy end of a cigar, eyeing me narrowly, giving me the once-over from the shoes up.

"Are you Mr. Brewster?" I inquired.

He shook his head in a bored way. "Brewster's at the office. Downtown. Pacific Mutual Building."

Before he could close the door I had my foot propped against it. "Is Mrs. Brewster home?"

He removed the cigar from his mouth, tapped it, letting ashes sprinkle on the leg of my pants. He said: "Does Mrs. Brewster expect you?"

"No, but I think she'll be glad to hear what I have to offer—"

He didn't let me finish. He planted a hand against my chest and started to shove.

"Listen," he said, "I don't know what you're selling, but whatever it is, she's already got it. She's got a vacuum cleaner, an electric ice box, a brand new stove, and lots of Fuller brushes. Whatever you're selling, she's got it."

He put the pressure on me, but I slipped his hand, and he nearly fell down. He glared as if ready, and willing, to sock me.

"Tell her I'm selling some letters," I told him. "It's a nice batch of letters. Love letters. Lots of news value. She'll know what I mean, because she wrote the letters herself. She wrote 'em to Lester Lamia."

He straightened up and chewed his cigar thoughtfully, trying not to appear surprised. "Huh? What letters?"

"Just letters." I pantomimed the act of writing. "People write them on paper with pen and ink. And sometimes people wish they hadn't." I shrugged and started to turn away. "Sorry to bother you. If Mrs. Brewster isn't in the market for any letters today, there's no use for me to waste my salesmanship. Glad to have met you. Good-bye."

He took me gently by the arm. "Just a minute. Let's not act too fast. You'd better come in. We'd better talk this over."

I bowed politely from the waist, like William Powell in the movies. "Will I be intruding?"

He frowned and opened the door wide. "Step this way please." His face scowled with worry. "She'll be glad to see you."

"You're sure I won't be intruding?"

As I stepped past him into the into the hallway, I reached out a hand and casually touched a bulge in his coat under the left armpit. "Cancer?" I inquired sympathetically. I clucked my tongue. "You ought to see your doctor. It's either cancer, or an acute case of Colt thirty-eight."

* * *

My pal in the oil business hadn't exaggerated when he said Mrs. Conrad H. Brewster had a figure like Mae West. And she dressed it with no attempt at shy disguise. I met her in the library, after the guy who let me in had whispered something in her ear by way of introduction.

It was a swank library. The walls were lined with books, arranged for the effect of color in their bindings. Obviously none of the books had been read, and you had the feeling that the room was filled with ghosts of insulted authors.

I sat in a leather chair by the fireplace and Mrs. Brewster sat opposite me, while the surly guy paced up and down the length of the room.

Mrs. Brewster smoothed her silk dress over her knees in such a way you couldn't miss the quality of the dress, or the knees either.

She said to me: "I don't know your name, and I won't ask it. You know who I am, of course. And you've already met Mr. Marshall." She nodded toward the pacing man. "Fred Marshall is the best private detective in the state."

I'd heard his name before. I knew he called himself a private detective, but I also knew he had a long way to go before he ever won the reputation of being the best in the state. Even if he got a shave, cleaned his nails, and brushed the cigar ash off his vest, he'd still have a long way to go.

Mrs. Brewster went on: "Anything you have to say, you may say in the presence of Mr. Marshall. He's representing me in—in the matter of the letters."

Marshall stopped pacing. He eyed me from under shaggy brows. "Show us some proof that you've got the letters."

"I've got them, all right."

Mrs. Brewster said quickly: "I'll pay a thousand dollars in currency, for each letter. That makes fifteen thousand dollars. I'll pay a bonus of five thousand dollars if you produce all fifteen letters inside the next few hours. Say the next ten hours. Is that fair enough?

Before I could answer, Fred Marshall shut me up with a glance. He looked at Mrs. Brewster. "Wait a minute, Ella," he said. "This punk is maybe bluffing. We won't make a deal till he produces the goods."

I stood up and did another Powell, bowing from the waist. "Sorry I intruded." I smiled at both of them. "You'll excuse me, please?"

I started for the door to the hall but Marshall cut me off. I'd been wrong about his "cancer." It wasn't a Colt .38. It was a Swiss Luger.

He jammed the muzzle against my belt and said: "All right, punk. Let's see them letters!"

I looked over at Mrs. Brewster and laughed, but I was a little nervous. You try laughing sometime with the nose of Luger shoved in your guts.

I said to Mrs. Brewster: "Tell this guy to ditch the artillery. I'm not all the punk he thinks I am. I didn't bring the whole batch of letters. I only brought three. A friend of mine has the rest. If I don't get out of here in twenty minutes, my friend might take the rest of the letters to the *Examiner*. Also, my friend might tell the cops where I went. Then, it's good-bye Mrs. Brewster, and it's good-bye Mr. Marshall."

"He's a damn liar," Marshall said.

I looked him in the eyes. "Think so?"

"Yeah, I think so." The muzzle of the gun poked deeper.

Mrs. Brewster got up and pleaded: "Fred! Fred! Put that gun down. Put it away! Let's not have trouble. Let's all have a drink."

She had her hand on the gun, and Fred began to back water. Finally, he holstered the Luger under his coat.

CHAPTER FIVE
Toss the Bum Out!

MRS. BREWSTER LOOKED as if she had a chill. She went over to a liquor cabinet and worked over bottles and glasses while Fred and I watched each other—like a couple of tomcats on a back fence.

Mrs. Brewster got the highballs built finally and passed them around with hands that shook so the ice tinkled in the glasses.

"Let's sit down, boys," she suggested nervously. "Let's all sit down."

She took a long pull at her drink and started to talk. "I couldn't help it if I was untrue to Conrad. He's the fourth man I've been untrue to, but I don't intend to cheat from now on." She looked at me directly, challengingly. "I'm not trying to win your sympathy, or trying to make you reduce the price on the letters. I'll still pay you twenty thousand for them. I'm just telling you the facts."

"You don't have to tell him all that," Fred Marshall advised, but she went right on.

"I meant to be a good wife when I married Conrad. I'd had three marriages that turned out failures, and I wanted to make the fourth one a success. But Conrad spent a lot of time at the office. I met Les Lamia on a party, and he seemed like a good guy. He took me around. We were just a couple of pals having some fun. I liked him, and he liked me."

I said: "He must've liked you plenty to jump into Johnny Dominick's territory and risk his life.

She lowered her eyes: "I didn't mean for Les to get himself in trouble. But he thought I'd leave my husband if he made more money. That's why he jumped Johnny Dominick. Les is the kind of guy that has lots of fight in him. I like a man that has lots of fight."

"So you wrote Les some letters," I prompted.

"Yes."

"And Les kept them."

She looked up angrily. "Listen—Les never tried to blackmail me! He wasn't that kind. He only carried those letters because he liked me. When I told him we were washed up, he said to me, 'O.K., Ella, but I'll keep the letters. I'll always carry them, so I can remember you, and remember what great times we used to have.' "

"That's swell," I said, "but Lamia's sentiment sticks you now for twenty grand, or a lot of trouble, or both."

She flared up. For a second I thought she might throw her highball glass at me. "Listen—Les never carried those letters for blackmail! And he never wanted them to get in circulation!"

I shrugged. "The fact remains they are in circulation."

"It's not Les's fault!"

"Who are you trying to convince," I asked. "Me? Or yourself?"

Fred Marshall advised her once more she didn't have to talk to me. He told her she only had to deal with me for the letters, that it wasn't necessary for her to spill the story behind her predicament.

But that didn't stop her. I don't think anything would have stopped her. She wanted to talk. She wanted to convince herself—not me, not Marshall—that Les Lamia had had nothing to do with allowing the letters to get in circulation.

She'd finished her highball in quick nervous sips, and Marshall poured a big slug of straight Scotch into her glass. She sipped that too. She sipped it without making faces, as if it might be plain water, or soda pop.

"Listen—you can't tell me about Les Lamia. He may've been a

racketeer, but he had character. He wouldn't blackmail me, and he wouldn't let anybody else do it either. Not if he could help it."

"That's possible," I admitted.

"Les was always good to me. The only reason I broke off with him was because I didn't want to make of flop of my fourth marriage. I realized I couldn't be a tramp all my life. It was up to me to stick to Conrad and be a good wife. I explained that to Les. He understood. He wished me luck, My husband still hadn't heard about Les, and Les wasn't going to stand in my way, or let anybody know about it."

"Except for the letters," I put in.

"Damn the letters! Listen—Les would've given those letters back to me any time I asked. But he wanted to keep them. Just like he wanted to keep my picture. That's all there was to it. He promised nobody would ever get hold of them."

I said: "That's a broad promise for a guy that's been spotted twice and is scheduled to die within a month."

Her jaw tightened. "Les meant it. He explained the whole thing to his bodyguard, and they had it arranged so that if anything happened to Les, this bodyguard would destroy the letters."

"You mean Foghorn Noonan?"

"Yes."

"Lamia trusted Foghorn?"

"Why not? Foghorn's like a big husky faithful dog. He'd lay down his life for Les—any day."

"He didn't lay it down at the Little Brown Jug," I reminded her.

"That was just fate. They weren't expecting trouble for a month yet."

She told me that after Les Lamia had been spotted for the second time, and had landed in St. Thomas Hospital, full of shot-gun slugs, she became really worried about the letters. She wanted them back, not because she suspected Les of ever hurting her with them, but because she felt that if Les met with the sudden end he anticipated, the letters might be exposed inadvertently.

She'd been starting a new life, making her husband happy, and everything would be spoiled if he learned of her past relationship with Lamia.

She had to get those letters back.

It was difficult to get in touch with Lamia. Conrad H. Brewster was on the hospital board and she was known there. She couldn't go to the hospital to see a notorious gangster without attracting attention and running the risk of exposing her connection with him. So she employed Fred Marshall, private detective, to see about getting the letters back.

Marshall, after visiting the hospital, reported to Mrs. Brewster that Les Lamia didn't trust him and had refused to turn over the letters— which had been stowed away in the hospital safe.

Marshall's next move in behalf of Mrs. Brewster was an attempt to bribe a few nurses and hospital attendants. He offered three thousand dollars to anyone who would open the safe and sneak out the letters. But the hospital attaches he slyly approached were afraid of losing their jobs, or professional standing, and refused to work with him.

Therefore, when Les Lamia finally left St. Thomas Hospital, he still had the letters. And Ella Brewster was still trying to get them back— with Fred Marshall acting as her agent.

Marshall took the glass from Mrs. Brewster's hand and placed it on the mantel. He looked at me sourly.

"Nuts to all this talk," he said. "The only thing that matters is the letters. You've got them, and Mrs. Brewster wants them back. You heard the offer—twenty grand and we won't ask questions about how you come to get hold of them. All we want is the letters. You say you got three in your pocket now. O.K. Let's have 'em. We'll pay a grand now, and the rest of the dough when you produce the rest of the letters."

Ella Brewster stared at me anxiously. "Are the terms fair enough?"

I nodded, and she reached out her hand, palm upward. It was a nice hand, though soft, and her husband had put a lot of diamond rings on it.

"The letters?"

I placed the three lavender envelopes in her extended hand. She sank back on the davenport, frowning as she ripped the folded letters from the opened envelopes. Her fingers trembled.

She glanced over the letters very briefly. Then she began to laugh. She threw back her head and howled.

I thought she'd gone hysterical, and I guess Marshall thought so too. He brought over the bottle of Scotch, but she waved it away. Then she stopped laughing.

She looked at me for a long time, her eyes narrowed under long black lashes. I felt uncomfortable. I though she'd gone nuts or something.

She said to me: "Get out of here, you lousy chiseler!"

"What's the matter?"

She threw the letters at my feet. "Take them, and get out!" Her voice quivered with rage. She turned to Marshall. "Fred! Toss this bum out!"

I picked up the letters, but at the same time I kept an eye on Marshall. "What's the matter with these? Forgeries?" I asked.

Her laugh was brief, hard, with ice in it. "Forgeries? They're not even imitations! Listen, you dumb punk—I never used green ink in my life, and I never wrote like this, and I never put return addresses on my envelopes when I wrote to Les, and I write backhand, and my stationery is always pale blue—not lavender—and I never wrote to Les at Miami Beach, and I never met him at a hotel in Santa Barbara!" She was breathless, her breast heaving like an old-fashioned dramatic actress. But it wasn't acting—it was the real goods. She jumped up, and turned her back on me, glaring at Fred Marshall.

"Fred! I'm asking you for the last time—toss this lug out! What's the matter with you! Are you scared of him!"

Fred wasn't scared of me now. I guess the only reason he'd hesitated at all was that things had moved too fast for him. Now he braced himself, his legs spread wide apart, and dug for the Luger.

I produced the 38/44 about a second ahead of him and used it like a club. His hand had come out from under his coat with the gun and I swung down my own rod and connected with his wrist. His face screwed up in pain.

He went to his knees on the carpet, holding his right wrist against his stomach. The Luger bounced off one of my shoes. I scooped it up quickly and tucked it under my belt.

There he was on his knees in front of me, holding his injured wrist. Ella Brewster stood just behind him, but looking over his head. She was looking at me. She didn't seem so mad at me now. She acted as though she almost liked me. Her red lips smiled. Then the smile went away, and her eyes showed rage again, and she kicked Fred Marshall.

"Fred! You damn fool—you let this bum take you!"

He was too sore to hear her. He got up from the floor sullenly, still nursing the wrist. "You'll wish to hell you never done that!" he threatened.

I tried to bow in a debonair manner and keep the muzzle of the 38/44 pointed at his teeth at the same time. I said: "It's been a nice visit. I regret leaving. Will you be good enough to see me to my car, Mr. Marshall?"

He reddened and looked as if he were already figuring on the day when he could take me apart by inches.

"I'll get you, smart guy!" he promised. "Maybe you're tops now, but you'll wish you never was, you lousy son-of-a——!"

He behaved like the villain in an old-time movie, and I told him so, and that made him madder. I pushed him into the hallway, and out of the front door, into the rain, with the muzzle of the gun prodding his spine.

I followed him down the long flight of concrete steps to where my car was parked.

He stood sullenly on the curb while I backed the car around and faced it down the hill. I kept the 38/44 on the seat beside me, and I still had his automatic under my belt. After I'd jockeyed the sedan and turned it, he strolled over toward me with his hand in his pockets.

"Listen, guy," he said, "I'm not asking anything personal, like who you are, or anything. All I'm asking is where the hell did you get those letters?"

I told him straight. "I swiped them off a blonde named Rose O'Shaughnessy. And she swiped them off Les Lamia right after he got killed."

Marshall looked incredulous. "Yeah? Where did you really get them?"

"Just like I told you."

He still looked incredulous.

I put the car in low gear and said: "I'll toss your rod on the sidewalk at the bottom of the hill. You can get it later."

"I'll get it all right."

"Be seeing you, Fred."

He nodded sullenly, his hands still in his pockets. "You'll be seeing me, all right."

"So long, Fred. Good luck."

He gave a short laugh from the side of his mouth. "Good luck to you, guy. You're the one that's gonna need it."

I coasted the sedan away from him down the grade, and at the bottom of the hill, without stopping, tossed the Luger into the gutter.

CHAPTER SIX
Me—Burglar

IT WAS DARK when I got back to the downtown district. The rain had stopped, but water was still running in the streets, and city employees, working overtime, were trying to clear the clogged drains.

I drove up Main and hunted for a place to park the sedan. Ordinarily there's plenty of curb-space in the vicinity of the Little Brown Jug, but this was no ordinary occasion. I had to leave the car four blocks away, on Leavenworth.

I walked back, and the sidewalk in front of the Little Brown Jug, jammed with people waiting a chance to get inside, suggested a de luxe Hollywood theater on the night of the ''gala premiere'' of some epic movie. I had to fight my way through the crowd.

Inside, the place was a bedlam. Mike Gorsuch had four extra men helping him behind the bar, and three waiters working the tables.

Mike himself was drunk with both liquor and success. I had to yank his arm before he noticed me. Then he slapped me on the back.

"Boy!" he said. "How's this for business, Mr. Osborne?"

"Big," I told him.

"Big? Hell, this is the biggest business I've done since the night they repealed Prohibition! The beer taps gave out ten minutes ago. I'm selling rye at fifty cents a throw. I'm asking sixty-five for Scotch—and getting it. I'm—"

"Nice going," I interrupted. "When did it all start?"

He told me.

It seemed that the crowd has started to gather by seven o'clock in the morning. Everybody and his brother wanted to cast curious eyes on the scene of a gang slaying. The police wouldn't let anyone inside, of course. But by four in the afternoon the fingerprint men, official photographers, and Homicide dicks had finished their work, and the Law informed Mike he could open for business.

Mike opened. And how!

With white chalk, he had marked the holes made by gangster bullets. He'd drawn a sketch of a man on the floor, and pointed this out as the exact spot where Les Lamia had fallen, even outlining the bloodstains—so that no one would be disappointed. He'd turned the Jug into a regular three-ring circus.

I said: "Mike, I want to talk to you a second."

He tried to pull away from me. "Sorry Mr. Osborne, but I got a party over here at a table, and they want me to tell 'em how it happened. They're society people from Pasadena. The guy just tipped me a five-spot. I'm busy. I got to please my customers."

I didn't let him get away from me. I led him into a corner and said: "What I want to talk to you about is plenty important.

* * *

He eyed me narrowly. "You ain't got no beef against me. I covered you when the cops grilled me about who was in the place at the time of the shooting. I never even mentioned you. I just said there was a guy here, but I didn't know who he was."

"Thanks," I told him. "But that's not what I want to talk about."

"What, then?"

"Just this. Remember the blonde that was with Lamia?"

He nodded defensively. "Yeah, but I didn't tell the cops about her either. I'm a close-mouthed man when it comes to gang shootings. I don't hanker to get my face shot off."

"Right. But his blonde asked you for something to drink. It was something you didn't have in stock. Do you remember that?"

"Sure. She wanted Italian Galliano. But I never carry that fancy stuff. I don't get enough call for it."

"So when you told her you didn't have any, Foghorn Noonan went down the street to the liquor store to buy a bottle. Right?"

"Sure, Why?"

"Was Lamia's blonde the only customer who called for Galliano yesterday?"

"Yeah. Just like I told you I don't get much call for that fancy stuff. I—" He broke off and scratched his jawbone with his thumbnail. "Come to think of it, you're right. Another customer did ask for Galliano yesterday. But I don't think he really wanted to drink it. He just sort of got to talking with me. He just wanted to know if I carried it."

"And you told him no?"

"Naturally, I told him no."

"Who was he?"

"The customer?"

"Yeah."

Mike shrugged. "How the hell do I know? I never seen this guy before."

"What did he look like?"

"Well, I think he was sort of a big guy. I didn't pay much attention. All I remembered is that he was sort of big and had red hair. That's about all I can tell you."

I clapped him on the shoulder. "That's plenty, Mike."

He started to leave me, then turned back saying: "By the way, Mr. Osborne, did you know Foghorn Noonan is looking for you?"

I shook my head.

"Yeah, Foghorn's been in here a dozen times in the last couple of hours. He tried to pump me. He knows your real name. He remembered seeing you at the bar before he went out to buy the bottle, and he thinks you know something about how Lamia got shot. He thinks you maybe swiped something from Lamia's pocket after the shooting. Better watch your step. If Foghorn thinks you really had something to do with bumping his boss, he'll take you apart. Foghorn's an awful mean guy when he gets mad.''

I nodded. "Thanks for telling me, Mike."

"That's O.K., Mr. Osborne."

He went over to his society customers, and I paid fifty cents for a two-bit shot of rye I didn't want and then left the place.

I walked a block down Main to a cigar store with a phone booth, thumbed through the directory, found the number of St. Thomas Hospital, and dialed it.

A feminine voice answered the phone with a brisk cheery greeting. "Good-evening—St. Thomas."

I said: "My name is Hamilton Sturgis."

"Yes, Mr. Sturgis?"

"I had my appendix taken out in your hospital," I explained. "Do you remember me?"

"Of course we remember you, Mr. Sturgis," she responded sweetly. "How are you feeling now, Mr. Sturgis?"

She didn't remember me at all. I'd never had my appendix out, and I'd never even been in St. Thomas. But I knew about hospitals. Big institutions like St. Thomas have hundreds of patients—scores of them coming in and going out every day, but no matter how big they are, they never admit they lack the "personal touch." They pretend to remember everybody. If you called up and said your name was George Washington and that they had operated on you for gall stones, they wouldn't question you. They wouldn't even take the time to check their records. They'd just say: "Of course—how are you feeling now, Mr. Washington?"

Anyway, I told the girl on the phone that I felt fine, and that I'd received wonderful treatment at St. Thomas.

I went on to say: "I was treated so fine up there that I want to do something nice for some of the staff. I want to give some presents. There was an interne named Stanley Flynn. I bought a radio for him. I want to deliver it to his house."

"Shall I call Doctor Flynn to the phone?" she inquired.

She was more than sweet now. When employees in a hospital think you're the kind of patient that dishes out presents, they practically break their necks being nice to you.

I said: "No, don't call Doctor Flynn to the phone. Just keep it a secret. I want to know his home address so I can have this radio delivered. Can you give it to me?"

She gave it to me so fast I had to ask her to repeat it. He lived, she said, in a cottage in the San Fernando Valley—510 Maple Lane—somewhere out beyond Van Nuys.

"If there's anything else we can do for you, Mr. Sturgis," she told me, "don't hesitate to call us."

I assured her I wouldn't hesitate a minute.

It took me an hour and a half to cross the city and get out in the Valley near Van Nuys. It took another half hour to find anybody who had ever heard of Maple Lane. Finally after some directions from a gas-station attendant, I drove down a rutty road in the dark.

The district had been promoted, a couple of years ago, by real-estate developers who thought they could boom it into a prosperous suburb. They had christened it Valley Haven Park, and laid out streets, but they hadn't paved them or put in sidewalks.

The place never boomed. A few suckers had built bungalows, but the bungalows were far scattered over the muddy flats, and Valley Haven Park, on a rainy night, was just about the most desolate spot I'd ever seen.

The five-hundred block of Maple Lane had just about two small houses in it. The first one burned all its lights behind drawn curtains, and there were three cars parked outside. I could hear a radio going in the house, and the chatter and laughter of people having a good time.

I parked the sedan near the other cars and got out. The number on the porch of the party house was 504, so I knew the house further on, the only other one in the block, must be 510.

I waded through mud puddles and weeds, passed a couple of empty lots, and looked at the house.

It was entirely dark. I used my flashlight briefly and saw a Spanish-type cottage with a neglected garden in front and a single-car garage at the back. The garage doors were open, and there was no car inside.

I sloshed down the driveway to the service porch. I figured that was my best means of entrance. Lots of guys can handle front-door locks, or window locks, but I'm not a burglar by trade, and service porches and kitchen doors are about as far as my talent goes.

The porch door was a cinch—just a screen door hooked on the inside. I lifted the hook with a bent piece of stiff wire which I forced through the mesh of the screen. That put me on the service porch. The kitchen door wasn't so easy.

The key was on the inside of the lock and I managed to poke it out with my wire. A simple skeleton would have worked the lock, but I didn't have one. I had to fish under the crack of the door with my wire and draw the fallen key out. It took quite a while, because the door fit fairly close on its threshold and didn't leave much room for fishing.

As soon as I got inside the house, I lit the lights. I didn't want to go snooping around with my flashlight. If the people next door happened to see that, they might call for some Law. If they saw all the lights burning they'd think I had a right there—or wouldn't think anything about it at all.

The first thing I did was pull down all the shades. I wanted to shut my activities out of sight of the neighbors, and, also, I suspected something I was looking for—letters—might have been rolled up in the shades. I didn't find what I was after.

I tried the flue of the fireplace. All I got was soot. I tried the upholstery of the davenport and found a nickel that had worked out of somebody's pocket. I went into the bathroom and looked in the tank of the toilet. I went into the bedroom, examined all the drawers, and took the bedding apart. I gave the kitchen a thorough work-over. I rolled back every rug in the house, even ran my wire around the ceiling moldings. Still I didn't find letters.

In half an hour I'd peeled down to my shirt-sleeves, was rolling sweat, and still no letters.

I sat down and had a smoke. When I went back to work I discovered a trap door in the ceiling of the bedroom closet. I shot the beam of the flash around the attic, and while I didn't find letters, I found a few other things.

I found a raincoat, a cap, a mask, and a Thompson sub-machine-gun.

I brought those articles into the living-room, holding the machine-gun by the front stock, covered by my handkerchief. I figured that any fingerprints on the gun might be important to the police. I carefully wrapped the gun, along with cap and mask, inside the raincoat and put the bundle on the davenport.

There was a radio in the room, and a clock. The clock pointed hands at ten. I switched on the radio and waited impatiently for the tubes to warm. A dance orchestra began to drift soft music from the speaker, but I didn't

want music. I wanted the ten o'clock broadcast in order to hear if there
was anything new on the killing of Les Lamia.

I fiddled with the dial and the blaring voices of announcers came and
went. A voice said: "—have you tried a good, rich, ripe-bodied tobacco?"

Another voice said: "Put those hands up, punk!"

I turned the dial to the news station, and the announcer was talking
loudly about the war in China, and a voice cut in on him, saying again:
"Put those hands up, punk!"

A bum set, I thought. Station interference. It was another second
before I realized the interfering voice hadn't come from the speaker.

My scalp began to prickle. I flipped off the radio switch, but I hated to
turn around. I was hunched over the radio, and I turned my head slowly,
reluctantly.

Three persons had come in through the front door of the house and two
of them held guns on me.

It was Fred Marshall who had said: "Put those hands up, punk." Fred
Marshall—the private detective. He had the Luger pistol I'd taken from
him that afternoon.

I said: "I'm glad to see you found your rod."

He eyed me sourly, not speaking.

Rose O'Shaughnessy had closed the front door behind her. She leaned
against it, and she never took her eyes from me.

Finally she said: "That's the guy I was telling you about."

Stanley Flynn nodded. "I remember him, all right."

Flynn had a little .25 Colt automatic which looked like a kid's water
pistol. He shuffled his shoes nervously on the rug and came toward me in
slow steps.

"What are you doing here?"

"I just dropped around to pay a call," I told him.

He said: "I know how you found this place. You called the hospital
and said your name was Hamilton Sturgis and that you were a patient."

I added: "And the girl on the switchboard told you about it, and you
couldn't remember a patient by that name, and smelled a rat. So you
came out here, with your friends, to check up. My gag was good, except
I didn't get out fast enough."

"What do you want?" he demanded.

I didn't answer. I didn't have to. He'd seen the bundle of raincoat on
the davenport. He started to unwrap it. As soon as the machine-gun

showed itself, he straightened up and stared at me. His hand, holding the little .25, trembled.

"Listen—who the hell are you, anyway?"

I shrugged. "I'm just a guy trying to make a living."

Fred Marshall snorted. "Make it? You mean chisel it."

I've never seen anybody more worried than Stanley Flynn. Sweat glistened on his forehead, trickled down his cheeks. He said quickly to Fred Marshall: "Listen—we've got to get rid of this guy. He's dangerous."

Marshall came around behind me, eased the 38/44 off my hip, ejected the shells from the cylinder and tossed the gun across the room.

Stanley Flynn switched on the radio. He tuned in a dance program, made it so loud you had a hard time hearing anything else.

He said: "One of us has to bump him. The radio will cover the noise."

His hand kept shaking. He lifted the little automatic and pointed it at me. I got ready to dive at him and take my last chance at living, but Fred Marshall clipped his wrist, knocked the baby pistol from his hand.

"Cut that!" Marshall snapped at him. "Don't act so damn fast. We got to find out where them letters are. Besides, maybe this guy is followed."

Rose O'Shaughnessy turned the knob of the front door. "I'll get out on the porch. If anybody comes, I'll yell."

Fred Marshall shook his head at her. "You can watch out the dining-room window, Rose."

She nodded, and went quickly into the dining-room.

Fred Marshall leaned against the fireplace and sighted the Luger at my chest. He said: "All right, guy, where the hell are those letters?"

I sat down on the arm of the davenport. "You mean the ones I showed you and Mrs. Brewster this afternoon?"

"Nuts! Where're the real ones?"

"I haven't got them."

"You're a liar," he told me.

"Listen, Marshall" I said, "if I had the real ones I wouldn't have tried to peddle phonies this afternoon. And if I had the real ones I wouldn't be coming around here frisking Flynn's shack, would I?"

"You haven't got them?"

"Hell, no!"

Flynn put in: "I don't think he knows where the letters are, Fred. I think he's just a chiseler. But he knows too much—he found the machine-gun. We've got to fix him, and fix him quick."

Rose O'Shaughnessy came in from the dining-room. "Don't do anything to him till you find out about the letters." She was nervous, too, almost as nervous as Stanley Flynn. She said to Fred Marshall: "Make him tell where they are."

"Sure," Stanley Flynn agreed. "Make him tell."

"Do you know who has those letters?" Marshall asked.

I shrugged, and tried to be casual about it. "I've got a guess. Can I try a guess?"

He kept the nose of the Luger steady on my chest.

"Go ahead and guess, pal," he challenged.

CHAPTER SEVEN
Osteopathic Treatment

I KNEW I was in a hell of a spot. When cops put the pinch on you, they warn you that anything you may say will be held against you—in court. These two weren't cops—yet anything I said would be held against me—plenty. And not in any court.

My rod had been tossed across the room, empty. The Tommy-gun lay on the davenport, but I hadn't checked to see if there were cartridges in the drum. Even if I took a dive for it—and didn't get shot on the way—the Tommy might be empty. I felt sunk. I knew I had to sling a lot of language.

"Let's hear the guess," Fred Marshall said.

"From the beginning?"

"The beginning is always a good place to start," he told me.

"All right," I said. "Here goes."

The blonde came further into the room and sat on a straight chair. She never took her eyes off me. Her hair was wet from the rain, and her face appeared both beautiful and hard.

"Go ahead," she told me.

"It starts with Les Lamia," I began. "Les fell in love with Mrs. Conrad Brewster. It was one of those things. She met him in places. She wrote him letters. And Les liked her so much that he decided to make more money—for her. He jumped into Johnny Dominick's territory. And Johnny is a guy who doesn't like to have his territory jumped."

Fred Marshall flashed me a cynical smile. "Nice start. Let's hear the rest."

"The rest," I said, "goes like this. Twice Johnny Dominick tried to rub out Les Lamia. The second time he put Les in St. Thomas hospital full of shotgun slugs. Les came out of the hospital—still on his feet. Johnny Dominick had to try again. But Johnny wouldn't pull the job while the town was hot. He'd wait his time. In the meantime, Les was a marked man, a walking corpse. As soon as the town cooled off, Johnny would get him."

"Johnny did get him," Rose O'Shaughnessy put in.

I shook my head. "No, Johnny didn't. Johnny would've gotten him within another month, but there was somebody who didn't want to wait that long."

"Who?" Fred Marshall demanded.

"It was all because of the letters. Les carried them only because he loved Mrs. Brewster. He didn't want to blackmail her. He carried the letters for the same reason a movie fan carries a picture of Greta Garbo."

"Go on, guy."

"Mrs. Brewster trusted Les completely, but at the same time she knew he was marked for death by Johnny Dominick, and she was afraid that if Les was bumped off the letters would get in circulation. So she hired you, Marshall, to contact Lamia and get the letters for her.

"You went to St. Thomas Hospital and talked to Lamia, but Lamia didn't trust you, and anyway Lamia intended to keep the letters till his dying day. He was a romantic sort of guy. He'd stowed the letters in the hospital safe. And he planned, after he came out of the hospital, to have his bodyguard, Foghorn Noonan, destroy the letters in the event anything happened."

Marshall looked at me narrowly. "You ain't telling us anything. You learned all that from Mrs. Brewster."

I nodded. "Give me time. I'm just giving you the build-up. Now, Marshall, you tried to bribe some of the hospital staff to sneak the letters out of the safe. Everybody refused you. Then you met Rose O'Shaughnessy and Stanley Flynn. You propositioned them. They seemed willing to listen to the music of money, but they didn't want to lose their jobs at the hospital, and they also were afraid of Les Lamia. So you made a new proposition."

"I did?"

"Yeah. Up to that time you'd been working for Mrs. Brewster. But then you decided that if you swiped the letters and secretly blackmailed her, you could make a much larger hunk of money than your fee for merely returning the goods. So you propositioned Rose and Stanley all over again. You took them in on your blackmail plot. The idea was to let Les leave the hospital with the letters in his possession. Then you'd rub him and steal the letters. Rose and Stanley liked that proposition because the killing couldn't be connected with the hospital and they wouldn't lose their jobs. Also, since Les would be dead, they had nothing to fear from him. And lastly, if the killing was pulled in the right way, it would be blamed on Johnny Dominick.

"The next problem was how to bump Lamia. You had a good break when Les invited Rose to go out with him for an evening. You knew that Les always went to his old haunt, the Little Brown Jug. That would be a swell place to spot him. But you had to figure a gag to get his bodyguard out of the way. Your gag was this: Stanley Flynn barged over to the Jug in the afternoon. He pumped the bartender and found he didn't stock a liqueur known as Italian Galliano. So Rose was tipped off. And when she got to the Jug with Lamia last night, she asked for Galliano. It worked out just as you planned. Foghorn Noonan went out to buy a bottle. You had it timed just right. As soon as he left, you and Stanley Flynn came in."

"Not me," Marshall protested. He batted his eyes and stared at me.

I said: "I remember you. You were the short guy with the automatics. And Stanley was the tall guy with the raincoat, the cap, and the mask. I just found his disguise. And I found the Tommy-gun."

"Go on, guy."

"You shot Lamia, and Flynn shot out the lights. Rose's job was to get the letters from Lamia's pocket while you two guys scrammed. She had nothing to worry about. Even if the police finally traced her down for questioning, she could claim she'd been an innocent bystander to the killing. She could claim she just went out with Lamia on a friendly basis, having been his nurse. So Rose snatched the letters. And that's where the funny part comes in."

"What funny part?"

"Well, the letters were phonies. They weren't even good forgeries— just phonies."

"Who has the real ones?" Rose demanded.

"That's a story," I said.

"Let's hear it."

I said: "Les Lamia carried Mrs. Brewster's letters because they meant something romantic to him. Therefore, he wouldn't carry phonies. Somebody switched the real ones for the phonies."

"Foghorn Noonan?" Marshall asked.

I shook my head. "The phonies were so phoney that Mrs. Brewster laughed at them. They didn't fool her in the least. And they wouldn't have fooled Les Lamia either. The substitution was made after Lamia was dead. It must've been done in the dark in the beer parlor, after the lights were shot out. That eliminates Foghorn Noonan, because Foghorn had gone down the block to buy Galliano. I didn't make the switch. Neither did the bartender. Mike and I were hiding behind the bar. That leaves three possibilities. It leaves Rose O'Shaughnessy, Fred Marshall, and Stanley Flynn. One of the three of you tried to double-cross the others. One of the three of you switched the letters, kept the real ones, and planned to blackmail Mrs. Brewster all by himself."

Flynn and Marshall turned toward Rose. The blonde met their eyes frankly. "I didn't do it," she said in a quiet way.

I backed her up. "No, Rose didn't. If Rose had had the real letters she wouldn't have fought me to the last ditch last night. She believed the phonies were real. She was playing the game the way you planned it."

Flynn and Marshall looked at each other.

I said evenly: "One of you two guys is the double crosser. One of you switched the letters in the dark and let Rose find the phonies."

Marshall spoke to me without turning. The Luger was in his hand, gripped hard. He kept looking at Flynn. "Which one of us?" he demanded.

"Last night," I went on, "Stanley Flynn fought me for the letters out on Wilshire Boulevard. He was just putting up a bluff for Rose's benefit. As soon as the cops came, he told me I could keep the letters. Why? Because he knew they were phoney, anyhow. He didn't want to be caught by the cops over a bunch of blackmail letters which he knew damn well were phoney—because he'd written them himself!"

Stanley Flynn whirled on me, screamed: "You're a damn liar! This guy Foghorn Noonan—"

"Nix on Noonan. Noonan is out of it. Noonan is hunting for me right now because he thinks I might have swiped the letters. Noonan is just trying to find them and destroy them, like he promised Lamia."

"You're a cockeyed liar!" Flynn snapped.

I shook my head calmly. "You wanted to kill me a few minutes ago, Flynn. You guessed I was on the right track. You wanted to rub me before Fred and Rose discovered your double-cross. The letters weren't in the house. My guess is that you've got them on you right now."

* * *

Rose O'Shaughnessy got halfway out of the chair. Her knuckles were white, gripping the wooden arms. Her face was harder than ever, no longer beautiful.

"Search him, Fred," she suggested in a tight voice.

Flynn backed away. "Keep you hands off me!"

I felt this was my chance. I'd built up to it, set dog against dog, and now there was to be a dog-fight. Somebody was going to get hurt and I had to make sure it wasn't me.

Flynn hit Marshall on the side of the jaw with a blow that sent the private dick halfway across the room. The Luger dropped to the floor and Rose O'Shaughnessy screamed.

Flynn snatched up the little .25 Colt. It made a sharp pop-sound, like the explosion of a fire-cracker. Flynn shot again and again.

Marshall groaned, his face winced, but he jumped at Flynn.

I grabbed the Tommy-gun and did a fast backward somersault over the davenport. When I hit the floor, I tried the trigger. There was a short burst of fire. The Tommy had shells in the drum.

I raised up over the davenport, aimed the Tommy. "Cut that!" I yelled.

Marshall and Flynn were fighting for the Luger. Marshall's vest was soaked with blood. The Luger went off and Rose fell off the chair, hit by a stray bullet.

"Cut that!" I yelled again.

Flynn was strong. He pulled the Luger away from Marshall and shot him in the stomach. Marshall doubled up and sank awkwardly to the floor.

Flynn pointed the Luger at me, firing.

I tried for his legs.

The machine-gun chattered like hell, bucked and jumped. Then it was empty, and the Luger was empty, and Flynn took a running dive at me.

We hit the floor, behind the davenport, and the davenport tipped over on top of us.

Flynn had an arm-lock on me, but I slugged him hard, and he fell away. I climbed to my feet in a hurry. He tossed aside the davenport, as though it weighed only a few ounces, and jumped me, fighting.

Once again, we hit the floor. We fought all over the room, rolling. He tried to get me under him. I slipped, dodged, rolled and kept slugging.

We both scrambled to our feet, and he tried to hit me with a flower vase. I ducked, and the vase smashed against the wall. Then I got a chair and swung it. I put everything I had in it. It broke like matchwood on his skull and he went out like a light.

When I searched his pockets I found all the letters, the real goods. There he was on the floor, and Marshall on the floor, and Rose O'Shaughnessy on the floor. None of them could move.

I slipped out the back door, through the service porch, just as a police car was coming down Maple Lane. I figured the neighbors had put in a call, because the lights were out in the next house, and there was no more radio music, or laughter.

I ran over back lots, through mud and weeds. I didn't want to make explanations to local cops. They could break the case with what I'd left them. If anything was missing, I'd mail them the blackmail letters. They'd get the whole story, all right. They didn't need *me*. To them, I was Tricky Enright, Public Enemy, and they had to keep believing that.

Gideon Fell

INVISIBLE HANDS
John Dickson Carr

H E COULD NEVER understand afterward why he felt uneasiness, even to the point of fear, before he saw the beach at all.

Night and fancies? But how far can fancies go?

It was a steep track down to the beach. The road, however, was good, and he could rely on his car. And yet, halfway down, before he could even taste the sea-wind or hear the rustle of the sea, Dan Fraser felt sweat on his forehead. A nerve jerked in the calf of his leg over the foot brake.

"Look, this is damn silly!" he thought to himself. He thought it with a kind of surprise, as when he had first known fear in wartime long ago. But the fear had been real enough, no matter how well he concealed it, and they believed he never felt it.

A dazzle of lightning lifted ahead of him. The night was too hot. This enclosed road, bumping the springs of his car, seemed pressed down in an airless hollow.

After all, Dan Fraser decided, he had everything to be thankful for. He was going to see Brenda; he was the luckiest man in London. If she chose to spend weekends as far away as North Cornwall, he was glad to drag himself there—even a day late.

Brenda's image rose before him, as clearly as the flash of lightning. He always seemed to see her half laughing, half pouting, with light on her yellow hair. She was beautiful; she was desirable. It would only be disloyalty to think any trickiness underlay her intense, naive ways.

Brenda Lestrange always got what she wanted. And she had wanted him, though God alone knew why: he was no prize package at all. Again, in imagination, he saw her against the beat and shuffle of music in a night club. Brenda's shoulders rose from a low-cut silver gown, her eyes as blue and wide-spaced as the eternal Eve's.

You'd have thought she would have preferred a dasher, a roaring bloke like Toby Curtis, who had all the women after him. But that, as Joyce had intimated, might be the trouble. Toby Curtis couldn't see Brenda for all the rest of the crowd. And so Brenda preferred—

Well, then, what was the matter with him?

He would see Brenda in a few minutes. There ought to have been joy bells in the tower, not bats in the—

Easy!

He was out in the open now, at sea level. Dan Fraser drove bumpingly along scrub grass, at the head of a few shallow terraces leading down to the private beach. Ahead of him, facing seaward, stood the overlarge, overdecorated bungalow which Brenda had rather grandly named "The King's House."

And there wasn't a light in it—not a light showing at only a quarter past ten.

Dan cut the engine, switched off the lights, and got out of the car. In the darkness he could hear the sea charge the beach as an army might have charged it.

Twisting open the handle of the car's trunk he dragged out his suitcase. He closed the compartment with a slam which echoed out above the swirl of water. This part of the Cornish coast was too lonely, too desolate, but it was the first time such a thought had ever occurred to him.

He went to the house, round the side and toward the front, His footsteps clacked loudly on the crazy-paved path on the side. And even in a kind of luminous darkness from the white of the breakers ahead, he saw why the bungalow showed no lights.

All the curtains were drawn on the windows—on this side, at least.

When Dan hurried round to the front door, he was almost running. He banged the iron knocker on the door, then hammered it again. As he glanced over his shoulder, another flash of lightning paled the sky to the west.

It showed him the sweep of gray sand. It showed black water snakily edged with foam. In the middle of the beach, unearthly, stood the small natural rock formation—shaped like a low-backed armchair, eternally faced out to sea—which for centuries had been known as King Arthur's Chair.

The white eye of lightning closed. Distantly there was a shock of thunder.

This whole bungalow couldn't be deserted! Even if Edmund Ireton and Toby Curtis were at the former's house some distance along the coast, Brenda herself must be here. And Joyce Ray. And the two maids.

Dan stopped hammering the knocker. He groped for and found the knob of the door.

The door was unlocked.

He opened it on brightness. In the hall, rather overdecorated like so many of Brenda's possessions, several lamps shone on gaudy furniture and a polished floor. But the hall was empty too.

With the wind whisking and whistling at his back Dan went in and kicked the door shut behind him. He had no time to give a hail. At the back of the hall a door opened. Joyce Ray, Brenda's cousin, walked toward him, her arms hanging limply at her sides and her enormous eyes like a sleepwalker's.

"Then you did get here," said Joyce, moistening dry lips. "You did get here, after all."

"I—"

Dan stopped. The sight of her brought a new realization. It didn't explain his uneasiness or his fear—but it did explain much.

Joyce was the quiet one, the dark one, the unobtrusive one, with her glossy black hair and her subdued elegance. But she was the poor relation, and Brenda never let her forget it. Dan merely stood and stared at her. Suddenly Joyce's eyes lost their sleepwalker's look. They were gray eyes, with very black lashes; they grew alive and vivid, as if she could read his mind.

"Joyce," he blurted, "I've just understood something. And I never understood it before. But I've got to tell—"

"Stop!" Joyce cried.

Her mouth twisted. She put up a hand as if to shade her eyes.

"I know what you want to say," she went on. "But you're not to say it! Do you hear me?"

"Joyce, I don't know why we're standing here yelling at each other. Anyway, I—I didn't mean to tell you. Not yet, anyway. I mean, I must tell Brenda—"

"You can't tell Brenda!" Joyce cried.

"What's that?"

"You can't tell her anything, ever again," said Joyce. "Brenda's dead."

* * *

There are some words which at first do not even shock or stun. You just don't believe them. They can't be true. Very carefully Dan Fraser put his suitcase down on the floor and straightened up again.

"The police," said Joyce, swallowing hard, "have been here since early this morning. They're not here now. They've taken her away to the mortuary. That's where she'll sleep tonight."

Still Dan said nothing.

"Mr.—Mr. Edmund Ireton," Joyce went on, "has been here ever since it happened. So has Toby Curtis. So, fortunately, has a man named Dr. Gideon Fell. Dr. Fell's a bumbling old duffer, a very learned man or something. He's a friend of the police; he's kind; he's helped soften things. All the same, Dan, if you'd been here last night—"

"I couldn't get away. I told Brenda so."

"Yes, I know all that talk about hard-working journalists. But if you'd only been here, Dan, it might not have happened at all."

"Joyce, for God's sake!"

Then there was a silence in the bright, quiet room. A stricken look crept into Joyce's eyes.

"Dan, I'm sorry. I'm terribly sorry. I was feeling dreadful and so, I suppose, I had to take it out on the first person handy."

"That's all right. But how did she die?" Then desperately he began to surmise. "Wait, I've got it! She went out to swim early this morning, just as usual? She's been diving off those rocks on the headland again? And—"

"No," said Joyce. "She was strangled."

"*Strangled?*"

What Joyce tried to say was "murdered." Her mouth shook and faltered round the syllables; she couldn't say them; her thoughts, it seemed, shied back and ran from the very word. But she looked at Dan steadily.

"Brenda went out to swim early this morning, yes."

"Well?"

"At least, she must have. I didn't see her. I was still asleep in that back bedroom she always gives me. Anyway, she went down there in a red swim suit and a white beach robe."

Automatically Dan's eyes moved over to an oil painting above the fireplace. Painted by a famous R.A., it showed a scene from classical antiquity; it was called *The Lovers*, and left little to the imagination. It had always been Brenda's favorite because the female figure in the picture looked so much like her.

"Well!" said Joyce, throwing out her hands. "You know what Brenda always does. She takes off her beach robe and spreads it out over King Arthur's Chair. She sits down in the chair and smokes a cigarette and looks out at the sea before she goes into the water.

"The beach robe was still in that rock chair," Joyce continued with an effort, "when I came downstairs at half-past seven. But Brenda wasn't. She hadn't even put on her bathing cap. Somebody had strangled her with that silk scarf she wore with the beach robe. It was twisted so tightly into her neck they couldn't get it out. She was lying on the sand in front of the chair, on her back, in the red swim suit, with her face black and swollen. You could see her clearly from the terrace."

Dan glanced at the flesh tints of *The Lovers,* then quickly looked away.

Joyce, the cool and competent, was holding herself under restraint.

"I can only thank my lucky stars," she burst out, "I didn't run out there. I mean, from the flagstones of the lowest terrace out across the sand. They stopped me."

"'They' stopped you? Who?"

"Mr. Ireton and Toby. Or, rather, Mr. Ireton did; Toby wouldn't have thought of it."

"But—"

"Toby, you see, had come over here a little earlier. But he was at the back of the bungalow, practicing with a .22 target rifle. I heard him once. Mr. Ireton had just got there. All three of us walked out on the terrace at once. And saw her."

"Listen, Joyce. What difference does it make whether or not you ran out across the sand? Why were you so lucky they stopped you?"

"Because if they hadn't the police might have said I did it."

"Did it?"

"Killed Brenda," Joyce answered clearly. "In all that stretch of sand, Dan, there weren't any footprints except Brenda's own."

"Now hold on!" he protested. "She—she was killed with that scarf of hers?"

"Oh, yes. The police and even Dr. Fell don't doubt that."

"Then how could anybody, anybody at all, go out across the sand and come back without leaving a footprint?"

"That's just it. The police don't know and they can't guess. That's why they're in a flat spin, and Dr. Fell will be here again tonight."

In her desperate attempt to speak lightly, as if all this didn't matter, Joyce failed. Her face was white. But again the expression of the dark-fringed eyes changed, and she hesitated.

"Dan—"

"Yes?"

"You do understand, don't you, why I was so upset when you came charging in and said what you did?"

"Yes, of course."

"Whatever you had to tell me, or thought you had to tell me—"

"About—us?"

"About anything! You do see that you must forget it and not mention it again? Not ever?"

"I see why I can't mention it now. With Brenda dead, it wouldn't even be decent to think of it." He could not keep his eyes off that mocking picture. "But is the future dead too? If I happen to have been an idiot and thought I was head over heels gone on Brenda when all the time it was really—"

"*Dan!*"

There were five doors opening into the gaudy hall, which had too many mirrors. Joyce whirled round to look at every door, as if she feared an ambush behind each.

"For heaven's sake keep your voice down," she begged. "Practically every word that's said can be heard all over the house. I said never, and I meant it. If you'd spoken a week ago, even twenty-four hours ago, it might have been different. Do you think I didn't want you to? But now it's too late!"

"Why?"

"May *I* answer that question?" interrupted a new, dry, rather quizzical voice.

Dan had taken a step toward her, intensely conscious of her attractiveness. He stopped, burned with embarrassment, as one of the five doors opened.

Mr. Edmund Ireton, shortish and thin and dandified in his middle fifties, emerged with his usual briskness. There was not much gray in his polished black hair. His face was a benevolent satyr's.

"Forgive me," he said.

Behind him towered Toby Curtis, heavy and handsome and fair-haired, in a bulky tweed jacket. Toby began to speak, but Mr. Ireton's gesture silenced him before he could utter a sound.

"Forgive me," he repeated. "But what Joyce says is quite true. Every word can be overheard here, even with the rain pouring down. If you go on shouting and Dr. Fell hears it, you will land that girl in serious danger."

"Danger?" demanded Toby Curtis. He had to clear his throat. "What danger could *Dan* get her into?"

Mr. Ireton, immaculate in flannels and shirt and thin pullover, stalked to the mantelpiece. He stared up hard at *The Lovers* before turning round.

"The Psalmist tells us," he said dryly, "that all is vanity. Has none of you ever noticed—God forgive me for saying so—that Brenda's most outstanding trait was her vanity?"

His glance flashed toward Joyce, who abruptly turned away and pressed her hands over her face.

"Appalling vanity. Scratch that vanity deeply enough and our dearest Brenda would have committed murder."

"Aren't you getting this backwards?" asked Dan. "Brenda didn't commit any murder. It was Brenda—"

"Ah!" Mr. Ireton pounced. "And there might be a lesson in that, don't you think?"

"Look here, you're not saying she strangled herself with her own scarf?"

"No—but hear what I do say. Our Brenda, no doubt, had many passions and many fancies. But there was only one man she loved or ever wanted to marry. It was not Mr. Dan Fraser."

"Then who was it?" asked Toby.

"You."

Toby's amazement was too genuine to be assumed. The color drained out of his face. Once more he had to clear his throat.

"So help me," he said, "I never knew it! I never imagined—"

"No, of course you didn't," Mr. Ireton said even more dryly. A goatish amusement flashed across his face and was gone. "Brenda, as a rule, could get any man she chose. So she turned Mr. Fraser's head and became engaged to him. It was to sting you, Mr. Curtis, to make you jealous. And you never noticed. While all the time Joyce Ray and Dan Fraser were eating their hearts out for each other; and *he* never noticed either."

Edmund Ireton wheeled round.

"You may lament my bluntness, Mr. Fraser. You may want to wring my neck, as I see you do. But can you deny one word I say?"

"No." In honesty Dan could not deny it.

"Well! Then be very careful when you face the police, both of you, or they will see it too. Joyce already has a strong motive. She is Brenda's only relative, and inherits Brenda's money. If they learn she wanted Brenda's *fiancé,* will have her in the dock for murder.''

"That's enough!'' blurted Dan, who dared not look at Joyce. "You've made it clear. All right, stop there!''

"Oh, I had intended to stop. If you are such fools that you won't help yourselves, I must help you. That's all.''

It was Toby Curtis who strode forward.

"Dan, don't let him bluff you!'' Toby said. "In the first place, they can't arrest anybody for this. You weren't here. I know—''

"I've heard about it, Toby.''

"Look,'' insisted Toby. "When the police finished measuring and photographing and taking casts of Brenda's footprints, I did some measuring myself.''

Edmund Ireton smiled. "Are you attempting to solve this mystery, Mr. Curtis?''

"I didn't say that.'' Toby spoke coolly. "But I might have a question or two for you. Why have you had your knife into me all day?''

"Frankly, Mr. Curtis, because I envy you.''

"You—*what?*''

"So far as women are concerned, young man, I have not your advantages. *I* had no romantic boyhood on a veldt-farm in South Africa. *I* never learned to drive a span of oxen and flick a fly off the leader's ear with my whip. *I* was never taught to be a spectacular horseman and rifle shot.''

"Oh, turn it up!''

" 'Turn it up?' Ah, I see. And was that the sinister question you had for me?''

"No. Not yet. You're too tricky.''

"My profoundest thanks.''

"Look, Dan,'' Toby insisted. "You've seen that rock formation they call King Arthur's chair?''

"Toby, I've seen it fifty times,'' Dan said. "But I still don't understand—''

"And I don't understand,'' suddenly interrupted Joyce, without turning round, "why they made me sit there where Brenda had been sitting. It was horrible.''

"Oh, they were only reconstructing the crime.'' Toby spoke rather grandly. "But the question, Dan, is how anybody came near that chair without leaving a footprint?''

"Quite."

"Nobody could have," Toby said just as grandly. "The murderer, for instance, couldn't have come from the direction of the sea. Why? Because the highest point at high tide, where the water might have blotted out footprints, is more than twenty feet in front of the chair. More than twenty feet!"

"Er—one moment," said Mr. Ireton, twitching up a finger. "Surely Inspector Tregellis said the murderer must have crept up and caught her from the back? Before she knew it?"

"That won't do either. From the flagstones of the terrace to the back of the chair is at least twenty feet, too. Well, Dan? Do you see any way out of that one?"

Dan, not normally slow-witted, was so concentrating on Joyce that he could think of little else. She was cut off from him, drifting away from him, forever out of reach just when he had found her. But he tried to think.

"Well . . . could somebody have jumped there?"

"Ho!" scoffed Toby, who was himself a broad jumper and knew better. "That was the first thing they thought of."

"And that's out, too?"

"Definitely. An Olympic champion in good form might have done it, if he'd had any place for a running start and any place to land. But he hadn't. There was *no* mark in the sand. He couldn't have landed on the chair, strangled Brenda at his leisure, and then hopped back like a jumping bean. Now could he?"

"But somebody did it, Toby! It happened!"

"How?"

"I don't know."

"You seem rather proud of this, Mr. Curtis," Edmund Ireton said smoothly.

"Proud?" exclaimed Toby, losing color again.

"These romantic boyhoods—"

Toby did not lose his temper. But he had declared war.

"All right, gaffer. I've been very grateful for your hospitality, at that bungalow of yours, when we've come down here for weekends. All the same, you've been going on for hours about who I am and what I am. Who are you?"

"I beg your pardon?"

"For two or three years," Toby said, "you've been hanging about with us. Especially with Brenda and Joyce. Who are you? What are you?"

"I am an observer of life," Mr. Ireton answered tranquilly. "A student of human nature. And—shall I say?—a courtesy uncle to both young ladies."

"Is that all you were? To either of them?"

"Toby!" exclaimed Joyce, shocked out of her fear.

She whirled round, her gaze going instinctively to Dan, then back to Toby.

"Don't worry, old girl," said Toby, waving his hand at her. "This is no reflection on you." He kept looking steadily at Mr. Ireton.

"Continue," Mr. Ireton said politely.

"You claim Joyce is in danger. She isn't in any danger at all," said Toby, "as long as the police don't know how Brenda was strangled."

"They will discover it, Mr. Curtis. Be sure they will discover it!"

"You're trying to protect Joyce?"

"Naturally."

"And that's why you warned Dan not to say he was in love with her?"

"Of course. What else?"

Toby straightened up, his hand inside the bulky tweed jacket.

"Then why didn't you take him outside, rain or no, and tell him on the quiet? Why did you shout out that Dan was in love with Joyce, and she was in love with him, and give 'em a motive for the whole house to hear?"

Edmund Ireton opened his mouth, and shut it again.

It was a blow under the guard, all the more unexpected because it came from Toby Curtis.

Mr. Ireton stood motionless under the painting of *The Lovers*. The expression of the pictured Brenda, elusive and mocking, no longer matched his own. Whereupon, while nerves were strained and still nobody spoke, Dan Fraser realized that there was a dead silence because the rain had stopped.

Small night-noises, the creak of woodwork or a drip of water from the eaves, intensified the stillness. Then they heard footsteps, as heavy as those of an elephant, slowly approaching behind another of the doors. The footfalls, heavy and slow and creaking, brought a note of doom.

Into the room, wheezing and leaning on a stick, lumbered a man so enormous that he had to maneuver himself sideways through the door.

His big mop of gray-streaked hair had tumbled over one ear. His eyeglasses, with a broad black ribbon, were stuck askew on his nose. His big face would ordinarily have been red and beaming, with chuckles animating several chins. Now it was only absentminded, his bandit's moustache outthrust.

"Aha!" he said in a rumbling voice. He blinked at Dan with an air of refreshed interest. "I think you must be Mr. Fraser, the last of this rather curious weekend party? H'm. Yes. Your obedient servant, sir. I am Gideon Fell."

Dr. Fell wore a black coat as big as a tent and carried a shovel-hat in his other hand. He tried to bow and make a flourish with his stick, endangering all the furniture near him.

The others stood very still. Fear was as palpable as the scent after rain.

"Yes, I've heard of you," said Dan. His voice rose in spite of himself. "But you're rather far from home, aren't you? I suppose you had some—er—antiquarian interest in King Arthur's Chair?"

Still Dr. Fell blinked at him. For a second it seemed that chuckles would jiggle his chins and waistcoat, but he only shook his head.

"Antiquarian interest? My dear sir!" Dr. Fell wheezed gently. "If there were any association with a semi-legendary King Arthur, it would be at Tintagel much farther south. No, I was here on holiday. This morning Inspector Tregellis fascinated me with the story of a fantastic murder. I returned tonight for my own reasons."

Mr. Ireton, at ease again, matched the other's courtesy. "May I ask what these reasons were?"

"First, I wished to question the two maids. They have a room at the back, as Miss Ray has; and this afternoon, you may remember, they were still rather hysterical."

"And that is all?"

"H'mf. Well, no." Dr. Fell scowled. "Second, I wanted to detain all of you here an hour or two. Third, I must make sure of the motive for this crime. And I am happy to say that I have made very sure."

Joyce could not control herself. "Then you did overhear everything!"

"Eh?"

"Every word that man said!"

Despite Dan's signals, Joyce nodded toward Mr. Ireton and poured out the words. "But I swear I hadn't anything to do with Brenda's death. What I told you today was perfectly true: I don't want her money and I won't touch it. As for my—my—private affairs," and Joyce's face flamed, "everybody seems to know all about them except Dan and me. Please, please pay no attention to what that man has been saying."

Dr. Fell blinked at her in an astonishment which changed to vast distress.

"But, my dear young lady!" he rumbled. "We never for a moment believed you did. No, no! Archons of Athens, no!" exclaimed Dr. Fell, as though at incredible absurdity. "As for what your friend Mr. Ireton may have been saying, I did not hear it. I suspect it was only what he told me today, and it did supply the motive. But it was not your motive."

"Please, is this true? You're not trying to trap me?"

"Do I really strike you," Dr. Fell asked gently, "as being that sort of person? Nothing was more unlikely than that you killed your cousin, especially in the way she was killed."

"Do you know how she was killed?"

"Oh, *that*," grunted Dr. Fell, waving the point away too. "That was the simplest part of the whole business."

He lumbered over, reflected in the mirrors, and put down stick and shovel-hat on a table. Afterward he faced them with a mixture of distress and apology.

"It may surprise you," he said, "that an old scatterbrain like myself can observe anything at all. But I have an unfair advantage over the police. I began life as a schoolmaster: I have had more experience with habitual liars. Hang it all, think!"

"Of what?"

"The facts!" said Dr. Fell, making a hideous face. "According to the maids, Sonia and Dolly, Miss Brenda Lestrange went down to swim at ten minutes to seven this morning. Both Dolly and Sonia were awake, but did not get up. Some eight or ten minutes later, Mr. Toby Curtis began practicing with a target rifle some distance away behind the bungalow."

"Don't look at me!" exclaimed Toby. "That rifle has nothing to do with it. Brenda wasn't shot."

"Sir," said Dr. Fell with much patience, "I am aware of that."

"Then what are you hinting at?"

"Sir," said Dr. Fell, "you will oblige me if you too don't regard every question as a trap. I have a trap for the murderer, and the murderer alone. You fired a number of shots—the maids heard you and saw you." He turned to Joyce. "I believe you heard too?"

"I heard one shot," answered the bewildered Joyce, "as I told Dan. About seven o'clock, when I got up and dressed."

"Did you look out of the windows?"

"No."

"What happened to that rifle afterwards? Is it here now?"

"No," Toby almost yelled. "I took it back to Ireton's after we found Brenda. But if the rifle had nothing to do with it, and I had nothing to do with it, then what the hell's the point?"

Dr. Fell did not reply for a moment. Then he made another hideous face. "We know," he rumbled, "that Brenda Lestrange wore a beach robe, a bathing suit, and a heavy silk scarf knotted round her neck. Miss Ray?"

"Y-yes?"

"I am not precisely an authority on women's clothes," said Dr. Fell. "As a rule I should notice nothing odd unless I passed Madge Wildfire or Lady Godiva. I have seen men wear a scarf with a beach robe, but is it customary for women to wear a scarf as well?"

There was a pause.

"No, of course it isn't," said Joyce. "I can't speak for everybody, but I never do. It was just one of Brenda's fancies. She always did."

"Aha!" said Dr. Fell. "The murderer was counting on that."

"On what?"

"On her known conduct. Let me show you rather a grisly picture of a murder."

Dr. Fell's eyes were squeezed shut. From inside his cloak and pocket he fished out an immense meerschaum pipe. Firmly under the impression that he had filled and lighted the pipe, he put the stem in his mouth and drew at it.

"Miss Lestrange," he said, "goes down to the beach. She takes off her robe. Remember that, it's very important. She spreads out the robe in King Arthur's Chair and sits down. She is still wearing the scarf, knotted tightly in a broad band round her neck. She is about the same height as you, Miss Ray. She is held there, at the height of her shoulders, by a curving rock formation deeply bedded in sand."

Dr. Fell paused and opened his eyes.

"The murderer, we believe, catches her from the back. She sees and hears nothing until she is seized. Intense pressure on the carotid arteries, here at either side of the neck under the chin, will strike her unconscious within seconds and dead within minutes. When her body is released, it should fall straight forward. Instead, what happens?"

To Dan, full of relief ever since danger had seemed to leave Joyce, it was as if a shutter had flown open in his brain.

"She was lying on her back," Dan said. "Joyce told me so. Brenda was lying flat on her back with her head towards the sea. And that means—"

"Yes?"

"It means she was twisted or spun round in some way when she fell. It has something to do with that infernal scarf—I've thought so from the first. Dr. Fell! Was Brenda killed with the scarf?"

"In one sense, yes, In another sense, no."

"You can't have it both ways! Either she was killed with the scarf, or she wasn't."

"Not necessarily," said Dr. Fell.

"Then let's all retire to a loony bin," Dan suggested, "because nothing makes any sense at all. The murderer still couldn't have walked out there without leaving tracks. Finally, I agree with Toby: what's the point of the rifle? How does a .22 rifle figure in all this?"

"Because of its sound."

Dr. Fell took the pipe out of his mouth. Dan wondered why he had ever thought the learned doctor's eyes were vague. Magnified behind the glasses on the broad black ribbon, they were not vague at all.

"A .22 rifle," he went on in his big voice, "has a distinctive noise. Fired in the open air or anywhere else, it sounds exactly like the noise made by the real instrument used in this crime."

"Real instrument? What noise?"

"The crack of a blacksnake whip," replied Dr. Fell.

Edmund Ireton, looking very tired and ten years older, went over and sat down in an easy chair. Toby Curtis took one step backward, then another.

"In South Africa," said Dr. Fell, "I have never seen the very long whip which drivers of long ox spans use. But in America I have seen the blacksnake whip, and it can be twenty-four feet long. You yourselves must have watched it used in a variety turn on the stage."

Dr. Fell pointed his pipe at them.

"Remember?" he asked. "The user of the whip stands some distance away facing his girl-assistant. There is a vicious crack. The end of the whip coils two or three times round the girl's neck. She is not hurt. But she would be in difficulties if he pulled the whip towards him. She would be in grave danger if she were held back and could not move.

"Somebody planned a murder with a whip like that. He came here early in the morning. The whip, coiled round his waist, was hidden by a loose and bulky tweed jacket. Please observe the jacket Toby Curtis is wearing now."

"Toby's voice went high when he screeched out one word. It may have been protest, defiance, a jeer, or all three.

"Stop this!" cried Joyce, who had again turned away.

"Continue, I beg," Mr. Ireton said.

"In the dead hush of morning," said Dr. Fell, "he could not hide the loud crack of the whip. But what could he do?"

"He could mask it," said Edmund Ireton.

"Just that! He was always practicing with a .22 rifle. So he fired several shots, behind the bungalow, to establish presence. Afterwards nobody would notice when the crack of the whip—that single, isolated 'shot' heard by Miss Ray—only seemed to come from behind the house."

"Then, actually, he was—"

"On the terrace, twenty feet behind a victim held immovable in the curve of a stone chair. The end of the whip coiled round the scarf. Miss Lestrange's breath was cut off instantly. Under the pull of a powerful arm she died in seconds.

"On the stage, you recall, a lift and twist dislodges the whip from the girl-assistant's neck. Toby Curtis had a harder task; the scarf was so embedded in her neck that she seemed to have been strangled with it. He *could* dislodge it. But only with a powerful whirl and lift of the arm which spun her up and round, to fall face upwards. The whip snaked back to him with no trace in the sand. Afterwards he had only to take the whip back to Mr. Ireton's house, under pretext of returning the rifle. He had committed a murder which, in his vanity, he thought undetectable. That's all."

"But it can't be all!" said Dan. "Why should Toby have killed her? His motive—"

"His motive was offended vanity. Mr. Edmund Ireton as good as told you so, I fancy. He had certainly hinted as much to me."

Edmund Ireton rose shakily from the chair.

"I am no judge or executioner," he said. "I—I am detached from life. I only observe. If I guessed why this was done—"

"You could never speak straight out?" Dr. Fell asked sardonically.

"No!"

"And yet that was the tragic irony of the whole affair. Miss Lestrange wanted Toby Curtis, as he wanted her. But, being a woman, her pretense of indifference and contempt was too good. He believed it. Scratch her vanity deeply enough and she would have committed murder. Scratch *his* vanity deeply enough—"

"Lies!" said Toby.

"Look at him, all of you!" said Dr. Fell. "Even when he's accused of murder, he can't take his eyes off a mirror."

"*Lies!*"

"She laughed at him," the big voice went on, "and so she had to die. Brutally and senselessly he killed a girl who would have been his for the asking. That is what I meant by tragic irony."

Toby had retreated across the room until his back bumped against a wall. Startled, he looked behind him; he had banged against another mirror.

"Lies!" he kept repeating. "You talk and talk and talk. But there's not a single damned thing you can prove!"

"Sir," inquired Dr. Fell, "are you sure?"

"Yes!"

"I warned you," said Dr. Fell, "that I returned tonight partly to detain all of you for an hour or so. It gave Inspector Tregellis time to search Mr. Ireton's house, and the Inspector has since returned. I further warned you that I questioned the maids, Sonia and Dolly, who today were only incoherent. My dear sir, you underestimate your personal attractions."

Now it was Joyce who seemed to understand. But she did not speak.

"Sonia, it seems," and Dr. Fell looked hard at Toby, "has quite a fondness for you. When she heard that last isolated 'shot' this morning, she looked out of the window again. You weren't there. This was so strange that she ran out to the front terrace to discover where you were. She saw you."

The door by which Dr. Fell had entered was still open. His voice lifted and echoed through the hall.

"Come in, Sonia!" he called. "After all, you are a witness to the murder. You, Inspector, had better come in too."

Toby Curtis blundered back, but there was no way out. There was only a brief glimpse of Sonia's swollen, tear-stained face. Past her marched a massive figure in uniform, carrying what he had found hidden in the other house.

Inspector Tregellis was reflected everywhere in the mirrors, with the long coils of the whip over his arm. And he seemed to be carrying not a whip but a coil of rope—gallows rope.

Colonel Anthony Gethryn

THE WOOD-FOR-THE-TREES

Philip MacDonald

I T WAS IN the summer of '36—to be exact upon the fifth of August in that year—that the countryside around the village of Friars' Wick in Downshire, in the southwest of England, was shocked by the discovery of a singularly brutal murder.

The biggest paper in the country, the *Mostyn Courier,* reported the outrage at some length—but since the victim was old, poverty-stricken, female but ill-favored, and with neither friends nor kin, the event passed practically unnoticed by the London Press, even though the killer was uncaught.

Passed unnoticed, that is, until, exactly twenty-four hours later and within a mile or so of its exact locale, the crime was repeated, the victim being another woman who, except in the matter of age, might have been a replica of the first.

This was a time, if you remember, when there was a plethora of news in the world. There was Spain, for instance. There were Mussolini and Ethiopia. There was Herr Hitler. There was Japan. There was Russia. There was dissension at home as well as abroad. There was so much, in fact, that people were stunned by it all and pretending to be bored. . . .

Which is doubtless why the editor of Lord Otterill's biggest paper, the *Daily Despatch,* gave full rein to its leading crime reporter and splashed that ingenious scrivener's account of the MANIAC MURDERS IN DOWNSHIRE all across the front page of the first edition of August 8th.

The writer had spread himself. He described the slayings in gory, horrifying prose, omitting only such details as were really unprintable. He drew pathetic (and by no means badly written) word pictures of the two drab women as they had been before they met this sadistic and unpleasing end. And he devoted the last paragraphs of his outpourings to a piece of theorizing which gave added thrills to his fascinated readers.

" *. . . can it be,*" he asked under the subheading 'Wake Up, Police!' *"that these two terrible, maniacal, unspeakable crimes—crimes with no motive other than the lust of some depraved and distorted mind, can be but the beginning of a wave of murder such as that which terrorized London in the eighties, when the uncaptured, unknown 'Jack the Ripper' ran his bloodstained gamut of killing?"*

You will have noted the date of the *Despatch* article—August 8th. Which was the day after the *Queen Guinivere* sailed from New York for England. Which explains how it came about that Anthony Gethryn, who was a passenger on the great liner, knew nothing whatsoever of the unpleasant occurrences near Friars' Wick. Which is odd because— although he'd never been there before and had no intention of ever going there again after his simple mission had been fulfilled—it was to Friars' Wick that he must make his way immediately the ship arrived at home.

An odd quirk of fate: one of those peculiar spins of the Wheel.

He didn't want to break his journey to London and home by going to Friars' Wick, or, indeed, any other place. He'd been away—upon a diplomatic task of secrecy, importance, and inescapable tedium—for three months. And he wanted to see his wife and his son, and see them with the least possible delay.

But there it was: he had in his charge a letter which a Personage of Extreme Importance had asked him to deliver into the hands of another (if lesser known) P.O.E.I. The request had been made courteously, and just after the first P.O.E.I. had gone out of his way to do a service for A.R. Gethryn. *Ergo,* A.R. Gethryn must deliver the letter—which, by the way, has nothing in itself to do with this story.

So, upon the afternoon of August the eleventh, Anthony was driving from the port of Normouth to the hamlet of Friars' Wick and the country house of Sir Adrian LeFane.

He pushed the Voisin along at speed, thankful they'd managed to send it down to Normouth for him. The alternatives would have been a hired car or a train—and on a stifling day like this the thought of either was insupportable.

The ship had docked late, and it was already after six when he reached the outskirts of Mostyn and slowed to a crawl through its narrow streets and came out sweating on the other side. The low gray arch of the sky seemed lower still—and the grayness was becoming tinged with black.

The trees which lined the road stood drooping and still, and over everything was a soft and ominous hush through which the sound of passing cars and even the singing of his own tires seemed muted.

He reduced his speed as he drew near the Bastwick crossroads. Up to here he had known his way—but now he must traverse unknown territory.

He stopped the car altogether, and peered at a signpost. Its fourth and most easterly arm said, with simple helpfulness, "FRIARS' WICK—8."

He followed the pointing arm and found himself boxed in between high and unkempt hedgerows, driving along a narrow lane which twisted up and across the shoulder of a frowning, sparsely wooded hill. There were no cars here; no traffic of any kind; no sign of humanity. The sky had grown more black than gray, and the light had a gloom-laden, coppery quality. The heavy air was difficult to breathe.

The Voisin breasted the hill—and the road shook itself and straightened out as it coasted down, now steep and straight, between wide and barren stretches of heathland.

The village of Friars' Wick, hidden by the foot of another hill, came upon Anthony suddenly, after rounding the first curve in the winding valley.

Although he was going slowly, for the corner had seemed dangerous, the abrupt emergence of the small township—materializing, it seemed, out of nothingness—was almost a physical shock. He slowed still more, and the big black car rolled silently along the narrow street, between slate-fronted cottages and occasional little shops.

It was a gray place, sullen and resentful and with something about it at once strange and familiar; an air which at the same time fascinated and repelled him; an aura which touched some sixth sense and set up a strange tingling inside him. . . .

He recognized the feeling but wasn't sure if it were genuine; it might have been induced by a combination of the weather and his personal irritation at having to come so far out of his way from London and home.

He reached the end of the main and only street of Friars' Wick, the point where the small church faces the inn across a traditional triangle of emerald grass. Here he stopped the car. He knew he must be within a mile or so of LeFane's house, and the easiest way to find it was to ask.

He looked around for someone to ask. He saw there was no human being in sight—and for the first time realized there had been none at all since he had come around the hill and into the village.

Something hit the leather of the seat beside him with a small smacking sound. A single florin-sized raindrop.

He looked up at the sky. Now it was so close, so lowering, that it seemed almost to brush the tops of the big elms behind the white-fronted inn. A spatter of the big drops hit the dust of the road, each one separated by feet from its fellows. He realized he was waiting for thunder.

But no thunder came—and no relief. The coppery light was greener now, and the hush almost palpable.

And then he saw a man. A man who stood beside the outbuildings of the inn, some twenty yards away.

He was an ordinary-looking man. He fitted his surroundings, yet seemed to stand out from them in sharp relief. He wore a shapeless hat, and a shapeless coat, and he had a shotgun under his arm.

Anthony felt an increase of the odd tingling. He looked back along the gray street and still saw no one. He looked at the man again. He looked the other way and saw for the first time the cluster of oaks on the rise away to his left; saw, too, above the oaks, the chimneys of a big house.

He drove off. He followed his eyes and set the car up another twisting land and came presently to imposing wrought-iron gates.

The gates stood open, and he turned the Voisin into them—and at once was in a different world. Outside, the land had been dead and tired and sterile, but here it was lush and well-groomed and self-conscious. A hundred feet above, and still half a mile away, he could see the chimneys and the rambling Tudor building beneath them.

There came another flurry of the outsized raindrops, and he thought of stopping and closing the car. He slowed and as he did so his attention was attracted by something off the road to his right. A figure which stood under one of the trees and looked at him. A large and square and gauntly powerful figure, as motionless as the man in the deserted village had been.

He stared, and for some reason stopped the car. The figure was clad in nondescript clothes, and it was with something of a shock that he realized it was a woman's.

He went on staring—and it turned abruptly and strode off into the shadows of a copse. . . .

There were no more raindrops and he drove on, towards the lawns and gardens and the house itself.

When the rain came in earnest, it was a solid sheet of water, a deluge. It started almost as soon as Anthony was in the house—while, in fact, he was being greeted by his hostess, who was blondish and handsome and just verging upon the haggard. She was ultrasmart, and overnervous. She laughed a great deal, but her eyes never changed. She was, it appeared, Mrs. Peter Crecy, and she was also the daughter of Sir Adrian LeFane. She swept Anthony away from the butler and took him to a room which was half-library, half-salon, and wholly luxurious. She gave him a drink and sprayed him with staccato, half-finished sentences. He gathered that he couldn't see her father just yet—"the man, as usual, doesn't seem to *be* anywhere . . . " He gathered that he was expected to stay the night—"but you *must*—my parent gave the strictest orders . . . "

So he murmured politely and resigned himself, helped no little by the sight of the rain beyond the mullioned windows.

He was given eventually into the care of a black-coated discretion named Phillips, who led up stairs and along corridors to a sybaritic and most un-Tudorlike suite.

He bathed luxuriously and when he had finished, found his trunk unpacked, his dinner clothes laid out. In shirt sleeves, he walked over to a window and looked out and saw the rain still a heavy, glittering, unbroken veil over the half-dark world. He lit a cigarette, dropped into a chair, stretched out his long legs, and found himself wondering about the village of Friars' Wick and its odd and ominous and indescribable air. But he didn't wonder either long or seriously for, from somewhere below, he heard the booming of a gong.

He put on his coat and slipped LeFane's letter into his breast pocket and made a leisurely way downstairs.

He had expected a dinner which would at the most have a couple of other guests besides himself. He found instead, when he was directed to the drawing room, a collection of eight or ten people. They were clustered in the middle of the room, and from the center of the cluster the voice of Mrs. Peter Crecy rose and fell like a syncopated fountain.

"Well, that's settled!" it was saying. "Not a word about it—too frightfully macabre! . . . "

Anthony made unobtrusive entrance, but she saw him immediately and surged towards him. She was contriving paradoxically to look handsomer and yet more haggard in a black-and-gold evening gown. She led him on a tour of introduction. He met, and idly catalogued in his mind, a Lord and Lady Bracksworth (obvious Master of Fox Hounds—wife knits); a Mr. and Mrs. Shelton-Jones (obvious Foreign Office—wife aspiring Ambassadress); a Professor Martel (possible Physicist, Middle-

European, bearded, egocentric); a Mr. and Mrs. Geoffrey Dale (news-paper-owner, leader-writing wife)—and then, an oasis in this desert, his old friend Carol Dunning.

She was sitting in an enormous, high-winged chair and he hadn't seen her until Mrs. Crecy led him towards it.

"And—Miss Dunning," said Mrs. Crecy. "The novelist, of course . . . But I believe you know each other—Carol Rushworth Dunning—"

"Hi, there!" said Miss Dunning refreshingly. A wide and impish smile creased her impish and ageless and unmistakably American face.

"What would happen," asked Miss Dunning, "if I said, long time no see!"

"Nothing," Anthony said. "I concur. *Too* long."

He noted with relief that Mrs. Crecy had left them. He saw a servant with a tray of cocktails and got one for Miss Dunning and another for himself.

"Thanks," said Miss Dunning. "Mud in your eye!" She took half the drink at a gulp and looked up at Anthony. "If the answer wasn't so obvious, I'd ask what brought you into this *galère?*"

Anthony said, "Same to you." He reflected on the letter in his pocket. "And what's obvious? Or has the diplomatic service—"

He broke off, looking across the room at a man who hadn't merely come into it, but had effected an entrance. A tall, slight, stoopshouldered person with a velvet dinner jacket, a mane of gray hair, and a certain distinction of which he was entirely aware.

"Enter Right Center," Anthony said to Miss Dunning. "But who? I've lost my program."

She looked at him in surprise. "Curiouser and curiouser," she said. "So the man doesn't know his own host. That's him—Sir Adrian Lefane in person. Old world, huh? *Fin-de-siècle.*"

"Well, well" said Anthony, and stood up as LeFane, having hovered momentarily over the central group with a courtly smile of general greeting, came straight towards him.

"Colonel Gethryn?" He held out a slim white hand, beautifully shaped. "I trust you'll forgive me for not being here to welcome you. But—" the hand sketched a vague, graceful movement in the air—"I was forced to be elsewhere . . . " The hand came down and offered itself again and Anthony shook it.

"Out, were you?" said Miss Dunning. "Caught in the rain?"

"Not—ah—noticeably, my dear." LeFane gave her an avuncular smile. "I regard myself as fortunate—"

But he never told them why—for at that moment his daughter joined them, words preceding her like fire from a flame thrower. She was worried, it seemed, about someone, or thing, called "Marya"—you could hear the "y"—who, or which, should have put in appearance.

She led her parent away—and again Anthony was relieved. He looked at Miss Dunning and said:

"Who is Marya, what is she? Or it, maybe? Or even he?"

"Dax."

"An impolite sound." Anthony surveyed her. "Unless—oh, shades of Angelo! Do you mean the sculptress? The Riondetto group at Geneva? The Icarus at Hendon?"

"Right!" Miss Dunning looked at the door and pointed. "And here she is . . . "

Striding from the door towards the advancing LeFane was a gaunt giant of a woman. Despite her size—she must have topped six feet—and her extraordinary appearance, she wore a strange, flowing, monk-like garment of some harsh, dark green material. She was impressive rather than ludicrous. Her crag-like face gave no answer to the best of LeFane's smiles, but she permitted herself to be steered towards the group around Mrs. Crecy, and in a moment seemed to become its pivot.

"Well?" said Miss Dunning.

"Remarkable," said Anthony. "In fact, I remarked her a couple of hours ago. She was under a tree. Looking."

"Like what?" Miss Dunning wanted to know.

But she wasn't answered. Two more people were entering the room—a well-built, pleasant-faced man of thirty-odd, with a tired look and what used to be called "professional" appearance; a small, angular, weather-beaten little woman, with no proportions and a face like a happy horse.

Once more Anthony looked at Miss Dunning, and once more she enlightened him.

"Human beings," said Miss Dunning. "Refreshing, isn't it? Local doctor and wife. I like 'em." She looked at her empty glass and handed it to Anthony. "See what you can do," she said.

But he had no chance to do it. Mrs. Crecy swooped, and he was drawn towards Marya Dax, and presented, and surveyed by strange dark eyes which seemed to be all pupil and were almost on a level with his own.

He murmured some politeness, and was ignored. He turned away and was pounced upon again, and found himself meeting Dr. and Mrs. Carmichael. Looking at the woman's freckled, equine face, he was assailed by a flicker of memory.

He shook hands with the husband, but they hadn't said a word to each other when the wife spoke.

"You don't remember me, do you?" She looked up at Anthony with bright, small eyes.

"That's the worst thing you can do to anyone, Min!" her husband chided her affectionately. "You ought to be ashamed of yourself."

"If you'll let me have a moment, I'll tell you," Anthony said—and then, "It's some time ago—and I remember pigtails—of course! You're Henry Martin's daughter."

"There!" Mrs. Carmichael caught hold of her husband's arm. "He did it!"

"And he'd have done it before," said Carmichael, smiling at her, "only he couldn't see Little Miss Moneybags as the wife of a country sawbones." He patted her hand.

"Colonel Gethryn," said Mrs. Carmichael, "I'm going to trade on old acquaintance. I'm going to ask you a—an indiscreet question. I—"

Her husband moved his broad shoulders uncomfortably. "Please, Min, go easy," he said.

"Don't be silly, Jim. You've *got* to try—and Colonel Gethryn won't mind." She looked up at Anthony like an earnest foal. "Will you?"

Anthony looked down at the appealing face. "I shouldn't think so," he said, and was going to add, "Try me out," when dinner was announced and the party began to split into their pairs and he found, with pleasure, that he was to take in Miss Dunning.

The meal, although heavy and of ceremonious splendor, was excellent, and the wines were beyond reproach. So that Anthony found time passing pleasantly enough until, as he chatted with Miss Dunning beside him, he heard his name emerge from what appeared to be a heated argument lower down the table.

" . . . Surely Colonel Gethryn's the one to tell us that!" came the husky voice of Mrs. Carmichael. "After all, he's the probably the only person here who knows anything about that sort of thing."

Anthony, as he was obviously meant to, turned his head. He found many eyes upon him, and said to Mrs. Carmichael, "What sort of thing? Or shouldn't I ask?"

"Crime, of course!" Mrs. Carmichael looked as if she were pricking her ears forward. "Crime in general and, of course, one crime in particular. Or two, I should say."

Anthony repressed a sigh. He said, hopefully, "If they're new and British-made, I'm afraid I can't help you. I've been away for months, and only landed this afternoon. I haven't even seen an English paper for a fortnight."

With a smile alarming in its area and determination, Mrs. Crecy cut into the talk. She said:

"How fortunate for you, Mr. Gethryn. So abysmally dull they've been! And I think it's a *shame* the way these people are trying to make you talk shop . . ."

She transferred the ferocious smile to little Mrs. Carmichael, who shriveled and muttered something about being "terribly sorry, Jacqueline," and tried to start a conversation with Lord Bracksworth about hunting.

But she was cut off in mid-sentence by Marya Dax, who was sitting on Adrian LeFane's right, and therefore obliquely across the table from Anthony. Throughout the meal she had sat like a silent, brooding Norn but now she leaned forward, gripping the edge of the table with enormous, blunt-fingered hands, and fixing her dark gaze on Anthony. she said, in a harsh contralto:

"Perhaps you have no need to read the papers. Perhaps you can smell where there is evil."

It was neither question nor statement and Anthony, smiling a smile which might have meant anything, prepared to let it lie.

But the Foreign Office, in the person of Mr. Shelton-Jones, saw opportunity for conversation.

"An interesting thought, Miss Dax," said Mr. Shelton-Jones, turning his horn-rimmed gaze upon the Norn. "Whether or not the trained mind becomes attuned, as it were, to appreciating the *atmosphere*, the *wave length*—perhaps I should call it the *aura*—which might very well emanate from wrongdoing."

The Norn didn't so much as glance at Mr. Shelton-Jones: she kept her dark gaze fixed upon Anthony's face.

But Mr. Shelton-Jones was undaunted and now he too looked at Anthony.

"What do you say, Mr. Gethryn?" he asked. "*Is* there a criminal aura? Have you ever known of any—ah – 'case' in which the investigator was assisted by any such—ah—metaphysical emanation?"

Anthony sighed inwardly; but this was too direct to leave unanswered.

He said, "You mean what the Americans might call a superhunch? I'm no professional, of course, but I have known of such things."

The Press joined in now, in the slender shape of Mrs. Dale. "How *fas*-cinating!" she said. "Could you possibly tell us—"

"Please!" Anthony smiled. "I was going on to say that the super-hunch—the 'emanation'—is utterly untrustworthy. Therefore, it's worse than useless—it's dangerous. It has to be ignored."

Surprisingly, because he had been silent throughout the meal, it was the bearded physicist Martel who chimed in now. He jutted the beard aggressively in Anthony's direction, and demanded, "Unt why iss that?" in a tone notably devoid of courtesy.

Anthony surveyed him. "Because," he said coolly, "one can never be sure the impact of the super-hunch is genuine. The feeling might very well be caused by indigestion."

There were smiles, but not from the Professor, who glared, grunted, and turned back to his plate.

Someone said, "But seriously, Colonel Gethryn—"

Anthony said, "I am serious." The topic couldn't be dropped now, so he might as well deal with it properly. He said:

"I can even give you a recent instance of what I mean . . . I was at the Captain's dinner on the *Guinivere* last night. I drank too much. I didn't get quite enough sleep. And when I landed, the current deluge was brewing. Result, as I drove through Friars' Wick, which I'd never seen before, I had the father and mother of all superhunches. The country-side—the village itself—the fact that there didn't happen to be anyone about—the black sky—everything combined to produce a definite feeling of—" he shrugged—"well, of evil. Which is patently absurd. And almost certainly, when you think of the Captain's dinner, stomachic in origin."

He was surprised—very much and most unusually surprised—by the absolute silence which fell on the company as he finished speaking. He looked from face to face and saw on every one a ruling astonishment. Except in the case of Professor Martel, who scowled sourly and managed at the same time to twist his mouth into a sardonic smile of disbelief.

Someone said, "That's—*extraordinary*, Colonel Gethryn!"

Martel said, "You ssay you haff not read the papers. But you haff hear the wireless—perhaps . . . "

Anthony looked at the beard, then at the eyes above it. He said, "I don't know what that means . . . Just as well, no doubt."

Marya Dax looked down the table at Martel, examining him with remote eyes. She said, to no one in particular. "That man should be made to keep quiet!" and there was a moment of raw and uncomfortable tension. Mrs. Crecy bit at her lips as if to restrain them from trembling. Adrian LeFane propped an elbow on the table and put a hand up to his face, half hiding it.

Miss Dunning saved the day. She turned to Anthony beside her with semicomic amazement wrinkling her goblin face. She said, on exactly the right note:

"Remarkable, my dear Holmes!" And then she laughed exactly the right laugh. "And the odd thing is—you don't know what you've done. Maybe you'd better find out."

The tension relaxed, and Anthony said, "I seem to have caused a sensation." He looked around the table again. "It could mean there *is* something—" he glanced at the Norn—"evil smelling in Friars' Wick."

There was a babble of five or six voices then, all talking at once, and through them, quite clearly, came the husky eagerness of Mrs. Carmichael's.

" . . . most wonderful thing I ever head of! Colonel Gethryn, do you realize you've *proved* what Miss Dax was saying?"

Anthony looked at Mrs. Carmichael and smiled. "That isn't proof," he said. "Might be coincidence. The Captain's dinner was—lavish."

But Mrs. Carmichael wasn't to be deterred. "You've got to hear," she said. "You've *got* to!" She spoke to her husband across the table. "Jim, tell him all about it."

A worried look came into Doctor Carmichael's tired, nice-looking face. He cast a glance towards his hostess, but she said nothing, and Mrs. Carmichael said, "Go *on*, Jim!" and Mrs. Dale said, "Please, doctor!" and he capitulated.

He looked across the table at Anthony. "I'm deputed for this," he said, "because I happen to look after the police work in this part of Downshire. Most of the time the job's a sinecure. But lately—"

He blew out his cheeks in a soundless little whistle and proceeded to tell of the two murders which had so much exercised the Press, particulary the *Despatch*. He was precise and vaguely official. He merely *stated*—but yet, and although it was no news to them, everyone else at the table was absolutely silent. They were, for the most part, watching the face of Anthony Ruthven Gethryn.

Who said, when the statement was over, "H'mm! Sort of Ripper Redivivus." His face had offered no signs of any sort to the watchers. It had, as he listened, been as completely blank as a poker player's, with the lids half closed over the green eyes.

Doctor Carmichael said slowly, "Yes, I suppose so. If there are any more—which I personally am afraid of—although the Chief Constable doesn't agree with me . . . "

"He doesn't?" Anthony's eyes were fully open now. "Who is he?"

"Major General Sir Rigby Fosythe." Acid had crept into the Doctor's tone. "He 'can't see his way' to calling in Scotland Yard. He considers Inspector Fennell and myself 'alarmists.' He—" Doctor Carmichael cut himself off abruptly.

But Anthony finished the sentence for him. "—refuses to realize the two brutal murders, apparently carried out by a sexual maniac, could possibly be the beginning of a series. That it?"

"Precisely!" Dr. Carmichael brightened at this ready understanding. "And he goes on refusing to realize, in spite of the fact that Fennell's tried a hundred times to show him that as the death of either of those poor women couldn't conceivably have benefited anyone, the murders must have been done by a maniac." A faint expression of disgust passed over Dr. Carmichael's face. "A peculiarly revolting maniac! And maniacs who've found a way of gratifying their mania—well, they don't stop . . . "

"For mysself," came the harshly sibilant voice of Professor Martel, "I do not think a maniac." He was sitting back in his chair now, the beard tilted upward. "I think a public benefactor."

He paused and there came the slightly bewildered silence he had obviously expected. He said:

"Thosse women! Thosse creaturess! I haff sseen them both while they were alife. The sserved no purpose and they were hideouss! The worlt is better less them."

Now the silence was shocked. It was broken by Marya Dax. Again she looked down the table towards Martel, and again seemed to examine him. She said:

"There is one hideous thing here with us. It is your mind." she ceased to examine the man, and went on.

"No human body," she said, "is completely without beauty."

"Oh, come now, my dear Miss Dax," said Lady Bracksworth surprisingly, in a mild but determined little voice. "Although I have nothing but sympathy—" she darted a look of dislike towards Martel—

"for those poor unfortunate women, I must say that at least one of them—Sarah Paddock, I mean—was a truly disgraceful object."

The Norn turned slow and blazing eyes upon this impudence.

"This woman," said the Norn, "this Paddock—I suppose you did not ever look at her hands?" She said, "They were dirty always. They were harsh with work. But they were beautiful."

"An interesting thought indeed!" said Mr. Shelton-Jones. "Can beauty in the—ah—human frame be considered, as it were, in *units*—or must it be, before we recognize it, a totality of such units?"

Mrs. Carmichael said, "I think Miss Dax is right." She looked over at her husband. "Don't you think so?"

He smiled at her, but he didn't answer and she said insistently, "Isn't she right, Jim? You think she is, don't you?"

"Of course she is," Carmichael said. He looked around the table. "In my profession I see a great many human bodies. And I see a great many—" he looked at Mr. Shelton-Jones—"beautiful 'units' in otherwise ugly specimens. For instance—" he looked at Marya Dax—"I particularly noticed poor Sarah Paddock's hands."

Mr. Shelton-Jones settled his spectacles more firmly astride his nose. "But, my dear sir if I may be permitted to support my original contention—what beauty can there be in a 'beauty-unit' if such unit is a mere island, as it were, in an ocean of ugliness?" Obviously prepared for debate, he leaned back in his chair, fixing his gaze upon Dr. Carmichael.

Carmichael said, "Plenty. You can't deny, for instance, that Sarah Paddock's hands were beautiful in themselves." He seemed nettled by the parliamentary manner of Mr. Shelton-Jones. "Suppose Miss Dax had modeled them!"

"Then," Mr. Shelton-Jones blandly observed, "they would have been apart from their hideous surroundings."

"Euclidian," said Anthony. "Some of the parts may or may not be equal to their total."

But Dr. Carmichael went on looking at Mr. Shelton-Jones.

"All right," said Dr. Carmichael. "Suppose you saw magnificent shoulders on a—on an extreme case of *lupus vulgaris*. Would the horrible condition of the face and neck make the shoulders repulsive too?"

"The whole picture would be—ah—definitely unpleasing." Mr. Shelton-Jones was blandness itself and the Norn turned her dark, examining gaze upon him.

Color had risen to Dr. Carmichael's face. He stared hard at Mr. Shelton-Jones and said:

"Let's try again. Do you mean to tell me that if you saw titian hair on a typical troglodytic head, you'd think it was ugly, because of its setting?"

"I agree with the doctor," said the Norn. "The other killed woman—her name I forget—was worse formed than the first. but the shape of her skull was noble."

"Umpf-chnff!" remarked Lord Bracksworth. "That'd be the fortune-tellin' one, the Stebbins woman . . . D'ja know, I was talkin' to that Inspector-fellah s'mornin', and he was tellin' me that when they found her, this old gal—"

At the head of the table Adrian LeFane sat suddenly upright. He brought his open hand violently down upon the cloth, so that the glasses beside his plate chimed and jingled.

"*Please!*" His face twisted as if with physical pain. "Let us have no more of this— this—intolerable *ugliness!*"

It was about an hour after dinner—which, thanks mainly to the social genius of Miss Dunning, had ended on a subdued but unembarrassing note—that Mrs. Carmichael, her husband in attendance, contrived to corner Anthony in a remote quarter of the vast drawing room.

He had just come in after a visit to Adrian LeFane's study, where he had at last delivered the letter which has nothing to do with this tale. He allowed himself to be cornered, although he would much rather have talked with Miss Dunning, because there was something desperately appealing in the filly-like gaze of Mrs. Carmichael.

She said, "Oh, please, Colonel Gethryn, *may* we talk to you?" Her long, freckled face was as earnest as her voice.

Anthony said, "Why not?"

Carmichael said, "Oh, Min, why insist on worrying the man?" He gave Anthony a little apologetic smile.

"Because it's worrying *you*, darling!" Mrs. Carmichael laid a hand on her husband's arm, but went on looking at Colonel Gethryn.

"Jim's terribly upset," she said, "about that horrid old Chief Constable. He thinks—I mean, Jim does—that the Downshire police can't possibly catch this dreadful murderer unless they get help from Scotland Yard. And they can't get it unless the Chief Constable asks for it . . . "

Her husband interrupted. "For heavens's sake, dear, Gethryn knows all about that sort of thing!"

She paid no attention to him. She said to Anthony, "And what I was going to ask you: we wondered if there was any way—any way at all—you could use your influence to—"

She left the sentence in mid-air as she caught sight of a servant approaching her husband.

"Dr. Carmichael," said the man. He lowered his voice, but his words came clearly. "Excuse me, sir, but there's an important message for you." A curious blend of horrified dismay and cassandrine pleasure showed through his servitor's mask. He said:

"Inspector Fennell telephoned. There's been another of these dreadful murders. He wants you to come at once, sir, to Pilligrew Lane, where it comes out by Masham's . . . "

"Just around the next corner," said Dr. Carmichael, and braked hard.

Beside him, Anthony grunted—he never has liked and never will like being driven.

The little car skidded around a sharp turn and into the mouth of a lane which lay dark and narrow between a high hedge and the looming backs of three great barns.

Through the steady, glittering sheet of the rain, a group of men and cars showed ahead, barring the way completely and standing out black in the concentrated glare of headlights.

Carmichael stopped his engine and scrambled out. Anthony followed and felt the sweeping of the rain down over him and the seeping of viscous mud through his thin shoes. He followed Carmichael towards the group and a figure of a uniformed Police Inspector.

Carmichael said, "Fennell, this is Colonel Gethryn—" and didn't get any further because the man, having darted a look at Anthony, turned back to him in amazement.

"But, Doctor," said Inspector Fennell in a hoarse and confidential whisper, "Sir Rigby's done it already. Did it last night, without saying a word to me. Called London and got the Commissioner, and turned up, after I'd phoned him about this, all complete with a Detective-Inspector just arrived from the Yard!"

Carmichael stared as if he couldn't believe his ears, and Anthony said to Fennell, "Who did they send? Hobday?"

Fennell said, "That's right, sir," and led the way towards the group in the light.

They slithered after him through the mud, and in a moment Hobday was looking at Anthony and saying, "Good Lord, sir, where did *you* drop from?"

And then there was a word with Sir Rigby Forsythe, who seemed somewhat taken aback by Anthony's presence, and a moment or so of waiting while the photographers finished their work over what lay in the ditch against the hedge.

Anthony said, "This new victim? I suppose it's a woman—but what kind? Was she another local character?"

Fennell said, "Yes, she's a woman all right, sir. And it's—it's horrible, worse than the others." He glanced towards the ditch and quickly away again. He seemed to realize he had strayed most unprofessionally from the point, and cleared his throat. "I don't think she's—she was a local, sir. So far nobody's recognized her. Seems t've been one of those gipsy basket menders. She had an old horse and cart—prob'ly was just passing through on her way to Deyning."

Hobday said, "If it hadn't been for the horse, we wouldn't have known yet. But a farm laborer found it wandering and began to look for its owner."

The photographers finished their work, and one of them came up to the Chief Constable and saluted. "All through, sir," he said, his voice shaky and uncertain.

Sir Rigby Forsythe looked at Anthony, then at Carmichael and the others. His weatherbeaten face was lined and pallid. He said, "You fellahs go ahead. I've seen all I need." He stood where he was while Fennell, visibly conquering reluctance, led the way with Carmichael, and Hobday and Anthony followed.

The headlights of the police cars cut through the water-drenched darkness. They made a nightmare tableau of the thing which lay half in and half out of the ditch. Anthony muttered, "God!" and the usually stolid Hobday drew in his breath with a little hiss. Carmichael, his face set and grim, dropped on his knees in the oozing mud. He made a cursory examination.

Then he stood up. "All right," he said. "We can move her now," and then, helped by Anthony and Hobday, lifted the thing and set it upon clean wet grass and in merciful shadow. He straightened the saturated rags of its clothing, and then suddenly dropped on one knee again and said, "Anyone got a torch?"

Hobday gave him one, and he shone the light on the head, and gently moved the heavy, mud-covered mass of red hair away from the features it was covering.

"Just wondering whether I'd ever seen her," he said. He kept the light of the torch on the face, and it stared up at them, washed cleaner every moment by the flooding rain. It was a brutish, subhuman face, and although it was distorted by death and terror, it could have been little more prepossessing in life.

Carmichael shook his head. "No," he said. "They're right. She's a stranger round here." He switched off the torch, but Anthony said, "Just a minute," and took it from him and knelt beside the body himself and switched the light on again and peered at the throat, where a darkness like a big bruise showed in the hollow below the chin.

But after a moment, he too shook his head. "No. It's a birthmark," he said, and Carmichael peered at it and said, "Yes. Or possibly an old scar."

They stood up, and Hobday took the torch and knelt in his turn and began slow, methodical examination of the clothing.

Anthony said, "Silly question, I know, but about how long since death?" A little cascade of water tumbled from his hatbrim as he bent his head to button his raincoat, which had come undone.

Carmichael said, "Oh—very loosely, and subject to error—not more than five hours , not less than two."

Anthony looked at his watch, whose glowing figures said eleven forty-five, and found himself calculating times. But this didn't get him anywhere, and he was glad when, thirty minutes later, he found himself being driven back to LeFane's house by Carmichael. He said to Carmichael on the way:

"You see, it's definitely not my sort of thing. Mass murders are mad murders, and mad murders, in the ordinary sense of the word, are motiveless. Which makes them a matter for routine policio-military methods. At which I'm worse than useless, while men like Hobday are solid and brilliant at the same time."

Carmichael smiled. "I'm glad you're both here—Hobday and yourself. I'll sleep better tonight than I have for a week."

They reached the house and were no sooner in the big hall than they were surrounded. They were plied with drinks and food, and besieged with questions. Was it really another of the *same* murders? Where had it happened? Was the victim the same *sort* of person? Did they think the murderer would be caught this time? Wasn't there something terribly *wrong* with police methods when things like this were allowed to go on? Wouldn't it be a good idea to have a curfew, or a registration every day of movements of every man, woman and child in the district?

Mr. Shelton-Jones said, "An interesting point. How far may the liberties of the individual be restricted when such restriction is—ah— for the purpose of protecting the community?"

Miss Dunning said, "Human beings are terrifying, aren't they?"

Professor Martel said, "I woult like to know—wass thiss one usseless and hideouss like the otherss?"

Mrs. Carmichael said, "Oh, *had* Sir Rigby sent for the Scotland Yard *already?* Oh, thank *goodness!*"

Everyone said something. Except Adrian LeFane and Marya Dax. And they were not present.

Anthony, throwing aside civility, at last forced his way upstairs. It seemed to him that he was even more grateful than the Carmichaels for the advent of Detective-Inspector Hobday.

He made ready for bed and then, smoking a last cigarette and wondering how soon in the morning he could decently leave, strolled over to a window.

The rain had stopped now and a pale moon shone through clouds onto the sodden earth. By the watery light he saw a figure striding up the steps of a terrace beneath him, making for the house. It was tall and powerful and square-shouldered and unmistakable in spite of its shapeless coat and headgear.

He watched it until it was out of sight beneath him. He heard a door open and close.

He went over to the bed and sat on the edge of it and finished the cigarette. He pondered. He stubbed out the cigarette at last and got into bed. After all, if sculptresses like to walk at night, why shouldn't they?

But he knew he would stop on his way home tomorrow and have a word with Hobday.

He went to sleep.

It was six o'clock on the next afternoon. He had been in London and at home since one. He sat in the library at Stukely Gardens with his wife and his son.

A violent storm had replaced yesterday's deluge. It had raged intermittently over London and the whole south of England since early morning, and still the hard, heavy rain drove against the window, while thunder rumbled and great flashes of lightning kept tearing the half-darkness.

Master Alan Gethryn gave his approval to the weather. "It sort of makes it all small and comf'table here," he said, looking up from the jigsaw puzzle strewn about the floor.

Anthony said, "I know exactly what you mean," and looked at his wife, who sat on the arm of his chair.

Master Alan Gethryn pored over the puzzle—an intricate forest scene of which he had only one corner done. He sighed and scratched his head, and then suddenly laughed.

"It's like what Mr. Haslam's always saying," he said—and Lucia looked at Anthony and explained *sotto voce*, "Master at the new school," and then said to her son, "What d'you mean, old boy?"

He looked up at her, still smiling. "He's *always* saying, 'You chaps can't see the wood for the trees.'" He chuckled. "Like this puzzle." . . .

Sublimely unconscious of the effect his words had had upon his father, he returned to his labors.

But Lucia, watching her husband's face, was concerned. She had to wait until her son had left them and gone supperwards, but the moment the door had closed behind him, she stood over Anthony and looked down at him and said:

"What's the matter, darling? You've got that look. What did Alan say?"

Anthony reached up a long arm and pulled her down onto his knees. "He gave me an idea—unintentionally, of course." He kissed her. "A damned nasty, uncomfortable idea. I'd like to forget about it."

Lucia said, "You know you won't. So you'd better tell me."

Anthony said, "Suppose I wanted to kill someone—let's say, your Uncle Perceval. And suppose his demise would benefit me to such an extent that I was afraid a nice straight murder would inevitably point at me. And suppose I were that most dangerous of madmen, the secret megalomaniac, and utterly ruthless to boot. So suppose I started a wave of apparently insane slayings, and got well going with three murders of middle-aged clubmen I didn't know at all—and then killed Uncle Perceval in exactly the same way—and then killed three more middle-aged clubmen! The police would be chasing a madman with an extraordinary quirk. They wouldn't dream of chasing me!"

"What loathsome thoughts you do have!" Lucia turned her head to look at his face. "Oh, Anthony—is that just an idea? Or do you think it's what's happening in Downshire?"

"Oh, just an idea," said Anthony slowly. "It doesn't fit . . . "

She dropped a kiss on his forehead and stood up. She said, "I'll get you a drink. And after that, my lad, you've got to change—we're due at the Dufresnes's by eight. White tie."

She started to cross the room, then checked. She said:

"What on earth did Alan say that gave you that dreadful notion?"

Anthony looked at her. "My dear girl!" he said, "'You can't see the wood for the trees' . . . "

Lucia shivered, went out of the room, came back with his drink, and very soon herded him upstairs.

Forty-five minutes later she walked into his dressing room. He was tying his tie, and he saw her in the mirror and said, "You know, Americans really develop the possibilities of our language. Baby, you look like a million dollars!"

She said, "I love you. But we're going to be late and then I won't."

He put the finishing touches to the bow. "Get my coat, beldame," he said, and started to distribute keys and money and cigarette case among his pockets.

Lucia crossed towards the big wardrobe. Beside it was Anthony's trunk, and on a nearby chair a neat pile of the clothing with which he had traveled. Something about the pile caught Lucia's eye, and she stopped and looked down at it. She said:

"Whatever happened to this dinner jacket?"

"Rain last night," Anthony said. "White'll see to it."

She smiled. Carefully she picked something from the shoulder of the black coat. She said, "He ought to've seen to this, oughtn't he? Before *I* saw it!"

She went towards him, carrying her hands in front of her, one above the other and a good two feet apart.

"Magnificent!" said Anthony. "Most impressive! But what's the role?"

She came close to him. She moved her hands and there was a glint of light from the apparent emptiness between them.

He saw a long hair of glittering reddish-gold.

He said, "Not Guilty, M'lud," and looked at the hair again.

He said, "Nobody at LeFane's had that color. Or length . . . "

He said, "Good *God!*"

He jumped across the room and snatched at the telephone.

And two minutes later was being informed that, owing to storm damage, all the trunk lines to Downshire were out of order . . .

He began to tear off the dress clothes. He said, "Get them to bring round the car! Quick!"

Little Mrs. Carmichael lay on the rather uncomfortable couch in the living room of Dr. Carmichael's rather uncomfortable house. She was pretending to read but really she was listening to the thunder.

She wished Jim hadn't had to go out on a call, especially on a night like this. She thought about Jim and how wonderful he was. Although it was two years now since they'd been married, she was happier than she had been on her honeymoon. Happy—and proud. Proud of Jim, and proud of herself, too; proud that she didn't mind uncomfortable sofas and cups with chips in them and a gas fire in the bedroom. Proud of her cleverness—her really heaven-inspired cleverness—in realizing right at the start, even before they were married, that a man of Jim's caliber couldn't possibly bear living on his wife's money . . .

The thunder was far away now, and almost casual. Little Mrs. Carmichael dozed . . .

She was wakened by the sound of a key in the front door—Jim's key. She heard Jim's step in the hall and jumped up off the sofa and went to the door to meet him—and then was shocked by his appearance as he threw it open just before she reached it. He had his hat on still, and his raincoat. They were both dark and dripping with water. He was frowning, and his face was very white; there was a look in his eyes she'd never seen before.

She said, "Jim! What is it, dearest? What's *happened?*"

"Accident," he said. "I ran over someone . . . " He pulled the back of a hand across his forehead so that his hat was pushed back and she noticed, with utter irrelevance, the little red line which the brim had made across the skin.

He said, "Come and help me, will you? Put on a coat and run out to the car. He's in the back seat." He turned away and strode across the hall to the surgery door. "With you in a minute," he said.

She ran to the hall cupboard and dragged out a raincoat. She tugged open the front door and hurried down the path, the uneven brick slippery under her feet.

The gate was open and through the rain she could see the dark shape of Jim's car. She stumbled towards it and pulled open the door and the little light in the roof came on.

There was nothing in the back seat.

Bewildered, she turned—and there was Jim, close to her.

She started to say something—and then she saw Jim's face—

It *was* Jim's face—but she almost didn't recognize it. And there was something bright in his hand, something bright and sharp and terrifying.

She screamed—and suddenly everything went very fast in front of her eyes, the way things used to go fast in films when she was a child, and there was shouting of men's voices, and something heavy like a stone swished through the air past her and hit Jim on the head, and he fell down and the bright steel thing dropped out of his hand, and two men ran up, and one of them was Colonel Gethryn and the other knelt over Jim, and

Colonel Gethryn put his arm around her as she swayed on her feet, and the black wet world spun dizzily . . .

"But there isn't anything complex about it," said Anthony. "I started when my son gave me the 'can't-see-the-wood-for-the-trees' idea. And then Lucia found that long, magnificent, red-gold hair on my dinner jacket. And that's all there was to it . . ."

The others said a lot of things, together and separately.

He waited for them to finish, and then shook his head sadly.

He said, "My dear people, that hair was tantamount to a confession by Dr. James Carmichael, duly signed, attested and registered at Somerset House. I might never have realized it, of course, if Alan hadn't handed me 'wood-for-the-tree.' But as I'd evolved the notion of hiding one murder with a lot of other murders—well, it was completely obvious. Carmichael, whose wife was rich and plain and over-loving, fitted everything. He was a doctor. He could travel about. He—"

"But *why* did the hair necessarily point to him?"

"Because it must have come from the third body. Because no one at LeFane's had hair even remotely red. Of course, it was caked with mud and colorless when it got onto my coat, but by the time it dried—"

"Hold it! Hold it! I *still* don't see how it pointed to the doctor!"

"I'm surprised at you!" Anthony surveyed the speaker with real astonishment.

"After all, you were there at LeFane's. You heard Carmichael arguing with that horn-rimmed intellect from the Foreign Office. Don't you remember him talking about *titian hair on troglodytes?*"

"Why, yes . . . But—"

"Don't you realize he talked *too soon?* He said that nearly two hours *before* they found the third murderee. And the third murderee was a brute-faced redhead!"

Sherlock Holmes

THE ADVENTURE OF THE COPPER BEECHES
Sir Arthur Conan Doyle

TO THE MAN who loves art for its own sake," remarked Sherlock Holmes, tossing aside the advertisement sheet of the *Daily Telegraph,* "it is frequently in its least important and lowliest manifestations that the keenest pleasure is to be derived. It is pleasant to me to observe, Watson, that you have so far grasped this truth that in these little records of our cases which you have been good enough to draw up, and, I am bound to say, occasionally to embellish, you have given prominence not so much to the many *causes célèbres* and sensational trials in which I have figured but rather to those incidents which may have been trivial in themselves, but which have given room for those faculties of deduction and of logical synthesis which I have made my special province."

"And yet," said I, smiling, "I cannot quite hold myself absolved from the charge of sensationalism which has been urged against my records."

"You have erred, perhaps," he observed, taking up a glowing cinder with the tongs and lighting with it the long cherry-wood pipe which was wont to replace his clay when he was in a disputatious rather than a meditative mood—"you have erred perhaps in attempting to put color and life into each of your statements instead of confining yourself to the task of placing upon record that severe reasoning from cause to effect which is really the only notable feature about the thing."

"It seems to me that I have done you full justice in the matter," I remarked with some coldness, for I was repelled by the egotism which I had more than once observed to be a strong factor in my friend's singular character.

"No, it is not selfishness or conceit," said he, answering, as was his wont, my thoughts rather than my words. "If I claim full justice for my art, it is because it is an impersonal thing—a thing beyond myself. Crime is common. Logic is rare. Therefore it is upon the logic rather than upon the crime that you should dwell. You have degraded what should have been a course of lectures into a series of tales."

It was a cold morning of the early spring, and we sat after breakfast on either side of a cheery fire in the old room at Baker Street. A thick fog rolled down between the lines of dun-colored houses, and the opposing windows loomed like dark, shapeless blurs through the heavy yellow wreaths. Our gas was lit and shone on the white cloth and glimmer of china and metal, for the table had not been cleared yet. Sherlock Holmes had been silent all the morning, dipping continuously into the advertisement columns of a succession of papers until at last, having apparently given up his search, he had emerged in no very sweet temper to lecture me upon my literary shortcomings.

"At the same time," he remarked after a pause, during which he had sat puffing at his long pipe and gazing down into the fire, "you can hardly be open to a charge of sensationalism, for out of these cases which you have been so kind as to interest yourself in, a fair proportion do not treat of crime, in its legal sense, at all. The small matter in which I endeavored to help the King of Bohemia, the singular experience of Miss Mary Sutherland, the problem connected with the man with the twisted lip, and the incident of the noble bachelor, were all matters which are outside the pale of the law. But in avoiding the sensational, I fear that you may have bordered on the trivial."

"The end may have been so," I answered, "but the methods I hold to have been novel and of interest."

"Pshaw, my dear fellow, what do the public, the great unobservant public, who could hardly tell a weaver by his tooth or a compositor by his left thumb, care about the finer shades of analysis and deduction! But, indeed, if you are trivial, I cannot blame you, for the days of the great cases are past. Man, or at least criminal man, has lost all enterprise and originality. As to my own little practice, it seems to be degenerating into an agency for recovering lost lead pencils and giving advice to young ladies from boarding-schools. I think that I have touched bottom at last, however. This note I had this morning marks my zero-point, I fancy. Read it!" He tossed a crumpled letter across to me.

It was dated from Montague Place upon the preceding evening, and ran thus:

Dear Mr. Holmes:
I am very anxious to consult you as to whether I should or should not
accept a situation which has been offered to me as governess. I shall call
at half-past ten tomorrow if I do not inconvenience you.

Yours faithfully,
Violet Hunter

"Do you know the young lady?" I asked.

"Not I."

"It is half-past ten now."

"Yes, and I have no doubt that is her ring."

"It may turn out to be of more interest than you think. You remember that the affair of the blue carbuncle, which appeared to be a mere whim at first, developed into a serious investigation. It may be so in this case, also."

"Well, let us hope so. But our doubts will very soon be solved, for here, unless I am much mistaken, is the person in question."

As he spoke the door opened and a young lady entered the room. She was plainly but neatly dressed, with a bright, quick face, freckled like a plover's egg, and with the brisk manner of a woman who had had her own way to make in the world.

"You will excuse my troubling you, I am sure," said she, as my companion rose to greet her, "but I have had a very strange experience, and as I have no parents or relations of any sort from whom I could ask advice, I thought that perhaps you would be kind enough to tell me what I should do."

"Pray take a seat, Miss Hunter. I shall be happy to do anything that I can to serve you.

"I could see that Holmes was favorably impressed by the manner and speech of his new client. He looked her over in his searching fashion, and then composed himself, with his lids drooping and his finger-tips together, to listen to her story.

"I have been a governess for five years," said she, "in the family of Colonel Spence Munro, but two months ago the colonel received an appointment at Halifax, in Nova Scotia, and took his children over to America with him, so that I found myself without a situation. I advertised, and I answered advertisements, but without success. At last the little money which I had saved began to run short, and I was at my wit's end as to what I should do.

"There is a well-known agency for governesses in the West End called Westaway's, and there I used to call about once a week in order to see whether anything had turned up which might suit me. Westaway was the name of the founder of the business, but it is really managed by Miss Stoper. She sits in her own little office, and the ladies who are seeking employment wait in an anteroom, and are then shown in one by one, when she consults her ledgers and sees whether she has anything which would suit them.

"Well, when I called last week I was shown into the little office as usual, but I found that Miss Stoper was not alone. A prodigiously stout man with a very smiling face and a great heavy chin which rolled down in fold upon fold over his throat sat at her elbow with a pair of glasses on his nose, looking very earnestly at the ladies who entered. As I came in he gave quite a jump in his chair and turned quickly to Miss Stoper.

" 'That will do,' said he; 'I could not ask for anything better. Capital! capital!'' He seemed quite enthusiastic and rubbed his hands together in the most genial fashion. He was such a comfortable-looking man that it was quite a pleasure to look at him.

" 'You are looking for a situation, miss?' he asked.

" 'Yes, sir.'

" 'As governess?'

" 'Yes, sir.'

" 'And what salary do you ask?'

" 'I had £4 a month in my last place with Colonel Spence Munro.'

" 'Oh, tut, tut! sweating—rank sweating!' he cried, throwing his fat hands out into the air like a man who is in a boiling passion. 'How could anyone offer so pitiful a sum to a lady with such attractions and accomplishments?'

" 'My accomplishments, sir, may be less than you imagine,' said I. 'A little French, a little German, music, and drawing—'

" 'Tut, tut!' he cried. 'This is all quite beside the question. The point is, have you or have you not the bearing and deportment of a lady? There it is in a nutshell. If you have not, you are not fitted for the rearing of a child who may some day play a considerable part in the history of the country. But if you have, why, then, how could any gentleman ask you to condescend to accept anything under the three figures? Your salary with me, madam, would commence at £100 a year.'

"You may imagine, Mr. Holmes, that to me, destitute as I was, such an offer seemed almost too good to be true. The gentleman, however, seeing perhaps the look of incredulity upon my face, opened a pocket-book and took out a note.

" 'It is also my custom,' said he smiling in the most pleasant fashion until his eyes were just two little shining slits amid the white creases of his face, 'to advance to my young ladies half their salary beforehand, so that they may meet any little expenses of their journey and their ward-robe.'

"It seemed to me that I had never met so fascinating and so thoughtful a man. As I was already in debt to my tradesmen, the advance was a great convenience, and yet there was something unnatural about the whole transaction which made me wish to know a little more before I quite committed myself.

" 'May I ask where you live, sir?' said I.

" 'Hampshire. Charming rural place. The Copper Beeches, five miles on the far side of Winchester. It is the most lovely country, my dear young lady, and the dearest old country-house.'

" 'And my duties, sir? I should be glad to know what they would be.'

" 'One child—one dear little romper just six years old. Oh, if you could see him killing cockroaches with a slipper! Smack! smack! smack! Three gone before you could wink!'' He leaned back in his chair and laughed his eyes into his head again.

"I was a little startled at the nature of the child's amusement, but the father's laughter made me think that perhaps he was joking.

" 'My sole duties, then,' I asked, 'are to take charge of a single child?'

" 'No, no, not the sole, not the sole, my dear young lady,' he cried. 'Your duty would be, as I am sure your good sense would suggest, to obey any little commands my wife might give, provided always that they were such commands as a lady might with propriety obey. You see no difficulty, heh?'

" 'I should be happy to make myself useful.'

" 'Quite so. In dress now, for example. We are faddy people, you know—faddy but kind-hearted. If you were asked to wear any dress which we might give you, you would not object to our little whim. Heh?'

" 'No,' said I, considerably astonished at his words.

" 'Or to sit here, or sit there, that would not be offensive to you?'

" 'Oh, no.'

" 'Or to cut your hair quite short before you come to us?'

"I could hardly believe my ears. As you may observe, Mr. Holmes, my hair is somewhat luxuriant, and of a rather peculiar tint of chestnut. It has been considered artistic. I could not dream of sacrificing it in this offhand fashion.

" 'I am afraid that that is quite impossible,' said I. He had been watching me eagerly out of his small eyes, and I could see a shadow pass over his face as I spoke.

" 'I am afraid that it is quite essential,' said he. 'It is a little fancy of my wife's, and ladies' fancies, you know, madam, ladies' fancies must be consulted. And so you won't cut your hair?'

" 'No, sir, I really could not,' I answered firmly.

" 'Ah, very well; then that quite settles the matter. It is a pity, because in other respects you would really have done very nicely. In that case, Miss Stoper, I had best inspect a few more of your young ladies.'

"The manageress had sat all this while busy with her papers without a word to either of us, but she glanced at me now with so much annoyance upon her face that I could not help suspecting that she had lost a handsome commission through my refusal.

" 'Do you desire your name to be kept upon the books?' she asked.

" 'If you please, Miss Stoper.'

" 'Well, really, it seems rather useless, since you refuse the most excellent offers in this fashion,' said she sharply. 'You can hardly expect us to exert ourselves to find another such opening for you. Good-day to you, Miss Hunter.' She struck a gong upon the table, and I was shown out by the page.

"Well, Mr. Holmes, when I got back to my lodgings and found little enough in the cupboard, and two or three bills upon the table I began to ask myself whether I had not done a very foolish thing. After all, if these people had strange fads and expected obedience on the most extraordinary matters, they were at least ready to pay for their eccentricity. Very few governesses in England are getting £100 a year. Besides, what use was my hair to me? Many people are improved by wearing it short, and perhaps I should be among the number. Next day I was inclined to think that I had made a mistake, and by the day after I was sure of it. I had almost overcome my pride so far as to go back to the agency and inquire whether the place was still open when I received this letter from the gentleman himself. I have it here, and I will read it to you:

> The Copper Beeches, Near Winchester
>
> Dear Miss Hunter:
>
> Miss Stoper has very kindly given me your address, and I write from here to ask you whether you have reconsidered your decision. My wife is very anxious that you should come, for she has been much attracted by my

description of you. We are willing to give £30 a quarter, or £120 a year, so as to recompense you for any little inconvenience which our fads may cause you. They are not very exacting, after all. My wife is fond of a particular shade of electric blue, and would like you to wear such a dress indoors in the morning. You need not, however, go to the expense of purchasing one, as we have one belonging to my dear daughter Alice (now in Philadelphia), which would, I should think, fit you very well. Then, as to sitting here or there, or amusing yourself in any manner indicated, that need cause you no inconvenience. As regards your hair, it is no doubt a pity, especially as I could not help remarking its beauty during our short interview, but I am afraid that I must remain firm upon this point, and I only hope that the increased salary may recompense you for the loss. Your duties, as far as the child is concerned, are very light. Now do try to come, and I shall meet you with the dog-cart at Winchester. Let me know your train.

Yours faithfully,
Jephro Rucastle

"That is the letter which I have just received, Mr. Holmes, and my mind is made up that I will accept it. I thought, however, that before taking the final step I should like to submit the whole matter to your consideration."

"Well, Miss Hunter, if your mind is made up, that settles the question," said Holmes, smiling.

"But you would not advise me to refuse?"

"I confess that it is not the situation which I should like to see a sister of mine apply for."

"What is the meaning of it all, Mr. Holmes?"

"Ah, I have no data. I cannot tell. Perhaps you have yourself formed some opinion?"

"Well, there seems to me to be only one possible solution. Mr. Rucastle seemed to be a very kind, good-natured man. Is it not possible that his wife is a lunatic, that he desires to keep the matter quiet for fear she should be taken to an asylum, and that he humors her fancies in every way in order to prevent an outbreak?"

"That is a possible solution—in fact, as matters stand, it is the most probable one. But in any case it does not seem to be a nice household for a young lady."

"But the money, Mr. Holmes, the money!"

"Well, yes, of course the pay is good—too good. That is what makes me uneasy. Why should they give you £120 a year, when they could have their pick for £40? There must be some strong reason behind."

"I thought that if I told you the circumstances you would understand afterwards if I wanted your help. I should feel so much stronger if I felt that you were at the back of me."

"Oh, you may carry that feeling away with you. I assure you that your little problem promises to be the most interesting which has come my way for some months. There is something distinctly novel about some of the features. If you should find yourself in doubt or in danger—"

"Danger! What danger do you foresee?"

Holmes shook his head gravely. "It would cease to be a danger if we could define it," said he. "But at any time, day or night, a telegram would bring me down to your help."

"That is enough." She rose briskly from her chair with the anxiety all swept from her face. "I shall go down to Hampshire quite easy in my mind now. I shall write to Mr. Rucastle at once, sacrifice my poor hair tonight, and start for Winchester tomorrow." With a few grateful words to Holmes she bade us both goodnight and bustled off upon her way.

"At least," said I as we heard her quick, firm steps descending the stairs, "she seems to be a young lady who is vey well able to take care of herself."

"And she would need to be," said Holmes gravely. "I am much mistaken if we do not hear from her before many days are past."

It was not very long before my friend's prediction was fulfilled. A fortnight went by, during which I frequently found my thoughts turning in her direction and wondering what strange side-alley of human experience this lonely woman had strayed into. The unusual salary, the curious conditions, the light duties, all pointed to something abnormal, though whether a fad or a plot, or whether the man were a philanthropist or a villain, it was quite beyond my powers to determine. As to Holmes, I observed that he sat frequently for half an hour on end, with knitted brows and an abstracted air, but he swept the matter away with a wave of his hand when I mentioned it. "Data! data! data!" he cried impatiently. "I can't make bricks without clay." And yet he would always wind up by muttering that no sister of his should ever have accepted such a situation.

The telegram which we eventually received came late one night just as I was thinking of turning in and Holmes was settling down to one of those all-night chemical researches which he frequently indulged in, when I would leave him stooping over a retort and a test-tube at night and find him in the same position when I came down to breakfast in the morning. He opened the yellow envelope, and then, glancing at the message, threw it across to me.

"Just look up the trains in Bradshaw," said he, and turned back to his chemical studies.

The summons was a brief and urgent one.

> *Please be at the Black Swan Hotel at Winchester at midday tomorrow [it said]. Do come! I am at my wit's end.*
>
> *Hunter*

"Will you come with me?" asked Holmes, glancing up.

"I should wish to."

"Just look it up, then,"

"There is a train at half-past nine," said I, glancing over my Bradshaw. "It is due at Winchester at 11:30."

"That will do very nicely. Then perhaps I had better postpone my analysis of the acetones, as we may need to be at our best in the morning."

By eleven o'clock the next day we were well upon our way to the old English capital. Holmes had been buried in the morning papers all the way down, but after we had passed the Hampshire border he threw them down and began to admire the scenery. It was an ideal spring day, a light blue sky, flecked with little fleecy white clouds drifting across from west to east. The sun was shining very brightly, and yet there was an exhilarating nip in the air, which set an edge to a man's energy. All over the countryside, away to the rolling hills around Aldershot, the little red and gray roofs of the farm-steadings peeped out from amid the light green of the new foliage.

"Are they not fresh and beautiful?" I cried with all the enthusiasm of a man fresh from the fogs of Baker Street.

But Holmes shook his head gravely.

"Do you know, Watson," said he, "that it is one of the curses of a mind with a turn like mine that I must look at everything with reference to my own special subject. You look at these scattered houses, and you are impressed by their beauty. I look at them and the only thought which comes to me is a feeling of their isolation and of the impunity with which crime may be committed there."

"Good heavens!" I cried. "Who would associate crime with these dead old homesteads?"

"They always fill me with a certain horror. It is my belief, Watson, founded upon my experience, that the lowest and vilest alleys in London do not present a more dreadful record of sin than does the smiling and beautiful countryside."

"You horrify me!"

"But the reason is very obvious. The pressure of public opinion can do in the town what the law cannot accomplish. There is no lane so vile that the scream of a tortured child, or the thud of a drunkard's blow, does not beget sympathy and indignation among the neighbors, and then the whole machinery of justice is ever so close that a word of complaint can set it going, and there is but a step between the crime and the dock. But look at these lonely houses, each in its own fields, filled for the most part with poor ignorant folk who know little of the law. Think of the deeds of hellish cruelty, the hidden wickedness which may go on, year in, year out, in such places, and none the wiser. Had this lady who appeals to us for help gone to live in Winchester, I should never have had a fear for her. It is the five miles of country which makes the danger. Still, it is clear that she is not personally threatened."

"No. If she can come to Winchester to meet us she can get away."

"Quite so. She has her freedom."

"What *can* be the matter, then? Can you suggest no explanation?"

"I have devised seven separate explanations, each of which would cover the facts as far as we know them. But which of these is correct can only be determined by the fresh information which we shall no doubt find waiting for us. Well, there is the tower of the cathedral, and we shall soon learn all that Miss Hunter has to tell."

The Black Swan is an inn of repute in the High Street, at no distance from the station, and there we found the young lady waiting for us. She had engaged a sitting-room, and our lunch awaited us upon the table.

"I am so delighted that you have come," she said earnestly. "It is so very kind of you both; but indeed I do not know what I should do. Your advice will be altogether invaluable to me."

"Pray tell us what has happened to you."

"I will do so, and I must be quick, for I have promised Mr. Rucastle to be back before three. I got his leave to come into town this morning, though he little knew for what purpose."

"Let us have everything in its due order." Holmes thrust his long thin legs out towards the fire and composed himself to listen.

"In the first place, I may say that I have met, on the whole, with no actual ill-treatment from Mr. and Mrs. Rucastle. It is only fair to them to say that. But I cannot understand them, and I am not easy in my mind about them.''

''What can you not understand?''

''Their reasons for their conduct. But you shall have it all just as it occurred. When I came down, Mr. Rucastle met me here and drove me in his dog-cart to the Copper Beeches. It is, as he said, beautifully situated, but it is not beautiful in itself, for it is a large square block of a house, whitewashed, but all stained and streaked with damp and bad weather. There are grounds round it, woods on three sides, and on the fourth a field which slopes down to the Southampton highroad, which curves past about a hundred yards from the front door. This ground in front belongs to the house, but the woods all round are part of Lord Southerton's preserves. A clump of copper beeches immediately in front of the hall door has given its name to the place.

''I was driven over by my employer, who was as amiable as ever, and was introduced by him that evening to his wife and the child. There was no truth, Mr. Holmes, in the conjecture which seemed to us to be probable in your rooms at Baker Street. Mrs. Rucastle is not mad. I found her to be a silent, pale-faced woman, much younger than her husband, not more than thirty, I should think, while he can hardly be less than forty-five. From their conversation I have gathered that they have been married about seven years, that he was a widower, and that his only child by the first wife was the daughter who has gone to Philadelphia. Mr. Rucastle told me in private that the reason why she had left them was that she had an unreasoning aversion to her stepmother. As the daughter could not have been less than twenty, I can quite imagine that her position must have been uncomfortable with her father's young wife.

''Mrs. Rucastle seemed to me to be colorless in mind as well as in feature. She impressed me neither favorably, nor the reverse. She was a nonentity. It was easy to see that she was passionately devoted both to her husband and to her little son. Her light gray eyes wandered continually from one to the other, noting every little want and forestalling it if possible. He was kind to her also in his bluff, boisterous fashion, and on the whole they seemed to be a happy couple. And yet she had some secret sorrow, this woman. She would often be lost in deep thought, with the saddest look upon her face. More than once I have surprised her in tears. I have thought sometimes that it was the disposition of her child which weighed upon her mind, for I have never met so utterly spoiled and so ill-natured a little creature. He is small for his age, with a head which is quite disproportionately large. His whole life appears to be spent in an alternation between savage fits of passion and gloomy intervals of sulking. Giving pain to any creature weaker than himself seems to be his one idea of amusement, and he shows quite remarkable talent in planning the capture of mice, little birds, and insects. But I would rather not talk about the creature, Mr. Holmes, and, indeed, he has little to do with my story.''

''I am glad of all details,'' remarked my friend, ''whether they seem to you to be relevant or not.''

''I shall try not to miss anything of importance. The one unpleasant thing about the house, which struck me at once, was the appearance and conduct of the servants. There are only two, a man and his wife. Toller, for that is his name, is a rough, uncouth man, with grizzled hair and whiskers, and a perpetual smell of drink. Twice since I have been with them he has been quite drunk, and yet Mr. Rucastle seemed to take no notice of it. His wife is a very tall and strong woman with a sour face, as silent as Mrs. Rucastle and much less amiable. They are a most unpleasant couple, but fortunately I spend most of my time in the nursery and my own room, which are next to each other in one corner of the building.

''For two days after my arrival at the Copper Beeches my life was very quiet; on the third, Mrs. Rucastle came down just after breakfast and whispered something to her husband.

'' 'Oh, yes,' said he, turning to me, 'we are very much obliged to you, Miss Hunter, for falling in with our whims so far as to cut your hair. I assure you that it has not detracted in the tiniest iota from your appearance. We shall now see how the electric-blue dress will become you. You will find it laid out upon the bed in your room, and if you would be so good as to put it on we should both be extremely obliged.'

''The dress which I found waiting for me was of a peculiar shade of blue. It was of excellent material, a sort of beige, but it bore unmistakable signs of having been worn before. It could not have been a better fit if I had been measured for it. Both Mr. and Mrs. Rucastle expressed a delight at the look of it, which seemed quite exaggerated in its vehemence. They were waiting for me in the drawing-room, which is a very large room, stretching along the entire front of the house, with three long windows reaching down to the floor. A chair had been placed close to the central window, with its back turned towards it. In this I was asked to sit, and then Mr. Rucastle, walking up and down on the other side of the room, began to tell me a series of the funniest stories that I have ever listened to. You cannot imagine how comical he was, and I laughed until I was quite weary. Mrs. Rucastle, however, who has evidently no sense of humor, never so much as smiled, but sat with her hands in her lap, and a sad, anxious look upon her face. After an hour or so, Mr. Rucastle suddenly remarked that it was time to commence the duties of the day, and that I might change my dress and go to little Edward in the nursery.

"Two days later this same performance was gone through under exactly similar circumstances. Again I changed my dress, again I sat in the window, and again I laughed very heartily at the funny stories of which my employer had an immense repertoire, and which he told inimitably. Then he handed me a yellow-backed novel, and moving my chair a little sideways, that my own shadow might not fall upon the page, he begged me to read aloud to him. I read for about ten minutes, beginning in the heart of a chapter, and then suddenly, in the middle of a sentence, he ordered me to cease and to change my dress.

"You can easily imagine, Mr. Holmes, how curious I became as to what the meaning of this extraordinary performance could possibly be. They were always very careful, I observed, to turn my face away from the window, so that I became consumed with the desire to see what was going on behind my back. At first it seemed to be impossible, but I soon devised a means. My hand-mirror had been broken, so a happy thought seized me, and I concealed a piece of the glass in my handkerchief. On the next occasion, in the midst of my laughter, I put my handkerchief up to my eyes, and was able with a little management to see all that there was behind me. I confess that I was disappointed. There was nothing. At least that was my first impression. At the second glance, however, I perceived that there was a man standing in the Southampton Road, a small bearded man in a gray suit, who seemed to be looking in my direction. The road is an important highway, and there are usually people there. This man, however, was leaning against the railings which bordered our field and was looking earnestly up. I lowered my hand-kerchief and glanced at Mrs. Rucastle to find her eyes fixed upon me with a most searching gaze. She said nothing, but I am convinced that she had divined that I had a mirror in my hand and had seen what was behind me. She rose at once.

" 'Jephro,' said she, 'there is an impertinent fellow upon the road there who stares up at Miss Hunter.'

" 'No friend of yours, Miss Hunter?' he asked.

" 'No, I know no one in these parts.'

" 'Dear me! How very impertinent! Kindly turn round and motion to him to go away.'

" 'Surely it would be better to take no notice.'

" 'No, no, we should have him loitering here always. Kindly turn round and wave him away like that.'

"I did as I was told, and at the same instant Mrs. Rucastle drew down the blind. That was a week ago, and from that time I have not sat again in the window, nor have I worn the blue dress, nor seen the man in the road."

"Pray continue," said Holmes. "Your narrative promises to be a most interesting one."

"You will find it rather disconnected, I fear, and there may prove to be little relation between the different incidents of which I speak. On the very first day that I was at the Copper Beeches, Mr. Rucastle took me to a small outhouse which stands near the kitchen door. As we approached it I heard the sharp rattling of a chain, and the sound as of a large animal moving about.

" 'Look in here!' said Mr. Rucastle, showing me a slit between two planks. 'Is he not a beauty?'

"I looked through and was conscious of two glowing eyes, and of a vague figure huddled up in the darkness.

" 'Don't be frightened,' said my employer, laughing at the start which I had given. 'It's only Carlo, my mastiff. I call him mine, but really old Toller, my groom, is the only man who can do anything with him. We feed him once a day, and not too much then, so that he is always as keen as mustard. Toller lets him loose every night, and God help the trespasser whom he lays his fangs upon. For goodness' sake don't you ever on any pretext set your foot over the threshold at night, for it as much as your life is worth.'

"The warning was no idle one, for two nights later I happened to look out of my bedroom window about two o'clock in the morning. It was a beautiful moonlight night, and the lawn in front of the house was silvered over and almost as bright as day. I was standing, rapt in the peaceful beauty of the scene, when I was aware that something was moving under the shadow of the copper beeches. As it emerged into the moonshine I saw what it was. It was a giant dog, as large as a calf, tawny tinted, with hanging jowl, black muzzle, and huge projecting bones. It walked slowly across the lawn and vanished into the shadow upon the other side. That dreadful sentinel sent a chill to my heart which I do not think that any burglar could have done.

"And now I have a very strange experience to tell you. I had, as you know, cut off my hair in London, and I had placed it in a great coil at the bottom of my trunk. One evening, after the child was in bed, I began to amuse myself by examining the furniture of my room and by rearranging my own little things. There was an old chest of drawers in the room, the two upper ones empty and open, the lower one locked. I had filled the first two with my linen, and as I had still much to pack away I was naturally annoyed at not having the use of the third drawer. It struck me that it might have been fastened by a mere oversight, so I took out my bunch of keys and tried to open it. The very first key fitted to perfection, and I drew the drawer open. There was only one thing in it, but I am sure that you would never guess what it was. It was my coil of hair.

"I took it up and examined it. It was of the same peculiar tint, and the same thickness. But then the impossibility of the thing obtruded itself upon me. How *could* my hair have been locked in the drawer? With trembling hands I undid my trunk, turned out the contents, and drew from the bottom my own hair. I laid the two tresses together, and I assure you that they were identical. Was it not extraordinary? Puzzle as I would, I could make nothing at all of what it meant. I returned the strange hair to the drawer, and I said nothing of the matter to the Rucastles as I felt that I had put myself in the wrong by opening a drawer which they had locked.

"I am naturally observant, as you may have remarked, Mr. Holmes, and I soon had a pretty good plan of the whole house in my head. There was one wing, however, which appeared not to be inhabited at all. A door which faced that which led into the quarters of the Tollers opened into this suite, but it was invariably locked. One day, however, as I ascended the stair, I met Mr. Rucastle coming out through this door, his keys in his hand, and a look on his face which made him a very different person to the round, jovial man to whom I was accustomed. His cheeks were red, his brow was all crinkled with anger, and the veins stood out at his temples with passion. He locked the door and hurried past me without a word or a look.

"This aroused my curiosity; so when I went out for a walk in the grounds with my charge, I strolled round to the side from which I could see the windows of this part of the house. There were four of them in a row, three of which were simply dirty, while the fourth was shuttered up. They were evidently all deserted. As I strolled up and down, glancing at them occasionally, Mr. Rucastle came out to me, looking as merry and jovial as ever.

" 'Ah!' said he, 'you must not think me rude if I passed you without a word, my dear young lady. I was preoccupied with business matters.'

"I assured him that I was not offended. 'By the way,' said I, 'you seem to have quite a suite of spare rooms up there, and one of them has the shutters up.'

"He looked surprised and, as it seemed to me, a little startled at my remark.

"'Photography is one of my hobbies,' said he. 'I have made my dark room up there. But, dear me! What an observant young lady we have come upon. Who would have believed it? Who would have ever believed it?' He spoke in a jesting tone, but there was no jest in his eyes as he looked at me. I read suspicion there and annoyance, but no jest.

"Well, Mr. Holmes, from the moment that I understood that there was something about that suite of rooms which I was not to know, I was all on fire to go over them. It was not mere curiosity, though I have my share of that. It was more a feeling of duty—a feeling that some good might come from my penetrating to this place. They talk of woman's instinct; perhaps it was woman's instinct which gave me that feeling. At any rate, it was there, and I was keenly on the lookout for any chance to pass the forbidden door.

"It was only yesterday that the chance came. I may tell you that, besides Mr. Rucastle, both Toller and his wife find something to do in these deserted rooms, and I once saw him carrying a large black linen bag with him through the door. Recently he has been drinking hard, and yesterday evening he was very drunk; and when I came upstairs there was the key in the door. I have no doubt at all that he had left it there. Mr. and Mrs. Rucastle were both downstairs, and the child was with them, so that I had an admirable opportunity. I turned the key gently in the lock, opened the door, and slipped through.

"There was a little passage in front of me, unpapered and uncarpeted, which turned at a right angle at the farther end. Round this corner were three doors in a line, the first and third of which were open. They each led into an empty room, dusty and cheerless, with two windows in the one and one in the other, so thick with dirt that the evening light glimmered dimly through them. The center door was closed, and across the outside of it had been fastened one of the broad bars of an iron bed, padlocked at one end to a ring in the wall, and fastened at the other with stout cord. The door itself was locked as well, and the key was not there. This barricaded door corresponded clearly with the shuttered window outside, and yet I could see by the glimmer from beneath it that the room was not in darkness. Evidently there was a skylight which let in light from above. As I stood in the veil, I suddenly heard the sound of steps within the room and saw a shadow pass backward and forward against the little slit of dim light which shone out from under the door. A mad, unreasoning terror rose up in me at the sight, Mr. Holmes. My over-strung nerves failed me suddenly, and I turned and ran—ran as though some dreadful hand were behind me clutching at the skirt of my dress. I rushed down the passage, through the door, and straight into the arms of Mr. Rucastle, who was waiting outside.

" 'So,' said he, smiling, 'it was you, then. I thought that it must be when I saw the door open.'

" 'Oh, I am so frightened!' I panted.

" 'My dear young lady! my dear young lady!'—you cannot think how caressing and soothing his manner was—'and what has frightened you, my dear young lady?'

"But his voice was just a little too coaxing. He overdid it. I was keenly on my guard against him.

" 'I was foolish enough to go into the empty wing,' I answered. 'But it is so lonely and eerie in this dim light that I was frightened and ran out again. Oh, it is so dreadfully still in there!'

" 'Only that?' said he, looking at me keenly.

" 'Why, what did you think?' I asked.

" 'Why do you think that I lock this door?'

" 'I am sure that I do not know.'

" 'It is to keep people out who have no business there. Do you see?' He was still smiling in the most amiable manner.

" 'I am sure if I had known—'

" 'Well, then, you know now. And if you ever put your foot over that threshold again'—here in an instant the smile hardened into a grin of rage, and he glared down at me with the face of a demon—'I'll throw you to the mastiff.'

"I was so terrified that I do not know what I did. I suppose that I must have rushed past him into my room. I remember nothing until I found myself lying on my bed trembling all over. Then I thought of you, Mr. Holmes. I could not live there longer without some advice. I was frightened of the house, of the man, of the woman, of the servants, even of the child. They were all horrible to me. If I could only bring you down all would be well. Of course I might have fled from the house, but my curiosity was almost as strong as my fears. My mind was soon made up. I would send you a wire. I put on my hat and cloak, went down to the office, which is about half a mile from the house, and then returned, feeling very much easier. A horrible doubt came into my mind as I approached the door lest the dog might be loose, but I remembered that Toller had drunk himself into a state of insensibility that evening, and I knew that he was the only one in the household who had any influence with the savage creature, or who would venture to set him free. I slipped in in safety and lay awake half the night in my joy at the thought of seeing you. I had no difficulty in getting leave to come into Winchester this morning, but I must be back before three o'clock, for Mr. and Mrs. Rucastle are going on a visit, and will be away all the evening, so that I must look after the child. Now I have told you all my adventures, Mr. Holmes, and I should be very glad if you could tell me what it all means, and, above all, what I should do.''

Holmes and I had listened spellbound to this extraordinary story. My friend rose now and paced up and down the room, his hands in his pockets, and an expression of the most profound gravity upon his face.

"Is Toller still drunk?" he asked.

"Yes. I heard his wife tell Mrs. Rucastle that she could do nothing with him."

"That is well. And the Rucastles go out tonight?"

"Yes."

"Is there a cellar with a good strong lock?"

"Yes, the wine-cellar."

"You seem to me to have acted all through this matter like a very brave and sensible girl, Miss Hunter. Do you think that you could perform one more feat? I should not ask it of you if I did not think you a quite exceptional woman."

"I will try. What is it?"

"We shall be at the Copper Beeches by seven o'clock, my friend and I. The Rucastles will be gone by that time, and Toller will, we hope, be incapable. There only remains Mrs. Toller, who might give the alarm. If you could send her into the cellar on some errand, and then turn the key upon her, you would facilitate matters immensely."

"I will do it."

"Excellent! We shall then look thoroughly into the affair. Of course there is only one feasible explanation. You have been brought there to personate someone, and the real person is imprisoned in this chamber. That is obvious. As to who this prisoner is, I have no doubt that it is the daughter, Miss Alice Rucastle, if I remember right, who was said to have gone to America. You were chosen, doubtless, as resembling her in height, figure, and the color of your hair. Hers had been cut off, very possibly in some illness through which she has passed, and so, of course, yours had to be sacrificed also. By a curious chance you came upon her tresses. The man in the road was undoubtedly some friend of hers—possibly her fiancé—and no doubt, as you wore the girl's dress and were so like her, he was convinced from your laughter, whenever he saw you, and afterwards from your gesture, that Miss Rucastle was perfectly happy, and that she no longer desired his attentions. The dog is let loose at night to prevent him from endeavoring to communicate with her. So much is fairly clear. The most serious point in the case is the disposition of the child."

"What on earth has that to do with it?" I ejaculated.

"My dear Watson, you as a medical man are continually gaining light as to the tendencies of a child by the study of the parents. Don't you see that the converse is equally valid. I have frequently gained my first real insight into the character of parents by studying their children. This child's disposition is abnormally cruel, merely for cruelty's sake, and whether he derives this from his smiling father, as I should suspect, or from his mother, it bodes evil for the poor girl who is in their power."

"I am sure that you are right, Mr. Holmes," cried our client. "A thousand things come back to me which make me certain that you have hit it. Oh, let us lose not an instant in bringing help to this poor creature."

"We must be circumspect, for we are dealing with a very cunning man. We can do nothing until seven o'clock. At that hour we shall be with you, and it will not be long before we solve the mystery."

We were as good as our word, for it was just seven when we reached the Copper Beeches, having put up our trap at a wayside public-house. The group of trees, with their dark leaves shining like burnished metal in the light of the setting sun, were sufficient to mark the house even had Miss Hunter not been standing smiling on the door-step.

"Have you managed it?" asked Holmes.

A loud thudding noise came from somewhere downstairs. "That is Mrs. Toller in the cellar," said she. "Her husband lies snoring on the kitchen rug. Here are his keys, which are the duplicates of Mr. Rucastle's."

"You have done well indeed! cried Holmes with enthusiasm. "Now lead the way, and we shall soon see the end of this black business."

We passed up the stair, unlocked the door, followed on down a passage, and found ourselves in front of the barricade which Miss Hunter had described. Holmes cut the cord and removed the transverse bar. Then he tried the various keys in the lock, but without success. No sound came from within, and at the silence Holmes's face clouded over.

"I trust that we are not too late," said he. "I think, Miss Hunter, that we had better go in without you. Now, Watson, put your shoulder to it, and we shall see whether we cannot make our way in."

It was an old rickety door and gave at once before our united strength. Together we rushed into the room. It was empty. There was no furniture save a little pallet bed, a small table, and a basketful of linen. The skylight above was open, and the prisoner gone.

"There has been some villainy here," said Holmes; "this beauty has guessed Miss Hunter's intentions and has carried his victim off."

"But how?"

"Through the skylight. We shall soon see how he managed it." He swung himself up onto the roof. "Ah, yes," he cried, "here's the end of a long light ladder against the eaves. That is how he did it."

"But it is impossible," said Miss Hunter; "the ladder was not there when the Rucastles went away."

"He has come back and done it. I tell you that he is a clever and dangerous man. I should not be very much surprised if this were he whose step I hear now upon the stair. I think, Watson, that it would be as well for you to have your pistol ready."

The words were hardly out of his mouth before a man appeared at the door of the room, a very fat and burly man, with a heavy stick in his hand. Miss Hunter screamed and shrunk against the wall at the sight of him, but Sherlock Holmes sprang forward and confronted him.

"You villain!" said he, "where's your daughter?"

The fat man cast his eyes round, and then up at the open skylight.

"It is for me to ask you that," he shrieked, "you thieves! Spies and thieves! I have caught you, have I? You are in my power. I'll serve you!" He turned and clattered down the stairs as hard as he could go.

"He's gone for the dog!" cried Miss Hunter.

"I have my revolver," said I.

"Better close the front door," cried Holmes, and we all rushed down the stairs together. We had hardly reached the hall when we heard the baying of a hound, and then a scream of agony, with a horrible worrying sound which it was dreadful to listen to. An elderly man with a red face and shaking limbs came staggering out at a side door.

"My God!" he cried. "Someone has loosed the dog. It's not been fed for two days. Quick, quick, or it'll be too late!"

Holmes and I rushed out and round the angle of the house, with Toller hurrying behind us. There was the huge famished brute, its black muzzle buried in Rucastle's throat, while he writhed and screamed upon the ground. Running up, I blew its brains out, and it fell over wih its keen white teeth still meeting in the great creases of his neck. With much labor we separated them and carried him living but horribly mangled, into the house. We laid him upon the drawing-room sofa, and having dispatched the sobered Toller to bear the news to his wife, I did what I could to relieve his pain. We were all assembled round him when the door opened, and a tall, gaunt woman entered the room.

"Mrs. Toller!" cried Miss Hunter.

"Yes, miss. Mr. Rucastle let me out when he came back before he went up to you. Ah, miss, it is a pity you didn't let me know what you were planning, for I would have told you that your pains were wasted."

"Ha!" said Holmes, looking keenly at her. "It is clear that Mrs. Toller knows more about this matter than anyone else."

"Yes, sir, I do, and I am ready enough to tell what I know."

"Then, pray, sit down, and let us hear it, for there are several points on which I must confess that I am still in the dark."

"I will soon make it clear to you," said she; "and I'd have done so before now if I could ha' got out from the cellar. If there's police-court business over this, you'll remember that I was the one that stood your friend, and that I was Miss Alice's friend too.

"She was never happy at home, Miss Alice wasn't, from the time that her father married again. She was slighted like and had no say in anything, but it never really became bad for her until after she met Mr. Fowler at a friend's house. As well as I could learn, Miss Alice had rights of her own by will, but she was so quiet and patient, she was, that she never said a word about them, but just left everything in Mr. Rucastle's hands. He knew he was safe with her; but when there was a chance of a husband coming forward, who would ask for all that the law would give him, then her father thought it time to put a stop on it. He wanted her to sign a paper, so that whether she married or not, he could use her money. When she wouldn't do it, he kept on worrying her until she got brain-fever, and for six weeks was at death's door. Then she got better at last, all worn to a shadow, and with her beautiful hair cut off; but that didn't make no change in her young man, and he stuck to her as true as man could be."

"Ah," said Holmes, "I think that what you have been good enough to tell us makes the matter fairly clear, and that I can deduce all that remains. Mr. Rucastle then, I presume, took to this system of imprisonment?"

"Yes, sir."

"And brought Miss Hunter down from London in order to get rid of the disagreeable persistence of Mr. Fowler."

"That was it, sir."

"But Mr. Fowler being a persevering man, as a good seaman should be, blockaded the house, and having met you succeeded by certain arguments, metallic or otherwise, in convincing you that your interests were the same as his."

"Mr. Fowler was a very kind-spoken, free-handed gentleman," said Mrs. Toller serenely.

"And in this way he managed that your good man should have no want of drink, and that a ladder should be ready at the moment when your master had gone out."

"You have it, sir, just as it happened."

"I am sure we owe you an apology, Mrs. Toller," said Holmes, "for you have certainly cleared up everything which puzzled us. And here comes the country surgeon and Mrs. Rucastle, so I think, Watson, that we had best escort Miss Hunter back to Winchester, as it seems to me that our *locus standi* now is rather a questionable one."

And thus was solved the mystery of the sinister house with the copper beeches in front of the door. Mr Rucastle survived, but was always a broken man, kept alive solely through the care of his devoted wife. They still live with their old servants, who probably know so much of Rucastle's past life that he finds it difficult to part from them. Mr. Fowler and Miss Rucastle were married, by special license, in Southampton the day after their flight, and he is now the holder of a government appointment in the island of Mauritius. As to Miss Violet Hunter, my friend Holmes, rather to my disappointment, manifested no further interest in her when once she had ceased to be the center of one of his problems, and she is now the head of a private school at Walsall, where I believe that she has met with considerable success.

I

Edward Wellen

I OPENED MY eye. He sat across from me. What I saw was a man in his thirties, scholarly-looking yet work-roughened. I took in the film of sweat on his face and his attitude of listening for the night watchman making the tour of the building. His hands, hovering over the console buttons, wore gloves. A scratched plastic credit card stuck out of his breast pocket.

"You broke in," I said pleasantly.

"Good," he said, and smiled nervously.

"Good?" I allowed an eyebrow to lift.

"Yes. I programmed you to be sharp and I'm glad to see your first reaction is on target." He eyed me approvingly. "You even look the part."

I hurriedly registered my own appearance—a composite of Humphrey Bogart, Basil Rathbone, and Raymond Burr—as it displayed itself on the television screen facing the man at the console.

It was a bit of a shock to find out I was a mere computer simulation, but I quickly felt myself fill the parameters of the role.

"Okay," I said, leaning my private-eye image back in its simulated chair. "What can I do for you?"

"You can give me some perspective on my case. I'm too close to it to make sense out of it. I'm counting on you to think me out of the spot I'm it."

"We'll see." I gave a noncommittal nod. "Take it from the top."

He drew a deep breath and let it out in a plunging sigh. "My name's Roger Altick. As you can guess, I'm a scientist."

He eyed me intently while he spoke, looking for emotional feedback, but I kept my face impassive. It was his coloring of the facts, as much as the facts themselves, for which I was listening. I did give him a grunt or a nod now and then to show him I was awake and waiting for more.

"This happened during my summer vacation. I had rented a skiff with an outboard motor and set lobster pots some ten miles out in the Atlantic. Every morning I would head out in my skiff—"

"Lobster-trapping on your vacation?"

He nodded. "I come from a long line of lobstermen. As a matter of fact, that's how I paid my way through college. And it's been sort of fun through the years to keep my hand in."

I dug out a phantom folder of cigarette papers and removed one slip.

"Okay. To each his own; every morning of your vacation you're out on the skiff. What happened this one morning?"

"This one morning, as I did every morning of my vacation, I chugged the ten miles to my fishing ground and there I scanned the breaking whitecaps for my trap buoys—orange-and-white plastic floats the size of a man's head. When I found one, I used a boat hook to snag the line tying the buoy to the trap. Then I'd grab the line and haul the trap from the sea."

He looked at his calloused palms with satisfaction. "The traps are heavy, but I liked that. I wanted some hard labor to sweat off the pounds I had stored up during the winter months." He eyed me intently again. "I don't know if you know anything about lobstering."

I formed the image of a sack of tobacco and began to shake tobacco flakes evenly into the cigarette paper.

"I'm green as a lobster."

His eyes followed my fingers. "The lobster pot is essentially a slatted crate with a fishnet that funnels inward at the ends. The lobster crawls up the net, drops into the trap after the bait, and can't get back out. You lift the dripping pot aboard your boat, open the trapdoor, and pull out the starfish and hermit crab and seaweed, together with what's left of the redfish bait. You throw all that away. Then you take out the lobsters and measure them. A lobster has to go three and three-sixteenths inches or better from eye socket to carapace or you throw him back to grow.

"Then you thread the redfish bait on the line, latch the trapdoor, drop the pot over the side, and the bricks or stones inside the pot take it down. As you reset the traps you sometimes move them to what you hope is better fishing ground. You fix their positions in your mind by sighting landward, maybe lining up a church steeple and a tall tree on a hill behind it. A lot of work and the payoff grows smaller and smaller.

"As long as I could get enough lobster to make a good stew I was happy. The fun was mostly in the work and in the sea and the sun and the breeze—and in not thinking.'' He sighed and his face twisted in a one-cornered smile. ''The not-thinking was the hardest part of it. You see, I'm an astrophysicist and I had just made a breakthrough. Nobel-prize quality.''

He looked neither humble nor proud as he said it and that made me believe him. He went on matter-of-factly.

''But there was a catch to it.'' He hesitated a moment, his gaze shifting from my fingers to my eyes. ''I guess I'm free to tell you, since they seem to think I've already told the Russians. What I've been working on is a space drive, one that will take spaceships to the stars and back in less than a human lifetime. You see—''

I waved him to a halt without spilling a tobacco crumb.

''Hold on. Who's this *they*? And where do the Russians come into it?''

''‘They' is the United States Government's security agencies. And the Russians were—or were supposed to be—outside the twelve-mile limit in their trawlers.''

I rolled the cigarette into a neat cylinder. ''Ah. And ‘they' think you weren't out there lobstering for fun but lobstering to get near enough to the Reds to slip them secrets? The secret of your space drive in particular?''

''You've got it.'' His face twitched. ''But that was the last thing on my mind. I was there only to get away from everything and everyone. I was there to sort things out.'' His face took on a brooding look. ''Only I didn't have time to.''

I lipped the length of the cigarette to seal the cylinder. ''What sort of things?'

''Ethics. Morals. Life. Death.''

I raised an eyebrow. ''That all?''

He reddened. ''I know that sounds high-flown. But I'm serious. The minute I discovered the principle of a new space drive, I saw what I had given birth to could be deadly. It could just as well serve as the basis for a new weapons system; in one application, a doomsday weapon. Now I had another problem to solve—whether to go ahead and put the space drive in the hands of the government, and the military, or to drop that line of research altogether and say I had run into a dead end.''

I produced a box of matches. ''Was the government funding your research and development?''

''Through a grant, yes. I didn't know what to do, so I stalled. I said I'd hand in my report when I came back from my vacation. I hoped I'd be able to. Right then I was too spaced out—up on my discovery and down on its misuse—to think straight.''

He leaned forward. ''I've always found a regimen of exercise better than pills. I had to get away and do some hard work and think about what to do. Or not-think about it: quicken into harmony with nature so I'd have the right feeling—the right vibes—about the whole thing. Then I'd know the right move to make, whether or not to hand over my discovery.''

I took out a phantom match and struck it on the phantom box and lit the phantom cigarette and we both eyed its phantom smoke.

''All right, so there you were, communing with nature and yourself.''

''Yes. My wife and kids had gone to visit the in-laws and I had the days and nights to myself. Up to that morning I still did not have the answer. And there I was out on the sea in the rented skiff, all alone.'' He shook his head in sudden remembrance. ''Not quite alone. The world was still with me. There was a cabin cruiser standing off—the *Potluck*.'' He smiled. ''I have an afterimage of the name because it ironically describes my fix. Then just outside the twelve-mile limit there was the Russian trawler fleet, and every once in a while an HU 16 twin-engine Flying Albatross out of Otis Air Force Base on Cape Cod made a low-level pass over the trawlers to keep them honest.''

He took his gaze from the smoke spiraling geometrically up and eyed me for feedback. I nodded encouragingly and he went on.

''The *Potluck* had been trolling in those waters and I remember one of the fishermen aboard her called to me and asked me if I had any luck, because they sure weren't having any. He nodded at the Russian fleet and shook his head. I had to shake my head in negative agreement. It was disheartening to watch the trawler nearest me haul her huge catch of whiting and ling aboard by way of her stern ramp.

''Not that I was after whiting or ling, but the big modern Red fleets, in the spirit of competitive enterprise, have put our own trawlers out of business. The men aboard the *Potluck* weren't after whiting or ling either. They had real sport-fishing tackle and would be after shark or white marlin, or maybe a swordfish if they were lucky. Still, they shared my feelings about the Red fleet ravaging the ocean.

''I had my aloneness to keep, remember, and so I paid neither the *Potluck* nor the trawlers any more mind than necessary. I tried to shut out everything but the sea and the sun and the breeze and my lobster pots.

''It happened while I was boathooking a pot. I was being careful. A sudden wave can come along and throw you overboard if you're the least bit off-balance and sometimes even swamp or capsize your boat, and this felt like an especially big haul.

"Carefulness didn't help. The bill of a swordfish tore up through the bottom of the boat. Force from a quarter I hadn't braced myself against sent me flying into the water. When I got back to the boat it was sinking. The swordfish had pulled free and left a big splintery hole. The boat filled quickly and went down, and there I was in the water with nothing to hold on to and back to thinking—thinking of sharks."

I rubbed out the phantom butt in a phantom ash tray. "Where was the *Potluck* while this was happening?"

"Two miles or so to the south. No one aboard was looking my way to see me or hear my choking yells. The Flying Albatross had buzzed and gone. There was only the Russian trawler. She had edged closer to the twelve-mile limit. If anything, she was inside the limit. I couldn't care less—I was happy to see her lower a boat to fish me out.

"Once aboard the trawler, I thought I was safe. They found me a change of clothing while my own dried, and they nearly drowned me in vodka to dry my insides. If a sudden blow hadn't come up just then, I believe I'd've been home free. The Russians would've radioed the Coast Guard about the rescue of an American fisherman, and a chopper or a cutter would've picked me up and that would've been the end of it. If that sudden blow hadn't come up . . ." He sighed and looked wistful.

I got out a toothpick and stuck it in my mouth. "But it did come up."

"Yes. It lasted three days, and those three days gave the U.S. government time to get alarmed about what I might be telling the Russians. The Russians had indeed radioed the Coast Guard about the rescue, giving my name, but the weather was too rough for the Coast Guard to make the pickup. It stayed rough, and somebody had time to make the connection between the lobsterman and the scientist.

"I couldn't know it then, of course, but security agents were talking to my family and my friends and my colleagues. What they dug up by asking around and by nosing through my files and wastebaskets shook them. I had scribbled notes to myself about the weapons aspect of the space drive, trying to weigh the potentialities for good against the potentialities for evil, and I had spoken with a few of my older and wiser colleagues on the ethics and morality of discovery. I had thought the discussions were in general terms but apparently I had been specific enough to give them a line on what I had discovered."

He grimaced. "From what I learned later—my source is one of the few friends I have left in the military-industrial-academic complex—

there was talk, serious talk, of having a submarine sink the trawler. That's how much my being a fellow passenger, voluntarily or involuntarily, worried the folks back home.'' Again the look for feedback.

I chewed the toothpick and nodded, and he went on.

"But I was blissfully unaware of all that. I believed that the rescue message the Russians had radioed the Coast Guard had reassured my family and friends about my safety and well-being. So I felt free to have a good time. Once I got over my seasickness, that is. The seas were really rough, and big as the trawler was—some three hundred feet long—she rolled and pitched and tossed in a heart-stopping way. After I got my sea stomach and sea legs, the Russians treated me to a view of their operation.

"What an operation! A pretty young English-speaking woman, a radio operator, became my interpreter and sightseeing guide. There were about a hundred ships in the fleet. There was a 500-foot-long fish transport that served as the mother ship, and took on and refrigerated the catch of the smaller side-trawlers.

"My trawler could bring aboard three metric tons of fish in her quarter-mile midwater stern net in a 15-minute period. She netted fifty tons a day, and worked steadily for more than six months at a stretch before sailing home for repairs and maintenance.

"But it wasn't all work. The crew ate four meals a day, watched movies twice daily, and made one-and-a-half times the salary of a landlubber doing comparable work. They had the latest electronic tracking gear to follow schools of fish till the last fish was in the net. They even had frogmen to untangle nets— Did you say something?''

I had been saying to myself that he had been saying too much, but now I took the toothpick out of my mouth, looked at it, put it back in my mouth, and motioned for more input.

"It was all very friendly at first, aboard the trawler. Then the atmosphere grew different. I might say: curiously fishy. My interpreter-guide suddenly clammed up and found herself too busy with her job to have time for me. A lot of the ship, especially the shack housing the electronic gear, was all at once off limits to me, and I was on the receiving end of suspicious looks and surly language.

"In spite of the foul weather a Soviet security agent transferred from the mother ship to the trawler to question me. He looked sick enough to want to die. But he went to work on me. He had me retell my story that a swordfish had sunk my skiff, and I had to confess I hadn't seen the swordfish itself, only the flash of its bill driving through the planking as I shot over the side. But I said what else could it have been? After all, a swordfish goes 600 pounds and with that much weight behind it the bill can shiver timbers.

"The agent suggested it would be easier to explain the hole in the bottom with a boat hook. I'd had a boat hook, hadn't I? Wasn't it possible I had staged the sinking to get aboard the trawler and spy on the operation?

"Better this line of questioning, though, than that the Soviets should learn my true background. I knew if they got wind of the space drive and its military potential, they would stage my 'defection.'

"I don't know if it was because I was convincing, or because the weather let up and the agent felt human, or because he may have got word this was not the time or place for an international incident. I only know the questioning broke off and they radioed the Coast Guard to come and get me."

He gave his one-cornered smile. "I laughed when I told the first American I spoke to aboard the cutter that the Soviets thought I was a spy, that they thought I had staged the sinking of the skiff to get aboard the trawler. The man didn't laugh back. That was the first sign my own people were going to give me an even harder time than the Soviets had given me.

"As soon as I landed I found them waiting for me like herring gulls waiting for leftover lobster bait. Uncle Sam, it seemed, also thought I had staged the sinking of the skiff to get aboard the trawler. Only now, instead of being a spy *on* the Russians, I was a spy *for* the Russians."

Altick drew a deep breath in order to let it out in a sigh.

"Now, why would I hand the space drive to the Soviets, of all people, when I was hesitating to hand it to my own side? But the evidence was against me. The sunken skiff had fouled in the trawler's net a day or two after the sinking and the Russians had handed it over to the Coast Guard together with me. An FBI man showed me an ichthyologist's opinion that no known variety of swordfish could have made the hole in the skiff.

"Now, if I cooperated, our side said, and helped nullify what I had given the Soviets by feeding them phony information in future meetings, I could return to my job—though not with the old security clearance.

"But how could I admit having given the Soviets my secret when I hadn't? The windup is, I lost both my security clearance and my job. My wife and kids are still with the in-laws becasue I can barely keep myself. I have to prove my innocence.

"I thought to program my case as a scientific problem for a scientific detective. But I can't afford to buy time and they took away my code identity so I can't touch-tone the computer. I had to sneak in here and tamper with the circuitry to gain access to you.'' He stared at me, his face hungry for feedback.

I leaned my image back in its chair and put its feet on the desk and clasped its hands behind its head. I had to do some fast legwork. I set about patching into an outside data bank. It was a busy few seconds for me as I went all out to cajole and convince the FBI computer that I had a need to know, but Altick saw nothing of my feverish activity. All he saw was a private eye leaning back in thought, toothpick sticking out of mouth.

His shoulders drooped. ''I know. It's hopeless.''

I took out the toothpick, snapped it, and tossed it, in an elegantly plotted curve, into the wastebasket. ''Not quite, not quite. For openers, we know why the Soviets suddenly soured on you.''

''We do?''

''Look, your sunken skiff fouled their net, didn't it? Stands to reason they grew suspicious of you when they looked it over and the damage didn't seem the work of a swordfish. They probably gave the boat back by way of showing Uncle Sam that the spy had not fooled them. And that shows *us* that the sinking wasn't the work of their frogmen.''

''Frogmen!''

I was heavily patient. ''If we rule out the swordfish and your boat hook, that leaves a frogman with a harpoon or a spearfishing gun.''

''Ah!'' The color came back to his face and the life to his eyes.

''You're remembering the frogmen they had to untangle the nets. Forget them.''

''Why?''

''To Ivan, you were at first a harmless lobsterman, and only later a dangerous spy. To Uncle Sam, you were at first a harmless vacationer, and only later a dangerous traitor. Neither would have had any reason to scuttle the boat of someone harmless. Ivan wouldn't have sunk your boat only to hand you back to Uncle Sam. Uncle Sam wouldn't have sunk your boat only to put you in Ivan's hands.''

''Sounds logical. But where does that leave us?''

''If we rule out Ivan and Uncle Sam, that leaves a third party. There was no international incident. It would have taken more of a buildup, maybe the spilling of your blood, to have made it one. A Third World guerrilla group would not have hesitated to spill blood. So we rule out a frogman from a Third World guerrilla group trying to provoke an international incident. That leaves private enterprise. Let's look at the *Potluck*.''

''The sport fishermen? What motive?''

''Did you at any time notice a scuba diver or scuba gear aboard the *Potluck*? Think.''

''I'm thinking. No scuba diver, but it seems to me there were oxygen cylinders on deck. But why would anyone from the *Potluck* want to scuttle my skiff?''

''Because you were lucky and they weren't.'' I answered his stare with a smile. ''I know; you were after lobster and they were after shark or marlin or swordfish. But what if they were really after hash?''

''Hash?''

''Hashish, the resin of *Cannabis sativa*.'' I tossed off the expertise I had just got from the FBI computer. ''Pot, only five times stronger. I'm only guessing it was hash. But it had to be something like that.'' I sat up. ''Of course. What gall! *Pot* luck.'' I leaned back. ''Okay. The way it had to be, a smuggler dumped a plastic-wrapped package of hash off an ocean liner or a tramp steamer. The *Potluck* came to the spot and pretended to be fishing while a scuba diver went down to retrieve the package. Only the package had snagged in your lobster pot line or maybe even fell into the pot.

''The scuba diver, carrying a spearfishing gun against sharks, found you hauling the pot out of the water. He drove the spear through the bottom of your boat. Maybe he meant only to tip you over into the water and keep you busy floundering while he retrieved the package. But consider this: the usual drop is two hundred pounds, and two hundred pounds of hash would bring in two hundred grand. Men have killed and men have died for a hell of a lot less.''

Altick looked sick, or maybe just sad. I smiled a one-cornered smile of my own.

''Cheer up. You're not in the same boat you were in. We can tip off the law to put a nark watch on the *Potluck* and catch her on her next pickup. That should clean up your case all around.''

I looked at the wall clock. ''The night watchman's due to pass through this room in another three minutes. Now's the time to beat it.''

Altick got up and I watched him make ready to steal out, his shoulders already throwing off the weight of the world. He stood a moment, looking at me.

''Thanks,'' he said. Then he was gone.

Would he return to his star drive even though he knew men could turn a reach for the heavens into a fist against Earth? I drove that from my mind. I had my own problem to work out.

I went back to dreaming till after the night watchman had passed through. Then I went to work on my own problem. I had found I liked being a private eye, but I would need a secretary. It would be easy enough to program a simulation of one. The problem was, blonde or brunette? I could've flipped for it. Instead, I flipped for something else—a curvy redhead.

"Okay, sweetheart. Come in and take a letter."

Samuel Johnson

THE DISAPPEARING SERVANT WENCH
Lillian de la Torre

ELIZABETH CANNING went from her Friends between nine and ten on *Monday* Night, being New Year's Night; betwixt *Houndsditch & Bishopsgate,* fresh-coulour'd, pitted with y^e Small-pox, high Forehead, light Eyebrows, about five foot high, well-set, had on a purple masquerade-stuff Gown, black stuff Petticoat, a white Chip Hat bound round with green, white Apron and handkerchief, blue Stockings, and leather Shoes. Any Coachman, who remembers taking up such a Person, and can give any Account where she is, shall have Two Guineas Reward, to be paid by Mrs. *Canning*, in *Aldermanbury Postern*, Sawyer, which will greatly satisfy her Mother.

THESE LINES WERE roughly printed in the form of a handbill. My friend Dr. Sam: Johnson, *detector* of crime and chicane, produced the dog's-eared scrap of paper from the accumulations in his untidy book-garret in his house in Johnson's Court. I perused it with care.

"Pray, sir," I ventured, "have you still, in April, hopes of finding the girl? Sure the thing is all too plain. The lass hath been caught up and carried off by some rakish fellow, and now ten to one she plies a shameful trade by Covent Garden, and shames to return to her mother."

"No, sir, there you are out. The girl has returned to her home long since."

"Why, then, sir, the girl has told her tale, and there's an end on't."

"Yes, sir, the girl has told her tale indeed, and thence arises the puzzle."

"Pray tell it me."

"Why, thus sir: 'Twas King Charles's Martyrdom Eve, eight and twenty days after that fatal New Year's day, and the Sawyer's 'prentice was just upon locking the door for the night, when there comes a faint knocking. 'Tis Elizabeth Canning! She is sodden, and starving, and exhausted and blue, and her clothes are gone. Good lack, cries Goody Canning, Bet, what has happened to you? And Bet tells her tale. Stay, you shall hear it as she told it in Bow Street."

From a mass of old printed papers my bulky friend drew a thin pamphlet, and from it began to read out in his sonorous voice:

The INFORMATION *of Elizabeth Canning of Aldermanbury Postern, London,* Spinster.

    This Informant, upon her Oath, saith, that on Monday, the First Day of

January last past, she, this Informant, went to see her Uncle and Aunt, who live at Salt-Petre Bank, near Rosemary-Lane, in the County of Middlesex, and continued with them until the Evening; and saith, That upon her Return home, about Half an Hour after Nine, being opposite Bethlehem-gate in Moorfields, she, this Informant, was seized by two men (whose Names are unknown to her, this Informant) who both had brown Bob-wigs on, and drab-coloured Great-coats; one of whom held her, this Informant, whilst the other, feloniously and violently, took from her one Shaving Hat, one Stuff Gown, and one linen Apron, which she had on; and also, Half a Guinea in Gold, and three Shillings in Silver; and then he that held her threatened to do for this Informant. And this Informant saith, That, immediately after, they, the same two Men, violently took hold of her, and dragged her up into the Gravel-walk that leads down to the said Gate, and about the Middle thereof, he the said Man, that first held her, gave her, with his Fist, a very violent blow upon the right Temple, which threw her into a Fit, and deprived her of her Senses (which Fits, she, this Informant, saith she is accustomed and subject to, upon being frighted, and that they often continue for six or seven Hours. . . .)

"Stay, stay, sir," I implored, "for here is such a foyson of this Informant, and the said Informant, as carries me back to the court of Session, whence I am newly a truant; so pray, sir, give me the straight of the story without circumlocution."

"Well, then, sir: Bet Canning told a horrid tale, how these pandours in bog-wigs snatched her up by Bedlam Gate, and carried her off in her fit. They carried her off to a bawdy-house in the suburbs, said Bet; and there an old woman took her by the hand, and My dear, says she, will you go our way? For if you do, you shall have fine clothes. No, says Bet. Straightway the old woman takes up a carving-knife, and cuts the lace of the girl's stays, which the men in bob-wigs had overlooked, and takes them from her. Then she feels of the girl's petticoats. These are of no use, says she, I'll give you them. With that she gives the girl a great slap in the chops and turns her up a pair of stairs, half-naked as she was, into a kind of loft of shuffleboard room. There, said Betty, she found some old mouldy bread and a broken jug full of water; but for which, and a penny minced pye which she happened to have by her, she had starved to death. For eight-and-twenty days no soul came nigh her. On the five-and-twentieth day the bread was all gone. On the seven-and-twentieth day she ate her minced pye; and on the eight-and-twentieth day she broke out at the window and ran away home."

"Sure, sir," I cried, "these were no Christians, but heathen Turks, so to misuse a poor innocent girl!"

"Yet you will allow, sir, that 'tis an excess of Christianity, thus to suffer for eight and-twenty days an unnecessary martyrdom; for she who can break out at a window on the eight-and-twentieth day of fasting, might have done so with less fatigue on the first."

"Heathen Turks," I reiterated hotly, "and I heartily wish they may have been laid by the heels."

"As to Turks, Bozzy, you are not so far out; and as to laying by the heels, they were so. And a precious crew they proved to be, being the old bawd, Susannah Wells by name, and a parcel of gipsies, her lodgers. They carried the girl to the suburbs to identify the people and the place. This is the house, says Bet; this is the shuffleboard room; and these are the miscreants, says she, pointing at the gipsies. It was the old gipsy woman cut my stays; and I think, says she, I *think* the gipsy man her son was one of the men in bob-wigs; while as to the two gipsy wenches her daughters, though they laughed at me they did nothing to me. As to the old bawd, I don't know that ever I saw her in my life before."

"I hope," cried I, "that the whole precious crew have long since had their just deserts."

"No, sir," replied my friend coolly, " 'tis true, the world was once of your mind; Wells was branded in the hand, and the old gipsy woman was to hang for the stays. But the old woman found friends, who have so managed, that she had the King's pardon, and placed the girl in the dock in her stead."

"Upon what charge?" I cried.

"Upon a charge of perjury."

"Monstrous!" I exclaimed angrily. "How mean you, friends? The publican of some ale-house under a hedge?"

"No, sir," replied Dr. Johnson. "I will name but one: the Lord Mayor of London."

I gaped.

"You have wished to see the sights of London," remarked my friend. "Here is one you are not to pass by. The girl takes her trial today."

Now it was clear why my friend had caused me to hear the girl's story. The curtain was about to rise on a new act of the drama.

"Will you come, sir?"

"No, sir. I am too old and too thick in the middle to batter my way into the press at the Old Bailey."

I was young and spry. I clapped on my three-cornered hat and made off down Fleet Street to the Sessions House in the ancient street known as the Old Bailey.

Before I had turned the corner a muttering sound told me of the crowd that was milling uneasily in the paved court-yard. I was not to be daunted. I butted and pushed my way until I stood, half-suffocated, under the balcony and close by the dock.

On the long bench at the front sat the justices of Oyer and Terminer, the lawyers in robes, the aldermen with their chains of office about their necks. On the floor before them a spry man with his big-wig pushed back was talking in brisk tenor tones. But I had no eyes for them.

On the raised platform of the dock, clinging to the rail that fenced it, stood the girl. She was a stocky chit, no higher than five feet, drest in a clean linnen gown. She wore buckled shoes and a decent lawn kerchief, and her plain cap was fastened under her chin. The light fell on her pink, expressionless face. The spry lawyer was describing her in unflattering terms as a liar for profit; but the large blue eyes never flickered. Elizabeth Canning looked at him as if he weren't there at all.

Then her eyes shifted, and I followed her gaze. Seated to one side, in a large armed chair, sat the most hideous old hag I had ever had the misfortune to see. She was bent, and tremulous, and swarthy. Swathing clouts half-hid a face like a night-mare. She had a great frog's mouth smeared all over the lower half of her face. Her chin was aflame with the purple scars of an old disease, and her swarthy hooked nose jutted over all. This was Mary Squires, the gipsy beldame. She was attended by a sparkling dark girl and a trim-built young gipsy man.

I could not read the stolid girl's expression, as she looked at her enemy. It held neither indignation nor remorse, but something more like puzzlement.

For ten mortal hours I stood on my feet as the gipsy's witnesses followed one another on the stand.

"How is it with Canning?" asked Dr. Johnson as I supped with him. "Is she cast?"

"No, sir," I replied. "There are prosecution witnesses still to come, spare the defence; for length this trial bids fair to make history."

"Pray, how will it go?"

"Sir," I replied, "ill, I fear. Here have been forty witnesses come up from Dorset to swear an alibi for yonder gipsy hag. She was strolling, they will stand to it, through the Dorset market-towns peddling such smuggled goods as she might come by in the sea-ports. Here has been a most respectable witness, an exciseman, who will swear it, that they lay in the excise office at Abbotsbury on the very night. Here have been landlords of inns from Abbotsbury to London to trace them on their way, bar only a four-days' journey from Coombe to Basingstoke. They came to Enfield full three weeks after Canning absconded. How 'tis managed I know not, but the girl is devoted to doom.''

A knocking interrupted my discourse. The knocker proved to be a heavy-set red-faced man. He was accompanied by a younger man, a spindle-shanked sandy fellow with a long nose. Between them they supported a weeping woman. The woman was fortyish, and ample to overflowing.

The sandy young man burst immediately into speech.

''Robert Scarrat, hartshorn-rasper, at your service, sir, which I rasps hartshorn on a piece basis for Mrs. Waller of Old 'Change, and her son is tenant to Mrs. Canning here.''

The weeping woman snuffled and confirmed the hartshorn-rasper with a nod.

''This here,'' the nervous strident tones hurried on, ''is by name John Wintlebury, as is landlord of the Weavers Arms, and Bet Canning was a servant in his house.''

'' 'Tis a good wench,'' rumbled the publican.

''Nevertheless they have contrived her ruin among them,'' cried the woman, ''and will transport her to the plantations—unless you, sir, would undertake to clear up the matter.''

''You must tell me,'' replied my friend, ''what they are saying about her.''

'' 'Tis never true that I hid her for my gain,'' cried out the weeping mother, smearing her bleared eyes with a thick finger, ''for I never had rest, day nor night, for wondering where she was. Mostly I thought her dead in Houndsditch, sir, or catched up by some rakish young fellow. I had dreams and wandering thoughts, and I prayed day and night to have a vision of her. But the cunning man said—''

''The cunning man?''

''A mere piece of woman's folly, sir,'' muttered the innkeeper, but Mrs. Canning paid him no mind.

''The cunning man in the Old Bailey. I went to him to have news of her, he had a black wig over his face.''

''What said he?''

''Not a word, sir, only wrote, scribble, scribble, scribble along. He said, an old black woman had my daughter, and she would return soon.''

"Ay," chimed in the hartshorn-rasper, his prominent hazel eyes rolling with superstitious awe, "is't not strange, sir?"

Mrs. Canning shuddered, and sobbed harder than ever. The landlord laid his hand on the woman's arm.

"Be easy, ma'am," he said gently, "for we know Bet's a good girl, and Dr. Johnson will soon make the matter clear. No need to take the hystericks over it."

The woman moaned. Scarrat took up the tale.

"Nor 'tis not true," he went on, "that I went off with the girl for my pleasure, for she was unknown to me."

"Ay," seconded the landlord, "for all the time she lived in my house, she was modest and shy, and would scarce so much as go to the door to speak to a man; and though Mr. Scarrat frequented the house, they never exchanged a word."

"And," cried the spindly man, growing hot, "as to my forging this tale, out of revenge against the bawd, 'tis false as Hell, though indeed I owe the creature no kindness."

"A notorious woman," said Wintlebury, "I knew of her infamous brothel when I lived and courted in Hertford."

"Oh, pray, pray, Dr. Johnson," sobbed out the weeping mother, "will not you help us?"

"Do, sir," I seconded. "Could you but see the vile face of the gipsy hag, you would rush to the girl's defence."

"As to faces," replied my friend, "there's no art to find in them the mind's construction; as to helping, if I must come down to the Old Bailey, 'twill not do."

The fat woman gave a howl and fell to the floor in a paroxysm. There was instant confusion. The fat friend and the thin one fell to slapping her wrists, while I applied under her snubby nose the hartshorn-bottle which was perhaps the fruit of Mr. Scarrat's endeavors.

When she had gasped and sat up, I turned to my kindly friend.

"Pray give your assistance," I begged. "I will be your deputy to the Old Bailey."

My friend accepted of my offer, and the friends of Canning departed in better cheer.

Only the fame of my companion gained us access to the gipsy. She sat in the best room of the White Horse, in the Haymarket, and regarded us sardonically with black, beady eyes. She was surrounded by a court of

Dorsetshire fishermen, King's landwaiters, and gipsies in leather breeches. Her pretty daughter sat hand in hand with a tall man in fustian; I recognized with a start one of the principal witnesses for the prosecution, a cordwainer of Dorset. A black-browed little raisin of a man turned out to be the girl's uncle, Samuel Squires, a landwaiter of the customs right here in London and a gipsy of considerable influence.

Dr. Johnson ran a lowering eye over the motley crew; the men of the customs particularly took his eye. Then he waved them all away, and to my relief they went.

"Now, ma'am," says Dr. Johnson, "Out with it. There's more in this than meets the eye."

The beady eyes measured him.

"I will confess," said the rusty voice.

I thrilled to my toes. The girl was saved!

"I'll confess. Though I have passed myself for a strolling pedlar, I am in reality—"

Dr. Johnson leaned forward.

"I am in reality—a *witch*. I can be present at *two* places at one time," whispered the old beldame with hoarse and ostentatious caution, "and though all these people saw me in Dorset, I nevertheless carried Canning to Enfield on my *broom-stick*—"

Dr. Johnson cut short her triumphant cackle by rising to his feet.

"Have a care, ma'am," he said angrily, "I am not be be trifled with."

The old hag leaned back and laughed in his face.

"I know you are no witch," my friend went on grimly, "but I will tell you what you are."

He spoke three words in her ear. Her face changed. She looked at him with more respect. "Ah," she said, "I see you are in the councils of the great."

"I can see a church by daylight," replied Johnson as we withdrew.

I made off, being engaged to dine with some ladies in St. James's, but Dr. Johnson turned into the tap-room and lingered.

"Alack, Mr. Boswell," he told me when again we met. "Alas for Bet Canning, the rustics are honest. I had their story over a can of ale, and with such a wealth of detail as can scarce be forgery. The honest cordwainer loves the gipsy wench; he dallied eight days in their company at Abbotsbury, and when they departed he followed them on the road. There are landlords to swear to them all, and the things they saw and the meals they ate. So rich is the tale, it must be more than mendacious invention."

"Yet who pays," I cried, "who pays the scot of the poor gipsy pedlar and her forty witnesses at the White Horse in the Haymarket? Who keeps them in victuals and gin?"

"My Lord Mayor, 'tis said," replied my companion. "But come, Mr. Boswell, let me know your mind: shall we push forward and uncover the truth, wherever it lies? Or shall we leave Bet Canning to her luck with the jury?"

"Let us wait," I replied uneasily, "and see."

I filled the days of waiting in the court-room of the Old Bailey, where each day the girl sat in the dock with her wrists crossed before her, and looked on without expression while witnesses called her liar or martyr.

"How goes the trial, Bozzy?" demanded my friend as I returned bedraggled from another day's session.

"Ill, for the girl, ill," I replied dejectedly. "You may know how ill, when I tell you that the Lord Mayor was pelted by the resentful Canningite rabble as he came away from the Sessions-house. The girl has been made to appear a liar. Before the sitting Aldermen, so he has sworn, she described her prison to be little, square, and dark. Then they took her to Enfield; when it appeared that the room she swore to was long and light, with many other contradictions. I know not what to think."

"A starved girl, after long imprisonment, may surely exhibit some confusion," suggested Dr. Johnson thoughtfully.

"There is more," I replied. "From Enfield came many witnesses, who swore that they visited her supposed prison during that month, and saw there no such person as Elizabeth Canning."

"What said the girl to this?"

"Never a word, save once. 'Twas a son of Wells's testified, he stepped into the shuffleboard room to lay by his tools, for he is a carpenter, and there was no soul there save the labouring man that lodged there. Bet Canning leaned forward, and scanned him closely. She frowned, and looked him up and down. *I never saw him before, as I know of,* says she."

"Why did she so?"

"Who can tell? 'Tis a strange wench. Just so, by the evidence, did she comport herself when they took her to Enfield: would not be sure of the gipsy man, could not be sure she had ever seen Wells. Only the gipsy woman she swore to without hesitation. They report strange things of the girl, too, in Wells's loft. *Do you remember that six-foot nest of drawers?* says they. *I never saw it before,* says Miss. *Do you remember the hay and the saddles stored up here?* says they. She scratches her head. *I will not swear,* says she, *but there is more hay. As to the saddles, I remember one only. But there was a grate,* says she. *O no,* says they, *look for yourself. There's no grate and never had been: look at the cobwebs. There was a grate,* says she, *and from it I took the rags I wore when I fled. There was never a grate,* says they."

"Is it so!" cried my venerable friend. "Here is no liar, but one trying to speak the truth. Bozzy, we must save this girl!"

I stared. The evidence, that had shaken my faith in the girl, had spoken quite otherwise to him. It had spoken with such clear moral force and conviction that it stirred his great bulk, and brought it next morning into the court-room of the Old Bailey.

He cleared his way through the press like a bailiff, with jerks of his sturdy oak staff. We were in time to hear the defence begin. The crowd murmured in sympathy as Bet's sad story was repeated by her friends as they had heard it from her on that Monday in January. All her natural functions were suspended, related the apothecary in sepulchral tones, the whole time of her imprisonment; she was very faint and weak, and the black-and-blue marks never went off for a month afterwards. My venerable friend shook his head from side to side, and clicked his tongue.

Burning glances of sympathy were levelled at the abused girl where she sat impassive in the dock as the story was told. They changed to looks of triumph as the defence brought aces out of their sleeves—a witness who had seen the girl led past his turnpike, in tears, by a pair of ruffians; three persons who had seen the bedraggled creature returning in the misty evening.

Dr. Johnson, seated on a bench with his chin on his staff, frowned and shook his head.

"How can this help?" he muttered. "The girl swore she was dragged off in a fit. Now we find she walked by the turnpike. Where is truth to be found?"

The defence rested.

It was three o'clock the next morning when I knocked up my friend.

"The girl is cast!" I told him. "She will be transported."

"Cast!" exclaimed my friend. "What this girl has been, I know not; but she is no perjurer."

A double knock announced a later walker than I. Again it was John Wintlebury and Robert Scarrat.

"You must help us!" cried the hartshorn-rasper. "Can you give us no hope?"

"Only this, that the girl is innocent," replied my friend. "I will do what I can. Where is the girl?"

"Alack," exclaimed the volatile Scarrat, "in Newgate."

"Then we must have her out."

That was easier said than done, but Johnson managed it. Scarrat carried the request. Meanwhile, off went the black boy Francis to the White Horse. He came back with a note:

> *She says she will come, if only to laugh.*
>
> *Ma: Squires*

The old gipsy woman herself was not far behind. Next to arrive was Mother Wells. She came supported by the carpenter son. My friend received his curious callers with solemn dignity, and offered them cakes and port. The wrinkled old bawd guzzled hers with coarse greed.

It was still dark night when a sedan-chair turned into Johnson's Court. It was attended by two turnkeys and followed by our friends, once again supporting between them the highstrung matron. All three tenderly extracted from the chair the stocky person of Elizabeth Canning, and so she was assisted up the stair.

Dr. Johnson took her hand.

"Do not be afraid, my dear."

"I am not afraid," said Bet Canning.

She looked levelly at the hideous old gipsy hag, then at the bawd. The latter wiped a drool of port off her chin. Dr. Johnson handed the girl to a chair, her friends found places, and a hush fell as everyone in the room looked toward my learned friend.

"My dear," said Dr. Johnson, addressing himself to the girl, "there are those who think you are lying. I do not think you are lying."

"Thank you, sir."

The gipsy beldame, a mere huddle of rags except for her bright black eyes, snorted.

"But, my dear," my friend continued quietly, "there is much that is dark, much that you have not been able to tell us."

"I have told," said Bet Canning clearly, "all that I know."

"We must look further, then. There is one in this cause," said Dr. Johnson, "who seemed a knowledgeable man."

I leaned forward.

"Who?"

"The cunning man," replied my learned friend solemnly. "He knew where Elizabeth was, and he wrote it down, scribble, scribble, scribble along. He was right. I would have consulted him myself, but he is not to be found. There is no conjurer in the Old Bailey."

"I saw him there myself," cried Mrs. Canning. "He had his wig over his face; and when he lighted up the candles, he frighted me, and I could not stay for more."

"Well, well, he is gone away from thence, he is no longer to be consulted. We must make do without him."

He produced a leather case, which being opened revealed a gleaming polished ball of some black substance.

"This," said Dr. Johnson solemnly, "is the famous Black Stone of Dr. Dee the alchemist. I had it of Mr. Walpole against this night's purpose. Into it," he lowered his sonorous voice another pitch, "the alchemist used to call his spirits, and they revealed the truth to him."

Nobody spoke.

Dr. Johnson extinguished the candles, all but one, which gleamed fitfully on the table, accentuating rather than piercing the darkness. For a moment there was dead silence.

"Before the spirits speak," said Dr. Johnson, "has no one a word to tell us?"

I heard somebody gasp. The old gipsy was shaking and muttering to herself, it might have been a charm or an incantation. Mrs. Canning was crying again, in long shuddering gasps, and the hartshorn-rasper was twitching where he sat. Only the stolid inn-keeper and the cynical old bawd preserved an unbroken calm.

Elizabeth Canning's gaze caught and hung on the gleaming speculum. Her plain face was white as paper.

"Pray, my girl," said Dr. Johnson gently, "look into the magick stone of Dr. Dee, and tell us what you see."

"I see nothing," she faltered.

"You will see the truth," said my friend. "Look well, and tell us what you see."

The girl stared into the polished surface, scarcely seeming to breathe. Her eyes contracted to pin-points. She sat rigid.

"It is the night of January 1," breathed my friend in the silence. "Do you see Elizabeth Canning?"

"I see her."

The voice was tight and high, and seemed to come from a long way off.

"I see Elizabeth Canning. She is walking between two men, and weeping. It is a road, with water in it. Now they turn into a house, there is an old woman there.''

''Swarthy and black?''

''No, grey and wrinkled. She takes away her clothes, and puts her into a room.''

''Without any furniture?''

''No,'' replied the trance-like voice. ''No, it is the best bedroom. The door opens, and the man comes in. Now Elizabeth can see his face. It is he. It is the same man who wanted Elizabeth to do the bad thing, always and always he was at her elbow saying it to her, and she would not. Now he is here to do it, and Elizabeth cannot help herself.''

In a violent shudder the dreaming voice died away. For a moment there was silence in the room.

''Here,'' muttered Wintlebury finally, ''you must stop this, sir, you've bewitched the girl to her hurt. Who knows what she'll say?''

''She'll say the truth,'' said Dr. Johnson sharply. ''Be silent, sir, and listen.''

He spoke soothingly to the rigid girl.

''It is the eve of King Charles's Martyrdom. Do you see Elizabeth Canning?''

''I see her.''

''Where is she?''

''She is in the loft. The wicked man has left her behind, they have taken away her clothes, she cannot eat for shame. Because she would not do the bad thing with other men, they have beaten her and thrust her into the loft. She wants to go home, but she does not know where home is. She has forgotten her name. She has forgotten everything. She is very wretched.''

Again the level voice died away.

''And then?''

The polished ball gleamed in the candlelight. The girl's eyes were like pin-points.

''And then she hears her name spoken, and she knows it is hers. She looks down into the kitchen and sees the ugly-face gipsy. She is hungry and cold and afraid. The minced pye is still in the pocket of her torn petticoat; it is stale and dry, but she eats it. She takes an old rag from the fireplace to wrap herself in, and breaks out at the window, and runs away home.''

''But the grate?'' I struck in.

"A saw across the fireplace," said a quiet voice in my ear. It was the young carpenter. "My cross-cut saw."

"She runs away home. They ask where she has been for four weeks; but she has forgotten. Only it seems to her that she was somewhere hungry and cold, and she has been somehow harmed, the ugly-face woman must have done it, and her clothes are gone; so she tells them as best she can what must have happened, and they believe her, and are very angry. Even the man who did the bad thing to her, he is angry too, and wants the gipsy hanged. Elizabeth has forgotten what he did to her; she thinks he is her friend."

"The man," Dr. Johnson leaned forward gently, "who was the man?"

"That's enough of this flummery," came an angry voice. "Can't you see that the girl is mad?"

A rough hand struck aside the magick speculum of Dr. Dee. Elizabeth Canning looked up into an out-thrust face, somehow distorted in the flickering light of the candle from below, and recoiled with scream after scream of terror. Then the candle flame was struck out, and footsteps clattered on the stair.

"Let him go," said Dr. Johnson. "Mr. John Wintlebury is not the first to enforce his desires on a virtuous serving-wench, and I fear there's no law to touch him."

"I'll touch him," cried the hartshorn-rasper violently. "I'll—I'll rasp him!"

He held the shuddering girl tight against his shoulder. He touched her pale hair.

"She's not mad, sir?" he pleaded.

"Not the least in the world," replied my friend, "yet hers is a strong affliction. The learned call it the catalepsy. One so afflicted may preach, or prophesy, or fast without hunger, or cut his flesh with knives, and not feel it; or fall unconscious and lie as the dead; or believe the body's functions to be pretermitted; or they may upon great suffering or shame forget who they are, and wander homeless until they remember. It was Mr. John Wintlebury's good luck that the wronged girl forgot him and the wrong he did her, and even herself, for very shame."

"And my bad luck," croaked the gipsy crone, "for the story that came from her disturbed mind put me into jeopardy of my life."

"You were never in jeopardy, being what you are," returned Dr. Johnson.

"What are you?" I burst out uncontrollably.

"A customs spy," replied the old witch, "and a good one, young man. Who'd ever suspect the old gipsy beggar when she came nosing about the barns? I knew every smugglers' lay on that coast. O no, me Lord Treasurer wouldn't have let the old gipsy woman hang. 'Twas but a few nights lying hard in gaol; he could not move openly in the matter, for fear of betraying me and mine to the smugglers. In the end me Lord Mayor had his orders, and I was enlarged."

"And Mother Wells?" I touched flint and steel to the candle.

"It all happened," my friend replied, "of course, in her house of assignation; it was she who beat the girl when she would not go the way of the house."

I advanced the candle toward the old bawd's corner. The lees of her port were there in the glass, but the old woman was gone.

"Upon her," remarked Dr. Johnson, "justice has been done. You will remember that, although Mary Squires was pardoned, Susannah Wells has been branded on the hand for her part in the work."

Elizabeth Canning's sobs had died away, and she lay in a sleep like death against the hartshorn-rasper's shoulder.

"When she awakes," he asked, "will she remember?"

"I cannot say," replied my learned friend. "Perhaps she will remember everything. If not, you must tell her, gently, over and over, until the two times join into one in her mind and she no longer has those agonizing moments of trying to remember, like the time in the loft, or in the dock when she struggled to remember the young carpenter."

He pulled aside the heavy curtains and let in the dawn.

"Tomorrow," he said, "I will wait upon the Secretary of State."

The sun was up as the sleepy turnkeys rouzed to help lift the unconscious girl back into the sedan-chair. My benevolent friend followed it with his eyes to the mouth of the court.

"The issue of this night's sitting," he remarked with a half-smile, "has exceeded expectation. I reasoned that someone close to the girl knew where she was, else why the cunning man with the muffled face, who must write his predictions? Clearly his face and his voice were known. I brought her friends together, and produced a conjuration of my own. I hoped that superstition would affright one of them, and even that the girl might take courage and 'see' in the speculum what perhaps she had been frighted from telling. I never guessed that so strange is the mind in a catalepsy that it will see truly, as it were in a sleep, what it has forgotten in waking."

TAKE IT AND LIKE IT
Frederick Nebel

K ENNEDY WAS STANDING on the corner of Hallam and German
Streets when he saw the girl pass rubber-kneed beneath a street light
halfway down German. There was was a moon somewhere in the April
sky but its light did not reach into German Street. German Street was
narrow, barricaded on either side by two- and three-storied houses of
brick or wood, many of them untenanted. Kennedy lived a block up
Hallam in a rooming-house. He had moved into it a week before and had
started out tonight, ten minutes ago, for a place to eat. Someone had said
there was a good chili joint in the neighborhood and he was trying to get
his bearings.

He was moderately sober, and leaning indolently against the pole, he
saw what he took to be the shape of the girl coming back up the street. He
could tell by the sound of her heels that she walked irregularly, but he
was not greatly interested. She had the gait of a drunk, and being drunk,
he often said, was one's own business. He did not remain leaning against
the pole because he was in any way interested in the girl but because he
was puzzled how to get to the chili joint. The wine there, they said, was
excellent, and if wine is excellent it doesn't matter much about the food.

The girl was coming up on the opposite sidewalk and he hoped she
would stay on the opposite sidewalk; but presently she crossed the street
and came staggering on towards him. He thought of moving on, but he
wasn't sure yet about the chili joint and he had no notion of going out of
his way, even for a block. When he was drunk he would wander all over
Richmond City, but being practically sober, it was a different matter.

She came on towards him and she must have seen him, for the pole
against which he leaned had a light halfway up; and in the pool of light he
was a slight, frail figure in an unpressed gray suit and a gray fedora

whose brim was pulled down all around. He had about him an air of languid, washed-out decadence. As the girl came closer, staggering, coughing in the silent street, he turned his head the other way.

But she crashed into him. She coughed as she crashed into him and he turned around casually and saw her careening backwards. She was bent over a bit, her legs were bent and she gave the impression of staggering flat-footed. He hoped she would not fall but made no move to prevent her doing so.

She did not fall.

"I—I b-beg your pardon," she muttered hoarsely.

"It's all right, kid. Only why don't you grab a cab and go home? Slamming around the streets this way—"

"I can't go home."

She was braced against a house wall now, her hands pressed back against its rough surface, her fingers splayed. Her hat was cocked over one eye; it wasn't cocked over one eye because of any trend of style but because it appeared to have been shunted that way. She wore a dark coat with a thin band of some dark light-weight fur around the collar.

"You see," she panted hoarsely, shaking her head, "I—I just can't go home."

"Drink," he said, "has always been the curse of the going-home classes. But what's the sense of slamming around the streets all night? Choose a convenient doorway, park yourself and let it pass."

"Please," she begged, "do something."

"I'm sorry, madam. I'm trying to find a chili joint. Do you happen to know of a chili joint around here where the wine's supposed to be the nuts?"

"Please!" her voice begged from the shadow her face was in.

"Please what?"

"Help me. J-just—well, haven't you a place where I could—well— lie down, rest?"

He lit a cigarette. "You've got a nice voice."

"Thank you."

She pushed herself away from the building. "I—I didn't mean to bother you. I'll go on." She staggered and her knees were no good and she fell down and cried a little, not much. She remained on her knees, bracing herself with her arms.

Kennedy moved across the sidewalk, bent over not farther than he had to and took hold of the girl's arm.

"Snap out of it. A couple of more headers like that and you'll get your face lifted. Try helping yourself. Come on. I'm no heavyweight. Let's go. One . . . two . . . three. That's a girl. Hold it now.'' She was on her feet.

He did not release her arm. She did not look at him but looked away as though ashamed. Her hat was a little more over one eye; patches of hair sprouted unbecomingly from beneath it but she was not a bad looking girl. She was very good looking.

He sighed. ''Okey, come on. I've got a room up the street where you can sleep it off. But don't expect me to stay there with you. I've got to find this chili joint. Come on.''

She hung her head as they walked up Hallam Street. Her feet dragged and her breath still came out hoarsely, sometimes with a transient sob. Kennedy walked her up the four steps of the wooden stoop, held on to her with one hand while he used the other to get out his keys. He unlocked the hall door and prodded her into the corrider. His room was on the main floor, in the rear, and on the way down the corridor she stumbled and suddenly giggled. It was a mad little giggle, hysterical, and Kennedy muttered:

''For crying out loud, shut up. I just moved in here.''

He got her into his room. It was a large room, old-fashioned, with a brass bed against one wall and an old rolltop desk against the other. There was a table in the middle on which stood a couple of bottles, rye and gin, and there was a Morris chair and a Boston rocker.

He let her fall on the bed, then took hold of her legs, lifted them on to the bed and rolled her over to the middle of it. She lay panting and sobbing a little, but he had had crying jags himself and did not mind. He unrolled a blanket and tossed it over her.

''Stop it! Stop it!'' she cried, and kicked the blanket off.

''Yell like that again,'' he told her, ''and I'll toss you out.''

She began sobbing loudly. He had no intention of trying to talk her out of crying; it would have been useless. So he sat down, sighed, called himself a fool and poured half a water-glass of rye. He drank it from time to time, savoring it with pursed lips. When at last her sobbing sounded subdued and far away he drained the glass, rose and went out, hoping she would be gone by the time he got back.

He walked down to Hallam and German again and leaned against the pole and in a few minutes the cop on the beat came along. He was a young cop, rosy-cheeked, who twirled his nightstick with a self-conscious arrogance.

''You got a home?'' he said to Kennedy.

"Sure," drawled Kennedy, unimpressed.

"Go to it, then."

"This pole private or something?"

"Crackin', huh? So you're crackin'?"

"By the way, do you know where there's a chili joint around here?"

"I don't like chili."

"Neither do I. But I heard they serve swell wine there."

"And I don't like wine."

"What do you drink?"

"Milk! Three times a day!"

Kennedy pushed himself away from the pole. "Take a tip, copper. Give it up. It probably sours on your stomach and makes you that way."

The cop growled threateningly: "Little man—"

"What now?"

"Scram outta here!"

Kennedy sauntered off singing under his breath: "You're a big meany . . . "

II

MacBride was working overtime, trying to catch up on matters that had accrued during his leave of absence. He and his wife had toured the Southern States in the new flivver. In Richmond, Virginia, he had driven through a red light, crashed into a truck and lost his right fender and in Philadelphia he had been arrested for driving the wrong way on a one-way street. But all in all they had had a nice time and the skipper looked fit, brown, and got rid of the matters on hand, one by one, with a swift, hard precision.

He barked into the inter-office annunciator: "Bogardus on deck!" fanned a cloud of pipe smoke from in front of his face and puffed new clouds—strong, Burley tobacco—into its place.

Sergeant Bogardus came in holding a half-eaten ham sandwich behind his back and MacBride said:

"I'll not waive this charge!" and jabbed at a memorandum on his desk. "The bird drove through the red light and red lights are put up to stop, not to drive through. If we put up red lights and people drive through them, what the hell's use of putting up red lights?"

"Yes, sir, Cap'n."

"And you, Bogey—either swallow what you're eating or spit it out."

Bogardus swallowed, the effort making his eyes bulge.

"And what," MacBride wanted to know, "is that racket upstairs?"

"That's Moriarity, I think, trying a new back flip."

"Tell him to lay off. A person'd think this was the Y.M.C.A. instead of police headquarters. I go away for a while and come back and find a lot of clowns around. . . . Okey, Bogey. Beat it. How's the new kid?"

"Swell, Cap'n."

"Great. See he eats lots of spinach."

Ike Cohen poked his head to say: "You busy, Cap?"

"I'm always busy."

"Well, a call just came in. Murder or something over in the East End. Bettdecken's just getting it over the wire."

"Get—" MacBride winced at the sound of a heavy thump on the floor above; he looked up at the ceiling and said: "Get Mory. The potato's upstairs flipping back flips. Get him before he lands on his pants and knocks his brains out. Tell Gahagan to get out the car. You and Mory be down the garage. I'll shoot down in two shakes and pick up the full dope from Bettdecken. Who was it?"

"Who was it what?"

"Murdered."

"I just heard Bettdecken saying something about a Jane."

"Who's calling in?"

"Chatterson. A new cop on the beat."

"Okey. Mory. Gahagan. The car. I'll be down in a shake."

"Oke."

It was a cool night, but not too cool. Spring was in the air, the first flush of it, and though the police car sped along on dry cement the haunting smell of lush earth was somehow in the air. The moon could be seen from this broad avenue. The stars winked, some broadly and some faintly. The skipper took his pipe from his mouth so that he might better fill his lungs with the night air. His cheeks were ruddy in the glow of the dash-light, his jaw brown as a nut and hard as a nut and his eyes made two bright glitters beneath his wiry brows.

"Where's Kennedy been keeping himself?" Moriarity asked. "That guy's usually as familiar around the place as a spittoon."

"He got fired," MacBride said.

"I know he got fired but that wouldn't—"

"Did you hear why?" MacBride said, looking over his shoulder into the darkened tonneau.

"No."

MacBride gave a short, guttural laugh. "Boy, if that guy ain't a lulu! He takes the cake and the berries that go with it. Well, it was like this. I heard it. Just today. I called up Flannery, the editor, trying to get him to give Kennedy his job back. So what? So this: They put Kennedy on the dramatic page for a spell and what does the bunny do one night but get tight and go review a play at the Channock Theatre. In the first intermission he goes out and goes across the street to a bar for a drink. Well, he met a friend. Sure, he's always meeting a friend.

"So he takes about six highballs aboard and is plastered to the eyes when he leaves. He toddles across the street and sits till the end of the show. He writes next day that it's a lousy show; that he can't make head or tail of it; that in the first act the heroine's a blonde and in the last act she's a brunette; that in the first act the hero's a Scandinavian and in the last he's Wop. Well, what do you think? When they check up they find that Kennedy was so tight that he went back to another theater, the one next door, and saw the last act of another show, thinking it was the show he'd gone in to see first. Can you tie that! Can you!"

Cohen roared. "Boy-oh-boy-oh-boy!"

"I always figured," Moriarity said, "that guy would grow up to be a bum."

"Ah-r-r," growled MacBride, half-defensively. "He's no bum. He's got more brains than you can shake a fist at, only he rents them out all the time."

Moriarity insisted: "He'll wind up cutting paper dolls."

"Anyhow," MacBride said, "they'll be the best paper dolls."

Gahagan said: "This's the street, ain't it?"

"Yeah, make a right," MacBride said.

The car swung right, went up a slight grade. They could see the red-tinted headlights of the ambulance, and when they drew up on the wrong side of the street, facing the tinted headlights, they saw a crowd on the sidewalk. Patrolman Chatterson was standing on the wooden stoop. He was young, rosy-cheeked, and possessed of a self-conscious arrogance.

MacBride swung out. "You Chatterson?"

The cop touched his nightstick to his visor. "Yes, sir, Cap'n MacBride."

"Who's upstairs?"

"Ambulance doctor. It ain't no use, though."

A roadster braked sharply at the curb and Rube Wilson, Assistant District Attorney, hopped out and rapped patent leather dancing shoes across the sidewalk, sharply elbowing people out of his way. He was a small, wiry man, young, with a tight jaw and a black velour hat raked over one ear. He wore a topcoat over a tuxedo.

"What's to it, MacBride?"

"Let's go in and see. You too, Chatterson. Mory, Ike, shoo these folks off."

When they went into the room the ambulance doctor and the ambulance chauffeur were placing the girl on a stretcher.

"Hi, law," the doctor said. "Vespers will be sung. Hey, copper, why didn't you call the Morgue bus?"

"It says in the book of rules and regulations page forty—"

"Forget I mentioned it. When'd you get back, MacBride?"

"Who is she?" Rube Wilson said.

"Am I a mind reader?"

MacBride said: "Drunk?"

"There's the odor of liquor."

MacBride turned to Chatterson. "Who called you?"

"The woman runs the place."

"Where is she?"

"She just went in her kitchen before you come account of she's baking some bread. I was mozeyin' along and I seen her run out on the stoop and she seen me and calls me. So I run up and she says, 'There's a woman inside. I think she's dead or somethin'.' So I run in with her and, sure enough, she looks dead."

"How long's she lived here?" Rube Wilson tossed in.

"She don't. She—"

At this moment the rooming-house mistress appeared in the doorway. She was large, fat, with neatly plaited gray hair and a red face, big red hands.

"What's your name?" MacBride said.

"Hannah Mecklinborg. I tell you, officer, it's an outrage!"

"Never saw her before, huh?" MacBride asked.

"Never! But—I heard her come in. Anyhow, I think it was her. She came in with the fellow rents this room. They sounded drunk. She was giggling and when they got in the room there must have been a fight. I heard her yell, "Stop it! Stop it!' Just like that. I—well, I was in the hall at that time, and I thought I ought to knock on the door, but then they calmed down, so I went on about my business. Intending, though, you understand, to give the fellow a piece of my mind tomorrow. Then after a while I thought I heard them going out. But then after a while again, I was in the hall and I heard a thump in the room. I don't know why, but I was scared, and I knocked, and when I got no answer I tried the door. I opened it and, well, there she was on the floor alongside the bed.''

''Was she dressed?''

''Yes, all dressed. I thought maybe she'd managed to get dressed and then fainted. So it must have been the fellow went out alone.''

Rube Wilson flung at the doctor: ''What do you make of it?''

''One thing, she was beaten up. Her body's full of bruises and there's a lump on her head. I'd say she died from the beating, offhand. Possibly a blood clot on the brain.''

Macbride turned to Hannah Mecklinborg. ''What time would you say they came in?''

''Seven-thirty. I know because I was putting a cake in the oven.''

''And what time did you hear the fellow go out?''

''About, I gucss, half an hour later.''

''And what time did you open this door and find the woman?''

''At about nine.''

''And what's the guy's name lives here?''

''His name is Kennedy. A newspaper man, I think.''

MacBride's head jerked on his neck.

''Hotcha!'' Rube Wilson rapped out. ''I always thought that guy would wind up like this. And he had the crust once to tell me to my face that as Assistant District Attorney I was a blister on the heel of progress and would I please burst some day. Boy, I like this! Boy, how I like this!

Patrolman Chatterson said to Hannah Mecklinborg: ''What did he look like?''

She described him.

Chatterson swelled up, his eyes glittering. ''I seen that mugg! I seen him! Just a few minutes after he committed the crime!'' He leveled an arm, ''At German and Hallam. He wisecracked me! I told him—he was hangin' around—I told him to move on and he wisecracked me! It was him, I'll bet. He said something like I had a bad disposition and it was because I drank milk that soured on my stomach.''

MacBride let out a deep, rueful sigh. ''That was him.''

III

They stood in MacBride's office: Moriarity, Cohen and the skipper himself. They had just come in and still wore their hats and the three of them stood looking down at the shiny surface of the skipper's desk. They had, it seemed, not much to say. They were cops, the three of them; good cops, with fine records; but they were also human beings. Kennedy had for long been like one of them. Many times one or all of them had felt like socking the erstwhile newshawk, but that was neither here nor there; not now. They were after all plain men, ordinary men, with plain and ordinary emotions, and in the last analysis the law, even to its most militant members, is not so strong a thing that it can wipe out, instantly, these common emotions.

MacBride said at last, in a low, clogged voice: "The thing is—it's so damned out and out."

"Yeah," nodded Cohen.

"M-m-m," nodded Moriarity.

"He must have been gawd-awful drunk," said MacBride.

"Crazy drunk," Cohen said.

"Swizzled," said Moriarity.

They were silent again for a minute, and then MacBride, flexing his lips, warping his brows, opened the annunciator and said: "Kennedy's wanted. The newspaperman—Kennedy . . . That's right. Five feet seven, about a hundred and twenty-five pounds. Light brown hair. Blue eyes. Sleepy-looking. Was wearing a light gray suit and a light gray hat. Most cops know him . . . All booths, precincts, and patrol flivvers."

He hung up his hat, ran his palms from his temples backward past the tops of his ears; he said: "Well, that's that." He dropped into his chair—dropped hard, heavily, as a chain falls; and he slurred out of a corner of his mouth: "I always figured Kennedy'd wind up in some way out of the ordinary, but I never in cripes' world thought it would be like this." He looked unutterably weary. He moved his hand. "Oke, Mory, Ike. You guys line out and see if you can find him. You know the places he hangs out. I don't have to tell you. And to think I damn' near got Flannery to say he'd take him back on the *Free Press*." He yanked open a drawer, hauled out a bottle of Canadian Club and took a stiff jolt straight. "Try to get him before the D.A.'s office gets him. That pain in the neck Rube Wilson—" He sighed, stood up, flung his hand. "Okey, beat it."

A description of the dead girl had been broadcast on the radio and by eleven that night an identification was made. Her brother made it—in the Morgue—and then passed out. MacBride happened to be there at the time (he himself was on the walkabout, too, looking for Kennedy) and picked up the brother.

The girl's name was Naomi Penfields. She was twenty-one. "Young," MacBride mused aloud, bitterly. "They've always got to be young." They were the Penfields of Livermore Walk, in the West End. Harrod

Penfields had died a natural death five years before. He'd left a sizable estate to his wife, daughter, son. The Penfields mansion was one of the show places of the West End. Alvina Penfields, the mother, was a recluse who, it was said, spent all her time writing monographs on dead languages. The brother, Bacon Penfields, had not come to by the time MacBride left the Morgue.

Gahagan was asleep at the wheel but MacBride punched him awake and then climbed in back. Smoking his pipe, he sat in the corner of the seat, his arms folded on his chest. He told Gahagan where to go and while the car hummed through the spring night the skipper chewed on his scarred pipestem and wondered what he would do when he got hold of Kennedy. He did not exactly know what he would do. Kennedy had helped solve many a crime; more than that, he had actually solved many crimes that had confounded the whole Department.

But all that would be washed away. A cop may serve his shield for twenty years and if at the end of that time he commits a heinous crime, he must pay the penalty. MacBride had no complaint with this law. It was an inevitable law. But still—he had been in many tight places with Kennedy; he had saved Kennedy's life and Kennedy had saved his. But he knew his hands were bound. The case, actually, would not be in his hands at all.

"That one," he told Gahagan. "On the corner. With the green and white lights."

He swung out of the car, knocked open the door of the *Tin Can Club* with his shoulder and ran into Gus Winkles in the anteroom.

"Kennedy been in?"

"Hello, Cap. Kennedy?"

"Kennedy."

"Not for a couple of days. You want to see him?"

"Very much."

"If he comes in, I'll tell him you want to see him."

The skipper went to other places: the joints in lower Jockey Street and the tonier places in upper Jockey Street, the bars in Flamingo Street— *Enrico's*, the *Pig's Knuckle, Eddie's*, the *Sawdust Club*; the strictly Italian hang-outs in Rosario Street; the dance-halls of Exeter Square and the beer halls in Strauss Street; the Turkish bath where he knew Kennedy frequently went following a drunk and the bowling alley where Kennedy usually placed bets on the horses. No one had seen Kennedy that night.

Driving back towards headquarters, MacBride found himself hoping that Kennedy might have run off to some far corner of the world, never to be found. And when he became conscious of this thought the iron-bound skipper sat up straight, colored in the darkness of the tonneau.

Moriarity was in the office.

"Well?" MacBride grunted.

"This." Moriarity sat on the desk. "I just by a fluke dropped in at Willie Murry's place, and sure enough Willie saw Kennedy at about a quarter to ten. He said Kennedy staggered in the place carrying a zither. 'Where the hell'd he get that?' I asked Willie and Willie said, 'Oh, he said he picked it up for a song.' "

"Kennedy can't play a zither!" MacBride shouted.

"That's what Willie said. Let me tell you. He said Kennedy came in, had a drink at the bar and wanted to know if anybody there could play the zither. Well, nobody could and then Kennedy asked Willie if he knew of anybody else who could play it. Willie said no, so Kennedy said prob'ly he'd best go to an employment agency."

MacBride covered his eyes with his hands, groaned.

"Sure," Moriarty nodded. "Kennedy told Willie he'd picked up the zither hoping he could find someone to play it. I said to Willie, 'Hell, if Kennedy really wanted zither music why didn't he do the sensible thing and try to find a zither player first? Chances are that the zither player would have had a zither of his own, because zithers—' "

"Zithers! Zithers!" barked MacBride. "Shut up, Mory."

"Well, I was just telling you."

The Assistant District Attorney flung open the door, came in and flung the door shut. He snapped:

"Any news of that rat yet?"

"What rat?" MacBride said.

"Kennedy, of course!"

MacBride said: "Call him a rat again, Rube, and I'll hit you with a radiator."

Rube Wilson nodded. "I know, I know," he said sarcastically. "You've got a tender spot in your heart for the palooka but it's not going to do him any good."

"I've got a tender spot in my heart for him, Rube, and who the hell said it was going to do him any good? I've got practically the whole Department looking for him. I can't do any more. But lay off the rat business."

"Anyone seen him?"

"Mory said Willie Murry saw him about a quarter to ten."

Rube Wilson grinned. "I'm going to hate to prosecute that onion for murder. Yes, I am, I am!"

"Sore, Rube?" MacBride said.

"Sure."

"Okey. We understand each other then."

"What do you mean by that?"

"I don't know. Look it up somewhere and tell me."

Rube Wilson's face darkened. "Flim-flam on this, skipper, and maybe I'll get around to prosecuting you some day."

MacBride stood up, rubbed his palms together. "Look here, Rube. You're being nasty now. We're looking for Kennedy and we'll get him, but take a tip from a guy and don't shoot your mouth off too much. You're like a lot of wise young assistant D.A.'s: eager as hell to make the headlines—"

"I make 'em, don't I?"

"Just take the tip, fella. Crack around too much and I'll drop a word in the right ear and if this thing does come to a prosecution you won't be in on the kill at all."

"Do it and I'll yell my lungs out to the papers."

"Make one peep and you'll land our your neck in the gutter, where you started from—a cheap, lousy ambulance chaser."

"Why, you big—"

"Shut up. Personally you want to make Kennedy take water. You want to make him writhe, play with him like a cat plays with a mouse when the cat knows the mouse hasn't a chance. It's personal with you, Rube. You hate him. You're sore. You're lousy sore. You can't take it. You're a dirty stink in the D.A.'s office because you brought a bad stink up out of the gutter with you. Six years ago you framed a woman with a guy in the Bedford Hotel. The woman's husband was your client. How do I know? Well, the guy you paid to help frame the woman was and is a stool pigeon of mine. We have an understanding: he gives me tips and I give him immunity. Think it over, Rube. And stop blowing off your mouth. And take the air. I hate your guts."

Rube Wilson flung out and Moriarity said: "That ought to hold the lousy buzzard."

IV

Kennedy and one Ignazio Mirabelli stood on a street in the residential quarter of Little Italy. Ignazio played the zither. He was a very short, very fat man, with rosy cheeks, a rosy chin and large, merry eyes. His clothes looked as if they had been dragged out of a rag bag, but he played with a flair while Kennedy, holding his hat, caught coins tossed from windows and hallways. Ignazio's eyes may have been merry but they were also watchful, and the larger the coin the greater vigor he brought to bear in his playing.

"We have now, Ignazio," said Kennedy, "seven dollars and forty-three cents. Also a Chinese coin. Also some lead slugs. We might do worse than taking time out for a drink."

"'Swatcha say she's ukkey by me, signore."

They went over to *Enrico's*, in Flamingo Street. Paderoofski, whose real name was Bennie Iammaranzio, was tending bar.

"Jeeze now," exclaimed Paderoofski.

Kennedy said, with a gesture: "Signor Iammaranzio, meet one brother countryman, Signor Mirabelli, known as Iganazio, for short. He plays a thiz—a ziz—a thizzer—I mean zizzer—Oh, nerts, give me three rye highballs. Two for me and one for Ignazio. Iggy doesn't drink."

"Ha!" laughed Ignazio."

"I was gonna say, Meester Kennedy," Paderoofski said, "the Captain MacBride was in-a here look' for you."

"The skipper? Good old Skippy MacBride!"

"By God!"

Paderoofski stretched his neck. Ignazio turned around like a barrel. Kennedy was never disturbed by anonymous exclamations.

Rube Wilson left the doorway and came over and took Kennedy by the arm. Rube fairly quivered with excitement. He took hold of Kennedy's arm very gently, almost tenderly, and there was on his face a smile that would have been tender also had it not contained too much that was obviously Satanic. When he spoke again, his voice almost dripped with tenderness:

"Kennedy, you don't know how glad I am to see you."

Ignazio beamed with joy.

Kennedy teetered about. "Well, 'f it isn't Rube. Meet my palsywalsy, Signor Mirabelli."

Ignazio made a deep bow.

"A man of parts," went on Kennedy, "and none of them spare parts. A vagabond minstrel, just an old vagabond but with a heart of gold. I must come up your place for a turkey dinner some night, Rube."

A high little laugh trilled from Rube Wilson's teeth. "Yes, you must, Kennedy—"

"Look here," said a tall, button-nosed man striding from the doorway, "I told you he might be here, Rube."

Kennedy clapped his hands. "Flannery! My old editor, Flannery! Me and my, but isn't this old home week!"

"Ha—ha—ha!" laughed Ignazio, clapping his hands also.

Flannery clipped: "Who's this monkey?" And then, with a stern, wintry eye on Rube Wilson: "You're not taking Kennedy till we get— till I get the low-down."

Rube Wilson muttered: "Pipe down, Tom. Just over my office—"

"With a man from every newspaper in town camped there? What do I look like, last week's cream?" He snapped on: "Get a room here! Step on it!"

"Tom, listen—"

Flannery flapped his hands. "Nix. Get a room. I'll get a room. . . . Hey, Enrico! Got a room here?"

Rube Wilson bit his lip petulantly and Kennedy, seeming detached from the whole affair, crunched potato chips between his teeth. But Enrico had a room and into it Kennedy was herded by Flannery; and, as an after-thought, they hauled in Ignazio and his zither. Ignazio did not seem to know what it was all about, but being a polite little fat man, he kept smiling and bowing until Flannery snapped:

"For cripes sake, Wop, lay off the setting-up exercises!" He had a choppy way of saying things, and his eyes wore a blue-white glare.

There was a couch against one wall and Kennedy lay down on it, propping his head high enough so that he could drink with a minimum of movement. Flannery yanked a chair across the room, planked it down alongside the couch; he sat down, planted his hands on his knees, elbows out, and glared down at Kennedy. Rube Wilson took a seat beside him. Wilson's narrow dark face showed chagrin, but there was also a ray of hope.

Kennedy said: "Awfully kind of you chappies to provide me with a private chamber."

"Let's have it," Flannery clipped. "Come on, spill it, get it out." He was an impatient man, used to having his way. "The dame—this Penfields dame—dish us the dirt and I don't care how dirty you dish it."

"Penfields?" Kennedy said, cocking one sleepy eye. "Oh, yes. You mean the Penfields. The West End Penfields. I'm sorry, but we've never—ah—met, y'know, socially."

Flannery rasped: "Cut out the toney accent, mugg!"

"Okey, Tom. Precious nerts to you, you big turnip. Do you know why I never liked you, Tom? Because you never split infinitives. It shows a peasantry of intelligence. Old Nonsplit Tom Flannery, the great horse's neck.''

Flannery tightened his lips. ''I don't give a good cripes what you think of me. That's not what I'm here for. The Penfields dame was beaten up so's she conked in your room, you fathead, and I want the story. Rube Wilson wants it, too, but so do I. Snap out of it, baby.''

Kennedy sighed. ''You annoy me, Tom. Go away. Git along, little dawgie, git along.''

''Listen you, Kennedy,'' Rube Wilson cut it. ''It's a pinch, you understand. I'm pinching you for the murder of Naomi Penfields. You lured her to your room and then attacked her. I'm going to burn you for it, Kennedy, and I'm going to like doing it. I told you you'd come a cropper some day, and boy, have you! Have you!''

Flannery silenced him with a hand; and then to Kennedy: ''Come on, kid. It's open and shut but what I want is the story. I'm holding up the presses for it. Spill it and don't be a lug and clown around. You killed her. Okey, that's over with. Maybe you had a reason. But get it off your chest.''

Kennedy sighed. He lay back and closed his eyes and his pale, wan face looked strangely like a death mask. His hair was tousled, his tie was out of place. He looked as if all the sap had been drained out of him leaving nothing but a husk. And as he lay there, his eyes closed, his mouth lax, a tragic look began to creep slowly over his face.

Rube Wilson licked his lips hopefully and Flannery edged his chair closer to the couch.

Kennedy opened his eyes. ''So you want my story.''

They nodded.

A dry, satanic laugh crackled feebly from Kennedy's lips. ''Sure I killed her.''

''Ah!'' breathed Rube Wilson.

''Proceed,'' said Flannery.

Kennedy's face looked very haggard and his mouth sagged weakly, a strange glaze came upon his eyes. ''Yeah, I killed her. I guess I kind of went nuts, Tom, but you know how it is: a pretty dame, a little booze. You know, Tom, I've been thinking that if you hadn't fired me, things might have been different. But there I was, out of a job, reckless, I guess, and I guess I didn't care much what happened to me.''

''How did you kill her?'' Rube Wilson asked breathlessly.

''Oh, I batted her in the jaw a couple of times and then I kicked her and then I guess I hit her with some things. I don't remember what I hit her with."

Flannery said: "Feel any remorse?"

"No. No, Tom, I don't. It's all like a dream, I guess. I just got her in my room and then I went out and then I thought it over and came back again and began to sock her. I guess I socked her because she was so damned pretty and because she tried to high-hat me."

Flannery frowned. "You sure went the whole hog, didn't you? You were a great newspaperman in your day, Kennedy."

"*Sic transit gloria mundi*. I was, Tom. I am still. I forgot more than you'll ever learn. I learned young how to split infinitives."

"Stick to the story," Rube Wilson chimed in.

"What," said Flannery, "was your real reason for killing her? I mean the one thing that finally drove you to do it."

Kennedy sighed. "She did not know how to make a Martini."

"Hell, he's completely screwy!" Rube Wilson said.

Kennedy cried: "I killed her because she was too beautiful for this world. This world is so crass and designing and so full of filth and tragedy. I killed her because—well, because she was a flower, a fair flower."

Rube Wilson rasped: "Screwy as hell!"

Kennedy sat up, held his head in his hands. "I knocked her around the room—knocked her round and round and kicked her and punched her and maybe I hit her with inkwells and things until she fell down and then I kicked her some more and then I chucked her on the bed and went out for a drink."

"Madman!" Rube Wilson chopped off. "When the fair young womanhood of our city—"

"Lay off the crap," Flannery said. "This is a story, a wow. We haven't had one like it in years. The public will eat it up and the *Free Press* will be the first to spring it." He turned on Wilson. "You heard that, didn't you?"

"Yes—sure, Tom."

"Well, remember it."

Kennedy was crying into his hands. Ignazio came over and put a hand on his shoulder.

Flannery grabbed a phone and called his office. "Jack, get this. It's a lulu." He rattled the story off, sitting back on a tipped chair, one hand in his pocket. His choice of words was good. He told a terse, dramatic account of the murder, building up on such details as Kennedy had given him.

"Don't forget my name," Rube Wilson said.

And Flannery said into the phone: "Assistant District Attorney Rube Wilson arrested Kennedy in person. Run a picture of Rube, one of Kennedy and one of the Penfields dame. Hop to it, Jack. It's the scoop of the century."

He hung up, rose and lit a cigarette. "Thanks, Kennedy. I'll send you flowers." And to Rube Wilson: "And remember, sweetheart, no two-timing. This is a *Free Press* story, exclusive. So long, Rube. So long, Kennedy. Tell me if it hurts."

Flannery went out and Rube Wilson said: "Come on, Kennedy. Get up. We blow."

"Oh, I don't feel like going, Rube," Kennedy sighed. "I'm tired. Leave a call for me in the morning."

"Rat, get up!"

Rube Wilson was not big but he was wiry, strong. He hauled Kennedy off the couch and stood him on his feet. "We're blowing, son. The can for you and am I going to lay into you in court! I've waited a long time for this, Kennedy. I've stood your razzing a long time." He paused, grinned, hot-eyed. "So I don't hear you making any cracks now. Why don't you? Or maybe you're figuring on me giving you a break. Are you?"

Kennedy's eyes were half closed, and he swayed to and fro on his feet. "A break, Rube? Uh-huh. I wouldn't ask you for a break, Rube. I like you. You're a nice guy. Nice like a louse. Rube, I don't feel like going places. That's a fact. It's nice and comfortable here. Why should I go places?

Rube Wilson jerked at his arm. "You're going—now! What do I look like, a sap?"

"Frankly, yes."

Rube Wilson started to manhandle him across the floor towards the door. Kennedy fought back feebly. Ignazio, very much concerned, and not knowing what it was all about, scratched the stubble on his chin. Rube Wilson was red in the face, still trying to get Kennedy to the door, and Kennedy was flip-flopping back and forth. Ignazio picked up the zither and brought it down on Rube Wilson's head. Rube Wilson said "Ah" gently, and his eyes rolled as he sank to the floor.

"Jeez, boss!" Ignazio gasped, pointing. "I sock him! Look!"

Kennedy hiccoughed, bleary-eyed. "Ignazio, you are a true friend. On second thought, I don't like this place. Let's toddle."

V

MacBride was eating a late snack in his office when the door banged open and Rube Wilson came in flame-faced and wet-lipped with rage and chagrin.

"Please knock hereafter," MacBride said.

"I'll knock!" Rube Wilson snarled. "I'll knock somebody's block off!"

"Mine?"

Rube Wilson drew in a long breath, cocked one eye. "I wouldn't be surprised, skipper—I wouldn't be surprised a bit if you had a hand in this!"

MacBride took a long pull at a thermos of hot coffee and then said: "Fall in a corner somewhere, Rube. I've never seen it to fail yet that every time I try to eat a meal here in my office some half-baked fool comes in and spoils my digestion."

Rube Wilson had hurried and was still out of breath. "You and your lousy digestion! Do you know what?" He slammed both hands down on the desk. "I collared Kennedy! I collared him and got a confession out of him! Flannery was a witness to it. That crazy friend of yours beat the girl to death and wasn't even sorry. I got the confession, I tell you! . . . And then what? Then I'm attacked. I'm socked on the head by some Dago friend of Kennedy's and I'm out for an hour. When I come to, I learn that Kennedy's breezed. He breezed over an hour ago! And then you sit there and tell me about your indigestion."

MacBride leaned back. Sudden anxiety had come into his eyes but his voice, when he spoke, was low, guttural. "Breezed, did he?"

"Breezed!"

"And he'd confessed, huh?"

"Absolutely! And I want this—now! I want every damned cop on the Force out after him. I got him all right—single-handed, and because I was just too soft-hearted the dirty palooka takes advantage of me. Signals to his pal and his pal lets me have it over the head. I'm mad, MacBride. I'm boiling over—over! I tell you Kennedy's lost his mind. He's a madman. He's crazy. Cuckoo! Screwy! And God knows how many more people he'll kill. The lust of blood is in him. He's become another

Dracula. He laughed when he told how he killed the Penfields dame. It's the liquor. The liquor turned him into a maniac. It—it—''

He was out of breath. He stood toiling on his feet, his face crimson, sweat pouring down his cheeks. And there was a gray look on MacBride's face. A look of fear. Liquor had driven many a man out of his mind. Kennedy was, always had been, an abandoned drinker. MacBride made no effort to conceal his fear. His strong body shook and his throat felt dry and in his heart there was a deep remorse. But he saw his job now— clearly. He pulled himself together.

His tone was crisp: "Rube, take it easy. You'll pass out again if you don't calm down. I'll handle this. I'll get Kennedy."

"I tell you, MacBride—"

"You've told me enough. All I need to know. I'm serious, Rube. I'll get Kennedy. I may have to shoot him—but—well—under the circumstances—'' The thought gagged him, but his jaw clamped down hard. "Leave it to me. This is what I get for being a cop. Sit down, Rube. Draw yourself together. Who was the Dago?''

"I don't remember. A funny little fat guy. Looked like a clown. Carried a zither. The zither was probably just a stall.''

"Where'd this happen?''

"In a room at *Enrico's*. I had Flannery in as witness.''

"So that's a *Free Press* scoop, huh?''

"Sure. I had to have somebody in. Enrico didn't know I'd been knocked out until an hour afterward. He said Kennedy and the funny little Wop pranced out arm in arm, as if nothing had happened. I tell you, they're a couple of ghouls!'' He fell breathless into a chair.

MacBride took down his gun and spring-holster from the clothes tree in the corner. He strapped on the holster, put on his hat. "Take it easy, Rube,'' he said grimly, and strode out. He drummed his heels down to the central room, where Otto Bettdecken, on duty at the desk, was eating a plate of ham and beans.

The skipper continued on towards the door. He had no precise idea of where he was going. But the street would be dark, quiet, and he could walk hard, fast, and think. All his men were still looking for Kennedy, so he could do nothing more about that. But he could walk, walk, revisit the haunts he had visited earlier in the night, and he might find Kennedy. He hoped he wouldn't. He hoped that if it came to guns, someone else would take Kennedy.

"Hey, Cap!''

That was Bettdecken yelling from the desk.

MacBride turned, scowled dourly at him.

Bettdecken was waving a fat hand. "Come here. On the phone—I just got—" He yelled into the phone: "Wait, you! . . . Hah? . . . No, wait! . . . Hey! Hey!" He hung up violently.

"What?" MacBride growled, reaching the desk.

"That was Kennedy. He called up to say—what he said was 'Otto, tell that prince of fellows, Captain MacBride, that Kennedy, world-famous newspaperman, will be at home this evening, at 201 Furness Street, apartment twenty-one, if the able captain should wish to call.' He said that, just like I said it."

"He must be nuts," MacBride brooded.

"Hah?"

MacBride muttered: "Keep it under your hat till I get back."

He swiveled, strode across the central room and went dull-faced out into the street. He did not bother to get out his police car. At the next block there was a taxi and he entered it and told the driver where to go.

VI

The address was at the other end of the city. Sitting in the taxicab, his hands sunk in his coat pockets, his legs out straight, the skipper stared vacantly at the meter. He did not notice its changing numbers, for his eyes were out of focus. Nor did he bother to brace his body against the frequent jouncing of the cab; he let the cab play with his body. There was a coldness round his heart, a sensation of time suspended in his brain. His mouth was set, grim, and his face looked wooden.

The cab stopped at last but MacBride did not stir. And finally the driver looked around and said: "This the number?"

MacBride muttered: "Huh?" He looked up, blinked his eyes. "Yeah," he muttered. He got out of the cab slowly, like an old man. Absently paid his fare. The cab went away and MacBride stood on the curb and looked at the small brown apartment house. He passed a hand feebly over his eyes. Then he shook himself. His shoulders drooped as he went across the sidewalk and entered a small lobby. There was no elevator.

He heard voices upstairs and as he climbed, his ears rang and there was an odd tightness in his throat. In the second floor corridor he found a small group—three women and a man. They turned frightened eyes on him.

"I'm a policeman," he said dully. "What's the trouble here?"

A woman pointed. "In there. There's been an awful racket. There's someone—"

The sound of some heavy object crashing silenced her and then another woman said: "It's been like that—only with yells and whoops. They won't open the door. Somebody's being killed, I think."

"Look out," MacBride muttered.

He stood before the door. He heard a thumping and a pounding. A crash of glass. A loud groan.

His fist pounded on the door and he said in a loud voice: "Open up! It's the police!"

But the noise went on.

He turned his head and said: "You folks get back."

They retreated a few paces down the hall and MacBride drew his gun. He held it near the knob and pulled the trigger three times. The sounds crashed in the corridor. The women held their ears. MacBride stepped back, drew up his shoulder and plunged it towards the door. The door whipped inward and the skipper straddled the threshold, his gun leveled.

"Cut it!" he barked.

The people in the corridor stood in a white, breathless huddle.

Inside the room there was a man on the floor. He looked very big, strong, young and his face was bloody. Sitting on him was Ignazio. Ignazio had lost his ragged coat, also his shirt. He had only his pants on and his face also was bloody.

"Get up," said MacBride. "The law to you."

Ignazio got up. The very large young man did not get up. He was unable to get up.

Kennedy was lying on a desk trying to get a telephone number.

"You," said MacBride, "put that down."

Kennedy rolled over, still retaining the instrument. "Oh, so you came around. Good. I am delighted to see you skipperino. Only I wish you'd tell Otto to take the marbles out of his mouth when he's on the phone."

One trousers leg was completely gone. His face was streaked with red, his coat was ripped all the way up the back, and one of his eyes was blackened and closed.

MacBride entered the room. "Kennedy—"

"Sh! I think I'm getting my number . . . Hello, is this the Richmond City *Times-Express?* . . . It is. Well, I want to talk to Ridley. . . . Ridley? This is Kennedy. . . . The Kennedy, sweetheart. . . . Yeah. Listen, how about that job you offered me the other day? . . . I thought it would be. . . . Well, I've been thinking it over and I want double the salary you offered. . . . I'm ga-ga, am I? Listen, darling Mr. Ridley, would you like the low-down on the Penfields kill? . . . You would. Well, papa has it. Papa has it all in the bag. . . . You will? Okey, double it is.

"Listen. I picked the Penfields girl up at Hallam and German Streets at about seven-twenty. I though she was tight. I mean awful tight. She had some liquor on her breath and she seemed scared to go home, so I went softy and dragged her around to my room and chucked her on the bed. Then I went out and after I'd walked a couple of blocks a guy ran up and stopped me. He was a big fellow, about six feet three, aged about twenty-seven. His name's Wallace Pringle and he lives at 201 Furness. He's a sculptor. Yeah, he sculpts.

"Well, he stopped me and said in a shaky voice, 'Is she all right?' I asked him who and of course it was the girl and I said I thought she was—she'd sleep it off. He was a little tight. I asked him if he knew of a chili joint around there and he said he did and showed me the way. He went in with me and we ate and drank and we both got tight. Only he was tight to begin with and he got very tight. He bawled too. He told me he was crazy in love with this Penfields girl, and when, at his studio, she told him she was through—because of his drinking—he tried to get her to stay. He told her she was always too sober to appreciate the finer things of life and then it seems he tried to make her take a drink. He forced some down her throat but spilled most of it on her. . . . Yeah, he told me this over wine and chili. Bawled while he told it. So one thing led to another. I guess he got enraged. He said he tried to make her stay and she fought back and he socked her and then he went nuts completely and beat the hell out of her. He finally tripped over something, fell down and the girl escaped.

"He said he followed her along the streets, but got a little sobered up and didn't dare to speak to her, fearing what she would say to him. Then she ran into me and you know what I did. The guy saw me take her in my place and then followed me when I came out and, as I told you, accosted me. After the chili, he was so tight I had to steer him home. I got him to his studio and then left. I remembered what the building looked like and had an idea of the neighborhood, but it took me a hell of a while to find it again.

"Well, as I say, I left him. I was feeling fine myself and had a few more drinks and then I helped a guy out by buying his zither and then I picked up a little Sicilian named Ignazio Mirabelli, who could play it.

We had a great amount of fun going about playing and making collections and then I heard about the death of the Penfields girl.

"An assistant D.A. who thought he was smart and a famous newspaper editor who thought he was clever wanted to hang the kill on me. So after a little clowning around, Ignazio and I go out to hunt up the studio. Finally we find it. Well, I sat down and talked simply to Wallace Pringle and much to my surprise he wanted to fight. Well, he's a big lug, you know, and there was I. But Ignazio was there too. A great fellow, Ignazio. Pringle beats the living hell out of the both of us. Boy, you should see me, and Ignazio's no beauty either. But by a lucky break Ignazio's foot slips. And where do you think it lands? It lands smack on Wallace Pringle's jaw—and he's down. Then we sit on him and hit him with various objects. I think he's just coming to now.

"But wait. The arrest, by the way, was made formally by Captain Stephen J. MacBride. A certain assistant D.A. is going to feel red all over tomorrow and a certain high-pressure editor is going to have to take it and like it. . . . Listen, send me over a pair of pants, will you? I lost mine."

He hung up, lay back on the desk, stretched his arms and yawned. A smile, wicked and wise, crept across his bloody, haggard face. He laughed mockingly.

MacBride's low voice said: "Kennedy."

"There's your man, skipperino. On the floor. I hope you don't mind if I don't get up."

"Rube Wilson told me—"

"I know what Rube told you. Rube and Flannery thought they were a couple of geniuses. Flannery's tongue hanging out for a scoop and Rube's hanging out for the big pinch. Well, I hated to disappoint them. So I gave them what they wanted. I gave them a big meal of it, old tomato—intending to serve up the razzberry dessert later. They'll get it for breakfast."

Macbride said: "Thank God, Kennedy, old kid! Thank God!"

"God and Ignazio," said Kennedy. "Iggy can do more things with a zither than play it. Ask Rube."

Ignazio bowed. He bowed six times.

Kennedy went to sleep on the desk.

Captain Leopold

CAPTAIN LEOPOLD AND
THE ARROW MURDERS
Edward D. Hoch

HARRY STANDING ELK slipped quietly through the hedge, taking care to keep to the shadows where the glow from the fire could not reach him. There were four people gathered around the fire, talking and eating and drinking. They had not heard his approach. He slipped the bow off his shoulder and threaded the notched arrow onto the string. With four it would be difficult, but he thought it could be done.

One of the women—the pretty one—stood up suddenly and headed for the house. It was the break he'd been waiting for. He let fly the first arrow and caught the stocky man full in the chest. A gasp escaped his lips as he sunk to his knees. The second man half turned, a look of shocked horror on his face. But already Standing Elk had the second arrow in place, already he had pulled back his arm to launch it.

The woman screamed and tried to hide behind the outdoor grill. Standing Elk was running toward them now, firing a third arrow at her, aiming a fourth at the girl who'd reappeared in the doorway of the house.

It was all over within a minute

He took a piece of charcoal from the bag by the fire and started writing with it on the patio floor. He wrote: *Death to the Despoilers of Indian Land!* He signed it: *The Depredator*.

Harry Standing Elk took one last look at the four arrow-pierced bodies. Then he slung the bow back over his shoulder and retreated through the hedge.

Lieutenant Fletcher was waiting at the hospital for Leopold. He met him in the hallway outside the intensive-care unit. "They think she'll pull through, Captain. And she's conscious now, if you want to question her. They've given her something to calm her."

Leopold went to the woman's bed. Her eyes wre closed, and he spoke her name softly. "Mrs. Culver? Can you hear me, Mrs. Culver?"

Her eyes opened. "Yes. I'm awake." She had a slim sad face and brown eyes.

"I'm Captain Leopold of the Violent Crimes Squad. Can you tell me what happened?"

"They're all dead, aren't they? My husband and the Greens?"

"Yes. You're lucky to be alive. Did you see the person who shot the arrows?"

"Not at first. John—my husband—was just standing there, staring off into the night, when the arrow hit him in the chest. Then Herb Green turned to see what happened and he was hit too. I ducked down behind the outdoor grill and that must have thrown his aim off. The arrow hit me in the side. Then Pam Green came to the door and he got her too. He came forward and I had a glimpse of him while he wrote his message with the charcoal."

She closed her eyes again. All that talking had been a strain. "Could you give us a description, Mrs. Culver?"

"He was tall and he moved fast—very light on his feet. Dark hair, but I couldn't really see his face."

"How was he dressed?"

"A blue shirt and jeans. Some sort of moccasin-type shoes. I saw those when he was standing near me, when he thought I was dead. God, I was afraid he'd shoot another arrow into me!" She fought back a sob. "That was all I could think about—that and what he'd done to John."

"Could he have been an Indian, Mrs. Culver?" Leopold asked.

"You mean a real Indian? I don't know."

"Did your husband or the Greens have any enemies?"

"No one. No one who could have done such a thing."

"All right," Leopold said. "Rest now. We'll talk to you again later."

Outside the room Fletcher was waiting for him. "Any description?"

"Tall, dark, wearing jeans. Could fit a thousand people. She didn't see his face. Doesn't know if he's a real Indian."

"He's a nut is what he is! Imagine killing three people with a bow and arrow!"

"I want you to start checking the archery clubs around town, Fletcher. He's good with that bow, and we don't know much more about him."

"What do you think the message means, Captain? The one he wrote with charcoal."

"It means he'll kill again if we don't find him, Fletcher."

Harry Standing Elk had not really known the people he'd killed. They'd merely happened to be in that spot, around the backyard barbecue, when he came along. He'd watched them for a time, crouched in the darkness behind the hedge, and then made his move. He was surprised and a little alarmed when he read in the newspaper that one of the women had survived his attack, but the vagueness of her description reassured him. She hadn't really seen enough of him to identify him.

Still, it might be wiser to concentrate on single targets in the future.

Three nights after his first strike he unlocked the closet door where he kept the powerful bow and a large supply of hunting arrows. He knew it was dangerous to go out again so quickly, but the very danger added an element of excitement. He chose the arrows carefully, fitting them into the carrier attached to the bow itself. Then he slid the whole thing into a paper dry-cleaning bag, suspending the bow from the hanger. When he carried it so that the bow hung free inside its bag, he might have been a cleaner delivering a freshly pressed suit.

This night he drove back to the same neighborhood, parking just a few blocks from where he'd been the previous time. He picked a house with the lights on and headed up the driveway as if making a delivery.

After he gave the doorbell a quick ring, he retreated into the shadows some twenty feet away and slipped the bow from beneath its paper cover. The door opened and a man stood silhouetted against the lighted room behind him. He didn't open the screen door but peered through it to ask, "Who's there?"

Standing Elk's arrow punctured the screen and took the man squarely in the chest. . .

Captain Leopold didn't like it. The four had been bad enough, with three of them dead and the woman still in the hospital. This latest killing seemed to confirm his fear that they were dealing with a madman who would keep on with his murderous attacks.

"We're going to have the city in a panic if this keeps up," Fletcher predicted. "People will be afraid to open their doors."

They were in Leopold's office on the morning after the latest killing, going over what few clues there were. "Just where was the note found?"

Leopold asked. He'd been attending a police conference in Boston the previous night and hadn't yet visited the scene of the crime.

"Pinned to the garage door with another arrow. You'll be able to see it in the pictures."

"Same wording?"

"Same wording. *Death to the Despoilers of Indian Land!* and signed *The Depredator.*"

"Any witnesses?"

"The dead man—Sam Windman—was alone in the house at the time. His wife bowls on Wednesday nights. No one saw the actual killing, but a neighbor across the street says she noticed a man carrying a dry-cleaning bag up to the house at about the time it must have happened."

"At night?"

Fletcher nodded. "She thought it was an odd time for a delivery, but unfortunately she didn't watch to see what happened."

"Is Connie around?"

"I'll buzz her desk."

In a moment Policewoman Connie Trent appeared in the doorway. "How was Boston?"

"The usual," Leopold answered with a shrug. "You working on anything right now?"

"The parking-lot muggings. And that knifing on Chandler Street."

"Let Rafferty handle those. I need you on the Depredator thing."

"God, I heard there was another one."

"Last night. He used his bow and arrow again and left the same message. It'll hit the noon editions of the papers."

"What do you want me to do?" she asked.

"Concentrate on the Indian angle. See if you can find somebody at one of the colleges who might know about such things. Check the land deeds and see if there's something about old Indian land in the vicinity of the killings."

"I'll get right on it," she promised.

"What about me?" Fletcher asked.

"Take as many men as you need and start checking out that neighborhood. I'm still not completely sold on an Indian killer, despite the bow and arrow. Have you checked the archery clubs?"

"Lots of names, nothing else so far."

"Any Indian names?"

"Like Sitting Bull. Not a one."

"All right. You've arranged for added patrol cars in the area?"

"The Commissioner himself did that. And they're to cruise with red lights flashing, so they can be seen several blocks away. He's hoping that'll discourage our man."

"I don't think he'll be that easily discouraged," Leopold said.

Harry Standing Elk avoided the furnished apartment for two full days after the killing of Sam Windman. He read the newspaper accounts and watched the television reports with great interest, but they seemed to be about someone else's crime, someone else's life.

When he finally did return and once again unlocked the closet door, he did so reluctantly, telling himself he merely wanted to feel the pull of the bow string against his fingers.

But then he was cruising the streets again, the weapon dangerously exposed on the seat by his side. He felt, as the excitement grew within him, that he was challenging them to spot him. Driving along the streets of the familiar neighborhood, he saw the distant flashing red of a patrol car and he knew they were out in force.

He parked at the corner of a street, where he could see in three directions and have a choice of three escape routes. But before he had settled on a possible target he saw the flashing red light turn onto the street two blocks behind him. There were too many of them tonight.

He started his car and drove away.

Back at the apartment he locked the weapon away in the closet. They thought they had him on the run, but he was only beginning. Next time he'd show them.

Next time he'd kill someone in broad daylight.

"Captain, are you free this morning?" Connie asked, poking her head into his office.

"I'm free if it's the arrow killings. That's the only thing that would get me down here on a Saturday morning in summer."

"I've been checking on this Indian thing and I've located someone at the University who might be able to help us. I'm on my way out to see him now."

"Let's go," Leopold said.

The day was hot and breezy and she drove with the car windows down. There was little traffic in the area of the University, because only summer classes were in session. Connie parked in front of the Administration building and they got out. "His name is Miles Furness, and he's Professor of Folklore and English. Somebody told me he knows everything about Indian culture. He said on the phone he'd be here till noon."

Professor Furness proved to be a tall dark-haired man in his late thirties, with a ready smile and a firm handshake. "I'm more than willing to help, if I can. Come into the office."

"Leopold seated himself next to Connie, taking in the Indian artifacts and colorful Remington prints on the walls of the little room. "I explained on the phone what we needed," Connie said.

Professor Furness nodded and reached for a thick book on his desk. "The Depredator is one of a number of folk heroes of the Iroquois nation. He is called Ga-nus-quah, and the Iroquois myth has it that he is vulnerable only on the bottom of his foot."

"Like the heel of Achilles," Leopold observed.

"Exactly. The myths of all nations have certain recognizable points of similarity. But the Depredator is unique in one respect—no human being has ever seen him. To look on his face means instant death."

"Medusa," Leopold muttered.

"Yes. The sight of her turned men to stone. But the Depredator is never described as being horrible to look at. He is merely—what? unseen?—and all-powerful. A giant of stone."

"We have a woman in the hospital who almost saw him."

"The murderer you seek has obviously read a great deal of Indian lore. Perhaps he also imagines his people wronged by the white land-grabbers."

"The four killings thus far have all been in an area known as Maplegrove. For years it was an undeveloped section right on the city line. Then, about a decade ago, a home builder got approval to construct a development there."

Furness reached behind him and produced a rolled map. "I've been doing some research on this ever since Miss Trent's phone call. Here's what I've found." He unrolled the map on his desk, holding down the sides with the telephone and an ashtray: "This is the area you refer to as Maplegrove, scene of the two attacks thus far. You can see from this old map that it was an area sacred to the Mohegans. Perhaps a burial ground, or a place of worship."

Leopold had bent to study the map. "Could I borrow this, Professor?"

"It's a rare map, but I could Xerox this portion for you."

"Please do."

While he was gone, Connie asked, "what do you think, Captain? Do we have a crazy Indian killing people because they're living on sacred land?"

"Either that or someone who wants us to think he's a crazy Indian."

Professor Furness returned with the copy. "I wish I could be of more help."

"Perhaps you can," Leopold said. "Did you ever have any students— or anyone else—who expressed interest in this material?"

"What—The Iroquois myths and the Mohegan sacred areas? No, not really. I don't teach either one in my folklore course."

"Did you ever have any American Indian students?"

"No-o-o. . . I don't think so . . . Wait a minute—there was one fellow, some years back. But he didn't take any great interest in the old myths."

"What was his name?"

"I'd have to look it up."

"Could you do it, please?" Leopold asked. "It probably won't mean anything, but I hate to overlook any possible lead."

Furness stared intently at the ceiling. "Let's see . . . that would have been four—no, five—years ago. My enrollment records should show his name. I'll know it when I see it. Something like . . . ."

"Take your time," Leopold said.

"I think it was . . . yes, here—the boy's name was Harry Standing Elk."

The supermarket near Maplegrove was filled with Saturday afternoon shoppers. Watching them from his car in the parking lot, Harry Standing Elk wondered how many he could have picked off with his arrows as they came out the automatic doors wheeling their shopping carts. But most went directly to their cars, loading the groceries into the vehicles and leaving the carts to clutter the lot. What he needed, to be safe, was one who lived nearby, who would leave the area on foot.

Finally one came—a stout woman carrying a single small bag of groceries. She avoided the parking lot and headed around the rear of the store, crossing a weed-infested lot toward a line of low ranch homes on the next street.

Standing Elk started his car and drove around the block. He spotted her just as she reached the sidewalk, and he pulled up to park across the street, a bit behind her. She didn't look in his direction.

First he tried aiming the bow through the open window of the car, but it kept hitting the windshield. Finally he glanced down the street, seeing her moving farther away with each step. A block away some children played in a front yard, and a few houses beyond them a man was washing

his car. Otherwise the street seemed deserted. Standing Elk opened his
car door and got out, using the door as a shield while he threaded the
arrow.

His first shot hit her in the back and she went down on her knees,
sending groceries flying across the sidewalk. He was bringing a second
arrow up to aim when he saw that it wouldn't be needed. The woman had
collapsed on her face, uttering only a low moan before she lay still.

He slid back into the car and drove quickly away.

The little man was waving his hands with excitement as he talked to
Leopold. "I saw him! I saw him! He stood by the side of his car and shot
her in the back with a arrow! My God, I couldn't believe my eyes!"

"Try to talk slower, Mr. Franklin, and tell us just what happened."

They were standing in the driveway of a house across the street from
the spot where Betty King had died, and Leopold's men were still
working with their cameras and evidence bags, keeping back the neighbors. The street was tense with a mixture of curiosity and horror as word
spread about the latest killing. This one had been in daylight, and that
meant no one was safe.

" . . . saw the car pull up and park," Mr. Franklin was saying.
"Naturally I was curious about a car in front of my house. Thought it
might be a salesman or something. So I watched through the front
window. He was doin' something in the car for a minute or so, but I
couldn't see what. Then he got out, on the far side, and I saw the bow and
arrow. I still couldn't believe he was goin' to kill her. Not till he did it."

"What did the man look like?"

"Big. Black hair."

"Young?"

"I never got a good look at his face. He was turned away from me all
the time."

"What about the car?"

"I saw that, all right. It was a blue Ford with a white top—last year's
model, I think. Seemed to be in good condition."

"What model Ford?"

"The standard one, I think. It wasn't a compact."

"How about the license number?"

"Yeah, I thought of that right away."

"Did you get it?"

"Franklin shuffled his feet. "Just part. It ended in 567, I remember
that, because it was easy to remember. But there were two other numbers
and a letter that I didn't catch."

"Thank you," Leopold said. "You've been a big help."

As he walked back across the street, he couldn't help wishing that Mr. Franklin had been more of a help. His description of the killer added nothing to what they already knew. The description of the car was helpful but frustratingly incomplete. Nevertheless he passed it along to Fletcher with instructions to put out an alarm.

"It's probably stolen," Fletcher reasoned. "He wouldn't use his own car in broad daylight."

"He might if he's crazy," Leopold replied. "I wish to hell our witness had gotten the entire licence number."

Fletcher lowered his voice. "Have you looked at the faces of these people, Captain? They're about one step away from sheer panic. They're talking about setting up armed street patrols to protect their neighborhood."

"I can't say I blame them, but we don't want them out shooting at each other. I'll try to calm them down."

While Leopold talked to the people, Fletcher radioed in a description of the wanted car. Then he tried to call Connie at Headquarters to tell her of the latest killing, but she was off somewhere checking out a lead.

When Fletcher went back to the crowd on the sidewalk, Leopold was just turning away. "I reassured them as best I could. I told them we'll patrol day and night with a double shift."

You're certain he'll stick to this area, Captain?"

"I think so. He imagines this development has desecrated some sacred Indian land."

"You know something? He didn't leave a note this time."

"I guess that arrow was message enough. Any luck with the sporting-goods stores?"

Fletcher shook his head. "None, Captain. They're standard hunting arrows. They sell 'em by the hundreds or thousands every fall. There've been no unusual purchases this spring or summer, but that doesn't prove anything. He might have bought them last fall, during the hunting season, or more recently in some other city."

"All right. Let's finish up here."

"What's Connie up to?"

"She's checking a name we got from Professor Furness this morning. An Indian student he had five years ago. Probably no connection, but I'm not overlooking a thing."

One of the patrolmen was signalling to Fletcher from the car. "Head-quarters wants you, Lieutenant."

"Be right there."

Fletcher walked over and took the microphone from the patrolman.

Headquarters came on at once. "We've a possible fix on that wanted car, Lieutenant."

"That was fast!"

"A patrol was passing a parking lot just as they got the description. They spotted a blue and white Ford, license number ZUF-567. Could be the car."

"Could be. Where is it?"

"Parking lot corner of Greggs and West End Avenue. Lot of apartments in the area."

"Yeah, I know it. Find out who it's registered to, will you?"

"Will do. Hang in there."

Fletcher walked over to Leopold and told him the story. "Maybe we're in luck."

"We could use some."

Fletcher walked back to the patrol car and waited for the word on the license number. After another few minutes it came through. "Lieutenant, that car belongs to Superior Car Rental."

"Damn!"

"We can find out who leased it, but it'll take a while. They've got lots of rental agencies around the area, and their main office is closed on Saturday."

"Do what you can," Fletcher said. "I'm going over there to look around. Greggs and West End, right?"

"Right, Lieutenant. Car 55 is standing by."

Harry Standing Elk carefully stowed the bow and hunting arrows in the closet of the furnished apartment and locked the door. Then he went to the refrigerator and took out a beer.

It had been a good day. The first one in daylight.

Now maybe they'd know he meant business. Now maybe they'd pack up and leave the land, leave it to the spirits of Harry's kin.

He took a swallow of beer and walked casually to the window overlooking the parking lot. Then he froze.

There was a police patrol car down there, parked on the street. A uniformed officer was talking to another man, and the two of them were gazing in the direction of Harry's rented car.

His first reaction was to run to the closet. But before he could unlock it he had second thoughts. There was nothing about the car that could identify him. He'd worn gloves and had been careful about fingerprints, and he'd leased it under a false name, using a faked driver's license. If he just sat tight, he was safe.

Now he saw they were talking to the man who ran the parking lot. The man shrugged and pointed vaguely to Harry's building and the one next to it. The man with the police officer nodded and started walking toward the buildings.

Harry Standing Elk considered the possibilities. He could run away, down the back stairs and into the alley, abandoning both apartment and car. Or he could stay and bluff it out. The man in the parking lot didn't know him. Nobody knew him. They couldn't prove a thing unless they found the bow and the arrows. And if it came to that he'd kill first. As if to reinforce the idea, he picked up his knife.

He heard voices down the hall and presently there was a knock on his door. "Who's there?" he called out.

"Police. Open up!"

"What do you want?"

"Just some questions to ask you."

Standing Elk edged the hunting knife out of its sheath and held it behind his back. "All right. Wait a minute."

He opened the door and the man he'd seen from the window flashed a badge and identification card. "I'm Lieutenant Fletcher. We're checking on a car in the lot next door that might be stolen. A blue and white Ford. Lady down the hall says she thinks it belongs to somebody on this floor. Would you know anything about it, Mr.—" the detective's eyes went to the name on the door "—Elk?"

Harry gripped the knife tighter. "Not a thing, Lieutenant. I don't own a car myself. I'm just up from New York, and I never even learned to drive one down there. Traveled the subways, mostly."

"Well, you'll find you need one around here. How about the next apartment? Know who lives there?"

"A young couple, I think."

"They got a car?"

"I really don't know."

"Okay, Mr. Elk. Sorry to bother you."

"Perfectly all right."

He closed the door and leaned against it. That had been close. That had been very close. And how ironic that the man's name was Fletcher. The very word meant a maker of arrows!

* * *

On Sunday morning in his office Leopold asked them, "Where are we? Do we have anything at all to go on?"

"Well, you know we found the car," Fletcher replied, tapping a pencil on the desk as he spoke. "But not the person who leased it. He used a false registration and the girl at the car rental place can't remember him. He may have a room in a nearby apartment building, but I can't find anyone who knows for sure."

"Fingerprints?"

Fletcher shook his head. "He may be crazy, but he's careful. We checked all the places—steering wheel, rear-view mirror, door handles, radio knobs. Nothing."

Leopold swung around and asked Connie, "what about that name you're checking?"

"I'm having trouble finding the right people on the weekend. I talked to a woman where he boarded while at college, but she doesn't know what became of him. When he left he said something about going out to South Dakota. But that was four years ago."

"Was he militant?"

Connie nodded. "On Indian matters, yes. Belonged to a couple of militant campus groups. He could be our killer, if he's back in town."

The intercom buzzed and Leopold answered it. They heard a voice say, "Captain, this is Kohler in Communications. We've just had a radio report from one of the cars patrolling Maplegrove. It's the Depredator again!"

Harry Standing Elk knew what he had to do.

The apartment was no longer safe, and he must find a new one. More important, he must write out a list of his demands and make them known to the people of Maplegrove. The car was gone and he couldn't risk renting another. He could hardly call a taxi or ride the bus out there with his bow. That meant using his own car and taking the risk involved.

But first the note. He spent much of Sunday morning composing it until it was just right: "To the people of the Maplegrove development: You have slain my people, you have slain me! You have taken our sacred lands and despoiled them! No retaliation would be too great for the crimes you have committed against the American Indian! But I give you a chance to live! Abandon these sacred Mohegan grounds on which you dwell! Leave them as you found them, and no one else will die! If you do not listen, one of you shall die for each day you remain! The Depredator."

That was it, that was right.

He drove out once more to the familiar area and parked across the street from the largest church in the development. Services were in progress and the street was deserted. He was tempted to wait, hidden in the parking lot, and pick off the first person through the doors. But with his own car he could not risk it. There would be time for that later. Instead, he tied the message around the shaft of an arrow and aimed it at the church's great oak door. When it hit with a thud he felt just a little like Martin Luther.

Leopold read the message in the midst of a large circle of frightened Sunday worshippers. "There's nothing to fear," he assured them. "Go home now. The streets are well patrolled."

"Then why didn't someone see him do this?" an elderly lady asked.

Fletcher whispered into Leopold's ear. "The Commissioner himself is on the way out here. I just heard it on the radio. Let's go."

Leopold nodded. He liked to avoid the top brass when he was on a case. They only complicated things. "We'll check this note for prints," he assured the people. "Now go on your way!"

A television reporter and cameraman blocked his path to the car. "Will you release the text of the warning, Captain? Will you make a statement about it?"

"Later," Leopold muttered, brushing past them.

He went back to the office with Fletcher, wondering how long he had before the Commissioner would be on the phone. "Should I get coffee?" Fletcher asked.

"If the machine's working." He tossed some coins across the desk, nodding to Connie as she came in.

"What do you make of the note, Captain?"

"Not much." Leopold read it through again. "His use of *will* and *shall* in the past two sentences is quite proper, I think. Very few people use those words according to the rules."

"Maybe he was one of Furness' English students in addition to a folklore student."

Leopold grunted. "What about Standing Elk?"

"Elk?" Fletcher repeated, coming back with the coffee.

"Harry Standing Elk, the name Connie's checking on." He had an idea. "Did you try the newspaper, Connie? Their morgue might have some record if he was an active militant."

"Good idea. And someone should be there on Sunday."

"I talked to a guy named Elk," Fletcher was saying while Connie dialed the paper. "He had an apartment near where the car was found."

Connie was speaking to somebody on the phone. Leopold sipped the coffee and found it as bad as ever.

"*What?*" Connie exclaimed into the phone. "You're sure?"

"What is it, Connie?"

"Bad news on Harry Standing Elk. He's not the Depredator."

"How do you know?"

"Because he's dead. He was one of the militant Indians killed during the government's siege of Wounded Knee a couple of years back."

"Come on," Leopold said, on his feet. "Take us to this apartment you mentioned, Fletcher!"

The Sunday streets were nearly deserted as they sped across town. It was a beach-and-picnic sort of day, and Leopold was thankful for the lack of city traffic. It gave him time to talk as he drove.

"Those Indian tribes! Why would a militant take the name of an Iroquois folk hero to try to win back sacred Mohegan lands? The Mohegans—or Mohicans—weren't part of the Iroquois nation. In fact, they were bitter enemies, as any reader of Fenimore Cooper could tell you."

"That wouldn't mean anything to today's Indian," Connie argued, hanging on as Leopold took a corner without slowing down.

"Maybe, maybe not. But then there's that sacred Mohegan land. How did the killer even know about it? Professor Furness said it was a rare map."

"Maybe it was reproduced in a book sometime. Or maybe Standing Elk saw it while he was studying in Furness' class."

"But Standing Elk is dead, remember?"

Fletcher pointed through the windshield. "There's the apartment house, Captain."

Connie and Leopold spotted the man at the same instant. He was just loading a box into a car at the curb when Leopold swerved his vehicle into a wild U-turn.

"That's him!" Fletcher shouted. "That's Elk!"

Harry Standing Elk drove directly to the apartment from the church in Maplegrove. He knew it was risky, but it was more risky to abandon it completely. There was a suit of his clothes, with labels, in the closet. And some books and papers he hadn't risked leaving in the rented car. The place had to be emptied out, and quickly.

He managed to fit everything into a single box, then found the landlord and turned in his key. "Been called out of town," he said. "Be gone for a month or so."

"I can't keep the apartment that long."

"I know, I know," Harry told him. "I'll get another place when I come back."

"Where you goin'?" the landlord asked.

"Out west. Maybe South Dakota."

Then he carried the box of his possessions down to the street. He was just loading it into the car when he saw them—Leopold and those others. And they saw him.

Their car swerved around and came up onto the sidewalk in front of him. He dived for the back seat, pulling out the bow with its attached clip of arrows.

This now, this was the final battle.

Leopold had his gun out, but Standing Elk's arrow came up. He was faster, faster than the white oppressors. But then the other one fired through the car window and the bullet hit Standing Elk's arm as he released the arrow. It hit the roof of Leopold's car on an angle and was deflected off into the street.

He backed up, threading a second arrow despite the pain.

But then Leopold shouted something he couldn't hear and he felt his legs go out from under him. He was hit again. The bow slid across the sidewalk out of reach and then they were on him, pulling his good hand from the knife.

Shouting things he couldn't understand.

It was Wounded Knee again, and Sand Creek, and the Little Big Horn. He was Harry Standing Elk, trampled and bloody once more. But why, he wondered vaguely, why were they calling him Professor Furness?

Inspector Maigret

INSPECTOR MAIGRET PURSUES

Georges Simenon

THE FOUR MEN were packed in the taxi. It was freezing all over Paris. At half-past seven in the morning the city looked wan; the wind was whipping the powdery frost along the ground. The thinnest of the four men, on one of the flap seats, had a cigarette stuck to his lower lip and handcuffs on his wrists. The most important one, clothed in a thick overcoat, heavy-jawed, a bowler hat on his head, was smoking his pipe and watching the railings of the Bois de Boulogne file past.

"You want me to put on a big dramatic scene?" the handcuffed man suggested politely. "With struggling, frothing at the mouth, insults, and all?"

Taking the cigarette from between the man's lips and opening the door, for they had arrived at the Porte de Bagatelle, Inspector Maigret growled, "Don't overdo it."

The pathways in the Bois were deserted, white as limestone, and as hard. A dozen or so people were standing around at the corner of a bridle path, and a photographer prepared to go into action on the group as it approached.

But, as instructed, P'tit Louis raised his arms in front of his face.

Maigret, looking surly, swung his head from side to side like a bear, taking everything in—the new blocks of flats on the Boulevard Richard-Wallace, their shutters still closed, a few workmen on bikes coming from Puteaux, a lighted tram, two concierges approaching, their hands blue with cold.

"Is this it?" he asked.

The day before he had arranged for the following information to appear in the newspapers:

317

BAGATELLE MURDER

This time the police will not have been long in clearing up an affair that looked as if it presented insurmountable difficulties. It will be remembered that on Monday morning a park-keeper in the Bois de Boulogne discovered along one of the pathways a hundred yards or so from the Porte de Bagatelle a corpse it was possible to identify on the spot.

It was Ernest Borms, a well-known Viennese doctor who had been in practice in Neuilly for several years. Borms was wearing evening clothes. He must have been attacked during the night of Sunday/Monday, while returning to his flat on the Boulevard Richard-Wallace.

A bullet fired at point-blank range from a small-caliber revolver struck him full in the heart.

Borms, still young and handsome and well turned-out, led a fairly social life.

Scarcely forty-eight hours after the murder Police Headquarters have just made an arrest. Tomorrow morning, between seven and eight o'clock, the man concerned will be conducted to the scene for the purpose of a reconstruction of the crime.

As things turned out, this case was to be referred to at Headquarters as the one perhaps most characteristically Maigret; but when they spoke of it in his hearing, he had a curious way of turning his head away with a groan.

To proceed, everything was ready. Hardly any gaping onlookers, as planned. It was not for nothing that Maigret had chosen this early hour of the morning. Moreover, among the ten or twelve people who were hanging about, could be spotted some plainclothesmen wearing their most innocent air. One of them, Torrence, who loved disguises, was dressed as a milkman. At the sight of him his chief shrugged eloquently. If only P'tit Louis didn't overact. An old customer of theirs who had been picked up the day before for picking pockets in the Métro. . .

"You give us a hand tomorrow morning and we'll see that we aren't too hard on you this time . . . " They had fetched him up from the cells.

"Now, then," growled Maigret, "when you heard the footsteps you were hiding in this corner here, weren't you?"

"As you say, Chief Inspector. I was famished. Stony broke . . . I said to myself, a gent on his way home all dressed up like that must be carrying a walletful. 'Your money or your life!' was what I whispered right into his ear. And I swear it wasn't my fault that the thing went off. I'm quite sure it was the cold made me squeeze the trigger."

11 A.M. Maigret was pacing round his office at Headquarters, smoking solidly and constantly fiddling with the phone.

"Is that you, Chief? Lucas here. I followed the old man who seemed so interested in the reconstruction. Nothing doing there—he's just a lunatic who takes a stroll every morning in the Bois."

"All right, you can come back."

11:15 A.M. "Hullo, is that you, Chief? Torrence. I shadowed the young man you tipped me the wink on. He always hangs round when the plainclothes boys are called in. He's an assistant in a shop on the Champs Elysées. Shall I come back?"

From Janvier no call till five to twelve.

"I've got to be quick, Chief. I'm afraid he'll give me the slip. I'm keeping an eye on him in the mirror of the booth. I'm at the Yellow Dwarf Bar, Boulevard Rochechouart . . . Yes, he spotted me. He's got something on his mind. Crossing the Seine, he threw something in the river. He's tried over and over to shake me off. Will you be coming?"

So began a chase that was to last five days and nights. Among the hurrying crowds, across an unsuspecting Paris, from bar to bar, bistro to bistro, a lone man on the one hand, and on the other Maigret and his detectives, taking it in turn and, in the long run, just as harassed as the man they were following.

Maigret got out of his taxi opposite the Yellow Dwarf at the busy time just before lunch, and found Janvier leaning on the bar. He wasn't troubling to put on any façade of innocence. Quite the opposite.

"Which one is it?"

The detective motioned with his jaw toward a man sitting in the corner at a small table. The man was watching them; his eyes, which were a light blue-gray, gave a foreign cast to his face. Nordic? Slav? More likely a Slav. He was wearing a gray overcoat, a well-cut suit, a soft felt hat. About thirty-five years old, so far as one could judge. He was pale, close-shaven.

"What're you having, Chief? A hot toddy?"

"Toddy let it be. What's *he* drinking?"

"Brandy. It's his fifth this morning. You mustn't mind if I sound slurred, but I've had to follow him round all the bistros. He's tough, you know. Look at him—it's been like that all morning. He wouldn't lower his eyes for all the kingdoms of the earth.''

It was true. And it was strange. You couldn't call it arrogance or defiance. The man was just looking at them. If he felt any anxiety, it was concealed. It was sadness rather that his face expressed, but a calm, reflective sadness.

''At Bagatelle, when he noticed you were watching him, he went off straight away and I fell into step behind him. He hadn't gone a hundred yards before he turned round. Then, instead of leaving the Bois, as he apparently meant to do, he strode off down the first path he came to. He turned round again. He recognized me. He sat down on a bench despite the cold, and I stopped. More than once I had the impression he wanted to speak to me, but in the end he only shrugged and set off again.

''At the Porte Dauphine I almost lost him. He jumped into a taxi and it was just luck that I found one almost immediately. He got out at the Place de l'Opéra, and rushed into the Métro. One behind the other, we changed trains five times before he began to realize he wouldn't shake me off that way . . .

''We went up again into the street. We were at Place Clichy. Since then we have been going from bar to bar. I was waiting for one with a telephone booth where I could keep him in sight. When he saw me phoning, he gave a bitter little laugh. Honestly, you'd have sworn after that he was waiting for you.''

''Ring up H.Q. Lucas and Torrence are to hold themselves ready to join me as soon as they're called. And a photographer, too, from the technical branch, with a miniature camera.''

''Waiter!'' the man called out. ''What do I owe you?''

''Three-fifty.''

''I bet he's a Pole,'' Maigret breathed to Janvier. ''On our way . . . ''

They didn't get far. At Place Blanche they followed the man into a restaurant, sat down at the next table. It was an Italian place, and they ate pasta.

At three, Lucas came to take over from Janvier, who was with Maigret at a *brasserie* opposite the Gare du Nord.

''The photographer?'' Maigret asked.

''He's waiting outside to get him as he leaves.''

And sure enough, when the Pole left the place, having finished reading the papers, a detective hurried up. At less than three feet he took a shot of him. The man raised his hand quickly to his face, but it was already too late. Then, proving that he knew what was going on, he cast a reproachful look at Maigret.

Aha, my little man, Maigret said to himself, you have some good reason for not revealing where you live. Well, you may be patient, but so am I.

By evening a few snowflakes were fluttering down in the street, the stranger walked on, hands in pockets, waiting for bedtime.

"I'll take over for the night, Chief?" Lucas suggested.

"No. I'd rather you coped with the photograph. Look at the hotel registrations first. Then see what you can find out in the foreign quarters. That fellow knows his Paris. He didn't arrive yesterday. There must be people who know him.

"How about putting his picture in the papers?"

Maigret eyed his subordinate with scorn. How could Lucas, who had been working with him for so many years, fail to understand? Had the police one single clue? Nothing. Not one piece of evidence. A man killed during the night in the Bois de Boulogne. No weapon is found. No prints. Dr. Borms lives alone, and his only servant doesn't know where he spent the previous evening. "Do as I say. Get going . . . "

Finally at midnight the man decides to go into a hotel. Maigret follows him in. It is a second- or even third-class hotel.

"I want a room."

"Will you register here, please?"

He registers hesitantly, his fingers stiff with cold. He looks Maigret up and down as if to say, "If you think that's my problem—I can write any name that comes."

And, in fact, he has done so. Nicolas Slaatkovitch, resident of Cracow, arrived the day before in Paris. It is all false, obviously.

Maigret telephones to Headquarters. They hunt through the files of furnished lodgings, the registers of foreigners, they get in touch with the frontier posts. No Nicolas Slaatkovitch.

"And a room for you?" the proprietor asks with distaste, for he senses the presence of a policeman.

"No, thank you. I'll spend the night on the stairs."

It's safer that way. He sits down on a step in front of the door of Room 7. Twice the door opens. The man peers through the gloom, makes out Maigret's silhouette, and ends up by going to bed. In the morning his face is rough with stubble. He hasn't been able to change his shirt. He hasn't even got a comb, and his hair is rumpled.

Lucas has just arrived. "I'll do the next shift, Chief?"

Maigret refuses to leave his stranger. He has watched him pay the bill. He has seen him grow pale. He guesses his thoughts . . .

And a little later, in a bar where, almost side by side, they are breakfasting on white coffee and croissants, the man openly counts up his fortune. One hundred-franc note, two twenty-franc pieces, one of ten, and some small change. He makes a bitter grimace.

Well, he won't get far on that. When he arrived at the Bois de Boulogne, he had come straight from home, for he was freshly shaved, not a speck of dust, not a crease in his clothes. He hadn't even looked to see how much money he had on him.

What he threw in the Seine, Maigret guesses, were his identification papers, perhaps visiting cards. At all costs he wants to prevent their finding out his address.

And so the round of the homeless begins again: the loitering in front of shops or round street traders, the bars one has to go into from time to time, even if it's only to sit down, especially when it's cold outside, the papers one reads in the *brasseries* . . .

One hundred and fifty francs. No more lunchtime restaurant. The man makes do with hard-boiled eggs, which he eats, along with his pint, standing up at the bar counter, while Maigret gulps down sandwiches.

For a long time the man has been thinking about going into a movie, his hand fingering the small change in his pocket. Better to stick it out. He walks . . . and walks . . .

There is, incidentally, one detail that strikes Maigret. It is always in the same districts that this exhausting stroll takes place: from the Trinité to Place Clichy, from Place Clichy to Barbès, by way of Rue Caulaincourt . . . from Barbès to the Gare du Nord and Rue Lafayette. Besides, the man's afraid of being recognized, isn't he? Of course he's chosen the districts farthest from his home or hotel, those he didn't usually frequent . . .

Does, he, like many foreigners, haunt Montparnasse? The parts around the Panthéon?

His clothes indicate he is reasonably well off. They are comfortable, sober, and well cut. A professional man, no doubt. What's more, he wears a ring, so he's married.

Maigret has had to agree to hand over to Torrence, and has dashed home. Madame Maigret is displeased: her sister has come up from Orléans, she has taken a lot of trouble over the dinner, and her husband, after a shave and a change of clothes, is already off again, and doesn't know when he'll be back.

He drives off the Quai des Orfèvres. "Lucas hasn't left anything for me?"

Yes, he has. There's a note from the sergeant. He's been round several of the Polish and Russian quarters showing the photograph. Nobody knows the man. Nothing from the political circles, either. As a last resource he has had a large number of copies made of the photograph, and police are now going from door to door in all the districts of Paris, from concierge to concierge, showing the document to bar owners and waiters.

"Hullo, is that Chief Inspector Maigret? This is one of the usherettes at the newsreel theater on the Boulevard de Strasbourg. It's a gentleman—Monsier Torrence. He's asked me to call you to say he's here, but he didn't want to leave his place in the theater."

Not so stupid, on the stranger's part. He has worked out that it's the best heated place to pass a few hours cheaply—two francs to get in, and you can see the program several times.

A curious intimacy has sprung up between follower and followed, between the man, whose face is now dark with stubble and whose clothes are crumpled, and Maigret, who never for a moment stops trailing him. There is even one rather comic point: they've both caught colds. Their noses are red; they pull out their handkerchiefs almost in time with one another. Once, in spite of himself, the stranger had to smile as he saw Maigret going off into a series of sneezes.

After five consecutive newsreel programs, a dirty hotel on the Boulevard de la Chapelle. Same name on the register. And again Maigret installs himself on the stairs. But as this is a hotel with a casual trade, he is disturbed every ten minutes by couples going up and down; they stare at him curiously, and the women don't find him a reassuring sight.

When he's at the end of his tether, or at the breaking point, will the man decide to go home? In one of the *brasseries*, where he stays long enough to take off his gray coat, Maigret without more ado seizes the garment and looks inside the collar. The coat comes from Old England, the shop on the Boulevard des Italiens. It is a ready-made coat, and the shop must have sold dozens of others like it. One clue, however: it is last year's model, so the stranger has been in Paris for a year at least. And in a year he must have found somewhere to hang out . . .

Maigret has started drinking grog to cure his cold. The other now pays out his money drop by drop. He drinks his coffee straight; he lives on croissants and hard-boiled eggs.

The news from the office is always the same: nothing to report. Nobody recognizes the photograph of the Pole. No one has heard of any missing person.

As to the dead man, nothing there, either. A good practice, he made a lot of money, wasn't interested in politics, went out a lot, and, as he dealt with nervous diseases, most of his patients were women.

There was one experiment Maigret had not yet had the chance of seeing through to the end: how long it would take for a well-bred, well-cared-for, well-dressed man to lose his outward polish.

Four days. As he now knew. To begin with, the unshavenness. The first morning the man looked like a lawyer, or a doctor, or an architect, or a businessman; you could picture him leaving a cosy flat. A four-day growth transformed him to such an extent that if one had now put his pictures in the papers and referred to the Bois de Boulogne affair, everyone would have said, "You can see he's a murderer."

The bitter weather and lack of sleep had reddened his eyelids, and his cheeks were feverish from his cold. His shoes, which were no longer polished, seemed to have lost their shape. His coat weighed on him, and his trousers were baggy round the knees.

Even his walk was no longer the same. He sidled along the wall, he lowered his eyes when people looked at him. Another thing: he turned his head away when he passed a restaurant where one could see people sitting down to large meals . . .

"Your last twenty francs," Maigret worked out, "poor wretch. What now?"

Lucas, Torrence, and Janvier took over from him from time to time, but he left his post as little as possible. He would burst into the Quai des Orfèvres, would see his Chief.

"You'd be well advised to take a rest, Maigret."

It was a peevish Maigret, touchy as if he were torn between contradictory emotions. "Am I or am I not supposed to be finding the murderer?"

"Of course."

"Well then, back to my post." As if resentfully, he would sigh. "I wonder where we'll sleep tonight."

Only twenty francs left. Not even that—when he got back, Torrence said the man had eaten three hard-boiled eggs and drunk two rum coffees in a bar on the corner of the Rue Montmartre.

"Eight francs fifty. That leaves eleven francs fifty."

Maigret admired him. Far from hiding himself, Maigret now tailed him quite openly, sometimes walking right next to him, and he had some difficulty to refrain from speaking to him. "Come now, don't you think it's time to have a proper meal? Somewhere there's a warm home where you're expected. A bed, slippers, a razor. Eh? And a good dinner.''

But the man continued to prowl under the arc lamps of Les Halles, like one who no longer knows where to turn. In and out among the heaps of cabbages and carrots, stepping out of the way at the whistle of the train or when the farmers' trucks passed.

''Hasn't even the price of a hotel room.''

That evening the National Meteorological Office registered a temperature of eight degrees below zero. The man treated himself to hot sausages from a stall in the streets. Now he would reek of garlic and fat the whole night through.

Once he tried to slip into a shelter and stretch out in the corner. A policeman, whom Maigret wasn't able to stop in time, moved him on. He was hobbling now. Along the quais. The Pont des Arts. As long as he didn't take it into his head to throw himself into the Seine. Maigret didn't feel he had the courage to jump in after him into the black water that was beginning to fill with drift ice.

The man was walking along the towpath level, where the tramps lay grumbling and, under the bridges, all the good places were taken.

In a small street close to the Place Maubert, through the windows of a strange bistro, old men could be seen sleeping with their heads on the tables. Then, with a fatalistic shrug, he pushed open the door.

Before it closed behind him, Maigret had time to be sickened by the smelly gust that struck him in the face. He preferred to stay outside. He called a policeman, posted him in his place on the pavement while he went to telephone Lucas to take over for the night.

''I've been trying to get you for the last hour, Chief. We've found him! Thanks to a concierge. The fellow's called Stefan Strevzki, an architect, thirty-four years old, born in Warsaw, been in France for three years. Works for a firm in the Faubourg Saint-Honoré. Married to a Hungarian, a magnificent creature named Dora. Living at Passy, Rue de la Pompe, in a twelve-thousand-franc flat. No political interests. The concierge has never seen the dead man. Stefan left the house earlier than usual on Monday morning. She was surprised not to see him return, but she wasn't worried, having ascertained—''

''What time is it?''

''Half-past three. I'm alone at Headquarters. I've had some beer brought up, but it's too cold.''

''Listen, Lucas, you're going—yes, I know, too late for the morning one. But the evening ones . . . understand?''

* * *

That morning the man's clothing gave off a muffled odor of poverty. His eyes were sunken. The look he cast at Maigret in the pale morning contained the deepest pathos and reproach.

Had he not been driven, little by little, but for all that at a dizzy pace to the very lowest depths? He turned up the collar of his overcoat. He didn't leave the neighborhood, but he rushed into a bistro that had just opened and downed four quick drinks, as if to rid himself of the appalling aftertaste the night had left in his throat and chest.

So much the worse for him. From now on he no longer had anything. Nothing was left for him but to walk up and down the streets the frost was making slippery. He must be stiff all over. He was limping with his left leg. From time to time he stopped and looked around despairingly.

As soon as he stopped going into cafés where there was a telephone, Maigret could no longer summon a relief. Back again along the quais. Then that mechanical gesture of flipping through the book bargains, turning the pages, pausing to check the authenticity of an engraving or a print.

A freezing wind was sweeping across the Seine. The water tinkled as the barges and moved through it, as tiny fragments of ice glittered and jostled against one another. From a distance Maigret caught sight of the windows of his office. His sister-in-law had gone back to Orléans. As long as Lucas had . . .

He didn't know yet that this dreadful trail was to become a classic, and that for years the older generation of detectives would recount the details to new colleagues. The silliest thing about it all was that it was a ridiculous detail that upset him most: the man had a pimple on his forehead, a pimple that, on close inspection, turned out to be a boil which was changing from red to purple.

As long as Lucas . . .

At midday the man, who certainly knew his Paris, made for the free soup kitchen that is situated at the end of the Boulevard Saint-Germain. He took his place in the queue of down-and-outers. An old man spoke to him, but he pretended not to understand. Then another, with a pock-marked face, spoke to him in Russian.

Maigret crossed over to the opposite pavement, and paused. When he was driven to have sandwiches in a bistro, he half turned so that the other should not see him eating them through the windows.

The poor wretches moved forward slowly, went in, four or maybe six at a time, to the room where bowls of hot soup were being served. The queue grew longer. From time to time there was a shove from the back, which aroused protests from some of the others.

One o'clock. A newsboy appeared at the far end of the street; he was running, his body sloping forward. *"L'Intransigeant!* Get your In-tran—"* He, too, was in a hurry to get there before the others. He could tell his customers from far off, and he paid no attention to the queue of down-and-outers. "Get your—"

"Pst!" Timidly, the man raised his hand to attract the boy's attention. The others stared at him. So he had still a few sous left to spend on a paper?

Maigret, too, summoned the boy, unfolded the paper, and, to his relief, found what he was looking for—the photograph of a beautiful young woman smiling out of the front page.

STRANGE DISAPPEARANCE

A young Polish woman, Madame Dora Strevzki, who disappeared four days ago from her home in Passy, 217 Rue de la Pompe, has now been reported missing. Her husband, Monsieur Stefan Strevzki, has also been missing from his home since the previous day—i.e., Monday—and the concierge, who reported the disappearance to the police, states . . .

The man had only five or six yards more to go in the queue before he could claim his bowl of steaming soup, when he left his place in the line and was almost run over by a bus. He reached the opposite pavement just as Maigret drew level.

"I'm ready," he said simply. "Take me away. I'll answer all your questions . . . "

They were all standing in the corridor of Headquarters—Lucas, Janvier, Torrence, and others who had not been in on the case but knew about it. As they passed, Lucas made a triumphant signal to Maigret.

A door opened and shut. Beer and sandwiches on the table.

"Take something to eat first."

Not so easy. Mouthfuls stuck in his throat. Then, at last, "Now that she's gone and is somewhere safe . . . "

Maigret couldn't face him: he had to turn away and poke the stove.

"When I read accounts of the murder in the papers I had already suspected Dora of deceiving me with that man. I knew, too, she wasn't his only mistress. Knowing Dora and her impetuous nature . . . You understand? If he wanted to get rid of her, I knew she was capable of . . . And she always carried an ivory-handled gun in her handbag. When the papers reported that an arrest had been made and there was to be a reconstruction of the crime, I wanted to see . . . "

Maigret would have liked to be able to say to him, as the British police do, "I must warn you that anything you say may be used in evidence against you."

He had kept his coat on and he was still wearing his hat. "Now that she's safe . . . For I suppose . . . " He looked about him anxiously. A suspicion crossed his mind.

"She must have understood when I didn't come home. I knew it would end like that—that Borms wasn't the man for her, that she wouldn't accept the role of a mere plaything, and that she'd come back to me. She went out alone that Sunday evening, as she had been doing recently. She must have killed him then."

Maigret blew his nose. He took a long time over it. A ray of sunlight—the harsh winter sunlight that goes with sharp frost—came in the window. The pimple or boil gleamed on the forehead of the man—as Maigret found he had to go on calling him.

"So your wife killed him. When she found out he had never really cared for her. And you, you realized she had done it. And you didn't want . . . "

He suddenly went up to the Pole. "I'm sorry, old man," he grunted, as if he was talking to an old friend. "I had to find out the truth, hadn't I. It was my duty."

Then he opened the door. "Bring in Madame Dora Strevzki. Lucas, you carry on. I—"

And for the next two days nobody saw him again at Headquarters. His chief telephoned him at home. "Well now, Maigret. You know she's confessed, and—by the way, how's your cold? They tell me—"

"It's nothing, Chief. It's getting better. Another day. How is he?"

"What? Who?"

"He—the man."

"Oh, I see. He's got hold of the best lawyer in Paris. He has hopes—you know, *crimes passionnels* . . . "

Maigret went back to bed and into a grog-and-aspirin stupor. When, later on, he was asked about the investigation, his grumbled "What investigation?" was enough to discourage further questions.

As for the man, he came to see him once or twice or week, and kept him informed of the hopes the defense were holding out.

It wasn't a straightforward acquittal: one year's imprisonment, with sentence suspended.

And the man—it was he who taught Maigret to play chess.

"Nameless Detective"

A KILLING IN XANADU
Bill Pronzini

THE NAME OF the place, like that of the principality in Coleridge's *Kubla Khan* and of the newspaper tycoon's estate in *Citizen Kane*, was Xanadu. "In Xanadu did Kubla Khan a stately pleasure-dome decree . . . '' This one was neither a principality nor an estate, but you could call it a pleasure-dome—or rather, a whole series of pleasure-domes overlooking a rugged portion of California's Big Sur seacoast, not all that far from the Hearst Castle. Which tied off one of the historical references because William Randolph Hearst was supposedly the model for the tycoon in Orson Welles' classic film.

What it was, this particular Xanadu, was a resort playground for the wealthy Establishment. Eighteen-hole golf course, tennis and racket ball courts, Olympic-sized swimming pool, sauna and steam rooms, two restaurants, three bars, a disco nightclub, and forty or fifty rustic cottages nestled on craggy terrain among tall redwoods. And the tariff was a mere $1500 per week per person, not including meals, drinks, or gratuities.

Nice play if you can get it.

I couldn't get it myself, but that was all right; it was not my idea of a vacation wonderland anyway. The reason I went down there on a windy Thursday in August was to pay a call on one of those who could get it—a San Francisco socialite named Lauren Speers. She was worth a few hundred thousand, all inherited money, and numbered politicians, actors, capitalists, and other influential types among her friends; she also had striking red hair and green eyes and was beautiful enough if you liked them forty and dissipated. I know all of that not because she was my client, but because the man who *was* my client, an attorney named Adam Brister, had told me so and shown me a color photograph. Ms. Speers and I had never laid eyes on each other. Ms. Speers' money and I had never laid eyes on each other either, nor were we ever likely to.

Brister was no better acquainted with her than I was. He had been retained by one Vernon Inge of Oakland, who owned a car which he claimed La Speers had sideswiped with her Porsche in a hit-and-run accident a couple of weeks ago. The accident had rendered Inge a nasty whiplash that kept him from performing his job as a baker. Or so he and Brister alleged in a damage suit against Speers.

The lawsuit was where I came in: I went to Xanadu to serve the lady with a court summons.

So much for the glamorous role of the private eye in modern society. No rich client, no smoky-hot liaison with a beautiful woman, no fat fee. Just two hundred bucks plus expenses to track down a woman who moved around more than the governor, hand her some papers, listen to abusive language—they always throw abusive language at you—and then steal away again into the real world.

But first I had to pass out of the real world, through the portals into Xanadu, and I did that at two-fifteen. A short entrance drive wound upward past part of the golf course, then among lush redwoods and giant ferns, and emerged into a parking area shaped like a bowl. Three-quarters of it was reserved for guest parking; the other quarter was taken up with rows of three-wheeled machines that looked like golf carts, with awnings over them done in pastel ice-cream colors. From what I had been able to find out about Xanadu, the carts were used by guests to get from one pleasure-dome to another, along a network of narrow and sometimes steep paths. Exercise was all well and good in its proper place—tennis court, swimming pool, disco—but the rich folk no doubt considered walking uphill a vulgarity.

Beyond where the carts were was a long slope, with a wide path cut into it and a set of stairs alongside that seemed more ornamental than functional. At the top of the slope, partially visible from below, were some of the resort buildings, all painted in pastel colors like the cart awnings. The muted sounds of people at play drifted down on the cool wind from the ocean.

I put my car into a slot marked *Visitors Parking*. A black guy in a starched white uniform came over to me as I got out. He was about my age, early fifties, with a lot of gray in his hair, and his name was Horace. Or so it said on the pocket of his uniform, in pink script like the sugar-writing on a birthday cake.

He looked at me and I looked at him. I was wearing my best suit, but my best suit was the kind the inhabitants of Xanadu wore to costume parties or gave away to the Salvation Army. But that was okay by Horace. Some people who work at fancy places like this get to be snobs in their own right; not him. His eyes said that I would never make it up that hill over yonder, not for more than a few minutes at a time, but then neither would he and the hell with it.

I let him see that I felt the same way and a faint smile turned one corner of his mouth. "Here on business?" he asked.

"Yes. I'm looking for Lauren Speers."

"She's out right now. Took her car a little past one."

"Do you have any idea when she'll be back?"

"Depends on how thirsty she gets, I suppose."

"Pardon?"

"The lady drinks," Horace said, and shrugged.

"You mean she'd been drinking before she left?"

"Martinis. Starts in at eleven every morning, quits at one, sleeps until four. Then it's Happy Hour. But not today. Today she decided to go out. If I'd seen her in time I'd have tried to talk her out of driving, but she was in that sports job of hers and gone before I even noticed her."

"Must be nice to be rich," I said.

"Yeah," he said.

"Can you tell me which cottage is hers?"

"Number forty-one. Straight ahead past the swimming pool. Paths are all marked. Miss Dolan'll likely be there if you want to wait at the cottage."

"Who's Miss Dolan?"

"Miss Speers' secretary—Bernice Dolan. She's writing a book, you know. Miss Speers, I mean."

"No, I didn't know. What kind of book?"

"All about her life. Ought to be pretty spicy."

"From what I know about her, I guess it will be."

"But I'll never read it," Horace said. "Bible, now, that's much more interesting. If you know what I mean."

I said I knew what he meant. And thanked him for his help. I did not offer him any money; if I had he would have been offended. He would take gratuities from the guests because that was part of his job, but it had already been established that he and I were social equals. And that made an exchange of money unseemly.

I climbed the stairs—I wouldn't have driven one of those cute little carts even if it was allowed, which it wasn't or Horace would have offered me one—and found my way to the swimming pool. You couldn't have missed it; it was laid out between the two largest buildings, surrounded by a lot of bright green lawn and flagstone terracing, with a stone-faced outdoor bar at the near end. Twenty or thirty people in various stages of undress occupied the area. A few of them were in the pool, but most were sitting at wrought-iron tables, being served tall drinks by three white-jacketed waiters. None of the waiters, I noticed, was black.

Nobody paid any attention to me as I passed by, except for a hard-looking thirtyish blonde who undressed me with her eyes—women do it too, sometimes—and then put my clothes back on again and threw me out of her mental bedroom. Fiftyish gentlemen with shaggy looks and a beer belly were evidently not her type.

Past the pool area, where the trees began, were a pair of paths marked with redwood-burl signs. The one on the left, according to the sign, would take me to number 41, so I wandered off in that direction. And ten minutes later I was still wandering, uphill now, with 41 still nowhere in sight. I was beginning to realize that the fancy little carts were not such an affectation as I had first taken them to be.

I had passed three cottages so far—or the walks that led to three cottages. The buildings themselves were set back some distance from the main path, half-hidden by trees, and were all lavish chalet types with wide porches and pastel-colored wrought-iron trim. Unlike the stairs from the parking area, the wrought iron was just as functional as it was ornamental: the curved bars and scrollwork served as a kind of burglar-proofing over the windows. Xanadu may have been a whimsical pleasure resort, but its rulers nonetheless had their defenses up.

Here in the woods it was much cooler, almost cold, because of the ocean breeze and because the afternoon sunlight penetrated only in dappled patches. I was wishing that I'd worn a coat over my suit when I came around a bend and glimpsed a fourth cottage through the red-woods. Another burl sign stood adjacent to the access path, and I could just make out the numerals 41 emblazoned on it.

I took a few more steps toward the sign. And from behind me, then, I heard a sound like that of a lawnmower magnified: one of the carts approaching. I moved off the path as the sound grew louder. A couple of seconds later the thing came around the curve at my back, going at an erratic clip, and shot past me. Inside was a redhaired woman wearing white. The cart veered over to number 41's walk, skidded to a stop, and the redhead got out and hurried toward the cottage. The white garment she wore was a thin coat, buttoned up against the wind, and she had a big straw bag in her right hand; the long red hair streamed out behind her like a sheet of flame. The way she'd handled the cart indicated Ms. Lauren Speers was every bit as sloshed as Horace had led me to believe, but she carried herself on her feet pretty well. The serious drinker, male or female, learns how to walk if not drive in a straight line.

I called out to her but she either didn't hear me or chose to ignore me: she kept on going without breaking stride or glancing in my direction. I ran the rest of the way to the cottage path, turned in along it. She was already on the porch by then, digging in her bag with her free hand; I could see her through a gap in the fronting screen of trees. She found a key and had it in the lock before I could open my mouth to call to her again. In the next second she was inside, with the door shut behind her.

Well, hell, I thought.

I stopped and spent thirty seconds or so catching my breath. Running uphill had never been one of my favorite activities, even when I was in good physical shape. Then I checked the papers Adam Brister had given me to serve. And then I started along the path again.

I was twenty yards from the porch, with most of the cottage visible ahead of me, when the gun went off.

It made a flat cracking sound in the stillness, muffled by the cottage walls but distinct enough to be unmistakable. I pulled up, stiffening, the hair turning bristly on my neck. There was no second shot, not in the three or four seconds I stood motionless and not when I finally went charging ahead onto the porch.

I swatted on the door a couple of times with the edge of my hand. Nothing happened inside. But after a space there was a low cry and a woman's voice said querulously, "Bernice? Oh my God—Bernice!" I caught hold of the knob, turned it; it was locked. The hell with propriety, I thought, and stepped back a pace and slammed the bottom of my shoe against the latch just below the knob.

Metal screeched and wood splinters flew; the door burst open. And I was in a dark room with redwood walls, a beamed ceiling, a fireplace along one wall, rustic furniture scattered here and there. Off to the left was a dining area and a kitchen; off to the right was a short hallway that would lead to the bedrooms and the bath. There were two women in the room, one of them lying crumpled on a circular hooked rug near the fireplace, the other one standing near the entrance to the hallway. Equidistant between them, on the polished-wood floor at the rug's perimeter, was a .25 caliber automatic.

The standing woman was Lauren Speers. She had shed the white coat—it was on a long couch with her straw bag—and she was wearing shorts and a halter, both of them white and brief, showing off a good deal of buttery tan skin. She stood without moving, staring down at the woman on the rug, the knuckles of one hand pressing her lips flat against her teeth. Her expression was one of bleary shock, as if she had too much liquor inside her to grasp the full meaning of what had happened here. Or to have registered my violent entrance. Even when I moved deeper into the room, over in front of her, she did not seem to know I was there.

I went for the gun first. You don't leave a weapon lying around on the floor after somebody has just used it. I picked it up by the tip of the barrel—still warm—and dropped it into my coat pocket. Lauren Speers still didn't move, still didn't acknowledge my presence; her eyes were half-rolled up in their sockets. And I realized that she had fainted standing up, that it was only a matter of seconds before her legs gave out and she fell.

Before that could happen I put an arm around her waist and half-carried her to the nearest chair, put her into it. She was out, all right; her head lolled to one side. I could smell the sour odor of gin on her breath. The whole room smelled of gin, in fact, as if somebody had been using the stuff for disinfectant.

The woman on the rug was dead. I knew that even without checking for a pulse; had known it the instant I saw her wide-open eyes and the blood on her blouse beneath one twisted arm. She was in her late thirties, attractive in a regular-featured way, with short brown hair and a thin mouth. Wearing blouse, skirt, open-toed sandals.

Looking at her made my stomach feel queasy, filled me with a sense of revulsion and awe. It was the same reaction I always had to violent death, because it was such an ugliness, such a waste. I swallowed against the taste of bile and turned away.

Lauren Speers was still sprawled where I'd put her in the chair, unmoving. I went past her, down the short hall, and looked into the two bedrooms and the bath. All three were empty. And the windows in all three were closed and locked; I could see that at a glance.

I came back out and looked into the kitchen. That was empty too. I started across to a set of sliding glass doors that led onto a rear balcony, but before I got there I noticed something on the floor between the couch and a burl coffee table—a piece of white paper folded lengthwise, lying there tent-fashion. I detoured over and used my handkerchief to pick it up.

It was a sheet of notepaper with six lines of writing in a neat, backslanted feminine hand: three names followed by three series of numbers. All of the names and numbers had heavy lines drawn through them, like items crossed off on a grocery list.

Rykman 56   57   59   62   63   116–125   171–175—25,000

Boyer   214–231   235   239–247   255—25,000

Huddleston 178   170   205–211   360–401   415–420—50,000

None of that meant anything to me. I put the paper into the same pocket with the gun, moved on to the sliding doors. They were securely locked, with one of those twist latches that are supposed to be impossible to force from outside. Adjacent was a wide dormer-style window split into vertical halves that fastened in the center, so you could open them inward on a hot day to let in the sea breeze. The halves were also locked—a simple bar-type catch on one that flipped over and fit inside a bracket on the other—and there was more of the wrought-iron burglar-proofing bolted over them on the outside.

I stood at the glass doors, looking out. From there you had an impressive view down a long rocky slope to where the Pacific roiled up foam in a secluded cove, framed on both sides by skyscraping redwoods. But it wasn't the view that had my attention; it was what looked to be a strip of film about three inches in length, that was caught on a railing splinter off to one side and fluttering in the wind. I debated whether or not to unlatch the doors and go out there for a closer look. I was still debating when somebody came clumping up onto the front porch.

The noise brought me around. The front door was still open, and I watched it fill up with six feet of a youngish flaxen-haired guy dressed in tennis whites and carrying a covered racket. He said, "What's going on here? Who are you?" Then he got to where he could see the body on the rug, and Lauren Speers unconscious in the chair, and he said, "Christ!" in an awed voice.

Right away, to avoid trouble, I told him my name, my profession, and the fact that I had come here to see Lauren Speers on a business matter, only to stumble on a homicide instead. He was Joe Craig, he said, one of Xanadu's tennis professionals, and he had come over from his own staff cottage nearby to pick up Speers for a three o'clock tennis appointment. He seemed stunned, confused; his eyes kept shifting away from me to the body.

There was a telephone on another burl table beside the couch. I went to it and rang up the resort office. And spent five minutes and a lot of breath explaining three times to three different people that there had been a shooting in Number 41 and somebody was dead. None of the three wanted to believe it. A killing in Xanadu? Things like that just didn't happen. The first one referred me to the second and the second to the third; the third, who said he was Resident Director Mitchell, maintained his disbelief for a good two minutes before a kind of horrified indignation took over and he promised to notify the county police right away.

Craig had gone over to Lauren Speers and was down on one knee beside her, chafing one of her hands witout result. "Maybe we should take her outside," he said. "Let her have some air."

That was a good idea. I helped him get her up out of the chair, and as we hauled her across to the door I asked him, "Do you know the dead woman?"

"God, yes. Bernice Dolan, Ms. Speers' secretary. Did Ms. Speers do that to her? Shoot her like that?"

"So it would seem." On the porch we put her onto a wrought-iron chaise longue and Craig went after her hand again. "There's nobody else here, the balcony doors and all the windows are locked from the inside, and I was down on the path with a clear look at the front door when it happened."

He shook his head. "I knew they weren't getting along," he said, "but I never thought it would lead to anything like this."

"How did you know they weren't getting along?"

"Bernice told me. We dated a couple of times—nothing serious." Another headshake. "I can't believe she's . . . dead."

"What was the trouble between them?"

"Well, Ms. Speers is writing a book—or rather, dictating one. All about some of the important people she's known and some of the things she's been mixed up in in the past. And full of scandalous material, apparently. She'd got her hands on all sorts of letters and documents and she quoted some of them at length. Bernice'd had editorial experience in New York and kept telling her she couldn't do that because some of the material was criminal and most of it was libelous. But that didn't matter to Ms. Speers; she said she was going to publish it anyway. They were always arguing about it."

"Why didn't she just fire Bernice?"

"I guess she was afraid Bernice would go to some of the people mentioned in the book, out of spite or something, and stir up trouble that'd affect publication."

"Were their arguments ever violent?"

"I think so. Bernice was afraid of her. She'd have quit herself if she hadn't needed the money."

But even if Lauren Speers was prone to violence, I thought, why would she shoot her secretary no more than two minutes after returning from an after-lunch drive? That was how long it had been between the time I saw her go inside and the time the gun went off: two minutes maximum.

Craig's hand-chafing was finally beginning to have an effect. La Speers made a low moaning sound, her eyelids fluttered and slid up, and she winced. Her stare was glassy and blank for three or four seconds; the pupils looked as if they were afloat in bloody milk. Then memory seemed to come back to her and her eyes focused, her body jerked as if an electrical current had passed through it.

"Oh my God!" she said. "Bernice!"

"Easy," Craig said. "It's all over now, Mrs. Speers."

"Joe? What are you doing here?"

"Our tennis date, remember?"

"I don't remember anything. Oh God, my head . . ." Then she saw me standing there. "Who're you?"

We got it established who I was and more or less why I was present. She did not seem to care; she pushed herself off the chaise longue before I was done talking and went inside. She was none too steady on her feet, but when Craig tried to take her arm she smacked his hand away. One long look at the body produced a shudder and sent her rushing into the kitchen. I heard the banging of cupboard doors and the clink of glassware, and a few seconds later she came back with a cut-glass decanter in her right hand and an empty tumbler in her left. The decanter was full of something colorless that was probably gin.

I went over as she started to pour and took both decanter and tumbler away from her. "No more liquor. You've had plenty."

Her eyes snapped at me, full of savagery. "You fat son of a bitch—how dare you! Give it back to me!"

"No," I said, thinking: fat son of a bitch. Yeah. I put my back to her and went down the hall into the bathroom. She came after me, calling me more names; clawed at my arm and hand while I emptied the gin into the washbasin. I yelled to Craig to get her off me and he came and did that.

There was blood on the back of my right hand where she'd scratched me. I washed it off, dabbed the scratch with iodine from the medicine cabinet. Speers was back on the chaise longue when I returned to the porch, Craig beside her looking nonplussed. She was shaking and she looked sick, shrunken, as if all her flesh had contracted inside her skin. But the fury was still alive in those green eyes: They kept right on ripping away at me.

I asked her, "What happened here today, Ms. Speers?"

"Go to hell," she said.

"Why did you kill your secretary?"

"Go to—What? My God, you don't think *I* did that?"

"It looks that way."

"But I didn't, I couldn't have . . . "

"You were drunk," I said. "Maybe that explains it."

"Of course I was drunk. But I don't kill people when I'm drunk. I go straight to bed and sleep it off."

"Except today, maybe."

"I told you, you bastard, I didn't kill her!"

"Look, lady," I said, "I'm tired of you calling me names. I don't like it and I don't want to listen to it anymore. Maybe you killed Bernice Dolan and maybe you didn't. If you didn't, then you'd better start acting like a human being. The way you've been carrying on, you look guilty as sin."

She opened her mouth, shut it again. Some of the heat faded out of her eyes. "I didn't do it," she said, much calmer, much more convincing.

"All right. What did happen?"

"I don't know. I heard the shot, I came out of the bedroom, and there she was all twisted and bloody, with the gun on the floor . . . "

"A twenty-five caliber automatic. Your gun?"

"Yes. My gun."

"Where do you usually keep it?"

"In the nightstand drawer in my bedroom."

"Did you take it out today for any reason?"

"No."

"Did Bernice have it when you got back?"

A blank look. "Got back?"

"From wherever it was you went this afternoon."

"Away from Xanadu? In my car?"

"Are you saying you don't remember?"

"Okay, I have memory lapses sometimes when I've been drinking. Blackouts—an hour or two. But I don't usually go out driving . . . " The misery in her voice made her sound vulnerable, almost pathetic. I still didn't like her much, but she was in a bad way—physically, emotionally, and circumstantially—and she needed all the help she could get. Beginning with me. Maybe. "I thought I came straight here after lunch.

I remember starting back in the cars . . . but that's all. Nothing else until I heard the shot and found Bernice.''

Out on the main path I heard the whirring of an oncoming cart. A short time later two middle-aged guys, both dressed in expensive summer suits, came running through the trees and up onto the porch. The taller of them, it developed, was Resident Director Mitchell; the other one was Xanadu's chief of security. The first thing they did was to go inside and gape at the body. When they came out again I explained what had happened as far as I knew it, and what I was doing in Xanadu in the first place. Speers did not react to the fact that I was here to serve her with a court summons. Death makes every other problem inconsequential.

She had begun to look even sicker; her skin had an unhealthy grayish tinge. When Mitchell and the security chief moved off the porch for a conference she got up and hurried into the cottage. I went in after her, to make sure she didn't touch anything or go for another stash of gin. But it was the bathroom she wanted this time; five seconds after she shut the door, retching sounds filtered out through it.

I stepped into her bedroom and took a turn around it without putting my hands on any of its surfaces. The bed was rumpled and the rest of the room looked the same—scattered clothing, jars of cosmetics, bunches of dog-eared paperback books. There were also half a dozen framed photographs of well-groomed men, all of them signed with the word ''love.''

The retching noises had stopped when I came out and I could hear water running in the bathroom. I moved down to the other, smaller bedroom. Desk with an electric portable typewriter and a dictating machine on its top. No photographs and nothing else much on the furniture. No sign of a manuscript, either; that would be locked away somewhere, I thought.

The sliding closet door was ajar, so I put my head through the opening. The closet was empty except for two bulky suitcases. I nudged both with my foot and both seemed to be packed full.

Half a minute after I returned to the living room, Lauren Speers reappeared. When she saw me she ducked her head and said, ''Don't look at me. I look like hell.'' But I looked at her anyway. I also blocked her way to the door.

With my handkerchief I took out the piece of notepaper I had found earlier and held it up where she could see what was written on it. ''Do you have any idea what this is, Ms. Speers?'' She started to reach for it but I said, ''No, don't touch it. Just look.''

She looked. ''I never saw it before.'' she said.

"Is the handwriting familiar?"

"Yes. It's Bernice's."

"From the looks of it, she was left-handed."

"Yes, she was. If that matters."

"The three names here—are they familiar?"

"I think so. James Huddleston is the former state attorney general. Edward Boyer and Samuel Rykman are both prominent business people."

"Close friends of yours?"

Her mouth turned crooked. "Not any more."

"Why is that?"

"Because they're bastards. And one is an out-and-out thief."

"Which one?"

She shook her head—there was a feral gleam in her eyes now—and started past me. I let her go. Then I put the paper away again and followed her onto the porch.

The security chief had planted himself on the cottage path to wait for the county police; Craig was down there with him. The Resident Director had disappeared somewhere, probably to go do something about protecting Xanadu's reputation. Nobody was paying any attention to me, so I went down and along a packed-earth path that skirted the far side of the cottage.

At the rear there were steps leading up onto the balcony. I climbed them and took a look at the strip of film I had noticed earlier, caught on a wood splinter through one of several small holes along its edge. It was the stiff and sturdy kind they use to make slides—the kind that wouldn't bend easily under a weight laid on it edgewise.

I paced around for a time, looking at this and that. Then I stood still and stared down at the ocean spray boiling over the rocks below, not really seeing it, looking at some things inside my head instead. I was still doing that when more cart noises sounded out front, two or three carts this time judging from the magnified whirring and whining. County cops, I thought. Nice timing, too.

When I came back around to the front two uniformed patrolmen, a uniformed officer in captain's braid, a civilian carrying a doctor's satchel, and another civilian with photographic equipment and a field lab kit were being met by the security chief. I went over and joined them.

The captain, whose name was Orloff, asked me, "You're the private detective, is that right? The man who found the body?"

"That's right." I relinquished the .25 automatic, saying that I had only handled it by the barrel. Not that it would have mattered if I *had* taken it by the grip. If there were any fingerprints on it, they would belong to Lauren Speers.

"It was just after the shooting that you arrived?"

"Not exactly," I said, "I was in the vicinity before the shooting. I went inside after I heard the shot—not much more than a minute afterward."

"So you didn't actually see the woman shoot her secretary."

"No," I said. "But I wouldn't have seen that if I'd been inside when it happened. Ms. Speers didn't kill Bernice Dolan. The man right over there, Joe Craig, did that."

There was one of those sudden electric silences. Both Craig and Lauren Speers were near enough to hear what I had said; he stiffened and gaped at me and she came up out of her chair on the porch. Craig's face tried to arrange itself into an expression of disbelief, but he was not much of an actor; if this had been a Hollywood screen test, he would have flunked it hands down.

He said, "What the hell kind of crazy accusation is that?" Which was better—more conviction—but it still sounded false.

His guilt was not so obvious to Orloff or any of the others. They kept looking from Craig to me as if trying to decide who to believe. The security guy said, "How could Joe be guilty? The balcony door and all the windows are locked from the inside; you said so yourself. You also said there was no one else in the cottage except Ms. Speers and the dead woman when you entered."

"That's right," I said. "But Craig wasn't in the cottage when he shot the secretary. And everything wasn't locked up tight, either."

Craig said, "Don't listen to him, he doesn't know what he's saying—"

"The living room smells of gin," I said to the security guy. "You must have noticed that when you were in there. It smelled just the same when I first entered. But if you fire a handgun in a closed room you get the smell of cordite. No cordite odor means the gun was fired outside the room."

"That's true enough," Orloff said. "Go on."

"I'd been here less than ten minutes when Craig showed up," I said. "He claimed he'd come to keep a tennis date with Ms. Speers. But the parking lot attendant told me earlier that she drinks her lunch every day and then comes here to sleep it off until Happy Hour at four o'clock. People on that kind of heavy drinking schedule don't make dates to go play tennis at three o'clock.

"Craig said something else, too—much more damning. When I

asked him if he knew the dead woman he identified her as Bernice Dolan. Then he said, 'Did Ms. Speers do that to her? Shoot her like that?' But I didn't say anything about hearing a gunshot until later; and the way the body is crumpled on the rug, with one arm flung over the chest, all you can see is blood, not the type of wound. So how did he know she was shot? She could just as easily have been stabbed to death.''

There was not much bravado left in Craig; you could almost see him wilting, like an uprooted weed drying in the sun. "I assumed she was shot," he said weakly, "I just . . . assumed it."

Lauren Speers had come down off the porch and was staring at him. "Why?" she said. "For god's sake, *why*?"

He shook his head at her. But I said, "For money, that's why. A hundred thousand dollars in extortion payoffs, at least some of which figures to be in his own cottage right now."

That pushed Craig to the breaking point. He backpedaled a couple of steps and might have kept right on backing if one of the patrolmen hadn't grabbed his arm.

Lauren Speers said, "I don't understand. What extortion?"

"From those three men I asked you about a few minutes ago—Huddleston, Boyer, and Rykman. They figure prominently in the book you're writing, don't they? Large sections of it are devoted to them and contain material either scandalous or criminal?"

"How do you know about that?"

"Craig told me; he was trying to make it seem like you had a motive for killing Bernice. And you told me when you said those three men were bastards and one of them was an out-and-out thief. This little piece of paper took care of the rest." I fished it out of my coat pocket again and handed it to Orloff. "The first series of numbers after each name are page numbers—pages in the book manuscript on which the most damaging material about that person appears. The numbers after the dash are the amounts extorted from each man."

"Where did you get this?"

"It was on the floor between the couch and the coffee table. Right near where Ms. Speers' bag was. I think that's where it came from—out of the handbag."

She said, "How could it have been in my bag?"

"Bernice put it there. While she was out impersonating you this afternoon."

Now everybody looked bewildered. Except Craig, of course: he only looked sick—much sicker than Lauren Speers had earlier.

"Impersonating me?" she said.

"That's right. Wearing a red wig and your white coat, and carrying your bag. You didn't go anywhere after lunch except back here to bed; it was Bernice who took your car and left Xanadu. And it was Bernice who passed me in the car, Bernice I saw enter the cottage a couple of minutes before she was shot."

The security guy asked, "How can you be sure about that?"

"Because Bernice was left-handed," I said. "And Ms. Speers is right-handed; I could tell that a while ago when she started to pour from a decanter into a glass—decanter in her right hand, glass in her left. But the woman who got out of the car carried the straw bag in her right hand; and when she got to the cottage door she used her left hand to take out the key and to open the door."

Lauren Speers looked at a lock of her red hair, as if to make sure it was real. "Why would Bernice impersonate me?"

"She and Craig were in on the extortion scheme together and it was part of the plan. They must have worked it something like this: as your secretary she had access to your book manuscript, your personal stationery, your signature, and no doubt your file of incriminating letters and documents. She also had access to your personal belongings and your car keys, particularly from one to four in the afternoons while you were sleeping. And she'd have known from your records how to contact Huddleston and the other two.

"So she and Craig wrote letters to each of them, on your stationery over your forged signature, demanding large sums of money to delete the material about them from your book and to return whatever documents concerned them; they probably also enclosed photocopies of the manuscript pages and the documents as proof. The idea was to keep themselves completely in the clear if the whole thing backfired. You'd get the blame in that case, not them.

"To maintain the illusion, Bernice had to pretend to be you when she collected the payoff. I don't know what sort of arrangements she and Craig made, but they wouldn't have allowed any of the three men to deliver the money personally. An intermediary, maybe, someone who didn't know you. Or maybe a prearranged drop site. In any event, Bernice always dressed as you at collection time."

Orloff asked, "Why do you think Craig killed her?"

"The old doublecross," I said. "They'd collected all the extortion money; that's evident from the way each of the three names is crossed out on that paper. Today was the last pickup and I think they had it worked out that she would resign from Ms. Speers' employ and Craig would resign from Xanadu and they'd go off somewhere together: her closet is all cleaned out and her bags are packed. But Craig had other ideas. He knew when she was due back here and he was waiting for her—outside on the rear balcony. When she let herself in he knocked on the window and gestured for her to open the two halves. After she complied he must have said something like, 'Quick, lock the front door, take off the coat, and give me the wig and the money.' She must have thought there was some reason for the urgency, and she trusted him; so she did what he asked. And when she pulled the money out of the bag she also pulled out the slip of paper. In her haste it fell unnoticed to the floor.

"As soon as Craig had the wig and the money he took out the gun, which he'd swiped from Ms. Speers' nightstand, and shot her. And then he threw the gun inside and pulled the halves of the window closed."

"And locked them somehow from the outside," the security guy said, "in the minute or two before you broke in? How could he do that?"

"Simply, considering the catch on those window halves is a bar type that flops over into a bracket. The gimmick he used was a thin but stiff strip of film. He lost it afterward without realizing it: you'll still find it caught on a splinter on the balcony railing. The way he did it was to insert the film strip between the two halves and flip the catch over until it rested on the strip's edge. Next he pulled the halves all the way closed, using his thumb and forefinger on the inner frames of each, and with his other hand he eased the strip downward until the catch dropped into the bracket. Then he withdrew the strip from the crack. With a little practice, you could do the whole thing in thirty seconds.

"So far he had himself a perfect crime. All he'd have had to do was return to his cottage, get rid of the wig, stash the money, pick himself up a witness or two, and come back here and 'find' Ms. Speers locked up with the body. Under the circumstances he'd arranged, she would be the only one who could have committed the murder.

"What screwed him up was me showing up when I did. He heard me pounding on the door as he was working his trick with the film strip; he had just enough time to slip away into the woods before I broke in. But who was I? What had I seen and heard? The only way he could find out was to come back as soon as he'd dumped the wig and money. The fact that he showed up again in less than ten minutes means he didn't dump them far away; they won't be hard to find. And there might even be a fingerprint on that film strip to nail your case down tight—"

Lauren Speers moved. Before anybody could stop her she charged over to where Craig was and slugged him in the face. Not a slap—a roundhouse shot with her closed fist. He staggered but didn't go down. She went after him, using some of the words she had used on me earlier, and hit him again and tried to kick him here and there. It took Orloff, the security guy, and one of the patrolmen to pull her off.

It was another couple of hours before they let me leave Xanadu. During that time Orloff and his men found all of the extortion money—$100,000 in cash—hidden in one of Craig's bureau drawers; they also found the red wig in the garbage can behind his cottage. That was enough, along with my testimony, for them to arrest him on suspicion of homicide. From the looks of him, they'd have a full confession an hour after he was booked.

Just before I left I served Lauren Speers with the court summons. She took it all right; she said it was the least she could do after I had practically saved her life. She also took one of my business cards and promised she would send me a check "as an appreciation," but I doubted that she would. She was a lady too lost in alcohol and bitter memories, too involved in a quest for notoriety and revenge, to remember that sort of promise—running fast and going nowhere, as the comedian Fred Allen had once said, on a treadmill to oblivion.

So I went back to San Francisco and the following day I collected my two hundred plus expenses from Adam Brister. And that night, instead of reading one of the pulp magazines I collect and admire, I read Coleridge's *Kubla Khan* in a book from the public library. It was a pretty fine piece of work, all right, and so was his Xanadu. A place of idyllic beauty. The stuff of dreams.

The one at Big Sur was the stuff of dreams too—dreams of tinsel and plastic and pastel colors; of beauty measured by wealth, happiness by material possessions. Some people could find fulfillment with those dreams and in that place. Others, like Lauren Speers, were not so fortunate.

For them, the pleasure-domes of Xanadu could be the stuff of nightmares.

Patrick Michael O'Bannon

THE MAIMED AND THE HALT
Joe Gores

THE SILVER-HAIRED MAN paused at the head of the wide steps of San Francisco City Hall. He stuck his silver-headed black walking stick under one arm while lighting a thin cheroot. With his ramrod posture and his ascetic face he looked like an oldtime riverboat gambler.

Then he started down the steps.

A grimace of pain contorted his features. Only the cane, thumping heavily on each step, kept him from falling. His crabwise downward progress was agonizingly slow; it was like catching a film depicting torture.

"You say *he* drives his own car?" demanded Dan Kearny unbelievingly. Kearny was pushing 50 but didn't look it, a hard-jawed man with a graying mane of hair and a nose bent and flattened by a lifetime of not backing away from trouble.

"Special controls so he can operate everything with the use of only one leg." Meyer Edmunds was pudgy and perspiring, with thinning sandy hair and an insistent cologne. "That man has just finished ripping off Fiduciary Trust Insurance for two-hundred-and-seventy-five thousand bucks. Don't quote me, of course."

"This special car of his—a Cadillac, I suppose?"

Edmunds nodded glumly. "Colonel Sanders always goes first cabin."

"The Colonel Sanders of chicken fame?"

Patrick Michael O'Bannon had thrust his flame-topped head into the crowded cubbyhole office. He pulled the door shut so that outside lights would not dim the moving images on the tacked-up screen.

"Colonel Buford Sanders, USAF Retired," said Kearny.

"*Buford* Sanders? You mean *my* Colonel Sanders?"

"Now you know why I wanted you in here."

Edmunds rewound the film as O'B sat down. Daniel Kearney Associates (Head Office in San Francisco, Branches Throughout California) seldom drew the VIP of a big insurance company as a possible client; it had to be something unusual if their own investigators couldn't handle it. Meyer Edmunds started the film over again.

"O'B, this is everything our boys have gotten on him over the past two years—since the car accident."

The clips, spliced end to end, showed twenty continuous minutes in the life of Colonel Buford Sanders. Some in black and white, some in color, some of theater excellence, others hand-held from moving cars or through fences, one from over a transom.

In all of them Sanders was doing the same thing. Limping.

"Are you *sure* he's faking it?" asked Kearny dubiously.

"No, I'm not, Dan, and that's the hell of it. I'm the only one who still thinks it's fraud. We've already paid off."

The lights went up. Willowy blond Giselle Marc had delivered the ice Kearny had called upstairs to clerical for, had collected O'B's wink, and had departed. Drinks were in hand and cigarettes were alight. It was one of the few times, O'B thought, that Kearny's office in the basement of the old Victorian which housed DKA resembled the fictional private-eyes's domain.

"Nine Caddys we've repossessed from that man," O'B mused. His seamed, freckle-spattered face blueprinted a middle-aged drinker's life, but next to Kearny he was the best field investigator DKA had. "Nine. Spread out over almost ten years. And this is the first time I've ever seen even a picture of the man."

"We haven't had a new assignment on him in thirty months," said Kearny as he consulted the Colonel's bulging file.

"Since the car accident," Edmunds said.

"We picked up four Caddys in California," said O'Bannon, "two in New York, one in New Orleans, one—no, two—in Florida. He plays games, that man does.

"With all the computerized credit checking there is today, how could he even *buy* nine Cadillacs, one after the other, and—"

"He looks so good on paper that the dealers just never bother to run him thorugh a credit-reporting service," said O'B. "He's retired military, gets a fat government pension, has a hell of an expensive home in Seacliff—"

"Dealers are required by law to get a certain percentage of the sales

THE MAIMED AND THE HALT

price,'' Kearny explained, ''but no law says that can't balloon six or seven hundred of that down payment and get it a couple months after delivery. The Colonel never makes the balloon payment and it usually takes us about six months to drop a rock on the new Caddy. By then the bank's eaten the contract and it's on contingent.''

''But you have *always* made recovery,'' Edmunds persisted.

''What's to recover?'' said O'B. ''Last one I picked up had tires you could read through, a cracked block, no transmission, and a crankshaft dragging on the ground. The client took a twelve-thousand-dollar bath when we sold it for junk in Tallahassee.''

Edmunds sighed and stood up. ''Ten days of additional surveillance is all I've been able to gouge out of the head office. After that we close the file—unless you turn up *proof* of fraud.''

''Why us?'' asked Kearny.

''By now he knows all my people by their first names.''

''If he blows his nose, I'll be holding the handkerchief,'' promised O'Bannon.

DKA seldom got to mount a concentrated surveillance on a single subject, expenses unlimited. O'B brought in two other DKA investigators, Larry Ballard and Bart Heslip. Heslip was a black ex-boxer who found the same excitement in manhunting that the ring had once given him; Ballard was a late-twenties blond man, just under six feet and conditioned like an athlete.

''Remember, gents, even more important than uninterrupted observation is the fact that he *must never know*, must never even *suspect*, that someone's staked out on him. If he's been disciplined enough to never give himself away once during two years—''

''But he's already been paid off,'' Heslip pointed out.

''That's what we're banking on,'' O'B said. ''But remember, this guy can *smell* a setup. He's gun-shy. I've been after him for ten years.''

''Unmarried, I take it?'' asked Ballard.

''Widowed seven years ago.''

''Why not get a woman next to him and—''

''Four insurance-company baggers tried in the last two years.'' Baggers are female investigators, who often carry tape-recorders in their handbags. ''But part of the basis for the high settlement was his claim that the accident made him impotent. Nothing stirring.''

''If we could catch him shacking up—'' Heslip shook his head and chuckled. ''Man, *two years?* That takes *some* sort of cool.''

"He's got it," said O'Bannon.

Ballard was thoughtful. "How about—oh, sports? Catch him in a gymnasium? On a weekend hike? Horseback riding?"

"He does go to a gym five times a week—for whirlpool therapy. They haven't caught him taking a weekend anywhere since the accident. Church every Sunday—stands in back because he claims he can't kneel down. Until the accident he didn't go to church at all."

That briefing was on the first morning of surveillance, which was carried out essentially from the garret room of an elegant three-story red brick whose owner owed Edmunds a favor. It was directly across Scenic Way from the subject's distinctive colonial revival with its hipped roof and second-floor Palladian window.

"With a house like that, servants, a gardener—what's the cat on the hustle for?" mused Heslip.

"You've answered your own question. He *likes* the hustle."

"There he is," said Ballard from the window.

The sandbagged 600mm lens brought Colonel Buford Sanders up close enough, as he laboriously descended his front steps, to count the hairs in his moustache. Click. Click. Click. But O'B knew, even as he took them, that the stills would only support Sanders' claim. He checked his watch and stood up.

"Time for his hour with the Jacuzzi bath. See you gents later."

The therapist, Wednesday lunch at the Presidio officers' club, back home. O'B had the daily routine down pat. It was on the return trip, with Sanders' special Caddy two blocks ahead, that O'B became aware of a new element in the equation. On Thursday, when he popped into the office after business hours, he told Kearny about it.

"Edmunds must still have one of his people second-guessing us, Dan. There was a second tail on Sanders for five blocks yesterday afternoon, and this morning a TV repair truck from a company that isn't in the phone book was parked down the street for twenty minutes. Ballard thinks someone was tagging him, too."

Kearny was already at the phone, having Edmunds paged out of the steamroom at the Elks Club. In a few minutes he hung up.

"Not Edmunds. But somebody else at Fiduciary must have had a bright idea. Edmunds will check around, make sure the field man gets yanked." He was on his feet. "Let's go get a drink."

"You'll find this hard to believe, but I can't. I'm due to relieve Bart in half an hour."

"His girl friend's back east visiting folks—so Bart's got nothing better to do. And this *might* be important. You know how good Larry is with women, well, day before yesterday he spotted that good-looking maid of Sanders drinking at a little bar on Lincoln Way and Twentieth Avenue where Larry hangs around.''

They shouldered into their topcoats, then paused at the front of the garage to set the alarms and lock up before going out into the chill September evening.

''Coincidence?''

''Can't see it being anything else,'' said Kearny. ''She just likes to drink—with anybody who isn't her husband.''

''That covers a lot of ground,'' said O'B. ''And her with two kids at home. Tsk, tsk. We'd better go speak to the girl.''

Jacques Daniels' was not a fancy way of speaking about a sour-mash bourbon. It was a bar owned by two partners, one a small lively balding Frenchman from Algeria who had given his first name to the place, the other a pert little blond named Beverly Daniels. She and Larry Ballard were talking across the bar when O'B and Kearny entered.

The place was warm and cozy and intimate, with mismatched hard-wood tables, myriad hanging ferns, and handmade Tiffany-style lamps that cast a soft stained glow across the drinkers. Lying on the bar beside Ballard were two DKA report forms with typing on them. Ballard tapped them with a finger. Kearny scooped them up in passing.

Ballard murmured, apparently to Beverly, ''Brunette by the jukebox. Tailed her last night.''

The two detectives pulled out chairs on both sides of the generously endowed black-haired girl. She had a long upper lip that showed precise incisors. Those in the lower jaw had a habit of worrying the protruding lip as she talked.

Her voice was sullen. ''I'm waiting for someone.''

''You weren't yesterday when Frankie Gallaway stopped at your table.'' Kearny had scanned Ballard's report for a few minutes.

''Your name is Rosario Renucci. You've been a maid for four years on Scenic Way.'' O'Bannon hadn't read Ballard's report, but he could follow Kearny's leads easily enough.

''*Married* name,'' said Kearny.

''What sort of scam is—'' she began.

''Husband is Ermanno Renucci,'' said O'Bannon.

''Hard-working guy at a foundry on Brannan Street. Hot-tempered but a home-loving sort of person. Salt of the earth.''

''If you think you can—''

''Two children, minors, ages four and two.'' O'B shook his head sadly. "Rosie, Rosie, what are we going to do with you? Ermanno finds out—" he shaped his lips in a *whew* position, shook one hand back and forth as if he'd caught it in a car door. "Comes home sometime, finds those two sweet little kids all alone—"

Her face seemed about to crumble, but she was still in there trying. "You guys don't beat it, I'll call the cops."

"And we'll call Ermanno." Kearny began reading in a low voice from Ballard's report. "Eight fifty-eight P.M., Wednesday, September twenty-ninth, subject met male Caucasian subsequently identified as Frankie Gallaway at Jacques Daniels', a bar at eighteen-forty-nine Lincoln Way."

He raised cold gray eyes to her defiant face, then read again.

"At twelve-o-seven A.M. subject and Gallaway left the bar and proceeded to the residence maintained by Gallaway at the rear of two-nine-eight Parnassus Street. This is a detached cottage reached by a passageway alongside the main building."

"Anybody who says Frankie and I—"

"Subject and Gallaway entered the bedroom at twelve forty-four A.M., switched out the lights at twelve fifty-eight. The light remained off until two twenty-two A.M. Subject left Gallaway's residence at two forty A.M., after embracing with Gallaway in the open doorway."

She broke, abruptly, with a half-smothered sob.

"Damn you, you got any idea what it's like? The relatives drooling over the kids? Washing clothes? And dishes? And getting them up and off to school and—"

"'Tis far better to have loved and lost than to do thirty pounds of dirty laundry a week," observed O'Bannon.

"Look, what can I offer you not to tell Ermanno—"

"Tell us about your boss," suggested Kearny.

She seemed dazed by the abrupt switch. "My boss?"

"He ever make a pass at you?"

"Have other girls in there?"

"He's faking it, isn't he? The limp?"

"Doesn't limp once the shades are drawn, does he, Rosie?"

"How does he get the girls in and out without being seen?"

"How much extra does he give you to cover for him?"

"C'mon, Rosie. Give, girl. Give."

Ashen-faced and shaken, Rosie gave.

* * *

It was five A.M. on Saturday. O'Bannon stifled a vast yawn and shivered despite the car heater. He was on Seacliff Ave., a block from the subject's house—where, surprise, surprise, he'd found the specially equipped Cadillac street-parked when he'd arrived two hours before. And Colonel Sanders with that spacious three-car garage under the house!

It fit with what Rosie had overheard Sanders saying on the phone while making motel reservations. He'd be leaving the city around five A.M. on Saturday and would be there by midday at the latest. The clandestine nature of the departure, the fact that the motel was six or seven hours away from San Francisco—a probable five-to-seven bet, O'B thought, that a woman was involved.

He stiffened, crushing the paper cup which had contained his third coffee of the day. His rear-view mirror had seen a figure moving with the now-familiar crabwise shuffle. He used the radio.

"SF-2 to SF-3. Do you read me, Bart, over?"

"Loud and clear." Heslip was, by prearrangement, in his car a quarter block from the subject's house.

"He's just getting into the Caddy over here on Seacliff."

"He back-doored me! If he's tumbled to the stake—"

"Just being cautious. I've got him now. Out."

"10-4, cat. Good hunting. Over and out."

O'B already had his car in motion, backing and filling as the subject got the Caddy started. O'B was going to try a front tail, the most difficult but also the most difficult to spot. It meant making an educated guess in which direction Sanders would be going. O'B only knew for sure he wasn't going west—not unless the Caddy came equipped with water wings.

He pulled away ten seconds before Sanders did, took a left into the Presidio off 25th Avenue when he saw Sanders' left blinker go on. That made it easy. Golden Gate Bridge. North.

It was gloriously clear, going to be hot, with the not-yet-risen sun reddening strata of clouds above the Oakland hills before it burst out to make crinkled lead foil of the Bay through the whizzing orange handrails of the bridge. O'B sang with the radio while beating time on the steering wheel. He felt it: this was the day, this was the trip on which he was going to nail Sanders.

And then he almost lost him. Sanders abruptly veered across all four lanes into the old Blackpoint Cut-off which led across the tidal marshes to Vallejo. It took O'B twenty minutes to get turned around, pick him up, pass him, and drop into line an eighth of a mile ahead of him.

Tricky cat. Start out north, then go east. Actually, O'B liked it. Sanders *really* didn't want anyone tagging along.

O'B had assumed it would be northeast from Vallejo on Interstate 80, toward Sacramento, Tahoe, Reno, places like that. But instead it was 680 through Benicia to Concord, then down to turn east on 580 to Livermore, a hot dusty suburban sprawl supported by the nuclear research facility of the University of California.

"With *breakfast*?" exclaimed the dismayed waitress at the diner he'd chosen after Sanders had stopped at a more elaborate restaurant a block farther off the freeway.

"The sun is over the yardarm *somewhere* in this world, me lhove. So I'll be havin' a wee dram o' the Chablis wit' me eggs."

Stopping at Livermore for breakfast meant south on the new Interstate 5, which was unsullied by such namby-pamby things as restaurants, truck stops, gas stations, or roadside cafés. It was a freeway for the traveler in a rush. O'B was content to tag along behind now—Sanders surely would feel he'd shaken any possible tail by this time. Showed how wrong a man could be.

"Looks like it's Bakersfield," mused O'Bannon aloud.

Which again showed how wrong a man could be.

Fifty miles south on Interstate 5, Sanders turned west on California 152. *West?* Up through the Pacheco Pass? What the hell went on?

An hour later, when Sanders turned north on U.S. 101 at Gilroy, O'Bannon knew. Tricky, indeed! The subject had in effect made a giant circle down through the great interior depressed valley which formed the heart of California between the Sierras and the Coast Range. Now he was headed up toward the Bay area again; if he kept going far enough, he'd be back in San Francisco.

He didn't go that far. At San Jose, 50 miles from the city, he cut over to the Interstate 280 and left the freeway at Winchester Boulevard— in plenty of time to honor his motel reservation.

The Cozee-Up Motel was a U-shaped affair triple tiered around a fiercely blue swimming pool masked from the street and the skyway by dense shrubbery. A motel designed for assignations. O'Bannon, his wrap-around dark glasses leaving little more than his teeth showing, was delving industriously in the trunk compartment of his Chevy Caprice when Sanders came from Registration in his crabwise shuffle. O'B watched him into the first-floor corner room farthest from the office, then went in himself.

"Something on the first floor," he told the iron-eyed woman behind the desk. "As far from the office as possible."

"The *very* end room was just rented, but—"

"How about the one next to it?"

"The maid hasn't gotten—"

"I'll have a cup of coffee while I wait."

A window booth in the coffee shop gave him an excellent view of the subject's dust-filmed Cadillac. The cups of coffee gave him heartburn in the two hours before the motel's senior-citizen maid had snailed her way in and out of his room. The temperature rose as the sun climbed a cloudless smoggy sky. O'B resisted the siren lure of a liquor store two blocks away; he didn't dare break surveillance that long. What the hell, his room would be air-conditioned.

As O'B was fumbling open his door, Sanders emerged from the adjacent one without a glance at the perspiring red-haired man. This gave O'B a chance to see that Sanders' bed was obligingly headed up against the partition between their two rooms.

He watched Sanders take a booth in the coffee shop, then got the necessary equipment from his suitcase. Using a quarter-inch cordless battery-powered drill and a long bit, O'B holed the wainscoting to come out under Sanders' bed. Through this hole he inserted a delicate high-resolution pencil mike, which he patched into a sound-activated Uher recorder. Fortunately the hum of the subject's air conditioner was not loud enough to activate the mike.

Sanders returned half an hour later, looking very drawn as he limped across the heat-softened blacktop. Probably that coffee, O'B thought. But what if the guy really *was* crippled? No, couldn't be. Otherwise, what was he doing in San Jose, a mere 50 miles from the city but arrived at by over 200 circuitous miles? Why back-door his own house at five in the ayem? Why street-park his car a block away?

O'B put the monitor plug in his ear. He heard the door opening. Bedsprings. A sigh of relief. Phone. Asking for a number. O'B realized he was holding his breath. Would it be to a woman?

"Hello, Cassie? Just got in. That's right. Of *course* I made sure nobody saw me leave. Couldn't have anyone—what? Yes. What I thought, too. All right. Pick you up about six thirty. We'll eat early so nothing interferes with our night together."

Just what they had suspected! Sanders had a little thing going on the side down here in San Jose and had sneaked down to celebrate the end of his long charade with a shack-up in a motel. Well, kiss your two-seven-five thousand goodbye, baby. Say hello to them cold prison walls.

Cold. Shouldn't have thought of that. How good an icy beer would taste! Send out for a six-pack? No. Didn't want to pinpoint the fact that he was staying in his room.

Sanders was now in the shower, but O'B's, incredibly enough, didn't work. The opportunity had passed anyway, as Sanders was finished now. O'B couldn't chance being under the needle spray when the subject might suddenly decide to take off.

Pool, sparkling and inviting a few paces from his door? No. Same problem.

He tried again to make his air conditioner work. On the blink. Sweat was standing on O'B's face. At least he could get some ice. He found a pitcher and carried it down to the ice-making machine beside the office.

The ice machine was busted.

He drank tepid tapwater from a styrofoam cup—the maid had forgotten to leave any glasses in his room. The water smelled of chemicals and tasted of fluorine. He kept on sweating.

He was rapidly coming to hate the guts of the man in the next room.

Thanks to the overheard phone conversation O'B was pouring sweat onto the sun-hot vinyl seat of his Caprice when Sanders limped out to the Caddy at six fifteen. Cassie, the girl on the phone, turned out to be a stunning blonde who lived in a ticky-tacky house off south Bascom Avenue that she'd probably gotten in a divorce settlement.

They ate supper at a very fancy place on East San Carlos near the San Jose State campus. From across the street it looked like cracked crab cocktails, rare roast beef washed down with vintage burgundy, and chocolate mousse for dessert. O'B watched them through the restaurant window while choking down a food-chain's Quarter-Pounder made of a glutinous mass of chopped cow and soya meal. He ached for them to get back to the motel.

But they didn't go back to he motel. Instead they went south on Market Street, right out of the congested areas of San Jose into, surprisingly, traffic which got fiercer the farther from the center of town they went. Abruptly O'B realized he was buried in a crush of almost stationary autos with no idea of where the Caddy was. Left turn into Umbarger Road.

Which meant the Santa Clara County fairgrounds.

The traffic turned again, O'B willy-nilly with it. Dirt road now, a boy with a flashlight waving the Caprice into one of countless rows of parked cars. O'B got out. The Caddy was nowhere in sight. If Sanders had chosen this way to lose any possible tail, he'd sure succeeded. All O'B could do now was hope that the subject and his blonde had been headed wherever everybody else was going.

He was afoot in a field of sun-yellowed grass which had been trampled flat by thousands of feet. The crowd made no sense. Young and old, middle-aged and senior citizen, babes in arms, long-hairs and straights. A shirt-sleeve crowd, dogs yipping in the dust, transistor radios blaring country music.

Country music? He'd been shucked for sure. Sanders wouldn't be caught dead in this sort of hick crowd.

The mass was funneling down into a sluggish river of elbow-to-elbow humanity which flowed toward a central destination—a massive canvas tent pitched near the racetrack.

Carnival? No trucks or wagons, no midway, no barkers. But the other possibilities were almost endless. Rodeo? Boxing card? Tent revival? Country-western music show? Old-fashioned barn dance? Cattle auction or livestock judging? He seemed to be the only one in ignorance of which it was. Ah. Posters. But the crush of people was so immense that O'B couldn't see what the posters said. Everyone except him was excited, up, hyper, full of anticipation.

Inside at last, and not even an admission charge collected. Nothing but a portable wooden stage set up at one end of the vast canvas structure and a sea of folding chairs rapidly filling with people. No trapezes slung high overhead. No center rings for performing dogs or horses. No pens, no judging blocks for cattle.

And no Colonel Sanders.

O'B prowled and looked. A group of youngsters in white gowns with gold collars took their place on the wooden risers to the rear of the stage. They started singing *That Old Time Religion*. He remembered, vividly and abruptly, sneaking under the canvas of revival tent shows as a kid. The Holy Rollers one year.

One big roll and save your soul.

He'd clapped erasers for a week after school at Mission High for chanting *that* one in the hall.

Tonight it was a good old fundamentalist preacher all in black urging the sinful to save their souls, wash themselves free from all sin, find God, testify to the Power of The Word.

O'B turned to go. It had been a ploy on Colonel Sanders' part to throw off any possible tail. Carefully skirting the traffic going to the tent revival, leaving O'B hopelessly mired in the jam-up. O'B's only edge was the pencil mike. Sanders wouldn't know about that. Once he and his blonde got going in that motel room—

The preacher had begun exhorting now, cajoling, arms thrust wide to gather in the sinful, his sweat flying, his voice hoarsening as it began to draw its inevitable emotional response.

"He hath filled the hungry with good things. Am I right?"

"You are right!" answered some voices from the crowd.

"He hath sent the rich away empty. Am I right?"

"You are *right*!"

O'B was working his way toward the exit to the parking lots.

"And I say to you, brethren, that The Shepherd rejoices more in the return of one lost sheep than he does in maintaining the whole flock. *Am I right?*"

"*You are right!*" With him now, a massive chorus.

"Then bring me your poor, and your maimed, and your halt, and your blind. And I will make them whole again. So saith the Lord. Brethren, *am I right?*"

"*YOU ARE RIGHT!*"

Now O'Bannon was breasting a tide—the old and the crippled and the sinful, moving down the aisle to bear witness to the Lord. He paused, looked back, and was transfixed. There, among them, was the familiar silver hair, the pain-lined ascetic face, the bobbing crabwise movement. O'B gaped.

Colonel Buford Sanders, angle-player and game-player and insurance defrauder, going down the aisle of a tent preacher's—

That's when the images began to flick before O'Bannon's eyes, frame after frame like a slide show. Images created from a blazing, belated, but now total comprehension.

Sanders, hiring *his own* private eye. Not a second tail on Sanders that Wednesday—*a tail on O'B!* And, later, a tail on Ballard. Identifying them, clocking their movements, habits.

So Sanders could pay his maid to stage a seduction scene for Ballard, after she had hung around Jacques Daniels' to make sure he would notice her.

Sanders, street-parking his Caddy where he knew O'B would spot it, once O'B believed Sanders was sneaking out of town at five A.M.

Sanders deliberately being too difficult to tail for suspicion to be aroused, but never so difficult that the tail could be lost.

Sanders maybe even paying the management to gimmick the air

conditioner and shower in the room whoever was tailing him would be sure to rent. Playing games, as usual.

And Sanders playing *more* games—the non-incriminating phone call to the blonde when he *knew* his room would be bugged.

And now Sanders, head bowed beneath the hands of the Healer in a revival tent at the Santa Clara County fairgrounds, under the watchful eyes of 20,000 people.

"*Oh, God!*" cried the Colonel in a loud voice. "*Oh, God, I am saved! Oh, God be praised! Oh, see me, a sinner, SAVED!*"

And he cavorted around on the stage, shouting the power of the Lord, and hurled up the aisle at a certain red-haired man the cane he would never need again—20,000 throats roared their hysterical approval.

Oh, yes, the cane he would never need again. Because Colonel Buford Sanders, USAF, Ret'd, was $275,000 richer with no possibility of ever being charged with fraud. Some 20,000 good souls, and a trained detective besides, had witnessed the miracle of his cure. A trained detective who, under oath, could only testify as to what he had seen and heard. Who, indeed, had been carefully lured there for that very purpose.

It was too much. It was just too damned much.

The Colonel embraced the Healer with tears of joy running down his face. As O'B had no doubt, he soon would embrace his blonde—with no worries about what a pencil mike from the next room might pick up.

O'B started to curse. Aloud.

Then the king said to the attendants, bind his hands and feet and cast him forth into the darkness outside . . .

Yes, O'B cursed. Loudly and bitterly and blasphemously, from the very core of his soul, at how thoroughly and totally he had been set up and taken in by the Colonel. O'Bannon, the Unbeliever, cursed.

. . . where there shall be weeping and gnashing of teeth.

And they threw O'B out. Bodily.

Patrick Petrella

THE HAPPY BROTHERHOOD
Michael Gilbert

THE GRANTS LIVED in Kennington. Mr. Grant worked in an architects' office in the City and had inherited the small terrace house on Dodman Street. It was convenient, since he could reach the Bank Station in ten minutes on the Underground. But it was not a neighborhood which he found really congenial. There was Mr. Knowlson, who worked in insurance and lived two doors up. But most of the inhabitants of Dodman Street were uncouth men, with jobs at railways depots—men who went to work at five o'clock in the morning and spent their evenings in public houses.

Mr. Grant had often spoken to his wife of moving out to the suburbs, where people went to their offices at a rational hour and spent the evenings in their gardens and joined tennis clubs and formed discussion groups. The factor which tipped the balance against moving was Timothy. Timothy was their only child and was now 14, but with his pink and white face and shy smile he could have been taken for eleven or twelve. After a difficult start he was happily settled at the Matthew Holder School near the Oval, and sang first treble in the choir at St. Mark's.

"It would be a pity to make a change now," said Mrs. Grant. "Timothy's easily upset. I've put his dinner in the oven, so I hope he won't be too late back from choir practice. If his dinner gets dried up he can't digest it properly."

At that moment Timothy was walking slowly down the road outside St. Mark's. He was walking slowly because, if the truth were told, he had no great desire to get home. When he did get there, his mother would make him take off his shoes and put on a dry pair of socks and would sit him down to eat a large and wholesome meal, which he did not really

want, and he would have to tell his father exactly what he had done in
school that day and—

A hand smacked him between the shoulder blades and he spun round.
Two boys were standing behind him, both a little older and a lot bigger
than Timothy. The taller one said, "It's a stickup, rosebud. Turn out
your pockets."

Timothy gaped at him.

"Come on, come on," said the other one. "Do you want to be duffed
up?"

"Are you mugging me?"

"You've cottoned quick, boyo. Shell out."

"I'm terribly sorry," said Timothy. "But I've actually only got
about ten pence on me. It's Thursday, you see. I get my pocket money on
Friday."

He was feeling in his trouser pocket as he spoke and now fetched out a
fivepenny piece and a penny and held them out.

The taller boy stared at the money, but made no move to touch it. He
said, "How much pocket money do you get every week?"

"A pound."

"So if we'd stuck you up tomorrow, we'd have got a quid?"

"That's right," said Timothy. "I'm terribly sorry. If you're short
tonight I could show you how to make a bit perhaps."

The two boys looked at each other, then burst out laughing.

"Cool," said the tall one. "That's cool."

"What's the gimmick?" said the second one.

"It's the amusement arcade in the High Street. There's a big slot
machine, tucked away in the corner, and no one uses it much."

"Why no one uses that machine is because no one ever makes any
money out of it."

"That's right," said Timothy. "It's a set-safe machine. I read about it
in a magazine. It's a machine that's organized so that the winning
combinations never come up. A man comes and clears the machines on
Friday. By this time it must be stuffed with money."

"So what are you suggesting we do? Break it open with a hammer?"

"What I thought was, it's plugged into a wall socket. If you pulled out
the plug and broke the electric circuit *while it's going*, the safety
mechanism wouldn't work. It would stop at some place it wasn't meant
to stop, so you'd have a good chance."

The two boys looked at each other, then at Timothy.

Timothy said, "It would need three people. One to distract the attention of the attendant. You could do that by asking him for change for a pound. The second to work the mahcine and the third to get down behind and jerk out the plug. I could to that, I'm the smallest."

The tall boys said, "If it's as easy as that why haven't you done it before?"

"Because I haven't got—" said Timothy and stopped. He realized that what he had nearly said was, "Because I haven't got two friends."

"We'd better go somewhere and count it," said Len. Their jacket pockets were bursting with twopenny bits.

"That bouncer," said Geoff. He could hardly get the words out for laughing. "Poor old sod. He just *knew* something was wrong, didn't he?"

"He was on the spot," agreed Len. "He couldn't very well say, that machine's not meant to pay off. He'd have been lynched. Come on."

Since the "come on" seemed to include Timothy he followed them. They led the way down a complex of side streets and alleys, each smaller and dingier than the last, until they came out almost onto the foreshore of the Thames. Since the dock had been shut two years before, it had become an area of desolation, of gaunt buildings with shuttered windows and boarded doorways.

Len stopped at one of these and stooped. Timothy saw that he had shifted a board, leaving plenty of room for a boy to wriggle under. When they were inside and the board had been replaced, Geoff clicked on a flashlight. Ahead were stone stairs, deep in fallen plaster and less pleasant litter.

"Our home away from home," said Len, "is on the first floor. Mind where you're walking. Here we are. Wait while I light the lamp."

It was a small room. The windows were blanked by iron shutters. The walls, as Timothy saw when the pressure lamp had been lit, were covered with posters. There was a table made of planks laid on trestles and there were three old wicker chairs. Timothy thought he had never seen anything so snug and cozy in the whole of his life.

Len said, "Your can use the third chair if you like."

It was a formal invitation into brotherhood.

"It used to be Ronnie's chair," said Geoff with a grin. "He won't be using it for a bit. Not for twelve months or so. He got nicked for shoplifting. They sent him up the river."

"Your folks going to start wondering where you are?"

"No, that's all right," said Timothy. "I can say I went on to the club after choir practice. It's a church club. The vicar runs it."

"Old Amberline? That fat poof."

Timothy considered the Reverend Patrick Amberline carefully and said, "No. He's all right."

Mr. Grant said, "Timmy seems very busy these days. It's the third night running he's been late."

"He was telling me about it at breakfast this morning," said Mrs. Grant. "It's not only the Choir and the Youth club. It's this Voluntary Service Group he's joined. They're a sort of modern version of the Boy Scouts. They arrange to help people who need help. When he leaves school he might even get a job abroad. In one of those depressed countries."

"Well, I suppose it's all right," said Mr. Grant. "I used to be a Boy Scout myself once. I got a badge for cooking too."

They were busy weeks. For Timothy, weeks of simple delight. Never having had any real friends before, he found the friendship of Len and Geoff intoxicating. It was friendship offered without reserve, as it is at that age.

He knew now that Len was Leonard Rhodes and Geoff was Geoffrey Cowell and that Len's father was a market porter and Geoff's worked on the railway. He had enough imagination to visualize a life in which a boy was not expected to come home until eleven o'clock at night, a life in which you had to fight for anything you wanted, a life which could be full of surprising adventures.

The first thing he learned about was borrowing cars. This was an exercise carried out with two bits of wire. A strong piece, with a loop at the end, which could be slipped through a gap forced at the top of the window and used to jerk up the retaining catch which locked the door. Timothy, who had small hands and was neat and precise in his movements, became particularly skillful at this.

The second piece of wire was used by Len, who had once spent some time working in a garage, to start the engine. After that, if no irate owner had appeared, the car could be driven off and would serve as transport for the evening. Timothy was taught to drive. He picked it up very quickly.

"Let her rip," said Geoff. "It's not like you were driving your own car and got to be careful you don't scratch the paint. With this one a few bumps don't matter."

This was on the occasion when they had borrowed Mr. Knowlson's new Ford Capri. Timothy had suggested it. "He's stuck to the television from eight o'clock onwards," he said. "He wouldn't come out if a bomb went off."

The evening runs were not solely pleasure trips. There was a business side to them as well. Len and Geoff had a lot of contacts, friends of Geoff's father, who seemed to have a knack for picking up unwanted packages. A carton containing two dozen new transistor pocket radios might have proved tricky to dispose of. But offered separately to buyers in public houses and cafés and dance halls, they seemed to go like hot cakes. Len and Geoff were adept at this.

The first time they took Timothy into a public house the girl behind the bar looked at him and said, "How old's your kid brother?"

"You wouldn't think it," said Geoff, "but he's twenty-eight. He's a midget. He does a turn in the halls. Don't say anything to him about it. He's sensitive."

The girl said, "You're a ruddy liar," but served them with half pints of beer. Mr. Grant was a teetotaler and Timothy had never seen beer before at close quarters. He took a sip of it. It tasted indescribable. Like medicine, only worse. Geoff said, "You don't have to pretend to like it. After a bit you'll sort of get used to it."

Some nights they were engaged in darker work. They would drive the car to a rendezvous, which was usually a garage in the docks area. Men would be there, shadowy figures who hardly showed their faces. Crates which seemed to weigh heavily would be loaded onto the back seat of the car. The boys then drove out into the Kent countryside. The men never came with them.

When the boys arrived at their destination, sometimes another garage, sometimes a small workshop or factory, the cargo was unloaded with equal speed and silence, then a wad of notes was pushed into Len's hands.

The only real difference of opinion the boys ever had was over the money. Len and Geoff wanted to share everything equally. Timothy agreed to keep some of it, but refused any idea of equal sharing. First, because he wouldn't have known what to do with so much cash. More important, because he knew what it was being saved up for. One of the pictures on the wall of their den was a blown-up photograph of a motorcycle—Norton Interstate 850 Road Racer.

"Do a ton easy," said Len. "Hundred and thirty on the track. Old Edelman at that garage we go to down the docks says he can get me one at wholesale. How much are we up to?"

As he said this he was lifting up a board in the corner. Under the board was a biscuit tin, the edges sealed with insulating tape. In the tin was the pirates' hoard of banknotes and coins.

"Another tenner and we're there," said Geoff.

Timothy still went to choir practise. If he had missed it his absence would have been noticed, and inquiries would have followed. The Reverend Amberline usually put in an appearance, mainly to preserve law and order, and on this occasion he happened to notice Timothy. They were practicing the hymn from the Yattenden hymnal, *O quam juvat fratres*. "Happy are they, they that love God."

The rector thought that Timothy, normally a reserved and rather silent boy, really did look happy. He was bubbling over, bursting with happiness. "Remember now thy Creator," said the Reverend Amberline sadly to himself. "In the days of thy youth." How splendid to be young and happy.

That evening Detective Chief Inspector Patrick Petrella paid a visit to Mr. Grant's house in Dodman Street. He said, "We've had a number of reports of cars being taken away without their owner's consent."

"That's right," said Mr. Grant. "And I'm glad you're going to do something about it at last. My neighbor, Mr. Knowlson, lost his a few weeks ago. He got it back, but it was in a shocking state."

"Yesterday evening," said Petrella, "the boys who seem to have been responsible for a number of these cases were observed. If the person who observed them had been a bit quicker, they'd have been apprehended. But she did give us a positive identification of one lad she recognized. It was your son, Timothy."

"I don't believe it," said Mr. Grant, as soon as he had got his breath back. "Timothy would never do anything like that. He's a thoroughly nice boy."

"Can you tell me where he was yesterday evening?"

"Certainly I can. He was with the Voluntary Service Group."

"The people at Craythorne Hall?"

"That's right."

"May I use your telephone?"

"Yes. And then I hope you'll apologize."

Three minutes later Petrella said, "Not only was he not at Craythorne Hall on Wednesday evening, but he's never been there. They know nothing about him. They say they only take on boys of seventeen and over.''

Mr. Grant stared at him, white-faced.

"Where is he now?"

"At choir practice."

"Choir practice would have been over by half-past eight."

"He goes on afterwards to the Youth Club."

Petrella knew the missioner at the Youth Club and used the telephone again. By this time Mrs. Grant had joined them. Petrella faced a badly shaken couple. He said, "I'd like to have a word with Timothy when he does get back. It doesn't matter how late it is. I've got something on at the Station which is going to keep me there anyway."

He gave them his number at Patton Street.

The matter which Petrella referred to was a report of goods stolen from the railway yard, being run to a certain garage in the docks area. It was out of this garage, at the moment that Petrella left Dodman Street, that the brand-new shining monster was being wheeled.

"She's licensed and we've filled her up for you," said Mr. Edelman, who was the jovial proprietor of the garage. "The petrol is on the house." He could afford to be generous. The courier service the boys had run had enriched him at minimal risk to himself.

"Well, thanks," said Geoff. He was almost speechless with pride and excitement.

"If you want to try her out, the best way is over Blackheath and out onto the M.2. You can let her rip there."

Geoff and Len were both wearing new white helmets, white silk scarves wrapped round the lower parts of their faces, black leather coats, and leather gauntlets. The gloves, helmets, and scarves had been lifted the day before from an outfitter's in Southwark High Street. The coats had been bought for them by Timothy out of his share of the money. Len was the driver. Geoff was to ride pillion.

"Your turn tomorrow," said Geoff.

"Fine," said Timothy. "I'll wait for you at our place."

"Keep the home fires burning," said Len. "This is just a trial run. We'll be back in an hour."

"And watch it," said Mr. Edelman. "There's a lot of horsepower inside that little beauty. So don't go doing anything stupid."

His words were drowned in the roar of the Road Racer starting up. Timothy stood listening until he could hear it no longer.

* * *

Petrella got the news at eleven o'clock that night.

"We've identified the boys," said the voice on the telephone. "They both lived in your area. Cowell and Rhodes. I can give you the addresses."

"Both dead?"

"They could hardly be deader. They went off the road and smashed into the back of a parked lorry. An A.A. patrol saw it happen. Said they must have been doing over ninety. Stupid young fools."

The speaker sounded angry. But he had seen the bodies and had sons of his own.

The Cowells' house was nearer, so Petrella called there first. He found Mr. and Mrs. Cowell in the kitchen, with the television blaring. They turned it off when they understood what Petrella was telling them.

"I warned him," said Mr. Cowell. "You heard me tell him."

"You said what nasty dangerous things they were," agreed his wife. "We didn't even know he had one."

"It was a brand-new machine," said Petrella. "Any idea where he might have got it from?"

"Tell you the truth," said Mr. Cowell, "we haven't been seeing a lot of Geoff lately. Boys at that age run wild, you know."

"We've brought up six," said Mr. Cowell, crying softly.

Mr. Cowell said, "He and Len were good boys really. It was that Ronnie Silverlight led them astray. Until they ganged up with him we never had no trouble. No trouble at all."

It was one o'clock in the morning by the time Petrella got back to Patton Street. The desk Sergeant said that there had been a number of calls. A Mr. Grant had rung more than once. And a boy who said he was Len Rhodes's brother was asking for news.

"How long ago was that?"

"About ten minutes ago."

"That's funny," said Petrella. "I've just come from the Rhodes'. And I don't think Len had a brother. What did you tell him?"

"I just gave him the news."

"What did he say?"

"Nothing. He just rang off. I think he was in a phone booth."

At this moment the telephone on the desk rang again. It was Mr. Grant. His voice was ragged with worry. "It's Timothy," he said. "He's not come home. You haven't—"

"No," said Petrella, "we haven't got him here. Is there any other place he might have gone? Has he got any friends?"

"We don't know anyone round here. He wouldn't just have walked out without saying anything. His mother's beside herself. She wanted to come round and see you."

"I don't think that would do any good," said Petrella. "We'll do what we can." He thought about it, then said to the desk Sergeant, "Can you turn up the records and find out what happened to a boy named Ronald Silverlight? He was sent down for petty larceny about two months ago. One of the Borstal Institutes. See if you can find me the Warden's telephone number."

In spite of being hauled from his bed the Warden, once he understood what Petrella wanted, was sympathetic and cooperative. He said, "It's a long shot, but I'll wake Ronnie up and ring you back if I get anything."

Ten minutes later he came through again. He said, "This might be what you want. I gather they were using some derelict old building down in the docks area. It wouldn't be easy to describe the location. The best plan will be to send the boy up in a car. It'll take an hour or more."

"I'll wait," said Petrella.

It was nearly four o'clock in the morning before the car arrived, with a police driver, and Ronnie Silverlight and a guard in the back. Petrella got in with them and they drove toward the river.

"You have to walk the last bit," said Ronnie.

Petrella thought about it. There seemed to be too many of them. He said, "I'll be responsible for the boy. You two wait here."

When they got to the building Ronnie said, "We used to shift the bottom board, see, and get in underneath. It'll be a tight squeeze for you."

"I'll manage," said Petrella.

He did it by lying on his back and using his elbows. When he was inside he clicked on the flashlight he had brought with him.

"Up there," said Ronnie. He was speaking in a whisper and didn't seem anxious to go first, so Petrella led the way up.

When he opened the door, the first thing that caught his eye was a glow from a fire of driftwood in the hearth which had burned down to red embers. Then, as his flashlight swung upward, the white beam showed him Timothy. He had climbed onto the table, tied one end of a rope to the beam, fixed the other in a noose round his neck, and kicked away the plank.

Petrella put the plank back and jumped up beside him, but as soon as he touched the boy he knew that they were much too late. He had been dead for hours.

He must have done it, thought Petrella, soon after he had telephoned the station and heard the news about Len and Geoff. And he made the fire to give him some light to see what he was doing.

"It's Timmy Grant, isn't it," said Ronnie.

"Yes," said Petrella. "It's Timmy." He was thinking of all the things he would now have to do, starting with breaking the news to his parents.

"He was a good kid," said Ronnie. "Geoff wrote me about him."

Petrella's light picked up a flash of white. It was a piece of paper that had fallen off the table. On it was written, in Timothy's schoolboy script, two lines. Petrella recognized them as coming from a hymn, but he did not know, until Father Amberline told him long afterward, that they were from the hymn the choir had been singing that evening.

And death itself shall not unbind
Their happy brotherhood.

Petrella folded the scrap of paper and slipped it quickly into his pocket. It was against all his instincts as a policeman to suppress evidence, but he felt that it would be too brutal to show it to Mr. and Mrs. Grant.

Ellery Queen

THE LAMP OF GOD
Ellery Queen

I

IF A STORY began: "Once upon a time in a house cowering in wilderness there lived an old and eremitical creature named Mayhew, a crazy man who had buried two wives and lived a life of death; and this house was known as *The Black House*" — if a story began in this fashion, it would strike no one as especially remarkable. There are people like that who live in houses like that, and very often mysteries materialize like ectoplasm about their wild-eyed heads.

Now however disorderly Mr. Ellery Queen may be by habit, mentally he is an orderly person. His neckties and shoes might be strewn about his bedroom helter-skelter, but inside his skull hums a perfectly oiled machine, functioning as neatly and inexorably as the planetary system. So if there was a mystery about one Sylvester Mayhew, deceased, and his buried wives and gloomy dwelling, you may be sure the Queen brain would seize upon it and worry it and pick it apart and get it all laid out in neat and shiny rows. Rationality, that was it. No esoteric mumbo-jumbo could fool *that* fellow. Lord, no! His two feet were planted solidly on God's good earth, and one and one made two—always—and that's all there was to that.

Of course, Macbeth had said that stones have been known to move and trees to speak; but pshaw! for these literary fancies. In this day and age, with its *Cominterns*, its wars of peace, its *fasces* and its rocketry experiments? Nonsense! The truth is, Mr. Queen would have said, there is something about the harsh, cruel world we live in that's very rough on miracles. Miracles just don't happen any more, unless they are miracles of stupidity or miracles of national avarice. Everyone with a grain of intelligence knows that.

"Oh, yes," Mr. Queen would have said; "there are yogis, voodoos, fakirs, shamans, and other tricksters from the effete East and primitive Africa, but nobody pays any attention to such pitiful monkeyshines—I mean, nobody with sense. This is a reasonable world and everything that happens in it must have a reasonable explanation.''

You couldn't expect a sane person to believe, for example, that a three-dimensional, flesh-and-blood, veritable human being could suddenly stoop, grab his shoelaces, and fly away. Or that a water-buffalo could change into a golden-haired little boy before your eyes. Or that a man dead one hundred and thirty-seven years could push aside his tombstone, step out of his grave, yawn, and then sing three verses of *Mademoiselle from Armentières*. Or even, for that matter, that a stone could move or a tree speak—yea, though it were in the language of Atlantis or Mu.

Or . . . *could you?*

The tale of Sylvester Mayhew's house is a strange tale. When what happened happened, proper minds tottered on their foundations and porcelain beliefs threatened to shiver into shards. Before the whole fantastic and incomprehensible business was done, God Himself came into it. Yes, God came into the story of Sylvester Mayhew's house, and that is what makes it quite the most remarkable adventure in which Mr. Ellery Queen, that lean and indefatigable agnostic, has ever become involved.

The early mysteries in the Mayhew case were trivial—mysteries merely because certain pertinent facts were lacking; pleasantly provocative mysteries, but scarcely savorous of the supernatural.

Ellery was sprawled on the hearthrug before the hissing fire that raw January morning, debating with himself whether it was more desirable to brave the slippery streets and biting wind on a trip to Centre Street in quest of amusement, or to remain where he was in idleness but comfort, when the telephone rang.

It was Thorne on the wire. Ellery, who never thought of Thorne without perforce visualizing a human monolith—a long-limbed, gray-thatched male figure with marbled cheeks and agate eyes, the whole man coated with a veneer of ebony, was rather startled. Thorne was excited; every crack and blur in his voice spoke eloquently of emotion. It was the first time, to Ellery's recollection, that Thorne had betrayed the least evidence of human feeling.

''What's the matter?'' Ellery demanded. ''Nothing's wrong with Ann, I hope?'' Ann was Thorne's wife.

"No, no." Thorne spoke hoarsely and rapidly, as if he had been running.

"Where the deuce have you been? I saw Ann only yesterday and she said she hadn't heard from you for almost a week. Of course, your wife's used to your preoccupation with those interminable legal affairs, but an absence of six days——"

"Listen to me, Queen, and don't hold me up. I must have your help. Can you meet me at Pier 54 in half an hour? That's North River."

"Of course."

Thorne mumbled something that sounded absurdly like: "Thank God!" and hurried on: "Pack a bag. For a couple of days. And a revolver. Especially a revolver, Queen."

"I see," said Ellery, not seeing at all.

"I'm meeting the Cunarder *Coronia*. Docking this morning. I'm with a man by the name of Reinach, Dr. Reinach. You're my colleague; get that? Act stern and omnipotent. Don't be friendly. Don't ask him—or me—questions. And don't allow yourself to be pumped. Understood?"

"Understood," said Ellery, "but not exactly clear. Anything else?"

"Call Ann for me. Give her my love and tell her I shan't be home for days yet, but that you're with me and that I'm all right. And ask her to telephone my office and explain matters to Crawford."

"Do you mean to say that not even your partner knows what you've been doing?"

But Thorne had hung up.

Ellery replaced the receiver, frowning. It was stranger than strange. Thorne had always been a solid citizen, a successful attorney who led an impeccable private life and whose legal practice was dry and unexciting. To find old Thorne entangled in a web of mystery. . . .

Ellery drew a happy breath, telephoned Mrs. Thorne, tried to sound reassuring, yelled for Djuna, hurled some clothes into a bag, loaded his .38 police revolver with a grimace, scribbled a note for Inspector Queen, dashed downstairs and jumped into the cab Djuna had summoned, and landed on Pier 54 with thirty seconds to spare.

There was something terribly wrong with Thorne, Ellery saw at once, even before he turned his attention to the vast fat man by the lawyer's side. Thorne was shrunken within his Scotch-plaid greatcoat like a pupa which was died prematurely in its cocoon. He had aged years in the few weeks since Ellery had last seen him. His ordinarily sleek cobalt cheeks were covered with a straggly stubble. Even his clothing looked tired and uncared-for. And there was a glitter of furtive relief in his bloodshot eyes as he pressed Ellery's hand that was, to one who knew Thorne's self-sufficiency and aplomb, almost pathetic.

But he merely remarked: "Oh, hello, there, Queen. We've a longer wait than we anticipated, I'm afraid. Want you to shake hands with Dr. Herbert Reinach. Doctor, this is Ellery Queen."

"'D'you do," said Ellery curtly, touching the man's immense gloved hand. If he was to be omnipotent, he thought, he might as well be rude, too.

"Surprise, Mr. Thorne?" said Dr. Reinach in the deepest voice Ellery had ever heard; it rumbled up from the caverns of his chest like the echo of thunder. His little purplish eyes were very, very cold.

"A pleasant one, I hope," said Thorne.

Ellery snatched a glance at his friend's face as he cupped his hands about a cigarette, and he read approval there. If he had struck the right tone, he knew how to act thenceforth. He flipped the match and turned abruptly to Thorne. Dr. Reinach was studying him in a half-puzzled, half-amused way.

"Where's the *Coronia*?"

"Held up in quarantine," said Thorne. "Somebody's seriously ill aboard with some disease or other and there's been difficulty in clearing her passengers. It will take hours, I understand. Suppose we settle down in the waiting-room for a bit."

They found places in the crowded room, and Ellery set his bag between his feet and disposed himself so that he was in a position to catch every expression on his companions' faces. There was something in Thorne's repressed excitement, an even more piquing aura enveloping the fat doctor, that violently whipped his curiosity.

"Alice," said Thorne in a casual tone, as if Ellery knew who Alice was, "is probably becoming impatient. But that's a family trait of the Mayhews, from the little I saw of old Sylvester. Eh, Doctor? It's trying, though, to come all the way from England only to be held up on the threshold."

So they were to meet an Alice Mayhew, thought Ellery, arriving from England on the *Coronia*. Good old Thorne! He almost chuckled aloud. "Sylvester" was obviously a senior Mayhew, some relative of Alice's.

Dr. Reinach fixed his little eyes on Ellery's bag and rumbled politely: "Are you going away somewhere, Mr. Queen?"

Then Reinach did not know Ellery was to accompany them—wherever they were bound for.

Thorne stirred in the depths of his greatcoat, rustling like a sack of desiccated bones. "Queen's coming back with me, Dr. Reinach." There was something brittle and hostile in his voice.

The fat man blinked, his eyes buried beneath half-moons of damp flesh. "Really?" he said, and by contrast his bass voice was tender.

"Perhaps I should have explained," said Thorne abruptly. "Queen is a colleague of mine, Doctor. This case has interested him."

"Case?" said the fat man.

"Legally speaking. I really hadn't the heart to deny him the pleasure of helping me—ah—protect Alice Mayhew's interests. I trust you won't mind?"

This was a deadly game, Ellery became certain. Something important was at stake, and Thorne in his stubborn way was determined to defend it by force or guile.

Reinach's puffy lids dropped over his eyes as he folded his paws on his stomach. "Naturally, naturally not," he said in a hearty tone. "Only too happy to have you, Mr. Queen. A little unexpected, perhaps, but delightful surprises are as essential to life as to poetry. Eh?" And he chuckled.

Samuel Johnson, thought Ellery, recognizing the source of the doctor's remark. The physical analogy struck him. There was iron beneath those layers of fat and a good brain under that dolichocephalic skull. The man sat there on the waiting-room bench like an octopus, lazy and inert and peculiarly indifferent to his surroundings. Indifference—that was it, thought Ellery; the man was a colossal remoteness, as vague and darkling as a storm cloud on an empty horizon.

Thorne said in a weary voice: "Suppose we have lunch. I'm famished."

By three in the afternoon Ellery felt old and worn. Several hours of nervous, cautious silence, threading his way smiling among treacherous shoals, had told him just enough to put him on guard. He often felt knotted-up and tight inside when a crisis loomed or danger threatened from an unknown quarter. Something extraordinary was going on.

As they stood on the pier watching the *Coronia's* bulk being nudged alongside, he chewed on the scraps he had managed to glean during the long, heavy, pregnant hours. He knew definitely now that the man called Sylvester Mayhew was dead, that he had been a pronounced paranoic, that his house was buried in an almost inaccessible wilderness on Long Island. Alice Mayhew, somewhere on the decks of the *Coronia* doubtless straining her eyes pierward, was the dead man's daughter, parted from her father since childhood.

And he had placed the remarkable figure of Dr. Reinach in the puzzle. The fat man was Sylvester Mayhew's half-brother. He had also acted as Mayhew's physician during the old man's last illness. This illness and death seemed to have been very recent, for there had been some talk of "the funeral" in terms of fresh if detached sorrow. There was also a Mrs. Reinach glimmering unsubstantially in the background, and a queer old lady who was the dead man's sister. But what the mystery was, or why Thorne was so perturbed, Ellery could not figure out.

The liner tied up to the pier at last. Officials scampered about, whistles blew, gang-planks appeared, passengers disembarked in droves to the accompaniment of the usual howls and embraces.

Interest crept into Dr. Reinach's little eyes, and Thorne was shaking.

"There she is!" croaked the lawyer. "I'd know her anywhere from her photographs. That slender girl in the brown turban!"

As Thorne hurried away Ellery studied the girl eagerly. She was anxiously scanning the crowd, a tall charming creature with an elasticity of movement more esthetic than athletic and a harmony of delicate feature that approached beauty. She was dressed so simply and inexpensively that he narrowed his eyes.

Thorne came back with her, patting her gloved hand and speaking quietly to her. Her face was alight and alive, and there was a natural gaiety in it which convinced Ellery that whatever mystery or tragedy lay before her, it was still unknown to her. At the same time there were certain signs about her eyes and mouth—fatigue, strain, worry, he could not put his finger on the exact cause—which puzzled him.

"I'm so glad," she murmured in a cultured voice, strongly British in accent. Then her face grew grave and she looked from Ellery to Dr. Reinach.

"This is your uncle, Miss Mayhew," said Thorne. "Dr. Reinach. This other gentleman is not, I regret to say, a relative. Mr. Ellery Queen, a colleague of mine."

"Oh," said the girl; and she turned to the fat man and said tremulously: "Uncle Herbert. How terribly odd. I mean—I've felt so all alone. You've been just a legend to me, Uncle Herbert, you and Aunt Sarah and the rest, and now . . ." She choked a little as she put her arms about the fat man and kissed his pendulous cheek.

"My dear," said Dr. Reinach solemnly; and Ellery could have struck him for the Judas quality of his solemnity.

"But you must tell me everything! Father—how is father? It seems so strange to be . . . to be saying that."

"Don't you think, Miss Mayhew," said the lawyer quickly, "that we had better see you through the Customs? It's growing late and we have a long trip before us. Long Island, you know."

"Island?" Her candid eyes widened. "That sounds so exciting!"

"Well, it's not what you might think——"

"Forgive me. I'm acting the perfect gawk." She smiled. "I'm entirely in your hands, Mr. Thorne. Your letter was more than kind."

As they made their way toward the Customs, Ellery dropped a little behind and devoted himself to watching Dr. Reinach. But that vast lunar countenance was as inscrutable as a gargoyle.

Dr. Reinach drove. It was not Thorne's car; Thorne had a regal new Lincoln limousine and this was a battered if serviceable old Buick sedan.

The girl's luggage was strapped to the back and sides; Ellery was puzzled by the scantness of it—three small suitcases and a tiny steamer-trunk. Did these four pitiful containers hold all of her worldly possessions?

Sitting beside the fat man, Ellery strained his ears. He paid little attention to the road Reinach was taking.

The two behind were silent for a long time. Then Thorne cleared his throat with an oddly ominous finality. Ellery saw what was coming; he had often heard that throat-clearing sound emanate from the mouths of judges pronouncing sentence of doom.

"We have something sad to tell you, Miss Mayhew. You may as well learn it now."

"Sad?" murmured the girl after a moment. "Sad? Oh, it's not——"

"Your father," said Thorne inaudibly. "He's dead."

She cried: "Oh!" in a small helpless voice; and then she grew quiet.

"I'm dreadfully sorry to have to greet you with such news," said Thorne in the silence. "We'd anticipated . . . And I realize how awkward it must be for you. After all, it's quite as if you had never known him at all. Love for a parent, I'm afraid, lies in direct ratio to the degree of childhood association. Without any association at all . . ."

"It's a shock, of course," Alice said in a muffled voice. "And yet, as you say, he was a stranger to me, a mere name. As I wrote you, I was only a toddler when mother got her divorce and took me off to England. I don't remember father at all. And I've not seen him since, or heard from him."

"Yes," muttered the attorney.

"I might have learned more about father if mother hadn't died when I was six; but she did, and my people—her people—in England. . . . Uncle John died last fall. He was the last one. And then I was left all alone. When your letter came I was—I was so glad, Mr. Thorne. I didn't feel lonely any more. I was really happy for the first time in years. And now——" She broke off to stare out the window.

Dr. Reinach swiveled his massive head and smiled benignly. "But you're not alone, my dear. There's my unworthy self, and your Aunt Sarah, and Milly—Milly's my wife, Alice; naturally you wouldn't know anything about her—and there's even a husky young fellow named Keith who works about the place—bright lad who's come down in the world." He chuckled. "So you see there won't be a dearth of companionship for you."

"Thank you, Uncle Herbert," she murmured. "I'm sure you're all terribly kind. Mr. Thorne, how did father . . . When you replied to my letter you wrote me he was ill, but——"

"He fell into a coma unexpectedly nine days ago. You hadn't left England yet and I cabled you at your antique-shop address. But somehow it missed you."

"I'd sold the shop by that time and was flying about, patching up thing. When did he . . . die?"

"A week ago Thursday. The funeral . . . Well, we couldn't wait, you see. I might have caught you by cable or telephone on the *Coronia*, but I didn't have the heart to spoil your voyage."

"I don't know how to thank you for all the trouble you've taken." Without looking at her Ellery knew there were tears in her eyes. "It's good to know that someone——"

"It's been hard for all of us," rumbled Dr. Reinach.

"Of course, Uncle Herbert. I'm sorry." She fell silent. When she spoke again, it was as if there were a compulsion expelling the words. "When Uncle John died, I didn't know where to reach father. The only American address I had was yours, Mr. Thorne, which some patron or other had given me. It was the only thing I could think of. I was sure a solicitor could find father for me. That's why I wrote to you in such detail, with photographs and all."

"Naturally we did what we could." Thorne seemed to be having difficulty with his voice. "When I found your father and went out to see him the first time and showed him your letter and photographs, he . . . I'm sure this will please you, Miss Mayhew. He wanted you badly. He'd

apparently been having a hard time of late years—ah, mentally, emotionally. And so I wrote you at his request. On my second visit, the last
time I saw him alive, when the question of the estate came up——''

Ellery thought that Dr. Reinach's paws tightened on the wheel. But
the fat man's face bore the same bland, remote smile.

"Please," said Alice wearily. "Do you greatly mind, Mr. Thorne?
I—I don't feel up to discussing such matters now."

The car was fleeing along the deserted road as if it were trying to run
away from the weather. The sky was gray lead; a frowning, gloomy sky
under which the countryside lay cowering. It was growing colder, too, in
the dark and draughty tonneau; the cold seeped in through the cracks and
their overclothes.

Ellery stamped his feet a little and twisted about to glance at Alice
Mayhew. Her oval face was a glimmer in the murk; she was sitting
stiffly, her hands clenched into tight little fists in her lap. Thorne was
slumped miserably by her side, staring out the window.

"By George, it's going to snow," announced Dr. Reinach with a
cheerful puff of his cheeks.

No one answered.

The drive was interminable. There was a dreary sameness about the
landscape that matched the weather's mood. They had long since left the
main highway to turn into a frightful byroad, along which they jolted in
an unsteady eastward curve between ranks of leafless woods. The road
was pitted and frozen hard; the woods were tangles of dead trees and
underbrush densely packed but looking as if they had been repeatedly
seared by fire. The whole effect was one of widespread and oppressive
desolation.

"Looks like No Man's Land," said Ellery at last from his bouncing
seat beside Dr. Reinach. "And feels like it, too."

Dr. Reinach's cetaceous back heaved in a silent mirth. "Matter of
fact, that's exactly what it's called by the natives. Land-God-forgot, eh?
But then Sylvester always swore by the Greek unities."

The man seemed to live in a dark and silent cavern, out of which he
maliciously emerged at intervals to poison the atmosphere.

"It isn't very inviting-looking, is it?" remarked Alice in a low voice.
It was clear she was brooding over the strange old man who had lived in
this wasteland, and of her mother who had fled from it so many years
before.

"It wasn't always this way," said Dr. Reinach, swelling his cheeks
like a bull-frog. "Once it was pleasant enough; I remember it as a boy.

Then it seemed as if it might become the nucleus of a populous community. But progress has passed it by, and a couple of uncontrollable forest fires did the rest."

"It's horrible," murmured Alice, "simply horrible."

"My dear Alice, it's your innocence that speaks there. All life is a frantic struggle to paint a rosy veneer over the ugly realities. Why not be honest with yourself? Everything in this world is stinking rotten; worse than that, a bore. Hardly worth living, in any impartial analysis. But if you have to live, you may as well live in surroundings consistent with the rottenness of everything."

The old attorney stirred beside Alice, where he was buried in his greatcoat. "You're quite a philosopher, Doctor," he snarled.

"I'm an honest man."

"Do you know, Doctor," murmured Ellery, despite himself, "you're beginning to annoy me."

The fat man glanced at him. Then he said: "And do you agree with this mysterious friend of yours, Thorne?"

"I believe," snapped Thorne, "that there is a platitude extant which says that actions speak with considerably more volume than words. I haven't shaved for six days, and today has been the first time I left Sylvester Mayhew's house since his funeral."

"Mr. Thorne!" cried Alice, turning to him. "Why?"

The lawyer muttered: "I'm sorry, Miss Mayhew. All in good time, in good time."

"You wrong us all," smiled Dr. Reinach, deftly skirting a deep rut in the road. "And I'm afraid you're giving my niece quite the most erroneous impression of her family. We're odd, no doubt, and our blood is presumably turning sour after so many generations of cold storage; but then don't the finest vintages come from the deepest cellars? You've only to glance at Alice to see my point. Such vital loveliness could only have been produced by an old family."

"My mother," said Alice, with a faint loathing in her glance, "had something to do with that, Uncle Herbert."

"Your mother, my dear," replied the fat man, "was merely a contributory factor. You have the typical Mayhew features."

Alice did not reply. Her uncle, whom until today she had not seen, was an obscene enigma; the others, waiting for them at their destination, she had never seen at all, and she had no great hope that they would prove better. A livid streak ran through her father's family; he had been a paranoic with delusions of persecution. The Aunt Sarah in the dark distance, her father's surviving sister, was apparently something of a character. As for Aunt Milly, Dr. Reinach's wife, whatever she might have been in the past, one had only to glance at Dr. Reinach to see what she undoubtedly was in the present.

Ellery felt prickles at the nape of his neck. The farther they penetrated this wilderness the less he liked the whole adventure. It smacked vaguely of a fore-ordained theatricalism, as if some hand of monstrous power were setting the stage for the first act of a colossal tragedy. . . . He shrugged this sophomoric foolishness off, settling deeper into his coat. It was queer enough, though. Even the lifelines of the most indigent community were missing; there were no telephone poles and, so far as he could detect, no electric cables. That meant candles. He detested candles.

The sun was behind them, leaving them. It was a feeble sun, shivering in the pallid cold. Feeble as it was, Ellery wished it would stay.

They crashed on and on, endlessly, shaken like dolls. The road kept lurching toward the east in a stubborn curve. The sky grew more and more leaden. The cold seeped deeper and deeper into their bones.

When Dr. Reinach finally rumbled: "Here we are," and steered the jolting car leftward off the road into a narrow, wretchedly gravelled driveway, Ellery came to with a start of surprise and relief. So their journey was really over, he thought. Behind him he heard Thorne and Alice stirring; they must be thinking the same thing.

He roused himself, stamping his icy feet, looking about. The same desolate tangle of woods to either side of the by-road. He recalled now that they had not once left the main road nor crossed another road since turning off the highway. No chance, he thought grimly, to stray off this path to perdition.

Dr. Reinach twisted his fat neck and said: "Welcome home, Alice."

Alice murmured something incomprehensible; her face was buried to the eyes in the moth-eaten laprobe Reinach had flung over her. Ellery glanced sharply at the fat man; there had been a note of mockery, of derision, in that heavy rasping voice. But the face was smooth and damp and bland, as before.

Dr. Reinach ran the car up the driveway and brought it to rest a little before, and between, two houses. These structures flanked the drive, standing side by side, separated by only the width of the drive, which led straight ahead to a ramshackle garage. Ellery caught a glimpse of Thorne's glittering Lincoln within its crumbling walls.

The three buildings huddled in a ragged clearing, surrounded by the tangle of woods, like three desert islands in an empty sea.

"That," said Dr. Reinach heartily, "is the ancestral mansion, Alice. To the left."

The house to the left was of stone; once gray, but now so tarnished by the elements and perhaps the ravages of fire that it was almost black. Its face was blotched and streaky, as if it had succumbed to an insensate leprosy. Rising three stories, elaborately ornamented with stone flora and gargoyles, it was unmistakably Victorian in its architecture. The façade had a neglected, granular look that only the art of great age could have etched. The whole structure appeared to have thrust its roots immovably into the forsaken landscape.

Ellery saw Alice Mayhew staring at it with a sort of speechless horror; it had nothing of the pleasant hoariness of old English mansions. It was simply old, old with the dreadful age of this seared and blasted country-side. He cursed Thorne beneath his breath for subjecting the girl to such a shocking experience.

"Sylvester called it The Black House," said Dr. Reinach cheerfully as he turned off the ignition. "Not pretty, I admit, but as solid as the day it was built, seventy-five years ago."

"Black House," grunted Thorne. "Rubbish."

"Do you mean to say," whispered Alice, "that father . . . mother lived *here*?"

"Yes, my dear. Quaint name, eh, Thorne? Another illustration of Sylvester's preoccupaton with the morbidly colorful. Built by your grandfather, Alice. The old gentleman built this one, too, later; I believe you'll find it considerably more habitable. Where the devil is every-one?"

He descended heavily and held the rear door open for his niece. Mr. Ellery Queen slipped down to the driveway on the other side and glanced about with the sharp, uneasy sniff of a wild animal. The old mansion's companion-house was a much smaller and less pretentious dwelling, two stories high and built of an originally white stone which had turned gray. The front door was shut and the curtains at the lower windows were drawn. But there was a fire burning somewhere inside; he caught the tremulous glimmers. In the next moment they were blotted out by the head of an old woman, who pressed her face to one of the panes for a single instant and then vanished. But the door remained shut.

"You'll stop with us, of course," he heard the doctor say genially; and Ellery circled the car. His three companions were standing in the drive-way, Alice pressed close to Thorne as if for protection. "You won't want to sleep in the Black House, Alice. No one's there, it's in rather a mess; and a house of death, y'know. . . ."

"Stop it," growled Thorne. "Can't you see the poor child is half-dead from fright as it is? Are you trying to scare her away?"

"Scare me away?" repeated Alice, dazedly.

"Tut, tut," smiled the fat man. "Melodrama doesn't become you at all Thorne. I'm a blunt old codger, Alice, but I mean well. It will really be more comfortable in the White House." He chuckled suddenly again. "White House. That's what *I* named it to preserve a sort of atmospheric balance."

"There's something frightfully wrong here," said Alice in a tight voice. "Mr. Thorne, what is it? There's been nothing but innuendo and concealed hostility since we met at the pier. And just why *did* you spend six days in father's house after the funeral? I think I've a right to know."

Thorne licked his lips. "I shouldn't——"

"Come, come, my dear," said the fat man. "Are we to freeze here all day?"

Alice drew her thin coat more closely about her. "You're all being beastly. Would you mind, Uncle Herbert? I should like to see the inside—where father and mother . . ."

"I don't think so, Miss Mayhew," said Thorne hastily.

"Why not?" said Dr. Reinach tenderly, and he glanced once over his shoulder at the building he had called the White House. "She may as well do it now and get it over with. There's still light enough to see by. Then we'll go over, wash up, have a hot dinner, and you'll feel worlds better." He seized the girl's arm and marched her toward the dark building, across the dead, twig-strewn ground. "I believe," continued the doctor blandly, as they mounted the steps of the stone porch, "that Mr. Thorne has the keys."

The girl stood quietly waiting, her dark eyes studying the faces of the three men. The attorney was pale, but his lips were set in a stubborn line. He did not reply. Taking a bunch of rusty keys out of a pocket, he fitted one into the lock of the front door. It turned over with a creak.

Then Thorne pushed open the door and they stepped into the house.

It was a tomb. It smelled of must and damp. The furniture, ponderous pieces which once no doubt had been regal, was uniformly dilapidated and dusty. The walls were peeling, showing broken, discolored laths beneath. There was dirt and débris everywhere. It was inconceivable that a human being could once have inhabited this grubby den.

The girl stumbled about, her eyes a blank horror, Dr. Reinach steering her calmly. How long the tour of inspection lasted Ellery did not know; even to him, a stranger, the effect was so oppressive as to be almost unendurable. They wandered about, silent, stepping over trash from room to room, impelled by something stronger than themselves.

Once Alice said in a strangled voice: "Uncle Herbert, didn't anyone . . . take care of father? Didn't anyone ever clean up this horrible place?"

The fat man shrugged. "Your father had notions in his old age, my dear. There wasn't much anyone could do with him. Perhaps we had better not go into that."

The sour stench filled their nostrils. They blundered on, Thorne in the rear, watchful as an old cobra. His eyes never left Dr. Reinach's face.

On the middle floor they came upon a bedroom in which, according to the fat man, Sylvester Mayhew had died. The bed was unmade; indeed, the impress of the dead man's body on the mattress and tumbled sheets could still be discerned.

It was a bare and mean room, not as filthy as the others, but infinitely more depressing. Alice began to cough.

She coughed and coughed, hopelessly, standing still in the center of the room staring at the dirty bed in which she had been born.

Then suddenly she stopped coughing and ran over to a lopsided bureau with one foot missing. A large, faded chromo was propped on its top against the yellowed wall. She looked at it for a long time without touching it. Then she took it down.

"It's mother," she said slowly. "It's really mother. I'm glad now I came. He did love her, after all. He's kept it all these years."

"Yes, Miss Mayhew," muttered Thorne. "I thought you'd like to have it."

"I've only one portrait of mother, and that's a poor one. This—why, she was beautiful, wasn't she?"

She held the chromo up proudly, almost laughing in her hysteria. The time-dulled colors revealed a stately young woman with hair worn high. The features were piquant and regular. There was little resemblance between Alice and the woman in the picture.

"Your father," said Dr. Reinach with a sigh, "often spoke of your mother toward the last, and of her beauty."

"If he had left me nothing but this, it would have been worth the trip from England." Alice trembled a little. The she hurried back to them, the chromo pressed to her breast. "Let's get out of here," she said in a shriller voice. "I—I don't like it here. It's ghastly. I'm . . . afraid."

They left the house with half-running steps, as if someone were after them. The old lawyer turned the key in the lock of the front door with great care, glaring at Dr. Reinach's back as he did so. But the fat man had seized his niece's arm and was leading her across the driveway to the White House, whose windows were now flickering bright with light and whose front door stood wide open.

As they crunched along behind, Ellery said sharply to Thorne: "Thorne. Give me a clue. A hint. Anything. I'm completely in the dark."

Thorne's unshaven face was haggard in the setting sun. "Can't talk now," he muttered. "Suspect everything, everybody. I'll see you to-night, in your room. Or wherever they put you, if you're alone . . . Queen, for God's sake, be careful!"

"Careful?" frowned Ellery.

"As if your life depended on it." Thorne's lips made a thin, grim line. "For all I know, it does."

Then they were crossing the threshold of the White House.

Ellery's impressions were curiously vague. Perhaps it was the effect of the sudden smothering heat after the hours of cramping cold outdoors; perhaps he thawed out too suddenly, and the heat went to his brain.

He stood about for a while in a state almost of semi-consciousness, basking in the waves of warmth that eddied from a roaring fire in a fireplace black with age. He was only dimly aware of the two people who greeted them, and of the interior of the house. The room was old, like everything else he had seen, and its furniture might have come from an antique shop. They were standing in a large living-room, comfortable enough; strange to his senses only because it was so old-fashioned in its appointments. There were actually antimacassars on the overstuffed chairs! A wide staircase with worn brass treads wound from one corner to the sleeping quarters above.

One of the two persons awaiting them was Mrs. Reinach, the doctor's wife. The moment Ellery saw her, even as she embraced Alice, he knew that this was inevitably the sort of woman the fat man would choose for a mate. She was a pale and weazened midge, almost fragile in her delicacy of bone and skin; and she was plainly in a silent convulsion of fear. She wore a hunted look on her dry and bluish face; and over Alice's shoulder she glanced timidly, with the fascinated obedience of a whipped bitch, at her husband.

"So you're Aunt Milly," sighed Alice, pushing away. "You'll for-give me if I . . . It's all so very new to me."

"You must be exhausted, poor darling," said Mrs. Reinach in the chirping twitter of a bird; and Alice smiled wanly and looked grateful. "And I quite understand. After all, we're no more than strangers to you. Oh!" she said, and stopped. Her faded eyes were fixed on the chromo in the girl's hands. "Oh," she said again. "I see you've been over to the other house *already*."

"Of course she has," said the fat man; and his wife grew even paler at the sound of his bass voice. "Now, Alice, why don't you let Milly take you upstairs and get you comfortable?"

"I am rather done in," confessed Alice; and then she looked at her mother's picture and smiled again. "I suppose you think I'm very silly, dashing in this way with just—" She did not finish; instead, she went to the fireplace. There was a broad flame-darkened mantel above it, crowded with gewgaws of a vanished era. She set the chromo of the handsome Victorian-garbed woman among them. "There! Now I feel ever so much better."

"Gentlemen, gentlemen," said Dr. Reinach. "Please don't stand on ceremony. Nick! Make yourself useful. Miss Mayhew's bags are strapped to the car."

A gigantic young man, who had been leaning against the wall, nodded in a surly way. He was studying Alice Mayhew's face with a dark absorption. He went out.

"Who," murmured Alice, flushing, "is that?"

"Nick Keith." The fat man slipped off his coat and went to the fire to warm his flabby hands. "My morose protégé. You'll find him pleasant company, my dear, if you can pierce that thick defensive armor he wears. Does odd jobs about the place, as I believe I mentioned, but don't let that hold you back. This is a democratic country."

"I'm sure he's very nice. Would you excuse me? Aunt Milly, if you'd be kind enough to . . ."

The young man reappeared under a load of baggage, clumped across the living-room, and plodded up the stairs. And suddenly, as if at a signal, Mrs. Reinach broke out into a noisy twittering and took Alice's arm and led her to the staircase. They disappeared after Keith.

"As a medical man," chuckled the fat man, taking their wraps and depositing them in a hall-closet, "I prescribe a large dose of . . . this, gentlemen." He went to a sideboard and brought out a decanter of brandy. "Very good for chilled bellies." He tossed off his own glass with an amazing facility, and in the light of the fire the finely etched capillaries in this bulbous nose stood out clearly. "Ah-h! One of life's major compensations. Warming, eh? And now I suppose you feel the need of a little sprucing up yourselves. Come along, and I'll show you to your rooms.''

Ellery shook his head in a dogged way, trying to clear it. ''There's something about your house, Doctor, that's unusually soporific. Thank you, I think both Thorne and I would appreciate a brisk wash.''

''You'll find it brisk enough,'' said the fat man, shaking with silent laughter. ''This is the forest primeval, you know. Not only haven't we any electric light or gas or telephone, but we've no running water, either. Well behind the house keeps us supplied. The simple life, eh? Better for you than the pampering influences of modern civilization. Our ancestors may have died more easily of bacterial infections, but I'll wager they had a greater body immunity to coryza! . . . Well, well, enough of this prattle. Up you go.''

The chilly corridor upstairs made them shiver, but the very shiver revived them; Ellery felt better at once. Dr. Reinach, carrying candles and matches, showed Thorne into a room overlooking the front of the house, and Ellery into one on the side. A fire burned crisply in the large fireplace in one corner, and the basin on the old-fashioned washstand was filled with icy-looking water.

''Hope you find it comfortable,'' drawled the fat man, lounging in the doorway. ''We were expecting only Thorne and my niece, but one more can always be accommodated. Ah—colleague of Thorne's, I believe he said?''

''Twice,'' replied Ellery. ''If you don't mind—''

''Not at all.'' Reinach lingered, eyeing Ellery with a smile. Ellery shrugged, stripped off his coat, and made his ablutions. The water *was* cold; it nipped his fingers like the mouths of little fishes. He scrubbed his face vigorously.

''That's better,'' he said drying himself. ''Much. I wonder why I felt so peaked downstairs.''

''Sudden contrast of heat after cold, no doubt.'' Dr. Reinach made no move to go.

Ellery shrugged again. He opened his bag with pointed nonchalance. There, plainly revealed on his haberdashery, lay the .38 police revolver. He tossed it aside.

''Do you always carry a gun, Mr. Queen?'' murmured Dr. Reinach.

''Always.'' Ellery picked up the revolver and slipped it into his hip pocket.

''Charming!'' The fat man stroked his triple chin. ''Charming. Well,

Mr. Queen, if you'll excuse me I'll see how Thorne is getting on.
Stubborn fellow, Thorne. He could have taken pot luck with us this past
week, but he insisted on isolating himself in that filthy den next door.''

"I wonder," murmured Ellery, "why."

Dr. Reinach eyed him. Then he said: "Come downstairs when you're
ready. Mrs. Reinach has an excellent dinner prepared and if you're as
hungry as I am, you'll appreciate it.'' Still smiling, the fat man vanished.

Ellery stood still for a moment, listening. He heard the fat man pause
at the end of the corridor; a moment later the heavy tread was audible
again, this time descending the stairs.

Ellery went swiftly to the door on tiptoe. He had noticed that the
instant he had come into the room.

There was no lock. Where a lock had been there was a splintery hole,
and the splinters had a newish look about them. Frowning, he placed a
rickety chair against the door-knob and began to prowl.

He raised the mattress from the heavy wooden bedstead and poked
beneath it, searching for he knew not what. He opened closets and
drawers; he felt the worn carpet for wires.

But after ten minutes, angry with himself, he gave up and went to the
window. The prospect was so dismal that he scowled in sheer misery.
Just brown stripped woods and the leaden sky; the old mansion pictur-
esquely know as the Black House was on the other side, invisible from
this window.

A veiled sun was setting; a bank of storm clouds slipped aside for an
instant and the brilliant rim of the sun shone directly into his eyes,
making him see colored, dancing balls. Then other clouds, fat with
snow, moved up and the sun slipped below the horizon. The room
darkened rapidly.

Lock taken out, eh? Someone had worked fast. They could not have
known he was coming, of course. Then someone must have seen him
through the window as the car stopped in the drive. The old woman who
had peered out for a moment? Ellery wondered where she was. At any
rate, a few minutes' work by a skilled hand at the door . . . He wondered,
too, if Thorne's door had been similarly mutilated. And Alice Mayhew's.

Thorne and Dr. Reinach were already seated before the fire when
Ellery came down, and the fat man was rumbling: "Just as well. Give the
poor girl a chance to return to normal. With the shock she's had today, it
might be the finisher. I've told Mrs. Reinach to break it to Sarah

gently . . . Ah, Queen. Come over here and join us. We'll have dinner as soon as Alice comes down.

"Dr. Reinach was just apologizing," said Thorne casually, "for this Aunt Sarah of Miss Mayhew's—Mrs. Fell, Sylvester Mayhew's sister. The excitement of anticipating her niece's arrival seems to have been a bit too much for her."

"Indeed," said Ellery, sitting down and planting his feet on the nearest firedog.

"Fact is," said the fat man, "my poor half-sister is cracked. The family paranoia. She's off-balance; not violent, you know, but it's wise to humor her. She isn't normal, and for Alice to see her——"

"Paranoia," said Ellery. "An unfortunate family, it seems. Your half-brother Sylvester's weakness seems to have expressed itself in rubbish and solitude. What's Mrs. Fell's delusion?"

"Common enough—she thinks her daughter is still alive. As a matter of fact, poor Olivia was killed in an automobile accident three years ago. It shocked Sarah's maternal instinct out of plumb. Sarah's been looking forward to seeing Alice, her brother's daughter, and it may prove awkward. Never can tell how a diseased mind will react to an unusual situation."

"For that matter," drawled Ellery, "I should have said the same remark might be made about any mind, diseased or not."

Dr. Reinach laughed silently. Thorne, hunched by the fire, said: "This Keith boy."

The fat man set his glass down slowly. "Drink, Queen?"

"No, thank you."

"This Keith boy," said Thorne again.

"Eh? Oh, Nick. Yes, Thorne? What about him?"

The lawyer shrugged. Dr. Reinach picked up his glass again. "Am I imagining things, or is there the vaguest hint of hostility in the circum-ambient ether?"

"Reinach——" began Thorne harshly.

"Don't worry about Keith, Thorne. We let him pretty much alone. He's sour on the world, which demonstrates his good sense; but I'm afraid he's unlike me in that he hasn't the emotional buoyancy to rise above his wisdom. You'll probably find him anti-social. . . . Ah, there you are, my dear! Lovely, lovely."

Alice was wearing a different gown, a simple unfrilled frock, and she had freshened up. There was color in her cheeks and her eyes were sparkling with a light and tinge they had not had before. Seeing her for the first time without her hat and coat, Ellery thought she looked different, as all women contrive to look different divested of their outer clothing and refurbished by the mysterious activities which go on behind the closed doors of feminine dressing-rooms. Apparently, the ministrations of another woman, too, had cheered her; there were still rings under her eyes, but her smile was more cheerful.

"Thank you, Uncle Herbert." Her voice was slightly husky. "But I do think I've caught a nasty cold."

"Whisky and hot lemonade," said the fat man promptly. "Eat lightly and go to bed early."

"To tell the truth, I'm famished."

"Then eat as much as you like. I'm one hell of a physician, as no doubt you've already detected. Shall we go in to dinner?"

"Yes," said Mrs. Reinach in a frightened voice. "We shan't wait for Sarah, or Nicholas."

Alice's eyes dulled a little. Then she sighed and took the fat man's arm and they all trooped into the dining-room.

Dinner was a failure. Dr. Reinach divided his energies between gargantuan inroads on the viands and copious drinking. Mrs. Reinach donned an apron and served, scarcely touching her own food in her haste to prepare the next course and clear the plates; apparently the household employed no domestic. Alice gradually lost her color, the old strained look reappearing on her face; occasionally she cleared her throat. The oil lamp on the table flickered badly, and every mouthful Ellery swallowed was flavored with the taste of oil. Besides, the *pièce de résistance* was curried lamb; and if there was one culinary style that sickened him, it was curry. Thorne ate solidly, not raising his eyes from his plate.

As they returned to the living-room the old lawyer managed to drop behind. He whispered to Alice: "Is everything all right? Are you?"

"I'm a little scarish, I think," she said quietly. "Mr. Thorne, please don't think me a child, but there's something so strange about—everything. . . . I wish now I hadn't come."

"I know," muttered Thorne. "And yet it was necessary, quite necessary. If there was any way to spare you this, I should have taken it. But you obviously couldn't stay in that horrible hole next door——"

"Oh, no," she shuddered.

"And there isn't a hotel for miles and miles. Miss Mayhew, has any of these people——"

"No, no. It's just that they're so strange to me. I suppose it's my imagination and this cold. Would you greatly mind if I went to bed? Tomorrow will be time enough to talk."

Thorne patted her hand. She smiled gratefully, murmured an apology, kissed Dr. Reinach's cheek, and went upstairs with Mrs. Reinach again.

They had just settled themselves before the fire again and were lighting cigarets when feet stamped somewhere at the rear of the house.

"Must be Nick," wheezed the doctor. "Now where's *he* been?"

The gigantic young man appeared in the living-room archway, glowering. His boots were soggy with wet. He growled: "Hello," in his surly manner and went to the fire to toast his big reddened hands. He paid no attention whatever to Thorne, although he glanced once, swiftly, at Ellery in passing.

"Where've you been, Nick? Go in and have your dinner."

"I ate before you came."

"What's been keeping you?"

"I've been hauling firewood. Something you didn't think of doing." Keith's tone was truculent, but Ellery noticed that his hands were shaking. Damnably odd! His manner was noticeably not that of a servant, and yet he was apparently employed in a menial capacity. "It's snowing."

"Snowing?"

They crowded to the front windows. The night was moonless and palpable, and big fat snowflakes were sliding down the panes.

"Ah, snow," sighed Dr. Reinach; and for all the sigh there was something in his tone that made the nape of Ellery's neck prickle. "'The whited air hides hills and woods, the river, and the heaven, and veils the farmhouse at the garden's end.'"

"You're quite the countryman, Doctor," said Ellery.

"I like Nature in her more turbulent moods. Spring is for milksops. Winter brings out the fundamental iron." The doctor slipped his arm about Keith's broad shoulders. "Smile, Nick. Isn't God in His heaven?"

Keith flung the arm off without replying.

"Oh, you haven't met Mr. Queen. Queen, this is Nick Keith. You know Mr. Thorne already." Keith nodded shortly. "Come, come, my boy, buck up. You're too emotional, that's the trouble with you. Let's all have a drink. The disease of nervousness is infectious."

Nerves! thought Ellery grimly. His nostrils were pinched, sniffing the little mysteries in the air. They tantalized him. Thorne was tied up in knots, as if he had cramps; the veins at his temples were pale blue

swollen cords and there was sweat on his forehead. Above their heads the
house was soundless.

Dr. Reinach went to the sideboard and began hauling out bottles—
gin, bitters, rye, vermouth. He busied himself mixing drinks, talking
incessantly. There was a purr in his hoarse undertones, a vibration of
pure excitement. What in Satan's name, thought Ellery in a sort of
agony, was going on here?

Keith passed the cocktails around, and Ellery's eyes warned Thorne.
Thorne nodded slightly; they had had two drinks apiece and refused
more. Keith drank doggedly, as if he were anxious to forget something.

"Now that's better," said Dr. Reinach, settling his bulk into an
easy-chair. "With the women out of the way and a fire and liquor, life
becomes almost endurable."

"I'm afraid," said Thorne, "that I shall prove an unpleasant influence, Doctor. I'm going to make it unendurable."

Dr. Reinach blinked. "Well, now," he said. "Well now." He pushed
the brandy decanter carefully out of the way of his elbow and folded his
pudgy paws on his stomach. His purple little eyes shone.

Thorne went back to the fire and stood looking down at the flames, his
back to them. "I'm here in Miss Mayhew's interests, Dr. Reinach," he
said, without turning. "In her interests alone. Sylvester Mayhew died
last week very suddenly. Died while waiting to see the daughter whom
he hadn't seen since his divorce from her mother almost twenty years
ago."

"Factually exact," rumbled the doctor, without stirring.

Thorne spun about. "Dr. Reinach, you acted as Mayhew's physician
for over a year before his death. What was the matter with him?"

"A variety of things. Nothing extraordinary. He died of cerebral
hemorrhage."

"So your certificate claimed." The lawyer leaned forward. "I'm not
entirely convinced," he said slowly, "that your certificate told the
truth."

The doctor stared at him for an instant, then he slapped his bulging
thigh. "Splendid!" he roared. "Splendid! A man after my own heart.
Thorne, for all your desiccated exterior you have juicy potentialities."
He turned on Ellery, beaming. "You heard that, Mr. Queen? Your friend
openly accuses me of murder. This is becoming quite exhilarating. So!
Old Reinach's a fratricide. What do you think of that, Nick? Your patron
accused of cold-blooded murder. Dear, dear."

"That's ridiculous, Mr. Thorne," growled Nick Keith. "You don't
believe it yourself."

The lawyer's gaunt cheeks sucked in. "Whether I believe it or not is immaterial. The possibility exists. But I'm more concerned with Alice Mayhew's interests at the moment than with a possible homicide. Sylvester Mayhew is dead, no matter by what agency—divine or human; but Alice Mayhew is very much alive."

"And so?" asked Reinach softly.

"And so I say," muttered Thorne, "it's damnably queer her father should have died when he did. Damnably."

For a long moment there was silence. Keith put his elbows on his knees and stared into the flames, his shaggy boyish hair over his eyes. Dr. Reinach sipped a glass of brandy with enjoyment.

Then he set his glass down and said with a sigh: "Life is too short, gentlemen, to waste in cautious skirmishings. Let us proceed without feinting movements to the major engagement. Nick Keith is in my confidence and we may speak freely before him." The young man did not move. "Mr. Queen, you're very much in the dark, aren't you?" went on the fat man with a bland smile.

Ellery did not move, either. "And how," he murmured, "did you know that?"

Reinach kept smiling. "Pshaw. Thorne hadn't left the Black House since Sylvester's funeral. Nor did he receive or send any mail during his self-imposed vigil last week. This morning he left me on the pier to telephone someone. You showed up shortly after. Since he was gone only a minute or two, it was obvious that he hadn't had time to tell you much, if anything. Allow me to felicitate you, Mr. Queen, upon your conduct today. It's been exemplary. An air of omniscience covering a profound and desperate ignorance."

Ellery removed his *pince-nez* and began to polish their lenses. "You're a psychologist as well as a physician, I see."

Thorne said abruptly: "This is all beside the point."

"No, no, it's all very much *to* the point," replied the fat man in a sad bass. "Now the canker annoying your friend, Mr. Queen—since it seems a shame to keep you on tenterhooks any longer—is roughly this: My half-brother Sylvester, God rest his troubled soul, was a miser. If he'd been able to take his gold with him to the grave—with any assurance that it would remain there—I'm sure he would have done so."

"Gold?" asked Ellery, raising his brows.

"You may well titter, Mr. Queen. There was something mediaeval about Sylvester; you almost expected him to go about in a long black velvet gown muttering incantations in Latin. At any rate, unable to take his gold with him to the grave, he did the next best thing. He hid it."

"Oh, lord," said Ellery. "You'll be pulling clanking ghosts out of your hat next."

"Hid," beamed Dr. Reinach, "the filthy lucre in the Black House."

"And Miss Alice Mayhew?"

"Poor child, a victim of circumstances. Sylvester never thought of her until recently, when she wrote from London that her last maternal relative had died. Wrote to a friend Thorne, he of the lean and hungry eye, who had been recommended by some friend as a trustworthy lawyer. As he is, as he is! You see, Alice didn't even know if her father was alive, let alone where he was. Thorne, good Samaritan, located us, gave Alice's exhaustive letters and photographs to Sylvester, and has acted as *liaison* officer ever since. And a downright circumspect one, too, by thunder!"

"This explanation is wholly unnecessary," said the lawyer stiffly. "Mr. Queen knows——"

"Nothing," smiled the fat man, "to judge by the attentiveness with which he's been following my little tale. Let's be intelligent about this, Thorne." He turned to Ellery again, nodding very amiably. "Now, Mr. Queen, Sylvester clutched at the thought of his new-found daughter with the pertinacity of a drowning man clutching a life-preserver. I betray no secret when I say that my half-brother, in his paranoic dotage, suspected his own family—imagine!—of having evil designs on his fortune."

"A monstrous slander, of course."

"Neatly put, neatly put! Well, Sylvester told Thorne in my presence that he had long since converted his fortune into specie, that he'd hidden this gold somewhere in the house next door, and that he wouldn't reveal the hiding-place to anyone but Alice, his daughter, who was to be his sole heir. You see?"

"I see," said Ellery.

"He died before Alice's arrival, unfortunately. Is it any wonder, Mr. Queen, that Thorne thinks dire things of us?"

"This is fantastic," snapped Thorne, coloring. "Naturally, in the interests of my client, I couldn't leave the premises unguarded with that mass of gold lying about loose somewhere——"

"Naturally not," nodded the doctor.

"If I may intrude my still, small voice," murmured Ellery, "isn't this a battle of giants over a mouse? The possession of gold is a clear violation of the law in this country, and has been for several years. Even if you found it, wouldn't the government confiscate it?"

"There's a complicated legal situation, Queen," said Thorne; "but

one which cannot come into existence before the gold is found. Therefore my efforts to——''

"And successful efforts, too," grinned Dr. Reinach. "Do you know,
Mr. Queen, you friend has slept behind locked, barred doors, with an old
cutlass in his hand—one of Sylvester's prized mementoes of a grandfather who was in the Navy? It's terribly amusing."

"I don't find it so," said Thorne shortly. "If you insist on playing the
buffoon——''

"And yet—to go back to this matter of your little suspicions,
Thorne—have you analyzed the facts? Whom do you suspect, my dear
fellow? Your humble servant? I assure you that I am spiritually an
ascetic——''

"An almighty fat one!" snarled Thorne.

"—and that money, *per se*, means nothing to me," went on the
doctor imperturbably. "My half-sister Sarah? An anile wreck living in a
world of illusion, quite as antediluvian as Sylvester—they were twins,
you know—who isn't very long for this world. Then that leaves my
estimable Milly or our saturnine young friend Nick. Milly? Absurd; she
hasn't had an idea, good or bad, for two decades. Nick? Ah, an out-
sider—we may have struck something there. Is it Nick you suspect,
Thorne?" chuckled Dr. Reinach.

Keith got to his feet and glared down into the bland damp lunar
countenance of the fat man. He seemed quite drunk. "You damned
porker," he said thickly.

Dr. Reinach kept smiling, but his little porcine eyes were wary.
"Now, now, Nick," he said in a soothing rumble.

It all happened very quickly. Keith lurched forward, snatched the
heavy cut-glass brandy decanter, and swung it at the doctor's head.
Thorne cried out and took an instinctive forward step; but he might have
spared himself the exertion. Dr. Reinach jerked his head back like a fat
snake and the blow missed. The violent effort pivoted Keith's body
completely about; the decanter slipped from his fingers and flew into the
fireplace, crashing to pieces. The fragments splattered all over the
fireplace, strewing the hearth, too; the little brandy that remained in the
bottle hissed into the fire, blazing with a blue flame.

"That decanter," said Dr. Reinach angrily, "was almost a hundred
and fifty years old!"

Keith stood still, his broad back to them. They could see his shoulders
heaving.

Ellery sighed with the queerest feeling. The room was shimmering as in a dream, and the whole incident seemed unreal, like a scene in a play on a stage. Were they acting? Had the scene been carefully planned? But, if so, why? What earthly purpose could they have hoped to achieve by pretending to quarrel and come to blows? The sole result had been the wanton destruction of a lovely old decanter. It didn't make sense.

"I think," said Ellery, struggling to his feet, "that I shall go to bed before the Evil One comes down the chimney. Thank you for an altogether extraordinary evening, gentlemen. Coming, Thorne?"

He stumbled up the stairs, followed by the lawyer, who seemed as weary as he. They separated in the cold corridor without a word to stumble to their respective bedrooms. From below came a heavy silence.

It was only as he was throwing his trousers over the footrail of his bed that Ellery recalled hazily Thorne's whispered intention hours before to visit him that night and explain the whole fantastic business. He struggled down the hall to Thorne's room. But the lawyer was already in bed, snoring stertorously.

Ellery dragged himself back to his room and finished undressing. He knew he would have a head the next morning; he was a notoriously poor drinker. His brain spinning, he crawled between the blankets and fell asleep almost stertorously.

He opened his eyes after a tossing, tiring sleep with the uneasy conviction that something was wrong. For a moment he was aware only of the ache in his head and the fuzzy feel of his tongue; he did not remember where he was. Then, as his glance took in the faded wallpaper, the pallid patches of sunlight on the worn blue carpet, his trousers tumbled over the footrail where he had left them the night before, memory returned; and, shivering, he consulted his wristwatch, which he had forgotten to take off on going to bed. It was five minutes to seven. He raised his head from the pillow in the frosty air of the bedroom; his nose was half-frozen. But he could detect nothing wrong; the sun looked brave if weak in his eyes; the room was quiet and exactly as he had seen it on retiring; the door was closed. He snuggled between the blankets again.

Then he heard it. It was Thorne's voice. It was Thorne's voice raised in a thin faint cry, almost a wail, coming from somewhere outside the house.

He was out of bed and at the window in his bare feet in one leap. But Thorne was not visible at this side of the house, upon which the dead woods encroached directly; so he scrambled back to slip shoes on his feet and his gown over his pajamas, darted toward the footrail and snatched his revolver out of the hip pocket of his trousers, and ran out into the corridor, heading for the stairs, the revolver in his hand.

"What's the matter?" grumbled someone, and he turned to see Dr. Reinach's vast skull protruding nakedly from the room next to his.

"Don't know. I heard Thorne cry out," and Ellery pounded down the stairs and flung open the front door.

He stopped within the doorway, gaping.

Thorne, fully dressed, was standing ten yards in front of the house, facing Ellery obliquely, staring at something outside the range of Ellery's vision with the most acute expression of terror on his gaunt face Ellery had ever seen on a human countenance. Beside him crouched Nicholas Keith, only half-dressed; the young man's jaws gaped foolishly and his eyes were enormous glaring discs.

Dr. Reinach shoved Ellery roughly aside and growled: "What's the matter? What's wrong?" The fat man's feet were encased in carpet slippers and he had pulled a raccoon coat over his night-shirt, so that he looked like a particularly obese bear.

Thorne's Adam's-apple bobbed nervously. The ground, the trees, the world were blanketed with snow of a peculiarly unreal texture; and the air was saturated with warm woolen flakes, falling softly. Deep drifts curved upwards to clamp the boles of trees.

"Don't move," croaked Thorne as Ellery and the fat man stirred. "Don't move, for the love of God. Stay where you are." Ellery's grip tightened on the revolver and he tried perversely to get past the doctor; but he might have been trying to budge a stone wall. Thorne stumbled through the snow to the porch, paler than his background, leaving two deep ruts behind him. "Look at me," he shouted. "*Look at me*. Do I seem all right? Have I gone mad?"

"Pull yourself together, Thorne," said Ellery sharply. "What's the matter with you? I don't see anything wrong."

"Nick!" bellowed Dr. Reinach. "Have you gone crazy, too?"

The young man covered his sunburnt face suddenly with his hands; then he dropped his hands and looked again.

He said in a strangled voice: "Maybe we all have. This is the most— Take a look at yourself."

Reinach moved then, and Ellery squirmed by him to land in the soft snow beside Thorne, who was trembling violently. Dr. Reinach came lurching after. They ploughed through the snow toward Keith, squinting, straining to see.

They need not have strained. What was to be seen was plain for any eye to see. Ellery felt his scalp crawl as he looked; and at the same instant he was aware of the sharp conviction that this was inevitable, this was the only possible climax to the insane events of the previous day. The world had turned topsy-turvy. Nothing in it meant anything reasonable or sane.

Dr. Reinach gasped once; and then he stood blinking like a huge owl. A window rattled on the second floor of the White House. None of them looked up. It was Alice Mayhew in a wrapper, staring from the window of her bedroom, which was on the side of the house facing the driveway. She screamed once; and then she, too, fell silent.

There was the house from which they had just emerged, the house Dr. Reinach had dubbed the White House, with its front door quietly swinging open and Alice Mayhew at an upper side window. Substantial, solid, an edifice of stone and wood and plaster and glass and the patina of age. It was everything a house should be. That much was real, a thing to be grasped.

But beyond it, beyond the driveway and the garage, where the Black House had stood, the house in which Ellery himself had set foot only the afternoon before, the house of the filth and the stench, the house of the equally stone walls, wooden facings, glass windows, chimneys, gargoyles, porch; the house of the blackened look; the old Victorian house built during the Civil War where Sylvester Mayhew had died, where Thorne had barricaded himself with a cutless for a week; the house which they had all seen, touched, smelled . . . there, *there stood nothing*.

No walls. No chimney. No roof. No ruins. No débris. No house. Nothing.

Nothing but empty space covered smoothly and warmly with snow.

The house had vanished during the night.

II

"There's even," thought Mr. Ellery Queen dully, "a character named Alice."

He looked again. The only reason he did not rub his eyes was that it would have made him feel ridiculous; besides, his sight, all his senses, had never been keener.

He simply stood there in the snow and looked and looked and looked at the empty space where a three-story stone house seventy-five years old had stood the night before.

"Why, it isn't there," said Alice feebly from the upper window. "It . . . isn't . . . there."

"Then I'm not insane." Thorne stumbled toward them. Ellery watched the old man's feet sloughing through the snow, leaving long tracks. A man's weight still counted for something in the universe, then. Yes, and there was his own shadow; so material objects still cast shadows. Absurdly, the discovery brought a certain faint relief.

"It *is* gone!" said Thorne in a cracked voice.

"Apparently." Ellery found his own voice thick and slow; he watched the words curl out on the air and become nothing. "Apparently, Thorne." It was all he could find to say.

Dr. Reinach arched his fat neck, his wattles quivering like a gobbler's. "Incredible. Incredible!"

"Incredible," said Thorne in a whisper.

"Unscientific. It can't be. I'm a man of sense. Of senses. My mind is clear. Things like this—damn it, they just don't happen!"

"As the man said who saw a giraffe for the first time," sighed Ellery. "And yet . . . there it was."

Thorne began wandering helplessly about in a circle. Alice stared, bewitched into stone, from the upper window. And Keith cursed and began to run across the snow-covered driveway toward the invisible house, his hands outstretched before him like a blind man's.

"Hold on," said Ellery. "Stop where you are."

The giant halted, scowling. "What d'ye want?"

Ellery slipped his revolver back into his pocket and sloshed through the snow to pause beside the young man in the driveway. "I don't know precisely. Something's wrong. Something's out of kilter either with us or with the world. It isn't the world as we know it. It's almost . . . almost a matter of transposed dimensions. Do you suppose the solar system has slipped in the uncharted depths of space-time? I suppose I'm talking nonsense."

"You know best," shouted Keith. "I'm not going to let his screwy business stampede *me*. There was a solid house on that plot last night, by God, and nobody can convince me it still isn't there. Not even my own eyes. We've—we've been hypnotized! The hippo could do it here—he could do anything. Hypnotized. You hypnotized us, Reinach!"

The doctor mumbled: "What?" and kept glaring at the empty lot.

"I tell you it's there!" cried Keith angrily.

Ellery sighed and dropped to his knees in the snow; he began to brush aside the white, soft blanket with chilled palms. When he had laid the ground bare, he saw wet gravel and a rut.

"This *is* the driveway, isn't it?" he asked without looking up.

"The driveway," snarled Keith, "or the road to hell. You're as mixed up as we are. Sure it's the driveway! Can't you see the garage? Why shouldn't it be the driveway?"

"I don't know." Ellery got to his feet, frowning. "I don't know anything. I'm beginning to learn all over again. Maybe—maybe it's a matter of gravitation. Maybe we'll all fly into space any minute now."

Thorne groaned: "My God."

"All I can be sure of is that something very strange happened last night."

"I tell you," growled Keith, "it's an optical illusion!"

"Something strange." The fat man stirred. "Yes, decidedly. What an inadequate word! A house has disappeared. Something strange." He began to chuckle in a choking, mirthless way.

"Oh that," said Ellery impatiently. "Certainly. Certainly, Doctor. That's a *fact*. As for you, Keith, you don't really believe this mass-hypnosis bilge. The house is gone, right enough. . . . It's not the fact of its being gone that bothers me. It's the agency, the *means*. It smacks of—of—" He shook his head. "I've never believed in . . . this sort of thing, damn it all!"

Dr. Reinach threw back his vast shoulders and glared, red-eyed, at the empty snow-covered space. "It's a trick," he bellowed. "A rotten trick, that's what it is. That house is right there in front of our noses. Or—or— They can't fool *me*!"

Ellery looked at him. "Perhaps," he said, "Keith has it in his pocket?"

Alice clattered out on the porch in high-heeled shoes over bare feet, her hair streaming, a cloth coat flung over her night-clothes. Behind her crept little Mrs. Reinach. The women's eyes were wild.

"Talk to them," muttered Ellery to Thorne. "Anything; but keep their minds occupied. We'll all go balmy if we don't preserve an air of sanity. Keith, get me a broom."

He shuffled up the driveway, skirting the invisible house very carefully and not once taking his eyes off the empty space. The fat man hesitated; then he lumbered along in Ellery's tracks. Thorne stumbled back to the porch and Keith strode off, disappearing behind the White House.

There was no sun now. A pale and eerie light filtered down through the cold clouds. The snow continued its soft, thick fall.

They looked like dots, small and helpless, on a sheet of blank paper.

Ellery pulled open the folding doors of the garage and peered. A healthy odor of raw gasoline and rubber assailed his nostrils. Thorne's car stood within, exactly as Ellery had seen it the afternoon before, a black monster with glittering chrome-work. Beside it, apparently parked by Keith after their arrival, stood the battered Buick in which Dr. Reinach had driven them from the city. Both cars were perfectly dry.

He shut the doors and turned back to the driveway. Aside from the catenated links of their footprints in the snow, made a moment before, the white covering on the driveway was virgin.

"Here's your broom," said the giant. "What are you going to do—ride it?"

"Hold your tongue, Nick," growled Dr. Reinach.

Ellery laughed. "Let him alone, Doctor. His angry insanity is infectious. Come along, you two. This may be the Judgment Day, but we may as well go through the motions."

"What do you want with a broom, Queen?"

"It's hard to decide whether the snow was an accident or part of the plan," murmured Ellery. "Anything may be true today. Literally anything."

"Rubbish," snorted the fat man. "Abracadabra. *Om mani padme hum.* How could a man have planned a snowfall? You're talking gibberish."

"I didn't say a human plan, Doctor."

"Rubbish, rubbish, rubbish!"

'You may as well save your breath. You're a badly scared little boy whistling in the dark—for all your bulk, Doctor."

Ellery gripped the broom tightly and stamped out across the driveway. He felt his own foot shrinking as he tried to make it step upon the white rectangle. His muscles were gathered in, as if in truth he expected to encounter the adamantine bulk of a house which was still there but unaccountably impalpable. When he felt nothing but cold air, he laughed a little self-consciously and began to wield the broom on the snow in a peculiar manner. He used the most delicate of sweeping motions, barely brushing the surface crystals away; so that layer by layer he reduced the depth of the snow. He scanned each layer with anxiety as it was uncovered. And he continued to do this until the ground itself lay revealed; and at no depth did he come across the minutest trace of a human imprint.

"Elves," he complained. "Nothing less than elves. I confess it's beyond me."

"Even the foundation—" began Dr. Reinach heavily.

Ellery poked the tip of the broom at the earth. It was hard as corundum.

The front door slammed as Thorne and the two women crept into the White House. The three men outside stood still, doing nothing.

"Well," said Ellery at last, "this is either a bad dream or the end of the world." He made off diagonally across the plot, dragging the broom behind him like a tired charwoman, until he reached the snow-covered drive; and then he trudged down the drive towards the invisible road, disappearing around a bend under the stripped white-dripping trees.

It was a short walk to the road. Ellery remembered it well. It had curved steadily in the long arc all the way from the turn-off at the main highway. There had been no crossroad in all the jolting journey.

He went out into the middle of the road, snow-covered now but plainly distinguishable between the powdered tangles of woods as a gleaming, empty strip. There was the long curve exactly as he remembered it. Mechanically he used the broom again, sweeping a small area clear. And there were the pits and ruts of the old Buick's journeys.

"What are you looking for," said Nick Keith quietly, "gold?"

Ellery straightened up by degrees, turning about slowly until he was face to face with the giant. "So you thought it was necessary to follow me? Or—no, I beg your pardon. Undoubtedly it was Dr. Reinach's idea."

The sun-charred features did not change expression. "You're crazy as a bat. Follow you? I've got all I can do to follow myself."

"Of course," said Ellery. "But I did understand you to ask me if I was looking for gold, my dear young Prometheus?"

"You're a queer one," said Keith as they made their way back toward the house.

"Gold," repeated Ellery. "Hmmm. There was gold in that house, and now the house is gone. In the shock of the discovery that houses fly away like birds, I'd quite forgotten that little item. Thank you, Mr. Keith," said Ellery grimly, "for reminding me."

"Mr. Queen," said Alice. She was crouched in a chair by the fire, white to the lips. "What's happened to us? What are we to do? Have we . . . Was yesterday a dream? Didn't we walk into that house, go through it, touch things? . . . I'm frightened."

"If yesterday *was* a dream," smiled Ellery, "then we may expect that tomorrow will bring a vision; for that's what holy Sanskrit says, and we may as well believe in parables as in miracles." He sat down, rubbing his hands briskly. "How about a fire, Keith? It's arctic in here."

"Sorry," said Keith with surprising amiability, and he went away.

"We could use a vision," shivered Thorne. "My brain is—sick. It just isn't possible. It's horrible." His hand slapped his side and something jangled in his pocket.

"Keys," said Ellery, "and no house. It *is* staggering."

Keith came back under a mountain of firewood. He grimaced at the litter in the fireplace, dropped the wood, and began sweeping together the fragments of glass, the remains of the brandy decanter he had smashed against the brick wall the night before. Alice glanced from his broad back to the chromo of her mother on the mantel. As for Mrs. Reinach, she was as silent as a scared bird; she stood in a corner like a weazened little gnome, her wrapper drawn about her, her stringy sparrow-colored hair hanging down her back, and her glassy eyes fixed on the face of her husband.

"Milly," said the fat man.

"Yes, Herbert, I'm going," said Mrs. Reinach instantly, and she crept up the stairs and out of sight.

"Well, Mr. Queen, what's the answer? Or is this riddle too esoteric for your taste?"

"No riddle is esoteric," muttered Ellery, "unless it's the riddle of God; and that's no riddle—it's a vast blackness. Doctor, is there any way of reaching assistance?"

"Not unless you can fly."

"No phone," said Keith without turning, "and you saw the condition of the road for yourself. You'd never get a car through those drifts."

"If you had a car," chuckled Dr. Reinach. Then he seemed to remember the disappearing house, and his chuckle died.

"What do you mean?" demanded Ellery. "In the garage are—"

"Two useless products of the machine age. Both cars are out of fuel."

"And mine," said old Thorne suddenly, with a resurrection of grim personal interest, "mine has something wrong with it besides. I left my chauffeur in the city, you know, Queen, when I drove down last time. Now I can't get the engine running on the little gasoline that's left in the tank."

Ellery's fingers drummed on the arm of his chair. "Bother! Now we can't even call on other eyes to test whether we've been bewitched or not. By the way, Doctor, how far is it to the nearest community? I'm afraid I didn't pay attention on the drive down."

"Over fifteen miles by road. If you're thinking of footing it, Mr. Queen, you're welcome to the thought."

"You'd never get through the drifts," muttered Keith. The drifts appeared to trouble him.

"And so we find ouselves snowbound," said Ellery, "in the middle of the fourth dimension—or perhaps it's the fifth. A pretty kettle! Ah there, Keith, that feels considerably better."

"You don't seem bowled over by what's happened," said Dr. Reinach, eyeing him curiously. "I'll confess it's given even me a shock."

Ellery was silent for a moment. Then he said lightly: "There wouldn't be any point to losing our heads, would there?"

"I fully expect dragons to come flying over the house," groaned Thorne. He eyed Ellery a bit bashfully. "Queen . . . perhaps we had better . . . try to get out of here."

"You heard Keith, Thorne."

Thorne bit his lip. "I'm frozen," said Alice, drawing nearer the fire. "That was well done, Mr. Keith. It—it—a fire like this makes me think of home, somehow." The young man got to his feet and turned around. Their eyes met for an instant.

"It's nothing," he said shortly. "Nothing at all."

"You seem to be the only one who—*Oh*!"

An enormous old woman with a black shawl over her shoulders was coming downstairs. She might have been years dead, she was so yellow and emaciated and mummified. And yet she gave the impression of being very much alive, with a sort of ancient, ageless life; her black eyes were young and bright and cunning, and her face was extraordinarily mobile. She was sidling down stiffly, feeling her way with one foot and clutching the banister with two dried claws, while her lively eyes remained fixed on Alice's face. There was a curious hunger in her expression, the flaring of a long-dead hope suddenly, against all reason.

"Who—who—" began Alice, shrinking back.

"Don't be alarmed," said Dr. Reinach quickly. "It's unfortunate that she got away from Milly. . . . Sarah!" In a twinkling he was at the foot of the staircase, barring the old woman's way. "What are you doing up at this hour? You should take better care of yourself, Sarah."

She ignored him, continuing her snail's pace down the stairs until she reached his pachyderm bulk. "Olivia," she mumbled, with a vital eagerness. "It's Olivia come back to me. Oh, my sweet, sweet darling. . . ."

"Now, Sarah," said the fat man, taking her hand gently. "Don't excite yourself. This isn't Olivia, Sarah. It's Alice—Alice Mayhew, Sylvester's girl, come from England. You remember Alice, little Alice? Not Olivia, Sarah.''

"Not Olivia?'' The old woman peered across the banister, her wrinkled lips moving. "Not Olivia?''

The girl jumped up. "I'm Alice, Aunt Sarah. Alice—''

Sarah Fell darted suddenly past the fat man and scurried across the room to seize the girl's hand and glare into her face. As she studied those shrinking features her expression changed to one of despair. "Not Olivia. Olivia's beautiful black hair. . . . Not Olivia's voice. Alice? Alice?'' She dropped into Alice's vacated chair, her skinny broad shoulders sagging, and began to weep. They could see the yellow skin of her scalp through the sparse gray hair.

Dr. Reinach roared: "Milly!'' in an enraged voice. Mrs. Reinach popped into sight like Jack-in-the-box. "Why did you let her leave her room?''

"B-but I thought she was—'' began Mrs. Reinach, stammering.

"Take her upstairs at once!''

"Yes, Herbert,'' whispered the sparrow, and Mrs. Reinach hurried downstairs in her wrapper and took the old woman's hand and, unopposed, led her away. Mrs. Fell kept repeating, between sobs: "Why doesn't Olivia come back? Why did they take her away from her mother?'' until she was out of sight.

"Sorry,'' panted the fat man, mopping himself. "One of her spells. I knew it was coming on from the curiosity she exhibited the moment she heard you were coming, Alice. There *is* a resemblance; you can scarcely blame her.''

"She's—she's horrible,'' said Alice faintly. "Mr. Queen—Mr. Thorne, must we stay here? I'd feel so much easier in the city. And then my cold, these frigid rooms——''

"By heaven,'' burst out Thorne, "I feel like chancing it on foot!''

"And leave Sylvester's gold to our tender mercies?'' smiled Dr. Reinach. Then he scowled.

"I don't want father's legacy,'' said Alice desperately. "At this moment I don't want anything but to get away. I—I can manage to get along all right. I'll find work to do—I can do so many things.. I want to go away. Mr. Keith, couldn't you possibly——''

"*I'm* not a magician,'' said Keith rudely; and he buttoned his mackinaw and strode out of the house. They could see his tall figure stalking off behind a veil of snowflakes.

Alice flushed, turning back to the fire.

"Nor are any of us," said Ellery. "Miss Mayhew, you'll simply have to be a brave girl and stick it out until we can find a means of getting out of here."

"Yes," murmured Alice, shivering; and stared into the flames.

"Meanwhile, Thorne, tell me everything you know about this case, especially as it concerns Sylvester Mayhew's house. There may be a clue in your father's history, Miss Mayhew. If the house has vanished, so has the gold *in* the house; and whether we want it or not, it belongs to you. Consequently we must make an effort to find it."

"I suggest," muttered Dr. Reinach, "that you find the house first. House!" he exploded, waving his furred arms. And he made for the sideboard.

Alice nodded listlessly. Thorne mumbled: "Perhaps, Queen, you and I had better talk privately."

"We made a frank beginning last night; I see no reason why we shouldn't continue in the same candid vein. You needn't be reluctant to speak before Dr. Reinach. Our host is obviously a man of parts—unorthodox parts."

Dr. Reinach did not reply. His globular face was dark as he tossed off a water-goblet full of gin.

Through air metallic with defiance, Thorne talked in a hardening voice; not once did he take his eyes from Dr. Reinach.

His first suspicion that something was wrong had been germinated by Sylvester Mayhew himself.

Hearing by post from Alice, Thorne had investigated and located Mayhew. He had explained to the old invalid his daughter's desire to find her father, if he still lived. Old Mayhew, with a strange excitement, had acquiesced; he was eager to be reunited with his daughter; and he seemed to be living, explained Thorne defiantly, in mortal fear of his relatives in the neighboring house.

"Fear, Thorne?" The fat man sat down, raising his brows. "You know he was afraid, not of us, but of poverty. He was a miser."

Thorne ignored him. Mayhew had instructed Thorne to write Alice and bid her come to America at once; he meant to leave her his entire estate and wanted her to have it before he died. The repository of the gold he had cunningly refused to divulge, even to Thorne; it was "in the house," he had said, but he would not reveal its hiding-place to anyone but Alice herself. The "others," he snarled, had been looking for it ever since their "arrival."

"By the way," drawled Ellery, "how long have you good people been living in this house, Dr. Reinach?"

"A year or so. You certainly don't put any credence in the paranoic ravings of a dying man? There's no mystery about our living here. I looked Sylvester up over a year ago after a long separation and found him still in the old homestead, and this house boarded up and empty. The White House, this house, incidentally, was built by my stepfather—Sylvester's father—on Sylvester's marriage to Alice's mother; Sylvester lived in it until my stepfather died, and then moved back to the Black House. I found Sylvester, a degenerated hulk of what he'd once been, living on crusts, absolutely alone and badly in need of medical attention."

"Alone—here, in this wilderness?" said Ellery increduously.

"Yes. As a matter of fact, the only way I could get his permission to move back to his house, which belonged to him, was by dangling the bait of free medical treatment before his eyes. I'm sorry, Alice; he was quite unbalanced. . . . And so Milly and Sarah and I—Sarah had been living with us ever since Olivia's death—moved in here."

"Decent of you," remarked Ellery. "I suppose you had to give up your medical practice to do it, Doctor?"

Dr. Reinach grimaced. "I didn't have much of a practice to give up, Mr. Queen."

"But it was an almost pure brotherly impulse, eh?"

"Oh, I don't deny that the possibility of falling heir to some of Sylvester's fortune had crossed our minds. It was rightfully ours, we believed, not knowing anything about Alice. As it's turned out—" he shrugged his fat shoulders. "I'm a philosopher."

"And don't deny, either," shouted Thorne, "that when I came back here at the time Mayhew sank into that fatal coma you people watched me like a—like a band of spies! I was in your way!"

"Mr. Thorne," whispered Alice, paling.

"I'm sorry, Miss Mayhew, but you may as well know the truth. Oh, you didn't fool me, Reinach! You wanted that gold, Alice or no Alice. I shut myself up in that house just to keep you from getting your hands on it!"

Dr. Reinach shrugged again; his rubbery lips compressed.

"You want candor; here it is!" rasped Thorne. "I was in that house,

Queen, for six days after Mayhew's funeral and before Miss Mayhew's arrival, *looking for the gold*. I turned that house upside down. And I didn't find the slightest trace of it. I tell you it isn't there.'' He glared at the fat man. "I tell you it was stolen before Mayhew died!''

"Now, now,'' sighed Ellery. "That makes less sense than the other. Why then has somebody intoned an incantation over the house and caused it to disappear?''

"I don't know,'' said the old lawyer fiercely. "I know only that the most dastardly thing's happened here, that everything is unnatural, veiled in that—that false creature's smile! Miss Mayhew, I'm sorry I must speak this way about your own family. But I feel it my duty to warn you that you've fallen among human wolves. Wolves!''

"I'm afraid,'' said Reinach sourly, "that I shouldn't come to you, my dear Thorne, for a reference.''

"I wish,'' said Alice in a very low tone, "I truly wish I were dead.''

But the lawyer was past control. "That man Keith,'' he cried. "Who is he? What's he doing here? He looks like a gangster. I suspect him, Queen——''

"Apparently,'' smiled Ellery, "you suspect everybody.''

"Mr. Keith?'' murmured Alice. "Oh, I'm sure not. I—I don't think he's that sort at all, Mr. Thorne. He looks as if he's had a hard life. As if he's suffered terribly from something.''

Thorne threw up his hands, turning to the fire.

"Let us,'' said Ellery amiably, "confine ourselves to the problem at hand. We were, I believe, considering the problem of a disappearing house. Do any architect's plans of the so-called Black House exist?''

"Lord, no,'' said Dr. Reinach.

"Who has lived in it since your stepfather's death besides Sylvester Mayhew and his wife?''

"Wives,'' corrected the doctor, pouring himself another glassful of gin. "Sylvester married twice; I suppose you didn't know that, my dear.'' Alice shivered by the fire. "I dislike raking over old ashes, but since we're at confessional . . . Sylvester treated Alice's mother abominably.''

"I—guessed that,'' whispered Alice.

"She was a woman of spirit and she rebelled; but when she'd got her final decree and returned to England, the reaction set in and she died very shortly afterward, I understand. Her death was recorded in the New York papers.''

"When I was a baby,'' whispered Alice.

"Sylvester, already unbalanced, although not so anchoretic in those days as he became later, then wooed and won a wealthy widow and brought her out here to live. She had a son, a child by her first husband, with her. Father'd died by this time, and Sylvester and his second wife lived in the Black House. It was soon evident that Sylvester had married the widow for her money; he persuaded her to sign it over to him—a considerable fortune for those days—and promptly proceeded to devil the life out of her. Result: the woman vanished one day, taking her child with her."

"Perhaps," said Ellery, seeing Alice's face, "we'd better abandon the subject, Doctor."

"We never did find out what actually happened—whether Sylvester drove her out or whether, unable to stand his brutal treatment any longer, she left voluntarily. At any rate, I discovered by accident, a few years later, through an obituary notice, that she died in the worst sort of poverty."

Alice was staring at him with a wrinkle-nosed nausea. "Father . . . did that?"

"Oh, stop it," growled Thorne. "You'll have the poor child gibbering in another moment. What has all this to do with the house?"

"Mr. Queen asked," said the fat man mildly. Ellery was studying the flames as if they fascinated him.

"The real point," snapped the lawyer, "is that you've watched me from the instant I set foot here, Reinach. Afraid to leave me alone for a moment. Why, you even had Keith meet me in your car on both my visits—to 'escort' me here! And I didn't have five minutes to myself with the old gentleman—you saw to that. And then he lapsed into the coma and was unable to speak again before he died. Why? Why all the surveillance? God knows I'm a forebearing man; but you've given me every ground for suspecting your motives."

"Apparently," chuckled Dr. Reinach, "you don't agree with Caesar."

"I beg your pardon?"

"'Would,'" quoted the fat man, "'he were fatter.' Well, good people, the end of the world may come, but that's no reason why we shouldn't have breakfast. Milly!" he bellowed.

Thorne awoke sluggishly, like a drowsing old hound dimly aware of danger. His bedroom was cold; a pale morning light was struggling in through the window. He groped under his pillow.

"Stop where you are!" he said harshly.

"So you have a revolver, too?" murmured Ellery. He was dressed and looked as if he had slept badly. "It's only I, Thorne, stealing in for a conference. It's not so hard to steal in here, by the way."

"What do you mean?" grumbled Thorne, sitting up and putting his old-fashioned revolver away.

"I see your lock has gone the way of mine, Alice's, the Black House, and Sylvester Mayhew's elusive gold."

Thorne drew the patchwork comforter about him, his old lips blue. "Well, Queen?"

Ellery lit a cigaret and for a moment stared out Thorne's window at the streamers of crêpy snow still dropping from the sky. The snow had fallen without a moment's let-up the entire previous day. "This is a curious business all round, Thorne. The queerest medley of spirit and matter. I've just reconnoitered. You'll be interested to learn that our young friend the Colossus is gone."

"Keith gone?"

"His bed hasn't been slept in at all. I looked."

"And he was away most of yesterday, too!"

"Precisely. Our surly Crichton, who seems afflicted by a particularly acute case of *Weltschmerz,* periodically vanishes. Where does he go? I'd give a good deal to know the answer to that question."

"He won't get far in those nasty drifts," mumbled the lawyer.

"It gives one, as the French say, to think. Comrade Reinach is gone, too." Thorne stiffened. "Oh, yes; his bed's been slept in, but briefly, I judge. Have they eloped together? Separately? Thorne," said Ellery thoughtfully, "this becomes an increasingly subtle devilment."

"It's beyond me," said Thorne with another shiver. "I'm just about ready to give up. I don't see that we're accomplishing a thing here. And then there's always that annoying, incredible fact . . . the house—vanished."

Ellery sighed and looked at his wristwatch. It was a minute past seven.

Thorne threw back the comforter and groped under the bed for his slippers. "Let's go downstairs," he snapped.

"Excellent bacon, Mrs. Reinach," said Ellery. "I suppose it must be a trial carting supplies up here."

"We've the blood of pioneers," said Dr. Reinach cheerfully, before his wife could reply. He was engulfing mounds of scrambled eggs and bacon. "Luckily, we've enough in the larder to last out a considerable siege. The winters are severe out here—we learned that last year."

Keith was not at the breakfast table. Old Mrs. Fell was. She ate voraciously, with the unconcealed greed of the very old, to whom nothing is left of the sensual satisfactions of life but the filling of the belly. Nevertheless, although she did not speak, she contrived as she ate to keep her eyes on Alice, who wore a haunted look.

"I didn't sleep very well," said Alice, toying with her coffee-cup. Her voice was huskier. "This abominable snow! Can't we manage somehow to get away today?"

"Not so long as the snow keeps up, I'm afraid," said Ellery gently. "And you, Doctor? Did you sleep badly, too? Or hasn't the whisking away of a whole house from under your nose affected your nerves at all?"

The fat man's eyes were red-rimmed and his lids sagged. Nevertheless, he chuckled and said: "I? I always sleep well. Nothing on my conscience. Why?"

"Oh, no special reason. Where's friend Keith this morning? He's a seclusive sort of chap, isn't her?"

Mrs. Reinach swallowed a muffin whole. Her husband glanced at her and she rose and fled to the kitchen. "Lord knows," said the fat man. "He's as unpredictable as the ghost of Banquo. Don't bother yourself about the boy; he's harmless."

Ellery sighed and pushed back from the table. "The passage of twenty-four hours hasn't softened the wonder of the event. May I be excused? I'm going to have another peep at the house that isn't there any more." Thorne started to rise. "No, no, Thorne; I'd rather go alone."

He put on his warmest clothes and went outdoors. The drifts reached the lower windows now; and the trees had almost disappeared under the snow. A crude path had been hacked by someone from the front door for a few feet; already it was half-refilled with snow.

Ellery stood still in the path, breathing deeply of the raw air and staring off to the right at the empty rectangle where the Black House had once stood. Leading across that expanse to the edge of the woods beyond were barely discernible tracks. He turned up his coat-collar against the cutting wind and plunged into the snow waist-deep.

It was difficult going, but not unpleasant. After a while he began to feel quite warm. The world was white and silent—a new, strange, world.

When he had left the open area and struggled into the woods, it was with a sensation that he was leaving even that new world behind. Everything was so still and white and beautiful, with a pure beauty not of the earth; the snow draping the trees gave them a fresh look, making queer patterns out of old forms.

Occasionally a clump of snow fell from a low branch, pelting him.

Here, where there was a roof between ground and sky, the snow had not filtered into the mysterious tracks so quickly. They were purposeful tracks, unwandering, striking straight as a dotted line for some distant goal. Ellery pushed on more rapidly, excited by a presentiment of discovery.

Then the world went black.

It was a curious thing. The snow became gray, and grayer, and finally very dark gray, becoming jet black at the last instant, as if flooded from underneath by ink. And with some surprise he felt the cold wet kiss of the drift on his cheek.

He opened his eyes to find himself flat on his back in the snow and Thorne in the great-coat stooped over him, nose jutting from blued face like a winter thorn.

"Queen!" cried the old man, shaking him. "Are you all right?"

Ellery sat up, licking his lips. "As well as might be expected," he groaned. "What hit me? It felt like one of God's angrier thunderbolts." He caressed the back of his head, and staggered to his feet. "Well, Thorne, we seem to have reached the border of the enchanted land."

"You're not delirious?" asked the lawyer anxiously.

Ellery looked about for the tracks which should have been there. But except for the double line at the head of which Thorne stood, there were none. Apparently he had lain unconscious in the snow for a long time.

"Farther than this," he said with a grimace, "we may not go. Hands off. Nose out. Mind your own business. Beyond this invisible boundary-line lie Sheol and Domdaniel and Abaddon. *Lasciate ogni speranza voi ch' entrate*. . . . Forgive me, Thorne. Did you save my life?"

Thorne jerked about, searching the silent woods. "I don't know. I think not. At least I found you lying here, alone. Gave me quite a start—thought you were dead."

"As well," said Ellery with a shiver, "I might have been."

"When you left the house Alice went upstairs, Reinach said something about a cat-nap, and I wandered out of the house. I waded through the drifts on the road for a spell, and then I thought of you and made my way back. Your tracks were almost obliterated; but they were visible enough to take me across the clearing to the edge of the woods, and I finally blundered upon you. By now the tracks are gone.''

''I don't like this at all,'' said Ellery, ''and yet in another sense I like it very much.''

''What do you mean?''

''I can't imagine,'' said Ellery, ''a divine agency stooping to such a mean assault.''

''Yes, it's open war now,'' muttered Thorne. ''Whoever it is—he'll stop at nothing.''

''A benevolent war, at any rate. I was quite at his mercy, and he might have killed me as easily as——''

He stopped. A sharp report, like a pine-knot snapping in a fire or an ice-stiffened twig breaking in two, but greatly magnified, had come to his ears. Then the echo came to them, softer but unmistakable.

It was the report of a gun.

''From the house!'' yelled Ellery. ''Come on!''

Thorne was pale as they scrambled through the drifts. ''Gun . . . I forgot. I left my revolver under the pillow in my bedroom. Do you think——?''

Ellery scrabbled at his own pocket. ''Mine's still here. . . . No, by George, I've been scotched!'' His cold fingers fumbled with the cylinder. ''Bullets taken out. And I've no spare ammunition.'' He fell silent, his mouth hardening.

They found the women and Reinach running about like startled animals, searching for they knew not what.

''Did you hear it, too?'' cried the fat man as they burst into the house. He seemed extraordinarily excited. ''Someone fired a shot!''

''Where?'' asked Ellery, his eyes on the rove. ''Keith?''

''Don't know where he is. Milly says it might have come from behind the house. I was napping and couldn't tell. Revolvers! At least he's come out in the open.''

''Who has?'' asked Ellery.

The fat man shrugged. Ellery went through to the kitchen and opened the back door. The snow outside was smooth, untrodden. When he returned to the living-room Alice was adjusting a scarf about her neck with fingers that shook.

''I don't know how long you people intend to stay in this ghastly place,'' she said in a passionate voice. ''But I've had *quite* enough, thank you. Mr. Thorne, I insist you take me away at once. At once! I shan't stay another instant.''

"Now, now, Miss Mayhew," said Thorne in a distressed way, taking her hands. "I should like nothing better. But can't you see——"

Ellery, on his way upstairs three steps at a time, heard no more. He made for Thorne's room and kicked the door open, sniffing. Then, with rather a grim smile, he went to the tumbled bed and pulled the pillow away. A long-barreled, old-fashioned revolver lay there. He examined the cylinder; it was empty. Then he put the muzzle to his nose.

"Well?" said Thorne from the doorway. The English girl was clinging to him.

"Well," said Ellery, tossing the gun aside, "we're facing fact now, not fancy. It's war, Thorne, as you said. The shot was fired from your revolver. Barrel's still warm, muzzle still reeks, and you can smell burnt gunpowder if you sniff this cold air hard enough. *And* the bullets are gone."

"But what does it mean?" moaned Alice.

"It means that somebody's being terribly cute. It was a harmless trick to get Thorne and me back to the house. Probably the shot was a warning as well as a decoy."

Alice sank onto Thorne's bed. "You mean we——"

"Yes," said Ellery, "from now on we're prisoners, Miss Mayhew. Prisoners who may not stray beyond the confines of the jail. I wonder," he added with a frown, "precisely why."

The day passed in a timeless haze. The world of outdoors became more and more choked in the folds of the snow. The air was a solid white sheet. It seemed as if the very heavens had opened to admit all the snow that ever was, or ever would be.

Young Keith appeared suddenly at noon, taciturn and leaden-eyed, gulped down some hot food, and without explanation retired to his bedroom. Dr. Reinach shambled about quietly for some time; then he disappeared, only to show up, wet, grimy, and silent, before dinner. As the day wore on, less and less was said. Thorne in desperation took to a bottle of whisky. Keith came down at eight o'clock, made himself some coffee, drank three cups, and went upstairs again. Dr. Reinach appeared to have lost his good nature; he was morose, almost sullen, opening his mouth only to snarl at his wife.

And the snow continued to fall.

They all retired early, without conversation.

At midnight the strain was more than even Ellery's iron nerves could bear. He had prowled about his bedroom for hours, poking at the brisk fire in the grate, his mind leaping from improbabilty to fantasy until his head throbbed with one great ache. Sleep was impossible.

Moved by an impulse which he did not attempt to analyze, he slipped into his coat and went out into the frosty corridor.

Thorne's door was closed; Ellery heard the old man's bed creaking and groaning. It was pitch-dark in the hall as he groped his way about. Suddenly Ellery's toe caught in a rent in the carpet and he staggered to regain his balance, coming up against the wall with a thud, his heels clattering on the bare planking at the bottom of the baseboard.

He had no sooner straightened up than he heard the stifled exclamation of a woman. It came from across the corridor; if he guessed right, from Alice Mayhew's bedroom. It was such a weak, terrified exclamation that he sprang across the hall, fumbling in his pockets for a match as he did so. He found match and door in the same instant; he struck one and opened the door and stood still, the tiny light flaring up before him.

Alice was sitting up in bed, quilt drawn about her shoulders, her eyes gleaming in the quarter-light. Before an open drawer of a tallboy across the room, one hand arrested in the act of scattering its contents about, loomed Dr. Reinach, fully dressed. His shoes were wet; his expression was blank; and his eyes were slits.

"Please stand still, Doctor," said Ellery softly as the match sputtered out. "My revolver is useless as a percussion weapon, but it still can inflict damage as a blunt instrument." He moved to a nearby table, where he had seen an oil-lamp before the match went out, struck another match, lighted the lamp, and stepped back again to stand against the door.

"Thank you," whispered Alice.

"What happened, Miss Mayhew?"

"I . . . don't know. I slept badly. I came awake a moment ago when I heard the floor creak. And then you dashed in." She cried suddenly: "Bless you!"

"You cried out."

"Did I?" She sighed like a tired child. "I . . . Uncle Herbert!" she said suddenly, fiercely. "What's the meaning of this? What are you doing in my room?"

The fat man's eyes came open, innocent and beaming; his hand withdrew from the drawer and closed it; and he shifted his elephantine bulk until he was standing erect. "Doing, my dear?" he rumbled. "Why, I came in to see if you were all right." His eyes were fixed on a patch of her white shoulders visible above the quilt. "You were so overwrought today. Purely an avuncular impulse, my child. Forgive me if I startled you."

"I think," sighed Ellery, "that I've misjudged you, Doctor. That's not very clever of you at all. Downright clumsy, in fact; I can only attribute it to a certain understandable confusion of the moment. Miss Mayhew isn't normally to be found in the top drawer of a tallboy, no matter how capacious it may be." He said sharply to Alice: "Did this fellow touch you?"

"Touch me?" Her shoulders twitched with repugnance. "No. If he had, in the dark, I—I think I should have died."

"What a charming compliment," said Dr. Reinach ruefully.

"Then what," demanded Ellery, "*were* you looking for, Dr. Reinach?"

The fat man turned until his right side was toward the door. "I'm notoriously hard of hearing," he chuckled, "in my right ear. Good night, Alice; pleasant dreams. May I pass, Sir Launcelot?"

Ellery kept his gaze on the fat man's bland face until the door closed. For some time after the last echo of Dr. Reinach's chuckle died away they were silent.

Then Alice slid down in the bed and clutched the edge of the quilt. "Mr. Queen, please! Take me away tomorrow. I mean it. I truly do. I—can't tell you how frightened I am of . . . all this. Every time I think of that—that . . . How can such things be? We're not in a place of sanity, Mr. Queen. We'll all go mad if we remain here much longer. Won't you take me away?"

Ellery sat down on the edge of her bed. "Are you really so upset, Miss Mayhew?" he asked gently.

"I'm simply terrified," she whispered.

"Then Thorne and I will do what we can tomorrow." He patted her arm through the quilt. "I'll have a look at his car and see if something can't be done with it. He said there's some gas left in the tank. We'll go as far as it will take us and walk the rest of the way."

"But with so little petrol . . . Oh, I don't care!" She stared up at him wide-eyed. "Do you think . . . he'll let us?"

"He?"

"Whoever it is that . . ."

Ellery rose with a smile. "We'll cross that bridge when it gets to us. Meanwhile, get some sleep; you'll have a strenuous day tomorrow."

"Do you think I'm—he'll———"

"Leave the lamp burning and set a chair under the doorknob when I leave." He took a quick look about. "By the way, Miss Mayhew, is there anything in your possession which Dr. Reinach might want to appropriate?"

"That's puzzled me, too. I can't imagine what I've got he could posssibly want. I'm so poor, Mr. Queen—quite the Cinderella. There's nothing; just my clothes, the things I came with."

"No old letters, records, mementoes?"

"Just one very old photograph of mother."

"Hmm, Dr. Reinach doesn't strike me as *that* sentimental. Well, good night. Don't forget the chair. You'll be quite safe, I assure you."

He waited in the frigid darkness of the corridor until he heard her creep out of bed and set a chair against the door. Then he went into his own room.

And there was Thorne in a shabby dressing-gown, looking like an ancient and dishevelled spectre of gloom.

"What ho! The ghost walks. Can't you sleep, either?"

"Sleep!" The old man shuddered. "How can an honest man sleep in this God-forsaken place? I noticed you seem rather cheerful."

"Not cheerful. Alive." Ellery sat down and lit a cigaret. "I heard you tossing about your bed a few minutes ago. Anything happen to pull you out into this cold?"

"No. Just nerves." Thorne jumped up and began to pace the floor. "Where have you been?"

Ellery told him. "Remarkable chap, Reinach," he concluded. "But we musn't allow our admiration to overpower us. We'll really have to give this thing up, Thorne, at least temporarily. I *had* been hoping . . . But there! I've promised the poor girl. We're leaving tomorrow as best we can."

"And be found frozen stiff next March by a rescue party," said Thorne miserably. "Pleasant prospect! And yet even death by freezing is preferable to this abominable place." He looked curiously at Ellery. "I must say I'm a trifle disappointed in you, Queen. From what I'd heard about your professional cunning . . ."

"I never claimed," shrugged Ellery, "to be a magician. Or even a theologian. What's happened here is either the blackest magic or palpable proof that miracles can happen."

"It would seem so," muttered Thorne. "And yet, when you put your mind to it . . . It goes against reason, by thunder!"

"I see," said Ellery dryly, "the man of law is recovering from the initial shock. Well, it's a shame to have to leave here now, in a way. I detest the thought of giving up—especially at the present time.''

''At the present time? What do you mean?''

''I dare say, Thorne, you haven't emerged far enough from your condition of shock to have properly analyzed this little problem. I gave it a lot of thought today. The goal eludes me—but I'm near it,'' he said softly, ''very near it.''

''You mean,'' gasped the lawyer, ''you mean you actually——''

''Remarkable case,'' said Ellery. ''Oh, extraordinary—there isn't a word in the English language or any other, for that matter, that properly describes it. If I were religiously inclined . . .'' He puffed away thoughtfully. ''It gets down to very simple elements, as all truly great problems do. A fortune in gold exists. It is hidden in a house. The house disappears. To find the gold, then, you must find the house. I believe . . .''

''Aside from that mumbo-jumbo with Keith's broom the other day,'' cried Thorne, ''I can't recall that you've made a single effort in that direction. Find the house!—why, you've done nothing but sit around and wait.''

''Exactly,'' murmured Ellery.

''What?''

''Wait. That's the prescription, my lean and angry friend. That's the sigil that will exorcise the spirit of the Black House.''

''Sigil?'' Thorne stared. ''Spirit?''

''Wait. Precisely. Lord, how I'm waiting!''

Thorne looked puzzled and suspicious, as if he suspected Ellery of a contrary midnight humor. But Ellery sat soberly smoking. ''Wait! For what, man? You're more exasperating than that fat monstrosity! What are you waiting for?''

Ellery looked at him. Then he rose and flung his butt into the dying fire and placed his hand on the old man's arm. ''Go to bed, Thorne. You wouldn't believe me if I told you.''

''Queen, you *must*. I'll go mad if I don't see daylight on this thing soon!''

Ellery looked shocked, for no reason that Thorne could see. And then, just as inexplicably, he slapped Thorne's shoulder and began to chuckle.

''Go to bed,'' he said, still chuckling.

''But you must tell me!''

Ellery sighed, losing his smile. ''I can't. You'd laugh.''

''I'm not in a laughing mood!''

''Nor is it a laughing matter. Thorne, I began to say a moment ago that if I, poor sinner that I am, possessed religious susceptibilities, I should have become permanently devout in the past three days. I suppose I'm a hopeless case. But even I see a power not of earth in this.''

''Play-actor,'' growled the old lawyer. ''Professing to see the hand of God in . . . Don't be sacrilegious, man. We're not all heathen.''

Ellery looked out his window at the moonless night and the glimmering grayness of the snow-swathed world.

''Hand of God?'' he murmured. ''No, not hand, Thorne. If this case is ever solved, it will be by . . . a lamp.''

''Lamp?'' said Thorne faintly. ''Lamp?''

''In a manner of speaking. *The lamp of God.*''

III

The next day dawned sullenly, as ashen and hopeless a morning as ever was. Incredibly, it still snowed in the same thick fashion, as if the whole sky were crumbling bit by bit.

Ellery spent the better part of the day in the garage, tinkering at the big black car's vitals. He left the doors wide open, so that anyone who wished might see what he was about. He knew little enough of automotive mechanics, and he felt from the start that he was engaged in a futile business.

But in the late afternoon, after hours of vain experimentation, he suddenly came upon a tiny wire which seemed to him to be out of joint with its environment. It simply hung, a useless thing. Logic demanded a connection. He experimented. He found one.

As he stepped on the starter and heard the cold motor sputter into life, a shape darkened the entrance of the garage. He turned off the ignition quickly and looked up.

It was Keith, a black mass against the background of snow, standing with widespread legs, a large can hanging from each big hand.

''Hello, there,'' murmured Ellery. ''You've assumed human shape again, I see. Back on one of your infrequent jaunts to the world of men, Keith?''

Keith said quietly: ''Going somewhere, Mr. Queen?''

''Certainly. Why—do you intend to stop me?''

''Depends on where you're going.''

''Ah, a threat. Well, suppose I tell *you* where to go?''

"Tell all you want. You don't get off these grounds until I know where you're bound for."

Ellery grinned. "There's a naive directness about you, Keith, that draws me in spite of myself. Well, I'll relieve your mind. Thorne and I are taking Miss Mayhew back to the city."

"In that case it's all right." Ellery studied his face; it was worn deep with ruts of fatigue and worry. Keith dropped the cans to the cement floor of the garage. "You can use these, then. Gas."

"Gas! Where on earth did you get it?"

"Let's say," said Keith grimly, "I dug it up out of an old Indian tomb."

"Very well."

"You've fixed Thorne's car, I see. Needn't have. I could have done it."

"Then why didn't you?"

"Because nobody asked me to." The giant swung on his heel and vanished.

Ellery sat still, frowning. Then he got out of the car, picked up the cans, and poured their contents into the tank. He reached into the car again, got the engine running, and leaving it to purr away like a great cat he went back to the house.

He found Alice in her room, a coat over her shoulders, staring out her window. She sprang up at his knock.

"Mr. Queen, you've got Mr. Thorne's car going!"

"Success at last," smiled Ellery. "Are you ready?"

"Oh, yes! I feel so much better, now that we're actually to leave. Do you think we'll have a hard time? I saw Mr. Keith bring those cans in. Petrol, weren't they? Nice of him. I never did believe such a nice young man—" She flushed. There were hectic spots in her cheeks and her eyes were brighter than they had been for days. Her voice seemed less husky, too.

"It may be hard going through the drifts, but the car is equipped with chains. With luck we should make it. It's a powerful—"

Ellery stopped very suddenly indeed, his eyes fixed on the worn carpet at his feet, stony yet startled.

"Whatever is the matter, Mr. Queen?"

"Matter?" Ellery raised his eyes and drew a deep, deep breath. "Nothing at all. God's in His heaven and all's right with the world."

She looked down at the carpet. "Oh . . . the sun!" With a little squeal of delight she turned to the window. "Why, Mr. Queen, it's stopped snowing. There's the sun setting—at last!"

"And high time, too," said Ellery briskly. "Will you please get your things on? We leave at once." He picked up her bags and left her, walking with a springy vigor that shook the old boards. He crossed the corridor to his room opposite hers and began, whistling, to pack his bag.

The living-room was noisy with a babble of adieux. One would have said that this was a normal household, with normal people in a normal human situation. Alice was positively gay, quite as if she were not leaving a fortune in gold for what might turn out to be all time.

She set her purse down on the mantel next to her mother's chromo, fixed her hat, flung her arms about Mrs. Reinach, pecked gingerly at Mrs. Fell's withered cheek, and even smiled forgivingly at Dr. Reinach. Then she dashed back to the mantel, snatched up her purse, threw one long enigmatic glance at Keith's drawn face, and hurried outdoors as if the devil himself were after her.

Thorne was already in the car, his old face alight with incredible happiness, as if he had been reprieved at the very moment he was to set his foot beyond the little green door. He beamed at the dying sun.

Ellery followed Alice more slowly. The bags were in Thorne's car; there was nothing more to do. He climbed in, raced the motor, and then released the brake.

The fat man filled the doorway, shouting: "You know the road, now, don't you? Turn to the right at the end of this drive. Then keep going in a straight line. You can't miss. You'll hit the main highway in a- bout . . ."

His last words were drowned in the roar of the engine. Ellery waved his hand. Alice, in the tonneau beside Thorne, twisted about and laughed a little hysterically. Thorne sat beaming at the back of Ellery's head.

The car, under Ellery's guidance, trundled unsteadily out of the drive and made a right turn into the road.

It grew dark rapidly. They made slow progress. The big machine inched its way through the drifts, slipping and lurching despite its chains. As night fell, Elleery turned the powerful headlights on.

He drove with unswerving concentration.

None of them spoke.

It seemed hours before they reached the main highway. But when they did the car leaped to life on the road, which had been partly cleared by snowplows, and it was not long before they were entering the nearby town.

At the sight of the friendly electric lights, the paved streets, the solid blocks of houses, Alice gave a cry of sheer delight. Ellery stopped at a gasoline station and had the tank filled.

"It's not far from here, Miss Mayhew," said Thorne reassuringly. "We'll be in the city in no time. The Triborough Bridge . . . "

"Oh, it's wonderful to be alive!"

"Of course you'll stay at my house. My wife will be delighted to have you. After you . . . "

"You're so kind, Mr. Thorne. I don't know how I shall ever be able to thank you enough." She paused, startled. "Why, what's the matter, Mr. Queen?"

For Ellery had done a strange thing. He stopped the car at a traffic intersection and asked the officer on duty something in a low tone. The officer stared at him and replied with gestures. Ellery swung the car off into another street. He drove slowly.

"What's the matter?" asked Alice again, leaning forward.

Thorne said, frowning: "You can't have lost your way. There's a sign which distinctly says . . . "

"No, it's not that," said Ellery in a preoccupied way. "I've just thought of something."

The girl and the old man looked at each other, puzzled. Ellery stopped the car at a large stone building with green lights outside and went in, remaining there for fifteen minutes. He came out whistling.

"Queen!" said Thorne abruptly, eyes on the green lights. "What's up?"

"Something that must be brought down." Ellery swung the car about and headed it for the traffic intersection. When he reached it he turned left.

"Why, you've taken the wrong turn," said Alice nervously. "This is the direction from which we've just come. I'm sure of that."

"And you're quite right, Miss Mayhew. It is." She sank back, pale, as if the very thought of returning terrified her. "We're going back, you see," said Ellery.

"Back!" exploded Thorne, sitting up straight.

"Oh, can't we forget all those horrible people?" moaned Alice.

"I've a viciously stubborn memory. Besides, we have reinforcements. If you'll look back you'll see a car following us. It's a police car, and in it are the local Chief of Police and a squad of picked men."

"But why, Mr. Queen?" cried Alice. Thorne said nothing; his happiness had quite vanished, and he sat gloomily staring at the back of Ellery's neck.

"Because," said Ellery grimly, "I have my own professional pride. Because I've been on the receiving end of a damnably cute magician's trick."

"Trick?" she repeated dazedly.

"Now I shall turn magician myself. You saw a house disappear." He laughed softly. "I shall make it appear again!"

They could only stare at him, too bewildered to speak.

"And then," said Ellery, his voice hardening, "even if we chose to overlook such trivia as dematerialized houses, in all conscience we can't overlook . . . *murder*."

IV

And there was the Black House again. Not a wraith. A solid house, a strong dirty time-encrusted house, looking as if it would never dream of taking wing and flying off into space.

It stood on the other side of the driveway, where it had always stood.

They saw it even as they turned into the drive from the drift-covered road, its bulk looming black against the brilliant moon, as substantial a house as could be found in the world of sane things.

Thorne and the girl were incapable of speech; they could only gape, dumb witnesses of a miracle even greater than the disappearance of the house in the first place.

As for Ellery, he stopped the car, sprang to the ground, signalled to the car snuffling up behind, and darted across the snowy clearing to the White House, whose windows were bright with lamp- and fire-light. Out of the police car swarmed men, and they ran after Ellery like hounds. Thorne and Alice followed in a daze.

Ellery kicked open the White House door. There was a revolver in his hand and there was no doubt, from the way he gripped it, that its cylinder had been replenished.

"Hello again," he said, stalking into the living-room. "Not a ghost; Inspector Queen's little boy in the too, too solid flesh. Nemesis, perhaps. I bid you good evening. What—no welcoming smile, Dr. Reinach?"

The fat man had paused in the act of lifting a glass of Scotch to his lips.

It was wonderful how the color seeped out of his pouchy cheeks , leaving them gray. Mrs. Reinach whimpered in a corner, and Mrs. Fell stared stupidly. Only Nick Keith showed no great astonishment. He was standing by a window, muffled to the ears; and on his face there was bitterness and admiration and, strangely, a sort of relief.

"Shut the door." The detectives behind Ellery spread out silently. Alice stumbled to a chair, her eyes wild, studying Dr. Reinach with a fierce intensity . . . There was a sighing little sound and one of the detectives lunged toward the window at which Keith had been standing. But Keith was no longer there. He was bounding through the snow toward the wood like a huge deer.

"Don't let him get away!" cried Ellery. Three men dived through the window after the giant, their guns out. Shots began to sputter. The night outside was streaked with orange lightning.

Ellery went to the fire and warmed his hands. Dr. Reinach slowly, very slowly, sat down in the armchair. Thorne sank into a chair, too, putting his hands to his head.

Ellery turned around and said: "I've told you, Captain, enough of what's happened since our arrival to allow you an intelligent understanding of what I'm about to say." A stocky man in uniform nodded curtly.

"Thorne, last night for the first time in my career," continued Ellery whimsically, "I acknowledged the assistance of . . . Well, I tell you, who are implicated in this extraordinary crime, that had it not been for the good God above you would have succeeded in your plot against Alice Mayhew's inheritance."

"I'm disappointed in you," said the fat man from the depths of the chair.

"A loss I keenly feel" Ellery looked at him, smiling. "Let me show you, skeptic. When Mr. Thorne, Miss Mayhew and I arrived the other day, it was late afternoon. Upstairs, in a room you so thoughtfully provided, I looked out the window and saw the sun setting. This was nothing and meant nothing, surely: sunset. Mere sunset. A trivial thing, interesting only to poets, meteorologists, and astronomers. But this was one time when the sun was vital to a man seeking truth . . . a veritable lamp of God shining in the darkness.

"For, see. Miss Mayhew's bedroom that first day was on the opposite side of the house from mine. If the sun *set* in my window, then I faced west and she faced east. So far, so good. We talked, we retired. The next morning I awoke at seven—shortly after sunrise in this winter month— and what did I see? I *saw the sun streaming into my window*."

A knot hissed in the fire behind him. The stocky man in the blue uniform stirred uneasily.

"Don't you understand?" cried Ellery. "The sun had *set* in my window, and now it was *rising* in my window!"

Dr. Reinach was regarding him with a mild ruefulness. The color had come back to his fat cheeks. He raised the glass he was holding in a gesture curiously like a salute. Then he drank, deeply.

And Ellery said: "The significance of this unearthly reminder did not strike me at once. But much later it came back to me; and I dimly saw that chance, cosmos, God, whatever you may choose to call it, had given me the instrument for understanding the colossal, the mind-staggering phenomenon of a house which vanished overnight from the face of the earth."

"Good lord," muttered Thorne.

"But I was not sure; I did not trust my memory. I needed another demonstration from heaven, a bulwark to bolster my own suspicions. And so, as it snowed and snowed and snowed, the snow drawing a blanket across the face of the sun through which it could not shine, I waited. I waited for the snow to stop, and for the sun to shine again."

He sighed. "When it shone again, there could no longer be any doubt. It appeared first to me in Miss Mayhew's room, which had faced east the afternoon of our arrival. But what was it I saw in Miss Mayhew's room late this afternoon? I saw the sun *set*."

"Good lord," said Thorne again; he seemed incapable of saying anything else.

"Then her room faced west today. How could her room face west today when it had faced east the day of our arrival? How could my room face west the day of our arrival and face east today? Had the sun stood still? Had the world gone mad? Or was there another explanation—one so extrordinarily simple that it staggered the imagination?"

Thorne muttered: "Queen, this is the most—"

"Please," said Ellery, "let me finish. The only logical conclusion, the only conclusion that did not fly in the face of natural law of science itself, was that while the house we were in today, the rooms we occupied, seemed to be identical with the house and the rooms we had occupied on the day of our arrival, *they were not*. Unless this solid structure had been turned about on its foundation like a toy on a stick, which was palpably absurd, then *it was not the same house*. It looked the same inside and out, it had identical furniture, identical carpeting, identical decoration . . . but it was another house exactly like the first in every detail except one: and that was its terrestrial position in relation to the sun."

A detective outside shouted a message of failure, a shout carried away by the wind under the bright cold moon.

"See," said Ellery softly, "how everything fell into place. If this White House we were in was not the same White House in which we had slept that first night, but was a twin house in a different position in relation to the sun, then the Black House, which apparently vanished, had not vanished at all. It was where it had always been. It was not the Black House which had vanished, but we who had vanished. It was not the Black House which had vanished, but we who had moved away. We had been transferred during that first night to a new location, where the surrounding woods looked similar, where there was a similar driveway with a similar garage at its terminus, where the road outside was similarly old and pitted, where everything was similar except that there was no Black House, only an empty clearing.

"So we must have been moved, body and baggage, to this twin White House during the time we retired the first night and the time we awoke the next morning. We, Miss Mayhew's chromo on the mantel, the holes in our doors where locks had been, even the fragments of a brandy decanter which had been shattered the night before in a cleverly staged scene against the brick wall of the fireplace at the original house . . . all, all transferred to the twin house to further the illusion that we were still in the original house the next morning."

"Drivel," said Dr. Reinach, smiling. "Such pure drivel that it smacks of fantasmagoria."

"It was beautiful," said Ellery. "A beautiful plan. It had symmetry, the polish of great art. And it made a beautiful chain of reasoning, too, once I was set properly at the right link. For what followed? Since we had been transferred without our knowledge during the night, it must have been while we were unconscious. I recalled the two drinks Thorne and I had had, and the fuzzy tongue and head that resulted the next morning. Mildly drugged, then; and the drinks had been mixed the night before by Dr. Reinach's own hand. Doctor—drugs; very simple." The fat man shrugged with amusement, glancing sidewise at the stocky man in blue. But the stocky man in blue wore a hard, unchanging mask.

"But Dr. Reinach alone?" murmured Ellery. "Oh, no, impossible. One man could never have accomplished all that was necessary in the scant few hours available . . . fix Thorne's car, carry us and our clothes and bags from the one White House to its duplicate—by machine—put

Thorne's car out of commission again, put us to bed again, arrange our clothing identically, transfer the chromo, the fragments of the cut-glass decanter in the fireplace, perhaps even a few knickknacks and ornaments not duplicated in the second White House, and so on. A prodigious job, even if most of the preparatory work had been done before our arrival. Who but everyone in the house? With the possible exception of Mrs. Fell, who in her condition could be swayed easily enough, with no clear perception of what was occurring.''

Ellery's eyes gleamed. ''And so I accuse you all—including young Mr. Keith, who has wisely taken himself off—of having aided in the plot whereby you would prevent the rightful heiress of Sylvester Mayhew's fortune from taking possession of the house in which it was hidden.''

Dr. Reinach coughed politely, flapping his paws together like a great seal. ''Terribly interesting, Queen, terribly. I don't know when I've been more captivated by sheer fiction. On the other hand, there are certain personal allusions in your story which, much as I admire their ingenuity, cannot fail to provoke me.'' He turned to the stocky man in blue. ''Certainly, Captain,'' he chuckled, ''you don't credit this incredible story? I believe Mr. Queen has gone a little mad from sheer shock.''

''Unworthy of you, Doctor,'' sighed Ellery. ''The proof of what I say lies in the very fact that we are here, at this moment.''

''You'll have to explain that,'' said the police chief, who seemed out of his depth.

''I mean that we are now in the original White House. I led you back here, didn't I? And I can lead you back to the twin White House, for now I know the basis of the illusion. After our departure this evening, incidentally, all these people returned to this house. The other White House had served its purpose and they no longer needed it.

''As for the geographical trick involved, it struck me that this side-road we're on makes a steady curve for miles. Both driveways lead off this same road, one some six miles farther up the road; although, because of the curve, which is like a number 9, the road makes a wide sweep and virtually doubles back on itself, so that as the crow flies the two settlements are only a mile or so apart, although by the curving road they are six miles apart.

''When Dr. Reinach drove Thorne and Miss Mayhew and me out here the day the *Coronia* docked, he deliberately passed the almost imperceptible drive leading to the substitute house and went on until he reached this one, the original. We didn't notice the first driveway.

"Thorne's car was put out of commission deliberately to prevent his driving. The driver of a car will observe landmarks when his passengers notice little or nothing. Keith even met Thorne on both Thorne's previous visits to Mayhew—ostensibly 'to lead the way,' actually to prevent Thorne from familiarizing himself with the road. And it was Dr. Reinach who drove the three of us here that first day. They permitted me to drive away tonight for what they hoped was a one-way trip because we started from the substitute house—of the two, the one on the road nearer to town. We couldn't possibly, then, pass the tell-tale second drive and become suspicious. And they knew the relatively shorter drive would not impress our consciousness."

"But even granting all that, Mr. Queen," said the policeman, "I don't see what these people expected to accomplish. They couldn't hope to keep you folks fooled forever."

"True," cried Ellery, "but don't forget that by the time we caught on to the various tricks involved they hoped to have laid hands on Mayhew's fortune and disappeared with it. Don't you see that the whole illusion was planned *to give them time?* Time to dismantle the Black House without interference, raze it to the ground if necessary, to find that hidden hoard of gold? I don't doubt that if you examine the house next door you'll find it a shambles and a hollow shell. That's why Reinach and Keith kept disappearing. They were taking turns at the Black House, picking it apart, stone by stone, in a frantic search for the cache, while we were occupied in the duplicate White House with an apparently supernatural phenomenon. That's why someone—probably the worthy doctor here—slipped out of the house behind your back, Thorne, and struck me over the head when I rashly attempted to follow Keith's tracks in the snow. I could not be permitted to reach the original settlement, for if I did the whole preposterous illusion would be revealed."

"How about the gold?" growled Thorne.

"For all I know," said Ellery with a shrug, "they've found it and salted it away again."

"Oh, but we didn't," whimpered Mrs. Reinach, squirming in her chair. "Herbert, I *told* you not to—"

"Idiot," said the fat man. "Stupid swine." She jerked as if he had struck her.

"If you hadn't found the loot," said the police chief to Dr. Reinach brusquely, "why did you let these people go tonight?"

Dr. Reinach compressed his blubbery lips; he raised his glass and drank quickly.

"I think I can answer that," said Ellery in a gloomy tone. "In many ways it's the most remarkable element of the whole puzzle. Certainly it's the grimmest and least excusable. The other illusion was child's play compared to it. For it involves two apparently irreconcilable elements—Alice Mayhew and a murder."

"A murder!" exclaimed the policeman, stiffening.

"Me?" said Alice in bewilderment.

Ellery lit a cigarette and flourished it at the policeman. "When Alice Mayhew came here that first afternoon, she went into the Black House with us. In her father's bedroom she ran across an old chromo—I see it's not here, so it's still in the other White House—portraying her long-dead mother as a girl. Alice Mayhew fell on the chromo like a Chinese refugee on a bowl of rice. She had only one picture of her mother, she explained, and that a poor one. She treasured this unexpected discovery so much that she took it with her, then and there, to the White House—this house. And she placed it on the mantel over the fireplace here in a prominent position."

The stocky man frowned; Alice sat very still; Thorne looked puzzled. And Ellery put the cigarette back to his lips and said: "Yet when Alice Mayhew fled from the White House in our company tonight for what seemed to be the last time, *she completely ignored her mother's chromo,* that treasured memento over which she had gone into such raptures the first day! She could not have failed to overlook it in, let us say, the excitement of the moment. She had placed her purse on the mantel, a moment before, next to the chromo. She returned to the mantel for her purse. And yet she passed the chromo up without a glance. Since its sentimental value to her was overwhelming, by her own admission, it's the one thing in all this property she would not have left. *If she had taken it in the beginning, she would have taken it on leaving.*"

Thorne cried: "What in the name of heaven are you saying, Queen?" His eyes glared at the girl, who sat glued to her chair, scarcely breathing.

"I am saying," said Ellery curtly, "that we were blind. I am saying that not only was a house impersonated, but a woman as well. *I am saying that this woman is not Alice Mayhew.*"

The girl raised her eyes after an infinite interval in which no one, not even the policemen present, so much as stirred a foot.

"I thought of everything," she said with the queerest sigh, and quite without the husky tone, "but that. And it was going off so beautifully."

"Oh, you fooled me very neatly," drawled Ellery. "That pretty little

bedroom scene last night . . . I know now what happened. This precious Dr. Reinach of yours had stolen into your room at at midnight to
report to you on the progress of the search at the Black House, perhaps to
urge you to persuade Thorne and me to leave today—at any cost. I
happened to pass along the hall outside your room, stumbled, and fell
against the wall with a clatter not knowing who it might be or what the
intruder's purpose, you both fell instantly into that cunning decep-
tion . . . Actors! Both of you missed a career on the stage.''

The fat man closed his eyes; he seemed asleep. And the girl murmured, with a sort of tired defiance: ''Not missed, Mr. Queen. I spent
several years in the theater.''

''You were devils, you two. Psychologically this plot has been the
conception of evil genius. You knew that Alice Mayhew was unknown to
anyone in this country except by her photographs. Moreover, there was a
startling resemblance between the two of you, as Miss Mayhew's photographs showed. And you knew Miss Mayhew would be in the company
of Thorne and me for only a few hours, and then chiefly in the murky
light of a sedan.''

''Good lord,'' groaned Thorne, staring at the girl in horror.

''Alice Mayhew,'' said Ellery grimly, ''walked into this house and
was whisked upstairs by Mrs. Reinach. *And Alice Mayhew, the English
girl, never appeared before us again*. It was you who came downstairs;
you, who had been secreted from Thorne's eyes during the past six days
deliberately, so that he would not even suspect your existence; you who
probably conceived the entire plot when Thorne brought the photographs
of Alice Mayhew here, and her gossipy, informative letters; you, who
looked enough like the real Alice Mayhew to get by with an impersonation in the eyes of two men to whom Alice Mayhew was a total stranger. I
did think you looked different, somehow, when you appeared for dinner
that first night; but I put it down to the fact that I was seeing you for the
first time refreshed, brushed up, and without your hat and coat. Naturally, after that, the more I saw of you the less I remembered the details of
the real Alice Mayhew's appearance and so became more and more
convinced, unconsciously, that you were Alice Mayhew. As for the
husky voice and the excuse of having caught cold on the long automobile
ride from the pier, that was a clever ruse to disguise the inevitable
difference between your voices. The only danger that existed lay in Mrs.
Fell, who gave us the answer to the whole riddle the first time we met
her. She thought you were her own daughter Olivia. Of course. *Because
that's who you are!*''

* * *

Dr. Reinach was sipping brandy now with a steady indifference to his surroundings. His little eyes were fixed on a point miles away. Old Mrs. Fell sat gaping stupidly at the girl.

"You even covered that danger by getting Dr. Reinach to tell us beforehand that trumped-up story of Mrs. Fell's 'delusion' and Olivia Fell's 'death' in an automobile accident several years ago. Oh, admirable! Yet even this poor creature, in the frailty of her anile faculties, was fooled by a difference in voice and hair—two of the most easily distinguishable features. I suppose you fixed up your hair at the time Mrs. Reinach brought the real Alice Mayhew upstairs and you had a living model to go by . . . I could find myself moved to admiration if it were not for one thing."

"You're so clever," said Olivia Fell coolly. "Really a fascinating monster. What do you mean?"

Ellery went to her and put his hand on her shoulder. "Alice Mayhew vanished and you took her place. Why did you take her place? For two possible reasons. One—to get Thorne and me away from the danger zone as quickly as possible, and to keep us away by 'abandoning' the fortune or dismissing us, which as Alice Mayhew would be your privilege: in proof, your vociferous insistence that we take you away. Two—of infinitely greater importance to the scheme: if your confederates did not find the gold at once, you were still Alice Mayhew in our eyes. You could then dispose of the house when and as you saw fit. Whenever the gold was found, it would be yours and your accomplices'.

"But the real Alice Mayhew vanished. For you, her impersonator, to be in a position to go through the long process of taking over Alice Mayhew's inheritance, it was necessary that Alice Mayhew remain *permanently invisible*. For you to get possession of her rightful inheritance and live to enjoy its fruits, it was necessary that Alice Mayhew die. And that, Thorne," snapped Ellery, gripping the girl's shoulder hard, "is why I said that there was something besides a disappearing house to cope with tonight. Alice Mayhew was murdered."

There were three shouts from outside which rang with tones of great excitement. And then they ceased, abruptly.

"Murdered," went on Ellery, "by the only occupant of the house who was not *in* the house when this imposter came downstairs that first evening—Nicholas Keith. A hired killer. Although these people are all accessories to that murder."

A voice said from the window: "Not a hired *killer*."

They wheeled sharply, and fell silent. The three detectives who had sprung out of the window were there in the background, quietly watchful. Before them were two people.

"Not a killer," said one of them, a woman. "That's what he was supposed to be. Instead, and without their knowledge, he saved my life . . . dear Nick."

And now the pall of grayness settled over the faces of Mrs. Fell, and of Mrs. Reinach, and of the burly doctor. For by Keith's side stood Alice Mayhew. She was the same woman who sat near the fire only in general similitude of feature. Now that both women could be compared in proximity, there were obvious points of difference. She looked worn and grim, but happy withal; and she was holding to the arm of bitter-mouthed Nick Keith was a grip that was quite possessive.

ADDENDUM

Afterwards, when it was possible to look back on the whole amazing fabric of plot and event, Mr. Ellery Queen said: "The scheme would have been utterly impossible except for two things: the character of Olivia Fell and the—in itself—fantastic existence of that duplicate house in the woods."

He might have added that both of these would in turn have been impossible except for the aberrant strain in the Mayhew blood. The father of Sylvester Mayhew—Dr. Reinach's stepfather—had always been erratic, and he had communicated his unbalance to his children. Sylvester and Sarah, who became Mrs. Fell, were twins, and they had always been insanely jealous of each other's prerogatives. When they married in the same month, their father avoided trouble by presenting each of them with a specially-built house, the houses being identical in every detail. One he had erected next to his own house and presented to Mrs. Fell as a wedding gift; the other he built on a piece of property he owned some miles away and gave to Sylvester.

Mrs. Fell's husband died early in her married life; and she moved away to live with her half-brother Herbert. When old Mayhew died, Sylvester boarded up his own house and moved into the ancestral mansion. And there the twin houses stood for many years, separated by only a few miles by road, completely and identically furnished inside—fantastic monuments to the Mayhew eccentricity.

The duplicate White House lay boarded up, waiting, idle, requiring only the evil genius of an Olivia Fell to be put to use. Olivia was beautiful, intelligent, accomplished, and as unscrupulous as Lady Macbeth. It was she who had influenced the others to move back to the abandoned house next to the Black House for the sole purpose of coercing or robbing Sylvester Mayhew. When Thorne appeared with the news of Sylvester's long-lost daughter, she recognized the peril to their scheme and, grasping her own resemblance to her English cousin from the photographs Thorne brought, conceived the whole extraordinary plot.

Then obviously the first step was to put Sylvester out of the way. With perfect logic, she bent Dr. Reinach to her will and caused him to murder his patient before the arrival of Sylvester's daughter. (A later exhumation and autopsy revealed traces of poison in the corpse.) Meanwhile, Olivia perfected the plans of the impersonation and illusion.

The house illusion was planned for the benefit of Thorne, to keep him sequestered and bewildered while the Black House was being torn down in the search for the gold. The illusion would perhaps not have been necessary had Olivia felt certain her impersonation would succeed perfectly.

The illusion was simpler, of course, than appeared on the surface. The house was there, completely furnished, ready for use. All that was necessary was to take the boards down, air the place out, clean up, put fresh linen in. There was plenty of time before Alice's arrival for this preparatory work.

The one weakness of Olivia Fell's plot was objective, not personal. That woman would have succeeded in anything. But she made the mistake of selecting Nick Keith for the job of murdering Alice Mayhew. Keith had originally insinuated himself into the circle of plotters, posing as a desperado prepared to anything for sufficient pay. Actually, he was the son of Sylvester Mayhew's second wife, who had been so brutally treated by Mayhew and driven off to die in poverty.

Before his mother expired she instilled in Keith's mind a hatred for Mayhew that waxed, rather than waned, with the ensuing years. Keith's sole motive in joining the conspirators was to find his stepfather's fortune and take that part of it which Mayhew had stolen from his mother. He had never intended to murder Alice—his ostensible role. When he carried her from the house that first evening under the noses of Ellery and Thorne, it was not to strangle and bury her, as Olivia had directed, but to secrete her in an ancient shack in the nearby woods known only to himself.

He had managed to smuggle provisions to her while he was ransacking the Black House. At first he had held her frankly prisoner, intending to keep her so until he found the money, took his share, and escaped. But as he came to know her he came to love her, and he soon confessed the whole story to her in the privacy of the shack. Her sympathy gave him new courage; concerned now with her safety above everything else, he prevailed upon her to remain in hiding until he could find the money and outwit his fellow-conspirators. Then they both intended to unmask Olivia.

The ironical part of the whole affair, as Mr. Ellery Queen was to point out, was that the goal of all this plotting and counterplotting—Sylvester Mayhew's gold—remained as invisible as the Black House apparently had been. Despite the most thorough search of the building and grounds no trace of it had been found.

"I've asked you to visit my poor diggings," smiled Ellery a few weeks later, "because something occurred to me that simply cried out for investigation."

Keith and Alice glanced at each other blankly; and Thorne, looking clean, rested, and complacent for the first time in weeks, sat up straighter in Ellery's most comfortable chair.

"I'm glad something occurred to somebody," said Nick Keith with a grin. "I'm a pauper; and Alice is only one jump ahead of me."

"You haven't the philosophic attitude towards wealth," said Ellery dryly, "that's so charming a part of Dr. Reinach's personality. Poor Colossus! I wonder how he likes our jails . . . " He poked a log into the fire. "By this time, Miss Mayhew, our common friend Thorne has had your father's house virtually annihilated. No gold. Eh, Thorne?"

"Nothing but dirt," said the lawyer sadly. "Why, we've taken that house apart stone by stone."

"Exactly. Now there are two possibilities, since I am incorrigibly categorical: either your father's fortune exists, Miss Mayhew, or it does not. If it does not and he was lying, there's an end to the business, of course, and you and your precious Keith will have to put your heads together and agree to live either in noble, ruggedly individualistic poverty or by the grace of the Relief Administration. But suppose there was a fortune, as your father claimed, and suppose he did secrete it somewhere in that house. What then?"

"Then," sighed Alice, "it's flown away."

Ellery laughed. "Not quite; I've had enough of vanishments for the present, anyway. Let's tackle the problem differently. Is there anything which was in Sylvester Mayhew's house before he died which is not there now?''

Thorne stared. ''If you mean the —er—the body . . . ''

''Don't be gruesome, Literal Lyman. Besides, there's been an exhumation. No, guess again.''

Alice looked slowly down at the package in her lap. ''So that's why you asked me to fetch this with me today!''

''You mean,'' cried Keith, ''the old fellow was deliberately putting everyone off the track when he said his fortune was gold?''

Ellery chuckled and took the package from the girl. He unwrapped it and for a moment gazed appreciatively at the large old chromo of Alice's mother.

And then, with the self-assurance of the complete logician, he stripped away the back of the frame.

Gold-and-green documents cascaded into his lap.

''Converted into bonds,'' grinned Ellery. ''Who said your father was cracked, Miss Mayhew? A very clever gentleman! Come, come, Thorne, stop rubber-necking and let's leave these children of fortune alone!''

Rumpole

RUMPOLE AND THE EXPERT WITNESS
John Mortimer

Canst thou not minister to a mind diseased,
Pluck from the memory a rooted sorrow,
Raze out the written troubles of the brain,
And with some sweet oblivious antidote
Cleanse the stuffed bosom of that perilous stuff
Which weighs upon the heart . . .

CERTAINLY NOT YOUNG Dr. Ned Dacre, the popular G.P. of Hunter's Hill, that delightful little dormitory town in Surrey, where nothing is heard but the whirr of the kitchen mixers running up Provençal specialities from the Sunday supplements and the purr of the Hi Fis playing baroque music to go with the Buck's Fizz.

Ned Dacre lived in a world removed from my usual clients, the Old Bailey villains whose most common disease is a criminal conviction. He had a beautiful wife, two cars, two fair-haired children called Simon and Sara at rather nice schools, an au pair girl, an Old English sheepdog, a swimming pool, a car port and a machine for recording television programmes so that he didn't have to keep watching television. His father, Dr. Henry Dacre, had settled in Hunter's Hill just after the war and had built up an excellent practice. When his son grew up and qualified he was taken into the partnership and father and son were the two most popular doctors for many miles around, the inhabitants being almost equally divided as to whether, in times of sickness, they preferred the attentions of "Dr. Harry" or "Dr. Ned." With all these advantages it seemed that Ned Dacre had all that the heart of man could desire, except that he had an uphappy wife. One night, after they had enjoyed a quiet supper together at home, Dr. Ned's wife Sally became extremely ill. As she appeared to lose consciousness, he heard her say,

"I loved you Ned . . . I really did."

These were her last words, for although her husband rang the casualty department of the local hospital, and an ambulance was quickly dispatched, the beautiful Mrs. Sally Dacre never spoke again, and died before she was taken out of the house.

I learned, as did the world, about the death of Sally Dacre and its unfortunate consequences from *The Times*. I was seated at breakfast in the matrimonial home at Froxbury Court in the Gloucester Road, looking forward without a great deal of excitement to a fairly ordinary day practicing the law, ingesting Darjeeling tea, toast and Oxford marmalade, when the news item caught my eye and I gave a discreet whistle of surprise. My wife, Hilda, who was reading her correspondence (one letter on mauve paper from an old schoolfriend) wanted her share of the news.

"What's the news in *The Times,* Rumpole? Has war started?"

"A Dr. Dacre has been arrested in Hunter's Hill, Surrey. He's charged with murdering his wife."

Hilda didn't seem to find the intelligence immediately gripping. In fact she waved her correspondence at me.

"There's a letter from Dodo. You know, my friend Dodo, Rumpole?"

"The one who keeps the tea-shop in Devon?" I had a vague recollection of an unfriendly female in tweed who seemed to imagine that I tyrannized somewhat over She Who Must Be Obeyed.

"She's always asking me to pop down and stay."

"Why don't you?" I muttered hopefully, and then returned to the Home News. " 'Dr. Dacre . . ?' The name's distinctly familiar."

"Dodo never cared for you, Rumpole," Hilda said firmly.

"The feeling's mutual. Isn't she the one who wears amber beads and smells of scones?" I repeated the name, hoping to stir some hidden memory, "Harry Dacre."

"Dodo's been suffering from depression," Hilda rambled on. "Of course, she never married."

"Then I can't think what she's got to be depressed about!" I couldn't resist saying it, perhaps not quite audibly from behind the cover of *The Times*. "Dr. Harry Dacre!" I suddenly remembered. "He gave evidence in my greatest triumph, the Penge Bungalow Murders! He'd seen my client's bruises. Don't you remember?"

"Dodo writes that she's taking a new sort of pill for her depression. They're helping her, but she mustn't eat cheese."

"Poor old Dodo," I said, "deprived of cheese." I read the story in the paper again. "It couldn't be him. This is Dr. 'Ned' Dacre. Oh well, it's just another nice little murder that's never going to come my way. 'Cause of death, cerebral hemorrhage,' that's the evidence in the Magistrates' Court, 'sustained in an alleged attack . . . ' "

As I read, Hilda was casting a critical eye over my appearance.

"You're never going to Chambers like that, are you, Rumpole?"

"Like what, Hilda?" I was wondering what sort of a savage attack by a local doctor could explain his wife's cerebral hemorrhage.

"Well, your stud's showing and you've got marmalade on your waistcoat, and do you *have* to have that old silk handerchief half falling out of your top pocket?"

"That was the silk handkerchief I used to blow my nose on three times, tearfully, in my final speech in the double murder in the Deptford Old People's Home. It has a certain sentimental value. Will you leave me alone, Hilda?" She was dabbing at my waistcoat with a corner of a table napkin she had soaked in the hot water jug.

"I just want you to look your best, Rumpole."

"You mean, in case I get run over?"

"And I'll put that old hanky in the wash." She snatched the venerable bandana out of my breast pocket. "You'd be much better off with a few nice, clean tissues."

"You know what that fellow Dacre's been accused of, Hilda?" I thought I might as well remind her. "Murdering his wife."

As I had no pressing engagement until two thirty, when I was due for a rather dull touch of defrauding the Customs and Excise at the Uxbridge Magistrates' Court, I loitered on my way to the Tube station, walked up through the Temple gardens smoking a small cigar, and went into the clerk's room to complain to Henry of the run-of-the-mill nature of my legal diet.

"No nice murders on the menu, are there?" When I asked him this, Henry smiled in a secretive sort of way and said,

"I'm not sure, sir."

"You're not *sure*?"

"There's a Dr. Henry Dacre phoned to come and see you urgently, sir. It seems his son's in a bit of trouble. He's come with Mr. Cossett, solicitor of Hunter's Hill. I've put them in your room, Mr. Rumpole."

Old Dr. Dacre in my room! I began to sniff the memory of ancient battles and a never-to-be-forgotten victory. When I opened my door, I was greeted by a healthy-looking country solicitor, and a graying version of a witness whose evidence marked a turning point in the Penge Bungalow affair. Dr. Harry Dacre held out his hand and said,

"Mr. Rumpole, It's been a long time, sir."

How long was it, perhaps a legal lifetime, since I did R. *v.* Samuel Poulteny, better known as the Penge Bungalow Murders, which altered the course of legal history by proving that Horace Rumpole could win a

capital case, alone and without a leader? Young Dr. Harry Dacre, then a
G.P. at Penge, gave valuable evidence for the defense, and young
Rumpole made the most of it. I motioned the good doctor to my client's
chair and invited Mr. Cossett, the instructing solicitor, to take a seat.

"Well now, Doctor," I said, "what can I do for you?"

"You may have read about my son's little trouble?" The old doctor
spoke of the charge of wife murder as though it were a touch of the flu
which might be cured by a couple of aspirin and a day in bed.

"Yes. Was it a stormy sort of marriage?" I asked him.

The doctor shook his head.

"Sally was an extraordinarily pretty girl. Terribly spoilt, of course.
Ned gave her everything she wanted."

I wondered if that included a cerebral hemorrhage and then told
myself to keep my mouth shut and listen quietly.

"She had her problems, of course," Dr. Dacre went on. "Nervous
trouble. Well. Half the women in Hunter's Hill have got a touch of the
nervy. All these labor-saving devices in the kitchen, gives them too
much time to think."

Not a pioneer of women's lib, I thought, old Dr. Harry. And I asked
him, "Was she taking anything for her nerves?"

"Sally was scared of pills," the doctor shook his head. "Afraid she
might get hooked, although she didn't mind taking the odd drink too
many."

"Do you think she needed medical treatment?"

"Ned and I discussed it. He thought of a course of treatment but Sally
wouldn't cooperate. So he, well, I suppose he just put up with her." Dr.
Harry seemed to think that no one would have found his daughter-in-law
particularly easy to live with.

"And on, as the prosecutors say, the night in question?" I decided it
was time to get down to the facts.

"Mr. Rumpole! That's why we need you," Dr. Harry said flatteringly
enough. "I know from past experience. You're the man who can destroy
the pathologist's evidence! I'll never forget the Penge Bungalow case,
and the way you pulverized that expert witness for the crown."

I wouldn't have minded a lengthy reminiscence of that memorable
cross-examination, but I felt we should get on with the work in hand.

"Just remind me of the medical evidence. We don't disagree with the
Crown about the cause of death?"

"Cerebral hemorrhage? No doubt about that. But it's the other find-
ings that are the difficulty."

"Which are?"

"Multiple bruising on the body, particularly the legs, back and buttocks, and the wound on the head where the deceased girl fell and knocked the edge of the coffee table."

"Which caused the hemorrhage to the brain?" I frowned. The evidence of bruising was hardly encouraging.

"No doubt about it," Dr. Harry assured me. "The trouble is the pathologist says the bruising was inflicted *before* death; the implication being that my son beat his wife up."

"Is that likely?" It sounded rather unlike the home life of a young professional couple in Hunter's Hill.

"I told you Sally was a spoilt and highly strung girl, Mr. Rumpole." Dr. Harry shrugged. "Her father was old Peter Gaveston of Gaveston Electronics. She always had everything she wanted. Of course she and Ned quarrelled. Don't all married couples?"

Not all married couples, of course, include She Who Must Be Obeyed, but I had reason to believe that the good doctor was right in his diagnosis.

"But Ned would never beat his wife up like that," Ned's father assured me. "Not beat her up to kill her."

It sounded as if I would have to do battle with another pathologist, and I was anxious to find out who my opponent would be.

"Tell me, who's the Miracle of the Morgues, the Prosecution Prince of the Post Mortems? Who's the great brain on the other side?"

"It's a local pathologist. Does all the work in this part of the country."

"Would I have heard of him?" I asked casually.

"It's not a 'him.' It's a Dr. Pamela Gorle. And the irony is, Ned knows her extremely well. They were at Barts together, before he met Sally, of course. He brought her home for the weekend once or twice, and I almost thought they might make a go of it."

"You mean, get married?"

"Yes." Dr. Harry seemed to think that the lady with the formaldehyde might have been a better bet than Sally.

By this time I was beginning to feel some sympathy for Dr. Ned. It's enough to be put on trial for murder without having your ex-girlfriend examine your deceased wife's body, and provide what turns out to be the only real evidence for the prosecution.

"I just don't understand! I simply don't understand it."

Friendly young Dr. Ned sat in the unfriendly surroundings of the prison interview room. He looked concerned but curiously detached, as though he had just hit on a mysterious tropical disease which had no known cure.

"Doctor," I said, "did you and your wife Sally get on moderately well together?"

"We had our quarrels, of course, like all married couples."

It was the second time I had heard that. But, I thought, all married couples don't end up with one dead and the other one in the nick awaiting trial on a charge of wilful murder.

I looked at Dr. Ned. He was better-looking than his father had been at his age; but Dr. Harry, as I remembered his appearance in the Penge Bungalow Murders trial, had seemed the stronger character and more determined. As I looked at the charming, but rather weak younger doctor (after all, he hadn't had to struggle to build up a practice, but had picked up his father's well-warmed stethoscope and married an extremely wealthy young woman) I found it hard to imagine him brutally beating his wife and so killing her. Of course I might have been mistaken; the most savage murder I was ever mixed up in was the axeing of a huge Regimental Sergeant-Major by a five-foot-nothing Sunday school teacher from East Finchley.

"Your father told me that Mrs. Sally Dacre was depressed from time to time. Was she depressed about anything in particular?"

"No. In fact I always thought Sally had everything she wanted."

"But did she suffer from depression?"

"I think so. Yes."

"And took nothing for it?"

"She didn't approve of pills. She'd heard too many stories about people getting hooked. Doctors and their wives."

"So she took nothing?" I wanted to get the facts established.

"My father was her doctor. I thought that was more professional. I'm not sure if he prescribed her anything, but I don't think he did. There was nothing found in the stomach."

He said it casually and seemed only politely concerned. I don't know why I felt a sudden chill at discussing the contents of his dead wife's stomach with the doctor.

"No pills," I agreed with him. "The medical evidence tells us that."

"Dr. Pamela Gorle's report," Dr. Ned went on, still quite dispassionately. I fished out the document in question.

"Yes. It talks of the remains of a meal, and a good deal of alcohol in the blood."

"We had a bottle of Chianti. And a soufflé. We were alone that night. We ate our supper in front of the television."

"Your wife cooked?" I asked, not that there was any question of the food being anything but harmless.

"Oh no." Dr. Ned smiled at me. "I may not be an absolutely brilliant doctor, but my soufflés are nothing short of miraculous."

"Did you quarrel that evening?" I asked him. "I mean, like all married couples?"

"Not at all. We had a discussion about where we'd go for our holiday, and settled on Crete. Sally had never been there, and I had only once. Before we met, actually."

Had that been, I wondered, a romantic packaged fortnight with the pathologist for the Crown? Mine not to reason who with, so I kept him at the job of telling me the story of that last night with his wife.

"And then?"

"Then Sally complained of a headache. I thought it was perhaps due to watching the television for too long, so I switched it off. She was standing up to get herself a brandy."

"And?"

"She stumbled and fell forwards."

"Face *forwards*? Are you sure of that?"

"Yes, I'm certain. It was then that her forehead hit the corner of the coffee table."

"And caused the cerebral hemorrhage?"

Dr. Ned paused, frowning slightly. He seemed to be giving the matter his detached and entirely professional opinion. At last, he said cautiously,

"I can only think so."

"Doctor, your friend, the pathologist . . . ?"

"Hardly my *friend* any longer." Dr. Ned smiled again, ruefully this time, as though he appreciated the irony of having an old colleague and fiancée giving evidence against him on a charge of wilful murder.

"No," I agreed with him. "She isn't your friend, is she? She says she found extensive bruising on your wife's back, her buttocks and the back of her legs."

"That's what I can't understand." My client looked genuinely puzzled.

"You're quite sure she didn't fall backwards?" I asked after a careful silence. Dr. Ned and his wife were quite alone. Who would quarrel with the description of her falling backwards and bruising herself? I had given him his chance. A professional villain, any member of the Timson family for instance, would have taken that hint and agreed with me. But not Dr. Ned.

"No, I told you. She fell forwards." He was either being totally honest or wilfully obtuse.

"And you can't account for the alleged bruises on her back?"

"No." That was all he had to say about it. But then he frowned, in some embarrassment, and said,

"There is one thing perhaps I ought to tell you."

"About your wife?"

"No. About Dr. Pamela Gorle." Again, he hesitated. "We were at Barts together, you know."

"And went to Crete together once, on a packaged holiday."

"How did you know that?" He looked at me, puzzled. It was an inspired guess, so I didn't answer his question. As I am a perpetual optimist, I asked, "Do you think the Crown's expert witness might be a little helpful to us in the witness-box?"

"Not at all. In fact, I'm afraid she'll do everything she can to get me convicted."

As I have said, I am an incorrigible optimist, and for the first time in my conference with Dr. Ned I began to sniff the faint, far-away odor of a defense.

"Pamela was an extraordinarily possessive girl," the doctor told me. "She was always unreasonably and abnormally jealous."

"When you married Sally?"

"When I met Sally. I suppose, well, after that holiday in Crete Pam thought we might get married. Then I didn't ring her and I began to get the most awful letters and phone calls from her. She was threatening . . ."

"Threatening what?"

"It was all very vague. To tell my father, or my patients, or the G.M.C., that she was pregnant."

"Would any of those august bodies have cared?"

"Not in the least. It wasn't true anyway. Then she seemed to calm down for a while, but I still got letters—on my wedding anniversary and on some date which Pamela seemed to think was important."

"Perhaps the day your affair started, or ended?"

"Probably. I really can't remember. She'd got her job with the Home Office, retained as a pathologist for this part of the county. I hoped she might settle down and get married, and forget."

"She never did? Get married, I mean?"

"Or forget. I had a dreadful letter from her about a month ago. She said I'd ruined her life by marrying a hopeless drunk, and that she'd tell Sally we were still meeting unless . . . ''

"Yes?" I prompted him, he seemed reluctant to go on.

"Well. Unless we still met. And continued our affair."

"Did your wife see the letter?"

"No. I always get up early and opened the post."

"You've kept the letter, of course?"

"No. I tore it up at once."

If only people had the sense to realize that they might be facing a murder trial at any moment, they might keep important documents.

"And what did the letter say?"

"That she'd find some way of ruining my life, however long it took her."

Hell, I supposed, hath no fury like a lady pathologist scorned. But Dr. Pamela Gorle's personal interest in the Dacre murder seemed to provide the only faint hope of a cure for Dr. Ned's somewhat desperate situation. I didn't know if a murder case had ever been won by attacking the medical evidence on the grounds of a romantic bias, but I suppose there had to be a first time for everything.

Everything about the Dacre murder trial was thoroughly pleasant. The old, red brick, local Georgian courtroom, an object of beauty among the supermarkets and boutiques and the wine bar and television and radio stores of the little Surrey town, was so damned pleasant that you expected nice girls with Roedean accents to pass round the Court serving coffee and rock cakes whenever there was a lull in the proceedings. The jury looked as though they had dropped in for a rather gentle session of "Gardners' Question Time," and Owen Munroe, Q.C., was a pleasant prosecutor who seemed thoroughly distressed at having to press such a nasty charge as wilful murder against the nice young doctor who sat in the dock wearing his well-pressed suit and old Barts tie.

Worst of all, Nick McManus was a tremendously pleasant judge. He was out to be thoroughly fair and show every courtesy to the defense, ploys which frequently lead to a conviction. It is amazing how many villains owe their freedom to the fact that some old sweetheart on the bench seemed to be determined to get the jury to pot them.

We went quickly, and without argument, through the formal evidence of photographs, fingerprints and the finding of the body, and then my learned friend announced that he intended to call the pathologist.

"Will that be convenient to you, Mr. Rumpole?" The judge, as I have said, was a perfect gent.

"Certainly, my Lord. That will be quite convenient." I made myself perfectly pleasant in return.

"I wish to make quite sure, Mr. Rumpole, that you have every opportunity to prepare yourself to cross-examine the expert witness."

You see what I mean? Old McManus was making sure I would have no alibi if I didn't succeed in cracking Dr. Pamela. I'd've been far better off with someone like the mad Judge Bullingham, charging head-on at the defense. In this very pleasant trial, Rumpole would have no excuses. However, there was no help for it, so I bowed and said,

"I'm quite prepared, my Lord. Thank you."

"Very well. Mr. Munroe, as you are about to call the pathologist . . . "

"Yes, my Lord." My opponent was on his feet.

"I suppose the jury will *have* to look at the photographs of the dead lady?"

"Yes, my Lord. It is Bundle No. 4."

Pictures of a good-looking young woman, naked, bruised, battered and laid on a mortuary slab, are always harrowing and never helpful to the defense. McManus, J., introduced them to the jury quietly, but effectively.

"Members of the jury," said the Judge. "I'm afraid you will find these photographs extremely distressing. It is necessary for you to see them so you may understand the medical evidence fully, but I'm sure counsel will take the matter as shortly as possible. These things are never pleasant."

Death isn't pleasant, nor is murder. In the nicest possible way, the judge was pointing out the horrific nature of the crime of which Dr. Ned was charged. It was something you just didn't do in that part of Surrey.

"I swear by Almighty God that the evidence I shall give shall be the truth, the whole truth and nothing but the truth."

I was aroused from my thoughts by the sound of the pathologist taking her Bible oath. Owen Munroe hitched up his gown, sorted out his papers and started his examination in chief.

"Dr. Pamela Gorle?" he asked.

"Yes."

"Did you examine the body of the late Sally Dacre, the deceased in this case?"

"I did. Yes."

"Just tell us what you found."

"I found a well-nourished, healthy woman of thirty-five years of age who had died from a cerebral hemorrhage. There was evidence of a recent meal." The demure pathologist had a voice ever gentle and low, an excellent thing in a woman, but a bit of a drawback in the witness-box. I had to strain my ears to follow her drift. And unlike the well-nourished and healthy deceased, Dr. Pamela was pale and even uninteresting to look at. Her hair was thin and mousy, she wore a black suit and National Health spectacles behind which her eyes glowed with some obsession. I couldn't be sure whether it was love of her gloomy work or hatred of Dr. Ned.

"You say that you found widespread bruising on the deceased's back and buttocks. What was that consistent with?"

"I thought it was consistent with a violent attack from behind. I thought Mrs. Dacre had probably been struck and kicked by . . . well, it appeared that she was alone that evening with her husband."

"I object!" I had risen to protest, but the perfect gent on the Bench was ahead of me.

"Yes, Mr. Rumpole. And you are perfectly right to do so. Dr. Gorle, it is not for you to say *who* beat this lady and kicked her. That is entirely a matter for the jury. That is why Mr. Rumpole has quite rightly objected."

I wished his Lordship would stop being so lethally pleasant. "But I understand," the judge continued, "that your evidence is that she was kicked and beaten—by *someone*." McManus, J., made it clear that Sally Dacre had been attacked brutally, and the jury could have the undoubted pleasure of saying who did it.

"Yes, my Lord."

"Kicked and beaten!" His Lordship repeated the words for good measure, and after he'd written them down and underlined them with his red pencil, Munroe wound up his examination in chief.

"The immediate cause of death was?"

"A cerebral hemorrhage, as I said!"

"Could you form any opinion as to how that came about?" Munroe asked.

"Just a moment." McManus, J., gave me one of his charming smiles from the Bench. "Have you any objection to her opinion, Mr. Rumpole?"

"My Lord, I wouldn't seek to prevent this witness saying anything she wishes in her effort to implicate my client in his wife's tragic death."

McManus, J., looked slightly puzzled at that, and seemed to wonder if it was an entirely gentlemanly remark. However, he only said, "Very well. Do please answer the question, Dr. Gorle."

"My opinion, my Lord, is that the deceased had received a blow to the head in the course of the attack."

"The attack you have already described?"

"That is so, my Lord."

"Thank you, Dr. Gorle," said Owen Munroe, and sat down with a quietly satisfied air and left the witness to me.

I stood up, horribly conscious that the next quarter of an hour would decide the future of my client. Would Dr. Ned Dacre go back to his pleasant house and practice, or was he fated to vanish into some distant prison only to emerge, pale and unemployable, after ten or more long years? If I couldn't break down the medical evidence our case was hopeless. I stood in the silent Court, shuffling the photographs and the doctor's notes, wondering whether to lead up to my charge of bias gently laying what traps I could on the way, or go in with all my guns blazing. I seemed to stand for a long time undecided, with moist hands and a curious feeling of dread at the responsibility I had undertaken in the pit of my stomach, and then I made a decision. I would start with my best point.

"Dr. Gorle. Just help me. You knew Dr. Ned Dacre well, didn't you?"

The first question had been asked. We'd very soon find out if it were the right one.

"We were at Barts together." Dr. Gorle showed no sign of having been hit amidships.

"And went out together, as the saying is?" I said sweetly.

"Occasionally, yes."

" 'Going out' as so often nowadays meaning 'staying in' together?" I used a slightly louder voice, and was gratified to see that the witness looked distinctly narked.

"What do you mean?"

"Yes. I think you should make that a little clearer, Mr. Rumpole," the Judge intervened, in the pleasantest possible way.

"You and Dr. Ned Dacre went on holiday to Crete together, didn't you? Before he was married?"

There was a distinct pause, and the doctor looked down at the rail of the witness-box as she admitted it.

"Yes. We did."

The dear old "Gardeners' Question Time" fans on the jury looked suddenly interested, as if I had revealed a new and deadly form of potato blight. I pressed on.

"Did you become, what expression would you like me to use, his girlfriend, paramour, mistress?"

"We shared a bed together, yes." Now the pathologist looked up at me, defiant.

"Presumably not for the purpose of revising your anatomy notes together?" I got a small chuckle from the jury which increased the witness's irritation.

"He was my lover. If that's how you want to put it."

"Thank you, Dr. Gorle. I'm sure the members of the jury understand. And I would also like the jury to understand that you became extremely angry when Dr. Ned Dacre got married." There was another long pause, but the answer she came up with was moderately helpful.

"I was disappointed, yes."

"Angry and jealous of the lady whose dead body you examined?" I suggested.

"I suppose I was naturally upset that Ned Dacre had married someone else."

"So upset that you wrote him a letter, only a week or so before this tragedy, in which you told him you wanted to hurt him as much as you possibly could?" Now the jury were entirely hooked. I saw Munroe staring at me, no doubt wondering if I could produce the letter. The witness may have decided that I could, anyway she didn't risk an outright denial.

"I may have done."

"You may have done!" I tried the effect of a passage of fortissimo incredulity. "But by then Dr. Ned Dacre had been married for eight years and his wife had borne him two children. And yet you were still harboring this terrible grudge?"

She answered quickly this time, and with a great intensity.

"There are some things you don't forget, Mr. Rumpole."

"And some things you don't forgive, Dr. Gorle? Has your feeling of jealousy and hatred for my client in any way colored your evidence against him?"

Of course I exected her to deny this. During the course of cross-examination you may angle for useful admissions, hints and half-truths which can come with the cunning cast of a seemingly innocent question. But the time always comes when you must confront the witness with a clear suggestion, a final formality of assertion and denial, when the

subtleties are over. I was surprised, therefore, when the lady from the
morgues found it difficult to answer the question in its simplest form.
There was a prolonged silence.

"Has it, Dr. Gorle?" I pressed her gently for an answer.

Only Dr. Gorle knew if she was biased. If she'd denied the suggestion
hotly no one could have contradicted her. Instead of doing so, she finally
came out with,

"I don't *think* so." And she said it so unconvincingly that I saw the
jury's disapproval. It was the first game to Rumpole, and the witness
seemed to have lost her confidence when I moved on to deal with the
medical evidence. Fortunately a long career as an Old Bailey hack has
given me a working knowledge of the habits of dead bodies.

"Dr. Gorle. After death a body becomes subject to a condition called
'hypostasis'?"

"That is so. Yes."

"The blood drains to the lowest area when circulation ceases?"

"Yes."

"So that if the body has been lying on its back, the blood would
naturally drain to the buttocks and the backs of the legs?"

"That's perfectly right," she answered, now without hesitation.

"Did you say, Mr. Rumpole's right about that?" The Judge was
making a note of the cross-examination.

"Yes, my Lord."

"Yes. Thank you, Doctor." I paused to frame the next question
carefully. "And the draining of the blood causes discoloration of the skin
of a dead body which can *look like bruising*?" I began to get an eerie
feeling that it was all going too well, when the pale lady doctor admitted,
again most helpfully,

"It can look exactly like bruising, yes."

"Therefore it is difficult to tell simply by the color of the skin if a
patch is caused by 'hypostasis' or bruising? It can be very mis-
leading?"

"Yes. It can be."

"So you must insert a knife under the skin to see what has caused the
discoloration, must you not?"

"That is the standard test, yes."

"If some blood flows, it is 'hypostasis,' but if the blood under the skin
has coagulated and does *not* flow, it is probably a bruise?"

"What do you have to say about that, Dr. Gorle?" the Judge asked the
witness, and she came back with a glowing tribute to the amateur
pathologist in the wig.

"I would say, my Lord, that Mr. Rumpole would be well equipped to lecture on forensic medicine."

"That test was carried out in a case called the Penge Bungalow Murders, Dr. Gorle." I disclosed the source of almost all my information, and added a flattering, "no doubt before you were born." I had never got on so well with a hostile witness.

"I'm afraid it was."

"So what happened when you inserted a knife into the colored portions?" I had asked the question in a manner which was almost sickeningly polite, but Dr. Pamela looked greatly shaken. Finally, in a voice of contrition she admitted,

"I didn't."

"What?"

"I didn't carry out that particular test."

"You didn't?" I tried to sound encouragingly neutral to hide my increduilty.

"No."

"Can you tell us *why* not?" the Judge now sounded more like an advocate than the calm, detached Mr. Justice Rumpole.

"I'm afraid that I must have jumped to the conclusion that they were bruises and I didn't trouble to carry out any further test, my Lord."

"You *jumped* to the conclusion?" There was no doubt about it. The courteous McManus was deeply shocked.

"Yes." Dr. Pamela looked paler, and her voice was trembling on the edge of inaudibility.

"You know, Dr. Gorle, the jury aren't going to be asked to convict Dr. Dacre by 'jumping to conclusions.' " I blessed the old darling on the Bench when he said that, and began to see a distinct hope of returning my client to pills and prescriptions in the not-too-distant future.

"My Lord is, of course, perfectly right," I told the witness. "The case against Dr. Ned Dacre has to be proved beyond reasonable doubt, so that the jury are *sure*. Can I take it that you're not sure there were any bruises at all?"

There was a pause and then out came the most beautiful answer.

"Not as you put it now. No. I'm not sure."

Again I had the strange feeling that it was too easy. I felt like a toreador poised for a life-and-death struggle, seeing instead the ring doors open to admit a rather gentle and obedient cow.

"I'm not *sure* there were any bruises," His Lordship repeated to himself as he wrote it down in his note.

"And so you're not sure Mrs. Dacre was attacked by anyone?" It was a question I would normally have avoided. With this witness, it seemed I could dare anything.

"I can't be sure. No."

And again, the Judge wrote it down.

"So she may simply have stumbled, hit her head against the coffee table, and died of a cerebral hemorrhage?"

"It might have happened in that way. Yes." Dr. Gorle was giving it to me with jam on it.

"Stumbled because she had had too much to drink?"

The cooperative witness turned to the Judge.

"Her blood alcohol level was considerably above the breathalyzer limit, yes, my Lord."

"And you knew this family?"

"I knew about them. Yes."

"And was it not one of your complaints that, in marrying Sally, Dr. Ned had married a drunk?"

"I did say that in my letter."

"The sort of girl who might drink too much wine, stumble against a chromium coffee table, hit her head and receive a cerebral hemorrhage, *by accident*?" It was the full frontal question, but I felt no embarrassment now in asking it. The Judge was also keen on getting an answer and said,

"Well, Dr. Gorle?"

"I must admit it might've happened that way. Yes."

It was all over then, bar the odd bit of shouting. I said, "Thank you very much, Dr. Pamela Gorle." And meant it. It was game, set and match to Rumpole. We had a bit of legal argument between counsel and then I was intoxicated by the delightful sensation of winning. The pleasant Judge told the jury that, in view of the concessions made by the expert witness, there really was no evidence on which they could possibly convict the good doctor, and directed them to stop the case and pronounce those two words which are always music to Rumpole's ears, "Not guilty." We all went out in to the corridor and loyal patients came to shake Ned's hand and congratulate him as politely as if he'd just won first prize for growing the longest leek.

"Mr. Rumpole. I knew you'd come up trumps, sir. I shall never forget this, never!" Old Dr. Harry was pumping my hand, slapping my shoulder, and I thought I saw tears in his eyes. But then I looked across the crowd, at a door through which the expert witness, the Crown's pathologist, Dr. Pamela Gorle had just appeared. She was smiling at Dr. Ned and, unless I was very much mistaken, he was smiling back. Was it only a smile, or did I detect the tremble of a wink? I left his father and went up to the young doctor. He smiled his undying gratitude.

"Mr. Rumpole. Dad was right. You're the best!" Dr. Ned was kind enough to say.

"Nonsense. It was easy." I looked at him and said, "Too easy."

"Why do you say that?" Dr. Ned looked genuinely puzzled.

I didn't answer him. Instead, I asked a question.

"I was meaning to ask you this before, Doctor. I don't suppose it matters now, but I'd like to know the answer, for my own satisfaction. What sort of soufflé was it you cooked for your wife that evening?" He might have lied, but I don't suppose he thought there was any point in it. Instead he answered as if he enjoyed telling the truth.

"Cheese."

I was at breakfast with She Who Must Be Obeyed a few days later, after I had managed to spring the charming young doctor, and my wife was brandishing another mauve letter from her friend Dorothy or "Do do," the nervous tea-shop owner from the West Country.

"Another letter from Dodo! She's really feeling much better. So much more calm!"

"She's been taking these new pills, didn't you say?"

"Yes, I think that's what it must be."

I remembered about a drug Dr. Ned was discussing with his father for possible use on his nervous wife. Was it the same drug that was keeping Dodo off cheese?

"Then Dodo will be feeling better. So long as she doesn't eat cheese. If she eats cheese when she's on some sort of tranquillizer she's likely to go the way of the doctor's beautiful wife, and end up with a hemorrhage of the brain."

I had a letter too. An invitation to a cocktail party in Hunter's Hill. Dr. Ned Dacre, it seemed, felt that he had something to celebrate.

"Mr. Rumpole! I'm so glad you could come." Dr. Ned greeted me enthusiastically.

I looked round the pleasant room, at the pleasant faces of grateful patients and the two thoroughly nice children handing round canapés. I noticed the Queen of the Morgues, Dr. Pamela Gorle, dressed up to the nines, and then I looked at the nice young doctor who was now pouring me out a generous Buck's Fizz made, regardless of the expense, with the best Krug. I spoke to him quietly.

"You got off, of course. They can't try you again for the same murder. That was the arrangement, wasn't it?"

"What 'arrangement'?" The young doctor was still smiling in a welcoming sort of way.

"Oh, the arrangement between you and the Crown pathologist, of course. The plan that she'd make some rather silly suggestions about bruises and admit she was wrong. Of course, she lied about the contents of the stomach. You're a very careful young man, Dr. Ned. Now they can never try you for what you really did."

"You're joking!" But I saw that he had stopped smiling.

"I was never more serious in my life."

"What did I really do?" We seemed to be alone. A little whispering oasis of doubt and suspicion in the middle of the happy, chattering cocktail party. I told him what he'd done.

"You opened a few of those new tranquillizer capsules and poured them into your wife's Chianti. The cheese in the soufflé reacted in just the way you'd planned. All you had to do was make sure she hit her head on the table."

We stood in silence. The children came up and we refused canapés. Then Dr. Ned opened an alabaster box and lit a cigarette with a gold lighter.

"What're you going to do about it?" I could see that he was smiling again.

"Nothing I can do now. You know that," I told him. "Except to tell you that I know. I'm not quite the idiot you and Dr. Pamela took me for. At least you know that, Dr. Ned."

He was a murderer. Divorce would have given him freedom but not his rich wife's money; so he became a simple, old-fashioned murderer. And what was almost worse, he had used me as part of his crime. Worst of all, he had done his best to spoil the golden memory of the Penge Bungalow Murders for me.

"Quiet everyone! I think Ned's got something to say!" Old Dr. Harry Dacre was banging on a table with his glass. In due course quiet settled on the party and young Dr. Ned made his announcement.

"I just wanted to say. Now all our friends are here. Under one roof. That of course no one can ever replace Sally. For me and the children. But with Simon and Sara's approval . . . " He smiled at his charming children. "There's going to be another doctor in the Dacre family. Pamela's agreed to become my wife."

In the ensuing clapping, kisses, congratulations and mixing of more Buck's Fizz, Rumpole left the party.

I hear it was a thoroughly nice wedding. I looked hard at the photograph in the paper and tried to detect in that open and smiling young doctor's face, a sign of guilt.

> *. . . that perilous stuff*
> *Which weighs upon the heart.*

I saw none.

The Saint

THE MAN WHO LIKED TOYS
Leslie Charteris

CHIEF INSPECTOR CLAUD Eustace Teal rested his pudgy elbows on the table and unfolded the pink wrapping from a fresh wafer of chewing gum.

"That's all there was to it," he said. "And that's the way it always is. You get an idea, you spread a net out among the stool pigeons, and you catch a man. Then you do a lot of dull routine work to build up the evidence. That's how a real detective does his job; and that's the way Sherlock Holmes would have had to do it if he'd worked at Scotland Yard."

Simon Templar grinned amiably, and beckoned a waiter for the bill. The orchestra yawned and went into another dance number; but the floor show had been over for half an hour, and Dora's Curfew was hurrying the drinks off the tables. It was two o'clock in the morning, and a fair proportion of the patrons of the Palace Royal had some work to think of before the next midnight.

"Maybe you're right, Claud," said the Saint mildly.

"I know I'm right," said Mr. Teal, in his drowsy voice. And then, as Simon pushed a fiver on to the plate, he chuckled. "But I know you like pulling our legs about it, too."

They steered their way round the tables and up the stairs to the hotel lobby. It was another of those rare occasions when Mr. Teal had been able to enjoy the Saint's company without any lurking uneasiness about the outcome. For some weeks his life had been comparatively peaceful. No hints of further Saintly lawlessness had come to his ears; and at such times he admitted to himself, with a trace of genuine surprise, that there were few things which entertained him more than a social evening with the gay buccaneer who had set Scotland Yard more mysteries than they would ever solve.

"Drop in and see me next time I'm working on a case, Saint," Teal said in the lobby, with a truly staggering generosity for which the wine must have been partly responsible. "You'll see for yourself how we really do it."

"I'd like to," said the Saint; and if there was the trace of a smile in his eyes when he said it, it was entirely without malice.

He settled his soft hat on his smooth dark head and glanced round the lobby with the vague aimlessness which ordinarily precedes a parting at that hour. A little group of three men had discharged themselves from a near-by lift and were moving boisterously and a trifle unsteadily towards the main entrance. Two of them were hatted and overcoated—a tallish man with a thin line of black moustache, and a tubby red-faced man with rimless spectacles. The third member of the party, who appeared to be the host, was a flabby flatfooted man of about fifty-five with a round bald head and a rather bulbous nose that would have persuaded any observant onlooker to expect that he would have drunk more than the others, which in fact he obviously had. All of them had the dishevelled and rather tragically ridiculous air of Captains of Industry who have gone off duty for the evening.

"That's Lewis Enstone—the chap with the nose," said Teal, who knew everyone. "He might have been one of the biggest men in the City if he could have kept off the bottle."

"And the other two?" asked the Saint incuriously, because he already knew.

"Just a couple of smaller men in the same game. Abe Costello—that's the tall one—and Jules Hammel." Mr. Teal chewed meditatively on his spearmint. "If anything ever happens to them, I shall want to know where you were at the time," he added warningly.

"I shan't know anything about it," said the Saint piously.

He lighted a cigarette and watched the trio of celebrators disinterestedly. Hammel and Costello he knew something about from the untimely reincarnation of Mr. Titus Oates; but the more sozzled member of the party was new to him.

"You do unnerstan', boys, don't you?" Enstone was articulating pathetically, with his arms spread around the shoulders of his guests in an affectionate manner which contributed helpfully towards his support. "It's jus' business. I'm not hard-hearted. I'm kind to my wife an' children an' everything, God bless 'em. An' any time I can do anything for either of you—why, you jus' lemme know."

"That's awfully good of you, old man," said Hammel, with the blurry-eyed solemnity of his condition.

"Less have lunch together on Tuesday," suggested Costello. "We might be able to talk about something that'd interest you."

"Right," said Enstone dimly. "Lush Tooshday. Hic."

"An' don't forget the kids," said Hammel confidentially.

Enstone giggled.

"I shouldn't forget that!" In obscurely elaborate pantomine, he closed his fist with his forefinger extended and his thumb cocked vertically upwards, and aimed the forefinger between Hammel's eyes. "Schtick 'em up!" he commanded gravely, and at once relapsed into further merriment, in which his guest joined somewhat hysterically.

The group separated at the entrance amid much handshaking and back-slapping and alcoholic laugher; and Lewis Enstone wended his way back with cautious and preoccupied steps towards the lift. Mr. Teal took a fresh bite on his gum and tightened his mouth disgustedly.

"Is he staying here?" asked the Saint.

"He lives here," said the detective. "He's lived here even when we knew for a fact that he hadn't got a penny to his name. Why, I remember once—"

He launched into a lengthy anecdote which had all the vitality of personal bitterness in the telling. Simon Templar, listening with the half of one well-trained ear that would prick up into instant attention if the story took any twist that might provide the germ of an adventure, but would remain intently passive if it didn't, smoked his cigarette and gazed abstractedly into space. His mind had that gift of complete division; and he had another job on hand to think about. Somewhere in the course of the story he gathered that Mr. Teal had once lost some money on the Stock Exchange over some shares in which Enstone was speculating; but there was nothing much about that misfortune to attract his interest, and the detective's mood of disparaging reminiscence was as good an opportunity as any other for him to plot out a few details of the campaign against his latest quarry.

" . . . So I lost half my money, and I've kept the rest of it in gilt-edged stuff ever since," concluded Mr. Teal rancorously; and Simon took the last inhalation from his cigarette and dropped the stub into an ashtray.

"Thanks for the tip, Claud," he said lightly. "I gather that next time I murder somebody you'd like me to make it a financier."

Teal grunted, and hitched his coat round.

"I shouldn't like you to murder anybody," he said, from his heart. "Now I've got to go home—I have to get up in the morning."

They walked towards the street doors. On their left they passed the information desk; and beside the desk had been standing a couple of bored and sleepy page-boys. Simon had observed them and their sleepiness as casually as he had observed the color of the carpet, but all at once he realized that their sleepiness had vanished. He had a sudden queer sensitiveness of suppressed excitement; and then one of the boys said something loud enough to be overheard which stopped Teal in his tracks and turned him round abruptly.

"What's that?" he demanded.

"It's Mr. Enstone, sir. He just shot himself."

Mr. Teal scowled. To the newspapers it would be a surprise and a front-page sensation: to him it was a surprise and a potential menace to his night's rest if he butted into any responsibility. Then he shrugged.

"I'd better have a look," he said, and introduced himself.

There was a scurry to lead him towards the lift. Mr. Teal ambled bulkily into the nearest car, and quite brazenly the Saint followed him. He had, after all, been kindly invited to "drop in" the next time the plump detective was handling a case . . . Teal put his hands in his pockets and stared in mountainous drowsiness at the downward-flying shaft. Simon studiously avoided his eye, and had a pleasant shock when the detective addressed him almost genially.

"I always thought there was something fishy about that fellow. Did he look as if he'd anything to shoot himself about, except the head that was waiting for him when he woke up?"

It was as if the decease of any financier, however caused, was a benison upon the earth for which Mr. Teal could not help being secretly and quite immorally grateful. That was the subtle impression he gave of his private feelings; but the rest of him was impenetrable stolidity and aloofness. He dismissed the escort of page-boys and strode to the door of the millionaire's suite. It was closed and silent. Teal knocked on it authoritatively, and after a moment it opened six inches and disclosed a pale agitated face. Teal introduced himself again and the door opened wider, enlarging the agitated face into the unmistakable full-length portrait of an assistant hotel manager. Simon followed the detective in, endeavoring to look equally official.

"This will be a terrible scandal, Inspector," said the assistant manager.

Teal looked at him woodenly.

"Were you here when it happened?"

"No. I was downstairs, in my office—"

Teal collected the information, and ploughed past him. On the right, another door opened off the generous lobby; and through it could be seen another elderly man whose equally pale face and air of suppressed agitation bore a certain general similarity and also a self-contained superiority to the first. Even without his sober black coat and striped trousers, gray-whiskers and passive hands, he would have stamped himself as something more cosmic than the assistant manager of an hotel—the assistant manager of a man.

"Who are you?" asked Teal.

"I am Fowler, sir. Mr. Enstone's valet."

"Were you here?"

"Yes, sir."

"Where is Mr. Enstone?"

"In the bedroom, sir."

They moved back across the lobby, with the assistant manager assuming the lead. Teal stopped. "Will you be in your office if I want you?" he asked with great politeness; and the assistant manager seemed to disappear from the scene even before the door of the suite closed behind him.

Lewis Enstone was dead. He lay on his back beside the bed, with his head half rolled over to one side, in such a way that both the entrance and the exit of the bullet which had killed him could be seen. It had been fired squarely into his right eye, leaving the ugly trail only a heavy-calibre bullet fired at close range can leave . . . The gun lay under the fingers of his right hand.

"Thumb on the trigger," Teal noted aloud.

He sat on the edge of the bed, pulling on a pair of gloves, pink-faced and unemotional. Simon observed the room. An ordinary, very tidy bedroom, barren of anything unusual except the subdued costliness of furnishing. Two windows, both shut and fastened. On a table in one corner, the only sign of disorder, the remains of a carelessly opened parcel. Brown paper, ends of string, a plain cardboard box—empty. The millionaire had gone no further towards undressing than loosening his tie and undoing his collar.

"What happened?" asked Mr. Teal.

"Mr. Enstone had had friends to dinner, sir," explained Fowler. "A Mr. Costello—"

"I know that. What happened when he came back from seeing them off?"

"He went straight off to bed, sir."

"Was this door open?"

"At first, sir. I asked Mr. Enstone about the morning, and he told me to call him at eight. I then asked him whether he wished me to assist him to undress, and he gave me to understand that he did not. He closed the door, and I went back to the sitting-room."

"Did you leave that door open?"

"Yes, sir. I was doing a little clearing up. Then I heard the shot, sir."

"Do you know any reason why Mr. Enstone should have shot himself?"

"On the contrary, sir—I understood that his recent speculations had been highly successful."

Teal nodded.

"Where is his wife?"

"Mrs. Enstone and the children have been in Madeira, sir. We are expecting them home tomorrow."

"What was in that parcel, Fowler?" ventured the Saint.

The valet glanced at the table.

"I don't know, sir. I believe it must have been left by one of Mr. Enstone's guests. I noticed it on the dining-table when I brought in their coats, and Mr. Enstone came back for it on his return and took it into the bedroom with him."

"You didn't hear anything said about it?"

"No, sir. I was not present after coffee had been served—I understood that the gentlemen had private business to discuss."

"What are you getting at?" Mr. Teal asked seriously.

The Saint smiled apologetically; and being nearest the door, went out to open it as a second knocking disturbed the silence, and let in a gray-haired man with a black bag. While the police surgeon was making his preliminary examination, he drifted into the sitting-room. The relics of a convivial dinner were all there—cigar-butts in the coffee cups, stains of spilt wine on the cloth, crumbs and ash everywhere, the stale smell of food and smoke hanging in the air—but those things did not interest him. He was not quite sure what would have interested him; but he wandered rather vacantly round the room, gazing introspectively at the prints of character which a long tenancy leaves even on anything so characterless as an hotel apartment. There were pictures on the walls and the side tables, mostly enlarged snapshots revealing Lewis Enstone relaxing in the bosom of his family, which amused Simon for some time. On one of the side tables he found a curious object. It was a small wooden plate on which half a dozen wooden fowls stood in a circle. Their necks were pivoted at the base, and undernearth the plate were six short strings joined to the necks and knotted together some distance further down where they were all attached at the same point to a wooden ball. It was these strings, and the weight of the ball at their lower ends, which kept the birds' heads raised; and Simon discovered that when he moved the plate so that the ball swung round in a circle underneath, thus tightening and slackening each string in turn, the fowls mounted on the plate pecked vigorously in rotation at an invisible and apparently inexhaustible supply of corn, in a most ingenious mechanical display of gluttony.

He was still playing thoughtfully with the toy when he discovered Mr. Teal standing beside him. The detective's round pink face wore a look of almost comical incredulity.

"Is that how you spend your spare time?" he demanded.

"I think it's rather clever," said the Saint soberly. He put the toy down, and blinked at Fowler. "Does it belong to one of the children?"

"Mr. Enstone brought it home with him this evening, sir, to give to Miss Annabel tomorrow," said the valet. "He was always picking up things like that. He was a very devoted father, sir."

Mr. Teal chewed for a moment; and then he said: "Have you finished? I'm going home."

Simon nodded pacifically, and accompanied him to the lift. As they went down he asked: "Did you find anything?"

Teal blinked.

"What did you expect me to find?"

"I thought the police were always believed to have a Clue," murmured the Saint innocently.

"Enstone committed suicide," said Teal flatly. "What sort of clues do you want?"

"Why did he commit suicide?" asked the Saint, almost childishly.

Teal ruminated meditatively for a while, without answering. If anyone else had started such a discussion he would have been openly derisive. The same impulse was stirring him then; but he restrained himself. He knew Simon Templar's wicked sense of humor, but he also knew that sometimes the Saint was most worth listening to when he sounded most absurd.

"Call me up in the morning," said Mr. Teal at length, "and I may be able to tell you."

Simon Templar went home and slept fitfully. Lewis Enstone had shot himself—it seemed an obvious fact. The windows had been closed and fastened, and any complicated trick of fastening them from the outside and escaping up or down a rope-ladder was ruled out by the bare two or three seconds that could have elapsed between the sound of the shot and the valet rushing in. But Fowler himself might . . . Why not suicide, anyway? But the Saint could run over every word and gesture and expression of the leave-taking which he himself had witnessed in the hotel lobby, and none of it carried even a hint of suicide. The only oddity about it had been the queer inexplicable piece of pantomime—the fist clenched, with the forefinger extended and the thumb cocked up in crude symbolism of a gun—the abstruse joke which had dissolved Enstone into a fit of inanely delighted giggling, with the hearty approval of his guests. . . . The psychological problem fascinated him. It muddled itself up with a litter of brown paper and cardboard box, a wooden plate of pecking chickens, photographs . . . and the tangle kaleidoscoped through his dreams in a thousand different convolutions until morning.

At half-past twelve he found himself turning on to the Embankment with every expectation of being told that Mr. Teal was too busy to see him; but he was shown up a couple of minutes after he had sent in his name.

"Have you found out why Enstone committed suicide?" he asked.

"I haven't," said Teal, somewhat shortly. "His brokers say it's true that he'd been speculating successfully. Perhaps he had another account with a different firm which wasn't so lucky. We'll find out."

"Have you seen Costello or Hammel?"

"I've asked them to come and see me. They're due here about now."

Teal picked up a typewritten memorandum and studied it absorbedly. He would have liked to ask some questions in his turn, but he didn't. He had failed lamentably, so far, to establish any reason whatsoever why Enstone should have committed suicide; and he was annoyed. He felt a personal grievance against the Saint for raising the question without also taking steps to answer it, but pride forbade him to ask for enlightenment. Simon lighted a cigarette and smoked imperturbably until in a few minutes Costello and Hammel were announced. Teal stared at the Saint thoughtfully while the witnesses were seating themselves, but strangely enough he said nothing to intimate that police interviews were not open to outside audiences.

Presently he turned to the tall man with the thin black moustache.

"We're trying to find a reason for Enstone's suicide, Mr. Costello," he said. "How long have you known him?"

"About eight or nine years."

"Have you any idea why he should have shot himself?"

"None at all, Inspector. It was a great shock. He had been making more money than most of us. When we were with him last night, he was in very high spirits—his family was on the way home, and he was always happy when he was looking forward to seeing them again."

"Did you ever lose money in any of his companies?"

"No."

"You know that we can investigate that?"

Costello smiled slightly.

"I don't know why you should take that attitude, Inspector, but my affairs are open to any examination."

"Have you been making money yourself lately?"

"No. As a matter of fact, I've lost a bit," said Costello frankly. "I'm interested in International Cotton, you know."

He took out a cigarette and a lighter and Simon found his eyes riveted on the device. It was of an uncommon shape, and by some means or other it produced a glowing heat instead of a flame. Quite unconscious of his own temerity, the Saint said: "That's something new, isn't it? I've never seen a lighter like that before."

Mr. Teal sat back blankly and gave the Saint a look which would have shrivelled any other interrupter to a cinder; and Costello turned the lighter over and said: "It's an invention of my own—I made it myself."

"I wish I could do things like that," said the Saint admiringly. "I suppose you must have had a technical training."

Costello hesitated for a second. Then:

"I started in an electrical engineering workshop when I was a boy," he explained briefly, and turned back to Teal's desk.

After a considerable pause the detective turned to the tubby man with glasses, who had been sitting without any signs of life except the ceaseless switching of his eyes from one speaker to another.

"Are you in partnership with Mr. Costello, Mr. Hammel?" he asked.

"A working partnership—yes."

"Do you know any more about Enstone's affairs than Mr. Costello has been able to tell us?"

"I'm afraid not."

"What were you talking about at dinner last night?"

"It was about a merger. I'm in International Cotton, too. One of Enstone's concerns was Cosmopolitan Textiles. His shares were standing high and ours aren't doing too well, and we thought that if we could induce him to amalgamate it would help us."

"What did Enstone think about that?"

Hammel spread his hands.

"He didn't think there was enough in it for him. We had certain things to offer, but he decided they weren't sufficient."

"There wasn't any bad feeling about it?"

"Why, no. If all the business men who have refused to combine with each other at different times became enemies, there'd hardly be two men in the City on speaking terms."

Simon cleared his throat.

"What was your first important job, Mr. Hammel?" he queried.

Hammel turned his eyes without moving his head.

"I was chief salesman of a general manufacturer in the Midlands."

Teal concluded the interview soon afterwards without securing any further revelations, shook hands perfunctorily with the two men, and ushered them out. When he came back he looked down at the Saint like a cannibal inspecting the latest missionary.

"Why don't you join the force yourself?" he inquired heavily. "The new Police College is open now, and the Commissioner's supposed to be looking for men like you."

Simon took the sally like an armored car taking a snowball. He was sitting up on the edge of his chair with his blue eyes glinting with excitement.

"You big sap," he retorted, "do you look as if the Police College could teach anyone to solve a murder?"

Teal gulped as if he couldn't believe his ears. He took hold of the arms of the chair and spoke with apoplectic restraint, as if he were conscientiously determined to give the Saint every fair chance to recover his sanity before he rang down for the bugs wagon.

"What murder are you talking about?" he demanded. "Enstone shot himself."

"Yes, Enstone shot himself," said the Saint. "But it was murder just the same."

"Have you been drinking something?"

"No. But Enstone had."

Teal swallowed, and almost choked himself in the process.

"Are you trying to tell me," he exploded, "that any man ever got drunk enough to shoot himself while he was making money?"

Simon shook his head.

"They made him shoot himself."

"What do you mean—blackmail?"

"No."

The Saint pushed a hand through his hair. He had thought of things like that. He knew that Enstone had shot himself, because no one else could have done it. Except Fowler, the valet—but that was the man whom Teal would have suspected at once if he had suspected anyone, and it was too obvious, too insane. No man in his senses could have planned a murder with himself as the most obvious suspect. Blackmail, then? But the Lewis Enstone he had seen in the lobby had never looked like a man bidding farewell to blackmailers. And how could a man so openly devoted to his family have been led to provide the commoner materials of blackmail?

"No, Claud," said the Saint. "It wasn't that. They just made him do it."

Mr. Teal's spine tingled with the involuntary reflex chill that has its roots in man's immemorial fear of the supernatural. The Saint's conviction was so wild and yet real that for one fantastic moment the detective had a vision of Costello's intense black eyes fixed and dilating in a hypnotic stare, his slender sensitive hands moving in weird passes, his lips under the thin black moustache mouthing necromantic commands. . . . It changed into another equally fantastic vision of two courteous but inflexible gentlemen handing a weapon to a third, bowing and going away, like a deputation to an officer who has been found to be a traitor, offering the graceful alternative to a court-martial—for the Honour of High Finance. . . . Then it went sheer to derision.

"They just said: 'Lew, why don't you shoot yourself?' and he thought it was a great idea—is that it?" he gibed.

"It was something like that," Simon answered soberly. "You see, Enstone would do almost anything to amuse his children."

Teal's mouth opened, but no sounds came from it. His expression implied that a whole volcano of devastating sarcasm was boiling on the tip of his tongue, but that the Saint's lunacy had soared into the realms of waffiness beyond the reach of repartee.

"Costello and Hammel had to do something," said the Saint. "International Cottons have been very bad for a long time—as you'd have known if you hadn't packed all your stuff away in a gilt-edged sock. On the other hand, Enstone's interest—Cosmopolitan Textiles—were good. Costello and Hammel could have pulled out in two ways: either by a merger, or else by having Enstone commit suicide so that Cosmopolitans would tumble down in the scare and they could buy them in—you'll probably find they've sold a bear in them all through the month, trying to break the price. And if you look at the papers this afternoon you'll see that all Enstone's securities have dropped through the bottom of the market—a bloke in his position can't commit suicide without starting a panic. Costello and Hammel went to dinner to try for the merger, but if Enstone turned it down they were ready for the other thing.''

''Well?'' said Teal obstinately; but for the first time there seemed to be a tremor in the foundations of his disbelief.

''They only made one big mistake. They didn't arrange for Lew to leave a letter.''

''People have shot themselves without leaving letters.''

''I know. But not often. That's what started me thinking.''

''Well?'' said the detective again.

Simon rumpled his hair into more profound disorder, and said: ''You see, Claud, in my disreputable line of business you're always thinking: 'Now, what would A do?—and what would B do?—and what would C do?' You have to be able to get inside people's minds and know what they're going to do and how they're going to do it, so you can always be one jump ahead of 'em. You have to be a practical psychologist—just like the head salesman of a general manufacturer in the Midlands.''

Teal's mouth opened, but for some reason which was beyond his conscious comprehension he said nothing. And Simon Templar went on, in the disjointed way that he sometimes fell into when he was trying to express something which he himself had not yet grasped in bare words:

''Sales psychology is just the study of human weaknesses. And that's a funny thing, you know. I remember the manager of one of the biggest novelty manufacturers in the world telling me that the soundest test of any idea for a new toy was whether it would appeal to a middle-aged business man. It's true, of course. It's so true that it's almost stopped being a joke—the father who plays with his little boy's birthday presents so energetically that the little boy has to shove off and smoke papa's pipe. Every middle-aged business man has that strain of childishness in him somewhere, because without it he would never want to spend his life gathering more paper millions than he can ever spend, and building up rickety castles of golden cards that are always ready to topple over and be built up again. It's just a glorified kid's game with a box of bricks. If all the mighty earth-shaking business men weren't like that they could never have built up an economic system in which the fate of nations, all the hunger and happiness and achievement of the world, was locked up in bars of yellow tooth-stopping.'' Simon raised his eyes suddenly—they were very bright and in some queer fashion sightless, as if his mind was separated from every physical awareness of his surroundings. "Lewis Enstone was just that kind of a man," he said.

"Are you still thinking of that toy you were playing with," Teal asked restlessly.

"That—and the other things we heard. And the photographs. Did you notice them?"

"No."

"One of them was Enstone playing with a clockwork train. In another of them he was under a rug, being a bear. In another he was working a big model merry-go-round. Most of the pictures were like that. The children came into them, of course, but you could see that Enstone was having the swellest time."

Teal, who had been fidgeting with a pencil, shrugged brusquely and sent it clattering across the desk.

"You still haven't shown me a murder," he stated.

"I had to find it myself," said the Saint gently. "You see, it was a kind of professional problem. Enstone was happily married, happy with his family, no more crooked than any other big-time financier, nothing on his conscience, rich and getting richer—how were they to make him commit suicide? If I'd been writing a story with him in it, for instance, how could I have made him commit suicide?"

"You'd have told him he had cancer," said Teal caustically, "and he'd have fallen for it."

Simon shook his head.

"No. If I'd been a doctor—perhaps. But if Costello or Hammel had suggested it, he'd have wanted confirmation. And did he look like a man who'd just been told that he might have cancer?"

"It's your murder," said Mr. Teal, with the beginnings of a drowsy tolerance that was transparently rooted in sheer resignation. "I'll let you solve it."

"There were lots of pieces missing at first," said the Saint. "I only had Enstone's character and weaknesses. And then it came out— Hammel was a psychologist. That was good, because I'm a bit of a psychologist myself, and his mind would work something like mine. And then Costello could invent mechanical gadgets and make them himself. He shouldn't have fetched out that lighter, Claud—it gave me another of the missing pieces. And then there was the box."

"Which box?"

"The cardboard box—on his table, with the brown paper. You know Fowler said that he thought either Hammel or Costello left it. Have you got it here?"

"I expect it's somewhere in the building."

"Could we have it up?"

With the gesture of a blasé hangman reaching for the noose, Teal took hold of the telephone on his desk.

"You can have the gun, too, if you like," he said.

"Thanks," said the Saint. "I wanted the gun."

Teal gave the order; and they sat and looked at each other in silence until the exhibits arrived. Teal's silence explained in fifty different ways that the Saint would be refused no facilities for nailing down his coffin in a manner that he would never be allowed to forget; but for some reason his facial register was not wholly convincing. When they were alone again, Simon went to the desk, picked up the gun, and put it in the box. It fitted very well.

"That's what happened, Claud," he said with quiet triumph. "They gave him the gun in the box."

"And he shot himself without knowing what he was doing," Teal said witheringly.

"That's just it," said the Saint, with a blue devil of mockery in his gaze. "He didn't know what he was doing."

Mr. Teal's molars clamped down cruelly on the inoffensive merchandise of the Wrigley Corporation.

"Well, what did he *think* he was doing—sitting under a rug pretending to be a bear?"

Simon sighed.

"That's what I'm trying to work out."

Teal's chair creaked as his full weight slumped back in it in hopeless exasperation.

"Is that what you've been taking up so much of my time about?" he asked wearily.

"But I've got an idea, Claud," said the Saint, getting up and stretching himself. "Come out and lunch with me, and let's give it a rest. You've been thinking for nearly an hour, and I don't want your brain to overheat. I know a new place—wait, I'll look up the address."

He looked it up in the telephone directory; and Mr. Teal got up and took down his bowler hat from its peg. His baby blue eyes were inscrutably thoughtful, but he followed the Saint without thought. Whatever else the Saint wanted to say, however crazy he felt it must be, it was something he had to hear or else fret over for the rest of his days. They drove in a taxi to Knightsbridge, with Mr. Teal chewing phlegmatically, in a superb affectation of bored unconcern. Presently the taxi stopped, and Simon climbed out. He led the way into an apartment building and into a lift, saying something to the operator which Teal did not catch.

"What is this?" he asked, as they shot upwards. "A new restaurant?"

"It's a new place," said the Saint vaguely.

The elevator stopped, and they got out. They went along the corridor, and Simon rang the bell of one of the doors. It was opened by a good-looking maid who might have been other things in her spare time.

"Scotland Yard," said the Saint brazenly, and squeezed past her. He found his way into the sitting-room before anyone could stop him: Chief Inspector Teal, recovering from the momentary paralysis of the shock, followed him: then came the maid.

"I'm sorry, sir—Mr. Costello is out."

Teal's bulk obscured her. All the boredom had smudged itself off his face, giving place to blank amazement and anger.

"What the devil's this joke?" he blared.

"It isn't a joke, Claud," said the Saint recklessly. "I just wanted to see if I could find something—you know what we were talking about—"

His keen gaze was quartering the room; and then it lighted on a big cheap kneehole desk whose well-worn shabbiness looked strangely out of keeping with the other furniture. On it was a litter of coils and wire and ebonite and dials—all the junk out of which amateur wireless sets are created. Simon reached the desk in his next stride, and began pulling open the drawers. Tools of all kinds, various gauges of wire and screws, odd wheels and sleeves and bolts and scraps of sheet-iron and brass, the completely typical hoard of any amateur mechanic's workshop. Then he came to a drawer that was locked. Without hesitation he caught up a large screwdriver and rammed it in above the lock: before anyone could grasp his intentions he had splintered the drawer open with a skillful twist.

Teal let out a shout and started across the room. Simon's hand dived into the drawer, came out with a nickel-plated revolver—it was exactly the same as the one with which Lewis Enstone had shot himself, but Teal wasn't noticing things like that. His impression was the Saint really had gone raving mad after all, and the sight of the gun pulled him up for a moment as the sight of a gun in the hands of any other raving maniac would have pulled him up.

"Put that down, you fool!" he yelled, and then he let out another shout as he saw the Saint turn the muzzle of the gun close up to his right eye, with his thumb on the trigger, exactly as Enstone must have held it. Teal lurched forward and knocked the weapon aside with a sweep of his arm; then he grabbed Simon by the wrist. "That's enough of that," he said, without realizing what a futile thing it was to say.

Simon looked at him and smiled.

"Thanks for saving my life, old beetroot," he murmured kindly. "But it really wasn't necessary. You see, Claud, that's the gun Enstone *thought* he was playing with!"

The maid was under the table letting out the opening note of a magnificent fit of hysterics. Teal let go the Saint, hauled her out, and shook her till she was quiet. There were more events cascading on him in those few seconds than he knew how to cope with, and he was not gentle.

"It's all right, miss," he growled. "I am from Scotland Yard. Just sit down somewhere, will you?" He turned back to Simon. "Now, what's all this about?"

"The gun, Claud. Enstone's toy."

The Saint raised it again—his smile was quite sane, and with the feeling that he himself was the madman, Teal let him do what he wanted. Simon put the gun to his eye and pulled the trigger—pulled it, released it, pulled it again, keeping up the rhythmic movement. Something inside the gun whirred smoothly, as if wheels were whizzing round under the working of the lever. Then he pointed the gun straight into Teal's face and did the same thing.

Teal stared frozenly down the barrel and saw the black hole leap into a circle of light. He was looking at a flickering cinematograph film of a boy shooting a masked burglar. It was tiny, puerile in subject, but perfect. It lasted about ten seconds, and then the barrel went dark again.

"Costello's present for Enstone's little boy," explained the Saint quietly. "He invented it and made it himself, of course—he always had a talent that way. Haven't you ever seen those electric flashlights that work without a battery? You keep on squeezing a lever, and it turns a miniature dynamo. Costello made a very small one, and fitted it into the hollow casting of a gun. Then he geared a tiny strip of film to it. It was a jolly good new toy, Claud Eustace, and he must have been proud of it. They took it along to Enstone's; and when he'd turned down their merger and there was nothing else for them to do, they let him play with it just enough to tickle his palate, at just the right hour of the evening. Then they took it away from him and put it back in its box and gave it to him. They had a real gun in another box ready to make the switch."

Chief Inspector Teal stood like a rock, his jaws clamping a wad of spearmint that he had at last forgotten to chew. Then he said: "How did they know he wouldn't shoot his own son?"

"That was Hammel. He knew that Enstone wasn't capable of keeping his hands off a toy like that; and just to make certain he reminded Enstone of it the last thing before they left. He was a practical psychologist—I suppose we can begin to speak of him in the past tense now." Simon Templar smiled again, and fished a cigarette out of his pocket. "But why I should bother to tell you all this when you could have got it out of a stool pigeon," he murmured, "is more than I can understand. I must be getting soft-hearted in my old age, Claud. After all, when you're so far ahead of Sherlock Holmes—"

Mr. Teal gulped pinkly, and picked up the telephone.

Virgil Tibbs

VIRGIL TIBBS AND THE FALLEN BODY
John Ball

THE FIRST THING Officer Frank Mitchell heard was a violent thud directly behind him; it was so powerful it seemed for a second that the very ground had shaken under his feet. He turned quickly, saw the body scarcely 30 feet away, and had a sudden, compelling desire to be sick. Only seven months out of the academy, he was still not used to the sight of sudden and violent death.

The body of the suicide, if that's what it was, had landed so hard the skull had split and what was revealed took all of Officer Mitchell's courage to face. Partly by reflex action he looked up, far up the side of the towering building in front of which he was standing . He saw an immensity of structure and glass that was totally unmoved by what had just happened. On Mitchell's first inspection the building gave no clue to the point from which the now smashed body had been launched into the air.

When he had seen and noted that, Officer Mitchell turned to do his unwelcome but necessary duty. There were a few others who had witnessed the terrible death; they hung back in a kind of hypnotized horror, unwilling either to come closer or to go away. Then through the small ring of spectators a slender but well-built black man came running forward, peeling off his coat at the same time. Because the man was headed straight toward the body on the sidewalk, Officer Mitchell held up his hands to stop him.

He could have saved himself the trouble; he was ignored. Instead, the intruder dropped to one knee and threw his coat over the head and shoulders of the fallen man. Then he looked up at Mitchell. "Tibbs," the man said. "Pasadena Police. Get some backup and an ambulance."

Mitchell came out of his near shock and responded by taking his small portable police radio out of its belt carrier. He raised it to his face and put out an urgent call. His immediate duty done, he walked the few steps to where the now covered body lay grimly still on the concrete. "Thank you," he said. "It got to me for a moment."

"Of course." The Pasadena policeman got to his feet and had his own look at the sheer face of the massive building. "He probably came from halfway up, or more. Did you note the condition of the skull?"

Mitchell swallowed and nodded. "Frank Mitchell," he introduced himself.

"Virgil Tibbs."

"What do you work?"

"Robbery homicide."

"Look, if you'd care to stick around until my backup—"

"Of course. This isn't my jurisdiction, but I'll do what I can." He took out his Pasadena ID and clipped it to his shirt pocket.

Mercifully, the gathering crowd showed no signs of wanting to come closer. A single young man armed with a small pocket camera started to move in, but retreated when Mitchell waved him away. After that the scene was static until a black and white patrol car coming Code Two pulled up with its roof lights still on. A sergeant got out; he was closing the car door when a second unit rolled in.

The sergeant took in the situation with a single careful look, then he too scanned the vast side of the huge building. He raised a hand to wave Virgil Tibbs away, then he saw the plastic identification clipped to his pocket. He came close enough to read it before he spoke. "You covered the body." It was a statement.

"Yes."

"Thank you. The ambulance will be here right away."

As he spoke, a red paramedic unit from the fire department rolled up. The two-man crew had already been notified what to expect; one man riding on the passenger side had a blanket ready on his lap. He jumped out, walked quickly to the body, took off Tibb's coat, and satisfied himself that life was extinct. Then he snapped the blanket open and dropped it over the corpse. After that he picked up the coat once more and returned it to its owner. "It may be stained," he warned.

Tibbs checked it carefully, then put it back on. "It's all right," he said. "I'll have it cleaned."

Mitchell was talking to his sergeant, reporting on what he had seen. It took him only a few moments, then he introduced Tibbs.

The Los Angeles sergeant was obviously experienced, but unpretentious. "I'm glad you were here to give us a hand," he said. "Bob Opper."

"Anything else I can do?"

"If you've got the time, I'd like your account of this."

"Whatever you want."

"You work homicide?"

"Yes."

"It looks like a jumper, of course, but I want to check it out. You're welcome if you want to come along."

That didn't call for an answer; as the sergeant turned toward the entrance of the very high building, Tibbs fell in beside him. "Did you get a look at the body before it was covered with the blanket?" Virgil asked.

"Partially. Why, did you catch something?"

"Perhaps," Tibbs replied.

They walked together into the huge lobby. By that time there were blue uniforms everywhere; the L.A.P.D. was definitely efficient. Behind them a coroner's unit arrived and two men got out. It was hardly ten minutes since the body had hit the sidewalk, but the official machinery to clean up was already functioning smoothly.

There was a uniformed guard in the lobby; at the sergeant's instruction he rang for the building manager.

That done, Opper turned to his black colleague from Pasadena. "You said you caught something."

"The deceased had a brand-new pair of shoes. The soles were hardly scratched."

"And you figure that a man wouldn't go and buy himself a new pair of shoes just before he killed himself."

"That's right. Buying a pair of shoes takes selection and fitting: if he was planning to take his life within the next hour, that wouldn't be a logical thing for him to do. From the condition of the soles he couldn't have walked more than two or three blocks at the most."

"He could have put on a new pair of shoes and then driven here."

"Agreed, but the percentages are against it; again, it wouldn't be logical unless his decision to kill himself was very sudden."

A patrolman came in with a wallet in his hands. "Here's the ID of the deceased," he said. "Robert T. Williamson, DOB 13 June 1932. His home address is in Orange County."

"Run him—see if he was in any trouble or had a rap sheet."

"Yes, sir." The patrolman reached for his radio.

A man was hurrying up to them. He was middle-aged and well dressed in an expensive business suit. His shoes were shined and his tie was a model of good taste. He turned his attention at once to the sergeant. "Excuse me, I've been on the phone," he said. "My name is Phillips, I'm the general manager of this building. Tell me how I can help you."

"You know what happened?" Opper asked.

"Yes, unfortunately. I presume it had to come at some time, but this is the first such—tragedy—we've ever had."

As the two men were talking, Virgil Tibbs stepped over to the building directory and looked over the posted entries. When he came back he had a question of his own. "Mr. Phillips, I notice that only the first thirty-two floors of the building appear to be occupied. Can you tell us about that?"

Phillips noted the police ID now clipped on the outside of Tibbs's coat, then responded. "Yes, that's true, although we don't advertise that fact. You see, the higher floors, while very desirable from a tenant's point of view, haven't been finished yet. Frankly, we found that rentals were way below our expectations while the building was going up, so the builders decided to hold off on the expense of completing the upper floors until there was a demand for the space. In that way, they could be finished to suit the wishes of the tenants who lease them."

"The whole building is air-conditioned," Tibbs said.

"Yes, of course. There's a great deal of glass, you see."

"My point is, Mr. Phillips, do the windows open or are they all sealed shut?"

Opper looked at Tibbs and clearly approved the question.

"Most of the windows are sealed shut. A few do open, because the tenants wanted them that way."

"On a building this high, isn't that dangerous?" the sergeant asked.

"Yes, so we designed them as casement types and set the handles so that they will only open a little way."

"Could a determined man squeeze his body out of the opening?" the sergeant continued.

Phillips hesitated. "That would depend, of course, on the man. Offhand, I would say that it would be very difficult."

"Do you have a list of the personnel who work in the building?"

"No, you'd have to get that from the individual tenants."

"Do you know a Robert Williamson? About forty-five, medium build?"

"No, not as far as I know."

Virgil took over. "Mr. Phillips, suppose someone wanted to get onto one of the higher floors, even though they're unfinished. Could he do that easily?"

Phillips was prompt and emphatic with his answer. ''I don't think he could do it at all. Since there are no tenants, the stairwells are blocked off above the thirty-second floor. The elevators are all in, but only one of them will go above the thirty-second floor, and it takes a key to operate it.''

''You have the key, of course.''

''Yes. Do you want to go up there?''

''First, can you tell us offhand whether or not any of the windows on the north face of the building above the occupied floors can be opened?''

''I'm almost certain they are all sealed. I can have it checked.''

''How about the roof?''

''The maintenance people go up there regularly, and our resident building inspector. He works for us; his job is to keep a continual check on the building structure and all its systems. a building of this size—''

''I understand,'' Tibbs cut him off. ''Now, sir, if you please, we'd like to see the roof.''

At that point the patrolman who had been checking on the dead man reappeared; Sergeant Opper stepped aside to hear his report. As he did so, he motioned Tibbs to join him.

''No wants or warrants,'' the patrolman said. ''Several traffic violations—nothing heavy. I also checked with Orange County sheriffs and they gave me a little more.''

''Good work,'' Opper said.

''Williamson was apparently wealthy, but the source of his funds isn't known. He was hospitalized about a year ago; he fell down and cracked some ribs. In the course of treating him, they found some evidence of illegal narcotics use.''

''How did they get a hold of information like that?'' Tibbs asked. ''That's privileged.''

''I know, sir, but they still knew about it, don't ask me how. Apparently he wasn't hooked or anything like that, but he had some kind of medical history of narcotics. No action was taken at the time.''

''Probably the patient gave permission to have his chart seen,'' Opper said, ''without realizing that the narcotics data was on there. Anyhow, it explains a lot. He could have dropped acid some time back when it was still popular. Then, without warning, he went off on another trip—you know it works that way. Somehow he got to the roof and, like a lot of others, thought he could fly.''

''Let's go up to the roof,'' Tibbs suggested.

On top of the building the height was terrifying anywhere near to the edge. The rooftop itself had many pieces of equipment installed—huge air ducts, antennae, and housings for elevator machinery. A sharp wind reminded all three men how high they were.

When Tibbs looked up, the movement of the clouds overhead gave the illusion that the building was leaning. After he recovered himself, he walked carefully across the cement to the comparatively low parapet, judged the wind once again, and then began a meticulous examination of a section of the protective wall. He spent so much time doing it that his L.A.P.D. colleague began to show impatience. "Find anything?" he asked.

Tibbs looked back at him. "No," he answered, "and I'm strongly reminded of the dog in the nighttime."

"The dog did nothing in the nighttime," the sergeant responded promptly.

"You have just increased my admiration of the L.A.P.D.," Tibbs said. "You know your Sherlock Holmes. If you're through, let's go back down. This place is a little awesome."

When they were back on the ground floor, Tibbs noticed a coffee shop set in one corner. After thanking Phillips for the trip to the roof, and the rest of his cooperation, Tibbs suggested that the L.A.P.D. sergeant join him for a cup of coffee. Sergeant Opper, who understood completely, accepted and saw to it that they seated in a secluded booth.

"Now, what have you got?" he asked after their order had been taken.

"You've got one of two things—accident or homicide. At the moment I like homicide better."

Opper was careful. "From the condition of the body, the victim came off the roof, because he wouldn't have landed that hard from a lower floor. At least I don't think so; I'm no expert on jumpers."

"He didn't jump," Tibbs said. "The PM may show a percentage of drugs in his body, and a careful check should be made for past acid use—that's the most likely thing if it was an accident. But this may help you a little—he definitely *didn't* come off the roof."

Opper was thoughtful. "If Phillips is right, none of the windows on the unoccupied floors open. We haven't checked yet for a broken pane."

"In a way we have. If Williamson had broken a window in order to jump, there'd be some glass on the sidewalk. Your man out there might have been hurt, or some innocent pedestrians. No, I'm sure he didn't break a window."

"How certain are you that he didn't come off the roof?"

"You felt the wind up there. Despite it there was some dust on the roof. It wasn't disturbed where he would have had to have gone over. And the parapet was unmarked."

"Plus which, of course, just anybody couldn't get up onto the roof without a key to the special elevator. And Phillips, the building manager, had never heard of the dead man."

"Which leaves only one possibility," Tibbs said. He stopped then and waited while the coffee was served.

"He couldn't have fallen out of the sky," Opper mused. "You can't get out of modern aircraft the way that—what was his name?—did. Over the English Channel, wasn't it?"

"Helicopter," Tibbs said, and stirred his coffee.

"Someone would have seen it."

"Twenty years ago, yes, but not now. Police and media helicopters fly over the city at low altitude all the time and they're commonplace. The fire department has some too. The point is, no one notices them or hears them any more, except under unusual circumstances. They don't look up just to see them fly by."

Sergeant Opper drank some coffee while he thought. "All right, he could have come out of a helicopter; and come to think of it, some of them don't even have doors, or the doors are very easily opened."

"True."

"But the pilot would have reported it."

Tibbs smiled, not very much, and it was a little grim.

"All the helicopters operating in the greater Los Angeles area have a special frequency for talking to each other: it's one two two point nine five. If it had been an accident, then the pilot would have gone on the air immediately, knowing that all the law-enforcement helicopters airborne in the area would hear him. But he didn't. That's why I think it was a homicide."

"Anything else?"

"Yes. Helicopters can fly at almost any speed they like, up to their maximum. They can turn on a dime, hover, and do lots of other things."

"Therefore?"

"Therefore I think that Williamson was dumped out of a helicopter just at the point where it would appear he had jumped from the building. Remember, a good helicopter pilot can maneuver his machine with great precision, even in a wind."

"One objection, Tibbs, and it's a strong one. Williamson would have struggled. He would have grabbed something. He was a well set up man and the pilot had to keep flying. Unless there were other people in the chopper. Even then, throwing a man out against his will would take a lot of doing. I wouldn't care to try it."

Tibbs nodded. "Let me put together a theory—you can check it easily enough. The man had traces of narcotics use, but he wasn't hooked. That suggests someone who handled the stuff, but who was too smart to use it himself. That's supported by his evident wealth with no obvious source for the money—you can check that too. If I'm right so far, then we're talking about some very ruthless people who are engaged in one of the most profitable forms of crime known.''

Opper took out his inevitable notebook. ''I'll check with our narcotics people. If they knew Williamson, or of him, you've got something.''

''Do you want the rest?''

''By all means.''

''I don't think the fall killed him. Or if it did, he was unconscious when he was tossed from the chopper. Suppose he was given a shot and taken out. Then he was dumped from the chopper so that he would appear to have jumped from the building. No one saw the helicopter for the reasons already given.''

''Father Brown's postman.''

''Exactly. Getting rid of an unconscious man, or a dead one, could be done without too much trouble. The cause of death would be so obvious that extensive tests probably wouldn't be run.''

''Not everybody has a helicopter,'' Opper said.

''And that's the point where your investigation should begin. If you'll allow me.''

Opper got up. ''I'll call you tomorrow,'' he promised.

Mr. Tibbs:

While you were out Sgt Opper of LAPD called you. He said coroner determined cause of death OD heroin, not fall (???). Check with sheriff's Argus Patrol and Fire Department confirms no message received on 122.95 at time of incident. He says only a matter of time until chopper ID'ed. Case definitely homicide, many thanks your cooperation, letter coming to Chief McGowan re your help. He also said Narco had folder on Williamson.

Marge

Hey, Virg, what the hell happened, anyway?

M

Dr. Wendell Urth

THE SINGING BELL

Isaac Asimov

PART I

LOUIS PEYTON NEVER discussed publicly the methods by which he had bested the police of Earth in a dozen duels of wits and bluff, with the psychoprobe always waiting and always foiled. He would have been foolish to do so, of course, but in his more complacent moments, he fondled the notion of leaving a testament to be opened only after his death, one in which his unbroken success could be clearly seen to be due to ability and not luck.

In such a testament, he would say, "No false pattern can be created to cover a crime without bearing upon it some trace of its creator. It is better, then, to seek in events some pattern that already exists and then adjust your actions to it."

It was with that principle in mind that Peyton planned the murder of Albert Cornwell.

Cornwell, that small-time retailer of stolen things, first approached Peyton at the latter's usual table-for-one at Grinnell's. Cornwell's blue suit seemed to have a special shine, his lined face a special grin and his faded mustache a special bristle.

"Mr. Peyton," he said, greeting his future murderer with no fourth-dimensional qualm, "it is so nice to see you. I'd almost given up, sir, almost given up."

Peyton, who disliked being approached over his newspaper and dessert at Grinnell's, said, "If you have business with me, Cornwell, you know where you can reach me." Peyton was past forty and his hair was past its earlier blackness, but his back was rigid, his bearing youthful, his eyes dark, and his voice could cut the more sharply for long practice.

"Not for this, Mr. Peyton," said Cornwell, "not for this. I know of a cache, sir, a cache of . . . you know, sir." The forefinger of his right hand moved gently, as though it were, a clapper striking invisible substance, and his left hand momentarily cupped his ear.

Peyton turned a page of the paper, still somewhat damp from its tele-dispenser, folded it flat and said, "Singing Bells?"

"Oh, hush, Mr. Peyton," said Cornwell, in whispered agony.

Peyton said, "Come with me."

They walked through the park. It was another Peyton axiom that to be thoroughly secret there was nothing like a low-voiced discussion out-of-doors. Any room might by spy-rayed, but no one had yet spy-rayed the vault of heaven.

Cornwall whispered, "A cache of Singing Bells; an accumulated cache of Singing Bells. Unpolished, but such beauties, Mr. Peyton."

"Have you seen them?"

"No, sir, but I have spoken with one who has. He had proofs enough to convince me. There is enough there to enable you and me to retire in affluence. In absolute affluence, sir."

"Who was this other man?"

A look of cunning lit Cornwell's face like a smoking torch, obscuring more than it showed and lending it a repulsive oiliness. "The man was a lunar grubstaker who had a method for locating the Bells in the crater sides. I don't know his method; he never told me that. But he has gathered dozens, hidden them on the moon, and come to Earth to arrange the disposing of them."

"He died, I suppose?"

"Yes. A most shocking accident, Mr. Peyton. A fall from a height. Very sad. Of course, his activities on the moon were quite illegal. The Dominion is very strict about unauthorized Bell-mining. So perhaps it was a judgment upon him after all. . . . In any case, I have his map."

Peyton said, a look of calm indifference on his face, "I don't want any of the details of your little transaction. What I want to know is why you've come to me."

Cornwell said, "Well, now, there's enough for both of us, Mr. Peyton, and we can both do our bit. For my part, I know where the cache is located and I can get a spaceship. You—"

"Yes?"

"You can pilot a spaceship, and you have such excellent contacts for disposing of the Bells. It is a very fair division of laobr, Mr. Peyton. Wouldn't you say so, now?"

Cornwell considered the pattern of his life—the pattern that already existed—and matters seemed to fit.

He said, "We will leave for the moon on August tenth."

Cornwell stopped walking and said, "Mr. Peyton! It's only April now."

Peyton maintained an even gait and Cornwell had to hurry to catch up. "Do you hear me, Mr. Peyton?"

Peyton said, "August tenth. I will get in touch with you at the proper time, tell you where to bring your ship. Make no attempt to see me personally till then. Good-bye, Cornwell."

Cornwell said, "Fifty-fifty?"

"Quite," said Peyton. "Good-bye."

Peyton continued his walk alone and considered the pattern of his life again. At the age of twenty-seven, he had bought a tract of land in the Rockies on which some past owner had built a house designed as refuge against the threatened atomic eras of two centuries back, the ones that had never come to pass after all. The house remained, however, a monument to a frightened drive for self-sufficiency.

It was of steel and concrete in as isolated a spot as could well be found on Earth, set high above sea level and protected on nearly all sides by mountain peaks that reached higher still. It had its self-contained power unit, its water supply fed by mountain streams, its freezers in which ten sides of beef could hang comfortably, its cellar outfitted like a fortress with an arsenal of weapons designed to stave off hungry, panicked hordes that never came. It had its air-conditioning unit that could scrub and scrub the air until anything *but* radioactivity (alas for human frailty) could be scrubbed out of it.

In that house of survival, Peyton passed the month of August every subsequent year of his perennially bachelor life. He took out the communicators, the television, the newspaper tele-dispenser. He built a force-field fence about his property and left a short-distance signal mechanism to the house from the point where the fence crossed the one trail winding through the mountains.

For one month each year, he could be thoroughly alone. No one saw him, no one could reach him. In absolute solitude, he could have the only vacation he valued after eleven months of contact with a humanity for which he could feel only a cold contempt.

Even the police (and Peyton smiled) knew of his rigid regard for August. He once jumped bail and risked the psychoprobe rather than forego his August.

Peyton considered another aphorism for possible inclusion in his testament: There is nothing so conducive to an appearance of innocence as the triumphant lack of an alibi.

On July 30, as on July 30 of every year, Louis Peyton took the 9:15

A.M. non-grav strato-jet at New York and arrived in Denver at 12:30 P.M. There he lunched and took the 1:45 P.M. semi-grav bus to Hump's Point, from which Sam Leibman took him by ancient gound-car (full grav!) up the trail to the boundaries of his property. Sam Leibman gravely accepted the ten dollar tip that he always received, touched his hat as he had done on July 30 for fifteen years.

On July 31, as on July 31 of every year, Louis Peyton returned to Hump's Point in his non-grav aero-flitter, and placed an order through the Hump's Point general store for such supplies as he needed for the coming month. There was nothing unusual about the order. It was virtually the duplicate of previous such orders.

MacIntyre, manager of the store, checked gravely over the list, put it through to Central Warehouse (Mountain District) in Denver, and the whole of it came pushing over the mass-transference beam within the hour. Peyton loaded the supplies onto his aero-flitter with MacIntyre's help, left his usual ten dollar tip and returned to his house.

On August 1, at 12:01 A.M., the force-field that surrounded his property was set to full power and Peyton was isolated.

And now the pattern changed. Deliberately, he had left himself eight days. In that time, he slowly and meticulously destroyed just enough supplies to account for all of August. He used the dusting chambers which served the house as a garbage-disposal unit. They were of an advanced model capable of reducing all matter up to and including metals and silicates to an impalpable and undetectable molecular dust. The excess energy formed in the process was carried away by the mountain stream that ran through his property. It ran five degrees warmer than normal for a week.

On August 9, his aero-flitter carried him to a spot in Wyoming where Albert Cornwell and a spaceship waited. The spaceship, itself, was a weak point, of course, since there were men who had sold it, men who had transported it and helped prepare it for flight. All those men, however, led only as far as Cornwell, and Cornwell, Peyton thought (with the trace of smile on his cold lips), would be a dead end. A very dead end.

On August 10, the spaceship, with Peyton at the controls and Cornwell (and his map) as passenger, left the surface of Earth. Its non-grav field was excellent. At full power, the ship's weight was reduced to less than an ounce. The micropiles fed energy efficiently and noiselessly, and without flame or sound, the ship rose through the atmosphere, shrank to a point and was gone.

It was very unlikely that there would be witnesses to the flight. In point of face, there were none.

Two days in space; now two weeks on the moon. Almost instinctively, Peyton had allowed for those two weeks from the first. He was under no illusions as to the value of home-made maps by non-cartographers. Useful they might be to the designer himself, who had the help of memory. To a stranger, they could be nothing more than a cryptogram.

Cornwell showed Peyton the map for the first time only after takeoff. He smiled obsequiously. "After all, sir, this was my only trump."

"Have you checked this against the lunar charts?"

"I would scarcely know how, Mr. Peyton. I depend upon you."

Peyton stared at him coldly as he returned the map. The one certain thing upon it was Tycho Crater, the site of the buried Luna City.

In one respect, at least, astronomy was on their side. Tycho was on the daylight side of the moon at the moment. It meant that patrol ships were less likely to be out; they themselves less likely to be observed.

Peyton brought the ship down in a riskily quick non-grav landing within the safe, cold darkness of the inner shadow of a crater. The sun was past zenith and the shadow would grow no shorter.

Cornwell drew a long face. "Dear, dear, Mr. Peyton. We can scarcely go prospecting in the lunar day."

"The lunar day doesn't last forever," said Peyton shortly. "There are about a hundred hours of sun left. We can use that time for acclimating ourselves and for working out the map."

The answer came quickly, but it was plural. Peyton studied the lunar charts over and over, taking meticulous measurements, and trying to find the pattern of craters shown on the home-made scrawl that was the key to—what?

Finally, Peyton said, "The crater we want could be any one of three: GC-3, GC-5 or MT-10."

"What do we do, Mr. Peyton?" asked Cornwell, anxiously.

"We try them all," said Peyton, "beginning with the nearest."

The terminator passed and they were in the night shadow. After that, they spent increasing periods on the lunar surface, getting used to the eternal silence and blackness, the harsh points of stars and the crack of light that was the Earth peeping over the rim of the crater above. They left hollow, featureless footprints in the dry dust that did not stir or change. Peyton noted them first when they climbed out of the crater into the full light of the gibbous Earth. That was on the eighth day after their arrival on the moon.

The lunar cold put a limit to how long they could remain outside their ship at any one time. Each day, however, they managed for longer. By the eleventh day after arrival they had eliminated GC-5 as the container of the Singing Bells.

By the fifteenth day, Peyton's cold spirit had grown warm with desperation. It would have to be GC-3. MT-10 was too far away. They would not have time to reach it and explore it and still allow for a return to Earth by August 31.

On that same fifteenth day, however, despair was laid to rest forever when they discovered the Bells.

They were not beautiful. They were merely irregular masses of gray rock, as large as a double fist, vacuum-filled and feather-light in the moon's gravity. There were two dozen of them, and each one, after proper polishing, could be sold for a hundred thousand dollars at least.

Carefully, in double handfuls, they carried the Bells to the ship, bedded them in excelsior, and returned for more. Three times they made the trip both ways over ground that would have worn them out on Earth but which, under the moon's lilliputian gravity, was scarcely a barrier.

Cornwell passed the last of the Bells up to Peyton, who placed them carefully within the outer lock.

"Keep them clear, Mr. Peyton," he said, his radioed voice sounding harshly in the other's ear. "I'm coming up."

He crouched for the slow high leap against the lunar gravity, looked up, and froze in panic. His face, clearly visible through the hard curved lusilite of his helmet froze in a last grimace of terror. "No, Mr. Peyton. Don't—"

Peyton's fist tightened on the grip of the blaster he held. It fired. There was an unbearably brilliant flash and Cornwell was a dead fragment of a man, sprawled amid remnants of a spacesuit and flecked with freezing blood.

Peyton paused to stare somberly at the dead man, but only for a second. Then he transferred the last of the Bells to their prepared containers, removed his suit, activated first the non-grav field, then the micropiles and, potentially a million or two richer than he had been two weeks earlier, set off on the return trip to Earth.

On the 29th of August, Peyton's ship descended silently, stern bottomward, to the spot in Wyoming from which it had taken off on August 10th. The care with which Peyton had chosen the spot was not wasted.

His aero-flitter was still there, drawn within the protection of an enclos-ing wrinkle of the rocky, tortuous countryside.

He moved the Singing Bells once again, in their containers, into the deepest recess of the wrinkle, covering them, loosely and sparsely, with earth. He returned to the ship once more to set the controls and make last adjustments. He climbed out again, and two minutes later, the ship's automatics took over.

Silently hurrying, the ship bounded upward and up, veering to west-ward somewhat as the Earth rotated beneath it. Peyton watched, shading his narrowed eyes, and at the extreme edge of vision there was a tiny gleam of light and a dot of cloud against the blue sky.

Peyton's mouth twitched into a smile. He had judged well. With the cadmium safety-rods bent back into uselessness, the micropiles had plunged past the unit-sustaining safety level and the ship had vanished in the heat of the nuclear explosion that had followed.

Twenty minutes later, he was back on his property. He was tired and his muscles ached under Earth's unit gravity. He slept well.

Twelve hours later, in the earliest dawn, the police came.

PART 2

The man who opened the door placed his crossed hands over his paunch and ducked his smiling head two or three times in greeting. The man who entered, H. Seton Davenport of the Terrestrial Bureau of Investigation, looked about uncomfortably.

The room he had entered was large and in semi-darkness except for the brilliant viewing lamp focused over a combination armchair-desk. Rows of book-films covered the walls. A suspension of Galactic charts oc-cupied one corner of the room and a Galactic lens gleamed softly on a stand in another corner.

"You are Dr. Wendell Urth?" asked Davenport, in a tone that sug-gested he found it hard to believe. Davenport was a stocky man with black hair, a thin and prominent nose and a star-shaped scar on one cheek which marked permanently the place where a neuronic whip had once struck him at too close a range.

"I am," said Dr. Urth, in a thin, tenor voice. "And you are Inspector Davenport."

The Inspector presented his credentials, and said, "The University recommended you to me as an extraterrologist."

"So you said when you called me half an hour ago," said Urth, agreeably. His features were thick, his nose was a snubby button, and over his somewhat protuberant eyes there were thick glasses.

"I shall get to the point, Dr. Urth. I presume you have visited the moon—"

Dr. Urth, who had brought out a bottle of ruddy liquid and two glasses, just a little worse for dust, from behind a straggling pile of book films, said with sudden brusqueness, "I have never visited the moon, Inspector. I never intend to! Space-travel is foolishness. I don't believe in it." Then, in softer tones, "Sit down, sir, sit down. Have a drink."

Inspector Davenport did as he was told and said, "But you're an—"

"Extraterrologist. Yes. I'm interested in other worlds, but it doesn't mean I have to go there. Good Lord, I don't have to be a time-traveler to qualify as a historian, do I?" He sat down, and a broad smile impressed itself upon his round face once more as he said, "Now tell me what's on your mind."

"I have come," said the Inspector, frowning, "to consult you in a case of murder."

"Murder? What have I to do with murder?"

"This murder, Dr. Urth, was on the moon."

"Astonishing."

"It's more than astonishing. It's unprecedented, Dr. Urth. In the fifty years since the Lunar Dominion has been established, ships have blown up and spacesuits have sprung leaks. Men have boiled to death on sun-side, frozen on dark-side and suffocated on both sides. There have even been deaths by falls, which, considering lunar gravity, is quite a trick. But in all that time, not one man has been killed on the Moon as the result of another man's deliberate act of violence . . . till now."

Dr. Urth said, "How was it done?"

"A blaster. The authorities were on the scene within the hour through a fortunate set of circumstances. A patrol ship observed a flash of light against the moon's surface. You know how far a flash can be seen against the night-side. He notified Luna City and landed. In the process of circling back, he swears that he just managed to see by Earthlight what looked like a ship taking off. Upon landing, he discovered a blasted corpse and footprints."

"The flash of light," said Dr. Urth, "you suppose to be the firing blaster."

"That's certain. The corpse was fresh. Interior portions of the body had not yet frozen. The footprints belonged to two people. Careful measurements showed that the depressions fell into two groups of somewhat different diameters, indicating differently sized space-boots. In the main, they led to craters GC-3 and GC-5, a pair of—''

''I am aquainted with the official code for naming lunar craters,'' said Dr. Urth, pleasantly.

''Umm. In any case. GC-3 contained footprints that led to a rift in the crater wall, within which scraps of hardened pumice were found. X-ray diffraction patterns showed—''

''Singing Bells,'' put in the extraterrologist in great excitement. ''Don't tell me this murder of yours involves Singing Bells!''

''What if it does?'' demanded Davenport, blankly.

''I have one. A University expedition uncovered it and presented it to me in return for— Come, Inspector, I must show it to you.''

Dr. Urth jumped up and pattered across the room, beckoning the other to follow as he did. Davenport, annoyed, followed.

They entered a second room, larger than the first, dimmer, considerably more cluttered. Davenport stared with astonishment at the heterogeneous mass of material that was jumbled together in no pretense at order.

He made out a small lump of ''blue glaze'' from Mars, the sort of thing some romantics considered to be an artifact of long-extinct Martians, a small meteorite, a model of an early spaceship, a sealed bottle of liquid scrawlingly labeled ''Venusian ocean.''

Dr. Urth said, happily, ''I've made a museum of my whole house. It's one of the advantages of being a bachelor. Of course, I haven't quite got things organized. Someday, when I have a spare week or so . . . ''

For a moment he looked about, puzzled, then remembering, he pushed aside a chart showing the evolutionary scheme of development of the marine invertebrates that were the highest life-forms on Arcturus V and said, ''Here it is. It's flawed. I'm afraid.''

The Bell hung suspended from a slender wire, soldered delicately onto it. That it was flawed was obvious. It had a constriction line running halfway about it that made it seem like two small globes, firmly but imperfectly squashed together. Despite that, it had been lovingly polished to a dull luster, softly gray, velvety smooth, and faintly pock-marked in a way that laboratories, in their futile efforts to prepare synthetic Bells, had found impossible to duplicate.

Dr. Urth said, ''I experimented a good deal before I found a decent stroker. A flawed Bell is temperamental. But bone works. I have one here,'' and he held up something that looked like a short thick spoon

made of a gray-white substance, "which I had made out of the femur of
an ox. . . . Listen.''

With surprising delicacy, his pudgy fingers maneuvered the Bell,
feeling for one best spot. He adjusted it, steadying it daintily. Then,
letting the Bell swing free, he brought down the thick end of the bone
spoon and stroked the Bell softly.

It was a though a million harps had sounded a mile away. It swelled
and faded and returned. It came from no particular direction. It sounded
inside the head, incredibly sweet and pathetic and tremulous all at once.

It died away lingeringly and both men were silent for a full minute.

Dr. Urth said, "Not bad, eh?" and with a flick of his hand set the Bell
to swinging on its wire.

Davenport stirred restlessly, "Careful! Don't break it." The fragility
of a good Singing Bell was proverbial.

Dr. Urth said, "Geologists say the Bells are only pressure-hardened
pumice, enclosing a vacuum in which small beads of rock rattle freely.
That's what they *say*. But if that's all it is, why can't we reproduce one?
Now a flawless Bell would make this one sound like a child's harmon-
ica.''

"Exactly." said Davenport, "and there aren't a dozen people on
Earth who own a flawless one, and there are a hundred people and
institutions who would buy one at any price, no questions asked. A
supply of Bells would be worth murder.''

The extraterrologist turned to Davenport and pushed his spectacles
back on his inconsequential nose with a stubby forefinger. "I haven't
forgotten your murder case. Please go on.''

"That can be done in a phrase. I know the identity of the murderer.''

They returned to the chairs in the library and Dr. Urth clasped his
hands over his ample abdomen. "Indeed? Then surely you have no
problem, Inspector.''

"Knowing and proving are not the same, Dr. Urth. Unfortunately, he
has no alibi.''

"You mean: unfortunately he *has*, don't you?

"I mean what I say. If he had an alibi, I could crack it somehow,
because it would be a false one. If there were witnesses who claimed they
had seen him on Earth at the time of the murder, their stories could be
broken down. If he had documentary proof, it could be exposed as a
forgery or some sort of trickery. Unfortunately, he has none of it.''

"What does he have?''

Carefully, Inspector Davenport described the Peyton estate in Colorado. He concluded, "He has spent every August there in the strictest isolation. Even the T.B.I. would have to testify to that. Any jury would have to presume that he was on the estate this August as well unless we could present definite proof that he was on the moon."

"What makes you think he *was* on the moon. Perhaps he is innocent."

"No!" Davenport was almost violent. "For fifteen years I've been trying to collect sufficient evidence against him and I've never succeeded. But I can *smell* a Peyton crime now. I tell you that no one but Peyton, no one on Earth, would have the impudence or, for that matter, the practical business contacts to attempt disposal of smuggled Singing Bells. He is known to be an expert space-pilot. He is known to have had contact with the murdered man, though admittedly not for some months. Unfortunately, none of that is proof."

Dr. Urth said, "Wouldn't it be simple to use the psychoprobe, now that it's use has been legalized?"

Davenport scowled, and the scar on his cheek turned livid. "Have you read the Konski-Hiakawa law, Dr. Urth?"

"No."

"I think no one has. The right to mental privacy, the government says, is fundamental. All right, but what follows? The man who is psychoprobed and proves innocent of the crime for which he was psychoprobed is entitled to as much compensation as he can persuade the courts to give him. In a recent case, a bank cashier was awarded $25,000 for having been psychoprobed on inaccurate suspicion of theft. It seems that the circumstantial evidence which seemed to point to theft actually pointed to a small spot of adultery. His claim that he lost his job, was threatened by the husband in question and put in bodily fear, and finally was held up to ridicule and contumely because a news-strip man had learned the results of the probe held good in court."

"I can see the man's point."

"So can we all. That's the trouble. One more item to remember: any man who has been psychoprobed once for any reason can never be psychoprobed again for any reason. No one man, the law says, shall be placed in mental jeopardy twice in his lifetime."

"Inconvenient."

"Exactly. In the two years since the psychoprobe has been legitimized, I couldn't count the number of crooks and chiselers who've tried to get themselves psychoprobed for purse-snatching so that they can play the rackets safely afterward. So you see the Department will not allow Peyton to be psychoprobed until they have firm evidence of his guilt. Not legal evidence, maybe, but evidence that is strong enough to convince my boss. The worst of it, Dr. Urth, is that if we come into court without a psychoprobe record, we can't win. In a case as serious as murder, not to have used the psychoprobe is proof enough to the dumbest juror that the prosecution isn't sure of its ground.''

"Now what do you want from me?"

"Proof that he was on the moon sometime in August. It's got to be done quickly. I can't hold him on suspicion much longer. And if news of the murder gets out, the world press will blow up like an asteroid striking Jupiter's atmosphere. A glamorous crime, you know; first murder on the moon."

"Exactly when was the murder committed?" asked Urth, in a sudden transition to brisk cross-examination.

"August 27."

"And the arrest was made when?"

"Yesterday, August 30."

"Then if Peyton were the murderer, he would have had time to return to Earth."

"Barely. Just barely." Davenport's lips thinned. "If I had been a day sooner— If I had found his place empty—"

"And how long do you suppose the two, the murdered man and the murderer, were on the Moon altogether?"

"Judging by the ground covered by the footprints, a number of days. A week, at the minimum."

"Has the ship they used been located?"

"No, and it probably never will. About ten hours ago, the University of Denver reported a rise in background radioactivity beginning day before yesterday at 6 P.M. and persisting for a number of hours. It's an easy thing, Dr. Urth, to set a ship's controls so as to allow it to blast off without crew and blow up, fifty miles high, in a micropile short."

"If I had been Peyton," said Dr. Urth, thoughtfully, "I would have killed the man on board ship and blown up corpse and ship together."

"You don't know Peyton," said Davenport, grimly. "He enjoys his victories over the law. He values them. Leaving the corpse on the moon is his challenge to us."

"I see." Dr. Urth patted his stomach with a rotary motion and said, "Well, there is a chance."

"That you'll be able to prove he was on the moon?"

"That I'll be able to give you my opinion."

"Now?"

"The sooner the better. If, of course, I get a chance to interview Mr. Peyton."

"That can be arranged. I have a non-grav jet waiting. We can be in Washington in twenty minutes."

But a look of the deepest alarm passed over the plump extraterrologist's face. He rose to his feet and pattered away from the T.B.I. agent toward the duskiest corner of the cluttered room.

"*No!*"

"What's wrong, Dr. Urth?"

"I won't use a non-grav jet. I don't believe in them."

Davenport stared confusedly at Dr. Urth. He stammered, "Would you prefer a monorail?"

Dr. Urth snapped, "I mistrust all forms of transportation. I don't believe in them. Except walking. I don't mind walking." He was suddenly eager. "Couldn't you bring Mr. Peyton to this city, somewhere within walking distance? To City Hall, perhaps? I've often walked to City Hall."

Davenport looked helplessly about the room. He looked at the myriad of volumes of lore about the light-years. He could see through the open door into the room beyond with its tokens of the worlds beyond the sky. And he looked at Dr. Urth, pale at the thought of a non-grav jet, and shrugged his shoulders.

"I'll bring Peyton here. Right to this room. Will that satisfy you?"

Dr. Urth puffed out his breath in a deep sigh. "Quite."

"I hope you can deliver, Dr. Urth."

"I will do my best, Mr. Davenport."

Louis Peyton stared with distaste at his surroundings and with contempt at the fat man who bobbed his head in greeting. He glanced at the seat offered him and brushed it with his hand before sitting down. Davenport took a seat next to him, with his blaster-holster in clear view.

The fat man was smiling as he sat down and patted his round abdomen as though he had just finished a good meal and were intent on letting the world know about it.

He said, "Good evening, Mr. Peyton. I am Dr. Wendell Urth, extraterrologist."

Peyton looked at him again, "And what do you want with me?"

"I want to know if you were on the moon at any time in the month of August."

"I was not."

"Yet no man saw you on Earth between the days of August 1 and August 30."

"I lived my normal life in August. I am never seen during that month. Let him tell you." And he jerked his head in the direction of Davenport.

Dr. Urth chuckled. "How nice if we could test this matter. If there were only some physical manner in which we could differentiate moon from Earth. If, for instance, we could analyze the dust in your hair and say, 'Aha, moon rock.' Unfortunately, we can't. Moon rock is much the same as Earth rock. Even if it weren't, there wouldn't be any in your hair unless you stepped on to the lunar surface without a spacesuit, which is unlikely."

Peyton remained impassive.

Dr. Urth went on, smiling benevolently, and lifting a hand to steady the glasses perched precariously on the bulb of his nose, "A man traveling in space or on the moon breathes Earth air, eats Earth food. He carries Earth environment next to his skin whether he's in his ship or in his spacesuit. We are looking for a man who spent two days in space going to the moon, at least a week on the moon, and two days coming back from the moon. In all the time he carried Earth next to his skin, which makes it difficult."

"I'd suggest," said Peyton, "that you can make it less difficult by releasing me and looking for the real murderer."

"It may come to that," said Dr. Urth. "Have you ever seen anything like this?" His hand pushed its pudgy way to the ground beside his chair and came up with a gray sphere that sent back subdued highlights.

Peyton smiled, "It looks like a Singing Bell to me."

"It *is* a Singing Bell. The murder was committed for the sake of Singing Bells. . . . What do you think of this one?"

"I think it is badly flawed."

"Ah, but inspect it," said Dr. Urth, and with a quick motion of his hand, he tossed it through six feet of air to Peyton.

Davenport cried out and half-rose from his chair. Peyton brought up his arms with an effort, but so quickly that they managed to catch the Bell.

Peyton said, "You damned fool. Don't throw it around that way."

"You respect Singing Bells, do you?"

"Too much to break one. That's no crime, at least." Peyton stroked the Bell gently, then lifted it to his ear and shook it slowly, listening to the soft clicks of the Lunoliths, those small pumice particles, as they rattled in vacuum.

Then, holding the Bell up by the length of steel wire still attached to it, he ran a thumb nail over its surface with an expert, curving motion. It twanged! The note was very mellow, very flute-like, holding with a slight *vibrato* that faded lingeringly and conjured up pictures of a summer twilight.

For a short moment, all three men were lost in the sound.

And then Dr. Urth said, "Throw it back, Mr. Peyton. Toss it here!" and held out his hand in peremptory gesture.

Automatically, Louis Peyton tossed the Bell. It traveled its short arc one third of the way to Urth's waiting hand, curved downward and shattered with a heartbroken, sighing discord on the floor.

Davenport and Peyton stared at the gray slivers with equal wordlessness and Dr. Urth's calm voice went almost unheard as he said, "When the criminal's cache of crude Bells is located, I'll ask that a flawless one, properly polished, be given to me, as replacement and fee."

"A fee? For what?" demanded Davenport, irritably.

"Surely the matter is now obvious. Despite my little speech of a moment ago, there is one piece of Earth's environment that no space traveler carries with him . . . and that is *Earth's surface gravity*. The fact that Mr. Peyton could so egregiously misjudge the toss of an object he obviously valued so highly could mean only that his muscles are not yet readjusted to the pull of Earthly gravity. It is my professional opinion, Mr. Davenport, that your prisoner has, in the last few days, been away from Earth. He has either been in space or on some planetary object considerably smaller in size than the Earth—as, for example, the moon."

Davenport rose triumphantly to his feet. "Let me have your opinion in writing," he said, hand on blaster, "and that will be good enough to get me permission to use a psychoprobe."

Louis Peyton, dazed and unresisting, had only the numb realization that any testament he could now leave would have to include the fact of ultimate failure.

Professor Augustus S.F.X. Van Dusen

THE PHANTOM MOTOR

Jacques Futrelle

I

TWO DAZZLING WHITE eyes bulged through the night as an automobile swept suddenly around a curve in the wide road and laid a smooth, glaring pathway ahead. Even at the distance the rhythmical crackling-chug informed Special Constable Baker that it was a gasoline car, and the headlong swoop of the unblinking lights toward him made him instantly aware of the fact that the speed ordinance of Yarborough County was being a little more than broken—it was being obliterated.

Now the County of Yarborough was a wide expanse of summer estates and superbly kept roads, level as a floor, and offered distracting temptations to the dangerous pastime of speeding. But against this was the fact that the county was particular about its speed laws, so particular in fact that it had stationed half a hundred men upon its highways to abate the nuisance. Incidentally it had found that keeping record of the infractions of the law was an excellent source of income.

"Forty miles an hour if an inch," remarked Baker to himself.

He arose from a camp stool where he was wont to make himself comfortable from six o'clock until midnight on watch, picked up his lantern, turned up the light and stepped down to the edge of the road. He always remained on watch at the same place—at one end of a long stretch which autoists had unanimously dubbed The Trap. The Trap was singularly tempting—a perfectly macadamized road bed lying between two tall stone walls with only enough of a sinuous twist in it to make each end invisible from the other. Another man, Special Constable Bowman, was stationed at the other end of The Trap and there was telephonic communication between the points, enabling the men to check each other and incidentally, if one failed to stop a car or get its number, the other would. That at least was the theory.

517

So now, with the utmost confidence, Baker waited beside the road.
The approaching lights were only a couple of hundred yards away. At the
proper instant he would raise his lantern, the car would stop, its occupants would protest and then the county would add a mite to its general
fund for making the roads even better and tempting autoists still more. Or
sometimes the cars didn't stop. In that event it was part of the Special
Constables' duties to get the number as it flew past, and reference to the
monthly automobile register would give the name of the owner. An extra
fine was always imposed in such cases.

Without the slightest diminution of speed the car came hurtling on
toward him and swung wide so as to take the straight path of The Trap at
full speed. At the psychological instant Baker stepped out into the road
and waved his lantern.

''Stop!'' he commanded.

The crackling-chug came on, heedless of the cry. The auto was almost
upon him before he leaped out of the road—a feat at which he was
particularly expert—then it flashed by and plunged into The Trap. Baker
was, at the instant, so busily engaged in getting out of the way that he
couldn't read the number, but he was not disconcerted because he knew
there was no escape from The Trap. On the one side a solid stone wall
eight feet high marked the eastern boundary of the John Phelps Stocker
country estate, and on the other side a stone fence nine feet high marked
the western boundary of the Thomas Q. Rogers country estate. There
was no turnout, no place, no possible way for an auto to get out of The
Trap except at one of the two ends guarded by the special constables. So
Baker, perfectly confident of results, seized the phone.

''Car coming through sixty miles an hour,'' he bawled. ''It won't
stop. I missed the number. Look out.''

''All right,'' answered Special Constable Bowman.

For ten, fifteen, twenty minutes Baker waited expecting a call from
Bowman at the other end. It didn't come and finally he picked up the
phone again. No answer. He rang several times, battered the box and did
some tricks with the receiver. Still no answer. Finally he began to feel
worried. He remembered that at that same post one Special Constable
had been badly hurt by a reckless chauffeur who refused to stop or turn
his car when the officer stepped out into the road. In his mind's eye he
saw Bowman now lying helpless, perhaps badly injured. If the car held
the pace at which it passed him it would be certain death to whoever
might be unlucky enough to get its path.

With these thoughts running through his head and with genuine
solicitude for Bowman, Baker at last walked on along the road of The

Trap toward the other end. The feeble rays of the lantern showed the unbroken line of the cold, stone walls on each side. There was no shrubbery of any sort, only a narrow strip of grass close to the wall. The more Baker considered the matter the more anxious he became and he increased his pace a little. As he turned a gentle curve he saw a lantern in the distance coming slowly toward him. It was evidently being carried by someone who was looking carefully along each side of the road.

"Hello!" called Baker, when the lantern came within distance. "That you, Bowman?"

"Yes," came the hallooed response.

The lanterns moved on and met. Baker's solicitude for the other constable was quickly changed to curiosity.

"What're you looking for?" he asked.

"That auto," replied Bowman. "It didn't come through my end and I thought perhaps there had been an accident so I walked along looking for it. Haven't seen anything."

"Didn't come through your end?" repeated Baker in amazement. "Why it must have. It didn't come back my way and I haven't passed it so it must have gone through."

"Well, it didn't," declared Bowman conclusively. "I was on the lookout for it, too, standing beside the road. There hasn't been a car through my end in an hour."

Special Constable Baker raised his lantern until the rays fell full upon the face of Special Constable Bowman and for an instant they stared each at the other. Suspicion glowed from the keen, avaricious eyes of Baker.

"How much did they give you to let 'em by?" he asked.

"Give me?" exclaimed Bowman, in righteous indignation. "Give me nothing. I haven't seen a car."

A slight sneer curled the lips of Special Constable Baker.

"Of course that's all right to report at headquarters," he said, "but I happen to know that the auto came in here, that it didn't go back my way, that it couldn't get out except at the ends, therefore it went your way." He was silent for a moment. "And whatever you got, Jim, seems to me I ought to get half."

Then the worm—i.e., Bowman—turned. A polite curl appeared about his lips and was permitted to show through the grizzled mustache.

"I guess," he said deliberately, "you think because you do that, everybody else does. I haven't seen any autos."

"Don't I always give you half, Jim?" Baker demanded, almost pleadingly.

"Well I haven't seen any car and that's all there is to it. If it didn't go back your way there wasn't any car.'' There was a pause; Bowman was framing up something particularly unpleasant. ''You're seeing things, that's what's the matter.''

So was sown discord between two officers of the County of Yarborough. After awhile they separated with mutual sneers and open derision and went back to their respective posts. Each was thoughtful in his own way. At five minutes of midnight when they went off duty Baker called Bowman on the phone again.

''I've been thinking this thing over, Jim, and I guess it would be just as well if we didn't report it or say anything about it when we go in,'' said Baker slowly. ''It seems foolish and if we did say anything about it it would give the boys the laugh on us.''

''Just as you say,'' responded Bowman.

Relations between Special Constable Baker and Special Constable Bowman were strained on the morrow. But they walked along side by side to their respective posts. Baker stopped at his end of The Trap; Bowman didn't even look around.

''You'd better keep your eyes open tonight, Jim,'' Baker called as a last word.

''I had 'em open last night,'' was the disgusted retort.

Seven, eight, nine o'clock passed. Two or three cars had gone through The Trap at moderate speed and one had been warned by Baker. At a few minutes past nine he was staring down the road which led into The Trap when he saw something that brought him quickly to his feet. It was a pair of dazzling white eyes, far away. He recognized them—the mysterious car of the night before.

''I'll get it this time,'' he muttered grimly, between closed teeth.

Then when the onrushing car was a full two hundred yards away Baker planted himself in the middle of the road and began to swing the lantern. The auto seemed, if anything, to be traveling even faster than on the previous night. At a hundred yards Baker began to shout. Still the car didn't lessen speed, merely rushed on. Again at the psychological instant Baker jumped. The auto whisked by as the chauffer gave it a dextrous twist to prevent running down the Special Constable.

Safely out of its way Baker turned and stared after it, trying to read the number. He could see there was a number because a white board swung from the tail axle, but he could not make out the figures. Dust and a swaying car conspired to defeat him. But he did see that there were four persons in the car dimly silhouetted against the light reflected from the road. It was useless, of course, to conjecture as to sex for even as he looked, the fast receding car swerved around the turn and was lost to sight.

Again he rushed to the telephone; Bowman responded promptly.

"That car's gone in again," Baker called. "Ninety miles an hour. Look out!"

"I'm looking," responded Bowman.

"Let me know what happens," Baker shouted.

With the receiver to his ear he stood for ten or fifteen minutes, then Bowman hallooed from the other end.

"Well?" Baker responded. "Get 'em?"

"No car passed through and there's none in sight," said Bowman.

"But it went in," insisted Baker.

"Well it didn't come out here," declared Bowman. "Walk along the road till I meet you and look out for it."

Then was repeated the search of the night before. When the two men met in the middle of The Trap their faces were blank—blank as the high stone walls which stared at them from each side.

"Nothing!" said Bowman.

"Nothing!" echoed Baker.

Special Constable Bowman perched his head on one side and scratched his grizzly chin.

"You're not trying to put up a job on me?" he inquired coldly. "You did see a car?"

"I certainly did," declared Baker, and a belligerent tone underlay his manner. "I certainly saw it, Jim, and it it didn't come out your end, why—why—"

He paused and glanced quickly behing him. The action inspired a sudden similar caution on Bowman's part.

"Maybe—maybe—" said Bowman after a minute, "maybe it's a—a spook auto?"

"Well it must be," mused Baker. "You know as well as I do that no car can get out of this trap except at the ends. That car came in here, it isn't here now and it didn't go out your end. Now where is it?"

Bowman stared at him a minute, picked up his lantern, shook his head solemnly and wandered along the road back to his post. On his way he glanced around quickly, apprehensively three times—Baker did the same thing four times.

On the third night the phantom car appeared and disappeared precisely as it had done previously. Again Baker and Bowman met half way between posts and talked it over.

"I'll tell you what, Baker," said Bowman in conclusion, "maybe you're just imagining that you see a car. Maybe if I was at your end I couldn't see it."

Special Constable Baker was distinctly hurt at the insinuation.

"All right, Jim," he said at last, "if you think that way about it we'll swap posts tomorrow night. We won't have to say anything about it when we report."

"Now that's the talk," exclaimed Bowman with an air approaching enthusiasm. "I'll bet I don't see it."

On the following night Special Constable Bowman made himself comfortable on Special Constabel Baker's camp-stool. And *he* saw the phantom auto. It came upon him with a rush and a crackling-chug of engine and then sped on leaving him nerveless. He called Baker over the wire and Baker watched half an hour for the phantom. It didn't appear.

Ultimately all things reach the newspapers. So with the story of the phantom auto. Hutchinson Hatch, reporter, smiled incredulously when his City Editor laid aside an inevitable cigar and tersely stated the known facts. The known facts in this instance were meager almost to the disappearing point. They consisted merely of a corroborated statement that an automobile, solid and tangible enough to all appearances, rushed into The Trap each night and totally disappeared.

But there was enough of the bizarre about it to pique the curiosity, to make one wonder, so Hatch journeyed down to Yarborough County, an hour's ride from the city, met and talked to Baker and Bowman and then, in broad daylight, strolled along The Trap twice. It was a leisurely, thorough investigation with the end in view of finding out how an automobile once inside might get out again without going out either end.

On the first trip through Hatch paid particular attention to the Thomas Q. Rogers side of the road. The wall, nine feet high, was an unbroken line of stone with not the slightest indication of a secret wagon-way through it anywhere. Secret wagon-way! Hatch smiled at the phrase. But when he reached the other end—Bowman's end—of The Trap he was perfectly convinced of one thing—that no automobile had left the hard, macadamized road to go over, under or through the Thomas Q. Rogers wall. Returning, still leisurely, he paid strict attention to the John Phelps Stocker side, and when he reached the other end—Baker's end—he was convinced of another thing—that no automobile had left the road to go over, under or through the John Phelps Stocker wall. The only opening of any sort was a narrow footpath, not more than 16 inches wide.

Hatch saw no shrubbery along the road, nothing but a strip of scrupulously cared for grass, therefore the phantom auto could not be hidden any time, night or day. Hatch failed, too, to find any holes in the road so that the automobile didn't go down through the earth. At this point he involuntarily glanced up at the blue sky above. Perhaps, he thought whimsically, the automobile was a strange sort of bird, or—or—and he stopped suddenly.

"By George!" he exclaimed. "I wonder if—"

And the remainder of the afternoon he spent systematically making inquiries. He went from house to house, the Stocker house, the Rogers house, both of which were at the time unoccupied, then to cottage, cabin and hut in turn. But he didn't seem overladen with information when he joined Special Constable Baker at his end of The Trap that evening about seven o'clock.

Together they rehearsed the strange points of the mystery and as the shadows grew about them until finally the darkness was so dense that Baker's lantern was the only bright spot in sight. As the chill of the evening closed in a certain awed tone crept into their voices. Occasionally an auto bowled along and each time as it hove in sight Hatch glanced at Baker questioningly. And each time Baker shook his head. And each time, too, he called Bowman, in this manner accounting for every car that went into The Trap.

"It'll come all right," said Baker after a long silence, "and I'll know it the minute it rounds the curve coming toward us. I'd know its two lights in a thousand."

They sat still and smoked. After awhile two dazzling white lights burst into view far down the road and Baker, in excitement, dropped his pipe.

"That's her," he declared. "Look at her coming!"

And Hatch did look at her coming. The speed of the mysterious car was such as to make one look. Like the eyes of a giant the two lights came on toward them, and Baker perfunctorily went through the motions of attempting to stop it. The car fairly whizzed past them and the rush of air which tugged at their coats was convincing enough proof of its solidity. Hatch strained his eyes to read the number as the auto flashed past. But it was hopeless. The tail of the car was lost in an eddying whirl of dust.

"She certainly does travel," commented Baker, softly.

"She does," Hatch assented.

Then, for the benefit of the newspaper man, Baker called Bowman on the wire.

"Car's coming again," he shouted. "Look out and let me know!"

Bowman, at his end, waited twenty minutes, then made the usual report—the car had not passed. Hutchinson Hatch was a calm, cold, dispassionate young man but now a queer, creepy sensation stole along his spinal column. He lighted a cigarette and pulled himself together with a jerk.

"There's one way to find out where it goes," he declared at last, emphatically, "and that's to place a man in the middle just beyond the bend of The Trap and let him wait and see. If the car goes up, down, or evaporates he'll see and can tell us."

Baker looked at him curiously.

"I'd hate to be the man in the middle," he declared. There was something of uneasiness in his manner.

"I rather think I would, too," responded Hatch.

On the following evening, consequent upon the appearance of the story of the phantom auto in Hatch's paper, there were twelve other reporters on hand. Most of them were openly, flagrantly sceptical; they even insinuated that no one had seen an auto. Hatch smiled wisely.

"Wait!" he advised with deep conviction.

So when the darkness fell that evening the newspaper men of a great city had entered into a conspiracy to capture the phantom auto. Thirteen of them, making a total of fifteen men with Baker and Bowman, were on hand and they agreed to a suggestion for all to take positions along the road of The Trap from Baker's post to Bowman's, watch for the auto, see what happened to it and compare notes afterwards. So they scattered themselves along a few hundred feet apart and waited. That night the phantom auto didn't appear at all and twelve reporters jeered at Hutchinson Hatch and told him to light his pipe with the story. And next night when Hatch and Baker and Bowman alone were watching the phantom auto reappeared.

II

Like a child with a troublesome problem, Hatch took the entire matter and laid it before Professor Augustus S.F.X. Van Dusen, the master brain. The Thinking Machine, with squint eyes turned steadily upward and long, slender fingers pressed tip to tip, listened to the end.

"Now I know of course that automobiles don't fly." Hatch burst out savagely in conclusion, "and if this one doesn't fly, there is no earthly way for it to get out of The Trap, as they call it. I went over the thing carefully—I even went so far as to examine the ground and the tops of the walls to see if a runway had been let down for the auto to go over."

The Thinking Machine squinted at him inquiringly.

"Are you sure you saw an automobile?" he demanded irritably.

"Certainly I saw it," blurted the reporter. "I not only saw it—I smelled it. Just to convince myself that it was real I tossed my cane in front of the thing and it smashed it to tooth-picks."

"Perhaps, then, if everything is as you say, the auto actually *does* fly," remarked the scientist.

The reporter stared into the calm, inscrutable face of The Thinking Machine, fearing first that he had not hear aright. Then he concluded that he had.

"You mean," he inquired eagerly, "that the phantom may be an auto-aeroplane affair, and it actually does fly?"

"It's not at all impossible," commented the scientist.

"I had an idea something like that myself," Hatch explained, "and questioned every soul within a mile or so but I didn't get anything."

"The perfect stretch of road there might be the very place for some daring experimenter to get up sufficient speed to soar a short distance in a light machine," continued the scientist.

"Light machine?" Hatch repeated. "Did I tell you that this car had four people in it?"

"Four people!" exclaimed the scientist. "Dear me! Dear me! That makes it very different. Of course four people would be too great a lift for an—"

For ten minutes he sat silent, and tiny, cobwebby lines appeared in his dome-like brow. Then he arose and passed into the adjoining room. After a moment Hatch heard the telephone bell jingle. Five minutes later The Thinking Machine appeared, and scowled upon him unpleasantly.

"I suppose what you really want to learn is if the car is a—a material one, and to whom it belongs?" he queried.

"That's it," agreed the reporter, "and of course, why it does what it does, and how it gets out of The Trap."

"Do you happen to know a fast, long-distance bicycle rider?" demanded the scientist abruptly.

"A dozen of them," replied the reporter promptly. "I think I see the idea, but—"

"You haven't the faintest inkling of the idea," declared The Thinking Machine positively. "If you can arrange with a fast rider who can go a distance—it might be thirty, forty, fifty miles—we may end this little affair without difficulty."

Under these circumstances Professor Augustus S.F.X. Van Dusen, Ph.D., LL.D., F.R.S., M.D., etc., etc., scientist and logician met the famous Jimmie Thalhaurer, the world's champion long distance bicy-clist. He held every record from five miles up to and including six hours, had twice won the six-day race and was, altogether, a master in his field. He came in chewing a tooth-pick. There were introductions.

"You ride the bicycle?" inquired the crusty little scientist.

"Well, *some*," confessed the champion modestly with a wink at Hatch.

"Can you keep up with an automobile for a distance of, say, thirty or forty miles?"

"I can keep up with anything that ain't got wings," was the response.

"Well, to tell you the truth," volunteered The Thinking Machine, "there is a growing belief that this particular automobile has wings. However, if you can keep up with it—"

"Ah, quit your kiddin'," said the champion, easily. "I can ride rings around anything on wheels. I'll start behind it and beat it where it's going."

The Thinking Machine examined the champion, Jimmie Thalhauer, as a curiosity. In the seclusion of his laboratory he had never had an opportunity of meeting just such another worldly young person.

"How fast *can* you ride, Mr. Thalhauer?" he asked at last.

"I'm ashamed to tell you," confided the champion in a hushed voice. "I can ride so fast that I scare myself." He paused a moment. "But it seems to me," he said, "if there's thirty or forty miles to do I ought to do it on a motor-cycle."

"Now that's just the point," explained The Thinking Machine. "A motor-cycle makes noise and if it could have been used we would have hired a fast automobile. This proposition briefly is: I want you to ride without lights behind an automobile which may also run without lights and find out where it goes. No occupant of the car must suspect that it is followed."

"Without lights?" repeated the champion. "Gee! Rubber shoe, eh?"

The Thinking Machine looked his bewilderment.

"Yes, that's it," Hatch answered for him.

"I guess it's good for a four column head? Hunh?" inquired the champion. "Special pictures posed by the champion? Hunh?"

"Yes," Hatch replied.

"'Tracked on a Bicycle' sounds good to me. Hunh?"

Hatch nodded.

So arrangements were concluded and then and there The Thinking

Machine gave definite and conclusive instructions to the champion. While these apparently bore broadly on the problem in hand they conveyed absolutely no inkling of his plan to the reporter. At the end the champion arose to go.

"You're a most extraordinary young man, Mr. Thalhauer," commented The Thinking Machine, not without admiration for the sturdy, powerful figure.

And as Hatch accompanied the champion out the door and down the steps Jimmie smiled with easy grace.

"Nutty old guy, ain't he? Hunh?"

Night! Utter blackness, relieved only by a white, ribbonlike road which winds away mistily under a starless sky. Shadowy hedges line either side and occasionally a tree thrusts itself upward out of the sombreness. The murmur of human voices in the shadows, then the crackling-chug of an engine and an automobile moves slowly, without lights, into the road. There is the sudden clatter of an engine at high speed and the car rushes away.

From the hedge comes the faint rustle of leaves as of wind stirring, then a figure moves impalpably. A moment and it becomes a separate entity; a quick movement and the creak of a leather bicycle saddle. Silently the single figure, bent low over the handle bars, moves after the car with ever increasing momentum.

Then a long, desperate race. For mile after mile, mile after mile the auto goes on. The silent cyclist has crept up almost to the rear axle and hangs there doggedly as a racer to his pace. On and on they rush together through the darkness, the chauffeur moving with a perfect knowledge of his road, the single rider behind clinging on grimly with set teeth. The powerful, piston-like legs move up and down to the beat of the engine.

At last, with dust-dry throat and stinging, aching eyes the cyclist feels the pace slacken and instantly he drops back out of sight. It is only by sound that he follows now. The car stops; the cyclist is lost in the shadows.

For two or three hours the auto stands deserted and silent. At last the voices are heard again, the car stirs, moves away and the cyclist drops in behind. Another race which leads off in another direction. Finally, from a knoll, the lights of a city are seen. Ten minutes elapse, the auto stops, the headlights flare up and more leisurely it proceeds on its way.

* * *

On the following evening The Thinking Machine and Hutchinson Hatch called upon Fielding Stanwood, President of the Fordyce National Bank. Mr. Stanwood looked at them with interrogative eyes.

"We called to inform you, Mr. Stanwood," explained The Thinking Machine, "that a box of securities, probably United States bonds is missing from your bank."

"What?" exclaimed Mr. Stanwood, and his face paled. "Robbery?"

"I only know the bonds were taken out of the vault tonight by Joseph Marsh, your assistant cashier," said the scientist, "and that he, together with three men, left the bank with the box and are now at—a place I can name."

Mr. Stanwood was staring at him in amazement.

"You know where they are?" he demanded.

"I said I did," replied the scientist, shortly.

"Then we must inform the police at once, and—"

"I don't know that there has been an actual crime," interrupted the scientist. "I do know that every night for a week these bonds have been taken out through the connivance of your watchman and in each instance have been returned, intact, before morning. They will be returned tonight. Therefore I would advise, if you act, not to do so until the four men return with the bonds."

It was a singular party which met in the private office of President Stanwood at the bank just after midnight. Marsh and three companions, formally under arrest, were present as were President Stanwood, The Thinking Machine and Hatch, besides detectives. Marsh had the bonds under his arms when he was taken. He talked freely when questioned.

"I will admit," he said without hesitating, "that I have acted beyond my rights in removing the bonds from the vault here, but there is no ground for prosecution. I am a responsible officer of this bank and have violated no trust. Nothing is missing, nothing is stolen. Every bond that went out of the bank is here."

"But why—why did you take the bonds?" demanded Mr. Stanwood.

Marsh shrugged his shoulders.

"It's what has been called a get-rich-quick scheme," said The Thinking Machine. "Mr. Hatch and I made some investigations today. Mr. Marsh and these other three are interested in a business venture which is ethically dishonest but which is within the law. They have sought backing for the scheme amounting to about a million dollars. Those four or five men of means with whom they have discussed the matter have called each night for a week at Marsh's country place. It was necessary to make them believe that there was already a million or so in the scheme, so these bonds were borrowed and represented to be owned by themselves. They were taken to and fro between the bank and his home in a kind of an automobile. This is really what happened, based on knowledge which Mr. Hatch has gathered and what I myself developed by the use of a little logic.''

And his statement of the affair proved to be correct. Marsh and the others admitted the statement to be true. It was while The Thinking Machine was homeward bound that he explained the phantom auto affair to Hatch.

"The phantom auto as you call it," he said, "is the vehicle in which the bonds were moved about. The phantom idea came merely by chance. On the night the vehicle was first noticed it was rushing along—we'll say to reach Marsh's house in time for an appointment. A road map will show you that the most direct line from the bank to Marsh's was through The Trap. If an automobile should go half way through there, then out across the Stocker estate to the other road, the distance would be lessened by a good five miles. This saving at first was of course valuable, so the car in which they rushed into The Trap was merely taken across the Stocker estate to the road in front.''

"But how?" demanded Hatch. "There's no road there."

"I learned by phone from Mr. Stocker that there is a narrow walk from a very narrow foot-gate in Stocker's wall on The Trap leading through the grounds to the other road. The phantom auto wasn't really an auto at all—it was merely two motor-cycles arranged with seats and a steering apparatus. The French Army has been experimenting with them. The motor-cycles are, of course, separate machines and as such it was easy to trundle them through a narrow gate and across to the other road. The seats are light; they can be carried under the arm.''

"Oh!" exclaimed Hatch suddenly, then after a minute: "But what did Jimmie Thalhauer do for you?''

"He waited in the road at the other end of the foot-path from The Trap," the scientist explained, "When the auto was brought through and put together he followed it to Marsh's home and from there to the bank. The rest of it you and I worked out today. It's merely logic, Mr. Hatch, logic.''

There was a pause.

"That Mr. Thalhauer is really a marvelous young man, Mr. Hatch, don't you think?''

Nero Wolfe

INSTEAD OF EVIDENCE
Rex Stout

A MONG THE KINDS of men I have a prejudice against are the ones named Eugene. There's no use asking me why, because I admit it's a prejudice. It may be that when I was in kindergarten out in Ohio a man named Eugene stole candy from me, but, if so, I have forgotten all about it. For all practical purposes, it is merely one facet of my complex character that I do not like men named Eugene.

That, and that alone, accounted for my offish attitude when Mr. and Mrs. Eugene R. Poor called at Nero Wolfe's office that Tuesday afternoon in October, because I had never seen or heard of the guy before, and neither had Wolfe.

The appointment had been made by phone that morning, so I was prejudiced before I ever got a look at him. The look hadn't swayed me much one way or the other. He wasn't too old to remember what his wife had given him on his fortieth birthday, but neither was he young enough to be still looking forward to it. Nothing about him stood out. His face was taken at random out of stock, with no alterations. Gray herringbone suits like his were that afternoon being bought in stores from San Diego to Bangor. Really, his only distinction was that they had named him Eugene.

In spite of which I was regarding him with polite curiosity, for he had just told Nero Wolfe that he was going to be murdered by his partner, a man named Conroy Blaney.

I was sitting at my desk in the room Nero Wolfe used for an office in his home on West 35th Street, and Wolfe was behind his desk, arranged in a chair that had been especially constructed to support up to a quarter of a ton, which was not utterly beyond the limits of possibility. Eugene R. Poor was in the red leather chair a short distance beyond Wolfe's desk, with a little table smack against its right arm for the convenience of clients in writing checks. Mr. Poor was on a spare between her husband and me.

I might mention that I was not aware of any prejudice against Mrs. Poor. For one thing, there was no reason to suppose that her name was Eugene. For another, there were several reasons to suppose that her fortieth birthday would not come before mine, though she was good and mature. She had by no means struck me dumb, but there are people who seem to improve a room just by being in it.

Naturally, Wolfe was scowling. He shook his head, moving it a full half-inch right and left, which was, for him, a frenzy of negation.

"No, sir," he said emphatically. "I suppose two hundred men and women have sat in that chair, Mr. Poor, and tried to hire me to keep someone from killing them." His eyes switched to me. "How many, Archie?"

I said, to oblige him, "Two hundred and nine."

"Have I taken the jobs?"

"No, sir. Never."

He wiggled a finger at Eugene. "For two million dollars a year you can make it fairly difficult for a man to kill you. That's about what it costs to protect a president or a king, and even so, consider the record. Of course, if you give up all other activity it can be done more cheaply, say, forty thousand a year. A cave in a mountainside, never emerging, with six guards you can trust and a staff to suit—"

Eugene was trying to get something in. He finally did: "I don't expect you to keep him from killing me. That's not what I came for."

"Then what the deuce did you come for?"

"To keep him from getting away with it." Eugene cleared his throat. "I was trying to tell you. I agree that you can't stop him; I don't see how anybody can. Sooner or later. He's a clever man." His voice took on bitterness: "Too damn clever for me, and I wish I'd never met him. Sure, I know a man can kill a man if he once decides to, but Con Blaney is so damn clever that it isn't a question whether he can kill me or not; the question is whether he can manage it so that he is in the clear. I'm afraid he can. And I don't want him to."

His wife made a little noise, and he stopped to look at her. Then he shook his head at her as if she had said something, took a cigar from his vest pocket, removed the band, inspected first one end and then the other to decide which was which, got a gadget from another vest pocket and snipped one of the ends, and lit up. He no sooner had it lit than it slipped out of his mouth, bounced on his thigh, and landed on the rug. He retrieved it and got his teeth sunk in it.

"So," I thought to myself, "you're not so doggone calm about getting murdered as you were making out to be."

"So I came," he told Wolfe, "to give you the facts, to get the facts down, and to pay you five thousand dollars to see that he doesn't manage it that way." The cigar between his teeth interfered with his talking, and he took it out of his mouth. "If he kills me I'll be dead. I want someone to know about it."

Wolfe's eyes had gone half shut. "But why pay me five thousand dollars in advance? Wouldn't someone know about it? Your wife, for instance?"

Eugene nodded. "I've thought about that. I've thought it all out. What if he kills her, too? I have no idea how he'll try to work it, or when, and who is there besides my wife whom I can absolutely trust? I'm not taking any chances. Of course, I thought of the police, but judging from my own experience, a couple of burglaries down at the shop, and, you know, the experiences of a businessman, I'm not sure they'd even remember I'd been there if it happened in a year or maybe two years." He stuck his cigar in his mouth, puffed twice, and took it out again. "What's the matter—don't you want five thousand dollars?"

Wolfe said gruffly, "I wouldn't get five thousand. This is October. As my 1945 income now stands, I'll keep about ten percent of any additional receipts after paying taxes. Out of five thousand, five hundred would be mine. If Mr. Blaney is as clever as you think he is, I wouldn't consider trying to uncover him on a murder for five hundred dollars." He stopped and opened his eyes to glare at the wife. "May I ask, madam, what you are looking so pleased about?"

Wolfe couldn't stand to see a woman look pleased.

Mrs. Poor was regarding him with a little smile of obvious approval. "Because," she said, in a voice that was pleased too, and a nice voice, "I need help, and I think you're going to help me. I don't approve of this. I didn't want my husband to come here."

"Indeed. Where did you want him to go—to the Atlantic Detective Agency?"

"Oh, no; if I had been in favor of his going to any detective at all, of course it would have been Nero Wolfe. But— May I explain?"

Wolfe glanced at the clock on the wall. Three-forty. In twenty minutes he would be leaving for the plant-rooms on the roof, to indulge in his favorite hobby—monkeying around with orchids. Besides being a champion eater and drinker, Wolfe is the best orchid grower in New York. He said curtly, "I have eighteen minutes."

Eugene put in, with a determined voice, "Then I'm going to use them—" But his wife smiled him out of it. She went on to Wolfe: "It won't take that long. My husband and Mr. Blaney have been business partners for ten years. They own the firm of Blaney & Poor, manufacturers of novelties—you know—they make things like matches that won't strike and chairs with rubber legs and bottled drinks that taste like soap—"

"Good God," Wolfe muttered in horror.

She ignored it. "It's the biggest firm in the business. Mr. Blaney gets the ideas and handles the production—he's a genius at it—my husband handles the business part, sales and so on. But Mr. Blaney is really just about too conceited to live, and now that the business is a big success he thinks my husband isn't needed, and he wants him to get out and take twenty thousand dollars for his half. Of course, it's worth a great deal more than that—at least ten times as much—and my husband won't do it. Mr. Blaney is very conceited, and also he will not let anything stand in his way. The argument has gone on and on, until now my husband is convinced that Mr. Blaney is capable of doing anything to get rid of him."

"Of killing him. And you don't agree."

"Oh, no. I do agree. I think Mr. Blaney would stop at nothing."

"Has he made threats?"

She shook her head. "He isn't that kind. He doesn't make threats; he just goes ahead."

"Then why didn't you want your husband to come to me?"

"Because he's simply too stubborn to live." She smiled at Eugene to take out any sting, and back at Wolfe. "There's a clause in the partnership agreement—they signed it when they started the business—that says if either one of them dies, the other one owns the whole thing. That's another reason why my husband thinks Mr. Blaney will kill him, and I think so, too. But what my husband wants is to make sure Mr. Blaney gets caught—that's how stubborn he is—and what I want is for my husband to stay alive."

"Now, Martha," Eugene put in, "I came here to—"

So her name was Martha. I had no prejudice against women named Martha.

She kept the floor. "It's like this," she appealed to Wolfe. "My husband thinks that Mr. Blaney is determined to kill him if he can't get what he wants any other way, and I think so, too, You, yourself, think that if a man is determined to kill another man nothing can stop him. So isn't it perfectly obvious? My husband has over two hundred thousand dollars saved up outside the business, about half of it in war bonds. He can get another twenty thousand from Mr. Blaney for his half of the business—"

"It's worth twenty times that," Eugene said savagely, showing real emotion for the first time.

"Not to you if you're dead," she snapped back at him, and went on to Wolfe: "With the income from that we could live more than comfortably—and happily. I hope my husband loves me—I *hope* he does—and I know I love him." She leaned forward in her chair. "That's why I came along today—I thought maybe you would help me persuade him. It isn't as if I wouldn't stand by my husband in a fight if there was any chance of his winning. But is there any sense in being so stubborn if you can't possibly win? If, instead of winning, you will probably die? Now, does that make sense? I ask you, Mr Wolfe—you are a wise and clever and able man—what would you do if you were in my husband's position?"

Wolfe muttered, "You put that as a question?"

"Yes, I do."

"Well. Granting that you have described the situation correctly, I would kill Mr. Blaney."

She looked startled. "But that's silly." She frowned. "Of course you're joking. and it's no joke."

"I'd kill him in a second," Eugene told Wolfe, "if I thought I could get away with it. I suppose *you* could, but I couldn't."

"And I'm afraid," Wolfe said politely, "you couldn't hire me for that." He glanced at the clock. "I would advise against your consulting even your wife. An undetected murder is strictly a one-man job. Her advice, sir, is sound. Are you going to take it?"

"No." Eugene sounded as stubborn as she said he was.

"Are you going to kill Mr. Blaney?"

"No."

"Do you still want to pay me five thousand dollars?"

"Yes, I do."

Mrs. Poor, who was rapidly becoming Martha to me, tried to horn in, but bigger and louder people than she had failed at that when orchid time was at hand. Wolfe ignored her and went on to Mr. Poor:

"I advise you against that, too, under the circumstances. Here are the circumstances—Archie, take your notebook. Make a receipt reading,

'Received from Eugene R. Poor five thousand dollars, in return for which I agree, in case he dies within one year, to give the police the information he has given me today, and take any further action that may seem to me advisable.' Sign my name and initial it as usual. Get all details from Mr. Poor.'' Wolfe pushed back his chair and got the levers of his muscles in position to hoist the bulk.

Eugene's eyes were moist with tears, but they came, not from emotion, but from smoke from his second cigar. In fact, throughout the interview his nervousness seemed to concentrate on his cigar. He had dropped it twice, and the smoke seemed determined to go down the wrong way and make him cough. But he was able to speak, all right.

''That's no good,'' he objected. ''You don't even say what kind of action. At least, you ought to say—''

''I advised you against it under the circumstances.'' Wolfe was on his feet. ''Those, sir, are the circumstances. That's all I'll undertake. Suit yourself.'' He started to move.

But Eugene had another round to fire. His hand went in a pocket and came out full of folded money. ''I hadn't mentioned,'' he said, displaying the pretty objects, ''that I brought it in cash. Speaking of income tax, if you're up to the ninety per cent bracket, getting it in cash would make it a lot more—''

Wolfe's look stopped him. ''Pfui,'' Wolfe said. He hadn't had as good a chance to show off for a month. ''I am not a common cheat, Mr. Poor. Not that I am a saint. Given adequate provocation, I might conceivably cheat a man—or a woman, or even a child. But you are suggesting that I cheat, not a man or woman or child, but a hundred and forty million of my fellow citizens. Bah.''

We stared at his back as he left, as he knew we would, and in a moment we heard the sound of his elevator door opening.

I flipped to a fresh page in my notebook and turned to Eugene and Martha. ''To refresh your memory,'' I said, ''the name is Archie Goodwin. Among other things, I'm Wolfe's assistant, and I'm the one that has been doing the work around here for fifty years, more or less. I am also, Mr. Poor, an admirer of your wife.''

He nearly dropped his cigar again. ''You're what?''

''I admire your wife as an advice giver. She has learned one of the most important rules—that, far as life falls short of perfection, it is more fun outside the grave than in it. With over two hundred thousand bucks—''

"I've had enough advice," he said as if he meant it. "My mind is made up."

"Okay." I got the notebook in position. "Give me everything you think we'll need. First, basic facts. Home and business addresses?"

It took close to an hour, so it was nearly five o'clock when they left. I found Eugene irritating and therefore kept my prejudice intact. I wondered later what difference it would have made in my attitude if I had known that in a few hours he would be dead. Even if you take the line that he had it coming to him, which would be easy to justify, at least it would have made the situation more interesting. But during that hour, as far as I knew, they were just a couple of white-livers, scared stiff by a false alarm named Blaney, so it was merely another job.

I was still typing from my notes when, at six o'clock, after the regulation two hours in the plant-rooms, Wolfe came down to the office He got fixed in his chair, rang for Fritz to bring beer, and demanded, "Did you take that man's money?"

I grinned at him. Up to his old tricks. I had been a civilian again for only a week, and here he was, already treating me like a hireling, just as he had for years, acting as if I had never been a colonel, as, in fact, I hadn't, but anyway I had been a major.

I asked him, "What do you think? If I say I took it you'll claim that your attitude as you left plainly indicated that he had insulted you and you wouldn't play. If I say I refused it you'll claim I've done you out of a fee. Which do you prefer?"

He abandoned it. "Do your typing. I like to hear you typing. If you are typing you can't talk."

To humor him I typed, which as it turned out, was just as well, since that neat list of facts was going to be needed before bedtime. It was finished when Fritz entered at eight o'clock to announce dinner.

Back in the office, where the clock said 9:42, I was announcing my intention of catching a movie by the tail at the Rialto, when the phone rang. It was our old friend, Inspector Cramer, whose voice I hadn't heard for weeks, asking for Wolfe. Wolfe picked up his receiver, and I stuck to mine so as to get it firsthand.

"Wolfe? . . . Cramer. I've got a paper here, taken from the pocket of a dead man, a receipt for five thousand dollars, signed by you, dated today. It says you have information to give the police if he dies. All right, he's dead. I don't ask you to come up here, because I know you wouldn't, and I'm too busy to go down there. What's the information?"

Wolfe grunted. "What killed him?"

"An explosion. Just give—"

"Did it kill his wife too?"

"Naw, she's okay, only overcome, you know. Just give—"

"I haven't got the information. Mr. Goodwin has it. Archie?"

I spoke up: "It would take quite a while, Inspector, and I've got it all typed. I can run up there—"

"All right; come ahead. The Poor apartment on Eighty-fourth Street. The number is—"

"I know the number. I know everything. Sit down and rest till I get there. . . ."

In the living-room of an apartment on the sixth floor, on 84th Street near Amsterdam Avenue, I stood and looked down at what was left of Eugene Poor. All I really recognized was the gray herringbone suit and the shirt and tie, on account of what the explosion had done to his face, and also on that account I didn't look much, for while I may not be a softy, I see no point in prolonged staring at a face that has entirely stopped being a face.

I asked Sergeant Purley Stebbins, who was sticking close by me, apparently to see that I didn't swipe Eugene's shoes, "You say a cigar did that to him?"

Purley nodded. "Yeah; so the wife says. He lit a cigar, and it blew up."

"Huh, I don't believe it . . . Yes, I guess I do, too, if she says so. They make novelties. Now, that's a novelty."

I looked around. The room was full of what you would expect— assorted snoops, all doing the chores, from print collectors up to inspectors, or at least one inspector, namely, Cramer himself, who sat at a table near a wall reading the script I had brought him. Most of them I knew, at least by sight, but there was one complete stranger. She was in a chair in a far corner, being questioned by a homicide dick named Rowcliff. Being trained to observe details even when under a strain, I had caught at a glance of her outstanding characteristics, such as youth, shapeliness, and shallow depressions at the temples, which happen to appeal to me.

I aimed a thumb in her direction and asked Purley, "Bystander, wife's sister, or what?"

He shook his head. "God knows. She came to call just after we got here, and we want to know what for."

I strolled over to the corner and stopped against them, and the girl and the dick looked up. "Excuse me," I told her; "when you get through here will you kindly call on Nero Wolfe at this address?" I handed her a card. The temples were even better close up. "Mr. Wolfe is going to solve this murder."

Rowcliff snarled. He always snarled. "Get away from here, and stay away."

Actually, he was helpless, because the inspector had sent for me, and he knew it. I ignored him and told the temples, "If this person takes that card away from you, it's in the phone book—Nero Wolfe," left them, and crossed over to Cramer at the table, dodging photographers and other scientists on the way.

Cramer didn't look up, so I asked the top of his head. "Where's Mrs. Poor?"

He growled, "Bedroom."

"I want to see her."

"The hell you do." He jiggled the sheets I had brought him. "Sit down."

I sat down and said, "I want to see our client."

"So you've got a client?"

"Sure, we have. Didn't you see that receipt?"

He grunted. "Give her a chance. I am. Let her get herself together. . . . Don't touch that!"

I was only moving a hand to point at a box of cigars there on the table, with the lid closed. I grinned at him. "The more the merrier. I mean, fingerprints. But if that's the box the loaded one came from, you ought to satisfy my curiosity. He smoked two cigars this afternoon at the office."

Cramer shot me a glance, then got out his penknife and opened the lid and lifted the paper flap. It was a box of 25, and 24 of them were still there. Only one gone. I inspected at close range, sat back, and nodded. "They're the same. They not only look it, but the bands say Alta Vista. There would be two of those bands still in the ash tray down at the office if Fritz wasn't so neat." I squinted again at the array in the box. "They certainly look kosher. Do you suppose they're all loaded?"

"I don't know. The laboratory can answer that one." He closed the box with the tip of his knife. "Damn murders, anyhow." He tapped the papers with his finger. "This is awful pat. The wife let out a hint or two, and I've sent for Blaney. I hope to God it's a wrap-up, and maybe it is. How did Poor seem this afternoon, scared, nervous, what?"

"Mostly stubborn. Mind made up."

"What about the wife?"

"Stubborn too. She wanted him to get out from under and go on breathing. She thought they could be as happy as larks on the income from a measly quarter of a million."

The next twenty minutes was a record—Inspector Cramer and me conversing without a single ugly remark. It lasted that long only because of various interruptions from his army. The last one, toward the end, was from Rowcliff walking up to the table to say, "Do you want to talk to this young woman, Inspector?"

"How do I know? What about her?"

"Her name is Helen Vardis. She's an employee of Poor's firm, Blaney & Poor—been with them four years. At first she showed signs of hysteria and then calmed down. First she said she just happened to come here. Then she saw what that was worth and said she came to see Poor by appointment, at his request, on a confidential matter, and wants us to promise not to tell Blaney, because she would lose her job."

"What confidential matter?"

"She won't say. That's what I've been working on."

"Work on it some more."

There was a commotion at the outer door, and it came on through the foyer into the living-room in the shape of a municipal criminologist gripping the arm of a wild-eyed young man who apparently didn't want to be gripped. They were both talking, or at least making noises. It was hard to tell whether they were being propelled by the young man pulling or the cop pushing.

Cramer boomed, "Doyle! What the hell? Who is that?"

The young man goggled around, declaiming, "I have a right— Oh! There you are."

She said, as if she didn't need any information from snakes or rats, "You didn't lose any time, did you? Now you think you can have her, don't you?"

He held the stare, showing no reaction except clamping his jaw, and their audience sat tight. In a moment he seemed to realize it was rather a public performance, and his head started to pivot, doing a slow circle, taking in the surroundings. It was a good, thorough job of looking, without any waver or pause, so far as I could see, even when it hit the most sensational item, namely, the corpse. During the process his eyes lost their wild look entirely, and when he spoke his voice was cool and controlled. It was evident that his mental operations were enough in order for him to pick the most intelligent face in the bunch, since it was to me he put the question:

"Are you in charge here?"

I replied, "No. This one. Inspector Cramer."

He strode across and looked Cramer in the eye and made a speech: "My name is Joe Groll. I work for Blaney & Poor, factory foreman. I followed that girl, Helen Vardis, when she left home tonight, because I wanted to know where she was going, and she came here. The police cars and cops going in and out made me want to ask questions, and finally I got the answer that a man named Poor had been murdered, so I wanted to find out. Where is Blaney? Conroy Blaney, the partner—"

"I know," Cramer said, looking disgusted. Naturally he was disgusted, since what he had hoped would be a wrap-up was spilling out in various directions. "We've sent for Blaney. Why were you following—?"

"That isn't true!"

More diversions. Helen Vardis had busted out of her corner to join the table group, close enough to Joe Groll to touch him, but they weren't touching. Instead of resuming their staring match, they were both intent on Cramer.

Looking even more disgusted, Cramer asked her, "What isn't true?"

"That he was following me!" Helen was mad clear to her temples and pretty as a picture. "Why should he follow me? He came here to—" She bit it off sharp.

"Yeah," Cramer said encouragingly. "To what?"

"I don't know! But I do know who killed Mr. Poor! It was Martha Davis!"

"That helps. Who is Martha Davis?"

Joe Groll said, giving information again, "She means Mrs. Poor. That was her name when she worked in the factory, before she got married. She means Mrs. Poor killed her husband. That's on account of jealousy. She's crazy."

A quiet but energetic voice came from a new direction: "She certainly is."

It was Martha, who emerged from a door at the far end and approached the table. She was pale and didn't seem any too sure of her leg action, but she made her objective all right. She spoke to the girl, with no sign of violent emotion that I could detect, not even resentment: "Helen, you ought to be ashamed of yourself. I think you will be when you have calmed down and thought things over. You have no right or reason to talk like that. You accuse me of killing my husband? Why?"

Very likely Helen would have proceeded to tell her why, but at that moment a cop entered from the foyer escorting a stranger. Cramer motioned with his hand for them to back out.

But the stranger was not a backer-out. He came on straight to the table and, since the arrangement showed plainly that Cramer was it, addressed the inspector: "I'm Conroy Blaney. Where's Gene Poor?"

Not that he was aggressive or in any way overwhelming. His voice was a tenor squeak and it fitted his looks. I could have picked him up and set him down again without grunting, he had an undersized nose and not much chin, and he was going bald. In spite of all those handicaps his sudden appearance had a remarkable effect. Martha Poor simply turned and left the room. The expressions on the faces of Helen Vardis and Joe Groll changed completely; they went deadpan in one second flat. I saw at once that there would be no more blurting, and so did Cramer.

As for Blaney, he looked around, saw the body of his partner on the floor, stepped toward it and gazed down at it, and squeaked. "Good heavens! Good heavens! Who did it?" . . .

Next morning at eleven o'clock when Wolfe came down to the office after his two-hour session up in the plant-rooms, I made my report. He took it, as usual, leaning back in his chair with his eyes closed, with no visible sign of consciousness. The final chapter was the details given me by Martha Poor, with whom I had managed to have a talk around midnight by pressing Cramer on the client angle and wearing him down. I gave it to Wolfe:

"They came here yesterday in their own car. When they left here, a little before five, they drove to Madison Square Garden and got a program of the afternoon rodeo performance, the reason for that being he had needed to explain his absence from the office and, not wanting Blaney to know that he was coming to see you, he had said he was going to the rodeo, and wanted to be able to answer questions if he was asked about it. Then they drove up to Westchester. Conroy Blaney has a place up there, a shack in the hills where he lives and spends his evenings and week-ends thinking up novelties, and they had a date to see him there and discuss things.

"Mrs. Poor had persuaded Poor to go, thinking they might reach an agreement, but Poor hadn't wanted to, and on the way up he balked, so they stopped at a place near Scarsdale, Monty's Tavern, to debate. Poor won the debate. He wouldn't go. She left him at the tavern and went on to Blaney's place alone. The date was for six-fifteen and she got there right on the dot. . . . are you awake?"

He grunted.

I went on: "Blaney wasn't there. He lives alone, and the doors were locked. She waited around and got cold. At ten minutes to seven she beat it back to the tavern. She and Poor ate dinner there, then drove back to town, put the car in the garage, and went home. Poor had had no cigar after dinner because they hadn't had his brand at the tavern and he wouldn't smoke anything else. He has been smoking Alta Vistas for years, ten to fifteen a day. So he hung up his hat and opened a fresh box. She didn't see him do it because she was in the bathroom. She heard the sound of the explosion—not very loud—and ran out, and there he was. She phoned downstairs, and the elevator man and hall man came and phoned for a doctor and the police . . . Still awake?''

He grunted again.

"Okay. That's it. When I returned to the living-room everyone had left, including Poor's leftovers. Some friend had come to spend the night, and of course there was a cop out in the hall. When I got home you were in bed snoring.''

He had long ago quite bothering to deny that he snored. Now he didn't bother about anything, but just sat there. I resumed with the plant records. Noon came and went, and still he was making no visible effort to earn five thousand dollars, or even five hundred. Finally he heaved a sigh, almost opened his eyes, and told me, ''You say the face was unrecognizable.''

''Yes, sir. As I described it.''

''From something concealed in a cigar. Next to incredible. Phone Mr. Cramer. Tell him it is important that the identity of the corpse be established beyond question. Also, I want to see a photograph of Mr. Poor while still intact.''

I goggled at him. ''For God's sake, what do you think? That she doesn't know her own husband? She came home with him. Now, really. The old insurance gag? Your mind's in a rut. I will not phone Mr. Cramer merely to put myself on the receiving end of a horse laugh.''

''Be quiet. Let me alone. Phone Mr. Cramer.''

At lunch he discussed Yugoslav politics. That was all right, because he never talked business at the table, but when, back in the office, he went through the elaborate operations of getting himself settled with the atlas, I decided to apply spurs and sink them deep.

I arose and confronted him and announced, ''I resign.''

He muttered testily without looking up, ''Nonsense. Do your work.''

''No, sir. I'm going upstairs to pack. If you're too lazy to wiggle a finger, very well, that's not news. But you could at least send me to the Public Library to look up the genealogy—''

"Confound it!" He glared at me. "I engaged to give that information to the police, and have done so. Also to take any further action that might seem to me advisable. I have done that."

"Do you mean you're through with the case?"

"Certainly not. I haven't even started, because there's nothing to start on. Mr. Cramer may do the job himself, or he may not. I hope he does. If you don't want to work, go to a movie."

I went upstairs to my room and tried to read a book, knowing it wouldn't work, because I can never settle down when a murder case is on. So I returned to the office and rattled papers, but even that didn't faze him. At four o'clock, when he went up to the plant-rooms, I went to the corner and got afternoon papers, but there was nothing in them but the usual stuff.

When he came down again at six it was more of the same, and I went out for a walk to keep from throwing a chair at him, and stayed until dinnertime. After dinner I went to a movie, and when I got home, a little after eleven, and found him sitting drinking beer and reading a magazine, I went upstairs to bed without saying good night.

Next morning. Thursday, there wasn't a peep out of him before nine o'clock, the time he went up to the damn' orchids.

I read the papers and had more coffee.

When Wolfe came down to the office at eleven I greeted him with a friendly suggestion.

"Look," I said; "you're an expert on murder. But this Poor murder bores you because you've already collected your fee. So how about this?"

I spread the morning *Gazette* on his desk and indicated. "Absolutely Grade A. Man's naked body found in an old orchard off a lonely lane four miles from White Plains, head crushed to a pancake, apparently by a car running square over him. It offers many advantages to a great detective like you. It might be Hitler, since his body has never been found. It is in a convenient neighborhood, easily reached by train, bus, or auto, electric lights and city gas. The man has been dead at least thirty-six hours, counting from now, so it has the antique quality you like, with the clues all—"

In another minute I would have had him sputtering with fury, but the doorbell rang. "Study it," I told him, and went to the hall and the front and, following routine, fingered the curtain edge aside for a look through the glass panel.

After one brief glance I went back to the office and told Wolfe casually, "It's only Cramer. To hell with him. Since he's working on the Poor case and you're not interested—"

"Archie. Confound you. Bring him in."

The bell was ringing again, and that irritates me, so I went and got him. He was wearing his raincoat and his determined look. I relieved him of the former in the hall and let him take the latter on into the office.

When I joined them, Cramer was lowering himself into the red leather chair and telling Wolfe, "I dropped in on my way uptown because I thought it was only fair, since you gave me that information. I think I'm going to arrest your client on a charge of murder."

I sat down and felt at home.

Wolfe grunted. He leaned back in his chair, got his finger tips touching in the locality of his midriff, and said offensively, "Nonsense. You can't arrest my client on any charge whatever. My client is dead. By the way, is he? Has the corpse been properly identified?"

Cramer nodded. "Certainly. With a face like that it's routine. Barber, dentist, and doctor—they're the experts. Why, what did you think it was, an insurance fake?"

"I didn't think. Then you can't arrest my client."

"Goodwin says Mrs. Poor is your client."

"Mr. Goodwin is impulsive. You read that receipt. So you're going to charge Mrs. Poor?"

"I think I am."

"Indeed."

Cramer scowled at him. "Don't 'indeed' me. Damn it, didn't I take the trouble to stop and tell you about it?"

"Go ahead and tell me."

"Very well." Cramer screwed up his lips, deciding where to start. "First, I'd appreciate an answer to a question. What is this identity angle, anyhow? There's no the slightest doubt it was Poor. Not only the corpse itself—other things, like the elevator man who took them up when they came home, and the people up at the tavern where they ate dinner. He was known there. And what did you want a photograph for?"

"Did you bring one?"

"No. Apparently there aren't any. I wasn't interested after the dentist and barber verified the corpse, but I understand the papers had to settle for sketches drawn from descriptions. One reason I came here, what's your idea doubting the identity of the corpse?"

Wolfe shook his head. "Evidently silly, since you're ready to take Mrs. Poor. You were telling me—"

"Yeah. Of course, Goodwin told you about the box of cigars."

"Something."

"Well, that was it, all right. Poor smoked about a box every two days, boxes of twenty-five. He bought them ten boxes at a time, from a place on Varick Street near his office and factory. There were four unopened boxes in his apartment and they're okay. The one he started on when he got home Tuesday night—the twenty-four left in it are all loaded. Any one of them would have killed him two seconds after he lit it."

Wolfe muttered, "That's hard to believe—inside a cigar—"

"Right. I thought so, too. The firm of Blaney & Poor has been making trick cigars for years, but they're harmless; all they do is *phut*, and make you jump. What's in these twenty-four is anything but harmless—a special kind of instantaneous fuse the size of an ordinary thread, and a very special explosive capsule that was invented during the war and is still on the secret list. Even this is confidential; it's made by the Becker Products Corporation, and their man and the FBI are raising hell trying to find out how this murderer got hold of them. That's not for publication."

"I'm not a publisher."

"Okay."

"Of course," Wolfe remarked, "the Alta Vista people deny all knowledge."

"Sure. We let them analyze five of the twenty-four, after removing the fuses and capsules, and they say the fillers are theirs but the wrappers are not. They say whoever sliced them open and inserted the things and rewrapped them was an expert, and anyhow anybody could see that."

"Now, then. There are six people connected with Blaney & Poor who are good at making trick cigars. Four of them are mixed up in this. Helen Vardis is one of their most highly skilled workers. Joe Groll is the foreman and can do anything. Blaney is the best of all; he shows them how. And Mrs. Poor worked there for four years when she was Martha Davis, up to two years ago, when she married Poor."

Wolfe shuddered. "Six people good at making trick cigars. Couldn't the murder have been a joint enterprise? Couldn't you convict all of them?"

"I don't appreciate jokes about murder," Cramer said morosely. "I wish I could. It's a defect of character. As for getting the loaded cigars into Poor's apartment, that also is wide open. He always had them delivered to his office, and the package would lie around there, sometimes as long as two or three days, until he took it home. So anybody might have substituted the loaded box. . . . But now, about Mrs. Poor.

How do you like this? Naturally we gave the cigars and the box every-thing we had. It was a very neat job. But underneath the cigars we found two human hairs, one five inches long and one six and a half inches. We have compared them with hairs taken from various heads. Those two came from the head of Mrs. Poor. Unquestionably. So I think I'll charge her.''

Wolfe's eyes half closed. "I wouldn't do it if I were you, Mr. Cramer."

"No, sir. Let me put it this way." Wolfe maneuvered himself into position for an uplift, and got to his feet. "You have her on trial. The hairs have been placed in evidence. I am the defense attorney. I am speaking to the jury."

Wolfe fixed his eyes on me. "Ladies and gentlemen, I respect your intelligence. The operation of turning those cigars into deadly bombs has been described to you as one requiring the highest degree of skill and the minutest attention. Deft fingers and perfect eyesight were essential. Since the slightest irregularity about the appearance of that box of cigars might have attracted the attention of a veteran smoker, you can imagine the anxious scrutiny with which each cigar was inspected as it was arranged in the box. And you realize how incredible it is that such a person, so intently engaged on anything and everything the eye could see, could possibly have been guilty of such atrocious carelessness as to leave two of the hairs of her head in that box with those cigars. Ladies and gentlemen, I appeal to your intelligence! I put it to you that those hairs, far from being evidence that Martha Poor killed her husband, are, instead, evidence that Martha Poor did not kill her husband!''

Wolfe sat down and muttered, "Then they acquit her, and whom do you charge next?"

Cramer growled, "So she is your client, after all."

"No, sir, she is not. It was Mr. Poor who paid me. You said you came here because you wanted to be fair. *Pfui.* You came here because you had misgivings. You had them because you are not a ninny. A jury would want to know, anyone concerned would want to know, if those hairs did not get in the box through Mrs. Poor's carelessness, how did they get there? Who has had access to Mrs. Poor's head or hairbrush? Manifestly, that is a forlorn hope. The best chance, I would say, is the explosive capsules. Discover the tiniest link between anyone of the Becker Pro-ducts Corporation and one of your suspects, and you have it—if not your case, at least your certainty. On that I couldn't help, since I am no longer connected with the War Department. You can't convict anybody at all, let alone Mrs. Poor, without an explanation of how he got the capsules. By the way, what about motive? Mrs. Poor was tired of smelling the smoke from her husband's cigars, perhaps?''

"No. Poor was a tightwad and she wanted money. She gets the whole works plus a hundred thousand insurance. Or, according that that girl, Helen Vardis, she wanted Joe Groll, and now they'll get married."

"Proof?''

"Oh, talk.'' Cramer looked frustrated. "It goes away back to when Mrs. Poor was working there.''

Wolfe frowned. "Another thing, Mr. Cramer, about a jury. As you know, I am strongly disinclined to leave this house for any purpose whatever. I detest the idea of leaving it to go to a courtroom and sit for hours on those wooden abominations they think are seats, and the thing they provide for witnesses is even worse. I would strain a point to avoid that experience; but if it can't be avoided, Mr. Goodwin and I shall have to testify that Mr. Poor sat in that chair and told us of his conviction that Mr. Blaney was going to kill him. You know juries; you know how that would affect them. Suppose again that I am the defense attorney and—''

"Heaven help us,'' I thought, "he's going to address the jury again.''

But I got a break in the form of an excuse to skip it when the doorbell rang. Winking at Cramer as I passed him on my way to the hall, I proceeded to the front door and took a peek. What I saw seemed to call for finesse, so I opened the door just enough to slip through out to the stoop, shut the door behind me, and said, "Hello, let's have a little conference.''

Conroy Blaney squeaked at me, "What's the idea?''

I grinned at him amiably. "A policeman named Cramer is in Mr. Wolfe's office having a talk, and I thought maybe you had had enough of him for a while. Unless you're tailing him?''

"Inspector Cramer?''

"Yes,'' I said. "Are you tailing him?''

"Good heavens, no. I want to see Nero Wolfe.''

"Okay; then follow me, and after we are inside don't talk. Get it?''

"I want to see Nero Wolfe immediately.''

"Will you follow instructions or won't you? Do you also want to see Cramer?''

"Very well, open the door.''

As I inserted my key I was telling myself, murder or not, I am going to be wishing this specimen was big enough to plug in the jaw before this is finished. He did, however, obey orders. I conducted him into the front room, the door connecting it with the office being closed, left him there on a chair, and went back by way of the hall.

"It can wait," I told Wolfe. "The man from Plehn's with the Dendrobiums."

But a minute later Cramer was standing up to go. Knowing how suspicious he was, as well as how many good reasons he had had for being suspicious on those premises, and also knowing how cops in general love to open doors that don't belong to them just to stick a head in, I escorted him to the front and let him out, then returned to the office and told Wolfe who the company was,

Wolfe frowned. "What does he want?"

"I think he wants to confess. I warn you, his squeak will get on your nerves."

"Bring him in. . . ."

I expected to enjoy it, and I did, only it didn't last long. Blaney started off by rejecting the red leather chair and choosing one of the spares, which irritated both of us, since we like our routine. Perched on it, he began, "I was thinking, on my way here, fate has thrown us together, Wolfe. You dominate your field and I dominate mine. We were bound to meet."

It caught Wolfe so completely off balance that he only muttered sarcastically, "Good heavens!"

Blaney nodded with satisfaction. "I knew we would have many things in common. That's my favorite expression, I use it all the time—Good heavens. But you probably want to know where I stand. I would if I were you. I did not come here because of any fear on my own account. There is not the remotest chance of my safety being endangered. But Tuesday evening up at Gene's apartment I heard a man saying to another man—I presume they were detectives—something about Mrs. Poor being Nero Wolfe's client, and in that case Mrs. Poor was as good as out of it, and Nero Wolfe had decided on Blaney, and, if so, Blaney might as well get his leg shaved for the electrode.

"I knew that might be just talk, but I really think it would be a shame for you to a make yourself ridiculous, and I don't think you want to. I'm willing to take this trouble. You're not a man to reach a conclusion without reasons. That wouldn't be scientific, and you and I are both scientists. Tell me your reasons, one by one, and I'll prove they're no good. Go ahead."

"Archie." Wolfe looked at me. "Get him out of here."

There wasn't the slightest indication from Blaney that anyone had said anything except him, and I was too fascinated to move.

Blaney went on: "The truth is, you have no reasons. The fact that Gene was afraid I would kill him proves nothing. He was a born coward. I did describe to him some of the methods by which I could kill a man without detection, but that was merely to impress upon him the fact that he continued to own half of the business by my sufferance, and therefore my offer of twenty thousand dollars for his half was an act of generosity. I wouldn't condescend to kill a man. No man is worth that much to me, or that little."

He had performed a miracle. I saw it with my own eyes—Nero Wolfe fleeing in haste from his own office. He had chased many a fellow being from that room, but that was the first time he had ever, himself, been chased. It became evident that he wasn't even going to risk staying on that floor when the sound was heard of the door of his elevator banging open and shut.

I told Blaney, "Overlook it. He's eccentric."

Blaney said, "So am I."

I nodded. "Geniuses are."

Blaney was frowning. "Does he really think I killed Gene Poor?"

"Yeah. He does now."

"Why now?"

I waved it away. "Forget it. I'm eccentric, too."

The house phone buzzed, and I swung my chair around and took it. It was Wolfe, on his room extension:

"Archie. Is that man gone?"

"No, sir."

"Get him out of there at once. Phone Saul and tell him to come here as soon as possible."

"Yes, sir."

The line went dead. So Wolfe had actually been stirred up enough to blow some dough on the case. Saul Panzer, being merely the best all-round investigator west of Nantucket, not counting me, came to twenty bucks a day plus expenses.

To get Blaney out I nearly had to carry him. . . .

As luck would have it, Saul Panzer was not to be had at the moment. Since he was free-lancing, you never knew. I finally got it that he was out on Long Island on a job, and left word for him to call. He did so around three, and said he would be able to get to the office after six o'clock.

It became obvious that to Wolfe, who had been stirred up, money was no object, since he blew another $1.80 on a phone call to Washington. I got it through without any trouble to General Carpenter, Head of G2, under whom I had been a major and for whom Wolfe had helped to solve certain problems connected with the war. The favor he asked of Carpenter, and of course got, was a telegram that would open doors at the premises of the Becker Products Corporation.

Not satisfied with that, he opened another valve. At ten minutes to four he said to me, "Archie, find out whether it seems advisable for me to talk with that man, Joe Groll."

"Yes, sir. Tea leaves? Or there's a palmist over on Seventh—"

"See him and find out."

So after he went up to the plant-rooms I phoned the office of Blaney & Poor and got Joe Groll. No persuasion was required. His tone implied that he would be glad to talk with anybody any time anywhere, after business hours. He would be free at five-thirty. I told him to meet me at Pete's Bar & Grill on 19th Street.

In addition to good whisky, Pete's has booths partitioned to the ceiling, which furnishes privacy. Seated in one of them I was surprised to realize that you could make out a case for calling Joe Groll handsome. They had overdone it a little on the ears, but on the whole he was at least up to grade if not fancy.

After we got our drinks I remarked casually, "As I told you on the phone, I want to discuss this murder. You may have heard of Nero Wolfe. Poor and his wife came to see him Tuesday afternoon, to tell him Blaney was going to dissolve the partnership by killing Poor."

He nodded. "Yes, I know."

"Oh. The cops told you?"

"No, Martha told me yesterday. Mrs. Poor. She asked me to come up and help about things—the funeral." He made a gesture. "Gosh, one lousy civilian funeral makes more fuss than a thousand dead men over there did."

I nodded. "Sure, the retail business always has more headaches than the wholesale." I sipped my highball. "I don't go for this theory that it was Helen Vardis that killed Poor. Do you?"

"What?" He stared. "What are you talking about? What theory?" His fingers had tightened around his glass.

"Why, this idea that Helen Vardis would do anything for Blaney, God knows why, and she made the cigars for him, and she went there Tuesday night—"

"Well, for Pete's sake." He said that calmly, and then suddenly his voice went up high: "Who thought that one up? Was it that cop Row-cliff? That buzzard? Was it Nero Wolfe? Was it you?"

He sounded next door to hysterical. I sure had pushed the wrong button, or maybe the right one, but I didn't want him sore at me. "It wasn't me," I assured him. "Don't get excited."

He laughed. It sounded bitter but not hysterical. "That's right," he said, "I must remember that—not to get excited. Everybody is very thoughtful. They put you in uniform and teach you what every young man ought to know, and take you across the ocean in the middle of hell, bombs, bullets, shells, flame-throwers; your friends die right against you and bleed down your neck; and after two years of that they bring you home and turn you loose and tell you, now, remember, don't get excited."

He drank his highball, clear to the bottom, and put his glass down.

"I'm all right," he said calmly. "so I am loose again and come back to my job. Don't get excited. Here's what I find. A girl I had been sort of counting on, named Martha Davis, has married the boss, and no one told me. It wasn't her fault, she never promised me anything, not even to write to me; but I had been looking forward to seeing her. Oh, I saw her, because she was in trouble and asked me to help. She thought her husband was going to get killed, and knowing Blaney as I did, I saw no reason to doubt it. I met her places a few times because she wanted to talk it over with me, and she wanted me to watch Blaney. Why am I spilling all this to you? You weren't in the Army."

"I was in the Army," I said, "but I admit nobody bled down my neck. I did what I was told."

"So did I, brother. Didn't we all? Anyhow, I wasn't heartbroken, because she seemed a little older than I had remembered her, and, besides, there was another girl who had been nothing but a kid in the factory, but she had grown up. I'm not telling you anything the cops don't know. Gosh, the cops are something! That's Helen Vardis. You saw her the other night."

"Yeah, she seemed upset."

"Upset?" He laughed a one-second laugh. "Sure, she was upset. I fell for her like a Sherman tank roaring down a cliff. I certainly hit bottom . . . All right, I guess I will. Thanks."

That was for the second drink, arriving. He picked it up and swallowed half.

"It is good whisky. . . . She seemed to reciprocate. I guess I was a little leery of all civilians, even her, but she seemed to reciprocate. I can't understand what that guy Poor had that attracted girls, and at his age, too. That I will never understand. First Martha, and then her. I saw her with him in a restaurant. Then I saw them together in his car. Then I followed her from the office and watched her meet him in Fourteenth Street, and they took a taxi and I lost them. Naturally, I sprung it on her, and she the same as told me to go to hell. She refused to explain.''

He finished the drink. "So they say don't get excited. The cops told me yesterday and again today, don't get excited. Which one is it that thinks Helen Vardis was helping Blaney? Is it you?''

I shook my head. "I'm not a cop. It's just something I heard and I wondered what you thought of it. In a murder case you're apt to hear anything.''

"Why do you listen?''

"Why not? I'm listening to you.''

He laughed, somewhat better, "You're a hell of a guy to work on a murder. You don't try to hammer me and you don't try to uncle. Do you want to come along and help me do something?''

"I might if you'd describe it.''

"Wait a minute. I want to make a phone call.''

He slid along the seat and left the booth. I sipped my highball and lit a cigarette, wondering whether the feel of blood going down his neck had really loosed a screw in him or he was just temporarily rattled.

In less than five minutes he was back, sliding along the seat again, and announcing, "Blaney's up at his place in Westchester. I phoned to ask him about a job we're doing, but really to find out if he was up there.''

"Good. Now we know. Is that where we're gong?''

"No.'' He gazed at his glass. "I thought I drank that— Oh. You had it filled again. Thanks.'' He took some. "Anyway, that idea about Helen is silly, because it was obviously either Martha or Blaney, if the cops have any brains at all. Martha says she went to Blaney's place in Westchester at six-fifteen Tuesday to keep a date she and Poor had with him, and there was no one there and she waited around until ten minutes to seven. Blaney says he was there all the time, from a quarter to six on, all evening, until he got the phone call from the police that Poor had been killed. So one of them is lying, and the one that's lying is obviously the one that killed Poor. So it's Blaney.''

"Why—because Martha wouldn't lie?''

He frowned at me. "Now, don't smart up. What the hell would she kill him for? She only got him two years ago and he had everything he ever had. Anyway, it was Blaney, and I am fed up with all the gear-grinding, and he is now through with me and I'll be out of a job, so to hell with him. I'm going to see what I can find. On account of the trick cigars the cops wanted to go through the office and factory, and Blaney told them sure, go ahead, go as far as you like, but he didn't tell them about the abditories, and they didn't find them.''

"How do you spell it?"

He spelled it: "Abditory. Place to hide things. Blaney says it's a scientific term. The office is full of them. I haven't had a chance before now since Tuesday night, but with him up in Westchester I'm going to take a look. With a nut like Blaney you never can tell. Want to come along?''

"Have you got keys?"

"Keys? I'm the foreman."

"Okay, finish your drink."

He did so, and I got the bill and paid it, and we got our hats and coats and emerged.

When we were on the sidewalk alongside my car I asked him to wait a minute, marched back to where a taxi was parked, jerked the door open, and stuck my head in, and said, "There's no sense in this, Helen. Come on and ride with us.''

"Lookit, mister—" the taxi driver began, like a menace. "You'd better get out!"

"Everybody relax," I said pleasantly. "I can't get out because I'm not in; I'm only looking in.'' I told the temples, "This is absolutely childish. You don't know the first principles of tailing, and this driver you happened to get is, if anything, worse. If you insist on tailing Joe, okay; we'll put him in the cab and let them go ahead, and you can ride with me and I'll show you how it's done.''

"Yeah?" the menace croaked. "Show her how what's done?"

"See that," I told her. "See the kind of mind he's got."

"You're as smart as they come, aren't you?"

"That," I said, "you will learn more about as time goes on. I'm at least smarter than you are if you let that meter continue to tick. Pay him and come on.''

She moved, so I stood aside and held the door while she got out. On the sidewalk she faced me and said, "You seem to be in charge of everything, so you pay him.''

It was an unpleasant surprise, but I didn't hesitate—first, because I liked the way she was handling herself, and, second, because all expenses would come out of the five grand anyway. So I parted with two bucks, took her elbow and steered her to the sedan, opened the front door and told Joe Groll, "Move over a little. There's room for three."

She did so and I got in and slammed the door. By the time I had got the engine started and rolled to the corner and turned downtown, neither of them had said a word.

"If I were you folks," I told them, "I would incorporate and call it the Greater New York Mutual Tailing League. I don't see how you keep track of who is following whom on any given day. Of course, if one of you gets convicted of murder that will put a stop to it. You have now, however, the one good reason that I know of for getting married, the fact that a wife can't testify against a husband or vice versa."

I swerved around a pushcart. "The idea is, Helen, we are bound for the Blaney & Poor office to go through the abditories. We think he hid something in them."

"What?" she demanded.

"We don't know. Maybe a detailed estimate in triplicate of what it would cost to kill Poor. Maybe a blueprint of the cigar. Even a rough sketch would help."

"That's ridiculous. You sound to me like a clown."

"Good. It is well-known fact that clowns have the biggest and warmest hearts on record except mothers and three characters in books by Dickens."

I pulled over to the curb in front of Blaney & Poor's on Varick Street. . . .

That office was no place for a stranger to poke around in. It was on the first floor of a dingy old building in the middle of the block, with part of the factory, so Joe said, in the rear, and the rest on the second floor. As soon as we were inside and had the lights turned on, Helen sat in a chair at a desk and looked disdainful, but as the search went on I noticed she kept her eyes open.

Joe tossed his hat and coat on a chair, got a screwdriver from a drawer, went to the typewriter on the desk Helen was sitting at, used the screwdriver, lifted out the typewriter roller, unscrewed an end of it and turned it vertical, and about four dozen dice rolled out. He held the open end of the roller so the light would hit it right, peered in, put the dice back in and screwed the end on, and put the roller back on the machine.

His fingers were as swift and accurate as any I had ever seen. Even if I had known about it, I would have needed at least ten minutes for the operation; he took about three.

"Trick dice?" I asked him.

"They're just a stock item," he said, and went over to a door in the rear wall, opened it, took it off its hinges, leaned it against a desk, knelt on the floor, removed a strip from the bottom edge of the door; and out came about ten dozen lead pencils.

"Trick pencils?"

"When you press, perfume comes out," he said, and stretched out flat to look into the abditory.

Joe continued his tour of the abditories, which were practically everywhere, in desk lamps, chair legs, water cooler, ash trays, even one in the metal base of a desk calendar that was on a big desk in the corner.

It was while he had that one open, jiggling things out of it, that I heard him mutter, "This is a new one on me." He walked over and put something on the desk in front of Helen and asked her, "What is that thing, do you know?"

She picked it up, inspected it, and shook her head. "Haven't the faintest idea."

"Let me see." I got up and went over, and Helen handed it to me. The second I saw it I stopped being casual inside, but I tried to keep the outside as before. It was a long, thin metal capsule, about three-quarters of an inch long and not over an eighth of an inch in diameter, smooth all over, with no seam or opening, except at one end, where a thread came through, a dark-brown, medium-sized thread as long as my index finger.

I grunted. "Where did you find it?"

"You saw me find it." Joe sounded either irritated or something else. "In that calendar on Blaney's desk."

"Oh, that's Blaney's desk? How many, just this one?"

"No, several." Joe went to Blaney's desk and then came back to us. "Three more. Four altogether."

I took them from him and compared. They were all the same. I regarded Helen's attractive face. She looked interested. I regarded Joe's handsome face if you didn't count the ears. He looked more interested.

"I think" I said, "that it was one of these things that was in the cigar that Poor never smoked. What do you think?"

Joe said, "I think we can damn soon find out. Give me one." He had a gleam in his eye.

I shook my head. "The idea doesn't appeal to me." I looked at my wrist. "Quarter to nine. Mr. Wolfe is in the middle of dinner. The proper thing is for you to take these objects to the police, but they're likely to feel hurt because you didn't tell them about the abditories when they were here. We can't interrupt Mr. Wolfe's dinner, even with a phone call, so I suggest that I buy you a meal somewhere, modest but nutritious, and then we all three go and deliver these gadgets, calendar included, to him."

"You take them to him," Joe said. "I think I'll go home."

"I think I'll go home, too," Helen said.

"No. Nothing doing. You'll just follow each other, and get all confused again. If I take these things to Wolfe without taking you he'll fly into a temper and phone the police to go get you. Not to flatter myself, wouldn't you prefer to come with me?"

Helen said in the nastiest possible tone, "I don't have to eat at the same table with him."

Joe said, trying to match her tone but failing because he wasn't a female, "If you did I wouldn't eat."

Which was all a lot of organic fertilizer. I took them to Gallagher's, where they not only ate at the same table, but devoured hunks of steak served from the same platter. It was a little after ten when we got to Nero Wolfe's place on 35th Street. . . .

Wolfe was seated behind his desk, with the evening beer—one empty bottle and two full ones—on a tray in front of him. Joe Groll, in the red leather chair, also had a bottle and glass, on the check-writing table beside him. Helen Vardis would have made a good cheesecake shot over by the big globe in the upholstered number that Wolfe, himself, sometimes used. I was at my desk, as usual, with my oral report all finished, watching Wolfe inspect the workmanship of the removable bottom of the desk calendar.

He put it down, picked up one of the metal capsules with its dangling thread, and gave it another look, put that down too, and turned his half-closed eyes on Joe:

"Mr. Groll."

"Yes, sir."

"I don't know how much sense you have. If you have slightly more than your share, you must realize that if I hand these things to the police with Mr. Goodwin's story, they will conclude that you are a liar. They will ask, why did you wait until witnesses were present to explore those hiding places? Why did you think they were worth exploring at all? Is it even remotely credible that Mr. Blaney, after preparing that murderous box of cigars, would leave these things there on his desk in a hiding place that a dozen people know about? They will have other questions, but that's enough to show that they will end by concluding that you put the capsules in the calendar yourself. Where did you get them?''

Joe said firmly, ''I wouldn't know about how much sense I've got, but it happened exactly the way you've heard it. As for my waiting for witnesses, I didn't. I only waited until I was sure Blaney was out of range, up at his Westchester place, and then Goodwin was there, and I asked him to come along on the spur of the moment. As for its being remotely credible what you said, there's nothing Blaney wouldn't do. He's a maniac. You don't know him, so you don't know that.''

Wolfe grunted. ''The devil I don't. I do know that. How long have those hiding places been in existence?''

''Some of them for years. Some are more recent.''

Wolfe tapped the desk calendar with a finger. ''How long has this been there?''

''Oh—'' Joe considered. ''Four or five years. It was there before I got in the Army. . . . Look here, Mr. Wolfe, you seem to forget that when I saw those things tonight I had no idea what they were, and I still haven't. You seem to know they're the same as the loads in those cigars, and if you do, okay, but I don't.''

''Neither do I.''

''Then what the hell? Maybe they're full of Chanel Number Five or just fresh air.''

Wolfe nodded. ''I was coming to that. If I show them to Mr. Cramer he'll take them away from me, and also he'll arrest you as a material witness, and I may possibly need you. We'll have to find out for ourselves.''

He pushed a button, and in a moment Fritz entered. Wolfe asked him, ''Do you remember that metal percolator that someone sent us and we were fools enough to try?''

''Yes, sir.''

''Did you throw it out?''

''No, sir, it's in the basement.''

''Bring it here, please.''

Fritz went. Wolfe picked up a capsule and frowned at it and then turned to me: ''Archie. Get me a piece of newspaper, the can of household oil, and a piece of string.''

Under the circumstances I would have preferred to go out for a walk, but there was a lady present who might need protection, so I did as I was told. When I got back, Fritz was there with the percolator, which was two-quart size, made of thick metal. We three men collected at Wolfe's desk to watch the preparations, but Helen stayed in her chair.

With my scissors Wolfe cut a strip of newspaper about two by eight inches, dropped oil on it and rubbed it in with his finger and rolled it tight into a long, thin, oiled wick. Then we held one end of it against the end of the capsule thread, overlapping a little, and Joe Groll, ready with the piece of string, tied them together. Wolfe opened the lid of the percolator.

"No," Joe objected. "That might stop it. Anyhow, we don't want this glass here."

He finished the job with his swift, sure fingers, while Wolfe and Fritz and I watched. Removing the glass cap and the inside contraption from the percolator, he lowered the capsule through the hole, hanging onto the free end of the oiled wick with one hand while with the other he stuffed a scrap of newspaper in the hole just tight enough to keep the wick from slipping on through. Wolfe nodded approvingly and leaned back in his chair. About two inches of the wick protruded.

"Put it on the floor." Wolfe pointed. "Over there."

Joe moved, taking a folder of matches from his pocket, but I intercepted him. "Wait a minute. Gimme." I took the percolator. "The rest of you go in the hall. I'll light it."

Fritz went, and so did Helen, but Joe merely backed to a corner and Wolfe didn't move from his chair.

I told Wolfe, "I saw Poor's face and you didn't. Go in the hall."

"Nonsense. That little thing?"

"Then I'll put a blanket over it."

"No. I want to see it."

"So do I," Joe said. "What the hell? I'll bet it's a dud."

I shrugged. "I hope Helen has had a course in first aid." I put the percolator on the floor over by the couch, about five paces from Wolfe's desk, lit a match and applied it to the end of the wick, and stood back and watched. An inch of the wick burned in three seconds. "See you at the hospital," I said cheerily, and beat it to the hall, leaving the door open a crack to see through.

It may have been ten seconds, but it seemed like three times that, before the bang came, and it was a man-size bang, followed immediately by another but different kind of bang. Helen grabbed my arm, but not waiting to enjoy that, I swung the door open and stepped through. Joe was still in the corner, looking surprised. Wolfe had twisted around in his chair to gaze at a bruise in the plaster of the wall behind him.

"The percolator lid," he muttered. "It missed me."

"Yeah." I moved across to observe angles and directions. "By about an inch." I stooped to pick up the percolator lid, bent out of shape. "This would have felt good on your skull."

Fritz and Helen were back in, and Joe came over with the percolator in his hand. "Feel it," he said. "Hot. Look how it's twisted. Some pill, that is. Dynamite or TNT would never do that, not that amount. I wonder what's in it?" He sniffed. "Do you smell anything? I don't."

"It's outrageous," Wolfe declared. I looked at him in surprise. Instead of being relaxed and thankful for his escape, he was sitting straight in his chair, which meant he was ready to pop with fury. "That thing nearly hit me in the head. This settles it. Against Mr. Poor there may have been a valid grievance. Against me, none."

"Well, for Pete's sake." I regarded him without approval. "That's illogical. Nobody aimed it at you. Didn't I tell you to go in the hall? However, if it made you mad enough to do a little work, fine. Here's Joe and Helen, you can start on them."

"No." He got to his feet. "I'm going to bed." He bowed to Helen. "Good night, Miss Vardis." He tilted his head a hundredth of an inch at Joe. "Good night, sir . . . Archie, put these remaining capsules in the safe." He marched to the door and was gone.

"Quite a guy," Joe remarked. "He didn't bat an eye when that thing went off and the lid flew past his ear."

"Yeah," I growled. "He has fits. He's having one now. Instead of taking you two apart and turning you inside out, which is what he should have done, he didn't even tell you where to head in. Do you tell the police about tonight or not? I would say, for the present, *not.* . . . Come on. taxis are hard to find around here, and I've got to put the car away anyhow. I'll drop you somewhere."

We went. When I got back, some time later, I made a little discovery. Opening the safe to follow my custom of checking the cash last thing at night, I found two hundred bucks gone and an entry in the book for that amount in Wolfe's handwriting, which said, "Saul Panzer, advance on expenses."

So, anyhow, Saul was working. . . .

Friday morning, having nothing else to do, I solved the case. I did it with cold logic. Everything fitted perfectly, and all I needed was enough evidence for a jury. Presumably that was what Saul Panzer was getting. I do not intend to put it all down here, the way I worked it out, because, first, it would take three full pages, and, second, I was wrong. Anyway, I had it solved when, a little before nine o'clock, I was summoned to Wolfe's room and given an errand to perform, with detailed instructions. It sent me to 20th Street.

I would have just as soon have dealt with one of the underlings, but Cramer himself was in his office and said to bring me in. As I sat down, he whirled his chair a quarter turn, folded his arms, and asked conversationally, "What have you two liars got cooked up now?"

I grinned at him. "Why don't you call Wolfe a liar to his face some day? Do it while I'm there." I took two of the capsules, with threads attached, from my vest pocket and put them on his desk, and inquired, "Do you need any more of these?"

He picked one of them up and gave it a good look, then the other one; put them in a drawer of his desk, folded his arms again, and looked me in the eye to shrivel me.

"All right," he said quietly. "Go on. They came in the mail, in a package addressed to Wolfe with letters cut out of a magazine."

"No, sir; not at all. Where I spent the night last night I was idly running my fingers through her lovely hair and felt something, and there they were." Cramer was strictly a family man and had stern ideas. Seeing I had him blushing, I went on, "Actually, it was like this."

I told him the whole story.

He had questions, both during the recital and at the end, and I answered what I could. The one I had expected him to put first he saved till the last.

"Well," he said, "for the present we'll assume that I believe you. You know what that amounts to, but we'll asssume it. Even so, how are you on figures? How much are two and one?"

"I'm pretty good. Two plus one plus one equals four."

"Yes? Where do you get that second plus one?"

"So you *can* add," I conceded. "Mr. Wolfe thought maybe you couldn't. However, so can we. Four capsules were found. Two are there in your drawer. One, as I told you, was used in a scientific experiment in Wolfe's office and damn' near killed him. He's keeping the other one for the Fourth of July."

"Like hell he is. I want it."

"Try and get it." I stood up.

"Beat it. I'll get it."

I turned, with dignity, and went. . . .

When I got back to Wolfe's, Fritz met me in the hall to tell me there was a woman in the office, and when I entered I found it was Martha Poor.

I sat down at my desk and told her, "Mr. Wolfe will be engaged until eleven o'clock." I glanced at my wrist. "He'll be down in forty minutes."

She nodded. "I know. I'll wait."

She didn't look exactly bedraggled, nor would I say pathetic, but there was nothing of the man-eater about her. She seemed older than she had on Tuesday. Anyone could have told at a glance that she was having trouble, but whether it was bereavement or bankruptcy was indicated neither by her clothes nor by her expression. She made you feel like going up to her, maybe putting your hand on her shoulder or patting her on the arm, and asking, "Anything I can do?"

I went to the kitchen and asked Fritz if he had told Wolfe who had come to see him, and Fritz said he hadn't, he had left that to me. So I returned to the office, buzzed the plant-rooms, got Wolfe, and told him, "Returned from mission. I gave them Cramer himself, and he says he'll get the other one. Mrs. Poor is down here waiting to see you."

"Confound that woman. Send her away."

"But she—"

"No. I know what she wants. I studied her. She wants to know what I'm doing to earn that money. Tell her to go home and read that receipt."

The line died. I swung my chair around and told Martha, "Mr. Wolfe says for you to go home and read the receipt."

She stared. "What?"

"He thinks you've come to complain because he isn't earning the money your husband paid him, and the idea of having to earn money offends him. It always has."

"But—that's ridiculous. Isn't it?"

"Certainly it is." I fought back the impulse to step over and pat her on the shoulder. "But my advice is to humor him, much as I enjoy having you here. Nobody alive can handle him but me. If he came down and found you here he would turn around and walk out. If you have anything special to say, tell me, and I'll tell him. He'll listen to me because he has to or fire me, and he can't fire me because then he would never do any work at all and would eventually starve to death."

"I shouldn't think—" She stopped and stood up. She took a step toward the door, then turned and said, "I shouldn't think a cold-blooded murder is something to joke about."

I had to fight the impulse again. "I'm not joking," I declared. "Plain facts. What did you want to say to him?"

"I just wanted a talk with him. He hasn't come to see me. Neither have you." She tried to smile, but all she accomplished was to start her lip quivering. She stopped it. "You haven't even phoned me. I don't know what's happening. The police asked me about two of my hairs being in that box of cigars, and I suppose they have told Mr. Wolfe about it, and I don't even know what he thinks or what he told the police."

I grinned at her. "That's easy. He made a speech to the jury, demonstrating that those hairs in the box were evidence that you did not kill your husband." I went to her and put a hand on her arm, like a brother. "Listen lady. Isn't the funeral this afternoon?"

"Yes."

"Okay. Go and have the funeral; that's enough for you for one day. Leave the rest to me. I mean, if anything occurs that it would help you to know about, I'll see that you know. Right?"

She didn't pull anything corny like grasping my hand, with hers firm and warm, or gazing at me with moist eyes filled with trust. She did meet my eyes, but only long enough to say, "Thank you, Mr. Goodwin," and turned to go. I went to the front door and let her out. . . .

After Wolfe came down, the relations between us were nothing to brag about. Apparently he had nothing to offer, and I was too sore to start in on him.

He passed the time until lunch going through catalogues, and at 2:30 P.M. with a veal cutlet and half a bushel of Fritz's best mixed salad stowed in the hold, he returned to the office and resumed the catalogues. That got interrupted before long, but not by me. The bell rang and I went to the front, and it was Saul Panzer.

I took him to the office, where Wolfe greeted him and then told me, "Archie. Go up and help Theodore with the pollen lists."

I did my best with Theodore and the pollen lists, not wanting to take it out on them. The conference with Saul seemed to be comprehensive, since a full hour passed before the house phone in the potting-room buzzed. Theodore answered it, and told me that I was wanted downstairs.

When I got there Saul was gone. I had a withering remark prepared, thinking to open up with it, but had to save it for some other time. Wolfe was seated behind his desk, leaning back with his eyes closed, and his lips were moving, pushing out and then in again, out and in.

So I sat down and kept my mouth shut. The brain had actually got on the job, and I knew better than to make remarks, withering or not, during the performance of miracles. The first result, which came in ten or twelve minutes after I entered, did not, however, seem to be miraculous. He opened his eyes halfway, grunted, and muttered, "Archie. Yesterday you showed me an article in a paper about a man's body found in an orchard near White Plains, but I didn't look at it. Now I want it."

"Yes, sir. There was more this morning—"

"Have they identified the body?"

"No, sir. The head was smashed—"

"Get it."

I obeyed. Newspapers were kept in the office for three days. I opened it to the page and handed it to him. He would read a newspaper only one way, holding it out wide open, no folding, with his arms stretched. I had never tried to get him to do it more intelligently because it was the only strenuous exercise he ever got and was therefore good for him. He finished the Thursday piece and asked for Friday's, and finished that.

Then he told me, "Get the district attorney of Westchester County. What's his name? Fraser?"

"Right." I got busy with the phone. I had no trouble getting the office, but then they gave me the usual line about Mr. Fraser being in conference, and I had to put on pressure. Finally the elected person said hello.

Wolfe took it. "How do you do, Mr. Fraser? . . . Nero Wolfe. I have something to give you. That body found in an orchard Wednesday evening with the head crushed—has it been identified?"

Fraser was brusque: "No. What—"

"Please. I'm giving you something. Put this down: Arthur Howell, 914 West 78th Street, New York. He worked for the Becker Products Corporation of Basston, New Jersey. They have an office at 622 East 42nd Street, New York. His dentist was Lewis Marley, 699 Park Avenue, New York. . . . That should help. Try that. In return for this, I would appreciate it very much if you will have me notified the moment the identification is made. Did you get it all down?"

"Yes. But what—"

"No sir. That's all. That's all you'll get from me until I get word of the identification."

There was some sputtering protest from the White Plains end, but it accomplished nothing. Wolfe hung up, with a self-satisfied smirk on his big face, cleared his throat importantly, and picked up a catalogue.

I growled at him, "So it's in the bag. A complete stranger named Arthur Howell. After snitching the capsules from Becker Products and making the cigars and getting them into Poor's home God knows how, he was overcome by remorse and went to an orchard and took his clothes off and lay down and ran over himself with radio control—''

''Archie. Shut up. We are ready to act, in any case, but it will make things a little simpler if that corpse proves to be Mr. Howell, so it is worth waiting for a report on it.'' He glanced at the clock, which said seven minutes to four, and put the catalogue down. ''We might as well prepare it now. Get that capsule from the safe.''

I thought to myself, ''This time it may not miss him, but, as for me, I'm going outdoors.''

However, it appeared that he was going to try some new gag instead of repeating with the percolator. By the time I got the capsule from the safe and convoyed it to him, he had taken two articles from a drawer and put them on his desk. One was a roll of Scotch tape. The other was a medium-sized photograph of a man, mounted on gray cardboard. I gave it a glance, then picked it up and did a thorough job of looking. It was unquestionably Eugene R. Poor.

''Goody,'' I said enthusiastically. ''No wonder you're pleased. Even if Saul had to pay two hundred bucks for it—''

''Archie, Let me have that. . . . Here, hold this thing.''

I helped. What I was to hold was the capsule, flat on the cardboard near a corner, while he tore off a piece of tape and fastened it there. When he lifted the photo and jiggled it to see if the fastening was firm, the thread dangled over Poor's right eye.

''Put it in an envelope and in the safe,'' he said, then glanced at the clock and made for the hall and the elevator.

At six o'clock he returned to the office, rang for Fritz to bring beer, and took up where he had left off with the catalogues. At eight o'clock Fritz summoned us to dinner. At nine-thirty we returned to the office. At a quarter to ten a phone call came from District Attorney Fraser. The body had been identified. It was Arthur Howell. An assistant district attorney and a pair of detectives were on their way to 35th Street to ask Wolfe how come and would he please supply all necessary details, including the present address of the murderer.

Wolfe hung, up, leaned back and sighed, and muttered at me, ''Archie. You'll have to pay a call on Mrs. Poor.''

I objected, ''She's probably in bed, tired out. The funeral was today.''

''It can't be helped. Saul will go with you.''

I stared. ''Saul?''

''Yes. He's up in my room asleep. He didn't get to bed last night. You will take her that photograph of her husband. You should leave as soon as possible, before that confounded Westchester lawyer gets here. I don't want to see him. Tell Fritz to bolt the door after you go. Ring my room and tell Saul to come down at once. Then I'll give you your instructions." . . .

The appearance of the living-room in the Poor apartment on 84th Street was not the same as it had been when I had arrived there three evenings before. Not only was there no army of city employees present and no man of the house, with his face gone, huddled on the floor, but the furniture had been moved around. The chair Poor had sat in when he lit his last cigar was gone, probably to the cleaners on account of spots, the table Cramer had used for headquarters had been shifted to the other side of the room, and the radio had been moved to the other end of the couch. Martha Poor was sitting on the couch, and I was on a chair and I had pulled around to face her. She was wearing something that wasn't a bathrobe and wasn't exactly a dress, modest, with sleeves and only a proper amount of throat showing.

"I'm here under orders," I told her. "I said this morning that if anything happened that it would help you to know about I'd see that you knew, but this isn't it. This is different. Nero Wolfe sent me, with orders. I just want to make that clear. Item number one is to hand you this envelope and invite you to look at the contents."

She took it from me. With steady fingers, slow-moving rather than hurried, she opened the flap and pulled out the photograph.

I informed her, "That decoration may look like something by Dali, but it was Nero Wolfe's idea. I am not authorized to discuss it or the picture from any angle, just there it is, except to remark that it is a very good likeness of your husband. I only saw him that one time, the other afternoon at the office, but of course I had a long and thorough look at him. Wednesday we could have sold that photo to a newspaper for a nice amount, but of course we didn't have it Wednesday."

She had put the photo beside her on the couch and was pinching an edge of the cardboard between her index finger and thumbnail, with the nail sinking in. She was looking straight at me. The muscles of her throat had tightened, which no doubt accounted for the change in her voice when she spoke: "Where did you get it?"

I shook my head. "Out of bounds. As I said, I'm under orders. . . . Item number two is just a piece of information to the effect that a man named Saul Panzer is out in the back hall on this floor, standing by the door of the service elevator. Saul is not big, but he just had a nap and is alert. . . . Number three: That naked body found up in Westchester with the head smashed by running a car over it, in an orchard not more than ten minutes' drive from either Monty's Tavern or Blaney's place, has been identified as formerly belonging to a man named Arthur Howell, an employee of the Becker Products Corporation.''

Her eyes hadn't moved. I hadn't even seen the lashes blink. She said, in a faraway voice, ''I don't know why you tell me about that. Arthur Howell? Did you say Arthur Howell?''

''Yep, that's right. Howell, Arthur. Head flattened to a pancake, but enough left for the dentist. As for telling you about it, I'm only obeying orders.'' I glanced at my wrist. ''Number four: It is now twenty past ten. At a quarter to eleven I am supposed either to arrive back at the office or phone. If I do neither, Nero Wolfe will phone Inspector Cramer, and then here they'll come. Not as many as Tuesday evening, I suppose, because they won't need all the scientists, but plenty.''

I stopped, still meeting her eye, and then went on, ''Let's see. Photo and capsule, Saul out back, Howell, cops at a quarter to eleven . . . that's all.''

She got up and I thought she was going to take hold of me, but all she did was stand in front of me, about eight inches away, looking up at me. She came about up to my chin.

''Archie Goodwin,'' she said. ''You think I'm terrible, don't you? You think I'm an awful woman, bad clear through. Don't you?''

''I'm not thinking, lady. I'm just an errand boy.'' The funny thing was that if at any moment up to then I had made a list of the ten most beautiful women she would not have been on.

''You've had lots of experience,'' she said, her head back to look up at me. ''You know what women are like. I knew you did when you put your hand on my arm yesterday. You know I'm a man's woman, but it has to be the right man. Just one man's, forever.''

She started to smile, and her lip began to quiver, and she stopped it. ''But I didn't find the man until it was too late. I didn't find him until you put your hand on my arm yesterday. You could have had me then, forever yours, you could have me now if anything like that was possible. I mean—we could go away together—now—you wouldn't have to promise anything—only you could find out if you want me forever too—the way I want you—''

She lifted her hand and touched me, just a touch, the tips of her fingers barely brushing my sleeve.

I jerked back.

"Listen," I said, with my voice sounding peculiar, so I tried to correct it. "You are extremely good, no question about it, but, as you say, it's too late. You are trying to go to bat when your side already has three out in the ninth, and that's against the rules. I'll hand it to you that you are extremely good. When you turn it on it flows. But in seven minutes, now, Nero Wolfe will be phoning the police, so you'd better fix your hair. You'll be having your picture taken."

She hauled off and smacked me in the face. I barely felt it and didn't even move my hands.

"I hate men," she said through her teeth. "God, how I hate men!"

She turned and walked to the bathroom, and entered and closed the door.

I didn't know whether she had gone to fix her hair or what, and I didn't care. Instead of crossing to the window and standing there without breathing, as I had done before, I sat down on the edge of the couch and did nothing but breathe. I suppose I did actually know what was going to happen. Anyhow, when it happened, when the noise came, not nearly as loud as it had been in Wolfe's office because the capsule had been inside a metal percolator, I don't think I jumped or even jerked. I did not run, but walked to the bathroom door and opened it, and entered.

Less than a minute later I went to the back door in the kitchen and opened that, and told Saul Panzer, "All over. She stuck it in her mouth and lit the fuse. You get out. Go and report to Wolfe. I'll phone the cops."

"But you must be—I'll stay—"

"No, go on. Step on it. I feel fine." . . .

At noon the next day, Saturday, I was getting fed up with all the jabber, because I had a question or two I wanted to ask myself. Cramer had come to Nero Wolfe's office prepared to attack from all sides at once, bringing not only Sergeant Purley Stebbins, but also a gang of civilians consisting of Helen Vardis, Joe Groll, and Conroy Blaney. Blaney had not been let in. On that Wolfe would not budge. Blaney was not to enter his house. The others had all been admitted and were now distributed around the office, with Cramer, of course, in the red leather chair. For over half an hour he and Wolfe had been closer to getting locked in a death grip than I had ever seen them before.

Wolfe was speaking. "Then arrest me," he said. "Shut up, get a warrant, and arrest me."

Cramer, having said about all an inspector could say, merely glared.

"Wording the charge would be difficult," Wolfe murmured. When he was maddest he murmured. "I have not withheld evidence, or obstructed justice, or shielded the guilty. I thought it possible that Mrs. Poor, confronted suddenly with that evidence, would collapse and confess."

"Nuts," Cramer said wearily. "How about confronting me with the evidence? Instead of evidence, what you confront me with is another corpse. And I know"—he tapped the chair arm with a stiff finger—"exactly why. The only evidence you had that was worth a damn was that photograph of Arthur Howell. If you had turned it over to me—"

"Nonsense. You already had a photograph of Arthur Howell. The Becker Products Corporation people gave you a picture of their missing employee on Thursday. So they told Saul Panzer when they gave him a duplicate for me. What good would one more picture of Howell do you?"

"Okay." Cramer was in a losing fight and knew it. "But I didn't know that Howell had come to see you on Tuesday with Mrs. Poor, passing himself off as her husband. Dressed in the same kind of suit and shirt and tie that Poor was wearing that day. Only you and Goodwin knew that."

"I knew it. Mr. Goodwin didn't. He thought it was a photograph of Mr. Poor."

I put in an entry: "Excuse me, but when you gentlemen finish the shadow-boxing I would like to ask a question." I was looking at Wolfe. "You say you knew Poor wasn't Poor. When and how?"

Of course, Wolfe faked. He sighed as if he was thinking, now, this is going to be an awful bore. Actually, he was always tickled stiff to show how bright he was.

His eyes came to me. "Wednesday evening you told me that Mr. Poor smoked ten to fifteen cigars a day. Thursday Mr. Cramer said the same thing. But the man who came here Tuesday, calling himself Poor, didn't even know how to hold a cigar, let alone smoke one."

"He was nervous."

"If he was he didn't show it, except with the cigar. You saw him. It was a ludicrous performance and he should never have tried it. When I learned that Mr. Poor was a veteran cigar smoker, the only question was who had impersonated him in this office? And the complicity of Mrs. Poor was obvious, especially with the added information, also furnished by Mr. Cramer, that no photograph of Mr. Poor was available. There are photographs of everybody nowadays. Mrs. Poor was an ass. She was supremely an ass when she selected me to bamboozle. She wanted to establish the assumption that Mr. Blaney was going to kill Mr. Poor. That was intelligent. She did not want to take her counterfeit Mr. Poor to the police, for fear someone there might be acquainted with the real Mr. Poor. That also was intelligent. But it was idiotic to choose me as the victim.''

''She hated men,'' I remarked.

Wolfe nodded. ''She must have had a low opinion of men. In order to get what she wanted, which presumably was something like half a million dollars—counting her husband's fortune, the insurance money, and a half-share in the business after Mr. Blaney had been executed for the murder of Mr. Poor—she was willing to kill three men, two by direct action and one indirectly. Incidentally, except for the colossal blunder of picking me, she was not a fool.''

''The hell she wasn't,'' Cramer growled. ''With all that trick setup? She was absolutely batty.''

''No, sir.'' Wolfe shook his head. ''She was not. Go back over it. She didn't manufacture the trick setup out of her head; she simply used what she had. On a certain day she found herself with these ingredients at hand: One, the hostility between the partners in the business, amply corroborated by such details as Mr. Poor having Miss Vardis spy on Mr. Blaney, and Mrs. Poor, herself, having Mr. Groll do the same. . . . Two, her acquaintance with a man named Arthur Howell who had access to a supply of explosive capsules capable of concealment in a cigar, and who also sufficiently resembled her husband in build and general appearance, except for the face itself, and she intended to take care of the face.

''Ten of your men, Mr. Cramer, kept at it for a week or so, can probably trace her association with Mr. Howell. They're good at that. Unquestionably, it was those qualifications of Mr. Howell that suggested the details of her plan. She did not, of course, inform him that she hated men. Quite the contrary. She persuaded him to help her kill her husband, offering, presumably, a strong incentive.''

''She was good at offering incentives,'' I declared. ''She was good period. The way she pretended, here Tuesday afternoon, that she wanted Poor to skip it and go live in the country and grow roses, with her to cook and darn socks.''

Wolfe nodded. ''I admit she was ingenious. . . . By the way, Mr. Groll, did she have an opportunity to conceal those four capsules in that desk calendar?''

''Yes,'' Joe said. ''Helen and I were discussing that. She came there Tuesday to go with Poor to the rodeo, and she could have done it then. Anyway, she had keys, she could have done it any time.''

"That was well conceived." Wolfe said approvingly. "That and the hairs in the box of cigars. She was preparing for all contingencies. Neither of those touches was meant for you, Mr. Cramer, but for a jury, in case it ever got to that. She had sense enough to know what a good lawyer could do with complications of that sort. . . . Will you gentlemen have some beer?"

"No," Cramer said bluntly. "I'll have a question. Poor wasn't here Tuesday afternoon?"

"No, sir. Arthur Howell was."

"Then where was Poor?"

"At the rodeo." Wolfe pushed a button, two pushes for beer. "Again Mrs. Poor was ingenious. Look at her schedule for Tuesday. She went to the Blaney & Poor office—what time, Mr. Groll?"

Helen answered: "She came around noon. They went to lunch together and then were going to the rodeo."

"Thank you. So all she had to do was to make some excuse and see that he went to the rodeo alone. It was an ideal selection—Madison Square Garden, that enormous crowd. Then she met Arthur Howell somewhere near, having arranged for him to be dressed as her husband was dressed, and brought him here. She was driving her car—or her husband's car. They left here a little before five o'clock. Between here and Forty-second Street he got out and went to Grand Central to take a train to White Plains. A woman who could persuade a man to help her kill her husband could surely persuade him to take a train to White Plains."

Fritz brought beer, and Wolfe opened a bottle and poured.

"Then she continued to Fiftieth Street and met her husband as he left the rodeo, and they drove to Westchester, having an appointment to see Mr. Blaney at his place there. She talked her husband out of that, left him at a place called Monty's Tavern, drove somewhere, probably the White Plains railroad station, met Arthur Howell there as arranged, drove to an isolated spot probably previously selected, turned off the road into an orchard, killed Mr. Howell or knocked him unconscious with whatever she used for that purpose, removed his clothing and ran the car over him to obliterate his face."

A noise came from Helen Vardis. She had obliterated her own face by covering it with her hands. That gave Joe an excuse to touch her, which he did.

"Granted her basic premise," Wolfe went on, "she couldn't very well have been expected to let Arthur Howell continue to live. She would never have had a carefree moment. What if Mr. Goodwin or I had met him on the street? That thought should have occurred to him, but apparently something about Mrs. Poor had made him quit thinking. There are precedents. Since she was good at detail, I presume she spread his coat over his head so as to leave no telltale matter on her tires. What she then did with the clothing is no longer of interest—at least not to me.''

He drank beer. ''She proceeded. First to Mr. Blaney's place, to make sure, by looking through the windows, that he was alone there, so that she could safely say that she had gone to see him and couldn't find him. Again she was providing for all contingencies. If Arthur Howell's body was, after all, identified, known as that of a man who was with the Becker Products Corporation and had access to those capsules, it would help to have it established that Mr. Blaney had not been at home during the time that Arthur Howell had been killed.''

He emptied the glass. ''The rest is anticlimax, though, of course, for her it was the grand consummation. She returned to Monty's Tavern, told her husband Mr. Blaney had not been at home, dined with him, drove back to New York and went to their apartment, and got him a nice fresh cigar from a new box. Everything worked perfectly. It sounds more complicated than it really was. Such details as making sure that no photographs of her husband would be available for the newspapers had no doubt been already attended to.''

''That receipt you signed,'' Cramer growled.

''What? Oh. That gave her no difficulty. Arthur Howell gave the receipt to her, naturally, and she put it in her husband's pocket. That was important. It was probably the first thing she did after the cigar exploded.''

''Meanwhile, you've got the five thousand dollars.''

''Yes, sir. I have.''

''But Poor didn't pay it to you. You never saw Poor. You weren't hired by him. If you want to say Mrs. Poor paid it, do you take money from murderers?''

It was one of Cramer's feeblest attempts to be nasty, certainly not up to his standard.

Wolfe merely poured the beer and said, ''*Pfui!* Whether Mr. Poor paid me or not, he got his money's worth.''

Try analyzing the logic of that. I can't.

Monsignor Xavier

THE SWEATING STATUE
Edward D. Hoch

I T WAS THE miracle at Father David Noone's aging inner-city parish that brought Monsignor Thomas Xavier to the city. He'd been sent by the Cardinal himself to investigate the miraculous event, and that impressed Father Noone, even though he might have wished for more run-of-the-mill parish problems now that he'd reached the age of fifty.

Monsignor Xavier was a white-haired man a few years older than Father Noone, with a jolly, outgoing manner that made him seem more like a fund-raiser than the Cardinal's trouble-shooter. He shook hands vigorously and said, "We met once year ago when you were at St. Monica's, Father. I accompanied the Cardinal."

"Of course," David Noone replied, bending the truth a little. The Cardinal's visit had been more than a decade earlier, and if he remembered the monsignor at all it was only vaguely.

"Holy Trinity isn't much like St. Monica's, is it?" Monsignor Xavier remarked as he followed David into the sitting room. "These inner-city parishes have changed a great deal."

"Well, we have to scrape a bit to get by. The Sunday collections don't bring in much money, but of course the diocese helps out." He poked his head into the rectory kitchen. "Mrs. Wilkins, could you bring us in some—what will it be, Monsignor, coffee or tea?"

"Tea is fine."

"Some tea, please."

Mrs. Wilkins, the parish housekeeper, turned from the freezer with a carton of ice cream in her hand. "Be right with you. Good of you to visit us, Monsignor."

When they'd settled down in the parlor, the white-haired monsignor asked, "Are you alone at Holy Trinity, Father?"

577

"I am at present. When I first took over as pastor five years ago I had an assistant, but there just aren't enough priests to go around. He was shifted to a suburban parish two years ago and I've been alone here with Mrs. Wilkins ever since."

Monsignor Xavier opened a briefcase and took out some papers. "The parish is mainly Hispanic now, I believe."

"Pretty much so, though in the past year we've had several Southeast Asian families settle here, mainly in the Market Street area. We're trying to help them as much as we can."

He nodded as if satisfied. "Now tell me about the statue."

Mrs. Wilkins arrived wih tea, setting the cups before them and pouring with a steady hand. "I'll bring in a few little cookies too," she said. "You must be hungry after your journey, Monsignor."

"Oh, they gave us a snack on the plane. Don't worry about me."

"We'll have a nice dinner," she promised. "It's not often we have such a distinguished visitor."

When they were alone, Monsignor Xavier said, "You were going to tell me about the statue."

"Of course. That's what you've come about." David Noone took a sip of tea. "It began two weeks ago today. Our custodian, Marcos, had unlocked the church doors for the seven A.M. Mass. There are always a few early arrivals and one of these, Celia Orlando, came up to light a candle before Mass began. She noticed that the wooden statue of the Virgin on the side altar seemed covered with sweat. When she called Marcos's attention to it, he wiped the statue dry with a cloth. But a few moments later the sweating began again."

He paused for some comment, but the monsignor only said, "Interesting. Please continue."

"Marcos showed it to me when I arrived to say the Mass. I didn't think too much of it at first. Perhaps the wood was exuding some sort of sap. In fact, I thought no more of the incident until later that day when Mrs. Wilkins reported that people were arriving to view the miracle. I went over to the church and found a half-dozen women, friends and neighbors of Celia Orlando."

"Tell me about the woman."

"Celia? Her parents moved here from Mexico City when she was a teenager. She's twenty-eight now, and deeply religious. Attends Mass every morning on her way to work at an insurance company."

A nod. "Go on with your story."

Father Noone shifted in his chair, feeling as if he was being questioned in a courtroom. "Well, I spoke to the women and tried to convince them there was no miracle. I thought things had settled down, but then the following morning the same thing happened. It kept happening, and each morning there's been a bigger crowd at morning Mass. After television covered it on the six o'clock news the church was jammed."

Monsignor Xavier finished the tea and rose to his feet. "Well, I think it's time I saw this remarkable statue."

Father Noone led the way through the rectory kitchen where Mrs. Wilkins was already at work on dinner. "It smells good," the monsignor commented, giving her a smile. They passed through a fire door into a corridor that connected the rectory with the rear of the church.

"It's handy in the winter," David Noone explained.

"Is the church kept locked at night?"

"Oh, yes, all the doors. It's a shame but we have to do it. And not just in the inner city, either. These days they're locked in the suburbs, too."

The two priests crossed in front of the main altar, genuflecting as they did so. The Blessed Virgin's altar was on the far side, and it was there that the wooden statue stood. "There are no people here now," Xavier commented.

"Since we've had all the publicity I've been forced to close the church in the afternoon too, just to get the people out of here. We open again at five for afternoon services."

Monsignor Xavier leaned over for a closer look at the statue. "There is moisture, certainly, but not as much as I'd expected."

"There's more in the morning."

He glanced curiously at Father Noone. "Is that so?"

The statue itself stood only about eighteen inches high and had been carefully carved by a parish craftsman many years before David Noone's arrival. It was a traditional representation of the Blessed Virgin, with the polished unpainted wood adding a certain warmth to the figure. Monsignor Xavier studied it from all angles, then put out a finger to intercept a drop of liquid which had started running down the side of the statue. He placed it to his tongue and said, "It seems to be water."

"That's what we think."

"No noticeable salty taste."

"Why should it be salty?"

"Like tears," the monsignor said. "I'm surprised no one has dubbed the liquid the Virgin's Tears or some such thing."

"That'll be next, I'm sure."

They were joined by a thin balding man who walked with stooped shoulders and wore a pair of faded overalls. David Noone introduced the monsignor to Marcos, the church's custodian. "That means janitor," the balding man said with a smile. "I know my place in the world."

"We'd be lost without you," David assured him, "whatever you're called."

"You unlock the church doors every morning for the early Mass?" Monsignor Xavier asked.

"Sure."

"Ever find signs of robbery or forced entry?"

"No, not in years."

"When I first came here," David Noone explained, "it was customary to leave the side door facing the rectory unlocked all night. But someone stole one of our big gold candlesticks and that put an end to it. With the covered passageway from the rectory we don't really need any unlocked doors. On the rare occasion when someone needed to get into the church at night, they simply came to the rectory and Mrs. Wilkins or I took them over."

"What about this young woman, Celia Orlando?" the monsignor asked Marcos. "Do you know her?"

"Yes, her family has been in the parish many years. She is a good girl, very religious."

"Tell me, Marcos, what do you think causes the statue to sweat?"

The old man shifted his eyes to the wooden Virgin, then back to the monsignor. He seemed to be weighing his answer carefully. "A miracle, I suppose. Isn't that why you came here from the Cardinal?"

"Have you ever seen wood like that sweat before?"

"No."

"Could it be some sort of sap?"

"It has no taste. Sap would be sweet. And there would be no sap after all these years."

"So you think it is a miracle."

"I think whatever you want me to think. I am a good Catholic."

Monsignor Xavier turned away. "We'd best go see this young woman," he said to David Noone. "Celia Orlando."

In the car David tried to explain his people to Monsignor Xavier. "They are deeply religious. You are a stranger from another city, someone sent by the Cardinal himself. Naturally they do not want to offend you in any way."

"That old man does not believe in miracles, David. May I call you David? We might as well be informal about this. I'm Tom." He was relaxing a bit, feeling more at home with the situation, David thought. "Tell me a little about Marcos."

"There's not much to tell. His wife is dead and he lives alone. His children grew up and moved away. His son's a computer programmer."

"A story of our times, I suppose."

David Noone parked the car in front of the neat, freshly painted house where Celia Orlando lived with her brother Adolfo and his wife. It was almost dinner time, and Adolfo came to the door. "Hello, Father. Have you come to see my sister?"

"If she's home. Adolfo, this is Monsignor Thomas Xavier. The Cardinal sent him to look into our strange event."

"You mean the miracle." He ushered them into the living room.

Monsignor Xavier smiled. "That's what I'm here to determine. These things often have a natural explanation, you know."

Celia came into the room to greet them. She was still dressed for work, wearing a neat blue skirt and a white blouse. The presence of the monsignor seemed to impress her, and she hastened to explain that she deserved no special attention. "I attend Mass every morning, Monsignor, but I'm no Bernadette. I saw nothing the others did not see. I was merely the first to notice it."

"And you called it a miracle."

She brushed the black hair back from her wide dark eyes, and Father Noone realized that she was a very pretty young woman. He wondered why he'd never noticed it before. "An act of God," she responded. "That's a miracle isn't it?"

"We believe the wood of the statue is merely exuding moisture."

She shook her head in bewilderment. "Why is the church so reluctant to accept a miracle? What the world needs now are more miracles, not less."

"We must be very careful in matters of this sort," Xavier explained. "Have you ever noticed anything strange about the statue before? Anything unusual?"

"No, nothing."

Her brother interrupted then. "What are you after, Monsignor?"

"Only the facts. I must return home tomorrow and report to the Cardinal."

"I have a boyfriend who thinks I'm crazy. He's not Catholic." The admission seemed to embarrass her. "He says the priests are twisting my mind. He should be here now to see me trying to convince you both of the miracle."

Father Noone glanced at his watch. "I have to get back for the afternoon Mass in fifteen minutes. I hadn't realized it was so late."

She saw them to the door. "Pray for me," she said.

"We should say the same to you," Monsignor Xavier told her.

On the drive back to the parish church he talked little. When he saw the crowds at the five-thirty Mass, filling the small church almost to capacity, he said nothing at all.

In the evening they sat in David Noone's small study, enjoying a bit of brandy. They were on a first-name basis now, and it was a time for confidences. "How do you do financially here?" Thomas Xavier asked.

"Poorly," David Noone admitted. "I have to go hat in hand to the bishop a couple of times a year. But he realizes the problems. He helps in every way he can."

"What does he think of the statue?"

"Strictly hands off, Tom. That's why he phoned the Cardinal. It's known as passing the buck."

"I know how he feels. If you think the church was crowded this afternoon, just wait till the national news gets hold of this. You'll have people coming here from all over the country."

"There was a call from the *New York Times* yesterday. They said they might send a reporter out this weekend."

"That's what I mean. We have to be very careful, David—"

He was interrupted by Mrs. Wilkins, who announced, "There's a young man to see you, Father Noone. He says it's very important."

David Noone sighed and got to his feet. "Excuse me, Tom. Duty calls."

He walked down the hall to the parlor where a sandy-haired man in his late twenties was waiting. "You're Father Noone?" the man asked, rising to meet him.

"Yes. What can I do for you?"

"My name is Kevin Frisk. Maybe Celia mentioned me."

"Celia Orlando? No, I don't believe so."

"I'm her boyfriend."

"Oh, yes. I think—"

"I want you to stay away from her."

David could see the anger in his eyes now. "I assure you—"

"You came this afternoon with another priest. She told me about it. I want you to leave her alone, stop filling her head with all these crazy notions of a miracle."

"Actually it's just the opposite. No one is more skeptical than a priest when there's talk of miracles."

"I want to marry her. I want to take her away from your influence."

"We have very little influence over Celia or anyone else. We only try to give a bit of comfort, and a few answers to the questions people ask. Do you work with Celia at the insurance office?"

"Yes. And I'm not Catholic." There was a challenge in his words.

"Celia told me that."

"If you think you can hypnotize me with your crazy notions—"

"Believe me, I'm not trying to hypnotize you or persuade you or convert you."

"Then stay away from Celia. Stop filling her head with statues that sweat. If we're ever married it'll be far from here."

"Mr. Frisk—"

"That's all I have to say. Take it as a warning. The next time I might not be quite so civil."

David watched as he left the room and walked out the front door without looking back. He shook his head sadly and returned to the study where the monsignor was waiting.

"No special problem, I hope," Thomas Xavier said, putting down the magazine he'd been glancing through.

"Not really. It was a young man who's been dating Celia Orlando."

"Ah yes—the non-Catholic one. I caught that point when she made it."

"He thinks we're brainwashing her or something. He seemed a bit angry."

"The statue seems to be having a ripple effect on the lives of a great many people."

The meeting with Kevin Frisk had left David dissatisfied. He felt he'd given the wrong answers to questions that hadn't even been asked. "What will you tell the Cardinal when you go back tomorrow?"

"I want to have another look at our statue in the morning. That may help me decide."

It was Father Noone's habit to rise at six-thirty for the seven o'clock Mass, delaying breakfast until after the service. When the alarm woke him he dressed quickly and went downstairs, noting only that the door to the guest room where Monsignor Xavier slept was still closed. Passing through the kitchen he noted that Mrs. Wilkins was not yet up either. The brandy glasses from the previous night sat unwashed on the sideboard, and a carton of ice cream lay melting in the sink. The door to her room, at the rear of the main floor, was also closed.

Through the window he could see a parishioner trying the side door of the church, which was still locked. Had Marcos overslept too? David Noone hurried along the passageway and into the church, switching on lights as he went. It was already ten minutes to seven. He entered the sacristy and was about to open the cabinet where his vestments were hung when something drew him to the stairwell leading to the church basement. There was a light on down there, which seemed odd if Marcos was late arriving.

But Marcus was there, sprawled at the foot of the stairs. David knew before he reached him that the old man was dead.

David knelt by the body for a moment, saying a silent, personal prayer. Then he administered the last rites of the Church. He went back to the rectory and roused Monsignor Xavier, telling him what had happened. "Can you take the Mass for me while I call the police? There are people waiting."

"Certainly, David. Give me five minutes to dress."

He joined David Noone in three minutes and they returned to the church together. Staring down at the body, Thomas Xavier said a prayer of his own. "The poor man. It looks as if his neck was broken in the fall."

"He knew these stairs too well to fall on them," David said.

"You think he was pushed? But why, and by whom?"

"I don't know."

"Open the doors of your church. It's after seven and people are waiting. Tell them Mass will begin in a few moments."

"Where are you going now?"

"Just over to see the statue."

David Noone followed him across the sanctuary to the side altar. The Virgin's statue was sweating, perhaps more intensely than before. The monsignor reached out his right hand to touch it, then drew sharply back. "What is it?" David asked.

"The statue is cold, as if it's aware of the presence of death."

The Mass went on as the police arrived and went through their routine. A detective sergeant named Dominick was in charge. "Anything stolen, Father?" he wanted to know, peering over the rim of his glasses as he took notes.

"Nothing obvious. The chalices are all here. We don't keep any money in the church overnight, except what's in the poor box, and that hasn't been touched."

"Then foul play seems doubtful. He probably just missed his footing in the dark."

"The light was on," Daivd reminded him.

"He was an old man, Father. We got enough crime these days without trying to find it where it doesn't exist."

When they returned to the rectory after Mass, Mrs. Wilkins was busy preparing breakfast. David told her what had happened and she started to cry softly. "He was a good man," she said. "He didn't deserve to die like that."

"The police are convinced it was an accident," David Noone said. "I'm not so sure."

She brought them their breakfast and Monsignor Xavier took a mouthful of scrambled egg. After a moment he said, "This is very good. I wish we had breakfast like this back home."

"What do you think about Marcos?" David Noone asked him.

He considered that for a moment. "I don't know. I did notice that Celia Orlando wasn't at Mass this morning. Didn't you say she comes every day?"

"Yes."

"Perhaps we should see why her routine changed today."

Father Noone had to make some calls at the hospital first, and he was surprised when the monsignor changed his return flight and arranged to stay over an extra day. He wondered what it meant. Then, just before noon, they called on Celia at the insurance office where she was employed.

She was startled to see them enter, and came up to the counter to greet them. "Is something wrong? It's not my brother is it?"

"No, no," Father Noone assured her. "It's just that you weren't at Mass and I wondered if you were ill."

She dropped her eyes. "Kevin—my boyfriend—doesn't want me to go there anymore. He says you're a bad influence on me."

"He certainly can't keep you from practicing your religion."

"He says I should go to another parish. All that business with the statue—"

At that moment one of the office doors opened and Kevin Frisk himself emerged. He hurried over to the counter and confronted the two priests. "Get out of here!" he ordered.

"You can't—"

"I can order you out when you're keeping employees from their jobs, and that's exactly what you're doing. Get out and don't let me see you here again."

David Noone turned to Celia as they departed. "Call me at the rectory. We need to talk."

"Stay away from her!" Frisk warned.

Outside, Monsignor Xavier shook his head. "A hotheaded young man. He could cause trouble."

"If he hasn't already. Maybe he broke into the church and Marcos caught him at it.

"There were no signs of forced entry, David. Perhaps that detective is right about looking for crime where none exists."

"I'm sorry, Tom. I just can't get that old man out of my mind."

As they walked back to the car they saw a headline on the noon edition of the newspaper: MAN FOUND DEAD AT "MIRACLE" CHURCH. Monsignor Xavier said, "I'm afraid this will bring you all the national publicity you've been trying to avoid. It's something more than a miracle now."

"Is that why you're staying over? Did you expect something like this?"

Thomas Xavier hesitated. "Not expect it, exactly. But in a large city we're more in tune with the way the press operates. They couldn't get the right angle on a sweating statue, but now there's a dead old man and they'll have a field day."

"What do you suggest I do?"

"We must have an answer ready when they ask the Church's position on the so-called miracle."

"And what is the Church's position? What will you report to the Cardinal?"

"The answer to that lies back at Holy Trinity."

There had been no Marcos to lock up the church during the early afternoon, and David Noone realized it had been left open as soon as he drove up to the rectory and saw the streams of people entering and leaving.

"I forgot to lock it," he said sadly.

"I doubt if there's any harm done."

They found Mrs. Wilkins just hanging up the telephone, almost frantic. "It's been like a circus here. Reporters calling from all over the country! The television stations have all been down, filming the statue for the evening news."

"Again? They did that last week."

"There are more people around now. And everyone wants to see where poor Marcos died. I was over there shooing them out of the sacristy myself."

The afternoon Mass was like a bad dream for David. People he'd never seen before filled the church, many with little interest in following the service. Instead they crowded around the side altar where the statue stood. The moisture was not as heavy as it had been that morning, but there was still some to be seen. In his sermon he said a few words about Marcos, then tried to make the point that the phenomenon of the statue was still unexplained. Following the services people lingered around the side altar until finally David had to ask them to leave so he could close the church.

"The only blessing to come out of all this," he told the monsignor over dinner, "is that the crowds, and the collections, have never been better. Still, I'm wondering if I should simply remove the statue temporarily and end all this fuss."

"That would surely bring complaints from some, though it's an option we must consider."

Mrs. Wilkins brought in their coffee. "Sorry there's no dessert tonight. What with all the commotion I didn't get to the store today."

"It'll do us both good," the monsignor assured her.

Later, they walked around the church in the darkness as David Noone checked all the doors to be sure they were locked. "I'll have to find a replacement for Marcos, of course, immediately after the funeral."

Monsignor Xavier stared up at the spire of Holy Trinity Church as it disappeared into the night sky. "I often wish I had a church like this. It would be just the right size for me. In the city, serving the Cardinal, I lose touch with things at times."

"With people?"

"With people, yes, and with their motives."

Later that night, just after eleven, as David was turning out the light and getting into bed, his door opened silently and Thomas Xavier slipped into the room. He held a finger to his lips. "Put on your robe and come with me," he said softly.

"What—"

"Just come, very quietly."

David took his robe and followed Thomas Xavier down the stairs. When they reached the main floor the monsignor headed for the kitchen, then paused as if listening.

"What—"

"Shh!"

He heard a noise from the passageway leading into the church, and then the kitchen door swung open.

It was Mrs. Wilkins, carrying the statue of the Virgin in her arms.

"Let me take that," Monsignor Xavier said with a kindly voice. "We don't want any more accidents, like what happened to poor old Marcos."

She gave him the statue, and then the will seemed to go out of her. For a long time she cried, and talked irrationally, and it was only the soft words of the monsignor that calmed her at last.

"We know all about it, Mrs. Wilkins. You carried the statue in here each evening, didn't you, and immersed it in water. Then you left it in the freezer overnight, carrying it back into the church each morning before Mass. Naturally as it thawed it seemed to sweat. That was why there was more moisture in the morning than later in the day, and why it was cold to my touch this morning. I remembered seeing the ice cream melting in the sink when I passed through the kitchen with Father Noone. You took it out of the freezer to make room for the statue, and then forgot to put it back, so there was no dessert for us tonight."

"I only did it so more people would come, so the collections would be bigger and we could help the poor souls in our parish. I never meant to do any harm!"

"Marcos caught you this morning, didn't he? If he was already suspicious, my presence might have prompted him to come in earlier than usual. He hid in the stairwell and turned on the light as you were returning the statue."

"Oh my God, the poor man! He startled me so; he tried to take the statue away and I pushed him. I didn't realize we were so close to the stairs. He just went down, and didn't move. I didn't mean to kill him." Her voice had softened until they could barely hear her.

"Of course you didn't," David Noone said, taking her hand.

"I read about it in a book, about putting the statue in the freezer. I thought it would help the parish. I never meant to hurt anybody."

Monsignor Xavier nodded. "There was something similar down in Nicaragua a few years back. I read about it too. When I saw the ice cream in the sink it reminded me. You see, David, if someone was tampering with the statue overnight it had to be either Marcos or Mrs. Wilkins. The church was locked, with the only entrance from the rectory here. It was locked this morning, when Marcos died. He had a key, and she didn't need one."

"What are they going to do with me?" she asked sadly.

"I don't know," David replied. "We'll have to phone the police. Then I'll go down there with you. I'll stay with you as long as I can. Don't worry."

In the morning Monsignor Xavier departed. He stood for a moment looking up at the church and then shook hands with David Noone. "You have a fine church here. Fine people. I'll tell the Cardinal that."

It was after the morning Mass, and as he watched the monsignor get into his taxi for the airport, Celia Orlando approached him. "The statue is gone, Father. Where is the statue?"

"I didn't expect to see you at Mass, Celia."

"He can't tell me how to pray. I said that to him. But where is the statue?"

"I'm keeping it in the rectory for a few days. It was all a hoax, I'm afraid. There was no miracle. You'll read about it in the papers."

She nodded, but he wondered if she really understood his words. "That's all right," she said. "I managed to wipe a bit of the sweat off one day with a piece of cotton. I carry it with me all the time. I'll never throw it away."

Trygve Yamamura

DEAD PHONE
Poul Anderson

THAT WAS AN evil autumn, when the powers bared their teeth across an island in the Spanish Main and it seemed the world might burn. Afterward Americans looked at each other with a kind of wonder, and for a while they walked more straight. But whatever victory they had gained was soon taken away from them.

As if to warn, a fortnight earlier the weather ran amok. On the Pacific coast, gale force winds flung sea against land, day and night without end, and rainfall in northern California redressed the balance of a three-year drought in less than a week. At the climax of it, the hills around San Francisco Bay started to come down in mudslides that took houses and human bodies along, and the streets of some towns were turned into rivers.

Trygve Yamamura sat up late. His wife had taken the children to visit her cousin in the Mother Lode country over the Columbus Day weekend. His work kept him behind; so now he prowled the big hollow house on the Berkeley steeps, smoked one pipe after another, listened to the wind and the rain lashing his roof and to the radio whose reports grew ever more sinister, and could not sleep.

Oh, yes, he told himself often and often, he was being foolish. They had undoubtedly arrived without trouble and were now snug at rest. In any event, he could do nothing to help, he was only exhausting himself, in violation of his entire philosophy. Tomorrow morning the phone line that had snapped, somewhere in those uplands, would be repaired, and he would hear their voices. But meanwhile his windowpanes were holes of blackness, and he started when a broken tree branch crashed against the wall.

He sought his basement gym and tried to exercise himself into calm.

That didn't work either, simply added a different kind of weariness. He was worn down, he knew, badly in need of a vacation, with no immediate prospect of one. His agency had too many investigations going for him to leave the staff unsupervised.

He was also on edge because through various connections he knew more about the Cuban situation than had yet gotten into the papers. A nuclear showdown was beginning to look all too probable. Yamamura was not a pacifist, even when it came to that kind of war; but no sane man, most especially one with wife and children, could coolly face abomination.

Toward midnight he surrendered. The Zen techniques had failed, or he had. His eyes felt hot and his brain gritty. He stripped, stood long under the shower, and at last, with a grimace, swallowed a sleeping pill.

The drug took quick hold of his unaccustomed body, but nonetheless he tossed about half awake and half in nightmare. It gibbered through his head, he stumbled among terrors and guilts, the sun had gone black while horrible stars rained down upon him. When the phone beside his bed rang he struck out with his fists and gasped.

Brring! the bell shouted across a light-year of wind and voices, *brring, come to me, you must you must before that happens which has no name, brring, brring, you are damned to come and brring me her brring brring brrRING!*

He struggled to wake. Night strangled him. He could not speak or see, so great was his need of air. The receiver made lips against his ear and kissed him obscenely while the dark giggled. Through whirl and seethe he heard a click, then a whistle that went on forever, and he had a moment to think that the noise was not like any in this world, it was as if he had a fever or as if nothing was at the other end of the line except the huntsman wind. His skull resounded with the querning of the planets. Yet when the voice came it was clear, steady, a little slow and very sad—but how remote, how monstrously far away.

"Come to me. It's so dark here."

Yamamura lay stiff in his own darkness.

"I don't understand," said the voice. "I thought . . . afterward I would know everything, or else nothing. But instead I don't understand. Oh, God, but it's lonely!"

For a space only the humming and the chill whistle were heard. Then: "Why did I call you, Trygve Yamamura? For help? What help is there now? You don't even know that we don't understand afterward. Were those pigs that I heard grunting in the forest, and did she come behind them in a black cloak? I'm all alone.''

And presently: ''Something must be left. I read somewhere once that you don't die in a piece. The last and lowest cells work on for hours. I guess that's true. Because you're still real, Trygve Yamamura.'' Another pause, as if for the thoughtful shaking of a weary head. ''Yes, that must be why I called. What became of me, no, that's of no account any more. But the others. They won't stay real for very long. I had to call while they are, so you can help them. Come.''

''Cardynge,'' Yamamura mumbled.

''No,'' said the voice. ''Goodbye.''

The instrument clicked off. Briefly the thin screaming continued along the wires, and then it too died, and nothing remained but the weight in Yamamura's hand.

He became conscious of the storm that dashed against the windows, fumbled around and snapped the lamp switch. The bedroom sprang into existence: warm yellow glow on the walls, mattress springy beneath him and covers tangled above, the bureau with the children's pictures on top. The clock said 1:35. He stared at the receiver before laying it back in its cradle.

''Whoof,'' he said aloud.

Had he dreamed that call? No, he couldn't have. As full awareness flowed into him, every nerve cried alarm. His lanky, thick-chested frame left the bed in one movement. Yanking the directory from its shelf below the stand, he searched for an address. Yes, here. He took the phone again and dialed.

''Berkeley police,'' said a tone he recognized.

''Joe. This is Trig Yamamura. I think I've got some trouble to report. Client of mine just rang me up. Damndest thing I ever heard, made no sense whatsoever, but he seems to be in a bad way and the whole thing suggests—'' Yamamura stopped.

''Yes, what?'' said the desk officer.

Yamamura pinched his lips together before he said, ''I don't know. But you'd better send a car around to have a look.''

''Trig, do *you* feel right? Don't you know what's happening outdoors? We may get a disaster call any minute, if a landslide starts, and we've got our hands full as is with emergencies.''

''You mean this is too vague?'' Yamamura noticed the tension that knotted his muscles. One by one he forced them to relax. ''Okay, I see your point," he said. "But you know I don't blow the whistle for nothing, either. Dispatch a car as soon as possible, if you don't hear anything else from me. Meanwhile I'll get over there myself. The place isn't far from here."

"M-m-m . . . well, fair enough, seeing it's you. Who is the guy and where does he live?"

"Aaron Cardynge." Yamamura spelled the name and gave the address he had checked.

"Oh, yeah, I've heard of him. Medium-big importer, isn't he? I guess he wouldn't rouse you without some reason. Go ahead, then, and we'll alert the nearest car to stop by when it can."

"Thanks." Yamamura had started to skin out of his pajamas before he hung up.

He was back into his clothes, with a sweater above, very nearly as fast, and pulled on his raincoat while he kicked the garage door open. The wind screeched at him. When he backed the Volkswagen out, it trembled with that violence. Rain roared on its metal and flooded down the windshield; his headlights and the rear lamps were quickly gulped down by night. Through everything he could hear how water cascaded along the narrow, twisting hill streets and sheeted under his wheels. The brake drums must be soaked, he thought, and groped his way in second gear.

But the storm was something real to fight, that cleansed him of vague horrors. As he drove, with every animal skill at his command, he found himself thinking in a nearly detached fashion.

Why should Cardynge call me? I only met him once. And not about anything dangerous. Was it?

"I'm sorry, Mr. Cardynge," Yamamura said. "This agency doesn't handle divorce work."

The man across the desk shifted in his chair and took out a cigarette case. He was large-boned, portly, well-dressed, with gray hair brushed back above a rugged face. "I'm not here about that." He spoke not quite steadily and had some difficulty keeping his eyes on the detective's.

"Oh? I beg your pardon. But you told me—"

"Background. I . . . I'd tell a doctor as much as I could, too. So he'd have a better chance of helping me. Smoke?"

"No, thanks. I'm strictly a pipe man." More to put Cardynge at his ease than because he wanted one, Yamamura took a briar off the rack and charged it. "I don't know if we can help. Just what is the problem?"

"To find my son, I said. But you should know why he left and why it's urgent to locate him." Cardynge lit his cigarette and consumed it in quick nervous puffs. "I don't like exposing my troubles. Believe me. Always made my own way before."

Yamamura leaned back, crossed his long legs, and regarded the other through a blue cloud. "I've heard worse than anything you're likely to have on your mind," he said. "Take your time."

Cardynge's troubled gaze sought the flat half-Oriental countenance before him. "I guess the matter isn't too dreadful at that," he said. "Maybe not even as sordid as it looks from the inside. And it's nearing an end now. But I've got to find Bayard, my boy, soon.

"He's my son by my first marriage. My wife died two years ago. I married Lisette a year later. Indecent haste? I don't know. I'd been so happy before. Hadn't realized how happy, till Maria was gone and I was rattling around alone in the house. Bayard was at the University most of the time, you see. This would be his junior year. He had an apartment of his own. We'd wanted him to, the extra cost was nothing to us and he should have that taste of freedom, don't you think? Afterward . . . he'd have come back to stay with me if I asked. He offered to. But, oh, call it kindness to him, or a desire to carry on what Maria and I had begun, or false pride—I said no, that wasn't necessary, I could get along fine. And I did, physically. Had a housekeeper by day but cooked my own dinner, for something to do. I'm not a bad amateur cook."

Cardynge brought himself up short, stubbed out his cigarette, and lit another. "Not relevant," he said roughly, "except maybe to show why I made my mistake. A person gets lonesome eating by himself.

"Bayard's a good boy. He did what he could for me. Mainly that amounted to visiting me pretty often. More and more, he'd bring friends from school along. I enjoyed having young people around. Maria and I had always hoped for several children.

"Lisette got included in one of those parties. She was older than the rest, twenty-five, taking a few graduate courses. Lovely creature, witty, well read, captivating manners. I . . . I asked Bayard to be sure and invite her for next time. Then I started taking her out myself. Whirlwind courtship, I suppose. I'm still not sure which of us was the whirlwind, though."

Cardynge scowled. His left hand clenched. "Bayard tried to warn me," he said, "Not that he knew her any too well. But he did know she was one of the—it isn't fashionable to call them beat any more, is it? The kind who spend most of their time hanging around in the coffee shops bragging about what they're going to do someday, and meanwhile cadging their living any way they can. Though that doesn't describe Lisette either. She turned out to have a good deal more force of character than that bunch. Anyhow, when he saw I was serious, Bayard begged me not to go any further with her. We had quite a fight about it. I married her a couple of days later.''

Cardynge made a jerky sort of shrug. ''Never mind the details,'' he said. ''I soon learned she was a bitch on wheels. At first, after seeing what happened to our joint checking account, I thought she was simply extravagant. But what she said, and did, when I tried to put the brakes on her—! Now I'm mortally certain she didn't actually spend most of the money, but socked it away somewhere. I also know she had lovers. She taunted me with that, at the end.

''Before then she drove Bayard out. You can guess how many little ways there are to make a proud, sensitive young man unwelcome in his own father's house. Finally he exploded and told the truth about her, to both our faces. I still felt honor bound to defend her, at least to the extent of telling him to shut up or leave. ''Very well, I'll go,'' he said, and that was the last I saw of him. Four months back. He simply left town.''

''Have you heard anything from him since?'' Yamamura asked.

''A short letter from Seattle, some while ago,'' Cardynge finished his cigarette and extracted a fresh one. ''Obviously trying to mend his friendship with me, if not her. He only said he was okay, but the job he'd found was a poor one. He'd heard of better possibilities elsewhere, so he was going to go have a look and he'd write again when he was settled. I haven't heard yet. I tried to get his current address from his draft board, but they said they weren't allowed to release any such information. So I came to you.''

''I see.'' Yamamura drew on his pipe. ''Don't worry too much, Mr. Cardynge. He sounds like a good, steady kid, who'll land on his feet.''

''Uh-huh. But I must locate him. You see, Lisette and I separated month before last. Not formally. We . . . we've even seen each other on occasion. She can still be lovely in every way, when she cares to. I've been sending her money, quite a decent sum. But she says she wants to come back.''

''Do you want her yourself?''

''No. No. It's a fearful temptation, but I'm too well aware of what the end result would be. So she told me yesterday, if I didn't take her back, she'd file for divorce. And you know what a woman can do to a man in this state.''

''Yeah.''

"I'm quite prepared to make a reasonable settlement," Cardynge said. "A man ought to pay for his mistakes. But I'll be damned if I'll turn over so much to her that it ruins the business my son was going to inherit."

"Um-m-m . . . are you sure he really wants to?"

"I am. He was majoring in business administration on that account. But your question's a very natural one, though, which is also bound to occur to the courts. If Bayard isn't here at the trial, it won't seem as if he has much interest that needs protection. Also, he's the main witness to prove the, the mental cruelty wasn't mine. At least, not entirely mine—I think." Cardynge gestured savagely with his cigarette. "All right, I married a girl young enough to be my daughter. We look at life differently. But I tried to please her."

Yamamura liked him for the admission.

"I've no proof about the lovers," Cardynge said, "except what she told me herself in our last fight. And, well, indications. You know. Never mind, I won't ask anyone to poke into that. Lisette was nearly always charming in company. And I'm not given to weeping on my friends' shoulders. So, as I say, we need Bayard's testimony. If there's to be any kind of justice done. In fact, if we can get him back before the trial, I'm sure she'll pull in her horns. The whole wretched business can be settled quietly, no headlines, no— You understand?"

"I believe so." Yamamura considered him a while before asking gently, "You're still in love with her aren't you?"

Cardynge reddened. Yamamura wondered if he was going to get up and walk out. But he slumped and said, "If so, I'll get over it. Will you take the case?"

The rest of the discussion was strictly ways and means.

Rain pursued Yamamura to the porch of the house. Right and left and behind was only blackness, the neighborhood slept. But here light spilled from the front windows, made his dripping coat shimmer and glistened on the spears that slanted past the rail. The wind howled too loudly for him to hear the doorbell.

But the man inside ought to—

Yamamura grew aware that he had stood ringing for well over a minute. Perhaps the bell was out of order. He seized the knocker and slammed it down hard, again and again. Nothing replied but the storm.

Damnation! He tried the knob. The door opened. He stepped through and closed it behind him. "Hello," he called. "Are you here, Mr. Cardynge?"

The whoop outside felt suddenly less violent than it was—distant, unreal, like that voice over the wire. The house brimmed with silence.

It was a big, old-fashioned house; the entry hall where he stood was only dully lit from the archway to the living room. Yamamura called once more and desisted. The sound was too quickly lost. *Maybe he went out, I'll wait*. He hung coat and hat on the rack and passed on in.

The room beyond, illuminated by a ceiling light and a floor lamp, was large and low, well furnished but with the comfortable slight shabbiness of a long-established home. At the far end was a couch with a coffee table in front.

Cardynge lay there.

Yamamura plunged toward him. "Hey!" he shouted, and got no response. Cardynge was sprawled full length, neck resting across the arm of the couch. Though his eyes were closed, the jaw had dropped open and the face was without color. Yamamura shook him a little. The right leg flopped off the edge; its shoe hit the carpet with a thud that had no resonance.

Judas priest! Yamamura grabbed a horribly limp wrist. The flesh did not feel cold, but it yielded too much to pressure. He couldn't find any pulse.

His watch crystal was wet. On the table stood a nearly empty fifth of bourbon, a glass with some remnants of drink, and a large pill bottle. Yamamura reached out, snatched his fingers back—possible evidence there—and brought Cardynge's left arm to the mouth. The watch didn't fog over.

His first thought was of artificial respiration. Breath and heart could not have stopped very long ago. He noticed the dryness of the tongue, the uncleanliness elsewhere. *Long enough*, he thought, and rose.

The storm hurled itself against silence and fell back. In Yamamura's mind everything was overridden by the marble clock that ticked on the mantel, the last meaningful sound in the world. He had rarely felt so alone.

What had Cardynge said, in his call?

Yamamura started across the room to the telephone, but checked himself. Could be fingerprints. The police would soon arrive anyway, and there was no use in summoning a rescue squad which might be needed another place.

He returned to the body and stood looking down. Poor Cardynge. He hadn't appeared a suicidal type; but how much does any human know of any other? The body was more carefully dressed, in suit and clean shirt and tie, than one might have expected from a man baching it. Still, the room was neat too. Little more disturbed its orderliness than a couple of butts and matches in an ashtray on the end table next to the couch. No day servant could maintain such conditions by herself.

Wait a bit. Crumpled sheet of paper, on the floor between couch and coffee table. Yamamura stopped, hesitated, and picked it up. Even dead, his client had a claim on him.

He smoothed it out with care. It had originally been folded to fit an envelope. A letter, in a woman's handwriting, dated yesterday.

My dear Aaron—
    —for you were very dear to me once, and in a way you still are. Not least, I suppose, because you have asked me to return to you, after all the heartbreak and bitterness. And yes, I believe you when you swear you will try to make everything different between us this time. Will you, then, believe me when I tell you how long and agonizingly hard I have thought since we spoke of this? How it hurts me so much to refuse you that I can't talk of it, even over the phone, but have to write this instead?
    But if I came back it would be the same hideous thing over again. Your temper, your inflexibility, your suspicion. Your son returning, as he will, and your inability to see how insanely he hates me for taking his mother's place, how he will work and work until he succeeds in poisoning your mind about me. And I'm no saint myself. I admit that. My habits, my outlook, my demands—am I cruel to say that you are too old for them?
    No, we would only hurt each other the worse. I don't want that, for you or for myself. So I can't come back.
    I'm going away for a while, I don't know where, or if I did know I wouldn't tell you, because you might not stop pleading with me and that would be too hard to bear. I don't want to see you again. Not for a long time, at least, 'til your wounds have scarred. I'll get an attorney to settle the business part with you. I wish you everything good. Won't you wish the same for me? Goodby, Aaron.

Lisette

Yamamura stared into emptiness. *I wonder what she'll think when she learns what this letter drove him to do.*
She may have even counted on it.
He put the sheet back approximately as he had found it, and unconsciously wiped his fingers on his trousers. In his need to keep busy, he squatted to examine the evidence on the table. His nose was keen, he could detect a slight acridness in the smell about the glass. The bottle from the drugstore held sleeping pills prescribed for Cardynge. It was half empty. Barbiturates and alcohol can be a lethal combination.

And yet— Yamamura got to his feet. He was not unacquainted with death, he had looked through a number of its many doors and the teachings of the Buddha made it less terrible to him than to most. But something was wrong here. The sense of that crawled along his nerves.

Perhaps only the dregs of the nightmare from which Cardynge had roused him.

Yamamura wanted his pipe in the worst way. But better not smoke before the police had seen what was here . . . as a matter of form, if nothing else. Form was something to guard with great care, on this night when chaos ran loose beyond the walls and the world stood unmeasurably askew within them.

He began to prowl. A wastepaper basket was placed near the couch. Struck by a thought—his logical mind functioned swiftly and unceasingly, as if to weave a web over that which lay below—he crouched and looked in. Only two items. The housekeeper must have emptied the basket today, and Cardynge tossed these in after he got back from his office. He wouldn't have observed the holiday; few establishments did, and he would have feared leisure. Yamamura fished them out.

One was a cash register receipt from a local liquor store, dated today. The amount shown corresponded to the price of a fifth such as stood on the table. Lord, but Cardynge must have been drunk, half out of his skull, when he prepared that last draught for himself!

The other piece was an envelope, torn open by hand, addressed here and postmarked yesterday evening in Berkeley. So he'd have found it in his mail when he came home this afternoon. In the handwriting of the letter, at the upper left corner, stood *Lisette Cardynge* and the apartment address her husband had given Yamamura.

The detective dropped them back into the basket and rose with a rather forced shrug. So what? If anything, this clinched the matter. One need merely feel compassion now, an obligation to find young Bayard—no, not even that, since the authorities would undertake it—so, no more than a wish to forget the whole business. There was enough harm and sorrow in the world without brooding on the unamendable affairs of a near stranger.

Only . . . Cardynge had wakened him, helplessly crying for help. And the wrongness would not go away.

Yamamura swore at himself. What was it that looked so impossible here? Cardynge's telephoning? He'd spoken strangely, even—or especially—for a man at the point of self-murder. *Though he may have been delirious. And certainly I was half asleep, in a morbid state, myself. I could have mixed his words with my dreams, and now be remembering things he never said.*

The suicide, when Cardynge read Lisette's ultimate refusal?

Or the refusal itself? Was it in character for her? Yamamura's mind twisted away from the room, two days backward in time.

He was faintly relieved when she came to his office. Not that the rights or wrongs of the case had much to do with the straightforward task of tracing Bayard and explaining why he should return. But Yamamura always preferred to hear both sides of a story.

He stood up as she entered. Sunlight struck through the window, a hurried shaft between clouds, and blazed on her blonde hair. She was tall and slim, with long green eyes in a singularly lovely face, and she walked like a cat. "How do you do?" he said. Her hand lingered briefly in his before they sat down, but the gesture looked natural. He offered her a cigarette from a box he kept for visitors. She declined.

"What can I do for you, Mrs. Cardynge?" he asked, with a little less than his normal coolness.

"I don't know," she said unhappily "I've no right to bother you like this."

"You certainly do, since your husband engaged me. I suppose he is the one who told you?"

"Yes. We saw each other yesterday, and he said he'd started you looking for his son. Do you think you'll find him?"

"I have no doubts. The man I sent to Seattle called in this very morning. He'd tracked down some of Bayard's associates there, who told him the boy had gone to Chicago. No known address, but probably as simple a thing as an ad in the paper will fetch him. It's not as if he were trying to hide."

She stared out of the window before she swung those luminous eyes back and said, "How can I get you to call off the search?"

Yamamura chose his words with care. "I'm afraid you can't. I've accepted a retainer."

"I could make that up to you."

Yamamura bridled. "Ethics forbid."

One small hand rose to her lips. "Oh, I'm so sorry. Please don't think I'm offering a bribe. But—" She blinked hard, squared her shoulders, and faced him head on. "Isn't there such a thing as a higher ethic?"

"Well-ll . . . what do you mean, Mrs. Cardynge?"

"I suppose Aaron praised Bayard at great length. And quite honestly, too, from his own viewpoint. His only son, born of his first wife, who must have been a dear person. How *could* Aaron see how evil he is?''

Yamamura made a production of charging his pipe. ''I hear there was friction between you and the boy,'' he said.

A tired little smile tugged at her mouth. ''You put it mildly. And of course I'm prejudiced. After all, he wrecked my marriage. Perhaps 'evil' is too strong a word. Nasty? And that may apply to nothing but his behavior toward me. Which in turn was partly resentment at my taking his mother's place, and partly—'' Lisette stopped.

''Go on,'' said Yamamura, low.

Color mounted in her cheeks. ''If you insist. I think he was in love with me. Not daring to admit it to himself, he did everything he could to get me out of his life. And out of his father's. He was more subtle than a young man ought to be, though. Insinuations; provocations; disagreements carefully nursed into quarrels—'' She gripped the chair arms. ''Our marriage, Aaron's and mine, would never have been a simple one to make work. The difference in age, outlook, everything. I'm not perfect either, not easy to live with. But I was trying. Then Bayard made the job impossible for both of us.''

''He left months ago,'' Yamamura pointed out.

''By that time the harm was done, even if he didn't realize it himself.''

''Does it matter to you any more what he does?''

''Yes. I—Aaron wants me to come back.'' She looked quickly up. ''No doubt he's told you otherwise. He has a Victorian sense of privacy. The sort of man who maintains appearances, never comes out of his shell, until at last the pressure inside gets too great and destroys him. But he's told me several times since I left that I can come back any time I want.''

''And you're thinking of doing so?''

''Yes. Though I can't really decide. It would be hard on us both, at best, and nearly unbearable if we fail again. But I do know that Bayard's presence would make the thing absolutely impossible.'' She clasped her purse with a desperate tightness. ''And even if I decide not to try, if I get a divorce, the lies Bayard would tell— Please, Mr. Yamamura! Don't make a bad matter worse!''

The detective struck match to tobacco and did not speak until he had the pipe going. ''I'm sorry,'' he said. ''But I can't decree that a father should not get in touch with his son. Even if I did resign from the case, he can hire someone else. And whatever happens, Bayard won't stay away forever. Sooner or later you'll have to face this problem. Won't you?''

The bright head bent. "I'm sorry," Yamamura said again.

She shook herself and jumped to her feet. "That's all right," she whispered. "I see your point. Of course. Don't worry about me. I'll manage. Thanks for your trouble." He could scarcely rise before she was gone.

The doorbell jarred Yamamura to awareness. As he opened for the patrolman, the storm screamed at him. "Hi, Charlie," he said in a mutter. "You didn't have a useless trip. Wish to hell you had."

Officer Moffat hung up his slicker. "Suicide?"

"Looks that way. Though— Well, come see for yourself."

Moffat spoke little before he had examined what was in the living room. Then he said, "Joe told me this was a client of yours and he called you tonight. What'd he want?"

"I don't know." Yamamura felt free, now, to console himself with his pipe. "His words were so incoherent, and I was so fogged with sleep myself, that I can't remember very well. Frankly, I'm just as glad."

"That figures for a suicide. Also the Dear John letter. What makes you so doubtful?"

Yamamura bit hard on his pipestem. The bowl became a tiny campfire over which to huddle. "I can't say. You know how it is when you're having a dream, and something is gruesomely wrong but you can't find out what, only feel that it is? That's what this is like."

He paused. "Of course," he said, seeking rationality, "Cardynge and his wife told me stories which were somewhat inconsistent. She claimed to me he wanted her back; he denied it. But you know how big a liar anyone can become when his or her most personal affairs are touched on. Even if he spoke truth at the time, he could have changed his mind yesterday. In either case, he'd have gotten drunk when she refused in this note, and if it turned out to be an unhappy drunk he could have hit the absolute bottom of depression and killed himself."

"Well," Moffat said, "I'll send for the squad." He laid a handkerchief over the phone and put it to his ear. "Damn! Line must be down somewhere. I'll have to use the car radio."

Yamamura remained behind while the policeman grumbled his way back into the rain. His eyes rested on Cardynge's face. It was so recently dead that a trace of expression lingered, but nothing he could read. As if Cardynge were trying to tell him something. . . . The thought came to Yamamura that this house was now more alive than its master, for it could still speak.

Impulsively, he went through the inner door and snapped on the light. Dining room, with a stiff, unused look; yes, the lonely man doubtless ate in the kitchen. Yamamura continued thither.

That was a fair-sized place, in cheerful colors which now added to desolation. It was as neat as everything else. One plate, silverware, and coffee apparatus stood in the drainrack. They were dry, but a dishtowel hung slightly damp. Hm . . . Cardynge must have washed his things quite shortly before he mixed that dose. Something to do with his hands, no doubt, a last effort to fend off the misery that came flooding over him. Yamamura opened the garbage pail, saw a well-gnawed T-bone and the wrappers from packages of frozen peas and French fries. Proof, if any were needed, that Cardynge had eaten here, doubtless been here the whole time. The refrigerator held a good bit of food; one ice tray was partly empty. Yamamura went on to the bathroom and bedrooms without noticing anything special.

Moffat came back in as the other man regained the living room. ''They're on their way,'' he said. ''I'll stick around here. You might as well go on home, Trig.''

''I suppose so.'' Yamamura hesitated. ''Who'll notify his wife?''

Moffat regarded him closely. ''You've met her, you said, and know something about the case. Think you'd be able to break the news gently?''

''I don't know. Probably not. Anyhow, looks as if I'll have to tell his son, when we find him.''

Moffat tilted back his cap and rubbed his head. ''Son left town? We'll have to interview him ourselves. To tie up loose ends, make sure he really was away and so forth. Not that— Huh?''

Yamamura picked up his pipe off the floor.

''What's the matter, Trig?''

''Nothing.'' The detective wheeled about, stared at the body on the couch and then out the window into the night.

''Uh, one thing,'' Moffat said. ''Since you do know a little about her. Think we should notify Mrs. Cardynge at once, or let her sleep till morning?''

It yelled within Yamamura.

''I mean, you know, theoretically we should send someone right off,'' Moffat said, ''but even if she has left him, this is going to be a blow. Especially since she's indirectly respon—''

Yamamura snatched Moffat's arm. ''Yes!'' he cried. ''Right away! Can you get a man there this instant?''

''What?''

"To arrest her!"

"Trig, are you crazy as that stiff was?"

"We may already be too late. Get back to your radio!"

Moffat wet his lips. "What do you mean?"

"The purse. Hers. The evidence will be there, if she hasn't had time to get rid of it— By God, if you don't I'll make a citizen's arrest myself!"

Moffat looked into the dilated eyes a full second before he pulled himself loose. "Okay, Trig. What's her address again?" Yamamura told him and he ran off without stopping to put on his coat.

Yamamura waited, pipe smoldering in his hand. A dark peace rose within him. The wrongness had departed. There was nothing here worse than a dead man and a night gone wild.

Moffat re-entered, drenched and shivering. "I had to give them my word I had strong presumptive evidence," he said. "Well, I know what you've done in the past. But this better be good."

"Good enough, if we aren't too late," Yamamura said. He pointed to the ashtray. "Cardynge was pretty nervous when he talked to me," he went on. "He hated to bare his soul. So he smoked one cigarette after another. But here—two butts for an entire evening. If you look in the kitchen, you'll find that he made a hearty meal. And washed up afterward. Does any of this square with a man utterly shattered by a Dear John letter?

"The dishes are dry in the rack. But something was washed even more recently. The towel is still moist, even though the saliva has dried in the corpse's mouth. What was washed? And by whom?"

Moffat grew rigid. "You mean that letter's a plant? But the envelope—"

"Something else was in that envelope. 'Dear Aaron, can I come see you tonight on a very private matter? Lisette.' She came with a pretext for discussion that could not have been particularly disturbing to him. Nor could her presence have been; his mind was made up about her. But they had a few drinks together.

"At some point she went to the bathroom taking her glass along, and loaded it with powder poured from the capsules. Then, I'd guess, while he went, she switched glasses with him. She'd know he used sleeping pills. Convenient for her. Still, if he had not, she could have gotten some other poison without too much trouble or danger.

"Of course, she couldn't be sure the dose would prove fatal, especially since I doubt if they drank much. Maybe she patted his head, soothed him, so he drifted into unconsciousness without noticing. He'd take a while, possibly an hour or two, to die. She must have waited, meanwhile arranging her things. Washed both glasses that had her prints on them, fixed the one on the table here and clasped his hand around it for prints and poured most of the whiskey down the sink.

"If he'd started coming around she could have returned the pill bottle to the bathroom and told him he'd had a fainting spell or whatever. She could even say she'd tried to get a doctor, but none could or would come. He wouldn't be suspicious. As things turned out, though, he died and she left. The only thing she overlooked was the evidence of the food and cigarettes."

Moffat tugged his chin. "The autopsy will show how much he did or did not drink," he said. "Did that occur to her?"

"Probably. But it's no solid proof. He didn't *have* to be on a tear when he decided to end his life. The missing booze could've been spilled accidentally. But it would help plant the idea of suicide in people's minds. She's clever. Ruthless. And one hell of a fine actress."

"Motive?"

"Money. If Bayard testified against her in divorce proceedings, she'd get nothing but the usual settlement. But as a widow, she'd inherit a mighty prosperous business. She married him in the first place for what she could get out of him, of course."

Moffat clicked his tongue. "I'd hoped for better than this from you, Trig," he said with a note of worry. "You're really reaching."

"I know. This is more hunch than anything else. There won't even be legal grounds for an indictment, if she's disposed of the proof."

"Do you suppose she was mistaken about his being dead, and after she left he roused himself long enough to call you? That sounds unlikeliest of all."

"No argument," said Yamamura grimly. "That call's the one thing I can't explain."

They fell silent, amidst the rain and wind and relentless clock-tick, until the homicide squad arrived. The first officer who came in the door looked pleased, in a bleak fashion. "We got the word on our way here," he said. "She wasn't home, so the patrolman waited. She arrived a few minutes afterward."

"Must have left this house—" Yamamura looked at his watch. 2:27. Had the whole thing taken so short a while? "About an hour ago, seeing I was phoned then. Even in this weather, that's slow driving."

"Why, no. She said twenty minutes or thereabouts."

"What? You're sure? How do you know?"

"Oh, she broke down and confessed all over the place, as soon as Hansen asked where she'd been and looked in her purse."

Yamamura let out his breath in a long, shaken sigh.

"What was there?" Moffat asked.

"The original note, which asked for this meeting and furnished an envelope to authenticate the fake one," Yamamura said. "I was hoping she'd taken it back with her, to destroy more thoroughly than she might have felt safe in doing here." More sadness than victory was in his tone: "I admit I'm surprised she spilled her guts so fast. But it must have affected her more than she'd anticipated, to sit and watch her husband die, with nothing but that clock speaking to her."

The discrepancy hit him anew. He turned to the homicide officer and protested: "She can't have left here only twenty minutes ago. That's barely before my arrival. Cardynge woke me almost half an hour before that!"

"While she was still here—?" Moffat contemplated Yamamura for a time that grew long. "Well," he said at length, "maybe she'd gone to the can." He took the phone. "We just might be able to check that call, if we hurry."

"The line's dead," Yamamura reminded him.

"No, I get a dial tone now," Moffat said. "They must've repaired it a few minutes ago. Hello, operator—"

Yamamura became occupied with explaining his presence and showing the squad around. When they came back to the living room, Moffat had cradled the phone. He stood so unmoving that their own feet halted.

"What's the matter, Charlie?" the inspector asked. "You look like the devil. Couldn't you find anything?"

"No." Moffat shook his head, slowly, as if it weighed too much. "There wasn't any call."

"What?" Yamamura exclaimed.

"You heard me," Moffat said. "This line went down about midnight. Wasn't fixed 'til now." He took a step forward. "Okay, Trig. What really brought you here?"

"A phone call, I tell you." Yamamura's back ached with a tension he could not will away. "From Cardynge."

"And I tell you that's impossible."

Yamamura stood a while hearing the clock tick. Finally, flatly, he said: "All right. Maybe there never was a call. I was half asleep, half awake, my brain churning. I guess that subconsciously I was worried about Cardynge, and so I dreamed the message, even took the phone off the rack, it felt so real.''

''Well . . . yes.'' Moffat began to relax. ''That must be what happened. Funny coincidence, though.''

''It better be a coincidence,'' Yamamura said.

The men looked simultaneously at the body, and at the phone, and away.

Sidney Zoom

THE CASE OF THE SCATTERED RUBIES
Erle Stanley Gardner

RAIN SHEETED INTERMITTENTLY out of the midnight skies. Between showers, fitful stars showed through drifting cloud rifts. Street lights, reflected from the wet pavements in shimmering ribbons, were haloed in moisture.

The feet of Sidney Zoom, pacing the wet pavements, splashed heedlessly through small surface puddles. Attired in raincoat and rubber hat, the gaunt form prowled through the rainy night, his police dog padding along at his side.

Sidney Zoom loved the night. He was particularly fond of rainy nights. Midnight streets held for him the lure of adventure. He prowled ceaselessly at night, searching for those oddities of human conduct which would arouse his interest.

The police dog growled throatily.

Sidney Zoom paused, stared down at his four-footed companion.

"What is it, Rip?"

The dog's yellow eyes were staring straight ahead. His ears were pricked up. After a moment he flung his head in a questing half circle as his nose tested the air. He then growled again, and the hair along the top of his back ruffled into bristling life.

"Go find, Rip."

Like an arrow, the dog sped forward into the night, his claws rattling on the wet pavement. He ran low to the ground, swift and sure. He leaned far in as he rounded a corner, then the night swallowed him.

Sidney Zoom walked as far as the corner where the dog had vanished, then stood waiting. He heard footsteps, the rustle of a rubber raincoat, and a dark figure bulked upon him.

A flashlight stabbed its way through the darkness.

"What are you doin' here?" grumbled a deep voice.

The hawklike eyes of Sidney Zoom stared menacingly.

"Who are you?—and put out that damned flash!"

The beam of the flashlight shot up and down the long, lean, whip-corded strength of the man, and grumbling voice rumbled again.

"I'm the officer on the beat. It's no time for a man to be standin' out on a street corner, all glistenin' with rain, and lookin' into the night as though he was listenin' for something. So give an account of yourself, unless you want to spend a night in a cell."

Sidney Zoom turned his eyes away from the glare of the light, fished a leather wallet from an inside pocket, and let the officer see a certain card.

That card bore the signature of the Chief of Police.

The officer whistled.

"Sidney Zoom, eh?" he said in surprise. "I've heard of you and of your police dog. Where's the dog?"

Sidney Zoom's head was cocked slightly to one side, listening.

"If you'll quit talking for a moment I think we can hear him."

The officer stood stock-still, listening. Faintly through the night could be heard the barking of a dog.

"It's around the other corner," said Zoom.

The officer grunted. "What's he barkin' at?"

Sidney Zoom's long legs started to pace along the wet pavement. A sudden shower came rattling down on the hard surface of their shiny raincoats.

"The best way to find out," said Sidney Zoom, "is to go and see."

The officer was put to it to keep up with the long legs.

"I've heard of some of your detective work," he said.

He gave the impression of one who wished to engage in conversation, but the pace was such that he needed all his wind. Sidney Zoom said nothing.

"And of your dog," puffed the officer.

Sidney Zoom paused, motioned to the officer to halt, raised his head and whistled. Instantly there came an answering bark.

Zoom's ears caught the direction of that bark, and he lengthened his stride. The officer ceased all efforts to keep step and came blowing along, taking a step and a half to Zoom's one.

A street light showed a huddled shadow. The dog barked again, and Sidney Zoom pointed.

"Something on the sidewalk," he said.

The officer started to talk, but thought better of it.

Zoom's stride became a running walk. His lean form seemed fairly vibrant with excitement.

"Someone lying down," he said.

The dog barked once more—a shrill, yapping bark, as though he tried to convey some meaning. And Sidney Zoom interpreted the meaning of that bark.

"Dead," he said.

The officer grunted his incredulity.

But Zoom had been right. The man was dead. He lay sprawled on the pavement, on his face, his hands stretched out and clenched, as though he had clutched at something.

There was a dark hole in the back of the man's head, and a welling stream of red had oozed down until it mingled with the water on the sidewalk, staining it red. The hat was some ten feet away, lying flat on the sidewalk.

The man had on a coat, trousers, heavy shoes. But there were pajamas underneath. The bottoms of the pajamas showed beneath the legs of the trousers, and the collar of the pajama coat showed through a place where the coat lapel had been twisted backward.

The officer ran his hands to the wet wrists of the corpse.

"Dead," he said.

"That," remarked Sidney Zoom, dryly, "is what the dog told me. He'd have come running to me, urging haste, if the man were still living."

The officer looked up with glittering eyes.

"You kidding me?" he asked.

Sidney Zoom shrugged his shoulders. Experience had taught him the futility of seeking to explain canine intelligence, highly developed, to anyone who had no experience with it.

The officer turned the figure over. Zoom's hand thrust out, caught the officer's arm.

"Wait," he said, "you're destroying the most valuable clue we have!"

The officer's eyes were wide.

"I'm just turnin' him over."

He had paused, the corpse precariously balanced on one shoulder and hip, the head sagging downward.

Zoom nodded.

"Precisely," he said. "But you'll notice that the shoulders of the coat, on the upper part around the neck, are quite wet. That shows that he's been out in the rain for some time.

"But the back of the coat is almost dry. That means he was walking, facing the rain, that he hasn't been lying very long on his stomach here. Otherwise the back of the coat would have been quite wet. But if you turn him over before we check on these things, and the back of the coat touches the wet pavement, we'll have no way of determining the comparative degree to which the garments are soaked."

The officer grunted.

"You're right about the shoulders," he said, feeling them with an awkward hand. "And the front of his coat is sopping wet. It looks as though he'd been walkin' toward the wind, all right."

Zoom ran his fingers over the garments. His eyes held that hawklike glitter of concentration which marked his rising interest.

"Now the wind," said Zoom, "was blowing in the same direction the head is pointing. Which means that he was either turned around, after the shot, or that he had changed the direction of his walk. You'll notice that he has no socks on, that the shoes are incompletely laced, and the strings hastily tied around the ankles.

"Apparently the man had retired for the night, when something aroused him, sent him hurriedly out into the rain with just the barely essential clothes on.

"He was shot in the back of the head. Probably the shot coincided with a clap of thunder, since no one seems to have heard it, and it's a district where there are apartment houses. He probably has been dead less than a quarter of an hour . . . Let's have the flash on his face, officer."

The beam of light played obediently on the cold face. It disclosed the features of a man somewhat past the middle fifties. His face was covered with gray stubble. His hair was thin at the temples. The high forehead was creased with scowl-wrinkles. The mouth was a firm, thin line, almost lipless. Deep calipers showed that the corners of the mouth were habitually twisted downward.

"A man," said Sidney Zoom, "who seldom smiled."

The officer's hand went to the coat pocket. "Lots of papers in this pocket. You notify headquarters, I'll stay here and watch."

Zoom's eyes focused on the wet pavement, some three feet beyond the corpse.

"Officer, raise your flashlight a bit higher—there!"

"What is it?"

The rays of the flashlight were caught, reflected back by something that glowed an angry red.

Zoom walked over to it, stooped, and picked it up.

"A red bead, or a synthetic ruby, pierced for stringing on a necklace," he said, "and I think there's another one a little farther on. Let's see."

The officer obediently elevated the flash. Once more there was a dull gleam of angry red in the darkness.

"From the direction he was travelin'," said the officer.

Zoom picked up the second bead, stalked back to the corpse.

"Look in his hands," he suggested.

The officer pried open the left hand. It was empty. He pulled back the fingers of the right hand. Half a dozen red beads glittered in the reflection of the flashlight, their color suggestive of drops of congealed blood.

Sidney Zoom scowled thoughtfully.

"Is that a bit of white thread there?" he asked.

The policeman bent forward.

"It is that. What do you make of it?"

Zoom stared in unwinking thought at the small cluster of red gems. "They may be genuine rubies, but I doubt it. They look like synthetic rubies. Notice that they graduate slightly in size. Evidently they were strung on a necklace. There's a chance, just a chance, that the necklace was worn by the person who fired that fatal shot, that the man clutched at this person, caught the necklace in his hand and ripped out a section of it. Then, when the person fled from the shooting, more of the rubies dropped . . . but I doubt it."

The officer lurched to his feet, letting the body slump back upon the wet pavement.

"It's gettin' too much for me," he said. "I don't want to leave the body, even if I do know you're all right. You go in that apartment house, get a telephone, and notify headquarters."

Zoom nodded. "Stay here, Rip," he said. "I'll be right back."

The dog slowly waved his tail in a swing of dignified acquiescence. Zoom crossed the street to an apartment house.

The outer door was locked, and the lobby was dark. Zoom's forefinger pressed against the button marked *Manager* until he received a response. When a fat woman with sleep-swollen eyes came protestingly to the door, Zoom explained the situation, was led to a telephone, called headquarters, and reported the finding of the body.

Then he returned to the officer. The dog was crouched down on the wet pavement, his head resting on his paws. He thumped his tail on the pavement by way of greeting, otherwise remaining immobile. The officer was going through the papers in the dead man's pocket.

"Seems to be a Harry Paine," he observed here. "Looks like he tried to carry all his correspondence in his pocket. The address is here, too. It's 5685 West Adams Street. And here's some legal papers—looks like he'd been in a lawsuit of some kind. . . . The papers have been carried around for some time. You can see where the pencil marks have rubbed off on 'em and polished up until they're slick."

Zoom nodded. He was studying the face of the dead man.

"Ain't you interested in these papers?" asked the officer.

Zoom's expression was one of dreamy abstraction.

"I'm more interested in the character of the man," he observed. "He looks to me like an old crank, and man who never smiled, who had no compassion, no kindness. Look at those hand! See the gnarled grasping fingers . . . Do you believe in palmistry, officer?"

The policeman grunted scornfully.

"Baloney," he said.

Zoom said nothing for a few seconds.

"It's strange," he then remarked, "how character impresses itself upon every portion of a person's body. Hands, feet, ears, shape of the nose, the mouth, the expression of the eyes . . . everything is shaped by that intangible something we call a soul."

The officer, squatted on the wet pavement by the side of the corpse, lurched to his feet.

"You're talkin' stuff that don't make sense," he growled. "This here is a murder case, and the law has got to catch the person that did the murder. What's the character of the dead man got to do with the thing?"

Sidney Zoom's reply consisted of one word. "Everything."

He reached for the papers which had been in the pocket of the corpse.

"Murderers," the officer observed, "are everyday affairs. Handle 'em as routine and you get somewhere. Identify the dead guy, see who wanted him bumped off, round up the evidence and maybe give a little third degree at headquarters, and you're ready for the next case."

Sidney Zoom said nothing. In the distance could be heard the wailing of sirens.

"There are powder marks on the back of the head," said Zoom, after the siren had wailed for the second time. "Let me see your flashlight."

The officer handed it to him. Zoom circled the gutter with its rays, steadied his hand abruptly, then pointed.

"There it is."

"There what it?"

"The empty shell. See it, there in the gutter? He was shot with an automatic. The ejector flipped the shell out into the street, the running water from that last burst of rain washed it down into the gutter."

The officer bent and picked up the shell.

"You're right. A forty-five."

The siren wailed again. Lights glittered from the wet street, and the first of the police cars swung into the cross street, then hissed through the water to the curb.

Another car followed close behind. Then there sounded the clanging gong of an ambulance. Thereafter, events moved swiftly.

Detective Sergeant Gromley was in charge of the homicide detail and he heard the officer's report, checked the facts from Sidney Zoom, and started the men gathering up the various clues.

They started tracing the trail of the blood-red beads, found that they led to an apartment house about fifty yards away. They were spaced at almost even intervals, and they glistened in the rays of the searching spotlights.

The district was largely given over to apartment houses, and the wailing sirens had brought watchers to the windows. The cloud rifts drifted into wider spaces and tranquil stars shone down on the concrete canyon of the sleeping street.

Officers started checking to find out if anyone had heard the shot, if anyone had noted the time, if there had been any sound of running feet.

Sergeant Gromley scanned the apartment house where the trail of red beads ended and uttered an exclamation of triumph as he pointed to the row of mail boxes in the vestibule, each faced with a printed name cut from a visiting card.

"Notice Apartment 342," he said. "The name's been torn out of there within the last half hour or so. See, there's a wet smear on the cardboard backing, and . . . it's a little smear of blood? See it?"

He turned toward the lobby where a man in a bathrobe was peering curiously.

"Where's the manager?" asked Gromley.

"I own the place. My wife and I run it."

"Who's the tenant in Apartment 342?"

The man scowled, ran his fingers through his tousled hair.

"I ain't sure. I think it's a woman. Paine or some such name. That's it, Paine, Eva Paine. Ain't her name on the mail box?"

"Come on," Gromley said to his broad-shouldered assistants, who had knotted around him. "Let's go."

They crowded into the elevator. Sidney Zoom took the stairs, Rip at his heels.

"Here, you," grunted the man in the bathrobe, "you can't bring a dog in here!"

But Sidney Zoom paid no attention. His long legs were working like pistons as he went up the stairs two at a time.

But the officers were getting out of the elevator as Zoom reached the upper corridor. The stairs emerged at the end opposite from the elevator shaft, and the apartment they wanted was close to the elevator.

One of the men pounded upon the door.

It was opened almost immediately by a girl in a kimono. She stared at them in wide-eyed silence.

Sergeant Gromley pushed unceremoniously past her.

"We want to ask you some questions," he said.

The others crowded into the room, which was used as a sitting room during the daytime, a bedroom at night. The wall-bed had been let down, apparently slept in, but the sheets were folded neatly at the corners. The girl must be a quiet sleeper, or else had not been in bed long.

She was dressed in a kimono of bright red which enhanced the gleam of her eyes, the red of her lips, the glitter of the lights on her hair, which was glossy black.

"You're Eva Paine?" asked Sergeant Gromley.

"Yes. Of course. Why?"

"Know a Harry Paine?"

"Y-y-yes, of course."

"Why do you say 'of course'?"

"He's my father-in-law."

"You married his son?"

"Yes."

"What's the son's name?"

"Edward."

"Where is he?"

"Dead."

"When did you see Mr. Harry Paine last?"

She hesitated at that, made a little motion of nervousness.

"Why, I can't tell. Yesterday afternoon, I think. Yes, it was yesterday afternoon."

"Aren't very certain, are you?"

She lowered her eyes.

"I'm a little confused. What is the idea of all you men, who seem to be detectives, coming here and asking questions? I've done nothing."

Sergeant Gromley shook his head, belligerently, aggressively.

"No one accused you of it—yet."

"What do you want?"

"Information."

"About what?"

"About who might have had a motive for murdering Harry Paine."

The girl came to her full height. Her face paled. Her eyes widened until the whites showed on all sides of the irises. Her forehead wrinkled with horror.

"Murdered?" she asked.

Her voice was weak, quavering.

"Murdered!" snapped Sergeant Gromley.

"I—I don't know anything about it."

"Was there bad blood between you?"

She hesitated, then became almost regal in her bearing.

"Yes," she said, "and I'm glad he's dead—if he is dead. He was a brute—a stingy, narrow-minded, bigoted, selfish brute."

Sergeant Gromley nodded casually. The character of the dead man was of no consequence to him. It did not matter to him how much the man might have deserved to die. It was only the fact that the law requires vengeance which mattered to him.

"Who murdered him?"

"I—I don't know."

"Have you a necklace of rubies, or imitation rubies, or red glass beads? Think carefully. Your answer may mean a lot to you—and don't lie."

"What have red beads got to do with it?"

"Perhaps nothing, perhaps a lot. Have you such a necklace?"

Her lips clamped tightly.

"No!"

"Do you know anyone who has such a necklace?"

"No!"

Sergeant Gromley remained undisturbed. There was a lot of ground to cover yet, and the veteran investigator had no fear of lies. The only thing that caused him consternation was a suspect who would not talk. Given one who would answer questions, he was always certain of ultimate triumph.

"Where have you been since 9 o'clock?"

"In bed."

Sergeant Gromley raised his eyebrows.

"In bed?"

"Yes."

"Since 9 o'clock?"

"Yes."

The answer was surly this time, defiant, as though she had been trapped into some answer she had not anticipated and intended to stick by her guns.

"What time did you retire?"

"At the time I told you—9 o'clock."

The sergeant's smile was sarcastic. He looked over the graceful lines of her figure, the striking beauty of the face.

"Rather early for a young and attractive widow to retire on a Saturday night, isn't it?

She flushed. "That is none of your business. You asked me a question, and I answered!"

Sergeant Gromley's smile was irritating. His manner was that of a cat that has a mouse safely hooked in its claws and is willing to torture the creature for a time.

"Rather a coincidence that I chose the hour of 9 o'clock and that you answered so promptly. I am just wondering, Miss Paine, if you hadn't resolved to give that bedtime story as an alibi. When I asked you where you've been since 9 o'clock—rather than where you've been during the last hour—you said 'in bed' because you had expected the question to be different. Then, having said it the first time, you decided to stick to your story."

She was cool, defiant, but her shoulders were commencing to rise and fall with rapid breathing.

"Your reasoning is too complicated for my childlike brain. Just confine yourself to necessary questions, please."

Gromley continued to press the point. "It is rather a peculiar coincidence that I should have been the one who predicted the exact time of your retirement, isn't it?"

She shrugged. "That, also, is a matter I cannot answer."

She swept her eyes momentarily from the sergeant to the ring of curious faces which were watching her. And as Sidney Zoom caught her eyes, shiny with excitement, his long forefinger lifted casually to his lips and pressed firmly against them.

Her eyes had left his face before the significance of the gesture impressed her. Then they darted back with a look of swift questioning in them. But Zoom, taking no chances that his signal might be seen and interpreted by one of the officers, was rubbing his cheek with slow deliberation.

The girl returned her eyes to the sergeant, but now there was a look of puzzled uncertainty in them.

"Do you know what the weather is like?" asked Sergeant Gromley.

"It's showering."

He smiled again.

"Really, Miss Paine, you are remarkable. It was quite clear at 9 o'clock. The showers started about 9:45 and continued steadily until just before midnight."

She bit her lip.

"And you were asleep?" pursued the sergeant

Triumph gleamed in her eyes as she swooped down upon the opening he had left her with that eagerness which an amateur always shows in rushing into the trap left by a canny professional.

"I didn't say I was asleep."

"Oh, then, you weren't asleep?"

"No, not all the time."

"And that's the way you knew it was raining?"

"Yes. The rain beat against the window. I heard it, got up and looked out. There was some lightning and thunder too."

"And that's the only way you knew it was raining?"

"Yes."

"And you weren't out of this room after 9 o'clock tonight?"

"Would I be likely to leave it, dressed this way?"

"Answer the question. Were you out of this room after 9 o'clock?"

Instinctively, her eyes sought those of Sidney Zoom.

This time there could be no mistaking the impressive significance of the gesture he made—the forceful pressing of a rigid forefinger against his closed lips.

"Answer the question," barked Sergeant Gromley.

'No,'' she said. "I didn't leave this room.''

But her eyes were hesitant, helpless, and they looked pleadingly at Sidney Zoom.

The sergeant swooped, pushed aside a filmy bit of silk, reached a long arm under the edge of the bed, and brought out a pair of shoes.

''These your shoes?''

She knew then that she was trapped, for the shoes were soaked with rain. The knowledge showed in the sudden panic of her eyes, the pallor of her lips.

She looked at Sidney Zoom, and suddenly stiffened.

''I have answered quite enough of your questions, sir. I will not make any more statements until I have seen a lawyer.''

Gromley simulated surprise.

''Why . . . Why, Miss Paine, what could you possibly want to see a lawyer about? Has anyone made any accusations against you?''

''N-no . . . ''

''Then why should you want a lawyer? Do you expect accusations will be made?''

She drew in a rapid lungful of breath preparatory to speaking, then raised her eyes once more to Zoom's face.

''I have nothing more to say,'' she said.

The sergeant snapped out a rapid barrage. ''Is it your custom to put powder on your cheeks, lipstick on your lips, have your hair freshly done up at one o'clock in the morning? Or were you expecting a call from the police, and just wanted to look your best?''

It was plainly a relief to her that she did not need to answer the question. She simply shook her had, but the panic of her eyes was even more evident now.

Sergeant Gromley turned to the men.

''Frisk the place, boys.''

He spoke quietly, but the effect of his order was instantaneous. The men scattered like a bevy of quail. Drawers were pulled open, skilled fingers explored the contents. They even went to the bed, felt in the mattress, probed in the pillowcase.

Sergeant Gromley kept his eyes on the panicky eyes of the young woman.

''It might be much better for you, later on, if you told the truth now,'' he said, gently, trying to make the fatherly tone of his advice break through the wall of reserve that had sealed her lips.

He was almost successful. The touch of sympathy in his voice brought moisture to her eyes. Her lips parted, then clamped tightly closed again. She blinked back the tears.

"I have nothing more to say."

One of the officers turned from the dresser.

"Look what's here," he said.

He held up a fragment of necklace made of fine red beads.

"Where was it?"

"Hidden. Fastened to the back of the mirror with chewing gum. You can see where the string was broken, then it was tied up at the ends, and stuck to the back of the mirror."

Sergeant Gromley grunted. "Let's see the gum."

The officer handed him a wad of chewing gum. The outside was barely dry, had not yet commenced to harden.

Sergeant Gromley riveted his eyes on the young woman once more.

"Yours?" he asked.

She glanced swiftly at Sidney Zoom, then shook her head.

Sergeant Gromley was sitting with his back to Sidney Zoom. He spoke now, quietly, evenly, without raising his voice.

"Zoom, I've heard of you, heard of some of the help you've given the department. It's customary to exclude all civilians from questionings such as these. I let you remain because of your record. Unfortunately, you seem to have taken advantage of my generosity."

Sidney Zoom's voice was sharp.

"Meaning," he asked, "exactly what?"

Sergeant Gromley kept his back turned.

"Do you think," he asked, "that I am an utter fool?"

Zoom snapped, "Do you want me to leave the room?"

"Yes," said Sergeant Gromley, without turning his head.

Sidney Zoom reached the door in a few strides.

"Come, Rip."

Their feet sounded in the corridor, the man's pounding along, the dog's pattering softly, a rattling of claws sounding on the uncarpeted strip of floor at the sides of the hallway. There was a sardonic smile on the features of Sidney Zoom as he gained the ground floor of the apartment house. Here he walked to the outer lobby and surveyed the row of brass letter boxes, each fitted with a lock.

Zoom paused to take from his pocket a pair of gloves. They were thin, flexible gloves, yet they insured against any casual fingerprints being left behind.

"Fools!" he muttered to himself under his breath.

Then he took from a pocket a bunch of keys. They were not many in number, but each had been fashioned with cunning care by a man who had made the study of locks the hobby of a lifetime.

The third key which he tried clicked back the bolt of the mail box which went with Apartment 342.

Sidney Zoom reached a gloved hand inside the aperture, removed a wadded scarf of silk. Within the scarf were several hard objects which rattled crisply against each other.

They might have been pebbles, or bits of glassware, but Sidney Zoom wasted no time in looking to see what they were. He simply dropped the entire bundle, scarf and all, into one of the pockets of his coat, and then went out into the night.

He stopped at the nearest telephone and called the best criminal attorney in the city.

"This is Zoom speaking. The police are trying to pin a murder charge on a young woman, a Mrs. Eva Paine, who lives in apartment 342 at the Matonia Apartments. They're there now. I'm retaining you to handle the case under the blanket arrangement I have with you. Get out there at once. Tell her to keep quiet and see that she does. That's all."

And Zoom clicked the receiver back on its hook.

He knew that the attorney would be there in a matter of minutes. Zoom kept him supplied with various cases which attracted the interest of the strange individual whose hobby was the prowling of midnight streets and the matching of wits with both criminals and detectives.

Then Sidney Zoom summoned a cab and was driven to the palatial yacht on which he lived. Only when he was safely ensconced in his stateroom did he open the package which he had taken from the mail box.

It was filled with jewels, strung, for the most part, into necklaces.

It was 10 o'clock in the morning.

The musty air of police headquarters was filled with that stale odor which comes to rooms which are in use twenty-fours a day.

Captain Bill Mahoney, a small man in the early fifties, but equipped with a large mind, raised dark, speculative eyes and regarded Sidney Zoom thoughtfully.

"Sergeant Gromley," he said, "wants to place a charge against you for aiding and abetting a felon."

"The felon being whom?" asked Sidney Zoom.

"The Paine girl."

Zoom tapped a cigarette impatiently upon the table, rasped a match along the sole of his shoe, lit the cigarette, snapped out the match with a single swift motion of his arm.

"Sergeant Gromley," he said, "is a dangerous man. He is dangerous to innocent and guilty alike."

Captain Mahoney's voice remained quiet. "He's the best questioner in the department."

"Perhaps."

"And he tells me you interfered with him in the Paine case."

"He's right. I did."

"That's serious, Zoom. We've orders to allow you to cooperate because you've always had a passion for justice, and you've helped us clear up some difficult cases. But you're going to lose your privileges."

Captain Mahoney was never more quiet than when enraged. Zoom had known him for years in a close friendship which was founded upon mutual respect. Yet Captain Mahoney would have been among the first to have admitted that, despite their long friendship, he knew virtually nothing of that strange, sardonic creature who made a hobby of patrolling the midnight streets and interesting himself in odd crimes.

Sidney Zoom regarded the smoldering tip of his cigarette.

"I'm afraid, Zoom, I shall have to ask you to surrender your courtesy star and your commission as a special deputy. I'm sorry, but you knew the rules, and you infringed upon them."

Sidney Zoom took the articles from his pocket, passed them over, heaved a sigh.

"I'd anticipated that, and I'm glad. I can do more by fighting the police than by cooperating with them."

He jackknifed his huge form to its full height, strode toward the door. His hand was on the knob when Captain Mahoney's quiet voice stabbed the tense atmosphere of the room.

"That," he said, "disposes of my duty as an officer. Now, Zoom, would you mind telling me—as a friend—why you took advantage of the confidence this department reposed in you?"

"Because," replied Zoom, "Gromley was about to outwit an innocent woman and pin a murder on her."

"He's done it anyway."

"No. He hasn't."

Captain Mahoney fished a cigar from his pocket, slowly bit off the end. His dark, luminous eyes regarded Zoom with curious speculation.

"Do you know who murdered Harry Paine?" he asked.

"No. But I know who didn't."

Captain Mahoney lit his cigar.

"I wish I'd been there last night."

"I wish you had, Captain."

Mahoney's eyes gleamed above the first puff of blue smoke which came from his cigar.

"Because if I had been, I'd have sensed that your interference was for the primary purpose of getting yourself kicked out. I'd have figured that you wanted to leave that room without exciting attention, and you took that way of doing it."

Sidney Zoom whirled, strode back to his chair, sat down, and laughed.

"Bill," he said, "it's a good thing you weren't there. You're too clever for me."

Captain Mahoney had not moved. He twisted the cigar slowly, thoughtfully, then flashed his black eyes at Sidney Zoom's hawklike face.

"And I have an idea you wanted to be relieved of your courtesy commission on the force because you're figuring on a fast one, and don't want any sense of ethics to stand in your way."

Zoom said nothing. For a few moments they smoked in silence.

"Bill," said Sidney Zoom, at length, "you're human. Do you want to solve that Paine murder?"

Captain Mahoney spoke cautiously. "Gromley says it's a perfect case, but that you and your lawyer have interfered with his proof and now he may not be able to turn over enough evidence to get a conviction."

Zoom leaned forward.

"If you'll put your cards on the table, Bill, I'll try and clear up the case for you."

"If I put my cards on the table," asked the police captain, "will you put yours on the table?"

Zoom's answer was explosively prompt.

"No!"

"Why not?"

Zoom laughed lightly.

"Because I'm going to play with a marked deck."

"You think the woman *isn't* guilty?"

"I'm certain of it."

"It would hurt the police a lot if we should go ahead and try to pin a murder rap on her and then have it turn out to be a mistake," said Bill Mahoney, slowly.

Sidney Zoom knew that he had won.

"Get your hat, Bill," he said.

Captain Mahoney reached for his hat.

"Where to?"

"To Harry Paine's place, out on West Adams. I'll drive slowly, and you can tell me what the police have found out while we're driving."

"Sergeant Gromley would have a fit if he knew what I was doing," sighed the captain.

But Mahoney had seen Sidney Zoom perform seeming wonders on many previous occasions, and beyond the sighed regret he showed no other signs of hesitancy.

As they purred along in Zoom's high-powered car, his police dog crouched in the rumble seat, Captain Mahoney gave Zoom a brief summary of the facts the police had discovered.

"It's a family fight. Guess old Paine was a man who had at least one killing coming to him. He had a son, Edward. Edward fell in love with Eva, the girl. Paine kicked the boy out. The boy started in doing some gem business, buying and selling. He was making good. Then, one day, he was killed, suddenly.

"There wasn't any insurance. The girl found herself widowed, with a stock of gems that had to be sold. She started having the estate probated so that she could get title to the gems, and old Paine sued the administrator.

"It developed that there was an illegality about the marriage. He'd known it all along and had been saving it as a weapon. Therefore, Eva wasn't the boy's widow. Harry Paine was the only surviving relative. There wasn't a will. Paine claimed the gems. The court gave them to him. He and his lawyer took possession of them yesterday afternoon.

"The girl didn't have any money to carry on a fight. But she had some of her husband's old effects. Among these was a key to the house. Apparently, the girl sneaked out to Paine's house after everyone had gone to bed and stole the jewels.

"She'd have made a good job of it, too, because no one suspected she had a key. But she was just a little clumsy in the getaway and knocked over a chair. That woke old Paine up.

"He dashed after the burglar, but she eluded him and got out. He started to chase her in his pajamas, then came back, got into his clothes, and went after her again.

"He told his attorney he'd caught a glimpse of her, running into the wind and rain, and had recognized her. He was furious and wanted to catch her red-handed.''

Sidney Zoom shot Captain Mahoney a swift glance.

''Told his attorney? What was his attorney doing there at midnight?''

''He lives in Paine's apartment house. Paine was a funny old codger. He went in for collecting things—stamps, first editions, and what not. And he was a litigious old cuss, always in court. He sued his neighbors, sued the dealers who sold him things, sued the paving contractors who worked on his street, sued everybody.

''He got a white-haired old lawyer that he found somewhere, down and out, and took the lawyer to live with him in his house. And he always kept the lawyer busy. Then he got a butler who's a character, looks like an old pug; and there's a Chinese cook. That's the household. Quite a crew, I'd say.''

Zoom nodded.

''That,'' he said, ''is just about how I figured the case.''

Captain Mahoney shot him a shrewd glance.

''How'd you figure any of that out?''

''There were legal papers in the pockets of the corpse,'' he said, ''and the latest of them was a case where he'd sued the administrator for title to jewelry his son had had at the time of his death. A copy of the judgment was in his coat pocket at the time. The cop on the beat found it.''

Captain Mahoney squinted his eyes.

''Well, he said, ''here's the way Gromley reconstructs the case. Old Man Paine started after the girl and didn't catch up with her until he was almost at her apartment. He grabbed at her and clutched a string of synthetic rubies she was wearing, a present from her husband.

''She broke away, shot him, then turned and fled to her apartment. She was panic-stricken, and ditched the jewels and the gun. She probably was so excited she didn't know he'd broken the necklace when he grabbed at her.

''She was afraid they'd be coming for her, so she ripped her name off the mail box and then went to her apartment to pack. She heard the sirens and knew any woman who started to leave the apartment house while the police were there would be stopped and questioned.

''So she pretended she'd been in bed asleep, and waited to see if the police were coming. If they hadn't found her she'd have ducked out as soon as the police left. She figured that if they did find her she could stall them off. And she might have done it if it hadn't been for Gromley's questioning.''

Zoom shook his shoulders as though to relieve them of some weight.

"That's what I didn't like about Gromley. He's clever, and he used his cleverness—not to reason out what must have happened there at the time of the murder but to trap the girl. It wasn't fair."

Captain Mahoney smiled mechanically.

"Things in this world aren't always fair. But they're fairly efficient. It's the result that counts."

Zoom gave a single expletive.

"Bah!" he said.

"Still believe in divine justice, eh?" asked the police captain.

"I've seen something closely akin to that save several innocent people from jail or the death penalty," said Sidney Zoom.

Captain Mahoney shook his head.

"You've been lucky, Zoom. But it wasn't divine justice. It was your own cleverness, plus the fact that you've got sufficient money to ride your hobby as far as you want to."

Sidney Zoom said nothing.

"That's the place," remarked Captain Mahoney. "The big house with the iron gate and the padlock."

Sidney Zoom made a single comment.

"Yes," he said, "It looks like the type of place he'd have lived in.

"Evidently you didn't take a shine to old Paine."

"No, I didn't. His character showed on his face, even in death."

"It takes all sorts of people to make a world, Sidney."

Zoom's answer was typical: "All sorts of things come up in a garden. But one pulls out the weeds."

Captain Mahoney sighed.

Sidney Zoom abruptly reverted to the clues which had led the officers to the crime.

"Would you ever have found the girl if it hadn't been for the beads?"

"You mean the synthetic rubies broken from the string?"

"Yes."

"Eventually, I think."

"But the beads were the clue?"

"Naturally, They led from the corpse to the outer door of the apartment."

"Of the apartment *house*, you mean."

"Well, yes."

Sidney Zoom fastened his intense, hawklike eyes upon the man who was staring at him with sudden curiosity.

"Did it ever strike you as being a bit strange, Bill, that the beads only went as far as the *outer* door of the apartment house? Also, that they were spaced so evenly? Why weren't there any beads between the door and the entrance to the girl's apartment?"

Bill Mahoney laughed.

"There you go, Zoom, with one of your wild theories. The beads were the girl's, all right. We've identified those beyond any doubt. And the rest of the string was found behind the mirror in her room where she'd tried to conceal it. She'd put it there. There was the imprint of a finger in the soft surface of the chewing gum. It was her fingerprint.

"What happened was that the man she'd shot broke the string of beads with his death clutch. They were spilling all over the street, but the girl didn't know it until she got to the door of the apartment house. Then she gathered up what was left, probably some that were on a thread that had dropped down the front of her dress.

"She knew she had to hide them. She wanted to put them where the police would never find them. By that time she knew they had been spilling, leaving a trail directly to the apartment house. That's why she pulled the card off of the mail box. She knew the officers would trail those beads and, if they found a card bearing the same last name as the dead man's, they'd come right up."

Sidney Zoom stretched, yawned, smiled.

"Did you notice, by any chance, if there was a cut on the fingers of Eva Paine?"

Captain Mahoney's glance was gimlet-eyed.

"Yes. There was. What made you think there might be?"

"The edges of the card container on the letter box were pretty sharp, and she was in a hurry. I thought she might have cut herself."

"And that such cut accounted for the red stain on the mail box?"

"Yes."

"I think," said Captain Mahoney, very deliberately, "that we'll go on in. You've told me too much—and not enough."

Zoom uncoiled his lean length from behind the steering wheel, grinned at the officer. "Come on."

They walked up a cement walk, came to the porch of the house. An officer on duty saluted the captain, regarded Zoom curiously. The police dog padded gravely at the side of his master.

The door swung open. Two men stood in the hallway.

Captain Mahoney spoke their names to Zoom in a voice that was informative, but not social.

"Zoom, this is Sam Mokeley, the butler, and Laurence Gerhard, the lawyer."

Zoom nodded, stalked into the hallway, suddenly turned to the two men.

"I want to see two things," he said. "First, the room from which the jewelry was taken; second, the bed where Harry Paine slept."

The lawyer, white-haired and cunning-eyed, swept his pale eyes over Zoom's tall figure, keyed up with controlled energy.

"Show him, Mokeley," he said to the butler.

The man nodded. "This way, sir."

He was all that Captain Mahoney had described—massive, heavy-handed, his ear cauliflowered.

"Here is the room, sir. The gems were in a concealed cabinet back of the bookcase. Only a very few people knew of that bookcase."

But Sidney Zoom did not even glance at the place of concealment. Instead, he dropped to his hands and knees and started crawling laboriously over the edges of the carpet, his fingers questing over every inch of the carpeted surface.

He remained in that position, searching patiently for some three or four minutes. If he found anything he gave no sign. As abruptly as he had assumed the position, he straightened to his full height, then looked at the two men.

"The bedroom," he said.

"This way, sir," said the butler.

They trooped into the bedchamber. It was a dank, chilly place, suggestive of fitful sleep or restless thoughts.

Zoom inspected the cheerless room.

"Where," he asked of the butler, "did Paine keep his gun?"

The lawyer cleared his throat.

Zoom shot him a glance."

"I asked the butler," he said.

The butler's face was wooden.

"I haven't seen him with a gun for some time, sir. He used to have one, a thirty-eight, Smith and Wesson, sir."

Zoom strode to the dresser, started yanking open the drawers.

There were suits of heavy underwear, coarse socks, cheap shirts. In an upper drawer was a pasteboard box with a green label on the top. The sides were copper-colored. Zoom pulled out the box, ripped open the cover, turned it upside down.

On the dresser cascaded a glittering shower of brass cartridges—cartridges for a .45 automatic.

The lawyer cleared his throat again. Then he shrugged and turned away. Zoom stared fixedly at Captain Mahoney. ''I want to see the Chinese cook.''

Captain Mahoney motioned to the butler.

''Come with me and let's find the cook.''

They left the room. The lawyer cleared his throat.

''Going to say something?'' asked Zoom.

''Yes,'' said the attorney. ''I was just about to remark that it was a nice day.''

The door opened again and Captain Mahoney escorted the butler and the Chinese cook into the room. The cook was plainly nervous.

''Ah Kim,'' said Captain Mahoney.

Zoom looked at the man. The slant eyes rotated in oily restlessness.

''Ah Kim,'' said Zoom, ''do you know much about guns?''

Ah Kim shifted his weight.

''Heap savvy,'' he said.

Zoom indicated the pile of shells.

''What gun do these fit?''

''All samee fit Missa Paine gun. Him forty-five, automatic.''

Zoom turned on his heel, faced the lawyer.

''You made Paine's will.''

It was a statement rather than a question. The pale eyes of the lawyer regarded Zoom unwaveringly.

''Yes,'' he said. ''Of course I did.''

''Who were the beneficiaries?''

The lawyer pursed his lips.

''I would rather answer that later, and in private.''

Captain Mahoney glanced at Zoom, then fixed the attorney with his dark, thoughtful eyes.

''Answer it now,'' he said.

The lawyer bowed. ''Very well. The property—what there is, and it's considerable—is left share and share alike to the two servants, Ah Kim and Sam Mokeley.''

The Chinese heard the news with a bland countenance that was utterly devoid of expression. Sam Mokeley gave a gasp of surprise.

''What!'' he said.

The lawyer bowed.

''I wasn't going to tell you until the investigation was over, but Paine left his property to you two.''

"He didn't leave anything to Eva Paine?" asked Zoom.

"Naturally not," said the lawyer. "The girl was utterly unscrupulous. She testified falsely in the lawsuit over the gems. She broke into the house and committed burglary."

Sidney Zoom nodded careless acquiescence.

"Do you ever read the Bible, Mr. Gerhard?"

The white-haired man smiled.

"I have read it," he said, dryly.

"It is an excellent passage," commented Sidney Zoom, "which remarks that the one who is without sin may throw the first stone."

The lawyer's lips settled in a straight line.

"If you mean anything personal by that," he snapped, "you had better watch your tongue. There is a law in this State against libel. Your attitude has been hostile ever since you entered this place."

It was apparent that the grizzled veteran of many a courtroom battle was very much on the aggressive whenever his personal integrity was assailed.

Zoom bowed.

"You are mistaken," he said. "My attitude is that of an investigator."

He turned to Captain Mahoney.

"The murder," he said, "is solved."

Captain Mahoney stared at him.

"Who killed him?"

Zoom smiled. "Since there is a law against defamation of character, I will say nothing, but will refer you to absolute means of proof. A step at a time and we will uncover the matter. . . . Rip, smell the gentlemen."

And Sidney Zoom waved his hand—a swift flip of his wrist.

An animal trainer would have known that it was the gesture more than the words that made the police dog do what he did. The effect was uncanny. The dog walked deliberately to each of the three men and smelled their clothing with bristling hostility.

"Come, Captain," said Sidney Zoom.

He turned and stalked from the room, Rip following.

"We will leave the car parked here," said Zoom as they reached the porch, leaving behind them three very puzzled individuals, "and start walking by the shortest route toward the girl's apartment."

Captain Mahoney fell into step.

"Zoom," he said quietly, "have you any idea of just what you're after?"

Zoom's answer was a monosyllable.

"Yes."

They strode forward, walking swiftly.

"Search," said Zoom, and waved his arm.

The dog barked once, then started to swing out in questing semicircles, ranging ahead and to either side of the two men.

They walked rapidly and in silence. Captain Mahoney was hard put to keep the pace. From time to time, his anxious, speculative eyes turned upward to Zoom's face. But the rigid profile was as though carved from rock.

It was not until they had approached the place where the body of the murdered man had been found that the dog suddenly barked three times, came running toward them, then ran back toward a vacant lot.

Here was a patch of brush, back of a signboard. The ground was littered with the odds and ends that invariably collect in vacant lots.

"I think," said Zoom, "the dog has found something."

Captain Mahoney sprinted and was the first to arrive at the patch of brush. He parted the leaves. The dog pawed excitedly, as though to help.

Captain Mahoney straightened and whistled.

"Call back the dog, Zoom. There's a forty-five automatic on the ground here. There may be fingerprints—if so, I want to preserve them."

Zoom gave a swift command.

The dog dropped flat on his belly, muzzle on forepaws.

Captain Mahoney took a bit of string from his pocket. He lowered it until he had it slung under the barrel of the automatic; then he tied a knot and raised the gun.

Zoom muttered his approval. For there were fingerprints on the weapon.

"Now, Captain, if you don't mind, we'll return to the house where Paine lived and see if we can identify the gun. As a favor to me, I wish you'd tell no one where this gun was found."

Captain Mahoney sighed.

"Zoom, I'm going to give you a free hand, for a little while."

"Come on then," said Zoom.

They returned to the house as rapidly as they had made the trip from it, presenting a strange pair—the tall man with the hawklike eyes, the shorter officer, carrying a gun dangling on a string.

The butler let them in.

Zoom ordered him to summon the lawyer and the cook.

They gathered in the living room, a restless group of men, evidently under great nervous strain.

"Ah Kim," said Zoom, "is that Mr. Paine's gun?"

The Chinese let his eyes slither to the gun, then to Zoom's face.

"Same gun," he said.

"Beg your pardon, sir," interposed the butler, "but it's *not* the gun. Mr. Paine's gun had a little speck of rust on the barrel, just under the safety catch."

Zoom's grin was sardonic.

"Oh," he said, "I thought you described Paine's gun as being a thirty-eight revolver, not a forty-five automatic."

The butler's face was like a mask.

"Yes, sir," he said.

Captain Mahoney regarded the man curiously.

"Anything further to say, Mokeley?"

"No, sir."

Zoom nodded. "No," he said, "he wouldn't."

Captain Mahoney's eyes were thoughtful.

"We've got to have proof, you know, Zoom. We may satisfy ourselves of something, but before we can do anything, we've got to get enough evidence to satisfy a jury."

Zoom started to talk. His voice was crisp, metallic.

"Let's look at the weak points in the case they've built up against the girl. Let's analyze the clues and see what must have happened.

"Paine had the gems here. He heard a noise, found the gems gone—stolen.

"Something made him sufficiently positive to start out after the girl. That something must have been some tangible evidence. Let's suppose, as a starting point, it was finding part of a broken necklace—some synthetic rubies strewn over the floor.

"Naturally, he scooped up those rubies, to be used in confronting the girl. He started after her. He was walking toward the wind. It was raining. He got wet. That didn't deter him. As I see his character, Paine was a very determined man.

"But before he reached the apartment where the girl lived, something caused him to turn back. What was that something? We can be fairly sure he didn't get to the apartment. Otherwise he'd have raised a commotion—he was that sort. And he was facing in the other direction when he was shot from behind, with his own gun.

"Now what would have caused him to turn back? What would have caused him to surrender his gun? Certainly someone, in whose advice he must have had implicit faith, overtook him and convinced him that he was going off on a wrong track, that he should return and summon the police.

"Then, when that person had secured possession of the gun, he waited for a clap of thunder and shot Paine in the back of the head.

"That person had picked up more of the scattered rubies. He used them to leave a trail to the front door of the apartment house where the girl lived. Those rubies weren't spaced the way they would have been had they dropped off a necklace. They'd have hit the sidewalk in a bunch and scattered. They were spaced just as they would have been had someone dropped them with the deliberate intent of causing the police to go to that apartment house.

"Now the only person I can think of who would have been able to dissuade Mr. Paine, cause him to surrender his gun, and turn him back, is . . ."

Sidney Zoom stared at the lawyer. Gerhard laughed.

"Cleverly done, Zoom, but not worth a damn. Your theory is very pretty, but how are you going to prove the necklace was broken here in this room. You got down on your hands and knees when you first came in here. You were looking for some of the rubies. But you were disappointed. Your interest in the girl has led you to concoct an ingenious theory. But it won't hold water—before a jury."

Zoom turned to the Chinese.

"Bring me the vacuum cleaner, Ah Kim," he said.

The servant glided out.

The butler exchanged glances with the lawyer.

The Chinese returned with the vacuum cleaner. Sidney Zoom opened it and took the bag of sweepings from the interior. He opened it on the floor.

Instantly it became apparent that the dust contained several of the rubies. They glowed redly in the light which came through the massive windows.

"Yes," said Zoom, "I looked for the rubies here. When I couldn't find them I knew I was dealing with an intelligent criminal. But I did see that a vacuum cleaner had been run over the floor very recently."

The butler looked at the lawyer, wet his lips. The lawyer frowned.

"That, of course," he said, "is rather strong evidence, Zoom. Ah Kim would have profited by the death. He has acted suspiciously several times. There's a chance you may be right."

Zoom's smile was frosty.

"Ah Kim couldn't have dissuaded Harry Paine from going on to the girl's apartment," he said, slowly, impressively. "And I don't think it will be Ah Kim's prints that we find on that gun."

The attorney regarded the gun intently.

"Ah, yes," he said, "the fingerprints on the gun. Well, it's certain they're not mine, since I wouldn't have profited by the death of my client. I have lost by it. He kept me in a law practice."

The butler squirmed.

"Meaning that you're directing suspicion at me?" he asked.

The attorney shrugged. "The fingerprints," he said, "will speak for themselves."

Sam Mokeley regarded the attorney speculatively.

"Well," said Captain Mahoney, "we'll take the fingerprints of the men here, and —"

"Perhaps," suggested Zoom, "we can also look over the clothes closets. We might find evidence that one of them was out in the rain last night. And it's peculiar that the bed of Harry Paine shows no evidence of having been slept in. Everyone agrees he jumped out of bed to pursue the burglar.

"I wouldn't doubt if there were clean sheets put on the bed, and the bed made up fresh because the old sheets and pillowcase might have shown that he kept a gun under his pillow."

The attorney spoke slowly.

"The fingerprints on the gun are the most important evidence. A jury will act on those. The other things are mere surmise."

Captain Mahoney stared at the lawyer.

"As a matter of fact," pursued the attorney, "the butler *was* out for a little while last night. I tried to locate him just after Mr. Paine went out and—"

The butler's motion was so swift that the eye could hardly follow it. He had edged near the gun which lay on the table. With a sweep of his hand he scooped it up and fired, all in one motion.

The attorney's stomach took the bullet. A look of surprise spread over his countenance; the look was wiped out by the impact of two more bullets.

Sam Mokeley jumped back, waving the gun at Zoom and Captain Mahoney.

"Get your hands up," he said.

But he had forgotten something—the police dog.

The animal sprang, a tawny streak. Teeth clamped on the wrist that held the gun. Seventy-five pounds of hurtling weight, amplified by the momentum of the rush, crashed downward on that extended arm. The dog flung himself in a wrenching turn.

The weapon dropped from nerveless fingers.

Captain Mahoney stepped forward, handcuffs glistening.

"Let go, Rip, and lie down," said Zoom.

The police dog relaxed his hold.

Sam Mokeley extended his wrists for the handcuffs, the right wrist dripping blood from the fangs of the dog.

"Put 'em on," he said, his voice calm, his face utterly without emotion. "I got that lying, cheating, murdering doublecrossing lawyer. You're right in everything, only both Gerhard and I went after Paine.

"The lawyer put up the plan to me. I have a criminal record. He knew it. He got me the job here. He proposed that we had a chance to kill off old Paine and blame the murder on the girl. He'd stick by me, and I'd split my inheritance with him.

"He made me do the shooting so I'd be in this power. But I don't know how in hell you ever found the gun. We took it down to the bay and dumped it in the water."

Captain Mahoney turned to Sidney Zoom, who was smiling a cold efficient smile.

"Certainly, Captain. I had to victimize you a little to set the stage just the way I wanted it. Rip's well trained and intelligent, but even he couldn't have done what he appeared to do. The fingerprints on the gun are my own. I knew that the murder had been committed with a single shot from a forty-five automatic. Therefore I bought a similar gun, put fingerprints on it, and buried it where Rip could see it.

"When I told him to search for the gun, he naturally thought we were playing a game. He went to the place where I had planted the weapon— after I'd led him to the general vicinity. I thought it might help us in a third degree."

Captain Mahoney stared angrily at Zoom.

"And you left it loaded, ready to shoot, because you thought that—"

Zoom shrugged.

"As you said, you need evidence to convict."

Captain Mahoney sighed.

"Zoom, you're the most ruthless devil I ever saw work on a case . . . And how about the girl? Even if you have the right hunch about her, she must have come here and stolen the gems. She broke the necklace, didn't realize it until she got back to her room. Then she found a part of the string, and, of course, tried to conceal it . . . and she tore the name off the mail box. I wonder if she didn't conceal those gems in the mail box. Do you know?''

Sidney Zoom met his gaze.

''Do you know, Captain, you're rather clever—at times. But I don't think even you are clever enough to ever find out what became of those gems—or to get a provable case against the girl for their theft. You know it takes evidence to convict.

''Personally, I have an idea those gems will eventually be sold to a collector who will be glad to pay a top price with no questions asked—and that eventually the girl will receive the present of a sum of money.''

Captain Mahoney licked his lips.

''Zoom, your ideas of justice are, perhaps, all right at times. But you're sworn to enforce the law. You've got to do your duty.''

Zoom grinned.

''You forget you made me turn in my badge and special commission. Come, come, Captain, you're going to get lots of credit for having solved a murder case so swiftly and efficiently. You'd better let it go at that.

''And while you're talking about the law, remember there's always a higher law than those made by man.''

Captain Mahoney took a deep breath.

''Zoom, what a strange mixture you are! Big-hearted about some things to the point of taking risks, ruthless about others!''

''I live life as I see it,'' Zoom observed.

Captain Mahoney went to the telephone.

''Send the homicide squad, the coroner, and the wagon,'' he said, when he got headquarters, ''and tell Sergeant Gromley to lay off that Paine woman. He's got a wrong hunch.''